I0762263

# THE WORKS OF SRI CHINMOY

# STORIES

## VOLUME II

THE WORKS OF SRI CHINMOY

# STORIES

## VOLUME II

★

IS YOUR MIND READY TO CRY?
IS YOUR HEART READY TO SMILE?

AMUSEMENT I ENJOY
ENLIGHTENMENT I STUDY

LIFE'S BLEEDING TEARS AND FLYING SMILES

LYON · OXFORD

GANAPATI PRESS

LXXXVII

ISBN 978-0-9933080-5-5

See appendix for notice regarding this edition.

FIRST EDITION WENT TO PRESS ON 13 APRIL 2017

STORIES

VOLUME II

# PART I

## IS YOUR MIND READY TO CRY?
## IS YOUR HEART READY TO SMILE?

IS YOUR MIND READY TO CRY?
IS YOUR HEART READY TO SMILE?

BOOK 1

## MRC 1. *China's foolish king*

Many, many years ago in China there lived a king who was always afraid of losing his prestige. The king thought that if his subjects had more information, knowledge or wisdom than he did, then they would not bow to him and obey him. So he asked his ministers to burn all the books in the schools, the libraries and everywhere in the kingdom. He did not want anybody to read books. The ministers carried out his orders and all the books were burned to ashes. Then the king was very, very happy because he thought nobody would be able to surpass him in information, knowledge or wisdom. O God, there were some scholars who had learned by heart some important books and who had also hidden their books. The king was very happy that others would become fools, and the scholars were so happy that they had made a fool of the king. They became even greater scholars than before because they learned many things by heart and also because they had kept the really good books in hiding. It is because of these great scholars that Laotzu's and others' works are still available in China.

## MRC 2. *The thief's new profession*

There was once a thief who used to commit theft every night. His wife was an honest woman. She would beg her husband not to commit theft. But her husband wouldn't listen, so she was miserable. Like this it went on for years.

At times the thief used to be caught. Surprisingly enough, his wife would outwardly show no sadness. She used to say that he deserved to be caught; he deserved to be punished. But inwardly she always felt sad and miserable. After all, he was her husband. But he would never, never listen to her when she asked him not to steal. He would tell her, "If you really do not want me to steal, then why do you keep taking my money?"

She would say, "What am I going to do? I take very little money from you, next to nothing, and it is only for my necessities. But I don't want you to do this kind of work. You can easily find some other profession. I am a village woman; otherwise, I myself would have found work. But now I have made a decision. If you continue stealing, I will go out and work. If I go out and work, then you will be embarrassed! You will be ashamed that your wife has gone out to work."

In India women don't usually work. It is beneath the dignity of the husbands to send their wives out to work. So when his wife threatened him in this way, the husband told her that he would stop stealing. The wife believed him because he started staying home at night. Previously he used to steal only at night, and now he was staying home at night. He told his wife that during the day he took jobs here and there and was making money. But he was actually stealing during the day and hiding all his stolen goods in a room that he had rented. The thief amassed lots of things in his rented room. But the wife thought that he had turned over a new leaf and become a good and honest man.

O God, one day he came to his rented room with something he had stolen and got the shock of his life. All the things that he had stolen over the months had been taken by some other thieves. He came home and cried and cried and cried. His wife asked him, "Why are you crying? Why are you crying? Has your boss fired you or has anything gone wrong today?"

The husband wouldn't tell her. She said, "Am I not your wife? Can you not tell me what is wrong with you?"

Finally he told her the story. He admitted that he hadn't stopped stealing. He had only lied to her. He had stolen thousands of rupees' worth of things, and now they were all stolen by some other thieves. He was so sad and miserable.

His wife said, "Now look, you are crying for things that were not even your own hard-earned possessions. You went somewhere and in a few minutes' time you stole things, and now you are miserable that they have been stolen from you. But look how hard the actual owners had to work to buy these things! It took them weeks and months of hard work to earn enough money to buy these expensive things. They saved money from their salaries for months. So if you feel sad now, think how much sadder the actual owners must have felt when their things were stolen."

The husband said, "This time I am telling you the absolute truth: I am not going to steal anymore. I will get a regular job so that I can make you happy and also make myself happy. Stealing is not only an embarrassing task; at times it is also very dangerous. I want to be worthy of you. You are a very honest wife. I want to be as good as you are. I am giving up stealing, this time for good."

### MRC 3. *The fool tries to become wise*

In a certain village there lived a stupid fellow. Everybody ridiculed him and he felt miserable. Since he was in his teens, he went to school, and in the class all the other students made fun of him. Even children who were in lower grades cut jokes at his expense. All the time they made fun of him, and he used to feel miserable. But what could he do? Only the teachers didn't ridicule him. They were wise and sympathetic and they showed him utmost compassion and affection. There was also another reason why they were so kind to him. He came of a very rich family. His father and sister were well-educated and his mother had a very big heart.

One day he said to his father, "Father, I know you are very wise. Although I am your son, I am not wise. I am so sorry. Please tell me how I can be wise like you."

His father said, "Always listen to me. If you listen to me, then everybody will think that you are wise. Now, do one thing. Still you have not learned how to make calculations. When you have to add or subtract, you make mistakes. So listen to me. In our family you have your mother, your father, yourself and your sister. If I say that your mother is the first member of the family, your sister is the second member of the family, you are the third member of the family and I am the fourth member, how many members are we?

The son said, "Four!"

The father continued, "Right, we are four! Don't say five or six or seven. Always listen to whatever I say!"

The son agreed to do this. Then, in a few minutes' time, he ran out of his house and went to the house of another boy from his class. "Look, look!" he said. "Now I am really wise and you won't be able to laugh at me anymore."

The boy said, "I won't be able to laugh at you anymore?"

The stupid fellow said, "No, no! I can easily tell you how many members you have in your family. I know how to calculate, how to add."

The boy said, "All right, tell me."

The stupid fellow said, "Let me examine you! You tell first how many members you have in your family. In case you make a mistake, I will correct you."

His friend laughed and laughed and said, "Look here, my brother is the first member of the family, I am the second member, my mother is the third and my father is the fourth."

The stupid fellow said, "No, no, it can't be. You are wrong. My father told me that he is the fourth member. My father has told me always to listen to him. So I am listening to him. You can say anything about your brother being the first member, you being the second member and your mother being the third. But the fourth member, no! My father is the fourth member. My father has told me that if I always listen to him, then I will become wise. So the fourth member cannot be anybody else but my father."

## MRC 4. *The king's three sons*

Once a king had three sons. The first and second sons were very good, but the third one was very bad. He was the worst possible rogue. In spite of knowing that the third one was bad, the king liked him. After all, he was his son.

The king was getting old. One day the third son said to his father, "You know, my two brothers are useless. Although they spend all their time reading books and following other kinds of scholarly pursuits, they are not as smart as I am. When you die, the oldest one will get the throne. Then your whole kingdom will immediately be ruined because he is not as clever and as smart as I am. Neither is your second son. So please make me the king after you leave the body."

The king said, "How can I do that?"

The son said, "If you don't do that, then your kingdom will be ruined."

The king said, "All right, let me see who can really please me. From now on I would like to see how well my sons can utilise my wealth. Let me give each of you one lakh of rupees and see how you use it, since money-power can easily corrupt. After giving you this money, I would like to know how you utilise it. From this I will know which of you three is the wisest."

With the money that his father gave him, the first brother bought many, many books and opened up a library so that not only he, but also others could study. He wanted both himself and others to be wise.

The second brother said, "The best thing is to give the money to charity. I am not doing this for name and fame, but because there are so many poor people on earth. Let this money go to them. If Father hadn't given me this money for a special purpose, I would not have got it at all. So actually it is not my money. Even if I feel it is my money, let me give it to the poor." So he gave away his money to charity.

The third one used the money to form an army, and he told some of the new recruits that when he became the king, he would give them very, very high posts. He said that he would easily be able to defeat his father's army with his own army.

In three months' time the father sent for his sons and asked them what they had done with the money.

The first one said that he had opened up a library and the second one said that he had given his money to charity. The third one, instead of saying anything, brought four hundred soldiers right in front of the king and said, "Now give me the throne, or I will kill you. Since you are an old man, the best thing is for you to leave with honour. Either say that you are giving me the kingdom because I am your wisest son and keep your honour, or I will kill you and get the kingdom that way. Make up your mind."

The king remained silent. Then he said, "Since my life is in your hands, you decide what you are going to do. Either you can kill me now or you can wait for a few years and then take the throne."

The son said, "If you promise that you will give me the throne, then I will wait until you die. But if you don't promise, then I will take it now by killing you."

The king said, "I have to be kind and just to my other two sons who really deserve this kingdom. The best thing is for you to kill me."

So the king was executed by his own son, who then declared himself king.

### MRC 5. *The burglar's signature*

Once there were two kings who were very good friends. They used to help each other all the time. One day one of the kings needed a large sum of money. He made a request to his friend, and his friend immediately agreed to give it to him. The first king said, "I will send my minister to you, so please give it to him."

The other king said, "Definitely I will give it to him."

So the first king sent his minister and three or four bodyguards to the other king. Now, in the first king's kingdom there was a burglar who used to steal money every night. He was a real rogue, but nobody could catch him. He had stolen lots of money, and with this money he had bribed certain palace officials to give him news of what was happening there. He hoped that one day he would be able to enter into the palace with their help and steal everything.

The thief heard from his palace friends that the minister was going to get money from the other king. That evening, as the minister and three guards set out from the palace, all of a sudden the burglar and three of his friends came and surrounded them. The thief said to them, "Now give us your clothes. I have brought some other clothes for you. I will wear the minister's clothes and my three friends will wear the guards' uniforms." Then the thief and his followers forced the minister and the guards to give up their clothes.

Now it happened that the thief did not know how to read and write. But he was very clever. Several days earlier, he had gone to a great scholar and asked him how to write the minister's name.

The scholar had asked him, "Why do you have to know how to write the minister's name?"

The thief told him, "I want to know for some special purpose."

The scholar said, "No, I won't teach you how to sign the minister's name."

Finally the burglar said, "You have to teach me; otherwise, I will kill you."

The scholar got frightened and said, "All right, don't kill me. I will teach you how to sign his name."

The burglar wanted to be able to sign the minister's name in case the other king asked for his signature on a receipt. He knew that he was going to get the minister's clothes, so he also wanted to be able to sign the minister's name.

After changing clothes the thief and his three followers went to the neighbouring king's palace and got the money. It was a very, very large amount. The burglar wanted to show off that he knew how to sign the minister's name, so he said, "Do you not need my signature?"

The king said, "Oh no, your king and I are such good friends. I don't need your signature."

The thief said, "Still it is good to get the signature."

The king said, "All right, if you want to sign, you can. But I really don't need any signature."

So the false minister wrote down "Junga the Burglar".

Immediately the king got a shock. He thought to himself, "O God, how could this happen?" He asked the minister and the three guards to wait for a while. Then he ordered his guards to go to the other king.

When they arrived, the guards said to the king, "We always hear that Junga is the worst possible burglar in your kingdom. How is it that your minister has signed Junga's name? Our king wants to know why your minister is making fun of him when he is giving you so much money."

By this time the real minister had returned to the palace with the three guards and had told his king that he had been forced to change clothes. Immediately the king sent the message to his friend. His friend arrested Junga and sent him back to the first king. Then he personally brought the money to the neighbouring king.

So the thief was caught because the scholar was so clever. Since Junga did not know how to read or write, the scholar taught him how to write his own name and told him that it was the minister's name.

### MRC 6. *The doctor and his assistant*

Once there was a village doctor whom everybody liked because he was always able to cure his patients. He was very smart and he also knew all about medicine.

One day a young man came up to him and said he wanted to be his assistant. The doctor said, "No, no, no, I don't think you are smart enough."

The young man said, "No, I will be able to please you. Please let me learn from you."

The doctor finally agreed, and soon the man began learning how to use medicine. After two years he started begging the doctor to let him come along to see some of his patients. The doctor said, "All right. Since you have been with me for two years, you may come with me today."

So they went to see a patient. The doctor felt the pulse of the patient and said, "I can see your fever has gone high."

The patient said, "Yes, I know that my fever has gone high."

The doctor asked, "Do you know why? It is because you have eaten some candy."

"Candy!" exclaimed the patient.

"Yes," said the doctor. "I can see that you have eaten a few pieces of candy."

The patient said, "It is true."

The doctor said, "I know, I know. When I feel the pulse, immediately the pulse tells me."

So the patient confessed that he had eaten candy. The doctor told him not to eat candy until he was totally cured and his fever had gone down.

When the doctor and assistant were coming back, the assistant said he was so amazed at how the doctor could tell what someone had eaten just by feeling the pulse. "How could you do it? How could you do it?" he asked.

The doctor said, "You fool, I saw at the door a few candy wrappers. I said to myself, 'Who else could have eaten the candy?' So immediately I challenged the man and he confessed. Otherwise, do you think that by feeling the pulse one can say who has eaten candy? But don't you do this kind of thing. You will be in trouble."

The doctor was a smart doctor, but he was also sincere. He told his assistant what he had done. A few days later, when the doctor was supposed to see another patient, it happened that he himself was sick. By this time he had a little faith in his assistant, so he told him, "Today I am feeling very sick. You go and see this patient. But be very careful, because this is the first time you are going to see someone."

"Definitely I will be careful," said the assistant. "When I come back, you will be very proud of me. You can rest assured that I will do everything correctly, and you will get a good report. The patient will say nice things about me."

When the assistant arrived at the patient's house, he saw that the patient had a very high fever. The assistant said, "I know why you have got such a high fever. I can see that you have eaten mangos."

The patient said, "No, I have not."

The assistant said, "Your pulse tells me that you have."

The patient said, "My pulse tells you? Those mangos I have kept for my wife and children. They eat mangos. I have got such a high fever. How can I eat mangos?"

The assistant said, "Your pulse tells me that this morning you ate four mangos. That's why your fever is so high."

The man got so furious that he asked his sons and servants to beat the assistant black and blue. He also got mad at the real doctor for sending such a horrible assistant, and he sent one of his servants to insult the doctor.

The assistant never returned to the doctor again. He was so badly beaten that he said, "No, no, I am not going to be a doctor anymore. It is too dangerous a profession."

The real doctor was very happy that he did not have to deal with that kind of idiot-assistant anymore.

### MRC 7. *The king and the three thieves*

In a certain kingdom there were three thieves. These three thieves used to steal like anything. The king was so sad that he was unable to do anything to punish these thieves. In so many ways his ministers had tried to catch them, but always they failed. The king was physically very strong and powerful. "In some way I will have to catch these thieves," he said.

So every night he went out of his palace in disguise, wearing most simple clothes like those a thief wears. During the night he went in search of the culprits. He would go by the houses of his friends, the way a thief does, moving around in a very secret manner. He told his friends not to tell anyone what he was doing.

One night it happened that the king, who was posing as a thief, actually saw the three thieves near the house that he was pretending to steal from. So he jumped in front of them and said, "Look, you are thieves. Let me join you. I will be the fourth."

They said, "Who needs you? We don't need you."

He said, "You don't need me? It is good to have one more. And I tell you, I shall always please you. I am a great thief, just like you are. I have been hearing so much about you. Now I would like to be a member of your group."

They said, "What kind of special capacity do you have?"

The king said, "Oh, I have no special capacity, but may I hear what special capacities you have?"

One thief said, "I can unlock any door in the twinkling of an eye. I have that kind of capacity."

Another one said, "I know where the wealth is. He can unlock any door, but I can easily tell in which room or in which place the wealth is."

The third one said, "I can remember people. Once I see someone, I can always recognise that person even if his face or his body has changed. Even if everything is changed, still I can recognise the person. I have that kind of retentive faculty."

Then they said to him, "Now you have to tell us what capacity you have. If you don't have any special capacity, why should we take you in our group?"

The king said, "Look, I have got a ring. If I press my ring, immediately I can kill people. And if I raise my hand, immediately I can save people."

They said, "Oh, you have that kind of capacity! Then we can use you."

The king said, "Today, let me take you to the King's palace. There is no need to be afraid. We have a silly king. Since you have the capacity to unlock doors and the capacity to know where the wealth is, today let us go to the palace and rob the king."

The three thieves agreed. "This is a wonderful idea, a wonderful idea," they said.

So in disguise the king brought them to the palace. Then the fellow who knew how to open the lock immediately opened the door. The other one who had the capacity to find the wealth, did so. Then immediately the king summoned the guards and the thieves were arrested.

The following morning the minister brought them before the king. The king said to the robbers, "I played this trick and caught you. Now you shall be executed. Yesterday I told you that if I press my ring, then whomever I want to kill will be killed. See, I am pressing my ring. Now you will be executed."

The three thieves started crying and crying. Now the three thieves realised that he was the king and he had caught them. They said, "But you told us that you also have another capacity. You said that if you raise your hand, then you can save anybody you want to. Will you not show us that capacity too? Will you not raise your hand and save us?"

So the king raised his hand and said, "All right, I will save you three. But now you have to take an oath that you will never steal again. Better yet, I will give you some work here in the palace. Then you will be always under supervision and you won't be able to steal from anybody else."

MRC 8. *The yogi's advice*

There was once a king who was very unhappy because he was unable to conquer the neighbouring king. He and the other king were friends, but at the same time they were rivals. When meanness, jealousy and ego came forward, the first king wanted to conquer his so-called friend and make him his subordinate. In so many ways he tried to increase his army and military power. But even then he could not compete with his rival-friend. Finally he said, "Now that physical power, military power, is not succeeding, let me try spiritual power."

So he went to a yogi and said, "Please, please help me out. I will give you everything that I have. All my money-power, everything, I will surrender to you. I will touch your feet; I will sit at your feet and wash your feet every day. Only please tell me how I can conquer the other king."

The yogi said, "It is so easy. Just conquer your anger. If you conquer your anger, then you will be able to easily conquer the other king."

So the king went home and followed the yogi's advice. No matter what people said or did, he did not get angry. For some time he practised this, until there was no anger at all in his life. After six months he was so happy. He went back to the sage and said, "Now that I have conquered anger, will I not be able to conquer that king?"

The sage said, "Just wait for a few more months. For another three months try to keep your temper under control. Don't get angry with anybody."

The king said, "All right, all right. For three more months I will do that."

After three months the king came back. The yogi said to him, "I am so sorry. It seems to me that you will need another two months."

The king said, "All right. I have already conquered my anger for six months and for three months, so I can easily do it for two more months."

After two months the king came back again. The yogi said, "Please wait one more month. This time it will be absolutely the last. If you can keep your temper under control for one more month, I tell you, you will be able to conquer the neighbouring king."

After one month the king came back once again. He was so happy and delighted and said, "Now tell me how I can really conquer my enemy. Now I am calling him my enemy because I have conquered my anger and am about to fight him."

The yogi said, "What do I know about fighting? What do I know about kings and armies and battles? What do I know about these things? I pray to God for peace, joy and love. How can I be of any help to those who want war and fighting? I try to save people and you try to kill people. In my case by giving new life to people I become happy. In your case you want to be happy by killing people. I am the last person to help you out, because you want violence and I want peace. You have come to the wrong person."

The king got mad and wanted to kill the yogi. He said, "You told me to come back to you when I had conquered my anger."

The yogi said, "Look, look! Who is angry now, who is angry now? Have you really conquered your anger? If you can't conquer your own anger, then how are you going to conquer the other king? I told you that if you conquer your anger, then easily you will be able to conquer that king. But you have not even conquered your own anger. So how are you going to conquer him? I cannot help you at all."

MRC 9. *The sculptor*

There was once a rich man who was also kind and generous. He had many friends and admirers. When he died, everybody felt sad and miserable. So some of his friends wanted to have a statue made of him to perpetuate his memory.

Unfortunately, everyone had a different opinion as to who should make the statue. One person said that a particular sculptor was the best. Another one said that someone else would be better. In this way they argued for several months. Finally they decided to take a vote. When they took a vote, they found that one person stood first. So all of them went to that particular sculptor and said, "You are the best according to us. Now please make a statue of our friend."

The sculptor said, "He was such a great and good man. He was not only rich but great and good as well, so it is a great honour for me to be requested to make a statue of him. I can start right away if you want me to."

They asked, "How much will you charge?"

The sculptor said, "I will charge one thousand dollars."

They said, "One thousand dollars? One thousand! That is too much. We shall find somebody else. There are many other good sculptors."

One person said, "Let us go to a certain young sculptor who is just rising in his career. I am sure he will ask for less money. He may not be well-established, but I tell you, he will do a much better job than this old man. Just because he is young, nobody knows him. But a day will come when he will become very well-known and famous."

They all agreed to go to the young sculptor. The young man was very happy, delighted and excited to get this kind of job. They asked, "How long will it take?"

He said, "It will take a long time. It will take at least six months."

They told him, "Don't worry. Only do a good job. You don't have to worry about your wages. We will please you."

After six months they came back and they were quite pleased with the statue. Then they asked, "How much do you want?"

The young man said, "Two thousand dollars."

They cried, "What! Two thousand? How dare you ask for two thousand when the old man who is so well-known only asked for one thousand."

The young man said, "That is his business. He can ask whatever he wants. He is my teacher and I bow to him in all artistic matters. But I don't ask him about the price. In this area I make my own decision. Whatever I feel is right, I ask for. So you have to give me two thousand dollars. Otherwise, I am not going to give you the sculpture."

They said, "All right, what can we do? Now we have to surrender. We are very pleased with your sculpture; it is so beautiful. But before we give you the two thousand dollars, let us go and ask your teacher how much your work deserves."

When they went to ask his teacher how much the young sculptor deserved, the teacher said, "How much did he ask for?"

They said, "He asked for two thousand dollars."

The old sculptor said, "He is right, he is right."

They said, "How can he be right? You are far better than he is. You are a great sculptor, an expert. You asked for one thousand dollars and he is asking for two thousand dollars. How can you say he is right?"

He said, "If I had done it, then I would have finished it in three months or even less. But he has taken six months. Doesn't he deserve to be paid for the three extra months he has spent on it? If I had done it, I would have taken three months and asked for one thousand dollars. But he has taken six months because he is not an expert like me. He told you it would take time and he has done a good job. So now for another three months' work you have to pay. Therefore he deserves the two thousand dollars."

### MRC 10. *The telltale mark*

A rich couple was blessed with a child who was born with a mark on his forehead. They were very happy and excited. The mother said that the mark was a sign that the boy was going to become a great writer. But the father said, "No, no! The mark means that he is going to be as strong and as powerful as I am. Physically he will be very, very strong and powerful."

Some of their friends said that the child would be a sailor and sail from one country to another. But everybody said that the mark meant that this little baby would be very great or good or both. So the parents were very pleased. They said, "Let us now see what happens to him when he grows up. Everybody is saying good things, exceptionally good things, about him."

One day a beggar came to their house for alms. The father happened to be at the gate and he noticed that the beggar had exactly the same kind of mark at the same spot as their little child.

The father immediately summoned his wife and said, "Now look, look! Here is a fellow who has the same mark as our child. And what is he doing? He is a beggar! So let us not boast anymore. Our son is definitely going to become a beggar. Here is the proof!"

The wife said, "You are right, you are right. This beggar has the same mark at the same spot. O God, what have You done, what have You done? When our son grows up, he will also become a beggar. That we don't want to see."

The husband said, "From now on, let us put as much money as possible in the bank for him. We are now old, and soon we shall die. But if he has money in the bank, then he will be able to live comfortably on earth. We don't want our son to become a beggar."

So they put lots of money in the bank in their son's name, so that he would not end up poverty-stricken like this beggar.

# IS YOUR MIND READY TO CRY?
# IS YOUR HEART READY TO SMILE?

## BOOK 2

## MRC 11. *The money-lender*

There was once an elderly village moneylender who was very rich. He was a very nice man, and many times he would give money to the needy. His name was Junga.

One day a young man took a loan from Junga. He promised that in six months' time he would return the money.

After six months had passed, the young man came to the rich man and said that he could not return the money. The rich man got mad. He said, "No, you have to return it!"

The young man said, "I don't have the money. What can I do?"

The old man started screaming and insulting him. "No, you have to return it!" he said.

The young man said, "When I have the money, I will give it back. But right now I don't have the money."

The old man said, "Then why did you take the money from me and why did you promise to return it in six months?"

The young man, who was badly insulted, said, "You donkey, you camel!"

The old man got furious and said, "You take money from me and you call me a donkey and a camel? I will sue you."

He sent for the village head and gave some money to him. Then he said, "Now you tell me what I should do. This young man took money from me and he is not returning it. What is worse, he is calling me a camel and a donkey."

The young man said, "I took money, true, and one day I will give it back to him. But how badly he was scolding and insulting me, you have no idea! So what could I do?"

The village head scolded the young man and said, "You should not call him names. He is of your father's age. You should always have respect for elderly people. Also, you should return his money as soon as possible."

The young man said, "All right, I will not call him names, and one day I promise I will return his money. But when I return the money, if at that time I have a camel and a donkey, may I not call my animals Junga?"

The village head said, "Do anything you like, but first give the money back. As long as you do not call Junga a camel and a donkey, whatever name you want to give to your camel and donkey is up to you."

In two weeks' time the young man borrowed money from somebody else and returned the money to Junga. Then he brought a camel and donkey right in front of the moneylender's house and started shouting, "Junga, Junga! What do you want? Do you want to have grass? Do you want water? Do you want something?"

The old moneylender got furious. But the young man said, "I have returned your money. Now I can do anything I want to. These are my animals. I have every right to name them Junga. It is none of your business!"

### MRC 12. *Saturn and Indra*

Indra, the king of the gods, and Saturn, another god, were one day quarreling bitterly over their supremacy. Each one felt that he was superior to the other. Indra said, "I am the king of the gods. Naturally I am superior to you. Everybody bows to me, so definitely I am superior."

Saturn said, "You! Everybody is afraid of me. Nobody wants to come under my influence. So, am I not superior if everybody is afraid of me?"

Indra said, "No, no, no! I am greater; I am the greatest of all because everybody surrenders to me."

Saturn said, "Everybody is afraid of me. Nobody wants to come near me."

Like this, Indra was bragging and Saturn was bragging. Finally Saturn said, "Look, tomorrow I am going to capture you and destroy you. Only if I fail to keep my promise will you be able to say that you are superior to me. Otherwise, the whole world will know that I am superior."

Indra said, "Don't brag, don't brag. Tomorrow I will see if you can capture and destroy me!"

The following day, in order to escape from Saturn, Indra went into the forest. The whole day he spent hiding in the forest. Then in the evening he came to Saturn and said, "Look, you could not capture me; you could not destroy me. So am I not superior?"

Saturn said, "You fool, you fool! Did I not tell you that everybody is afraid of me? If you were as strong as I am, then why did you hide in the forest? If you had been superior or even equal to me, you would not have hidden in the forest. So here is the proof that you are afraid of me and acknowledge my supremacy!"

### MRC 13. *The village zamindar*

There was a village zamindar who was nice, kind and honest. He had lots of land and also a very large barn, where he used to keep grain. One day, while walking in front of his house, he saw a few pieces of grain on the ground. He bent down and started picking them up.

Two travellers happened to be passing by. They said, "We heard that you are a very, very rich man, a very kind man and a very generous man. Now what are you doing? Why are you not asking your servants to pick up these bits of grain? Again, it is only very few kernels — six or seven. It is not even worth asking your servants to do it. Why are you picking up this grain at all? On the one hand you are so generous, but now you are acting like a miserly man."

The zamindar said, "I am not miserly; I am generous. But why do I have to waste anything? I don't want to waste even a single kernel of grain. When it is necessary, I show my generosity. But when it is a matter of being economical, why should I waste even one piece of grain? Today I will waste ten bits of grain, tomorrow twenty and the day after tomorrow many more."

One of the travellers said, "Yes, but we thought that you were collecting the pieces of grain as if they were the most precious jewellery, most precious gold coins. So inwardly we were laughing at you. But we see that you are right. It is good to be economical. Now we shall go."

The zamindar said, "Since you are passing by my house and you have said that I am kind and so forth, let me be hospitable to you. Why not stay and eat with me, and then go?"

The travellers went to eat in the zamindar's house. He said to his guests, "Usually I don't serve anyone because I have so many servants. But I like you two; you seem to be very nice people. So let me serve you." Then the zamindar brought them a plate containing ten gold coins instead of food.

The travellers said to him, "What are you doing? How can we eat gold coins? Have you brought this by mistake or for some other special reason? Is it out of your generosity that you are doing this? You are really kindhearted and compassionate. We are so grateful. But the thing is that now we are very hungry. This is not the time to get gold coins. We can't eat them."

The zamindar said, "Oh no, I am showing you fools something. When I was collecting the pieces of grain, you laughed at me. You acted as though they were not valuable whereas gold coins were valuable. I have brought you these gold coins to show you that everything has its own value at the proper time. Gold coins are valuable, true. But you can't eat them. When you are hungry, you don't think of gold coins — you want to eat food. At that time, grain is even more precious than gold coins."

MRC 14. *The transformation of iron into gold*

There was once a spiritual Master who was the leader of a spiritual community. Everybody in the community was leading an honest life except for one person. This person was a businessman who cared only about making money and becoming rich. He did not pay any attention to his spiritual life. Everybody else wanted to become spiritually rich. Of course, some unfortunate disciples wanted to become spiritually rich without praying or meditating. But this man did not even want spiritual wealth. He wanted only to become materially rich. That was his goal. Everybody laughed at the businessman because he was not spiritual, but out of compassion the Master continued to keep him in the community. "As long as he wants to stay in my boat, I will keep him," the Master said.

The Master occasionally would tell him, "Don't pay so much attention to money-power. Pay attention to your heart-power, your soul-power." But he never listened to his Master. This went on and on for years.

One day the Master said, "My days are numbered. I will be leaving the body soon."

Everybody was so sad and shocked. They all loved the Master very much and appreciated his compassion and forgiveness. How could the Master say all of a sudden that he was going to leave the body?

The Master said, "Since I am going to leave the body soon, I want you people to come to me one by one privately. I will bless you, and if you have any special desire, then I will fulfil it."

One by one they all came up to him for a last blessing and said, "To hear that you have forgiven us — that is our only desire. During this lifetime so many things we have done wrong. If you have not yet forgiven us, please do so. From the soul's world think of us and bless us all the time." Each one had the same prayer, and the Master was very, very pleased.

When the businessman came, he looked around and said, "I have a very special prayer. You have fulfilled others' prayers. Will you not fulfil my prayer?"

The Master said, "Yes, today I will fulfil everybody's prayer. Now what is your prayer?"

The man said, "Everybody says that you have occult power. Can you not give me some occult power?"

The Master said, "What will you do with occult power?"

The businessman said, "With my occult power I will be able to make more money and become richer. When I become very rich, then I will talk to many people and tell them all about you."

The Guru said, "Oh no, I don't need people to hear about me from you. If you want to have occult power to make more money, then I will give it to you. But don't pretend that you are asking for it to help my mission. All right, now tell me what kind of occult power you want."

The man said, "In my business I get the most profit from my steel factory. I buy iron at one price and sell it at a higher price as steel. Now, with my occult power if I can transform the iron into gold, then I will have even more money. I will become rich overnight. Please give me the capacity to transform iron into gold."

The Guru said, "Yes, I want to keep my promise. I will give you this power. But who knows, some day you will feel miserable that you have asked for occult power."

The disciple said, "No, no, I will never be miserable."

The Guru gave him the power. Then, in a few days, the Guru died. Everybody felt so sad. The businessman shed crocodile tears, but secretly he was very pleased with his new occult power.

Soon the businessman became very, very rich, and people came to know that it was all because of the occult power that he had got. But the sincere ones still did not care for occult power. They said, "No, we want peace, peace, peace. Let us see what will happen at the end of his life. We want only peace and joy."

So for two or three years the man went on transforming iron into gold with his occult power. But even though he had become very, very rich, still he always tried to get the people selling him iron to lower the price. Sometimes they said that they would lower the price after three or four months, and he would wait until that time before buying. He would say to himself, "Now that I have got from my Master the mantra that turns iron into gold, there is no rush to use it. So why not wait until I can buy iron at a much cheaper price? Then my profit will be even higher."

Then, all of a sudden the price of iron went down considerably. The businessman kept buying more and more. The more the price of iron went down, the greater was his joy. For he knew he could turn it into most valuable gold. "In every way I am the happiest person," he said.

In this way he kept accumulating iron, and for two years he did not use the mantra at all. When he had finally filled up a large warehouse, he said to himself, "All right, before I buy another supply of iron, let me transform what I now have into gold. I have accumulated a very large quantity."

He was so excited at the thought of transforming all his iron into gold, and he tried to chant the mantra that his Guru had given him. O God, since he had not used the mantra for two years, he had totally forgotten it. He tried desperately to remember it, but to no avail. Naturally the iron was not transformed into gold, and he was feeling miserable, miserable, miserable.

The next day in the market he heard that iron had become absolutely worthless. So now what could he do? All his iron he would have to practically give away because he didn't want to keep it. So he went to the market and had to sell his iron below cost because the price had gone down so much. The businessman cursed his fate and said, "So this is what occult power can do!"

### MRC 15. *The king's new astrologer*

A certain king had three astrologers. He relied on astrology for everything. But for a few months the predictions of the astrologers were not coming true. The king became extremely displeased with them and eventually he dispensed with their services.

Then he asked his prime minister to get a new astrologer. He said, "I don't need three. One will be enough. But I want an astrologer who will always be able to tell me about my future and about the world's future so that I can always take advantage of what I know is going to happen. If I know beforehand what is going to happen, then definitely I will be able to be successful in everything that I undertake."

The minister made an announcement that he would interview any astrologers who would like to get the post at the palace. The minister found seven astrologers who wanted the post, and the king decided that he would personally see all of them and make the choice.

After interviewing them, the king casually said, "It seems that all of you are great astrologers. Do you know of any astrologers in the kingdom who have not come here because they know that you are greater and feel that they do not have a chance?"

One astrologer said to the king, "Your Highness, I have a friend who is an astrologer. But I know infinitely more than he does. Therefore, he did not dare to come to the palace."

The king said, "Tell me his name and address and I will summon him."

When the other astrologer was brought before the king, the king asked him, "Why didn't you come here to apply for this post?"

The man was very clever. First he remained silent. Then he said, "Your Majesty, these astrologers are all fools. How could any of them be your astrologer? Did any of them know who was going to be appointed? I knew all along that I would be appointed. Therefore, I did not bother coming. It is I who was destined to be your astrologer."

The king said to him, "You are right. I am making you my new astrologer." Then the king asked all the other astrologers to leave the palace.

### MRC 16. *The swordmaker's son*

There was a craftsman who used to make swords for all the soldiers in the kingdom. One day he made some extraordinary swords and he took them to the king, hoping to get a reward. As soon as the king saw the swords, he took one and started hammering a stone with it. Immediately the sword broke into pieces. So the king said, "I don't need that kind of sword. It is useless!" The craftsman was very sad.

A few days later he came to the palace again with a new sword. This time he said to the king, "This sword is far better than the previous one."

The king took it and again started striking it against a solid stone. In no time it broke in two. The king said, "Don't come to me any more. I will give you money, since that is what you want. But don't bother me with any more swords. Don't come again!"

A few days later the craftsman's son came to the king with another sword. The son was very clever. He didn't tell the king that he was the craftsman's son. He simply said, "I have heard that somebody brought you swords twice and you didn't like them. Now I am sure that you will like this sword that I have made. It will take anybody's life in a twinkling of an eye."

Immediately the king took the sword and was about to strike it against a stone. The boy, who had been warned about this, said, "Please, please, wait! Swords are not meant for stones. They are meant for men. What use is it to strike a stone if you want to test a sword? You use a sword to kill someone or to defend yourself. You can apply it on me and see if it is really powerful."

The king said, "All right, I am ready. I am going to use it."

The king picked up the sword and was about to strike the boy when the boy said, "O King, you are a noble ruler. Will you not allow me to use a shield to protect myself? If you fight someone, will you not allow that person to at least have armour?"

The boy put on armour and then said, "Now you strike me and see if the sword breaks or not."

As the king lifted the sword, suddenly the boy pulled out another sword to defend himself. "What are you doing?" cried the king.

"O King," replied the boy, "you are attacking me. Should I not defend myself? This sword is my protection. You are a noble King and I am a noble soldier."

The king, who was very pleased with the boy's intelligence, said to the boy, "Then you are ready to be one of my knights." So he made the boy a knight.

## MRC 17. *Two horses*

One day a businessman was riding his horse to the marketplace. After covering quite a distance he became tired. So he got down from his horse and tied it to a mango tree. At the foot of the mango tree he lay down and took rest.

In a few minutes' time, a high-ranking officer came passing by. He was also riding his horse to the marketplace to perform some duty. When he saw that the businessman was lying under the tree, he also felt tired. If one sees someone else lying down, one also becomes tired. So the officer decided to tie his horse to the same mango tree and also take rest.

The businessman said to the officer, "What are you doing? Why are you tying your horse to the same tree that I have tied my horse to?"

The officer replied, "Shut up!"

The businessman said, "My horse is much more powerful, much stronger than yours. If it fights with your horse, it may injure or even kill your horse. You have to take your horse somewhere else. Otherwise, if anything happens to your horse, I will not be responsible. I came here before you. I am tired and want some rest. Is this the kind of justice one finds in this kingdom?"

"Yes!" said the officer. "Might is right."

"You may be stronger than I am," said the businessman, "but my horse is stronger than your horse. I am going to lie down here again, but if my horse attacks yours, I won't be responsible."

In a few minutes' time the businessman's horse attacked the other horse and badly injured it. The poor horse was miserable and badly hurt.

The following day the officer went to the king and made a complaint against the businessman, and the businessman was summoned before the king. The king was very fond of the officer's horse, so he was very, very mad. He started scolding and insulting the businessman. "Why did you not take your horse to another place?" he asked.

The man did not answer him. He remained absolutely silent. The king again and again asked him the question, but the man would not answer him. Finally, the king said to the officer, "You are a fool. You brought me a dumb man. He can't even speak. I don't know what happened yesterday, but you should have told me that he could not speak. Why should I have to deal with a dumb person?"

The officer said, "No, no! Today he is dumb, but yesterday he was arguing with me and threatening me. He told me to move my horse, since he had been there first."

The king said, "If he was there first, and he asked you to keep your horse somewhere else, then it is your fault." Then the king immediately dismissed the case.

### MRC 18. *The gold coins*

Once a poor man came to a rich man and begged him to give him an acre of land that was not being used. He said that he would cultivate the land and then sell the grain at a cheap price to the poor people. Although the rich man was not using the land, he did not trust the poor man. He told him, "No, you have to pay me for the land."

A few months later the poor man's son came to the rich man and said, "Sir, I had a dream, a most powerful dream. In the dream a beautiful goddess appeared before me and showed me a particular plot of land. She said that if I dug deep enough at that particular place, I would find an earthen pot with one hundred gold coins." The son didn't disclose that the man who had asked for the land was his father. He only said that he had

had a dream, and the rich man was very pleased to hear about it.

The rich man asked, "Then what shall we do?"

The son said, "I don't have any money, so I won't be able to buy thc land. But if you want me to, I will be able to dig up the pot and give you the money. Then, if you are kind to me, you will give me the land."

"You can certainly have the land if you get a hundred gold coins!" exclaimed the rich man. "If you find the earthen pot and give the coins to me, I shall give you the land."

"Yes, I shall do that," said the young man. "Or you can give me a few gold coins instead of the land," he added. "You have got thousands of golden coins. You can give me a few."

The rich man said, "No, only take the land."

"All right," agreed the young man. "Now I have to dig up the earthen pot. But it is not safe to dig during the day. People will see me. So I will start at night. You can stay with me — but nobody else."

The rich man agreed because he didn't want to share the gold coins even with his wife and children. He said, "I don't want to share this with anybody."

That night the rich man watched the young man dig for some time. After a while he got tired and asked the young man, "Are you sure that you will find this earthen pot?"

"Absolutely sure," replied the man. "There is definitely something here!"

Finally the rich man went back home. "When you find it, call me," he said. "But be sure you don't call anybody else — not my children or wife or anybody."

"Certainly! I will call only you," agreed the young man.

As soon as the rich man left, the young man went home and brought back a small earthen pot. In it he put a hundred ordinary copper coins, and then he sealed the vessel. On the top he put a note that said, "Do not open this until three years have passed. After three years if you open it, then you will have gold coins. But if you open it before that, you may not get gold coins."

He put the pot in the hole that he had been digging and then pretended that he had just found it. He started screaming, "I have found it! I have found it!"

The rich man and his whole family came running. "What has happened? What has happened?" they cried.

The young man told them that he had discovered the earthen pot with the gold coins. The rich man became very forceful and said, "Nobody except me can touch this pot." When he read the message on the top, he was not disappointed at all. "Three years? That will pass by very quickly," he said. Then he asked the young man, "What would you like as your reward?"

"Just this acre of land," answered the young man.

"All right," said the rich man, "but you won't get anything from this earthen pot."

The rich man brought the pot home and put it near his bed so nobody would be able to touch it. O God, his eldest son was so clever and greedy. He said, "If there are golden coins in this pot, then why do we have to wait for three years?" Then he shook the pot and heard the coins rattling inside. "Definitely there is something inside. Why do I have to wait for three years?" he said. He was so anxious and eager to open it. He stole the pot from his father's room and opened it. As soon as he opened it, he saw the simple copper coins.

He ran to his father, crying, "That fellow is a liar. Let us kill him!"

"How can I kill him?" asked the father. "The note said that the pot should not be opened for three years."

The son was so angry that he went and got the young man and dragged him to see his father. The young man said, "Sir, it was written that one had to wait for three years. Why did you open it now?"

Then the father got mad at his son and started thrashing him.

The young man said, "What am I going to do? You didn't want to give me any gold. Instead you gave me the land because you were so pleased with me. Now you are going to take away the land."

"No," said the rich man. "This is my fate. I promised you that I would give you the land. It is yours."

So the young man started cultivating the land. He raised vegetables and grains. In six months' time he asked the rich man, "How much do you want me to pay for the land?"

"Why do you have to pay?" asked the rich man.

"Suppose you wanted to sell it to someone else," said the poor man. "How much would you sell it for?"

"I would ask for only two hundred rupees," said the rich man.

"Then take these two hundred rupees that I have made from selling vegetables and grains," said the young man.

This is how the young man was able to get money to buy the rich man's land.

### MRC 19. *The drunkard's promises*

There was a woodcutter who was a real drunkard. Since he never brought any money home, his poor wife lived a destitute life. The wife begged the husband to give up drinking, but he wouldn't listen.

One day the goddess Lakshmi appeared before the drunkard and said, "Look, everybody ridicules you. Nobody appreciates you, whereas your own brother is appreciated by everyone because he is simple, pure and honest. But everybody dislikes you — almost hates you. Why don't you give up drinking?"

"No, I can't give it up!" said the man.

"Do you like people to say nasty things about you?" the goddess asked.

"That I don't like, but how can I give up drinking?" the woodcutter said.

The goddess told him, "You can give it up if you want to."

"All right," said the drunkard. "I am ready to give it up if you will bring me free of charge a very large amount of wine."

"I can do that easily," said the goddess. "Then will you give up drinking?"

"Certainly!" said the drunkard. "I will take the wine home and it will last for a long time — perhaps a week. Then after that I will give up drinking altogether."

"Are you sure?" asked the goddess.

"I am sure," said the man. "For one week only I will drink. After one week I will give it up."

"Then I will bring the wine," said the goddess. "But you must drink only for one week and then give up drinking."

So the goddess brought him a large supply of wine. After one week of drinking at home, the woodcutter went into the woods and continued drinking. The goddess came to him again and scolded him. She said, "You didn't keep your promise. Still you are drinking."

The drunkard said, "I am so sorry that I could not keep my promise."

"Will you make another promise?" asked the goddess.

"Certainly I will make another promise," the man said. "Now, since you are the presiding deity of this forest, can you make a small pond that has not water but wine? I will stay by the pond and drink and drink. After three nights I will be fed up with drinking. Then I will go home and give it up."

The goddess said, "Yes, I will do it with my occult power."

Then the goddess made a pond filled with wine. She told the man, "In three days you have to give up drinking."

He promised again, "Certainly I will give it up."

Three days passed, but the man did not leave the pond. His poor wife did not see him for days. The goddess came to him again and said, "What are you doing here? You promised that you would go home after three days and stop drinking. You are not keeping your promise."

The man said, "Mother, when did you ever hear of a drunkard telling the truth? How can you expect any truth from a drunkard? Only he who has lost his brains can drink like this. Am I not insane? If I were sane, I would not have drunk so much. Since I am insane, how can you expect me to tell the truth? I am extremely grateful to you for the pond. For the rest of my life I will drink this wine."

The goddess said, "I will take care of you and your drunkard life. If you have to drink, then at least let me take care of you."

So the man stayed in the forest by the pond and never returned home. Although the woodcutter had been a useless drunkard, his poor wife still missed him because, after all, he was her husband.

### MRC 20. *The loafer who gave advice*

There was a bad fellow who was a real loafer. His poor wife was suffering like anything because her husband wouldn't work. But what could she do? He kept saying that soon he would get a nice job and then they would lead a luxurious life. But he never got a job. Finally she got mad at him and started insulting him. "I have heard that story too many times," she said.

The husband said, "I am not going to put up with your insults. I am going to leave you."

The wife could not believe her ears.

He said to her, "Previously you could say that at least you had a husband. Now you can consider yourself a widow."

She became furious and said, "It is better to be a widow than to have a husband like you!"

So the husband left the house and walked and walked. He said to himself, "It is beneath my dignity to be insulted by a woman. I am not going back there!"

As he was walking he saw a moneylender with his clients. So he said to himself, "My wife used to tell me that I am a good adviser. Let me start giving advice right now."

The loafer went up to the moneylender and said, "There is something called sin and there is a place called hell. To ask for interest is a sin. Because you are asking for interest, you will go to hell, whereas I will go to Heaven."

The moneylender said, "I am taking only my due. I am not asking for high interest. I am asking for only what I deserve. My interest is not exorbitant."

"No!" the man insisted. "What you are doing is very bad."

The moneylender looked at him and then said, "Perhaps you are a beggar. My wife is very kind-hearted. She always thinks of vagabonds. She has a special fondness for them. You can come to my house and my wife will definitely feed you."

The moneylender was right. The loafer went to his house and the moneylender's wife prepared a very delicious meal for him. This made the loafer very happy.

As he was leaving he said, "Don't forget my advice. There will come a time when you will feel the necessity of giving up this business entirely. Then you will pray to God for peace and love. But if you always deal in money and ask for interest, then you won't be happy."

The wife said, "He is right, he is right."

The husband said, "Yes, he is right, but he should keep his advice to himself."

The loafer felt sorry that he had been insulted, so he left the moneylender's house and again started walking. Then he saw a lawyer and a group of people. He said to the lawyer, "You are a lawyer. Do you ever tell the truth?"

The lawyer got mad. He said, "What are you saying? Who are you?"

The loafer said, "You are a lawyer and these people are your clients. You are teaching them falsehood and asking them to tell lies. For a lawyer there is no Heaven — only hell."

The lawyer got even more furious and he started beating the loafer. He shouted, "Granted, we tell lies, but it is only to save honest people."

"Yes," said the loafer, "honest people hire you. But for what? Only to see you tell lies so that you can win the case."

The lawyer said, "Go home peacefully. If you argue with me, I will thrash you even more."

The man went away and said, "First I gave advice to the moneylender and told him that he shouldn't ask for interest. He didn't appreciate my advice. Then I asked the lawyer to give up his profession and he became mad. That means the world does not need my advice. They will all definitely go to hell, and I shall go to Heaven. But where is my Heaven?"

Then he thought of his wife. Inwardly he saw that his wife was crying for him. So he said, "Let me go back to my wife, my Heaven, and let these people go to hell!"

# IS YOUR MIND READY TO CRY?
# IS YOUR HEART READY TO SMILE?

## BOOK 3

## MRC 21. *The wonderful singer*

There once was a singer who put everybody to sleep when he sang. As soon as he started singing, his audience would fall asleep for an hour or two. Then they would wake up when the power of his singing had worn off.

Some said that he was such an excellent singer that he was putting everyone's soul to sleep. Others said that he was such a horrible singer that people went to sleep rather than listen to him — they spontaneously invoked the goddess of sleep so that they could fall asleep. So there were two schools of thought about the singer. One deeply appreciated his musical talent; the other did not appreciate him at all. But they all went to hear him sing.

One day, two burglars came to the singer and said, "You are such a great singer. We want to hire you. If we give you a very large amount of money, will you be able to sing at a particular place?"

The singer said, "Of course! As long as I get the money, I will sing. I don't trust you two, but if you give me the money beforehand, then I will go wherever you want me to."

The two burglars gave the singer a very large amount of money and then asked him to follow them. They brought him in front of a small bank and asked him to sing there. It was early evening, and there was only one guard watching this bank. As soon as the singer started singing, immediately the guard fell asleep. Then the two burglars entered into the bank and began collecting all the money.

After some time the singer stopped singing, because the guard was fast asleep. He said, "There is nobody to listen. This man doesn't care for my music."

For a long time the singer stood waiting for the two burglars to come out of the bank. Finally he went inside and told them, "You have already given me my money. Now I am going away."

The burglars said, "Yes, you can go away now," and they thanked him profusely.

As the singer was about to leave, all of a sudden he got the inspiration to start singing. Immediately both of the burglars fell asleep. In the meantime the guard who was outside woke up since he was not in earshot of the singing.

When the guard saw the singer coming out of the bank, he said, "What were you doing inside the bank? What's going on in there?"

The singer said, "I don't know," and he ran away.

When the guard went inside, he found the two burglars sleeping and he caught them.

## MRC 22. *The miser's commitment*

There was once a rich man who was a real miser. He didn't trust anyone. He didn't love anyone. He wouldn't give anything to anyone as a gift. The man's wife was quite generous. Although she didn't have access to her husband's wealth and money-power, with her very limited resources she used to help people and give money to the poor.

Some people were very sympathetic to the wife because they knew that she had only limited means to help others. Others thought that she should have forced her husband to become a generous man or to give her more money so that she could use it in her own way. There were other people who were so callous that they used to ridicule her for having such a miserly husband. They didn't dare say anything to the rich man himself since they were afraid of him and his money-power. They felt that with his money-power he could create problems for them if he wanted to. Therefore, they didn't say anything to him directly, but they used to ridicule his wife mercilessly at times.

One day the wife was watering her garden when some neighbours happened to pass by and began making fun of her. They said, "Wc have heard that tomorrow your husband is going to give a big feast for hundreds of people. We shall come to his feast without fail."

The wife said, "I don't know a thing about it. Where did you hear it?"

They said, "You are telling a lie! Don't you know what is going to happen tomorrow in your own house? Anyway, tomorrow we shall come and hundreds of people will also come. Tomorrow your husband will really use his money-power in a proper way."

The wife answered, "Oh no, he will be generous only after his death."

The neighbours laughed and laughed at her and then went away. She went inside and told her husband, "Some neighbours told me that you are going to feed hundreds of people tomorrow. Is it true?"

He said, "Impossible! Impossible! What did you say to them?"

She said, "I told them that you would be generous only after your death."

This made the husband mad.

The wife asked, "Why are you mad? I said that you would be generous only after your death."

The husband said, "But that is a specific date. Why did you make a commitment? Now after I die I will have to think of people and feed them from Heaven. I am really angry and disappointed with you. You should never make any commitment on my behalf!"

MRC 23. *The thief's protector*

Once a thief was being chased by two policemen. They were running after him but they could not catch him. Finally, the thief entered into a house and asked the owner for protection. He told the owner, "I have lots of money. I will give you half if you save me."

The owner said, "Definitely I will save you, but you have to keep your promise."

It was evening, and the policemen had been two hundred metres behind the thief, so they did not see where he had gone. When they came to the house where the thief was hiding, they asked the owner, "Did you see a thief come in here?"

The man immediately said, "Where? On which side of the street did he come?" Then he started screaming loudly, "Thief! Thief!" The neighbours came out and joined the police in looking for him around the neighbourhood. The thief was not to be found anywhere, so the police were about to leave.

The owner of the house said, "I feel that one day the culprit will be caught. In God's creation if anybody does anything wrong, he will be caught. How I hate thieves. We work so hard to earn money. With greatest difficulty we earn money and then thieves come and steal it. Of all crimes I hate theft the most."

Then everyone went home, including the policemen. The man went back into his home and told the thief: "Look, everybody has gone away. I joined the party looking for the thief and I played my role most successfully. Now you have to give me half of the money you have."

The thief said, "A new idea has entered into my brain. From now on, I will never tell a lie or have anything to do with anybody who tells lies. I hate to see people telling lies. From now on if I see anyone telling lies, I will punish that person. Now, you are the first person I have seen telling lies."

The man said, "What? I have saved you!"

The thief said, "Yes, you told those people that you did not see me. You protected me, but you told them a lie. So you are the first person I have seen telling lies." Then the thief took out his revolver and said, "Now I am going to kill you."

The man started crying and the thief said, "Either allow me to kill you or let me leave your place peacefully."

The owner said, "Go away peacefully. I don't need your money. Please, just go."

### MRC 24. *The king and the traveller*

One day a king said to his minister, "I do not know what is actually happening in my kingdom. Unless I move around incognito, I will not know what my subjects are really thinking. People come and bow down to me and show me all kinds of respect, but their true nature I do not know. Let me try to find out the true nature of my subjects."

The minister said, "That is an excellent idea."

The king said, "This evening I am going to walk around my kingdom and I would like you to accompany me. We will move around in disguise like two ordinary men. Nobody will follow us. Only you and I will go."

The minister agreed. "That is a good idea. Then we will know what people are like in their true nature."

So that evening the king and the minister went out. As they were walking along, they happened to see a traveller. The traveller said to them, "I am very tired. Please tell me if there are any guest houses here where I can stay. I have no money."

The king said to him, "We don't know of any guest houses in our city."

The traveller exclaimed, "You do not have any guest houses? What kind of place is this? If you were to come to my city, you could easily find a place to stay!"

A middle-aged man was passing by and asked, "What is happening? May I take part in this conversation?" The man did not recognise the king at all.

The traveller said, "I am from another town and I am asking these two men if there is a guest house where I can take shelter tonight. They say there is no place. If you were to come to my city, there would be places for you to stay."

The man said, "These two are fools. They have no knowledge of our kingdom. Our king is so kind and generous. He has made us so good that we don't need any special guest houses. All the houses serve as guest houses. If you come with me, you will see what a nice host I am. Like that, you can go to any house. If you don't believe me, come with me and spend the night. These two are fools."

Then the man turned to the king and the minister and said, "You two live here and you do not know how kind and generous our king is? Our king would be shocked if he heard that a traveller could find no shelter here. Perhaps you two come from another city and that is why you don't know about our hospitality."

The king and the minister remained totally silent. Finally they said, "Can you tell us your name in case some other people ask for shelter? Then we will be able to recommend you. We have never seen such a kind-hearted man."

The man said, "I am sorry that the king has such fools in his kingdom like you two."

The man gave the king and minister his name and address and then brought the traveller with him to his house. The man kept his promise and offered the traveller excellent treatment.

The following day the king summoned the man to his palace. O God, when the soldiers arrived at his house to bring him to the palace, he got so frightened. He said, "What have I done wrong?"

When the man reached the palace the king said to him, "I was so moved by your kindness." The king told him the whole story and gave him a very large amount of money. Then he said, "I am ordering my workers to build many guest houses in my kingdom. I want my kingdom to be a place of hospitality. People should feel that I am really generous, which I am, but until now I haven't provided shelter for visitors. You have opened my eyes. From now on we shall have guest houses for all the travellers."

### MRC 25. *The minister's test*

There was a king who wanted to become really great. He said, "I shall conquer my neighbouring king."

His minister said to him, "O King, it is always good to remain peaceful. Why do you want to conquer another king?"

The king said, "If you speak to me like this, I will dispense with your services and get a new minister. Only a minister who listens to me and carries out all my wishes will I keep. Only tell me how I can conquer the other king."

The minister said, "But what has he done wrong?"

The king said, "The very fact that he is another king makes him a rival. I want only myself to be king and nobody else."

The minister told the king, "Whether or not you can conquer the other king entirely depends on the wisdom of the other king's minister."

"Yes, yes," said the king, "you are right. As I depend on your wisdom, the other king also has to depend on his minister. All right, tell me what you are going to do."

The minister said, "Let us make a test. Let us send a letter to the other king saying that we shall be extremely grateful if he could send us two men — one who makes his living by giving life to others, by helping others to have a sound life, and one who depends on the death of human beings to make his living. We will say that we have been looking everywhere in our kingdom for two men like this but have not been able to find them. If the king passes this test, then I tell you, it is useless to fight against him, for that king is really powerful."

The king got mad and said, "You are always saying that others are powerful and I am useless. You get out of my kingdom!"

The minister begged him, "O King, don't throw me out at my age. Allow me to make this test and see how the other king answers our letter."

So they sent the letter to the neighbouring king. When the other king received the letter he asked his minister what to do. The minister advised him to send a doctor and an undertaker. He said, "A doctor earns his livelihood by giving strength and life to people. He lives by helping others to have a sound life. An undertaker comes when people die, when they have to be buried. It is by the death of people that an undertaker lives."

So instead of answering the letter, the other king sent a doctor and an undertaker to the first king's palace.

When they arrived at the palace, the minister said to the king, "Don't try to conquer the other king. You will not succeed because that king is really wise. When a king can answer a question like this one, it is impossible to conquer him. Such wise people he has in his kingdom. With wise people you can't fight.

"O King, you can fire me if you wish. But no matter whom you take in my place, if that person advises you to fight against that other king, he will be making a very serious mistake. If you fight against intelligent people you will always lose."

### MRC 26. *Money-power surrenders to wisdom-power*

There was once a man who was very miserly, whereas his wife was very generous. But the wife did not have access to her husband's money. They had so much money that they could have easily helped the village that they lived in. For months people were suffering from drought and famine. Because of the drought, there was not enough food and people were dying of starvation. The wife begged the husband to dig some wells so that at least their neighbours could have water. But the husband did not want to spend money to dig wells.

The wife said, "Who knows, by digging in the ground, perhaps even I can find water."

So she asked their one servant to help her dig a well at a particular place. The wife, herself a respectable lady, also joined the servant in digging. Every day they would dig, but they did not find water at all. The husband laughed and laughed and said, "Yes, you will dig for a year and still there will be nothing. Only your stupidity-hole is becoming bigger."

One day the servant had a clever idea. He said, "Mother, we are trying so hard, but your husband is being so unkind and cruel. Let us play a trick."

"What kind of trick?" the wife asked.

The servant said, "Every morning your husband comes and laughs at us. Tomorrow also he will come. Let us put some oil on the ground where we are digging. When he sees the oil on the ground, he will get very excited. He will employ many workers and servants, thinking that oil may be found here. They will dig and dig. Who knows, perhaps there will be some water here."

The following day the husband came and saw the oil on the ground. He was so excited and said to himself, "I want to take the full credit for discovering oil." Then he said to his wife and servant, "Can you do me a favour today? Can you bring me something from the market? I will give you anything you want if you do me this favour."

His wife and servant went to the market to buy a few things for the husband. The wife was totally innocent. She had totally forgotten about the oil trick. She was just doing a favour for her husband. In the meantime, the husband brought twenty workers to continue digging at the same place so that he could get all the credit for discovering oil. They worked for a few hours and finally they found water.

The workers were so happy to find water, but the owner of the house was very disappointed. He said, "Who wanted to have water? I wanted to have oil so that I could sell it and become richer. How can I sell water? I can only give it away to my neighbours."

The wife and the servant came back from the market and they were so delighted and excited to see that water had been found. The husband said to them, "How can it be? This morning I actually saw oil on the ground. That's why I hired so many workers. This morning there was oil, but now there is only water."

The wife said, "Money-power surrenders to wisdom-power."

"What are you talking about?" asked the husband.

"This is all due to our servant's wisdom. We tried so hard to find water but we failed. Then he had a brilliant idea. He knows how miserly you are. He knew that if you saw oil on the ground where we were digging, then you would start digging a well looking for oil. God wanted you to help the needy. God didn't want you to become richer by discovering oil."

## MRC 27. *The kingdom's worst liar*

There was once a king's minister who was very jealous of the court jester because the king used to pay much attention to the jester and everybody used to appreciate the jester. It pained the king that although the minister held such a high post, still he was so jealous of the jester. The king said to himself, "Why should he be so insecure and jealous of this man?"

One day the king wanted to play a trick on the minister and humiliate him. He said to the minister, "I would like to have some entertainment. I would like the court jester to bring me the worst possible liar in my entire kingdom."

So the minister asked the court jester to bring the worst possible liar and said that the king would reward that person. The court jester went here and there and brought many different people to the palace.

One person told the king, "I have seen a lion flying in the sky."

Another person said, "I saw the sun and moon fighting like cats and dogs."

A third one said, "For the last few months my wife has not remembered my name. Many of my friends ask her what my name is, but she has totally forgotten, although she remembers everybody else's name."

The queen said, "I don't like this kind of entertainment. Why do people have to tell these kinds of lies? It is not good. You are the worst liar. You have been telling me for years that you will give me a new crown, but still you have not given me one. So you are a true liar."

The king said, "All right, I will give you a crown. But you can't be the worst possible liar because you have just stated a fact."

The queen said, "I don't want to be the worst liar. Again, I don't want to have such a stupid husband who enjoys trying to find the worst possible liar. This kind of game does not become you."

So the king and queen were arguing and everybody was enjoying it. Then the jester said, "Still I am not satisfied. Let us ask the minister." He turned to the minister and said, "You are the wisest of all. You don't know how much I admire you. Do you think you could tell us a lie?"

The minister became furious. He said, "How dare you ask me to tell a lie. I have never told a lie. My father and mother never told lies. My grandfather and grandmother and my great-grandfather and great-grandmother never told lies. I come from a family where there were no lies — only the truth. How do you dare to ask me to tell a lie!"

The jester turned to the king and said, "Your Highness, now I have found the man you are looking for. If you have real faith in me, then I wish to say that there can be no liar worse than this minister. He says that he has never told a lie and that his parents, grandparents and great-grandparents have never told a lie. Is it possible?"

So the king gave a prize to the court jester because he had discovered the greatest liar and another prize to the minister who had unconsciously proven himself to be the worst possible liar. One found the worst liar and the other unfortunately was caught.

## MRC 28. *The royal exhibition*

Once a king personally arranged an exhibition of all his wealth. All the jewels that he had collected during his life and also those that he had inherited from his parents and grandparents were displayed. Included in the exhibition was a most beautiful and valuable diamond ring called the Kohinoor diamond, which was displayed on a plate decorated with diamonds.

Ordinary subjects were not allowed to see the exhibition. Only those who were wealthy were allowed to go. Many distinguished people went.

One evening, many people were looking at the many beautiful objects and enjoying the display. All of a sudden, somebody noticed that the Kohinoor diamond ring was missing. The king was horrified to think that one of his many distinguished friends and relatives could have stolen the diamond. He asked his minister, "What should we do? This is so embarrassing."

The minister said, "We don't want to search anybody, because all the people here are your friends and relatives. Let us turn off all the lights, so that nobody will be able to see. Then, in the dark we can make an announcement asking whoever has taken the ring to quietly put it back. Let us not use the word 'stolen'. We will say, 'Whoever has taken the ring by mistake should quietly put it back on the plate'."

The king agreed that it was best not to expose the culprit. So they turned off all the lights and the minister said, "In five minutes I hope the one who has taken the ring by mistake will put it back." After five minutes the minister said, "Let us give a few more minutes for the person to return the diamond. Who knows, that person may not be near the place where the diamond was supposed to be."

After five more minutes the minister said, "Now we are turning on the lights, and to our deep joy I am sure we shall find that the ring has been returned."

They turned on the lights and all eyes turned to the place where the ring had been. O God, now the plate was also gone! The king got furious with the minister. He said, "Here I tried to avoid embarrassing my friends and relatives, and this is what has happened!"

The minister said, "I am sure at least that the fellow who has taken the plate is still here. The person who has taken the ring may not be here, but the fellow who has taken the plate must be here. Let us search everybody."

The king said, "No, I am now closing down the exhibition. God wants me to be wise. God wants me to know that I don't live with honest people. If even my friends and relatives are not honest, then I have to be careful."

### MRC 29. *The minister's trick*

There was once a kingdom where everybody had been living peacefully for years and years. One day a thief came into the kingdom and began creating problems for everyone. Every day reports would come in that something else had been stolen. The peace of the kingdom disappeared.

The king asked his minister to find the thief, but he could not find him. Finally, the king said to the minister, "If you can't find him, I will have to get another minister. Previously this was such a peaceful kingdom. Now it is full of suffering. Every day more people come to me and say that their things have been stolen."

The minister was afraid of losing his job, so he began praying to God to give him some Light from above. Then he went to the king and said, "Tomorrow I will catch the thief."

The king said, "Tomorrow?"

"Yes," said the minister. "I will catch him tomorrow."

The king was so delighted. The following day the minister ordered that an announcement be made throughout the kingdom that the thief would finally be caught. Then the minister bribed someone to say that he was the thief. He told him, "I will arrest you and bring you before the king. You will confess that you are the culprit. Don't worry, I will save you from any punishment. You take this money from me."

Everybody in the kingdom was talking about the minister's announcement. They were so happy and excited that the thief would finally be caught. Many people came to the palace so that they could see the bandit when the minister brought him to the king.

The next day, the minister rushed to the place with the "thief", acting so happy and excited that he had caught him. The king said to the man, "You have created so many problems. Such joy we once had in my kingdom. Now you deserve severe punishment."

The man said, "Whatever you want to do with me, I am ready, O King." Inwardly he had faith that the minister would save him.

The king said, "I am sentencing you to twenty years in jail."

Everybody in the palace applauded the king's decision. The minister said, "It is absolutely right that this fellow deserves a long punishment. But I have another idea."

"I am very interested to hear of another kind of punishment," said the king. "Please tell me your idea."

"You always tell me," said the minister, "that you want your kingdom to be the only peaceful kingdom. In other kingdoms you say you want unrest, unhappiness and misery. You want other subjects to suffer and your subjects alone to be happy."

"That is absolutely correct," said the king.

The minister continued, "Let us send this fellow into your worst enemy's kingdom. Let him create there the same problems that he has been creating here. Your kingdom will be full of peace again, just like before, and your enemy's kingdom will be full of suffering."

"It is an excellent idea!" exclaimed the king. "Let me give him lots of money since he will be doing us a favour."

The man was so excited to receive so much money from the king, and the king was so excited with the minister's new plan. All the people watching in the palace were happy that their kingdom would be peaceful once again, while the enemy's kingdom would be full of unrest and unhappiness.

So the minister, the thief and two guards set out to go to the other kingdom. When they reached the neutral territory between the two kingdoms, they let the thief go.

All of a sudden a very big, strong and stout bandit came out and attacked the so-called thief.

He said, "I was in the crowd at the palace observing everything that happened. How dare you get so much attention and money by saying you were the thief! It was I who used to steal and create all the problems. Now you have got so much money just to go to another kingdom. It is I who have stolen, but compared to what you have just received, I have got next to nothing. What you have got from the king you have to give me. Otherwise, I will kill you."

Immediately the guards who had been following the fake thief arrested the real one and brought him to the king. The minister said to the king, "Now we have got the real thief. We have caught him red-handed."

The king said, "What shall we do? Do you think we should kill him?"

The minister said, "If we send him to the enemy kingdom, it is not going to help us. God alone knows what he is going to do there. Since he is such a bad fellow, the best thing is for us to kill him."

So this is how the minister caught the thief and saved the kingdom. The minister knew that when the real thief came to learn how much attention the false thief was getting and how much money the king had given him, at that time he would not be able to remain silent.

### MRC 30. *The mistaken invitation*

There was once a king who had a big heart. Every month he used to invite some of his friends, a few of his ministers and selected officials from his cities to a special meal. He always gave them good meals and was happy that they enjoyed his food.

Once an invitation was sent to the wrong person — not to one of the officials of a city, but to a poor man. He came to the dinner and, O God, what did he do? He deliberately threw all the food off the expensive plate and started licking and biting the plate. The man didn't say a word. He refused to touch the food and just went on biting the plate. Everybody thought he was a crazy fellow and that something was wrong with him. Afterwards, as the man was leaving, the king followed him and asked him, "Why did you do this?"

The man said, "I am a poor man. There are thousands of poor people just like me. The ministers take your money and tell you that they are supplying us with food. But it is all lies. Like me, many are extremely poor. I have never seen that kind of plate or that kind of food. That is why I would not eat the food, and instead I was only biting the plate."

The king investigated and found that the man was telling the truth. He used to give money to his friends, to his ministers and to the city officials to give to these people, but they were all corrupt. After that he appointed new ministers and officials and he made this poor fellow who ate the plate his prime minister.

# IS YOUR MIND READY TO CRY?
# IS YOUR HEART READY TO SMILE?

## BOOK 4

## MRC 31. *The poet's head*

Once a king was very displeased with a particular poet because the poet was no longer writing flattering poems about him.

The king said to his guard, "I want his head."

So the guard went to the poet's house and said, "The king wants your head. I have come here to cut off your head and take it back to the king."

"What!" said the poet.

"I have come to kill you and place your head at the feet of the king," the guard said.

The poet started trembling. He said, "The king wants my head? To me, my most precious possession is my head. How can I give such a precious thing to you to give to the king? I must give it to him personally. Yes, I think that it would be better if I brought my head personally."

So he went to the king and said, "Now I have come with my head. Here is my head. You can do anything you want with it."

The king was pleased at how smart the poet was and he forgave him. "Now write better poems about me than you have written in the past few months!" he said.

## MRC 32. *The king and the sage*

Once there was a king who was always fighting. One day the king was severely wounded in a battle. A sage passed by and touched him, and the king was cured. The king wanted to give the sage a reward for saving him, but the sage didn't want anything. He was just happy to save the king.

The king said, "I don't want to remain indebted to you for saving my life."

The sage said, "In the future I will definitely come to you and ask for something. I do not need anything now, but one day I will come to you."

Months passed by and the sage was only praying to God for Peace, Light and Bliss. Then a desire entered into the sage's mind. For the past few months his cow had not been giving milk. "My cow is old," he said. "Let me ask the king to give me a cow. He will definitely give me a cow."

He went to see the king and found him inside a temple. The king was praying for more wealth and more name and fame.

The sage said to himself, "I won't ask him for a cow. He is also a beggar like me." Then he was about to go away.

The king stopped him and said, "Sage, you saved my life. Please tell me what you want. I will give you anything you want."

The sage said, "I pray to God and meditate on God. He is the only thing that I need. I don't want to take anything from anyone in need. You say you took an oath that you would not remain indebted to anyone. I have also taken an oath. My oath is that if anyone is in need, then I will not take anything from that person. That is why I won't take anything from you. You are praying to God for all kinds of material things. You are begging God to give you wealth and name and fame. So how can I ask anything of you? God has shown me that everyone is a beggar. So if I need something, I will get that thing only from Him. God is the only one I will go to get whatever I need."

## MRC 33. *The doctor's satchel*

In a particular village in India there was only one doctor, so naturally all those in the village held the doctor in great esteem. One day the doctor was called upon to visit a villager who was quite ill. In addition to fever and other ailments, the man had pains around the navel. He had been suffering for a long time.

When the doctor arrived at the man's house, all the members of the family were surrounding the patient, very worried. The doctor saw that the illness might be serious and he ordered them all to leave the room. "Out, out!" he said. "You can't stay in the room while I examine the patient. The case is serious."

So the members of the family left the room and waited anxiously in the next room for news about the patient. After a few minutes, the doctor was heard unlocking the bedroom door and his head appeared through the doorway looking grave. He said, "Bring me a chisel."

The son ran and got a chisel and delivered it to the doctor while the rest of the family wept. The doctor once again closed and locked the door.

Five minutes later, the doctor again broke the silence. He put his head through the doorway and this time demanded a hammer. "This case is more serious than I had thought," he said. After being given the hammer, the doctor again closed and locked the door.

The son turned to the uncle and said, "O God, something is wrong with his ribs. Uncle, it's so serious!" With that the whole family began weeping again.

Then the door opened and the doctor said, "Crowbar! Bring me a crowbar!" Upon receiving the crowbar, the doctor disappeared behind the locked door.

Quite some time passed and still there was no news from the doctor. The family became very uneasy and restless. The son said to the mother, "Mother, how is it that the doctor is not coming out? How is it that he is not asking for something? What if Father is dead? Why should the doctor be the only one to see Father when he is dying? We should also be with him. Father has not even written a will!"

Suddenly the boy went to the door and said, "We want to be able to see our father." And with that he broke the door down.

Upon entering the room they all saw the doctor bending over his satchel, trying fervently to open the malfunctioning lock on it. He had not even begun to treat the patient. Looking up quite embarrassed, the doctor ran out of the house, leaving satchel and all.

The family called in another doctor from a neighbouring village to treat the man.

## MRC 34. *The roaring tiger*

Once a young man was returning after visiting his maternal uncle's home. It was getting dark and he still had to cover five more miles, so he was getting a little worried. Then he saw a carriage and a driver about a hundred metres in front of him. The driver was sleeping inside the coach and his boss was resting in a field nearby.

The young man said to the driver, "Will you give me a ride in the carriage? Still my home is quite far and it is getting dark."

The driver said, "How dare you even ask such a thing! I have to stay with my boss. What kind of audacity you have!"

The young man said, "Will you take me if I pay you?"

The driver asked, "How much can you pay me?"

"One rupee," said the young man.

The driver laughed and laughed and laughed. Then the young man said, "Can you not ask your boss? Your boss may be generous."

The driver saw that his boss was still sleeping and he didn't dare to disturb him. So he told the young man, "I am sorry, but how can I wake up my boss? I can't ask him."

Then the young man started coughing uncontrollably. The boss heard the coughing and woke up. With folded hands the young man went to him and said, "Please forgive me for waking you, but I have no control over my cough. I understand that you are going past my village. You live a little farther away than I do. Will you be able to take me? I will give you money."

The boss laughed at the young man. He was such a rich man that he certainly didn't need this poor man's money. But he didn't want this fellow to go with him, so he asked him, "How much can you give me?"

The young man said, "One rupee."

Again the rich man laughed and laughed. Then he said, "Unless you give me a hundred rupees, I will not take you."

"How can you ask for a hundred rupees?" said the young man. "At most I can pay only three or four rupees. I have very little money. That's why I am offering you only one rupee." Then the young man said, "I tell you, I have a very special capacity. If you take me, I will be able to show you this capacity."

The rich man asked, "What special capacity do you have? Why don't you show me now?"

The young man said, "No! Only if you take me in your carriage will I show you."

The rich man said, "Either you have to show me the capacity now or pay one hundred rupees if you want me to take you home."

The young man said, "I don't have one hundred rupees and I will show you the capacity only after we are in the coach."

By this time it was quite dark. The rich man said, "Then I am going away." Then he said to his driver, "Let me take a little more rest. Don't bother me again with this kind of rascal! For half an hour I will lie down in the field and get some proper rest. In half an hour wake me up and then we shall go home."

After five minutes, all of a sudden the rich man and his coachman heard a tiger roaring nearby and they started trembling. They looked around to see where the noise was coming from. The tiger roared more and more powerfully. The carriage was about a hundred and fifty metres away from them, so they didn't dare run to it.

At one point the roaring stopped. The rich man said, "This is the time for us to enter into the coach. Then please drive as fast as possible before the tiger comes back and attacks us."

They ran to the coach and drove away as fast as possible. When they came to the village where the young man lived, all of a sudden they saw the young man jump off the rear of the carriage. He had been secretly standing there while they were driving.

As the young man jumped off, he started roaring like a tiger. The young man said, "Now you have found the tiger. I told you that I had a special capacity. My special capacity is that I can roar like a tiger." Then he threw one rupee into the carriage.

### MRC 35. *The businessman's punishment*

Once there was a businessman who was a real rogue. He used to sell clarified butter or ghee. But he would sell adulterated butter and the people who ate it would get sick. Many people actually died from the butter. So some people sued him and the case went to the village head.

The village head said, "Get a jar of his butter and I will make him drink it in front of us. Since his ghee has caused so many people to suffer, he must drink some of it himself."

They brought the clarified butter for him to drink, but the businessman said, "I am going to the magistrate, the higher court. Let him decide what I should do."

When the magistrate heard the story he said, "Either drink this ghee, or you will be whipped five hundred times. Choose one of the two."

The businessman said, "Oh no, I am not going to drink this and I do not want to be whipped. I am now going to bring my case to the governor. The governor has to decide my punishment."

When the governor heard the case he said, "If you pay a fine of two thousand rupees, then you don't have to drink the ghee or be whipped. You make the choice."

The businessman said, "I don't want to pay anything and I don't want to be whipped. So I shall drink the butter." He started drinking the ghee, but after drinking only half of it, he was feeling so miserable that he could not finish it.

The governor said, "Look, this is what you used to give others to eat!

The businessman said, "Since I can't finish the butter and I don't want to pay any money, let me be whipped. But since I have drunk half the ghee, let me take only half the whipping. Let me be whipped two hundred and fifty times instead of five hundred."

After being whipped a hundred times, the man was crying and screaming. He said, "Now I am ready to pay. But let it be only a thousand rupees, since I have already got part of the punishment."

So the businessman drank the butter, suffered a whipping and had to pay money. In the end he got the punishment of the village head, the magistrate and the governor.

## MRC 36. *The three braggarts*

Once three friends were bragging about their younger days in the army. Two of them were saying that when they were soldiers they had killed many, many people. All three of them were at a friend's house and all the members of the friend's family — the parents, children and grandchildren — were all listening to them with deep admiration.

One of the men said that he had cut off the legs of a giant who was extremely powerful. The other one said, "True, I saw it. But just before he cut off his legs I cut off his arms."

The first one said, "It was much more important to cut off his legs. Because I cut off his legs, the giant could no longer move around and appreciate the beauty of nature. Without hands and arms, one can still see the beautiful and vast world. But because of me, this extremely powerful giant could no longer walk!"

The second one said, "That is true. But even without legs one can still grasp things. Because I cut off his arms, the giant could no longer eat food or in any way lead a useful life. What I did was infinitely more significant than cutting off his legs."

The third one had all along remained silent. Finally he said, "It is true that one of them cut off the arms and the other cut off the legs. But do you know how they were able to do this? They were able to do this because I cut off the giant's head first. Once I cut off his head, naturally they could easily cut off his arms and legs."

## MRC 37. *The two dreamers*

Once there were two wonderful dreamers. One was the head of the village and the other was a tax collector. They used to dream every night about the king. The king used to come to the village chief in his dreams and tell him what to do every day with regard to the village. The king also would come to the tax collector in his dreams and say how much money he should collect every day from the villagers. Very peacefully this went on for some time. The villagers had great faith in these two.

One day the village chief was crying and crying because he hadn't dreamt about the king that night and he didn't know how to guide the villagers. He said, "Last night I didn't have any dream, so today I will do everything wrong. Please don't listen to me."

The villagers said, "Since you have been listening to the king so regularly, if for one day he doesn't come, no harm. We are sure that you will do what the king would have wanted you to do."

The chief replied, "The king has always come before. That is how I am able to guide you. But now what am I going to do?"

Everyone was very sad because they were not getting any guidance from the village chief, and nobody was working. When the tax collector came to know what had happened, he became worried. Since the taxes were collected on a daily basis, if nobody worked that day there would be no tax collections.

The tax collector was very clever. He went to the chief and said, "Do you know why the king did not come to you last night? It is because he spent the whole night with me. He was giving me so much advice about taxes that he was not able to come to your house."

Everybody was so happy that the king had spent the whole night with the tax collector. Still, the people were asking the chief, "What should we do today? The day is passing and you haven't given any of us jobs. If we don't make money, how can we pay the taxes?"

The chief said again, "No, I can't give you jobs today because I have not seen the king. I will not be able to give you any work."

The tax collector said, "The king has told me how much money to collect today. Even if you don't work and get paid, the king said you still have to pay taxes."

The people had such faith in the tax collector because they had so much faith in the king. They said, "Whatever the king has said, we shall do. Let us pay the taxes." So they had to pay taxes even though they were not working that day.

### MRC 38. *The rich mendicant*

There was once a businessman who had become a millionaire by adopting both fair means and foul means. He did not always do the right thing, but he did become very rich. When he reached the age of sixty he decided he wanted to change his life. In India, sixty is considered very old. When he told his wife, his children and his relatives that he wanted to become a religious mendicant, the members of his family all started crying.

His wife said, "If you are leaving, then you have to take me. Without my husband, how can I exist?"

His son said, "How will we be able to reach you when we need you? How can one get in touch with a mendicant roaming from one place to another? If you get a special place to stay, then several times a week we will be able to visit you. I will build you a cottage where you will be able to lead a spiritual life peacefully. Even if it is only a cottage, let me build it for you."

So the son made a very comfortable home for his father. Since his son had made it, what could the mendicant do? He had to use it.

Daily the wife used to send food for the husband. One day he said, "This is too much luxury. I don't want to eat the food that my wife sends. If this continues, I will end up having a comfortable life again. Whatever I get from begging on the street, I will eat." But his wife played a trick on him. She gave money to all the families living near his cottage and told them, "Every day he will go from door to door begging for food and I wish you to be very generous to him." So every day the villagers gave him lots of food, sweets and nice things.

The mendicant said, "I thought that I would be leading a very simple life. But whenever I go begging, everyone gives me most expensive things. O God, still I am leading such a comfortable life. Did I leave my house only to lead this same kind of life?"

Then one night he dreamt that Lord Indra sent a chariot to come for him. His time had come. But his wife said, "I must go also." The son also wanted to come and said, "But how can I go without my wife?" He had been recently married and he could not bear to be away from his new bride. The mendicant's mother also wanted to come. But she said, "O God, I also have another son. If I go away with this one, what will he think of me? Let him also come with us and his wife and children too." So everyone piled into the chariot. As soon as they all sat down, the chariot gave way; it broke into pieces. In the dream he jumped up and his own life-cord broke. What actually happened is that he jumped up from the bed and his own bed collapsed.

He said, "From this dream I see that God wants me to go alone to Heaven. That means God wants me to become a real mendicant." This time he left the village without telling his family where he was going and he lived the life of a true mendicant.

MRC 39. *The saintly scholar*

There was a great scholar who was very saintly. His wife was nice, but she was earthly whereas the scholar was all the time talking about philosophy, spirituality and all kinds of religious things. Although he was such a great scholar, he was very poor because he wouldn't take money from anyone. Whenever he taught he wouldn't accept money from his students. In wisdom he was like the Pacific Ocean, but he was absolutely poverty-stricken.

One day some of his students went to the king and said, "Your kingdom has such a great scholar. Other kings would die to have such a great scholar in their kingdom. Can you not give this man lots of money so that he will not have to live such a poor life? Then he will be able to concentrate more on his studies and become more learned. There is not a single scholar anywhere who is as great as he is."

The king was very happy to have this kind of scholar in his kingdom. So he sent a very large amount of money to the scholar through one of the scholar's admirers. The king also sent a message appreciating the scholar very highly.

When the scholar received the gift from the king, he said to his admirer, "I can never accept the king's money."

His wife immediately said, "You fool! If you take the king's money, you won't have to work any more. We are so poor. You must take his gift!"

The scholar said, "If my admirer doesn't take it back, I will take it back personally."

The wife said, "You are such a fool. You spend so many hours helping others and you take next to nothing for it. Now the king has given you money so that you can lead a comfortable life and not worry about ordinary necessities. Why won't you accept his gift and appreciation?"

The scholar said, "Look what kind of king we have. The king has given me money because some people have spoken highly of me. Before my admirers went to him, he had never heard of me. He didn't even know that there was a great scholar in his kingdom. Today he heard from someone that I am very great, so he gave me a reward. But he just sent the money; he did not even want to make any direct contact. He could have invited me to come to his palace so that he could see me, but he believed my admirers. Tomorrow some people may speak ill of me and he will hear that I am really very bad. Then he may punish me. Therefore, I will not accept his money."

### MRC 40. *The pirate and the king*

There was once a pirate who used to rob, torture and kill people who were voyaging on the sea. Everybody was very afraid of him. Many complaints went to the king about him, but nobody could catch him. Finally the king said, "I am going to go and capture him myself." So he went to sea with many bodyguards and sailors and finally caught the pirate.

The king told the pirate, "You are such a useless fellow. You have tortured so many people for so many years. Now you should be hanged."

The pirate said, "I am going to be hanged? Before I am hanged, you should be hanged."

Everybody was shocked. The pirate continued, "I have killed a few people here and there. But you are a far greater rogue than I am. You are not satisfied with ruling your own country. You go and conquer other countries and kill thousands of people. You do infinitely worse things than I do."

The king said nothing. Then he gave the pirate a large sum of money and said, "For God's sake, give up this pilferage. If money is what you need, here is money. But if what you want is to torture and kill people, then I can't be of any help. If I hear any more complaints, I will arrest you and definitely have you killed."

The pirate said, "Remember, you are doing the same thing."

Again the king remained silent. Then he said, "Come with me. I want you to work at the palace. Since you are physically so strong, you can be my bodyguard."

# IS YOUR MIND READY TO CRY?
# IS YOUR HEART READY TO SMILE?

## BOOK 5

## MRC 41. *Two brothers*

There were two brothers who were very fond of each other. One of them was a hard worker. The other was a very lazy fellow who always stayed home and slept. But the hard worker never blamed the lazy one. He always said, "God made him like that. What can he do? God also made me kind and affectionate to him. I will always work and do everything for him."

Both of them were married. The wife of the lazy one did not appreciate the fact that her husband did nothing for her. He did nothing for the family either, and the relatives always ridiculed the wife. The wife felt miserable that her husband was so useless, whereas his brother worked so hard. Everybody always appreciated the brother.

The wife repeatedly begged her husband to start working. Finally he agreed and found a job. Soon he was working day and night. Everybody was pleased with him and appreciated him.

Suddenly the nice brother who had always worked hard stopped working. Now he began wasting his time just like his brother used to do.

This brother's wife became sad and mad. She said, "Everybody is appreciating your brother now and not you." She begged her husband to go back to work.

He said, "No! In this world we share our good and bad qualities. When I am perfect, he is imperfect. When he is perfect, I am imperfect. Since we are one, it has to be that way. This is how the world goes on.

"It is like day and night, light and darkness. When there is darkness, then only will people appreciate light. If there is only light, nobody is going to appreciate it. When my brother is darkness and I am light, at that time everybody appreciates how good I am. And when I am darkness and he is light, everybody appreciates how good he is.

"So in order to get real appreciation, one of us has to play the role of ignorance and the other has to play the role of wisdom. We share these roles equally. We are close brothers. This is how we want to go on. After some time if he becomes lazy again, then I will go back to work. Wisdom and ignorance must go together, just as darkness and light must go together."

### MRC 42. *The hermit and the king's wealth*

A king once wanted to go hunting in the forest. On the way he stopped at a hermit's cottage. The king gave the hermit some expensive jewels and other things and said, "Now I am entering into the forest to hunt and I don't want to take these expensive things with me. Will you take care of them for me?"

The hermit said, "I will, because you are such a nice king."

The king said, "Do you want me to leave some guards to protect you?"

The hermit said, "It is a good idea to have guards. But I would appreciate it if the guards do not stay near my house. I would like them to stand so that I cannot see them. I don't want to be bothered by them. I want only to pray and meditate. I am only a simple hermit. If people see your guards near my house, they may think that I have got expensive things here. Why not give your belongings to your guards in the first place? Then I won't have to worry. Money creates such worries and anxieties!"

The king said, "I would like you, and not my guards, to keep my jewels. I am not pure, but I would like my possessions to become pure by remaining with you. You are a saint. If I give these things to you, then my golden rings and diamonds will become pure."

So the saint agreed to keep the expensive things until the king came back. O God, in two hours' time four hooligans passed by. They had never been to the hermit's house, but when they saw the king's guards moving around, the hooligans thought that perhaps the hermit had something valuable. They decided to wait a few hours. Then, if the guards fell asleep, that would be the time for them to enter into the hermit's house and see what was there. After all, if there was nothing expensive, why would there be guards?

In three hours the guards fell asleep on the ground outside the house. The four hooligans went inside the hermit's cottage and asked the hermit to give them whatever he had. They said, "We are sure you have expensive things because we saw those guards. If you have got anything from the king, give it to us. But if you make any noise, then we shall kill you!"

The hermit said, "I don't want to hide anything from you. Here are the king's jewels. You take them. But mind you, you are only four persons. The king has many soldiers and one day you will be caught."

The hooligans laughed and laughed. While they were laughing so loudly at what the hermit had said, the guards woke up and caught them.

The hermit said, "What can I do? The king gave these jewels to me and these hooligans wanted them. They didn't believe me when I said they would be caught."

The guards wanted to thrash the bandits. Although they had got back the jewels, still they wanted to punish the hooligans. But the hermit said, "Please do me a favour. Since they were unable to take anything, you must forgive them. The king has got his possessions back, so the best thing is to forgive them.

"It is really your fault that these hooligans came into my house. It is only because you were asleep that they were able to enter. What were you doing when they came in? Who asked you to fall asleep? Since you were not dependable, since you did not do your duty, how can you expect these hooligans to be good?

"If the king finds out that they came into the house because you were asleep, he will be very mad at you. So if you punish the thieves, you yourselves will be punished. In every way it is better for them to go away without being punished."

The guards listened to the hermit's judgement.

### MRC 43. *The three hosts*

One day a king and his minister went out for a walk incognito. The king said to the minister, "I really want to give something nice to everyone who is nice to us during our walk. I will give some reward to anyone who is hospitable."

The king and the minister went up to one man and said, "We are two travellers. This is such a nice town and we would like to spend the night here. Do you think we could stay at your house as guests?"

The man insulted them, saying, "How do I know that you are not bad people?"

Then the king and the minister went up and knocked on somebody else's door. When the man opened the door they asked, "Do you think we can spend the night here? We are travellers and now it is getting dark."

The man said, "First tell me how many of you there are. Then I will say if I can allow you to stay."

The king said, "You see that we are only two. We do not have much money, but if you allow us to stay with you, before we leave tomorrow morning we will give you some money."

Then the king said, "Still it is somewhat light out, and your country is so beautiful. We will just walk around a little more and come back in an hour or so."

So the king and minister continued walking. They approached another house and knocked on the door. The king said, "We are two travellers. It is getting dark. Could we spend the night at your house?"

The man said, "Certainly! Just tell me how many of you there are."

The king said, "You can see that we are only two." The king told that person also that they would come back in an hour or two. Then they went back to the palace.

The minister had taken down the address of each person to whom they had spoken, and the following day the king summoned all three persons to the palace. To the one who had insulted him the king said, "I don't need you in my kingdom. When travellers come from a different kingdom, if you don't give them shelter it is very bad. You could see that we were respectable people. We were not thieves." So the king threw the man out of his kingdom.

To the second man the king gave a very large amount of money. To the third one, who immediately offered shelter and only afterwards asked how many were in their party, the king gave his crown.

He told the man, "In this kingdom we need the kind of people who offer everything without any hesitation and only then seek to determine how much is necessary. When we approached you, you didn't ask how many were in our party. You just said, 'Come, come!' The other man first asked how many we had. If we had had more people, he might not have agreed to shelter us. We need more people like you."

So the third man received the crown from the king and took it home as his most treasured possession.

## MRC 44. *The two wild ducks*

A hunter once took his wife hunting with him in a forest, and there he killed two wild ducks. Both he and his wife were very happy and excited. The wife said, "I will make a most delicious meal from these two ducks."

While they were on their way home, the head of the village saw them and asked, "Where are you going? I see you have two ducks. You have to sell them to me!"

Since he was the village head, what could they do? They couldn't argue with him; otherwise, he would create such problems for them! After the village head bought the ducks for a large amount of money, the wife said to him, "Since these are most special ducks, I hope your cook knows how to cook them in a very special way." Inwardly she was very sad and mad that they had met the village head.

The village head said, "You are saying these ducks are very special, but my wife died about a year ago and my cook does not cook well. Do you think you would be able to cook them for me? I will pay you."

The woman said to herself, "If I say no, then we will be in trouble." So she told the village head, "I will cook on the condition that you make everything ready for me, and also that your cook does not stay in the kitchen while I am preparing the duck. I don't want him to learn from me. I want to be the only good cook."

The village head said, "My cook will leave the ingredients for you and he will not stay in the kitchen."

So the wife agreed. The village head took the ducks home and the husband and wife went to their own house. The husband was cursing his wife. He said, "Why did you agree? This is an insult to my pride. First of all, I had to give the ducks to him.

Secondly, my wife now has to go and work at somebody else's house like a servant."

The wife said, "I am not acting like a servant. I am only doing him a favour. But don't worry. You will eat the duck."

The man said, "I do not think that he will give me any."

The wife said, "I tell you, you will get the full amount."

The husband said, "All right, let me see your capacity."

The following day the wife went to the village head's home and started cooking a most delicious meal. The cook was not there. The village head came in from time to time to watch.

He asked, "In an hour will I be able to eat?"

She said, "That is absolutely true."

At one point the husband came to see if everything was going well. At that time the village head was upstairs. The wife asked her husband, "Did you see anybody on the street?"

The husband said, "Yes, I saw a soldier sleeping by the side of the road."

The wife said, "When the village head comes back downstairs, tell him that a high-ranking officer is sleeping nearby. Say that if he invites that man to eat here, the officer will be so pleased that he will tell the king about him. He will say that this village head is a very nice man and the king will definitely give him a higher post. The king may even make him head of a city rather than just a village."

In a few minutes, when the village head came downstairs, the husband said, "I came here to ask my wife if everything is going all right. On my way, I saw a high-ranking officer sleeping. He would be so pleased with you if you invited him to eat, especially since my wife is such an excellent cook. If he tells the king, the king may give you a very high post."

The village head agreed. So the husband went and woke up the officer and invited him to eat. Then the husband went back home.

After the village head welcomed the officer, he went into the kitchen to ask the wife to bring the food. She told him, "I have been cooking here for such a long time. My clothes are now dirty and filthy and I didn't bring an extra change of clothes. Do you not think it will look nicer if I serve the food in clean clothes? Then the officer will feel that your maid is clean and beautiful. Then in every way you will be able to please him."

The village head said, "Then let me hurry to your house and bring you a change of clothes from your husband."

As soon as he left, the wife went to the officer and started crying. "What is the matter?" asked the officer.

"I am not crying for myself, but for you," she said.

"I am a great officer," he said. "Nothing is going to happen to me."

The wife said, "Do not be so sure. This man is physically very strong. Of course, you know your own capacity. But every year on this particular day, this man invites one or two guests. And what does he do?" Then the wife started crying again.

"Please tell me," said the officer.

The wife said, "He takes out their eyes. Everybody has a hobby. This is his hobby!"

"Is this a joke?" asked the officer.

"No," said the wife. "If I ask my husband, my husband will be able to tell you the names of all the people that he has done this to. When he becomes mad, he can easily handle three or four persons. If you feel that you are stronger than he is, then stay and fight. You are such a big officer."

The officer asked, "Why do you work here?"

The wife said, "I don't work here. Only today the servant has not come and because he is the village head, I had to help him. But you do not have to stay. It may hurt your pride to leave, but that would be the wise thing."

The officer said, "Wisdom is always best. The best thing is to leave."

The village head was just returning as the officer was leaving. "Have you eaten?" asked the village head.

The officer immediately began running away. The village head said, "He should at least take one of the ducks," and he started running after him. He shouted at the officer, "Wait, wait, I will only take one." The officer thought he meant that he would take only one eye instead of both, and he ran even faster.

While the village head was chasing the officer, the wife packed up both ducks and took them to her own house.

When the village head came back, after getting disgusted at having to chase the officer, to his surprise he saw that nothing was left. The wife said to him, "I am so sorry that the soldier ate everything. When I asked him to wait, he didn't listen to me and ate everything himself. I am only a woman, so what could I do?"

## MRC 45. *The man without desires*

Once a king wanted to know who was the happiest person on earth. Although everybody always flattered him, he knew how unhappy he was. When his subjects didn't listen to him, he felt miserable. So the king asked one of his ministers, "Who is the happiest person on earth?"

The minister answered, "He who can drink nectar. He who can bring down Heaven to earth."

The king said, "I am disgusted with you! What kind of answer is this?"

The minister said, "He who can see God is the happiest person."

"Yes," said the king. "But who can see God? Give me a better answer."

This time the minister said, "He who has conquered desire."

The king said, "This is all philosophy."

"Then," said the minister, "he who has fulfilled his desires."

"Yes," said the king. "When our desires are fulfilled, we are very, very happy."

"But he is really the happiest," said the minister, "who has conquered his desires. You may say this is all philosophy, but perhaps there are some sages who have actually conquered their desires. There are people on earth who are praying and meditating. Perhaps for them this is not philosophy at all; it is reality."

"Go and bring them!" said the king.

So the minister left the palace in search of some holy men. He saw some persons very sincerely praying and meditating. He went over to one man and begged him to come to see the king. He said, "The king wants to see a man who has conquered his desires. Please come to show the king that you don't care for earthly pleasures."

The sage said, "All right, if he wants me to come, I have to go."

The man came with the minister and the king was very pleased with him. The sage was very simple, very innocent and very pure.

Another minister, who was very shrewd, became jealous of the first minister. He did not want the first minister to be admired by the king. So he said to the king, "I am so happy that my friend has brought you someone who has conquered his desires. But I forgot to tell you that just now the Queen has sent a message that she needs you desperately for something. She wants to know if it would be possible for you to come and see her privately. Since you have to go and see her, perhaps this man can come back tomorrow."

The king said, "Yes, the best thing is for me to see him tomorrow."

The minister who had brought the sage asked the man if he could come back the next day and the sage agreed.

The following day, when the sage again came before the king, the rogue minister greeted him before the other minister arrived. He said, "So you have come!"

"Why not?" asked the sage.

"We are glad to see that you have conquered your desires," said the minister. "But why have you come here? What for?" In this way the rogue minister challenged the sage.

The sage finally got annoyed and said, "Yesterday the king invited me and I promised that I would come here to prove that I am a desireless man. I am a desireless man and I want to prove it."

The minister said to the king, "That means that he still has an eagerness to prove that he is desireless. He has this desire. Otherwise, why would he care about what you think? His desire is to prove that he is without desire. So he is not a desireless person."

The king said, "It is true. He has not conquered his desires."

The sage could have said that the king had invited him to come, so he was listening to the king's request, or he could have said that it was the king's desire that he was fulfilling. But instead the man got annoyed with the minister and didn't think about what he was saying. Then he was caught.

MRC 46. *The prince and the battle*

Once there was a king who was very jealous of another king. So the jealous king increased the size of his army and asked his minister to get ready to fight. He said, "In a few days' time we shall go to conquer our enemy."

The minister said, "O King, that king is very powerful. Even in summer it would be difficult to conquer him. Now it is winter. We will have such trouble! Can you not wait for winter to pass by?"

The king became angry. He said, "You have to listen to me! Otherwise, I will find another minister."

"I am giving you good advice," said the minister. "If we fight during the winter we may lose. But I am always at your command. You know what is best for your kingdom. I shall work very, very hard and in a few days' time everything will be ready."

Then the minister went to the prince. He showed him a very sad face and started weeping. The prince said, "My father likes you very much. But if you weep, what will people think of you?"

The minister said to the prince, "What should I do?"

The prince said, "You are my father's advisor, and you want me to be your advisor?"

The minister said, "Your father wants to wage war against a neighbouring king. But in winter it is always cold and raining. So how is your father going to win? He says he will fire me if I don't prepare for battle. But I have such love for your father that I want to stop him from waging war now even if he fires me. If he fights now, he will definitely lose."

The prince said, "Tomorrow I will save you. My father is always very affectionate to me, and he always listens to my loving demands." The minister was so happy that the prince was going to save him.

The following morning the prince dug a small hole in the ground and put a mango seed inside the hole. Then he covered it with dirt and started watering it.

When the king saw him he said, "Why are you watering the ground?"

The prince explained, "There is a mango seed there."

The father said, "Since it is winter there will be plenty of water. It rains so many times during winter."

The son said, "Father, if I do this, then it will expedite its growth. If the mango plant ordinarily comes up in three months' time, will it not come up in two or three days if I water it more?"

The father said, "You fool! In the rainy season more water is not needed at all. If you continue to water it, the hole will fill up with water and perhaps the mango seed will come out of the ground."

The prince said, "Father, in winter every day it rains. When it is pouring people can't see anything at all. Yet this is the time you are planning to attack somebody else's kingdom. The enemy has shelter and food supplies, whereas you will have no shelter or supplies at all. So how are you going to conquer his kingdom? You will see that you will lose because of the rain.

"It is like watering this mango seed. I can't expedite the growth of the plant no matter how much water I put on it. The seed will only come out of the ground instead of growing into a plant. The water will work to my disadvantage. Similarly, if it is raining and your soldiers attack the other king, they will be destroyed. No matter how many soldiers you send, they will all be killed.

"If you show your capacity in the spring, then you will be able to win. But if you go in the winter, you will only bring disgrace to your kingdom."

The father believed the son and called off the attack.

## MRC 47. *Donkeys and dreamers*

Once there was a king who asked his minister to bring to the court as many people as possible who could tell him fascinating dreams. He wanted to get joy from hearing their dreams. He said, "There are so many people who have had inspiring and challenging dreams. I will reward them if they tell me their wonderful dreams. Bring hundreds of dreamers to the palace!"

The minister said, "But your Highness, it will take days to hear all of their dreams."

The king said, "No harm. From now on I will spend every minute listening to people's dreams."

The following morning the minister brought in front of the palace seven hundred donkeys. He said to the king, "O King, I went to these donkeys and asked them what their special talents were. All these donkeys told me that they can sing and play music well. Now I am very curious to hear them, and you also must be very curious to hear them."

"You won't like the music or get joy from it," said the king.

"Why not?" asked the minister. "The hundreds of idle dreamers you have asked for are in no way better than these donkeys. These donkeys at least are useful to others since they carry all kinds of loads. But these idiots I am going to bring tonight are absolutely useless people. Their dreams have nothing to do with reality. It is all fabrication. Do you not think that those dreamers are worse than these donkeys? Why do you want to bring useless people to your court? Only if you bring useful people will your subjects be proud of you. Otherwise, what will people think of you?"

The king said, "You are wise. Let us not invite those dreamers to the palace. Now take away your donkeys."

MRC 48. *The gods gain Immortality*

Brihaspati is the Guru of the gods and Sukaracharya is the Guru of the demons. Brihaspati's and Sukaracharya's disciples often used to fight. At that time Sukaracharya had a special power that Brihaspati did not have. Sukaracharya knew a particular mantra that could bring his soldiers back to life after they had been killed on the battlefield. The cosmic gods felt miserable that Brihaspati did not have that capacity. In other ways — in wisdom, compassion, forgiveness and other good qualities — Brihaspati was far superior to Sukaracharya. In wisdom-light he was superior to everybody. But in this one thing Sukaracharya surpassed him.

So the gods said to Brihaspati, "Your son Coch is so brilliant. Can he not go and learn that mantra from Sukaracharya? He can become Sukaracharya's student and please him in every way. Then Sukaracharya will teach him the mantra."

The gods were very tricky. They didn't tell Coch the real reason they were sending him to Sukaracharya. They said they were sending him there to become a devoted student and to learn how to use weapons and other things. Coch was an innocent fellow and he had no idea of what the gods had in mind. So he went to Sukaracharya and asked to become his student. In those days, even if someone was your enemy, if you went to him as a student that person would still teach you. Sukaracharya had an especially big heart. So he said to Coch, "Yes, I will accept you as my student."

In time, Coch became the favourite student of Sukaracharya. The other disciples of Sukaracharya became very jealous because their Master was paying so much attention to the son of their enemy. They also saw that Sukaracharya's daughter, Debajani, had a tremendous fondness for Coch. The two were the same age and Sukaracharya's disciples felt that she was hoping to marry Coch when they grew up.

Sukaracharya knew about his daughter's love for Coch and he didn't have any objection to their marriage. He said, "With all my heart I love my daughter and this boy I also love so much. He is such a nice boy." Sukaracharya was just waiting for the day when they would be old enough to get married.

One of Coch's main jobs was to take the cattle out to graze every morning. One day while Coch was with the cattle, the disciples of Sukaracharya killed him. When the young boy did not come back in the evening, Debajani became worried and went looking for him. She found him lying in the field and ran back home crying to her father. Sukaracharya went to where the boy was lying and uttered his special mantra in silence. Immediately the boy was revived.

Sukaracharya and his daughter were so happy, but the jealous disciples who had killed Coch felt very sad and miserable. Now what could they do? Once more they tried to kill him. This time, while he was in the field, they grabbed him and set fire to him, so that he was burned to ashes. Then they made a special drink and put his ashes into it. They brought the drink to Sukaracharya and said, "We have made a very special drink for you. Will you not have a taste of it?"

Sukaracharya said, "Fine. I will have a taste of it." When he drank it, he felt a little bit uneasy. Then his daughter came running up and cried, "What have you done? I have just heard that your disciples put the ashes of Coch into a special drink. Now you have drunk it and he is totally gone! You will not be able to revive him."

Sukaracharya said, "It is true. If I revive him, he will have to come out of me and then I will die. So either you have to accept the fact that he is dead, or if I revive him and bring him out of my body, then you will lose me. What shall we do?"

The daughter began crying uncontrollably. Sukaracharya said, "All right, I am an old man. I have enjoyed life and I have done many things, good and bad. What is the use of staying on earth any longer? Now is the time for me to retire. All of you leave me here. Secretly I will chant my special mantra. Then, since a portion of Coch still exists inside my body, I am sure he will be revived and come out of me and I will die."

Sukaracharya chanted the mantra in silence and immediately Coch was revived. As soon as Coch came out of his Master's body, Sukaracharya died.

It happened that when he had been inside Sukaracharya, Coch had heard him chant the mantra inwardly — although Sukaracharya never chanted it out loud. In this way Coch learned the secret mantra. As soon as Coch was revived, out of his sincere gratitude he immediately touched his Master's feet and said, "Master, you have saved me." Then he used the same mantra to revive his Master. Sukaracharya immediately blessed Coch and said to him, "You have learned the mantra from me, and now you have saved me with it."

Coch said, "Previously when you revived me, I did not learn it. Only when you were using the mantra in silence and I was inside you did I learn it."

So both Sukaracharya and Coch were alive and they were all so happy. Then a sadness dawned on Debajani. Because Coch had come out of her father, he was now her brother, and they could not get married. But at least she had got back her father.

So everything started with love. If the daughter had not loved Coch, then these things would not have happened, for the disciples of Sukaracharya would not have been so jealous. Then Coch showed his magnanimity when he revived his father's enemy, Sukaracharya. But, in his willingness to sacrifice his own life for Coch, Sukaracharya was the one who really showed his heart's nobility and generosity, like a real Master.

Here the actual winners were the cosmic gods. Now both Sukaracharya and Coch had the power to revive the dead. From that time on the demon-disciples of Sukaracharya could not defeat the gods because both parties knew how to revive their dead soldiers.

The cosmic gods justified their sending Coch to learn the mantra by saying, "As long as we got the badge of Immortality, even if by hook or by crook, then we did the right thing. Now our two sides are equally strong. This is the only way we will stop fighting."

When Sukaracharya's disciples came to know that the cosmic gods also had the same power, they didn't want to fight any more since now both parties were equally strong. This is how the fighting between the gods and the demons came to an end.

### MRC 49. *The king's sincere workers*

There was once a king who had two ministers. One day he said to his ministers, "Please submit to me the names of all the palace workers who are working sincerely. There are about five hundred workers altogether, so I would like to know which ones are sincere."

The first minister brought the king a list of twelve workers. He said these twelve workers were very sincere whereas the rest were not sincere. The other minister brought a list of three hundred sincere workers.

The king said, "The insincere people may be needed a little, but they often cheat me. Only the sincere people deserve my special attention. I never get a chance to give the sincere ones a reward, so now I would like to reward them."

To the one who had submitted only twelve names the king said, "How can we have only twelve people who are sincere out of five hundred?"

The minister said, "Many people are insincere. Some people work for just an hour or a half hour daily. Some don't work at all. But you still keep them. You don't want to fire them because you have a big heart."

The other minister said, "King, O King, he is wrong. Without these three hundred people on my list, you could not manage. They are absolutely sincere. You try keeping only those twelve and you will see that it is impossible to manage."

The first minister said, "I am not saying that the king should keep only these twelve people. I am only saying that the others are insincere. These twelve will never deceive the king. They do much work with utmost sincerity."

The king said, "Let all of the five hundred workers pass by me one by one. I will look at each one and come to my own opinion."

So one by one the five hundred workers passed by the king. As each one passed by, the king said, "I am sorry. I cannot give you a reward."

At one point five workers came by in a row who were all very surprised that the king did not give them a reward. "It is quite unexpected," each one of them said.

When everything was over, the king was confused. "Why did these five say that it was quite unexpected?" he asked. "All the others just remained silent."

The king told the story to a very, very wise friend who, quite unexpectedly, had come to see him. "I don't understand what it means," he said.

The friend answered, "I tell you, O King, the minister who said that only twelve workers are sincere is right. But the one who said that three hundred are sincere, you should investigate."

The king started his investigation by sending for the five who had been so surprised when he didn't give them a reward. He said to them, "You five all said that it was 'quite unexpected' when I didn't give you a reward. Why did you say that? I will give you lots of money if you tell me the truth. I assure you that I will not fire you or punish you if you tell me the truth."

One of them said, "O King, all three hundred of us bribed the minister, but we paid him the most. Since we never work, we had to pay him more than the others. Then he promised that he would say we were among the good workers. Since we were paying him so much more than the others, he assured us that we would definitely get a reward from you and we were expecting it. This minister is very bad. On many occasions we bribe him. The other minister is the sincere one. He won't accept bribes from anyone."

The king immediately fired the bad minister. Then he gave a reward to the good minister and to the twelve sincere workers. He also gave money to the five who had confessed that they had bribed the bad minister and said, "From now on all my workers will work under strict supervision. This time if they don't work sincerely, I will definitely fire them." Then he gave his friend all his gratitude.

### MRC 50. *The scholar's four questions*

There was once a great scholar. Everybody in the kingdom appreciated him because he was so learned. Unfortunately, although he was very learned, he also had great pride.

One day this scholar put on a gold necklace and went to the palace of another king. He said, "Whoever can defeat me in wisdom will get this necklace. I will challenge everybody!"

All the scholars in that particular kingdom had heard about this scholar, and they were afraid that they would lose. So they would not accept his challenge. The king was very sad that nobody would accept the challenge.

Finally, the court jester said, "I will accept the challenge."

The king had practically surrendered to the scholar but he thought it would be amusing if his jester challenged him. He thought that he was just a joker and would not be able to win the necklace.

The court jester said, "I will ask you four questions. If you answer any of my questions correctly, then you will lose, but if all your answers are incorrect, then I will accept defeat and the king will give you anything you want."

Then the court jester asked his first question: "Where do you come from?"

The scholar said, "I live here." This was incorrect, since he came from another kingdom. So by giving the wrong answer the scholar passed the first test.

The jester's second question was, "How long have you been here?"

"Three years," the scholar said, which was also incorrect. Still the court jester was not able to trick him.

The third time the jester asked, "Our king is very nice, kind and generous. Do you agree?"

The scholar said, "Your king? What you are saying is totally wrong. Your king is very undivine, very unkind." So again the scholar passed the test.

The court jester said, "It seems that I can't defeat you. How many questions have I asked you so far?"

The scholar said, "You have asked me three questions and you have one more question. If I do not answer it correctly, then you will lose."

The court jester cried out, "Look! The scholar has lost. He has answered this question correctly."

So the scholar gave his necklace to the court jester, and the jester immediately gave it to the king. The scholar's pride was totally smashed. He said, "I will never come to your kingdom to challenge anybody again."

All the scholars were very impressed by the court jester's cleverness. They knew that they would not have been able to defeat the great scholar. The jester said, "You see, when great scholars are not alert, they lose. Otherwise, had he been alert, he would have saved himself."

# IS YOUR MIND READY TO CRY?
# IS YOUR HEART READY TO SMILE?

## BOOK 6

## MRC 51. *The noisy rich man*

There was a rich man who was very miserly and, at the same time, very mischievous. He never gave a penny to anyone. Always he would show haughtiness and pride because of his wealth. He used to get tremendous joy at the expense of others. He wanted only himself to be happy.

Even at night he didn't want anybody to have joy or peace. In order to destroy the peace of others, he used to order his servants to move things around in his house in the middle of the night. Every night he would pretend that some thieves had entered his house and he would shout and scream and create a big commotion. He would strike his dogs so they would start barking. In every way he would make noise so that his neighbours who were trying to sleep could not have a peaceful night.

This went on for months and years. One day a man came to stay at the home of one of the rich man's neighbours. If this particular man didn't get sleep even for one night, he would become practically insane. That night, as usual, there was so much noise in the rich man's house that the man could not sleep.

Finally the man asked his host, "Why do you not go next door and stop the noise?"

The neighbour said, "How can I stop it? He pretends there are thieves in his house. Therefore, he has every right to shout at his servants and instigate his dogs to bark. We all know that this story is false, but we can't prove it. So we can never get proper sleep at night."

The guest said, "Don't worry. I will solve the problem."

The man said, "How?"

"You will see," said his friend.

The following morning he went to the rich man's house. He knew that the rich man never wanted to see anyone, so he presented something very beautiful and expensive to the rich man's servant as a bribe. He said, "I have only good news for your master. I just want to tell him that I am so grateful to him and proud of him."

The servant believed the man and went to his master and said, "Someone has come who is all admiration for you. He does not need anything from you, so you do not have to worry."

The rich man agreed to see him, and the servant brought the man before his master. The man said, "I don't need anything from you. I am coming here only to give you some good news. Last night I stayed at the home of one of your neighbours. You can't imagine how many of your neighbours admire and adore you. Many of them keep considerable amounts of money in their homes. At night you keep them awake, so nothing can ever be stolen. When there is so much commotion going on in your house, naturally thieves will never dare to come to your neighbours' houses. Therefore, they are so happy and grateful that you are living in their neighbourhood."

The rich man couldn't believe his ears. "They are really happy?" he said.

"Yes," said the man, "they are so grateful to you. They have real peace of mind because they know that their valuable possessions are safe at night."

From that night on, the rich man stopped banging doors, telling his servants to move everything around in his house and beating his dogs so they would bark. Why? He didn't want his neighbours to be happy and have peace of mind because they felt there would be no robberies. He wanted them to be miserable and to suffer from worries and anxieties. The rich man said, "I don't want them to be happy in any way. Why should I make them happy by keeping the neighbourhood free from thieves? I know that I have many dogs and servants, so nothing will be taken from my house. Let my neighbours suffer, while I have peace of mind. In this way I will again make myself happy."

## MRC 52. *The notorious son*

Once a young boy was notorious for quarrelling with people and insulting them. His father had died several years earlier, so his mother had to take care of him. She was very sad and miserable that he would not behave. The villagers used to speak ill not only of him, but also of his mother because they thought that the mother was indulgent. Actually, it was just the opposite. His mother was very strict with him, but he would never listen to her.

One day he insulted an elderly man and the villagers wanted to thrash him. The mother came and pleaded with the villagers. She said, "True, my son is totally wrong, but please forgive him and forgive me as well. I am trying to help him."

The village head was kind enough to release the son because of the mother's pleas. The mother brought the boy home and said, "I will soon die because I am old. After my death, perhaps you will start listening to my advice and become a good boy. I will leave some money for you when I die. So use the money and think of me. Right now, because you are mischievous and naughty, I am miserable. So I am going to send you away to a boarding school."

When the boy went to the boarding school, again he started arguing with the teachers and the students. Then one day he got a message that his mother had died. He returned to his village, shedding bitter tears, and said, "Mother, I could not please you when you were alive. But now I am taking an oath. I will become an excellent boy." From then on he never quarrelled with anyone. He became simple, honest and kind-hearted.

Although his mother had left him some money, it was not enough for him to continue his studies for very long. Since he didn't have any real interest in school, after studying for a year or two, he started looking for a job. Finally, the village zamindar gave him some work taking care of the zamindar's garden and also looking after his children.

One day the boy was holding the garden hose in one arm and the zamindar's youngest child in his other arm. The zamindar happened to pass by and said, "Look, if you want to water the garden, keep my child on the ground. For everything there is a time. Now you can water the garden and afterwards you can show your affection to the child. For everything there is a time."

The boy very obediently put the child on the ground and continued watering the garden. In ten minutes' time the zamindar's wife came by and got furious. She said, "How dare you keep my child on the ground. Can't you keep him in one arm? With one arm you can water the garden and with the other you can carry my child. Besides, who wants you to water the plants? Right now you should just take care of my youngest child and stop watering the garden."

The boy kept silent and stopped watering the garden to take care of the child. In this way he pleased both his master and his master's wife.

By this time everybody in the village appreciated the zamindar's servant because he was always kind-hearted and such a good worker. Now, it happened that in the school where he used to study, a younger student had developed the same kind of mischievous nature that he used to have. This younger student always fought with his teachers and the other students and did all kinds of wrong things. His mother was in distress all the time because of her son's bad behaviour.

This naughty student was very jealous of the zamindar's servant. The mother of the naughty student said to her son, "I know you are jealous of the zamindar's servant. But by being jealous you are not going to get his good qualities. Only by admiring him and doing what he does will you be able to get the same qualities one day."

The son didn't listen to his mother. He continued to do all kinds of undivine things, arguing with people and striking them. One day some stronger boys got angry with him and beat him up. The mischievous boy returned home crying. He was so miserable!

The naughty boy decided to go to the zamindar's servant to see how he could change his nature. He said to the servant, "You are so kind, so good, so modest. You have no pride, anger or restlessness. How did you develop your good qualities?"

The servant told him, "My mother always begged me to be good, but I wouldn't listen. When she died, I changed my nature. When my mother left the body, I took an oath that I would be good. Always one has to try to please people. Then they become grateful to you and proud of you."

The servant continued: "This morning I was watering the plants, holding the hose in one arm and my master's youngest child in the other arm. My master got mad and said I should not try to do two things at once. He said I should put the child on the ground while I watered the garden with both hands. So I put down the child with utmost humility and began watering the garden. The master was very pleased that I had listened to him.

"In a few minutes' time my master's wife saw me watering the garden. She insulted me brutally and said, 'Why are you leaving the child on the ground? Is he inferior to the plants?' She wanted me to lift up the child immediately. She said she would be happy if I stopped watering the plants and just took care of the child. So I stopped watering the garden.

"I didn't lose anything by making both my master and his wife happy. Like this, in every way I try to please my master and his wife. Now they are so fond of me. In your case also, if you always try to keep everything peaceful and harmonious with your mother, your teachers and friends, then they will be happy. And only by giving happiness to others can you become happy yourself.

"I feel miserable that I waited until my mother died before I tried to please her. I advise you to change your nature now and please your mother while she is still alive. Then you will see how much joy you will get. The joy you are getting now by being mischievous is all false joy. It is all stupidity. If you give others joy, if you are divine, then only you will be really happy."

The young boy went and told his mother what the servant had said. His mother went to the zamindar's house and literally grabbed the servant. She told him, "I won't allow you to be anybody's servant. From now on I want you to be my oldest son. I will take care of you and you can continue your studies. Your mother is not on earth, so I want to be your mother and offer you the same kind of affection and love."

The woman brought the boy home and sent both her sons to school to complete their higher studies.

### MRC 53. *The pilgrimage*

Once there were two neighbours who were friends and, at the same time, rivals. Both of them were very shrewd and miserly. At times they were absolutely, unthinkably undivine.

One day they decided to go on a pilgrimage. So their wives made delicious food for them and they left very early in the morning.

After they had walked for two hours, it was breakfast time. One of them said, "Let us not stop to eat breakfast. It is not necessary."

The other one said, "I agree. Let us keep walking and then stop for lunch instead."

So they continued walking. When lunch time came, one of them said, "I am not hungry. If you want to eat, you can eat. But I am not hungry in the least."

The other one said, "I am not hungry either. Let us walk further until we are tired. Then we can stop and eat."

Both of them were perfect rogues. Each one thought that his own wife had made most delicious food and did not want to share it with the other. Each one thought, "If we walk for some time, then my friend will become tired and fall asleep. Then I will be able to eat my food all by myself. I don't want to share any of it with him."

They walked until it was evening and they were both very tired. After they stopped, each one was waiting for the other to fall asleep. They were waiting and waiting. Finally, both of them fell asleep.

The following morning when they woke up, they saw that their food was crawling with ants. They were so mad at their wives! "We didn't examine the food when they gave it to us. Now we see that there are ants inside the food. When we go home, we will insult them like anything," they said.

Then they said, "Since we are extremely tired, let us take rest here for another few hours." When they woke up a few hours later, they saw that rats were eating their food. They were so disgusted that they immediately went home and insulted and scolded their wives.

Their wives said, "Why didn't you eat the food we gave you during the day?"

Each one told his wife, "I didn't want to share any of your most delicious food with that other rascal. Then it took him so long to fall asleep. In the meantime, I too fell asleep."

Each wife told her husband, "This time when you start on your pilgrimage again, I will give you special food. Since both of you are so greedy and miserly, this time I will give you simple food — a loaf of bread — which you can easily share with your friend. Your friend will be very pleased if you share it. Since both of you are going together, you can at least have this much friendship."

One wife made bread that was very salty and the other made bread with no salt at all. Since their wives had told them that the food was very simple, both the men suddenly became extremely generous. One of them said, "I am sure your wife is a good cook. Let us exchange our food. You give me your food and I will give you my food."

The other one said, "It is an excellent idea."

So they exchanged their food and started eating. O God, the one who got the salty bread became mad and disgusted. He said, "Your wife does not know how to cook!"

The other one also became mad and said, "Your wife also does not know how to cook! There is no salt in this bread. It is tasteless."

The first man said, "My wife is an excellent cook."

The other one said, "Your wife! Then how is it that she forgot to put salt in this bread?"

The first one said, "How is it that your wife put too much salt in her bread?"

Like this they fought and fought. Again their pilgrimage came to an end, and again they went home and insulted their wives.

Each of them said to his wife, "You made horrible food. I was ashamed of your preparation."

Their wives said, "We thought that you were good friends. If you had shared your food with each other, there would have been no problem. One loaf of bread had too much salt and the other had no salt. If you had shared, it would have been most delicious for both of you."

So the wives gave them illumination. The husbands said to each other, "We are fools. We should have put our food together and then eaten."

### MRC 54. *Akbar and the sword*

The greatest Mogul Emperor was Akbar. It was he who wanted both the Hindus and Muslims to be united. He was generous to the extreme and just to the extreme. Among the Mogul Emperors, he was the true ideal.

One day Akbar was walking incognito in the street. He was incognito because he wanted to be alone. Always people were around him and he never had his freedom. But this time he was all alone.

While he was walking, he saw an old lady holding a dagger. He asked her, "What are you doing with a dagger? Let me see what it looks like and how sharp it is."

The old lady gave him the dagger and he held it for a few seconds. "Oh, I am so sorry," she said. "Had you been the Emperor, then this metal dagger would have been transformed into a gold dagger. Now it is just a metal dagger, but I had a dream that if ever the Emperor touches it, then definitely it will be transformed into gold. I have been waiting and waiting for the Emperor to appear. I am praying to Allah that he will come. For years I have been here, waiting in the street for Akbar. I am so sorry that still I have not been blessed with Akbar's presence."

The following day Akbar summoned the old lady to the court. Now he was wearing his robes and his crown. He said, "Here is Akbar. He does not have the capacity to transform a metal dagger into a gold one, but he does have the capacity to change your life for good. How much money do you want?"

The lady was overwhelmed. She couldn't believe her eyes; she couldn't believe her ears. She told the Emperor that she wanted a particular amount of money. But Akbar gave her much, much more, saying, "I don't have the capacity to turn metal into gold, but I have another capacity."

So the lady became extremely rich because of Akbar the Great.

### MRC 55. *The honesty diploma*

There was a very rich village zamindar who was a great philanthropist. Everybody liked him. Once he decided that for three days he would give away things, including money, to the poor — only to the poor. People were getting rice, vegetables, money and all kinds of things.

One poor man got a very heavy sack of rice. Since he was such a poor man, he was very happy. O God, when he came home and emptied the sack, he found inside the rice twenty gold coins. His wife was delighted.

The husband said, "The zamindar didn't intend to give me these gold coins. He wanted to give me rice. This was a mistake. I should return these coins."

The wife said, "You fool! You fool! We are so poor. This is the time to take the gold to the market and exchange it for lots of money."

The husband said, "No, I can't do that. I have to go and return them." The wife and husband had a fight about the gold. Of course, the husband won because it was he who had brought the rice home.

The following day he went back and said to the rich man, "You were so kind to give all of us so many things. I have found these twenty gold coins that were in the rice sack by mistake. Now I have come to return them to you. If you want to give them to me, all right. But although I am only a beggar, I can never accept this kind of gift if it was a mistake." The rich man was so moved by his sincerity. He said, "No, you take them. And because of your sincerity, I am giving you double the amount. You brought me twenty gold coins and now you are getting forty. This time I am giving these to you personally so you don't have to come back again. You are such an honest man. I need honest men like you."

A greedy businessman happened to overhear the story and he came up with a brilliant idea. He went to the beggar and said, "I heard that you have got lots of gold coins. Do you want to sell a few to me?"

The poor man said, "Certainly. I can sell them to you. Since I have not received them by mistake nor stolen them, they are mine to sell."

The businessman bought six gold coins from the poor man.

Then he put on beggar's clothes and went to the rich man's house. "I will do the same thing that this beggar did and I will be able to double my wealth," he thought. "Since over the past three days hundreds and hundreds of beggars have received bags of food from the zamindar, I am sure that he will not remember that I was not one of those beggars."

So the businessman went to the zamindar and said, "Yesterday you gave me three gold coins but by some magic today it has become six gold coins. So now I have come to give you back the original ones, while I am keeping the extra ones. I got these extra ones by the magic of the previous ones, so I am giving you back the original ones free."

The zamindar said, "That means that you are the only person to whom I gave coins whose wealth has increased. I gave coins to others, but in their case the number did not increase. One man brought back the same amount that I gave him. But in your case the amount increased. I am so proud of you. I am so grateful to you. What do you want from me?"

The businessman-beggar said, "If you are pleased with my honesty because I am returning these three coins, you can give me a little more. If I had not returned these three coins, you would not have known that the original coins produced three more. So if you value honesty, then please give me a few more. But if you don't want to, then you are under no obligation."

The rich man said, "You really deserve much more. Since from three coins you have got six, let me do one thing. I will give you something much more important than a few more gold coins."

The businessman was so happy. He said, "Please, please tell me what it is."

The zamindar asked his servant to write out an 'honesty diploma'. The servant wrote it out and the zamindar put it on this fellow's back and signed it. Then he told the businessman-beggar, "See, with this diploma you can tell the whole world that the zamindar has said that you are the most honest person. This kind of 'honesty diploma' I have not given to anybody. But you deserve it."

## MRC 56. *Two neighbours*

There were two neighbours who were at times good friends and at times worst enemies. It happened that one of them needed some money, and he became extremely nice to the other one, so that he would then be in a position to ask for money. The man borrowed twenty rupees, which is equal to about two and a half American dollars. He said it would take him only a month to return the money.

His friend said, "Don't worry. Whenever you can, you will give it back."

Several months passed and still the neighbour did not return the money. Instead, the neighbour was always trying to avoid his so-called friend.

Finally, after six months the friend became disappointed and disgusted. A few times he went to his neighbour's house, but the neighbour was never at home. Actually, his wife would say that her husband was not at home even if he was. She would always tell lies. This happened seven or eight times.

One day the fellow who had lent the money told a mutual friend what a bad fellow his neighbour was because he was not returning the money. The friend said, "I tell you, you will get the money without fail."

The friend went to the culprit's house and scolded both the husband and the wife. He said, "You two are such liars! You are bringing disgrace to our village. Who asked you to borrow money, and why are you not returning it? If you do not return it, I will tell each and every person in the entire village. Then everyone will have a low opinion of you."

The friend said, "Please don't tell anyone. I shall give you a rupee if you promise not to tell anyone."

The man took the rupee and left. A few days later he came again and asked, "Have you returned the money?"

The neighbour said, "No!"

His friend said, "This time I am definitely going to tell everyone what a bad fellow you are."

Again the man begged him, "Please don't tell anyone." This time he gave him ten rupees so that he would not tell others.

In a few days' time the friend went to the man's house again. When he found out that still the man had not returned the money, he became furious. The man said, "I will give you another ten rupees if you remain silent." The man had borrowed only twenty rupees, but he had paid his friend twenty-one rupees in bribes. The friend assured him that he would never tell anyone about the debt.

In a few months' time, the man who borrowed the money and the one who lent the money accidentally met on the street. The one who borrowed the money was most apologetic. He said, "I promise that tomorrow without fail I will come to you with the money. Please believe me."

The friend said, "You don't owe me anything. You have already paid me."

The neighbour couldn't believe his ears. "How?" he asked.

"Our mutual friend gave me all the money that you gave him as a bribe," the man explained.

So the mutual friend had not actually taken any bribes. He had only wanted the bad fellow to return the money. He had threatened and frightened him so that he could get the bribe money and then return it to his friend.

## MRC 57. *The rich man's sons*

A rich man once said to a friend, "I am so sorry that neither of my sons is pleasing me. One is a fool. The other is extra smart, but because of his smartness he is always getting into trouble."

His friend asked, "In what way is one a fool and the other so smart?"

The rich man said, "One only remains in silence. The other one mixes with everyone and then creates all kinds of problems. Can you advise me what I should do about my sons? One is too smart for his own good, and the other one seems to be only a fool."

The friend said, "An ordinary crow mixes with many other crows, but a cuckoo mixes with very few birds."

The rich man said, "What do you mean?"

The friend explained, "Your son who does not mix with others is wise. He knows that this world is full of corruption, so he remains silent. He is very simple, kind and sincere. He remains quiet and always prays and meditates, for he knows that this world has nothing to give him. Again, the one that mixes all the time is truly intelligent. He knows that he will be able to accept the world's corruption because he is your son. Even if he falls into bad company, he feels that because his father is rich and great, he will be saved. He will be able to escape any problems because of your money-power. One thinks only of God, because God alone is happiness, Truth and Light. The other feels that he will never get in trouble because of his father's wealth."

The rich man said, "So I have one son who is kind-hearted and sincere, and I have another son who is extra smart in the inner and outer sense. He knows that he will be able to fool society. God wants one son to be happy by being pure and wise and the other to be happy by being extremely intelligent. And God wants me to be happy by playing the role of the fool. God always has to complete the family. If there is a wise member in the family and an intelligent member, then there must be a fool in the family as well. So God has made me the foolish member."

MRC 58. *The seeker's bargain with God*

There was once a seeker who was praying to God for years and years. In the beginning he was sincere, but he could not maintain his sincerity and purity. So after a while he started praying to God only for money, money and more money. Finally God came to him.

The seeker said, "God, why have You taken such a long time to come to me? Could You not have come earlier to make me rich? I have been praying and meditating for twelve long years!

God said to him, "You say that you have been praying for material wealth for twelve years. But in My Vision your twelve years is no more than one minute."

The seeker said, "O God, You are really cruel! But since You have come, are You going to make me rich?"

God said, "Definitely! What do you want?"

The seeker said, "You know that on earth we have rupees. Do You have rupees in Heaven also?"

"Yes," answered God.

The seeker said, "With an earthly rupee I know how much I can buy. Will You tell me how much I can buy with a Heavenly rupee?"

God said, "With an earthly rupee you can buy only one tiny little thing, but with a Heavenly rupee you can get hundreds of things."

The seeker said, "God, You say that my twelve years of prayer are equal to only one minute in Your Vision. Therefore, if I pray to You for one minute, will You not give me Heavenly wealth for twelve years? True, for twelve years I prayed for earthly wealth, but now I am changing my mind. Can You not change the reward? Can You not give me a Heavenly rupee instead of earthly rupees? If You give me just one Heavenly rupee, will it not last for twelve years?"

God said, "Certainly it will last for at least twelve years. If I give you one Heavenly rupee, you will be able to buy whatever you want for twelve years."

The seeker said, "Can You not give me the Heavenly rupee now?"

God said, "Just wait a minute. I am going to Heaven to get it. Since you will be able to use it for twelve years, can you not wait one minute?" The seeker said, "O God, have You taken down my address?"

God said, "Don't worry! I never make a mistake. I will come back to your house. Even if I am a little delayed, don't worry. I will definitely come back to give the rupee to your children or grandchildren."

God left, but He did not come back.

Here the seeker was arguing with God and trying to deceive God. Perhaps the seeker could have got earthly, material wealth since he had prayed so long for it. But he started bargaining with God. He tried to trick God into giving him Heavenly wealth. He felt that since he was definitely going to get earthly wealth, he could trick God into giving him the equivalent in Heavenly wealth instead. But if one tries to trick God, God will trick him first.

MRC 59. *The heaviest load*

Once a spiritual Master went out for a picnic with a group of twenty disciples. The disciples were so happy that they were going out with their Master. The Master told his disciples, "I have twenty bags for you to carry. These contain things which we are going to use today. Please each choose a bag to carry." Then the Master added, "But mind you, you will not be able to change the bag once you take it. Once you choose it, you won't be able to change with anyone."

The disciples started lifting up all the bags to find the lightest ones. All of them were looking for the light, lighter, lightest bag except one fellow who was looking for the heavy, heavier, heaviest one. The other disciples thought he was a real fool. They were so happy that this fool was carrying the heaviest load, while their bags were comparatively light.

After they had walked for four or five hours the Master said, "Let us sit down and eat. Please empty the bag that has the food in it. The other bags we will carry to our next destination. There we shall see the most beautiful trees and flowers. Then we shall go back home."

All the disciples sat down to eat. O God, when they opened the bags, they discovered that only the heavy one had food in it. The other ones contained only sand, clay, broken pots and all kinds of worthless things. The disciple with the heaviest bag emptied it at the request of the Master and everybody ate the food. When they set out for their second destination, the disciple who had had the heaviest load was now carrying a totally empty bag.

When they reached the second destination, an orchard, they picked fruits and admired the beautiful scenery. They spent quite a few hours there and then they walked to a museum. Finally, they had a six-hour walk back home.

Afterwards the Master said, "I told you that you could not change your bags. The one who had the heaviest load in the beginning, later had the lightest bag. While walking to the second and third destinations, and also on the way home, he had nothing to carry. As for the rest of you, your bags were lighter to start with, but then you had to carry them much, much farther. The one who chose the heaviest bag was good and kind-hearted. The rest of you wanted to find the lightest bag. So you rogues had to carry bags that contained only rubbish for the entire trip!"

The Master said to his rogue disciples, "You are my third-class disciples and he is my first-class disciple. The one who wants to carry everybody's load is the one who is really a first-class disciple!"

### MRC 60. *The brass pot*

There was a village diver to whom everybody turned whenever something valuable fell into the pond. He was the one who would find the object for them, and the villagers would pay him for his work. This is how he earned his living.

One day the wife of the village head saw the diver carrying a very beautiful brass vessel. Somebody had given him that beautiful brass pot as payment for his finding something in the pond. As soon as she saw the pot, the wife of the village head became very excited and said, "Will you give me that beautiful vessel? Tonight many people are coming to my house for a special dinner, and I want them to see that I have such an expensive vessel. I will keep the pot only for two or three days, and then I will return it to you." Because her husband was the head of the village, the diver had to give it to her if he wanted to stay out of trouble.

O God, two or three days passed and the lady still did not return the pot. The diver was afraid and embarrassed to ask her for it because she was the wife of the village head. He said, "Something has to be done, but what can I do? I am helpless."

Finally, the wife of the village head sent a vessel back to the diver. It was not a brass pot but an earthen pot, with a note inside. The note said, "One of my servants washed the pot and as soon as water touched it, it became earthen. I am very sorry that I am unable to return the pot to you the way I got it."

When the diver got the note, he felt miserable. He said, "O God, she has played a trick! But how can I fight with the wife of the head of the village?"

Two years passed. One day, the wife of the village head was showing off her beautiful brass pot to her friends. She had just had another dinner and she was bragging to her friends while washing the pot in the pond, when all of a sudden the vessel dropped into the water.

Now it was necessary for somebody to dive into the water and find the pot. The village head was very clever. He told his wife, "If we call the village diver and he finds it, he will know that we told a lie." So they called in another diver to look for the brass vessel. The diver spent hours and hours, but he was not as expert as the village diver and he could not find it. The village head was very mad at him and didn't want to pay him.

The diver said, "I have spent so many hours looking for the pot. You didn't say that you wouldn't pay me if I didn't find it. No! You must pay me."

Finally the village head threw some money at him and said, "Get out! You are useless!"

The wife was feeling sad. She told her husband, "By this time I am sure that the village diver has forgotten that I took his pot. Anyway, he won't be able to prove that it is the same vessel, and if our guards are watching him when he dives, how will he be able to take it back?"

So the village head called the diver and said, "Can you help us? We have dropped a beautiful brass vessel into the pond."

The diver, who felt certain that it was the vessel they had taken from him, said, "Certainly I can help you. There is only one problem. Today I am running a very high fever. Do you think that tomorrow I will be able to do it? If you insist, I can do it today, but I am quite sick. If I go into the water, my condition will become infinitely worse."

The village head said, "Already it has been sitting in the pond for a week. We can wait one more night."

The diver said, "I will come back tomorrow without fail to find it!"

When the diver left, the wife of the village head began trembling. She said, "O God, what will happen if he tells people that we have taken this pot?" But after thinking for a moment, she continued, "We are so rich and powerful. We will easily be able to silence him if he argues with us."

That night the diver secretly entered into the pond and found the lost brass vessel. Then he put into the water the earthen pot that the wife of the village head had given him two years before and took the brass pot home.

The following day the diver came to the village head and said, "Do you still want me to try to find the pot?"

"Yes," said the village head.

The diver said, "I can't assure you that I will be able to find it. In this world nobody is such an expert. If it is God's Will, then only will I be able to find it."

The village head said, "It is not God's Will; it is my will that you find it. That is enough!"

"Certainly," said the diver. "You are my lord, so there is no difference between your will and God's Will."

The village head was so flattered! He and his wife and children all went to the pond to watch the diver look for the pot. In ten or fifteen minutes the diver brought up the earthen pot.

The wife cried, "How can the pot be earthen? It was brass. How could this happen?"

The diver said, "I am sorry. This is what I found. You can ask somebody else to look if you like. Anyway, two years ago, when you were washing a brass pot that you had borrowed from me, it became earthen. If a brass pot turned earthen just from being washed, how can you expect a pot to remain brass after staying in water for a week? If you still feel that your brass vessel is inside the pond, then send someone else to find it!"

The village head and his wife got the point. That night, the village head went to the diver's house and said, "What can I do? My wife is so fond of that brass vessel. I know my wife told you a lie about the pot two years ago, and I had to stand up for her. Now, for God's sake, I want to keep my prestige. Take money from me, as much as you want. But just give me back the brass pot. I know it is yours, but let me buy it from you."

The village head bought the pot and took it home. The following day he asked his friends and neighbours to come to his house to see the pot. He was such a rogue! He told them, "I gave the diver a very large amount of money to go look in the pond once more. You people were not there, but he went there and found the one that we had lost."

The village head showed the pot to his wife and their friends and they all agreed that it was the same brass pot. "You see," said the village head, "money talks!"

Deception started with the village head and his wife. The poor diver thought, "Tit for tat." Afterwards, the village head made everybody think that the diver was a rogue, but the village head was the real rogue!

# IS YOUR MIND READY TO CRY?
# IS YOUR HEART READY TO SMILE?

## BOOK 7

## MRC 61. *The two friends*

There were once two friends who first became rivals and eventually became worst enemies. This is human life: first friendship, then rivalry, then enmity and finally the desire to kill one another. That is the revelation of human friendship.

These two friends were disciples of a spiritual Master. The spiritual Master felt miserable at the way they were always fighting. One day he asked them, "Why do you quarrel and fight? Don't you remember that once upon a time you were good friends?"

The two friends answered, "Yes, but now we have become bitter enemies and we don't think that we will ever be able to revive our friendship. What can we do?"

The spiritual Master soon appeared in a dream before both of his disciples. To the first one he said, "Tell me how you expect to be happy in this life. Are you not miserable now that you and your friend have become enemies?"

In the dream the disciple replied, "I am really miserable. I don't want to hate him. At the same time, I can't prevent myself from hating him."

The Master said, "I have discovered a way for you to become happy. If you do what I ask, you will find happiness."

The disciple said, "Master, I promise to do whatever you ask. Please tell me how I can be happy."

The Master said, "You can be happy if you can make your friend happy. Then only will you be happy. Tomorrow, as soon as you see him, the first thing you will do is embrace him. The moment you embrace him, all the wealth of Heaven will descend on him and he will be happy. Then, you yourself will also become happy."

The disciple said, "All right. I will do it since I want to keep my promise to you. After all, once upon a time he was my close friend. If he becomes rich, then I am sure he will give me some of his wealth and make me rich also."

The same night, the Master also appeared before the other disciple in a dream and said, "Are you not unhappy now that you and your friend have become worst enemies?"

The disciple replied, "It is true that I am miserable, but I can't help hating him. I will be happy only if I see him die."

"So that is how you want to be happy?" the Master asked. "That is the only way?"

"Yes," said the disciple. "There is only one way — if I can kill him."

The Master said, "All right, I will make you happy. Tomorrow, as soon as you see him, you will embrace him. As soon as you touch him, he will immediately die."

The second disciple was so excited that he would be able to kill the first one and couldn't wait for morning to dawn.

These dreams all took place in the inner world, and both disciples kept them quite secret. The following day each of them ran towards the other's house so that he could embrace the other one and make himself happy.

As soon as they saw each other, the one who was given the capacity to kill his friend all of a sudden thought, "Once upon a time he was my friend. How am I going to touch him and kill him? Am I doing the right thing?"

While he was hesitating, the other disciple came and embraced him. Immediately all the wealth of Heaven descended into him. He said, "What have you done? What have you done? Had I been able to embrace you first, I would have killed you. Now you have embraced me first. How am I going to become happy in my own way? You are trying to make me happy in your way, not my way."

With his occult power the spiritual Master came and stood in front of them. The Master said, "You fool, you wanted to be happy by killing your friend. But look at his friendship! He was willing to make you happy and then become happy in your happiness. He is definitely superior. But I want both the superior and inferior to go together. Then only will I be happy.

"You have received all the wealth of Heaven. Now give him half of your wealth. Then both of you become friends once again. In this way you will become excellent disciples."

### MRC 62. *The hooligan's son*

Once there was a hooligan who was destroying the peace and joy of an entire kingdom. The king was so sad and miserable because he wanted to have only peace, joy and harmony in his kingdom. In so many ways the king's soldiers tried to capture this hooligan, but they always failed.

The hooligan's wife had previously committed suicide because her husband would not give up stealing. At first the hooligan was very sad and miserable that he had lost his wife, but even then he would not stop stealing. The only other member left in his family was his little three-year-old son, his only child.

The king said, "Since everybody else is failing, I will try to catch the culprit myself." So one night the king disguised himself as a thief, broke into the hooligan's house and kidnapped the hooligan's son.

When the hooligan returned home the following day and saw that his only son was missing, his heart was completely broken. He said, "My wife warned me not to continue this kind of life, but I didn't listen to her. Now my only child is gone. What is the use of continuing to steal and torture people?"

So the hooligan became a mendicant and began leading a very simple, ascetic life. Often he thought of his wife and child, especially his child. He kept asking himself, "Who could have kidnapped my only son? I don't have the heart or the capacity even to try to find him again. Whoever has stolen him will never return him to me." He continued to lead a very pure and pious life and in six months' time he was totally changed.

In the meantime the king was keeping the child in his palace. He happened to have a son of the same age and he started showing both of them the same affection and love. One day both the children fell extremely sick and no physician was able to cure them. As a last resort one of the physicians said, "I know of a particular herb which will cure them. It is very difficult to procure, but I shall try."

In the meantime, the ascetic hooligan happened to come near the palace to pray and meditate for his illumination. Somebody reported to the king that a saint was praying and meditating nearby. The king said, "I need the prayer of a saint. Ask him to come here, and I will beg him to help me."

So, at the request of the king, the saint came to the palace. His consciousness had totally changed and nobody could recognise him as the former hooligan. The king told him, "I have two little children. Both are dying. Would you kindly come to see them and pray to God for their recovery? I will give you whatever you want."

The saint said, "I will pray to God to save them, but I will take nothing from you."

The king took him into a private chamber and showed him the children. The hooligan could not recognise his own child because the child had received such good care. He had got excellent nourishment and, even though he was sick, he looked totally changed.

The doctor then entered the room and quite happily told the king, "I have procured the herb, but I have enough for only one child. Who cares for the other child! Let your child be cured."

The king said, "Oh no, I can't do that. If we have enough only for one child, please give it to the other child."

The ascetic asked, "Why?"

The king said, "Although he is not my own child, I want him to be cured. Like me, his father too has a heart. Already I have stolen his child. I know that his heart is totally broken because he has lost his son. But what could I do? I had no alternative. His father was the worst possible hooligan. He was destroying the whole kingdom, robbing and killing people. When I captured his son, inwardly he was totally destroyed. He has never been seen again. This was the only way I could put an end to my kingdom's suffering. But I will never forgive myself if I allow his child to die, since already I have killed his father inwardly."

The king turned to the physician and said, "I order you to give the medicine to the other child and let my child die in front of my eyes. I do hope that one day the hooligan will find his child, even if by that time his son is a young man. If the hooligan gives up his profession, then I will gladly go to his house and return his son."

The sage immediately fell down at the feet of the king and would not get up. "What is the matter?" the king asked. "I asked you to pray and meditate."

The saint said, "O King, I am the hooligan you are speaking of and this is my child. I caused so much trouble for your subjects. I deserved the punishment you gave me. Today you have proved what kind of heart you have. Please keep my child. I promise that I will never steal again. I have taken to an ascetic life, but if you want to, you can throw me out of your kingdom or kill me."

The king said, "I now consider you a sage and I will gladly take care of your child. You will remain in the palace as my court sage. I am so grateful that you have come to pray and meditate for the recovery of the two children."

The two sons were both cured, and the hooligan and the king shed tears of gratitude.

MRC 63. *The bet*

Once there were two friends. One of them felt sorry for the other one because he did not have a good job. He said, "Let us make a bet. I am sure that I will definitely be able to find a good job for you."

The second one said, "What will you give me if you fail?"

The first one said, "All right, if I cannot find a good job for you, I will give you two hundred rupees from my salary. And if I find a job for you, what will you give me from your salary?"

The second one said, "I will give you four!"

So the first one looked for a job for his friend here, there and everywhere. Finally he found a good job for him that paid five hundred rupees per month. He was very excited that he had found this kind of job for his friend and said to him, "So, I have won the bet. When you get your first month's salary, you have to give me four hundred rupees."

The friend just handed him four rupees and started walking away.

The first one said, "Wait! Why are you giving me four rupees? You are supposed to give me four hundred."

The friend said, "Did I tell you four hundred? I said four."

The first one said, "You fool, I said that I would give you two hundred rupees if I didn't get you a job and you said you would give me four if I did. It was understood that it was four hundred."

The second friend said, "I said four. I didn't say four hundred."

The second one already had the job, so what could the first one do? Instead of winning four hundred rupees, he had to be satisfied with four. He was furious because he had worked so hard to find his friend a job, so he sued his friend.

When the case came before the king, the king asked the second friend, "Is it true that you were supposed to give this man four hundred rupees?"

The man replied, "O King, that is wrong. He told me that if he lost the bet, he would give me two hundred rupees. Then I told him I would give him four if he won. I lost the bet and I kept my promise; I gave him four rupees."

The king turned to the first one and said, "He is right. He didn't say four hundred." Then the king gave the first one four hundred rupees and he accepted it gratefully. Next the king turned to the second one and said, "I need clever people like you in my court." He gave a job to the fellow who had fooled his friend.

The clever fellow worked in the court and the king was very pleased with him. After some time the king told him, "People say that you are very good and wise and that you have many good qualities. Only one bad quality they find in you — that you do not admire others."

The man said, "O King, I admire only two persons. The first person is your noble self. You gave me this job. You are so good, so kind, so great. There is nobody as great as you. Therefore, I admire you and I am extremely grateful to you."

The king was very pleased with him. Then he asked, "And who is the other person you admire?"

The man said, "It is my friend whom I fooled about the four hundred rupees. He was my closest friend. I had led a vagabond life for so many years and he worked very, very hard to find me a job. I really admire him and I feel very sorry that I deceived him. Of course, there is a vast difference between you and my friend. But compared to others, my friend is by far the best. Therefore, I sincerely admire him."

The king said, "Since you admire him so much and he is an honest man, bring him to me. I will give him a job in my court as well." In this way the king brought the two friends together again.

One day the king asked them, "So, are both of you satisfied?"

They answered, "We are satisfied, but it is not because of our capacity. We are satisfied with you. We are satisfied with your wisdom. We are sincerely pleased with our lives because you care for us. Otherwise, we would not have become good friends again. It is you who have made us good. It is you who have made us great. It is you who care for us infinitely more than you care for yourself. Therefore, we are extremely, extremely grateful to you."

## MRC 64. *The father's lesson*

A man once had a beautiful daughter. His wife had died when their daughter was just a child, so the father lavished all his affection on the daughter. Unfortunately, the daughter was very careless. She would always forget to lock the doors and windows properly. At night she would go to sleep and leave everything open.

Her father was very sad because she was so careless. He thought, "When she gets married, her husband and relatives will scold her like anything."

Many times he told his daughter, "It is one thing to be fearless and another thing to be careless. It is one thing to show bravery and another thing to show bravado. You must be fearless and, at the same time, careful. Always lock the doors and windows, especially at night."

One day the father had to go out of town on business. He told his daughter, "Tonight I won't be here. You have to lock the doors and windows properly!"

His daughter said, "Yes, of course I will do it." But as usual, she did not lock the doors and windows properly when she went to bed. In the middle of the night a thief entered into her room and showed her a dagger. "Tell me where your father keeps his money!" he said.

The daughter screamed, "I don't know, I don't know! Otherwise, I would tell you."

Then the thief snatched her necklace and ran away.

She was frightened to death and said, "Father is right. From now on I will lock the doors and windows properly."

When the father returned the next day, he said, "Fortunately you are all right. But look what an expensive thing you have lost! At least you didn't tell the thief where I keep my money and jewellery."

She said, "I don't know where it is. Otherwise, the way he was showing me the dagger, I would have told him immediately."

The father said, "I am lucky that I never told you. Anyway, I am grateful that you were not hurt."

In few months' time the father said to the daughter, "The time has come for you to get married."

The daughter said, "Whomever you choose, I will gladly marry. You have good taste. I leave it all up to you."

The father said, "I will select several people. Let them come and see you one by one, and you can make a choice."

So the father brought five candidates. The first one the daughter didn't like at all. The second one didn't like her and she also didn't like him. Like this, the third and fourth candidates came and left. When the fifth one came, the daughter felt something respond inside her. But outwardly she gave no sign that this would be her future husband.

Before the young man left the house, the girl went to her father and said to him, "Father, I really love this man. This is the one for me. I hope that he likes me as well. Could you go and ask him?"

Her father said, "I will ask him, but I am sure that he likes you. Otherwise, why would he have come and asked to marry you?"

The father approached the young man and said, "Do you really love my daughter?"

He answered, "Of course. I would not have taken the trouble of coming here if I did not love her."

So the date was fixed for their wedding. On the day of their wedding, the bridegroom said to his bride, "I have a special present for my future wife," and he placed a necklace around her neck.

O God, it was the same necklace that the thief had stolen a few months earlier. The bride was confused. She cried out, "Where did you get this necklace? Who sold it to you? This necklace was stolen from me. I felt miserable that I had lost it. Now you have bought it from someone. If you can tell us who sold it to you, we will be able to catch the thief."

The father smiled and smiled. Finally he said to his daughter, "It was I who asked him to disguise himself as a thief and take your necklace away because you were not listening to me. I knew that one day you would get married and you would still be very careless. I knew that he was a very nice young man, and I felt that you two would fall in love and one day get married. So he listened to me and stole your necklace. In this way you learned to be careful. Now you will be going to his house. Always be careful and lock the windows and doors properly. Carelessness is not a good thing!"

The wife went to her husband's house and was always very careful. She and her husband lived a very happy, prosperous life.

## MRC 65. *The stingy rich man*

There was once a rich man who was very stingy. He had lots of money, but he wanted to have much more money. He used to pray to God to give him all kinds of wealth and riches. One day God came to him and said, "I will give you more money, but how will you use it?"

The rich man said, "If You give me more money, I will give some away to charity. Giving to charity means that I am giving it to You, for I am seeing You inside human beings. So I will give You some of the money."

Then God said, "Then can you tell everybody now that one day you will be giving away money to charity?"

"Of course," answered the man. "I can tell the whole world that some day I will definitely give away money to charity. But right now, please, by Your Grace, let me keep all the money intact so that nobody can steal it. If You listen to my request, then I will fulfil Your request to give money away to the poor and needy."

So God gave the man more money and the man kept the money for some time. Then God came to him and said, "You have kept your money safe. Now you can give some money away to Me — that is, to the poor and needy."

The rich man said, "Yes, but can You not do me a favour? At least for ten years I wish to keep the money intact. Then I will give some away."

God said, "No, I want you to give money now to the poor."

The man said, "O God, if I give money away, then my wealth will not remain intact. I will lose some money. But if You allow me to keep the money for ten years, then I promise I will give You a very large sum."

After ten years God came back to the rich man and said, "Now ten years are over. Will you not start giving some of your money to the poor and needy?"

The man said to God, "At least for thirty years more let me keep the money for myself."

God said, "Now you want to keep it for thirty years! Previously you said only ten years."

The man said, "True, I said only ten years, but now I want to keep the money for another thirty years. Otherwise, I am not going to give a thing to the poor."

God said, "When will thirty years ever come? It will take such a long time."

After thirty years God came again. The man was very old and couldn't even see properly. Even then he hadn't given any money to the poor.

God said to him, "What are you doing? Even at this time you won't give money to the poor?"

The man said, "Still I am hiding the money under my bed."

God said, "What will happen when you die? Do you want to give your money to your children or to the poor?"

The rich man said, "To be very honest, I don't want to do either."

"Why, why?" God asked.

"If my children get the money," the man said, "nobody will know that they got the money from me. They will be very rich, but very few people will know that they are useless people and it is I who have given it to them. I have always been very jealous of both my sons. If they put the money in the bank and get interest, naturally they will become richer than I now am. After ten years, people will say that the children are richer than their father was. At that time I will feel very sad in Heaven. I will feel jealous that my children have surpassed me. O God, I don't want my children to be richer than I am, and I don't want to help the poor. I want everybody to say that I was the richest man, even though they hate me because of my stinginess. Who cares for generosity? I want everybody to say I was the richest member of my family."

### MRC 66. *The foolish servants*

There were two close friends who were very fond of each other. They were very nice to each other and gave one another immense joy. One day one friend told the other, "I really want to give you innocent joy by bringing my servant to you. I am sure you have never seen such an idiot in your entire life."

The friend said, "Stop, stop! I have a servant who has to be infinitely worse than yours in stupidity."

So they said, "Then let us have a competition. Let us bring both our servants and see which is more stupid. Let us invite our friends and relatives to observe their stupidity."

They found a place to meet and invited all their friends and relatives. When the contest began, one friend said to his servant, "Look, I badly need a diamond ring. Do you think you can buy me one?"

"Of course," said the servant, "if you give me money."

The master gave him one paisa. One hundred paisas equal one rupee and nine rupees equal approximately one dollar. But the servant took the money without saying anything and left for the market.

Then the other master said to his servant, "Can you please go to my garden and see if I am there or not?"

The servant said, "Certainly, I will go there right away."

Everybody laughed and laughed. Now it happened that the two servants met on the way to perform their respective tasks. They were very good friends and one of them said, "What can we do with our masters? They are such idiots. Because of my master, I also have to become a fool. I have such respect for my master that I carry out his orders, even if they are stupid. Today is Sunday. On Sunday he has asked me to bring back a diamond ring for him. He has given me money, but today is Sunday. How can I buy a diamond on Sunday when the stores are closed?"

The other servant said, "Look at my master! He does not know whom to ask when he wants to know if he is in the garden. Should he not ask the gardener? The gardener should find out if the master is in the garden or not. Why is he asking me? Now I have to go there to see if he is there or not."

So both of them had made their own discoveries. They said, "They always make fun of us. They say we are fools. Now many, many people are waiting for us to return with the answers. They are waiting to see if one of us can buy the ring and the other can find out if the master is in the garden. But let us today make fools of our masters. Let us go back there in front of many people and expose our masters as fools."

So the servants returned with folded hands. One of them said to his master, "You always laugh at me. But today you are acting like a fool."

The master said, "Why? Did I not give you money to buy the diamond ring?"

"Yes," the servant said. "You gave me the money. That is no problem. But don't you know that today is Sunday? Today the stores are closed."

Everybody laughed and laughed. Then the other servant said with folded hands, "I am so sorry. Every day you laugh at me. But today you have asked me to go into your garden to see if you are there. I wish to say that the right person to ask would be the gardener who works in the garden, and not me. The gardener will be able to see if you are there better than I can."

All the friends and relatives laughed and laughed. Then they took a vote and the servant who asked about the gardener won.

### MRC 67. *The rich man's clothes*

A rich man was very fond of a particular servant. He had many servants, but this particular servant he used to take everywhere he went.

One day the rich man wanted to walk along the street in his own village and he asked his servant to follow him. It was a puja day, a festive occasion. The servant was so happy and proud that he was walking with his master on such a special day. Everybody would see that he was with his master that day.

The rich man was generous to others, but with regard to himself he was very strict. So he was wearing very simple clothes, even simpler than the servant's. The servant said, "Master, what will people think of me if I have on more expensive clothes than you? With your money I have bought these clothes. You are rich and great. Can you not wear something nicer?"

The rich man said, "No! Everybody knows me in this village. Who cares whether I wear simple or beautiful clothes? Since everybody likes me, I don't have to wear anything expensive. These simple clothes that I have put on are sufficient."

So the master and servant went from one place to another in the village. They saw many people, some of whom they had never met before. Everyone was nice to them.

The rich man and servant stayed overnight at a friend's house. The following day the rich man wanted to go to another village, wearing the same clothes.

The servant said, "Let me run back to your house and bring extra clothes for you. Otherwise, what will people think? I am your servant. Even if I wear the same clothes for two days, nobody will mind. I don't need clean and ironed clothes. But you do need a change of clothes. You are an important man."

The rich man said, "No, I don't want to waste time. We are going to another village, so who cares what I wear? Nobody knows me in that village. I can wear simple things or expensive things and nobody is going to know who I am. So it is useless for you to go and bring nice clothes."

The servant said, "Here people know you, so you don't have to wear beautiful clothes. There people don't know you, so you don't have to wear nice things."

The master said, "If you have wisdom, then you can manage with next to nothing. But if you are a fool, then you feel that you need many things. If you wear expensive things to please other people, then you are a fool. If you want to show off to your friends and neighbours, you are a fool. Again, you are a greater fool if you go to some other town and want to show absolute strangers how great you are.

"You have to be wise! Seek wisdom and not stupidity. In my own village I do not need anything since everyone knows who I am. And in another village they don't care for me, so why do I have to impress them?"

### MRC 68. *The priest and the three hooligans*

After performing a religious ceremony, a priest was returning home quite late at night. It was very dark. He had received a large sum of money from the people who had asked him to perform the ceremony. Also, someone had given him a golden necklace, which he was wearing around his neck.

All of a sudden he was surrounded by three hooligans who shouted, "What have you got?" When they saw the necklace, they started strangling the priest and taking away the necklace.

It was very easy for the three of them to take the necklace away from the poor priest.

The priest said, "Wait! You can have my necklace, but why do you have to strangle me? Why do you have to kill me? I am not resisting."

When they stopped strangling him he said, "This necklace is just stolen loot anyway. I am giving it to you cheerfully. I am not begging you to let me keep it. You are so strong. The best thing is for you to just take it.

"I don't feel sorry because somebody just gave this to me while I was coming back from my puja ceremony. I saw three or four people like you who had just stolen some things. They were showing what they had stolen to each other. As soon as they saw me, they said, 'Don't bother us. If you tell anybody that you have seen us, we shall kill you'. So I said, 'I am not going to tell anybody'.

"They thought that I was going to send the village chief, who would bring guards and arrest them. So they threw this necklace at me to make me keep quiet.

"Now I am going home. You can have the necklace."

The hooligans asked, "Where are these people with all the stolen things?"

The priest said, "They are straight ahead. They have very beautiful, expensive things. You perhaps cannot even imagine so much wealth!"

The hooligans said, "We are much stronger than they are. We will go and attack them.

The priest said, "I see that you people are much stronger."

Then, out of joy and gratitude, the hooligans threw the necklace which they had just taken from the priest back at him.

MRC 69. *The court jester and the eggplants*

A king and his court jester were walking through the kingdom. The king wanted to enjoy the scenery in the countryside around the palace. That day the king saw many places. He saw all kinds of mango trees and fields. He was so pleased that his kingdom was so beautiful and that there were so many trees and flowers.

At one spot he saw a green field with brinjals or eggplants. When he saw the brinjals he said to his court jester, "Look, such huge and beautiful brinjals! I have never seen such big and beautiful brinjals in my life."

The court jester said, "You are right, you are right. They are so beautiful. I can see that they are also very good, very tasty."

The king said, "Brinjals have countless seeds. Because of the seeds, I hate brinjals."

The servant immediately said, "I too hate brinjals. Because of the seeds I never liked them. The taste is horrible."

The king turned to the court jester and said, "A moment ago you said that they were so nice, good and tasty. Now you are saying that they are not tasty. Why are you changing your mind?"

The court jester said, "King, you have to know that I am your servant, not the servant of a brinjal. If you say 'good', then I say 'better and best'. If you say 'bad', then I say 'worse and worst'. I am your perfect slave. Whatever you say, I just add to it. I want to be your perfect servant. I don't want to become a servant of a brinjal. Who wants it, who needs it? I need only my Master, not an eggplant!"

## MRC 70. *The king's offering*

One day a king said to his minister, "In my kingdom I have many poor people. I feel sorry for them. After all, they are also human beings, just like me, only God has made me a king. I am so rich and I am living in a palace. I have so many servants and everybody is at my command. I enjoy all kinds of earthly pleasures. I feel sorry for these people who do not even have a house to live in. I really want them to have decent homes. I don't want homeless people in my kingdom. I want to give the poor people money to build houses."

So the king asked the minister to make an announcement about what he wanted to do. Thousands of people came to the palace to get money to build a house. They all said they were homeless, and the king believed them because he knew that there were many poor people in his kingdom.

The minister was very wise. He said to the king, "You do so many things for your subjects, but many times they don't properly use the things that you have given them out of your compassion. Often they misuse what you give them."

"Explain this to me further," said the king.

"Certainly I will," said the minister. "But first I would like to ask you a question. Do you not think that if you do something for me, then I will do something for you?"

"Certainly!" said the king. "It is give and take."

The minister said, "There are many times when we want to do things for others. But first we have to know whether or not they deserve it."

"What do you mean?" asked the king.

The minister said, "Thousands of people have come here to get money to build houses. But let us see how many of them actually deserve it. Will you listen to my request? I want to tell them that if they work for you for two hours a day for only one week, then you will give them money for a house."

The king said, "Who is such a fool that he will not work for two hours a day for one week to get a house? Everybody will agree. I am very happy that this is your request. I am more than ready to give them everything free, but if you want them to prove that they deserve it, I am happy that you are making such a simple request."

"Yes," said the minister. "One week will fly away in no time. Then we will give them money to build a house."

O God, after the minister made the announcement, out of the thousands of people who had come, only one hundred stayed to work. The others all left because they didn't want to work for two hours a day for one week.

The minister said to the king, "It is only these hundred who really deserve the money. I don't really want them to work. I just wanted to see if they were willing to work. Please give them the money. These people really need the money and truly deserve it."

So the king gave money to the hundred people who had stayed.

# IS YOUR MIND READY TO CRY? IS YOUR HEART READY TO SMILE?

## BOOK 8

## MRC 71. *The king's treasurer*

One day a king's minister said to him, "O King, you never take me seriously. But, your Highness, I have something to tell you. The man who used to be in charge of your treasury was not sincere. You always thought that he was very sincere, but I tell you, he was not."

The king said, "How do you know? Can you prove this?"

The minister said, "Two months ago he died. Now I see that his sons have opened very big and expensive shops. When their father was alive, they lived simple lives. Now they are getting married and are spending large amounts of money."

"What does that prove?" the king asked.

The minister said, "This proves that the treasurer was stealing things from you and saving them for his sons. This shows that he was not an honest man."

The king asked, "Now what should we do?"

The minister said, "Let us transfer our hidden treasures to some other place."

The king said, "No, no, don't worry! It is not necessary to transfer them."

The minister said, "Perhaps he has told someone the secrets of the treasury."

The king said, "Don't waste my time telling me what he might have done. Investigate more!"

The minister said, "I have investigated. Quite recently I asked someone to pretend he was a spy and tell your rival, the neighbouring king, that he would be willing to offer him the secrets of your treasury. But the neighbouring king was not at all interested in hearing the secrets."

The king said, "What does this prove?"

The minister said, "You two are rivals and you are richer than he is. For him not to want to learn the secrets of your treasury is very strange. It means that he had already been told the secrets by your former treasurer. That is why he was not at all interested in learning them."

The king understood what the minister was trying to tell him. He said, "Let us put our wealth somewhere else. And let us investigate his sons who are now leading a very, very luxurious life — a life of great pomp."

### MRC 72. *The well-intentioned youth*

There was a young man who was always getting in trouble because of the good things that he did for others. Usually when someone does bad things he gets in trouble. But in this young man's case, whenever he did something good he got in trouble.

His parents were very sad that he kept getting in trouble despite his good intentions. Because they were worried about him, they saved up lots of money so he would have some security when they died. But they were still worried that when they were no longer around to help their son, he would do stupid things and lose all his money. Then there would be nobody to take care of him. While they were alive they would always support him and there would be no financial difficulty. But they were concerned about what would happen after their death.

What kinds of stupid things would he do? One day he was walking along the bank of a river on his way to school when he saw an elderly woman fetching water from the river with a jar. The woman put the jar on her back and started carrying it back home. Since it was quite heavy, after a short while she put it on the ground and took rest. The young man was watching her and when she was about to lift it up again, he said to himself, "Since it is so heavy, let me help her. I will tell her that if she wants my service free of charge, I will carry the pot to her house."

The boy lifted up the jar for the old woman, only to get a slap from her. She said, "You! How dare you touch my jar! You have now polluted it. I am a brahmin. What class do you come from?"

He said, "I am just a kshatriya."

She gave him a few more slaps and said, "Now I have to throw this jar away and go home to get another one. Then I have to come all the way back to fetch water again. You have ruined my day."

The next day he saw an old man chasing a little boy and screaming, "Thief! Thief! Thief! If I can catch you, I will kill you."

The young man thought, "What can such a little boy have stolen? Even if he is a thief, I won't kill him. But I will at least catch him for the man who is chasing him."

So he chased and caught the boy. The little boy was very strong and he struck the young man. The young man said, "You are a thief! Why do you have to strike me?" Then he gave the boy a smart slap.

Just then the old man came running up and said, "How dare you touch my grandson! Out of affection I was calling him a thief. His grandmother made sweetmeats and we thought we would eat them together. But he was so greedy that he took them and ran away. So I was playing with my grandson, calling 'Thief! Thief!' Who asked you to come and grab him and give him a slap?" Then the grandfather started beating the poor young man black and blue.

Another day the boy saw an old man and old lady swimming. After some time, the old man got tired so he came out and started reading the newspaper, while the old lady continued swimming. After a little while the old lady said to her husband, "Now I am tired. Can you give me a hand?"

The old man was absorbed in reading the newspaper and he paid no attention to her. The young man, who was nearby, said, "Oh, since this lady is asking for help and her husband is reading, why bother him? Let me go and give her a hand."

So he went to the edge of the water and offered the lady his hand. The lady screamed as soon as she saw him extend his hand to help her out. immediately the old man said, "What are you doing?"

The young man said, "She needed a hand and you were reading the newspaper."

He said, "You idiot! She is my wife. How dare you touch my wife!"

Then he started beating the young man.

After getting such a bad beating, the young man went and lay down in a nearby field. The village head happened to be passing by and asked, "What are you doing there? Why are you lying down there?"

The young man said, "I am miserable, miserable! Every day I go out and try to help people. But despite my good intentions, people only beat me."

The village head asked, "What do you mean?"

The boy told the stories of all that had happened to him. The village head felt very sorry for him and said, "You come with me. I will inform your parents that I am hiring you. You don't have to go to school any more. I will put you in charge of my garden, and you will tell me every day how many mangos, guavas, apples and so forth I have. And you can eat as much as you want to.

"You are an honest person, I know. But sometimes honest people can be stupid. I want to save you from your stupidity. I will save you from your stupidity and you will save me from thievery. Your stupidity I will take care of and you will be able to help me when people come to steal things from my garden."

## MRC 73. *The gentleman shoots a burglar*

There was a gentleman who had a bad habit of drinking. He never drank at home or at the office; in these places he was a perfect gentleman. But sometimes he would drink on his way home from work.

One night the man came home late from the office, and on that particular night he was heavily drunk. His wife had been waiting up for him, but finally she had fallen asleep. When the man arrived, he didn't want to disturb his wife, his son or his servant. He just wanted to get into his bed very quietly. So very softly he opened the side door and he didn't turn on the light.

When he entered into his house, he saw a man standing in one corner of his living room. The gentleman always kept a revolver in his pocket. So he took out the revolver and shot the intruder. The gun made a very loud noise and his son, wife and servant came running. They cried, "What has happened? What has happened?"

He said, "I just shot a burglar."

O God, when they turned on the lights they saw it was just a coat hanging in the living room. His wife had bought a new suit for him and the jacket and trousers were hanging there. She was going to give it to him the next day as a gift for his birthday.

The wife said, "What have you done? I took so much time shopping for this and I spent so much money on it! Why didn't you call us and wake us up if you thought there was a burglar in the house?"

The gentleman said, "You are such a fool! Luckily it was not a man. Otherwise, I would be in jail by now!"

## MRC 74. *Three fools and a rogue*

When the head of a particular village passed away, many people came to his house to mourn. All of them were crying and saying how nice he had been. Some were bad and were only shedding crocodile tears, but some were shedding sincere tears.

A businessman wanted to go, but he himself was very sick. He told his eldest son, "Go there and console the members of the family."

The son said, "I don't know how to console anybody. I have never done this kind of thing. You are always the one who goes to mourn if someone dies. I don't know what to say."

The father said, "Just say what others are saying. Just imitate what others say and what others do."

Many people were gathered at the deceased man's house. Some were talking loudly and some were whispering. The son thought, "I am sure that the people speaking quietly are the ones who know the correct thing to say."

He went closer and heard one man telling his two friends, "It is good that the rogue has died at last."

So the businessman's son went to the oldest son of the village head and asked, "Why are you crying?"

The son said, "My father has just died. Why shouldn't I cry?"

The businessman's son said, "It is good that the rogue has finally died."

The son said, "What!" Then he and all the others in the house thrashed the businessman's son. So the boy went home crying.

His father said, "What has happened?"

The boy said, "You told me to say what others said. I overheard somebody say, 'It is good that the rogue has died at last'. When I said the same thing to his son, O God, he and many others beat me so badly."

The father was afraid that something would happen because his son had said this to the village head's son. He said, "Now they will think ill of me and my family, and then we will be in serious trouble."

The businessman's second eldest son said, "Father, I will make up for it. Please allow me to go there and I will say something to compensate."

The father said, "Just do the right thing. I don't have to tell you what to say or whom to talk to. Just go there and say something to the eldest son so that he doesn't hold anything against us. I have such a stupid eldest son. Look what he has done. Now go there and compensate for your older brother."

So the businessman's second eldest son went to the village head's house and said to the eldest son, "I am so sorry. I have such a stupid older brother. He is useless, useless, useless. Please forgive our family. I promise you that when you die, I will be the first person to come to your house and cry for you. And I will cry much more than anyone has ever cried."

The son got furious. He said, "My father has just died and we are all crying. Why do you now have to think of my death?"

The son of the village head's eldest son overheard the conversation and he also got mad. He said, "My grandfather has just died and we are all mourning. Is this the time to talk about my father's death?" Then he started beating the businessman's son.

This son was also beaten very badly, and he came back home crying and crying. The father said, "You idiot! Did you have to say, 'When you die?' His father has just died and you had to speak of the son's death!"

The third son of the businessman said, "Father, don't worry. I will be able to compensate for my brothers."

When the third son went to the village head's house, he said to the eldest son, "My brothers are such fools. Please forgive our family. I tell you, as soon as I hear that you have fallen sick,

I will come and cry for you. Even long before you die, I will start crying for you."

The son of the village head again became furious. He said, "Even long before I die, you will be thinking of my death!" Then he and all the members of his family beat the third son of the businessman.

When the third son returned home badly beaten, the father said, "I have such idiot sons! What will they think of our family?"

Finally the youngest son said, "Father, please let me go and compensate."

By this time the father had lost all faith in his sons, but he said, "All right, then go there."

The youngest son went to the house of the village head and saw that many people were crying and suffering. He went to the son of the deceased man and said, "I had a dream last night that I would like to tell you about. In the dream I felt miserable because I saw that your father had died. And now it is true; I see that your father has died."

The son said, "I don't want to hear about your dream."

The businessman's son said, "The next thing is very important. Your father said to me that you are immortal. You won't die."

The son said, "Everybody else will die, but I will not die?"

The businessman's son said, "Your father told me in my dream that he himself had a dream. His dream told him that if he died today, then you would be able to live as long as you wanted to."

The son said, "Do you mean that if he had died on another day, then I would live only for a short time like everybody else?"

The businessman's son said, "That is between your father and my dream. Whatever I heard I am telling you. One final thing! In my dream your father told me that definitely one day you will become king. Now you are a village head, but because of your big heart, wisdom and love for mankind, soon you will become king. In the village nobody is as good, as kind and as forgiving as you are. Because of all these good qualities, some day you will become king. So you will be immortal and you will be king."

The village head's son knew that because the first three brothers had been fools, this one was trying to flatter him. He thought, "At least one brother has some sense. Of course, he has come to flatter me, but at least he is not a fool. The other three were real fools!

So he said to the fourth brother, "Go home peacefully and tell your father that I don't hold anything against him or his other sons. I know that to take care of foolish sons is such a hard task. I am sure that those three foolish brothers of yours have done many foolish things in their lives. Your father has to put up with them, but I could not. So I thrashed them.

"You, at least, are not a fool. But I see that you are a rogue. You have come here only to flatter me. I don't need stupid people and, again, a rogue like you I don't need either. Go back to your father and tell him that I send my regards. Then I will mourn the loss of my father in peace."

### MRC 75. *The village meeting*

A meeting was held in a village to reform society. Many villagers came, because they all wanted to have a better society. But everybody was talking and nobody was listening to anybody else. It was absolutely like a village market. Everybody was shouting and screaming about how to reform the village, and nobody could hear anything.

Finally one man said, "My dear brothers, I have been trying to tell you something nice, good and inspiring. But since you are not paying any attention to me, from now on I will call you my brothers-in-laws."

Everybody started screaming, "What! Brothers-in-laws?" Then they laughed and laughed.

The man said, "What is wrong? Brothers-in-laws are all rascals, so I am saying that you people are all rascals."

Another person stood up and said, "Yes, we may be rascals, but you are an idiot."

"What!" said the man. "I am an idiot?"

The second man continued, "Rascals can thrash idiots but idiots cannot thrash rascals."

The man said, "What do you mean?"

The second man said, "We are all rascals, so we can thrash you. But you cannot thrash us because you are an idiot. Where did you learn to say 'laws?' It is not brothers-in-laws, but brothers-in-law. What kind of English are you speaking? You are a real idiot!"

### MRC 76. *The king's washerman*

Once a king was very dissatisfied with his washerman. The washerman usually did a good job with the king's clothes, but on one particular occasion he did not do a good job. The king was very dissatisfied and he sent a court officer to summon him.

When the officer went to the washerman's house, he found the man talking to his donkey with folded hands. He was saying, "Your highness, you are so great, you are so kind, you are so good. The world does not understand you. I myself cannot begin to understand how great you are. But so many of your subjects do not even want to know how great you are. They are such ungrateful people."

The officer told the washerman to come quickly to the king's palace. Then the officer returned to the king and reported, "He is such a crazy fellow. He was talking to his donkey!"

An hour passed, but still the washerman did not come to the palace. The king got mad at his officer and said, "Why did you come back without him? This time go and bring him personally."

The officer went back to the washerman's house and saw that the man was still speaking to his donkey with folded hands, saying, "Your highness, you are good and great. We have no humility. We don't show you enough humility."

This time the court officer grabbed the washerman and said, "Now stop this nonsense!" He brought him to the king and told the king, "He was literally praying to his donkey. What can you expect from this donkey?"

The king asked, "Why were you praying to your donkey? What is wrong with you?"

The washerman said, " I thought that if someday you were to summon me to the palace because I was doing such a good job on your clothes, then I would have to be humble. I have heard that there are people who are not humble to you and you do not like them. I wanted you to like me, so I was practising humility by praying to my donkey. I was practising the things that I wanted to tell you to express my appreciation and admiration. O King, there are many who come to you but do not show you due respect. So I am very sad."

The king was very pleased with the washerman. He knew that there were many who did not show him enough respect. Since the washerman had been practising humility, respectfulness and devotion, the king forgave him and gave him lots of money. He told him, "For God's sake, wash my clothes well. This time you have not done a good job, but otherwise you have been doing quite well. Now you have said very nice things to me. I see that it is not just flattery and I am deeply moved."

## MRC 77. *The crazy philosopher*

Once there was a philosopher who was very well known in the kingdom. On the one hand, he had such wisdom and everybody admired him. On the other hand, at times he was very, very crazy. But people forgave him because of his inner wisdom. They always saw only his good side. The king cared for men of wisdom, so he also liked the philosopher. He knew that sometimes people who are geniuses can act crazy. The king felt that he needed this philosopher and he greatly admired him.

One day the philosopher left his house for good. At night he would stay inside a cave and during the day he would roam the streets, always trying to hide from people. Everybody asked him, "Why do you always roam around alone? Why do you not allow anyone to accompany you?"

The philosopher would answer, "I roam around alone for only one reason: because all you people are dishonest. I am looking for an honest man. You may be my friends, but you are not honest."

Everybody was shocked at the philosopher's rude behaviour, for each one considered himself to be an honest person. But the philosopher said, "I myself am not honest. I am looking for an honest man."

One day a court officer brought the philosopher before the king and said, "Today a thief stole something and with great difficulty we chased him and arrested him. When we were bringing him to jail we passed this crazy philosopher. He said to us, 'Two big thieves have caught a little thief'."

The officer was very mad at the philosopher. He said to the king, "He called us thieves! With great difficulty we caught the real thief, and look what he said!"

The king looked at the officer and then at the philosopher. He thought for a few seconds and then he said, "He is right, he is right. We are all dishonest."

Then the king said, "Had I not been king, I would definitely have given up everything and lived the same kind of life that this philosopher is living. I too would have lived a simple life and I too would have looked for an honest person on earth. I am king, but even for me honesty is a far cry. No matter how hard one tries to be honest, it is extremely difficult. The philosopher is looking for honesty in others. This is also what I would have liked to do, but I cannot because of my position. I would have tried much more sincerely to be honest had I not been king."

## MRC 78. *The thief becomes a sage*

Once a thief entered into a tiny shop, stole a wristwatch and then started running away. The owner saw him stealing and began chasing him. He ran and ran and ran. While chasing the thief, the owner saw two young men who were just fooling around. He shouted to them, "Please help me, help me!"

The two men grabbed the thief and they all brought him to the police station. The police officer asked the thief, "Is it true that you have stolen something?"

The thief said, "Yes, I stole a wristwatch."

Then the police officer gave the thief three hard kicks. Each time the officer kicked harder. The thief was rolling on the ground in pain. After the third kick, he started running away. The two young men who had caught him were laughing and laughing. They were not in the mood to run after him again. They said, "We don't feel like chasing him again. We caught him once and that is enough. Besides, the police officer has already punished him."

The shopkeeper was pleased that he had got the wristwatch back and the thief had been punished. So everyone left the police station.

The thief felt sorry for himself. He said, "Did I come into the world to be kicked by a police officer? My life has no meaning."

He entered into the forest and began walking. After some time he saw a small hut. By then it was evening. He looked inside and saw two candles burning, but nobody was there. He said, "I am getting such a peaceful feeling from looking into this cottage. When I steal things, I don't get peace. I am always worrying that I will be caught. This small hut is so peaceful. Let me go inside."

When he entered the hut he saw a table with a few pieces of fruit and a small bowl of milk. He drank the milk and ate the fruit. Afterwards, he fell asleep. After an hour the owner of the cottage, a hermit, came back from his evening walk. The hermit had conquered anger, so when he saw the thief he said, "O my friend, I am very happy that you have come. I think that you needed the food more than I did."

The thief fell at the feet of the hermit and said, "There is such a difference between your life and my life. Will you accept me as your disciple?" Then he told the hermit all about his life as a thief.

The hermit said, "I will accept you on the condition that you never steal again."

The young man promised, "No, I will never steal again. If I become your disciple, how can I steal?"

The hermit accepted him and taught him how to pray and meditate. From time to time people used to come to the hermit for blessings. They could not recognise the thief because he had changed so much.

In a few years' time the hermit died. Some of the hermit's followers had such admiration for his disciple that they begged the young man to come to the neighbouring village and officiate at a puja.

The young man refused. "I am illiterate," he said. "I can't conduct the ceremonies."

The followers insisted. They said, "You have such faith in God and love for God! There are many scholars, but we don't need them. We need you."

Finally the man agreed. He felt that nobody would recognise him as the former thief. By that time he had grown long hair and a beard and he was quite saintly looking. So he went to the village and in a very simple way conducted the village puja.

The police officer who had kicked him several years before happened to be in the crowd attending the puja. The officer was very well-respected in the village, but by this time he was retired. During the ceremony he said to one of his friends, "This young man is very sincere. Whether he has occult power or not I do not know. But he is drawing my affection and love and even my admiration. I have seen many so-called saints, but they are all frauds. However, I can tell that this man is very sincere, although I do not know whether he has the capacity to perform miracles or not." The young man overheard the officer but remained silent.

After the young man finished performing the puja, everyone came and bowed down and touched his feet. They all felt that he was a great sage. The police officer also touched his feet very devotedly. When the officer touched his feet, the man said, "A little while ago you were talking about occult power. Occult power creates miracles, but you yourself have also performed a miracle."

The officer was surprised. "When?" he asked. "It can't be possible!"

The man insisted, "You have performed a miracle."

The police officer was so eager to hear what he had done.

The man said, "Only two or three years ago, do you remember when you kicked someone who had stolen a wristwatch?"

"So many thieves I have kicked so mercilessly," the officer said.

The man related the particular incident to the officer. He said, "On that day you kicked me so hard that I still remember it! Just because you kicked me so hard, I went to the hermit and became a seeker. By God's Grace I stopped stealing and became a spiritual person. It was your kick that began my inner life. And now you are touching my feet!"

### MRC 79. *The guest house*

There was a rich man who had a very big heart. He wanted to have a guest house named after him where everything would be free. So he built a guest house on the outskirts of his village and he hired three persons to look after it: a clerk, a cook and a maid. He paid them well and told them that everything was to be free of charge.

Everything went well for a couple of months. Everything was given for free by the clerk, the cook and the maid. O God, one day a brilliant scheme entered into their minds. They said to each other, "Let us very cleverly start charging something when the next guests come. Although it is free of charge, let us charge something just for 'wear and tear'. We will say that we would be grateful if they make a donation to pay for wear and tear. But we will tell them that they are under no obligation to pay anything. People will be willing to pay because we are taking such good care of the guest house."

As time passed, the clerk, the cook and the maid began demanding fees from their guests for overnight accommodations and for food, just like many other guest houses. If someone didn't give the money, then he was not allowed to stay there.

The rich man was totally ignorant of what was happening and he continued sending money to keep the guest house running. The guests didn't take the trouble to inform the rich man. They said, "We will stay here only overnight. If we stayed somewhere else, we would have to pay. So we may as well pay here."

One night a shrewd man came to the guest house. When he was given a bill for food and lodging, he became furious. "How can you do this?" he said.

The clerk answered, "We do it!"

He asked him, "What if someone makes complaints against you?"

The clerk answered, "Let them make complaints. We were advised by the owner just the other day to ask for money."

The traveller didn't believe it. So he went to the village where the rich man lived and casually said to a friend he had there, "Once upon a time that rich man was very generous. Now I understand that he has become mercenary. He used to allow travellers to stay for free at his guest house, but now the workers are saying that he wants them to charge money."

His friend couldn't believe his ears. "The rich man is still very kind-hearted," he said. "Who told you this?"

The man said, "I was there last night and they made me pay."

His friend said, "Please tell some of the villagers that you saw the king's brother-in-law in the guest house last night. Say that he was appreciating the guest house like anything and that he is planning to stay there for a week."

When the news reached the rich man, he said, "My guest house is such a humble place, and the king's brother-in-law is staying there! I must go and honour him."

In the meantime the traveller went back to the guest house. As usual the clerk asked him, "Did you make a reservation?"

The man said, "No, I do not have a reservation."

The clerk said, "You have to pay twenty rupees if you want to stay here overnight."

The man said, "I don't need any money in this guest house. Here one doesn't have to pay."

The clerk said, "If you won't pay, then go away from here."

The man ignored him and went into the restaurant. He sat at a table and ordered a meal. At the restaurant there was a sign saying that one didn't have to pay. But after the cook served him, he asked him for money. The man said, "The sign says that you don't have to pay for anything." By that time he had finished eating, so what could they do? They were so mad at him. They were cursing him and they wanted to throw him out.

The man ran upstairs and found a room that was unoccupied. He entered inside and pretended to fall asleep on the bed. When the man who was actually supposed to be in that room came in, he was shocked to find somebody else in his bed. He went downstairs and told the maid, "Look, somebody is in my room!"

The maid came and started insulting the man. She said, "You have not paid. What are you doing here?"

The man said, "Everything is supposed to be free of charge here from the beginning to the end."

The clerk, the cook and the maid were all about to thrash the man when the rich man arrived at the guest house. He was very surprised to find all the workers arguing with the guest who wouldn't pay.

The guest said to the rich man, "Sir, you are extremely kind and rich, but your affluence cannot bring you happiness."

"What do you mean?" asked the rich man.

"You also need wisdom," said the man.

"In what way?" he asked.

"You are kind and rich," the man explained, "but you are not wise. These workers of yours are rogues. They have been exploiting your kindness and charging all the guests who come here. I am the eyewitness. I can tell you firsthand how they tried to exploit me. There are other guests here also. You can ask them if I am telling the truth!"

The rich man spoke to the other guests. Some of them said, "We have visited this place quite a few times. Each time we have had to pay for everything."

The rich man got so disgusted that he fired the three workers and handed over the guest house to the government. He said, "Let the government take care of it!"

### MRC 80. *Shyama's husband*

There was once a man named Kiran who was very idle, while his wife, Shyama, was very active. Kiran wouldn't do anything. Shyama had to work and support him. Every day the wife would milk the cow and then take the milk to the market to sell. All kinds of things the wife had to make and sell to support her husband. In Indian villages the husband always works and the wife looks after the house. But in this case it was just the opposite. After some time, nobody would call the husband Kiran. They would always refer to him as 'Shyama's husband'.

One day, an old friend of his came to the village and asked one of his neighbours, "Do you know where Kiran lives?"

The man said, "I have never heard of him. He must not live around here."

It happened that Kiran was enjoying his afternoon siesta nearby. He woke up and overheard his neighbour saying that there was no one by the name of Kiran in the village. Kiran said, "What? Am I not Kiran?"

He and his friend were so happy to see each other. The friend said to the neighbour, "Why did you say that Kiran did not live here?

The man said, "I know him only as Shyama's husband."

When the man left, Kiran's friend said to him, "What an insult! Nowhere have I ever heard anyone called by his wife's name. It is always just the opposite."

Kiran felt miserable. He thought to himself, "This can't go on."

The following day he said, "How can I bring back my name and reputation?" He knew that his wife sold milk at the market every day. So this time he himself went to sell the milk.

One villager said to him, "Oh, it is so good to see you. You look wonderful, Shyama's husband. You look wonderful."

Kiran said, "Here I am selling the milk, and still the man has to call me 'Shyama's husband'."

Then Kiran went to another place to sell the milk. A little girl saw him and cried, "Mother, Mother, today Shyama's husband has come to sell milk, not Shyama."

Kiran said, "Even this little girl calls me 'Shyama's husband'." He became so furious. He said, "The only thing I can do now is become a merchant. I will borrow money from someone and open up a business. Then people will come to know me as Kiran and my deplorable fate will come to an end."

He went to a moneylender, but the moneylender said, "I don't know you well. Do you have property?"

The clerk said, "Sir, you don't have to worry because he is Shyama's husband. If he doesn't give you the money back, Shyama will."

Kiran was so angry that he left the moneylender's shop and said, "I am renouncing the world." He went into a forest to take up a life of prayer and meditation. He grew a beard and moustache and ate only the fruits that grew in the forest. At times he would go begging door to door as a mendicant.

Shyama felt miserable that she had lost her husband. One day there was a fair in the village and hundreds of people came. Kiran was begging for food from person to person, but nobody recognised him. Kiran went up to his wife, for he was absolutely sure that she would not be able to recognise him. As soon as Shyama looked at him, she immediately burst into tears. Everybody thought that this fellow had said something undivine to hcr.

Then in front of everyone, she said to the beggar, "How can you fool me? Are you not my husband? I promise you, if you come back home, from now on people will call you by your own name. I have saved up some money. With this money you can open up a business. Everybody will come to you, and I will only work at home as your servant. Nobody will call you by a servant's name. Everybody will call you Kiran."

The husband believed her and came back home. From then on, everybody called him Kiran and not 'Shyama's husband'.

IS YOUR MIND READY TO CRY?
IS YOUR HEART READY TO SMILE?

# BOOK 9

## MRC 81. *The brother's inheritance*

There were two brothers. One was very good and one was very bad, as quite often happens in a family. The father was quite old and about to die.

On his deathbed, the father said to his sons, "I wish both of you to be happy after my passing. Always be together and be peaceful. Be kind to each other. If one of you needs something, the other one should help him. I am distributing my property and land equally to each of you. Also I am keeping a large amount of money in the bank for both of you whenever you need it for an emergency."

Since the older one was the kinder and wiser of the two, the father wanted him to be responsible for the money. He told the older brother, "Since the older one is more responsible for things in a family, you will be the one to judge when either of you really needs the money. At the time of your real need, you yourself will use it, and you will give the younger one money when he needs it."

Soon the father died. Both the sons got large portions of land. The younger one was a real lazybones. He was a good talker but not a doer. The older one was a hard worker and he cultivated his fields. Since the younger one was not doing anything, eventually he became poverty-stricken.

The younger brother went to the older brother and said, "I am so poor. Can you not help me?"

The older brother said to him, "I can give you money, but your real problem is that you do not work. You have to work. Otherwise, people will ridicule you."

The younger one said, "Certainly I will work. But first, can you not do me a favour?"

"What is it?" asked the older brother.

He said, "Your fields are now yielding a bumper crop, whereas mine are growing nothing. Can you exchange fields with me? You take my land and I will take yours. My land you will cultivate. Then, once it starts growing fruits and vegetables, at that time I will take it back and give you back your land. From that time on, I will be extremely careful and work as hard as you are working now. In every way I will become a good and diligent person."

"All right," the brother finally agreed, "Father asked us to be kind to each other, so I will do it. But remember, you promised that as soon as your fields are cultivated and everything is in proper shape, you will return my land to me."

The younger brother said, "I promise you, I promise you!"

So the older brother started cultivating the younger one's fields. One day he was feeling sorry for the younger brother. He said to himself, "True, my brother has got my land. But perhaps he will need a little more money since he is still poor. Let me go and give him half the money that Father has left for us."

He went to his younger brother and said, "I feel that this is an emergency. Although I have given you my fields, it will take a long time for me to make your fields as fruitful as mine. So take half the money that Father has left for us."

The younger one said, "I have some special news to tell you. You will be very pleased to know that I have sold all your fields. So you don't have to worry about my money problems. Now I am really rich. You can do anything that you want to with my fields."

The older brother buried his head in his hands.

## MRC 82. *The gold necklace*

Once there were two brothers, and each one had a very good nature. Both brothers were very good, but one had a very good wife and one had a very bad wife. The one who had the very bad wife was the poorer of the two.

One day the rich brother's wife was wearing a beautiful gold necklace. Her husband had lots of money, so naturally she could afford expensive things. The wife of the poor brother was very jealous of her. When she saw the necklace, she went home and insulted her husband because he did not have as much money as his brother.

Then the poor wife went to her sister-in-law and said, "I have invited some guests over tonight, and I would like to wear your beautiful gold necklace. Could you possibly give it to me for one or two days, and then I will return it to you?"

The rich wife said, "Of course, I will gladly lend it to you."

The poor wife took the necklace home and wore it that night when her guests came. They all appreciated the necklace, but she didn't tell them it was borrowed.

Two days, three days and then a week passed, but still the poor wife didn't return the necklace. The rich wife felt sad that she didn't have her necklace back, so very apologetically she went to her sister-in-law and said, "Could you kindly return my necklace?"

The poor wife said, "What! When did you give me your necklace? You are just telling lies to make me feel that I am very poor and you are very rich. I have no idea what you are talking about."

The poor brother begged his wife to return the necklace. He said, "We are poor, but we can't be dishonest." But his wife wouldn't listen to him.

When the rich wife told her husband what had happened, he said, "O God, keep your mouth shut. If the villagers come to know that my brother's wife is such a liar, it will bring terrible disgrace to the family

The wife said, "No, I have to get this necklace back."

The next day she went back to her sister-in-law. Before she could even mention the necklace, the poor wife said, "This time, if you tell any lies, I will insult you. I have not taken anything from you!"

When the rich wife told her husband what had happened this time, he said, "She is right. Stop telling lies."

The wife got mad. "She has to give me the necklace," she said.

The husband said, "What can I do? I don't want to hear that my brother's wife is so bad. I will give you another necklace. If we say anything about this, it will reflect on our family."

A few days later the rich wife's daughter came to visit her. The mother was still very, very sad about the necklace. Her daughter asked her why she was so sad, and the mother told her.

The daughter said to her mother, "Don't worry, my aunt knows that I have come to visit you. She likes me very much, and she will definitely come here to see me." Then the daughter instructed her mother to say a few things when the aunt came.

The poor brother's wife arrived, and her sister-in-law served her a very nice meal. Everyone was having a wonderful time. Then the daughter said to her mother, "You wrote to me a few weeks ago that you had a most beautiful necklace. Where is it? Why are you not wearing it to show off?"

The mother said, "It was a stolen necklace. I bought it from someone who had stolen it. The police caught the thief and he told them that he had sold it to someone in this neighbourhood. Fortunately, the thief couldn't remember the exact house where he sold it. Now the police are making an investigation."

The daughter said, "So what has happened to the necklace?"

The mother said, "In the meantime, your aunt came to my house and borrowed it, because she was having guests over. But after the guests left, she misplaced it. She would gladly have given it back, but she misplaced it. Anyway, I am so glad that I do not have it anymore."

"Why is that?" asked the daughter.

The mother continued, "The police can come and search my house, and still they won't find it. At the same time, even if they go to your aunt's place, they won't find it there either. I am so glad that the stolen necklace is now lost."

When the aunt heard this story, she ran out of the house and went home. Then she put the necklace in a box and gave it to her servant. "Go and give this to my sister-in-law, but don't put it in her hand. Just throw it at her," she said.

The servant said, "How can I do that?"

The lady said, "Such disrespect! You must obey me!"

So the servant went to the rich woman's house. But instead of throwing the box at her, he threw it at her feet. This is how the rich wife got back her gold necklace.

### MRC 83. *The king and the salt*

A Muslim king once decided to go out with a few guards and ministers to a very distant place to see the poorest village in his kingdom. The people in that village had never seen the king before. They were so excited to hear that he was coming to visit them, and they decorated the village according to their poor capacity.

When the king arrived with his entourage, he asked his cook to prepare a delicious meal. The cook prepared the meal, but he did not have enough salt. The king said to the cook, "Go and get some salt from one of the villagers, but make sure you pay for it."

The cook said, "O King, how will the villagers accept money for the salt if I tell them that it is for you? Even if I don't say it is for you, if I ask them for a small quantity of salt, they will not ask for money."

The king said, "If they don't ask for money, no harm. Just ask for the salt and then give them double the amount of money that you would pay for it at the market."

The cook said, "I will do it, O King, but I can't understand why I should pay them. You are the King and you are coming here to visit them. They are deeply honoured that you have come."

The king said, "These are poor people. You have to pay them! I have to think of my son and my kingdom. To protect my kingdom I have to make my son wise. No matter what I do, my son always imitates me inwardly and outwardly and tries to surpass me. If I take some salt without paying for it, then one day my son will come here and take something that is very expensive without paying. If I take something for free, then he will force these people to give him something for free that is very expensive.

"That is why I am paying double the amount for the salt. I tell you, one day my son will come here and pay four times the amount that something costs. That is what I want. I want my son to be generous. I want my son to surpass me in every way in good qualities, but not in bad qualities. Now I am showing my generosity, so that one day my son will come and show even more generosity."

## MRC 84. *The diamond ring*

Once a princess, her maids and a few guards were by the side of a river. The princess entered into the river to swim and left her diamond ring on the bank. She didn't give the ring to any particular person; she just left it inside a jewellery box on the shore. Some of the maids were watching her swim, while others were just enjoying the day. The guards were not standing near the princess and her maids, because they knew that the princess was quite safe.

When the princess came out of the river, she saw that the diamond ring was missing from the box. She looked around and asked, "Who has taken my ring?"

Nobody wanted to confess. The princess said, "The two or three guards were quite far from the box. I know that they didn't do it. My maids have all been with me for years. But one of them must have taken it. This is such an embarrassing situation. How am I going to catch the thief?

"My father has such faith in astrologers. Some astrologer will be able to tell us secretly which maid has taken the ring. Then that person will have to give it back. But I don't want to embarrass that maid. Once I get it back, I won't blame the thief. I will be happy just to have my diamond ring back."

Then the princess said to the maids, "I am giving you one last chance. Tonight whoever has stolen the ring can put it in my room. Otherwise, tomorrow I will ask an astrologer who the culprit is."

The princess thought that since the maids had such faith in astrologers, the culprit would return the ring. But the following day the ring was still nowhere to be found. So the princess called in an astrologer and said, "Yesterday I was swimming, and when I came out of the river I discovered that my diamond necklace was missing. But nobody wants to confess that they have taken it. This is a very embarrassing situation. Can you tell me who has taken my necklace?"

The astrologer looked around and said, "Your maids are all nice people. They are very faithful and devoted. The thief was somebody else who was walking by. I can see him. He is now in another village. If you want, I will be able to concentrate on this person and catch him."

The princess got mad at the astrologer. She said, "I didn't lose a necklace. It was a diamond ring! What kind of astrologer are you?"

The princess told her father what had happened and the king told his guards to thrash this useless astrologer. The astrologer cried out, "Please don't thrash me. I will be very sincere. The maids bribed me. That is why I said that somebody else was the thief. Since I could not save them, the best thing is for me to give them their money back."

The king immediately fired all the maids and ordered the astrologer to leave the palace. Then the king sent for a different astrologer.

This time the princess said to the astrologer, "I had a necklace and also a diamond ring in a box near the river where I was swimming. There were a few more items in the box, but these two things were missing when I came out of the river. Please tell me if one of my maids was the thief or if the thief was somebody else. Although father has fired the maids, they have not yet left the palace. We want to know who the culprit is."

The astrologer went deep within and said, "Princess, you are wrong. You didn't lose a necklace. Your necklace is still inside the box. But your diamond ring is missing. Please look inside the jewellery box. I am sure your necklace is there."

The princess knew that the necklace was there, but she pretended to go to her room and look in the box. She returned to the astrologer, pretending to be quite happy that she had found her necklace. Now she had all faith that this astrologer would be able to tell her who the actual culprit was.

The astrologer said, "The culprit is in the palace. But before I embarrass that person, will it not be advisable for us to leave the room so that whoever has stolen the ring can secretly put it here? Then the princess will get her ring back."

The king got furious. "The maids are such bad people. They bribed the first astrologer because they thought that I would be angry at their negligence. If any one of them saw the culprit stealing, why is she not telling us?"

At that time the real culprit came and fell at the feet of the king and placed the diamond ring before him. She said, "O King, forgive me, forgive me."

The king said, "Now I have got my daughter's ring back. Either I can continue my anger or I can forgive you. Now that I am happy and the princess is happy, I will forgive all of you. You can again work at the palace. But never steal again!"

So the king forgave the maids and allowed them to work at the palace once again.

### MRC 85. *The zamindar's servant*

A village zamindar and his wife had a number of goats, and they had a servant who looked after them. The zamindar liked the boy very much, but his wife suspected him. The zamindar was sad that his wife didn't trust the servant, but fortunately the young boy did not know this. The wife was very clever. Outwardly she was very kind, polite and affectionate to him, but inwardly she was very hostile to him.

One day a friend came to the zamindar's home and saw that he was very sad. The friend asked, "Why are you sad?"

The zamindar answered, "I am sad that my wife and I are not getting along because of this servant. Both of us have different opinions about him."

The friend said, "Don't worry. I will be able to solve the problem and tell you whether he is good or bad."

One day while the servant was watching the goats in a field, the master's friend came up to him and said, "This particular goat is so beautiful. Will you sell it to me for five rupees?"

The boy answered, "No, I am sorry. I cannot sell it."

The friend asked again, "Will you sell it for ten rupees?"

The boy said, "No, I am sorry."

"Twenty rupees?" the friend asked.

The servant said, "If you want to buy the goat, you will have to go to my master and give him the twenty rupees. If my master says he will sell it, then I will give it to you."

The friend said, "Who wants to go to your master? His house is quite far. Let me give you thirty rupees. I am sure that your master does not give you enough salary. Keep the thirty rupees and tell your master that the goat was stolen. Your master has so many goats. He won't even know it is gone."

"Oh no," the boy said, "I can't do that. My master will know. And even if he didn't notice, I know how many goats my master has, so I would know if one were missing."

The friend said, "Just take thirty rupees and give me the goat. Then go and give your master the money and tell him you have sold it."

The boy said, "No, I am sorry. I can't sell it without my master's permission."

"If I give you one hundred rupees, will you give me the goat?" the friend said. "Then you can keep all the money."

"I am not a thief," the servant said. "I could never keep the money."

The friend said, "You could give him seventy rupees and keep thirty for yourself. Or you could just tell him the goat was stolen and keep all the money for yourself."

"That I could never do," the young man said.

Since the man was insisting, the servant finally said, "If you really want to give me a hundred rupees for one goat, then I will accept the money and give it to my master."

The zamindar's friend was very curious to see what the servant would do with the money. He thought, "Either he will give his master a little less or tell him the goat was stolen. No matter what he does, I will be able to tell his master the true story."

The servant went to his master and gave him the hundred rupees. He said, "Master, forgive me. Without your permission I sold a goat for a hundred rupees. I knew that the goat was only worth five rupees, but this man insisted on giving me one hundred rupees for it. I thought that you would be very happy to get one hundred rupees for a goat that is worth only five rupees. Now you can buy many more goats."

The wife said to the servant, "I wish to speak to my husband privately for a minute. Would you please go away from here now?"

Then the wife said to her husband, "I suspect him. I tell you, he must have sold it at an even higher price and he is giving us only part of it." She did not know that it was the zamindar's friend who had bought the goat.

Just then the zamindar's friend arrived at his house and asked, "What is happening?"

The zamindar said, "Our servant says that he has sold a goat for a hundred rupees. I don't suspect my servant, but my wife, as usual, suspects him. She feels that he has sold the goat for a still higher price and kept some money for himself."

The friend said, "You will never find anybody in your lifetime as honest and sincere as this servant. It was I who bought the goat for one hundred rupees. I tested him in so many ways. In so many tricky ways I tried to persuade him to keep the money for himself. But each and every time he proved to me that he is extremely sincere. I have examined him thoroughly. He is sincerity incarnate."

The zamindar said to his wife, "I told you so!"

The wife said, "It is always good to test people in this way. Now I am changing my opinion. From now on, I will take this boy as my own son."

The zamindar said, "I have already taken him as my own son. Unfortunately, my son is not and will never be as faithful to us as this servant is."

## MRC 86. *The miserly king*

There once was a king who was very miserly. People were dying of starvation in his kingdom, but he would not give away any of his huge supply of grain. He would not give anything free, even to the poor.

One of the king's ministers was very sad and miserable. He said to himself, "He is such a rich king and he has got so much food. He has everything in boundless measure, but he won't give anything away free."

The minister decided to play a trick on the king. He said to him, "O King, since you won't give anything away free, do you not think that people are criticising you?"

The king said, "Who cares?"

The minister said, "It is good to get appreciation and admiration from people. Then you get joy. If people criticise you, do you get joy?"

The king said, "No, I don't get joy."

The minister said, "If you want admiration, then do one thing. People are dying of starvation. Can you not sell them your excess grain at a low price?"

"Of course, of course!" said the king.

The minister continued, "In the neighbouring kingdom they also need food badly. Can we not also sell them grain at a low price? Then they will be eternally grateful to you."

The king said, "Certainly, we can do this."

"Then let us send the grain on a few ships," the minister said, "and inform the neighbouring king that it is coming. Let us say that whatever price he can pay, we will be very happy to accept."

The minister arranged for the king's extra grain to be brought to the pier. At the same time, he informed all the poor people to also come to the pier. Then the minister freely distributed all the grain to the poor people.

Then the minister returned to the king and said, "O King, something terrible has happened!"

The king said, "What has happened?"

The minister told him, "We put all the grain on the ships, but the ships sank. I feel so sad. Our neighbouring king didn't get the food, and we didn't get any money. Here our own poor people who are starving didn't get anything either. We are so unlucky that our ships sank."

The king said, "Don't feel sorry. Perhaps God is punishing me because I have not been kind and generous."

The minister said, "O King, God doesn't punish us; He only illumines us slowly and steadily. God has already illumined you by inwardly telling you to sell the grain at a very low price. Previously you didn't want to part with any of your grain. Then you agreed to sell your grain to the other king at a low price. A day will come when you will want to give everything for free. So God never punishes us; He only illumines us."

MRC 87. *The merchant's daughter*

There was a merchant who was a very good man. He was very nice and very kind and everybody liked him and appreciated him. He was also very well known as a philanthropist.

When his wife died, he lavished all his affection and love on his only daughter. The daughter also lavished much affection and love on her father. When the daughter came of age, the father wanted to find a suitable person for her to marry.

The daughter told him, "Oh, I have already chosen my future husband. In fact, I am in love with him."

The father was surprised. He said, "Please let me meet the young man."

After the father met the young man, he said to his daughter, "He seems to be a good person, but how can I trust him since I haven't known him very long? The best thing is for me to observe him for six months. If I am pleased with him, then you can marry him. Even if I am not pleased with him, if you still love him, there is every possibility that I will allow you to marry him. Since you are my only daughter, my love for you is blind."

Now the father had three or four ships, which he used to import and export merchandise. One day he came to his daughter and the young man shedding bitter tears. He told them, "There was a hurricane and two of my ships have sunk. I have lost thousands and thousands of rupees' worth of merchandise! What am I going to do? Soon the people who paid me for the merchandise that they ordered will start asking me for their money back, and I have nothing to give them."

Just as he had said, his clients started coming to his house and asking him to return the money they had paid in advance. The merchant was in a very deplorable financial situation.

After a few days the young man said to him, "I am so sorry that this has happened. You are suffering so much. When my father died he left me a small estate with a large house. I am going to sell my estate and also my house and give you all the money. I don't want you to be embarrassed like this. I want you to be happy and I want your daughter to be happy. Please don't feel that I am trying to bribe you in any way. What I have I will give you, but you are under no obligation to give your daughter to me."

The merchant immediately shook hands with the man and said, "You are the only one who deserves my daughter. This whole story about my ships sinking was all lies. My ships are in good condition, and those people who came to me for money are my friends. It was all a plot to test you, and you have indeed passed the test."

So the merchant's daughter and the young man were married, and the family was very, very happy.

### MRC 88. *The thief's gold cup*

There were two thieves who were good friends and, at the same time, were very jealous of each other. That is human life. Friendship and jealousy go together.

One night, after they had gone out stealing, they met in the street. One of them had a beautiful golden cup. The other thief said, "How did you get that?"

His friend said, "I stole it from a hermit's house."

The first thief said, "How could a hermit have such a beautiful gold cup?"

His friend said, "That I don't know, but the hermit has many disciples. Perhaps one of his disciples gave him this. The hermit does not care if he has a gold cup or an earthen pot. Most of the time he just stays at the foot of a tree near his small house and prays and meditates. He doesn't care about his possessions.

His disciples put expensive things in his house, but he is above all that. He is not attached to any material things."

The first thief was very jealous that his friend had got such a beautiful gold cup. Finally he said, "Well, I have decided that I will give up stealing."

His friend said, "What! What are you talking about?"

The first thief continued, "Stealing is not a good thing. I have decided to return all the things that I have stolen to their rightful owners. True, some things I have already sold, and those I cannot give back. But whatever I have that I know belongs to certain individuals, I am planning to return. And I shall confess that I have stolen it.

"Everybody looks down on me because they know I am a thief. Therefore, I have decided that I want to give up stealing. Then people will appreciate me and love me. I want appreciation from people, so I will become a good person. This is a new idea for me, and I am going to start tomorrow."

The other thief was amazed and jealous that his friend had thought of this idea first. He said, "You are starting tomorrow?"

"Yes," said the first thief.

"Then I am starting right now," said his friend. He ran to the hermit's hut and entered into it. Bowing down, he said, "Please give me some advice. During the day I was very busy. That is why I am coming at night to ask for your advice. Actually, it is not my problem; it is somebody else's problem. If you can solve my friend's problem, I will be very grateful."

"What is his problem?" asked the hermit.

The man said, "My friend is a thief. Now he says that he is going to return the things that he has stolen and lead a new and better life. What should he do now?"

"What do you mean?" asked the hermit.

"Suppose I have stolen something from someone. If I want to give it back, am I doing the right thing by telling him that I have stolen it and making a confession?"

The hermit said, "You are doing the right thing if you make a confession and give back the things that you have taken. Then God will forgive you."

The thief said, "In case the owner does not want to take it back, what should the person do? The owner may get disgusted and think that the object is polluted because it had been stolen by a low-class thief. A thief is impurity incarnate."

"In that case," said the hermit, "the thief can keep it. It is up to the owner whether he takes it back or not. If the owner does not take it back, then the thief cannot be blamed for keeping it."

The thief then took out the cup and gave it to the hermit. The hermit asked, "Where is it from?"

The thief said, "From your house."

The hermit was always in trance so he did not recognise it. He said, "You have taken it from my house?"

"Yes," said the thief. "Now please take it back."

The hermit said, "Since you have got it now, it is your possession. You need it more than I do. Otherwise, you would not have taken it. I pray to God and meditate on God. Why do I need this kind of expensive thing? Any kind of earthen cup is more than enough for me. I am not saying that you are impure. You are also God's child. I want to see purity in everyone. But I didn't know this cup was mine and I don't need it. In every way it should be yours. I don't have any claim on it."

When the thief returned, his friend was still waiting for him. The friend was surprised to see that he still had the beautiful gold cup. The thief said, "I went back, but the saint didn't want to take it back. He said he did not need it and that I need it more than he does."

The friend felt miserable that the other thief still had the beautiful gold cup. He had not really been planning to turn over a new leaf and return all his stolen goods the next day. It was only out of jealousy that he had tried to trick his friend into returning the cup by making him feel that he himself was planning to become good. But his philosophy didn't work.

### MRC 89. *The Muslim healer*

There was once a Muslim servant who, although he had never got any advanced medical degree, knew a lot about herbs and simple medicinal cures. One day one of his master's relatives developed a large boil or carbunkle which was very painful. The village doctor said it was necessary to open the carbunkle with a knife.

The relative was frightened to death. Even though the pain was unbearable, the relative said that he was ready to suffer the pain rather than undergo the operation. "Perhaps it will burst on its own and I will be cured," he said. But the carbunkle was not bursting at all and everybody was quite worried.

The Muslim servant went to his master and said that he could cure the relative. The master said to him, "Nobody trusts you, but you are so confident. Do you really think that you will be able to cure him?"

The servant had such respect for his master. With folded hands he said, "How can I tell you lies?" So the master agreed to let the servant try.

The servant got an eggplant and scooped out the pulp. Then inside the eggplant he put all kinds of things: leaves, mustard oil, ginger and other things that one can get in the kitchen. Then he took the whole concoction and placed it not on top of the carbuncle, but around it. Then he said his own mantra.

What happened? The carbunkle burst. It didn't even take ten minutes!

The patient's family wanted to give the servant some money, but he said, "I can't take anything."

The servant's master said, "You have to take something!"

The servant's master was like the head of the village and everybody appreciated him. So the servant said to his master, "If you want to do me a favour, then please tell others that I know a little bit of medicine. I am always ridiculed and insulted because people think I am ignorant. Whenever anybody criticises me, if you just say that I know a little bit of medicine, then that will be more than enough."

So the master told everyone how the servant had cured his relative, and from then on people in the village took the servant seriously.

### MRC 90. *The family heirloom*

There was an old man who always bragged to his children and grandchildren about their family history. He would say that his father, his grandfather and his great-grandfather were all very nice, kind-hearted and pure. One day he said that he had something that had been passed down for five generations. He said it was invaluable, but if someone wanted to buy it, he would sell it for fifty thousand rupees.

Many people heard about what the old man had said. But who could afford to spend fifty thousand rupees, except someone very, very rich? Finally the king himself heard the story. He said, "If it is something truly invaluable, then fifty thousand rupees is nothing for me. I will buy it."

His minister asked, "What is it?"

The king said, "What does it matter? The old man is selling something for fifty thousand rupees. I want to buy his invaluable heirloom. Then it will be my possession and he won't be able to brag any more. Anything really precious I should have. Who else should have it? Now go and bring the man to me."

When the minister brought the man, the king asked, "What is the thing that you have that is worth fifty thousand rupees? I have heard that you are bragging and bragging about it. Now I want it."

The man said, "O King, it is absolutely true that what I have is worth at least fifty thousand rupees. But will you not have faith in my judgement? If I am asking fifty thousand rupees, then I must have something very great."

The king said, "Why do you have to waste my time? If I give you fifty thousand rupees now, will you give it to me?"

The man said, "Of course, of course. If you give me fifty thousand rupees and I do not give this heirloom to you, then I know that you will punish me."

The king said, "You are right. I will hang you."

The man said, "Then will you give me the money first?"

The king said, "Take it!" and immediately gave the man fifty thousand rupees.

The man was carrying a bag with him. He opened up the bag and took out a blanket which was full of holes where rats had eaten it. He said, "O King, I have been preserving this blanket for many years. My father's father told me that it had been passed down for three generations before him. If one can preserve something for five generations, then naturally it is invaluable. So King, you take it. I give it to you. You will have blessings from five generations of my ancestors. They will all bless you."

The king said, "O God, I am not a king. I should go out in the street and tell everyone that I am this kingdom's worst possible fool for giving you fifty thousand rupees before even seeing your invaluable treasure. Since I am king, I always brag about how wise I am. Now you have fooled me. I should get a prize for my stupidity."

The king didn't take the money back. He said, "I deserve to lose the money for my stupidity. Once I give money to someone, I don't take it back. But now that I have pleased you by giving you the money, will you please me by doing me a favour?"

The man said, "Certainly I will please you."

The king said, "Take back your five-generation-old blanket full of rat holes. Give it to your sons and let them preserve it for generation after generation. I cannot pass this down to my own children and grandchildren. My children and grandchildren will not be so stupid as to want a blanket full of rat holes, and I don't want them to preserve the memory of this foolish thing that I have done!"

# IS YOUR MIND READY TO CRY?
# IS YOUR HEART READY TO SMILE?

## BOOK 10

## MRC 91. *The astrologer fulfils his prophecies*

When a young man's parents died they left him a very large amount of money. He became very rich and didn't have to work at all. Instead of working, he used to enjoy all kinds of hobbies. One day he would become interested in music. The next day he would want to become a great tennis player. And the day after he would want to be something else. Each day he wanted to become something else. But because he couldn't stick to anything, he was not becoming anything at all. In this way he wallowed in the pleasures of wealth and wasted lots of money. But he didn't have to worry at all because he still had plenty of money left.

One day he started casting horoscopes and telling people what would happen in the future. Nobody took him seriously because astrology was only another hobby for him, but everybody liked to hear what he had to say. As long as he didn't create any problems, nobody minded.

One day his uncle came to visit him, looking very sad. The young man asked his uncle, "Why are you so sad?"

His uncle said, "I am sad because I don't have money. I am in tremendous financial difficulty."

The young man said, "Let me take a look at your horoscope. Let us see what the future holds for you."

When the astrologer looked at his uncle's horoscope he said, "I see that in a month's time, by a stroke of luck, you will get lots of money."

The uncle said, "Oh, you are so kind. Are you sure?"

The rich young man said, "Your horoscope clearly indicates that you will. I can see it. I know your financial difficulties will definitely be over in a month's time."

The uncle was very, very happy to hear that he would get some money. Every day the uncle expected to get a large sum of money, but nothing happened.

On the last day of the month the uncle happened to be passing by his nephew's house. His nephew was in front of his house and the uncle said to him, "A month has passed and it seems that I am not going to get any money. Why do you have to fool people in this way? For God's sake, give up this astrology business. You were not meant to be an astrologer."

The young man said, "Uncle, I told you to wait for one month. The month is not yet over."

The uncle said, "You are so stupid! Today is the last day. Who is going to give me the money? No one! Either you are a fool or you are a liar. You know nothing about astrology!"

The young man said, "I do know about astrology. And I do know that you will get a large amount of money. Still the day has not passed."

Then the so-called astrologer went into another room and came back with a large amount of money. He handed it to his uncle and said, "Look, my prophecy is correct."

The uncle said, "Oh, yes! Your prophecy has come true. I am so grateful to you, so grateful to you."

At that moment a schoolteacher happened to be passing by. The schoolteacher didn't see the nephew giving his uncle money. He only overheard the uncle appreciating his astrologer-nephew because his prophecy had come true.

Now for some time the teacher had been thinking of going to this astrologer to have his daughter's horoscope cast. So the teacher approached the young man and said, "I am in such trouble. It is now time for my daughter's marriage. Can you tell me if there is a chance for her to get a good husband? I would like my daughter to marry a well-educated, rich person so that she won't have to worry and I won't have to worry about her future."

The young man looked at the daughter's horoscope and said, "In two months' time you will find a good, rich husband for your daughter. From her horoscope I can see that she is a very nice girl. You will definitely get a rich person to marry her."

The teacher was very excited and started all kinds of preparations for his daughter's wedding. He even hired a special cook and servants for the ceremony. Meanwhile, the days were passing by, and still he was not getting any suitable husband for his daughter. But he had such faith in the young astrologer that he still thought that something would happen.

Finally, when the two months were almost up, the man went back to the astrologer and said, "Are you sure that my daughter will be married? I have spent so much money for the preparations. I have arranged for a priest and hired extra servants. So much jewellery we have got for my daughter for her wedding. But still I am not getting a rich person for a bridegroom. What will happen if your prophecy does not come true?"

The astrologer said, "Why do you have to worry? In this village is there anybody who is richer than I am? And do you not think I am handsome? Do you not think I am well-educated?"

The teacher said, "You? How can I expect you to marry my daughter?"

The astrologer said, "Why not?"

The teacher said, "Since you are the richest person and you are also very handsome and kind-hearted, will you marry my daughter?"

The young man said, "Of course, of course! You don't have to worry. Tomorrow we shall get married, since you are fully prepared."

So the astrologer married the teacher's daughter, and in this way he kept his promise and made his prophecy perfect.

Now, the wife was very smart. She had heard how her husband had given money to his uncle because his prophecy was not coming true. And she knew that he had to marry her in order to make his prophecy come true. So she said, "I won't allow you to continue with this occupation. Since you have so much money, you don't have to work. But you do have to give up casting horoscopes because you don't know anything about astrology. If you really love me, then you have to give it up.

"You are the richest person in the village, the zamindar. You have so many servants. If occasionally you go to the fields to supervise, then our servants will do a better job and we will have a bumper crop. This can be your job."

So every day the young man would spend a few hours looking after the fields. The workers were very happy that he was showing such an interest in their work.

About three months later his uncle came again to him and said, "Nephew, again I am in need of money. Can you cast my horoscope and see if there is any hope for me to get some money?" The uncle was hoping that his nephew would again give him money to fulfil his own prophecy.

The young man said, "Sorry, sorry, sorry. I have given up casting horoscopes. My wife said I was no good in astrology, so I had to give it up."

### MRC 92. *The court poet and the king*

There was a court poet who used to write very nice verses. During the day he was a good man, but at night he used to drink like anything. One night the king left his palace and went to see his court poet. Very often the king used to visit his subjects at night. On this occasion, as usual, the poet was quite drunk. He did not even stand up when he saw the king.

The king's assistants told him, "O King, what can you expect? He is drunk."

But the king was mad at the poet's lack of respect. He said to the poet, "In my kingdom I have three categories of people. One is the commander-type. Another is the slave or donkey-type. And the third is in the fool category. To which category do you belong?"

The poet said to the king in a very commanding voice, "Sit down!"

"What!" shouted the king. "Nobody speaks to the king like that!"

"I want to be the commander-type," said the poet. "That's why I told you to sit down."

The king said, "Come to the palace in the morning. Tomorrow I hope you will be all right."

The next day the poet went to the palace. By now he was sober. As usual, the poet composed a poem. That day's poem was very nice, and everybody was appreciating it, except the king. The king was still sad and miserable that he had been insulted by the poet.

The king said to the poet, "Yesterday you insulted me like anything. I am still angry and I want to punish you. I want you to wear a donkey skin with a donkey's head and shoes. From top to bottom I want you to dress like a donkey — because you are an ass."

The poet said, "Fine." So the king's assistants gave the poet a donkey uniform and began parading him around the kingdom.

People were surprised and they asked the poet, "What is the matter with you?"

The poet was a rogue. He answered, "Today I composed a most beautiful poem for the king and he was very pleased with me. When the king saw that I had given him the best thing that I had, he also wanted to give me the best thing that he had. So he gave me all the things that I am wearing. These are the things that the king treasures most, just as I treasure my poems."

## MRC 93. *The escaped convict*

One night a middle-aged woman was cooking in her kitchen. All of a sudden, somebody started banging on her door and crying, "Save me, save me!"

The lady opened the door and asked, "What's the matter?"

The man said, "Two policemen are chasing me." Then he forced his way into the house. He said, "If it looks as if I am going to be caught, just before I am arrested I will strangle you."

The lady said, "Don't worry; I will help you." So the lady didn't open the door when the policemen came, and they didn't know the man was inside the house. After half an hour the lady went out of the house to see if the policemen were still there and she didn't see anyone. Still, the man was afraid that the police would find him.

Some time passed and the lady offered the man something to eat. While he was eating the man said, "I have escaped from jail. People were very unkind to me in the prison. But now that I am out of jail, the police are after me and I will have no peace. I don't know what I am going to do."

The lady said, "Well, you have to know what is best for yourself. But I will tell you something absolutely true. My brother...."

Then the lady started crying.

"What about your brother?" asked the man.

The lady continued, "Many years ago my brother got angry with his best friend. He kicked his friend so hard that his friend had a heart attack and died. My brother didn't kill his friend intentionally, but he was arrested. While he was in jail he was always thinking that he would be the happiest person when he was finally freed. After fourteen years my brother was released."

"Where is your brother now?" asked the man.

The lady said, "My brother stayed here for three months, but during that time he didn't have any peace. He was always afraid that again he would do something wrong and be returned to jail. He was afraid that he would do something wrong by accident. That kind of fear entered into his mind."

The lady turned to her guest and said, "I hope you will not have that kind of fear. Perhaps you too will be haunted by the thought that the police will always be after you."

Then the lady started crying again. "What happened?" asked the man.

"One day," said the woman, "he committed suicide by jumping off the second floor of our house." And the woman started crying again.

The man was horrified.

"Before he died, my brother said it would have been far better for him to have remained in jail. He would have had more peace in prison. I really don't want this kind of thing to happen in your life."

The man said, "I don't want to have the same problem!"

He was so shocked and afraid that he would have the same fate that he ran out of the house and went back to the jail on his own.

The superintendent had sent many policemen out looking for the escaped convict, but the search had been all in vain. The superintendent was so happy that the man had come back on his own.

The superintendent happened to be the father of the woman who had inspired the convict to turn himself in. When he came home, he told his daughter what had happened. He said, "So you see, my daughter, in this world there are still nice people. You always say that we don't treat people well. But now somebody has come back on his own. He was telling us that he will have better rest and peace with us. So never say that we torture people in our jail. Here is the proof that we treat the inmates well."

The daughter said, "Father, you know that I don't have a brother. I am your only child."

"Of course," said the superintendent.

"To make that culprit go back to your jail," the daughter said, "I had to invent a brother. Not only that, I had to make my brother a murderer who was arrested and thrown in jail. I had to say that when he came out of jail, he was haunted by the thought that the police would again arrest him. Then I made him commit suicide. Now he is dead."

The father said, "What are you talking about?"

The daughter told her father the whole story. Then she said, "When I told that story, the thief ran back to the jail because he didn't want to have that kind of miserable life. You always brag that you treat the prisoners so well, but I had to play all kinds of tricks to get that man to go back. It was only out of utter fear that he went back."

### MRC 94. *The strict village head*

A head of a particular village was very nice and, at the same time, very strict. He would not allow anyone to be idle in his village. He said, "Idleness is a very serious crime. If anybody is idle, then that person will be punished."

The village head was especially strict with the members of his own family. Early in the morning, at five o'clock, his wife and children had to get up to pray and meditate. Then they had to start working. If they did not get up on time, he would have his servants insult them badly. He himself also used to scold them and punish them in various ways. The villagers all loved the village head dearly because they knew that it was for their own good that he was so strict. The neighbouring villages also used to appreciate him. They especially admired the villagers' dynamic qualities. This particular village was superior to the other villages in every way and everyone gave all the credit to the head of the village.

Every month the village head used to give a special talk about the village activities. He would say that what the villagers were doing was absolutely necessary for them to make progress and please God in His own Way. Everybody admired him and was fond of him.

One very cold winter evening he gave a very excellent talk. Afterwards, many villagers gave him gifts. Although he was very rich, they gave him gifts as tokens of their appreciation and admiration. They started throwing warm winter garments at him because they felt he might need them. Some were their own coats and shawls and some were presents. The poor man was suddenly buried under all the clothes. Then all the people in the audience started pushing towards him so that they could express their gratitude to him. Suddenly the crowd fell on the village head, and he suffocated to death.

All of the villagers were so shocked when they found out what had happened. Then the son of the village head took up the challenge. He said, "Now I will follow in the footsteps of my father. Like my father, I will also be very strict with the villagers. But I will also be very careful, especially if they ever throw gifts at me."

The villagers were very sad that they had killed the village head and happy that his son had forgiven them and would take over his father's job. The son told them, "You meant well. It was not that you wanted to kill him. You did this out of admiration."

MRC 95. *The grammar lesson*

One day there was a hurricane in a small Indian village. Many students could not come to school because of the rain and wind. Very few students were present. The English teacher said to one of the students, "It is raining so heavily. How did you manage to come?"

The student said, "I came in a taxi."

The teacher said, "Your parents are rich and you are a good student. I appreciate your parents."

She asked another student and he said, "I came on my bicycle."

The teacher said, "You are very brave."

Then she asked a third boy, "How did you come?"

This boy didn't know English grammar very well. He always repeated what others said because he was afraid of his own grammar. In this case, he wanted to follow the previous student's way of speaking, only changing it a little. So he said, "I came on my train."

Everybody started laughing and the boy was very sad. He said, "What is wrong? The teacher asked me and I said I came on my train. If your grammar was correct, why is mine wrong?"

The teacher said, "You can say, 'I came in a taxi' or 'I came on my bicycle'. But you can't say, 'I came on my train'. You have to say, 'I came by train' or 'I came on the train'. If somebody walks to school, one does not say, 'I came on my feet'. One says, 'I came by foot'. You are using your feet, but you can't say, 'I came by my feet' or 'I came on my feet'. You say, 'I came by foot'. English grammar may seem peculiar and ridiculous, but you have to learn it. You must say, 'I came by train', 'I came by car', 'I came by taxi', or 'I came in a taxi'. Don't say, 'I came by a taxi' or 'I came by the car' or 'by the taxi'."

The teacher continued, "You are children. Therefore you have to learn English grammar, although it can seem peculiar at times.

If you are learning English, you have to learn the grammar and usage of the language and you have to learn it the way it is spoken."

## MRC 96. *The dowry*

A well-to-do man had two daughters. The man was very kind and affectionate to his daughters and both of them were very nice and very beautiful. The older one was extremely beautiful and she also knew how to sing and dance. In the Indian system we have something called a dowry, which is money that the bride's family has to give to the bridegroom. In India, nobody will take someone's daughter without a dowry. The young men are so proud. They will say, "Unless you give a dowry, I don't need your daughter."

When the time came for the older daughter to get married, the father gave ten thousand rupees to his future son-in-law. The young man took the money and he was quite happy. Since his father-in-law had given him so much money, he thought that he would not have to work for several years. The young man started leading a vagabond life, and everybody started saying nasty things about him.

The elder daughter was miserable and blamed her father for giving her husband so much money. Previously her husband had worked in a bank, but once he got the dowry he stopped working. The wife felt he should have kept at least some of the dowry in the bank to earn interest. But the husband was such a fool. He wanted to show off. So he resigned from the bank and tried to make the bank manager feel that he was richer than he was. He was spending money like anything and making everybody feel he was so rich that he didn't have to work.

In a few months' time he squandered all the money. Then again he had to go back to work at the bank as a clerk. The wife was happy that at least he was working and leading a modest life.

Several years passed by and the time came for the younger sister to get married. This time the father gave his future son-in-law fifteen thousand rupees. After the marriage took place, the daughter moved to her husband's house, and they were living happily together.

The husband of the elder daughter had a few bad friends. They said to him, "Shame, shame, shame! Look, you are a third class son-in-law. You got only ten thousand rupees, whereas the fellow who married your sister-in-law got fifteen thousand. You are a useless fool. That is why you got only ten thousand rupees."

The husband said, "If I am an idiot, then my father-in-law is a rogue. In what way am I inferior to my brother-in-law?" He got furious and insulted his father-in-law. He said, "You are such a rogue! Do you think I am inferior to your second son-in-law? I am working in a bank. I am a well-educated person. You deceived me. Who wants your daughter? I don't need her. Unless you immediately give me five thousand rupees more, I will throw your daughter out of my house like a filthy rag."

The father-in-law said, "It is too late. I won't give you even one more rupee!"

The husband said, "Then I will sue you for having deceived me."

The first daughter was miserable that her husband was suing her father, but what could she do? Finally the judge handed down his decision. He said to the husband, "Yes, you have a good case. Fifteen years ago you got only ten thousand rupees and now the second son-in-law has got fifteen thousand rupees. My decision is that your father-in-law shall give you five thousand rupees — but only on the condition that you give him the interest the ten thousand rupees would have earned, starting from the day of your wedding."

The husband looked at the judge with eyes and mouth wide open. The judge said, "I am telling you to look at the goddess Lakshmi with your eyes and to keep your mouth shut. Since you are looking up with your eyes wide open, the goddess of wealth is descending. And since your mouth is wide open, I am telling you to keep it shut."

### MRC 97. *The haunted house*

There was once an old man whose daughter had grown up and he wanted to find her a husband. Since he didn't have enough money for a proper dowry, he went to the village moneylender. The moneylender was a real rogue. Whenever somebody was in serious difficulty, he would always raise the interest. In this case he asked the old man to pay a very high interest rate.

The old man said, "Already I am in serious trouble, since my daughter is unmarried. What will society say if I keep a mature girl home without letting her marry? That is why I need the money. Can you not at least ask for the regular interest?"

The moneylender said, "No, no, no! For each person I have a different rate of interest."

So the old man said, "All right, then I can do only one thing. I have an old house that my grandfather left for me. Now I am living in a smaller house. I was planning to keep my grandfather's house so that when my daughter got married, she and her husband could go and live there. But now, since I am unable to get money, I will sell the house."

Again the moneylender proved himself to be a rogue. When the old man put an advertisement in the newspaper telling people that he was going to sell his house, the moneylender spread the gossip everywhere that it was a haunted house. He warned people, "Don't buy it, don't buy it!"

The villagers liked the house. It was big and in good condition. Unlike the moneylender, the old man was not asking for an exorbitant amount of money. He was asking for only fifty thousand rupees, which was almost nothing, since it was a very big house. But people wouldn't go near the house because they all thought that it was haunted.

One day a rich man came to this particular village. The moneylender was hoping this rich man would ask him for money, because he knew he would be able to charge a very high rate of interest. The rich man did not need money from the moneylender, but still the moneylender was talking to him, saying how nice the village was and other things.

The rich man said to the moneylender, "I see in your village a very big house for sale. I am going to buy this house, even if the owner asks for one hundred thousand rupees. Then I will turn it into a factory and make lots of profit. I won't buy it now, but next time I come I will bring my assistant and negotiate to buy it."

The moneylender said, "Yes, yes, it is a nice house. You should try to buy it. Are you definitely willing to spend one hundred thousand rupees?"

"Yes," said the rich man. "I am definitely willing to buy it for that price."

The moneylender said, "It is a fine idea. Good luck."

As soon as the rich man left the village, the moneylender went to the old man and said, "I understand that you want to sell your house. People are saying that it is a haunted house, but they are fools. How much are you asking for the house?"

The old man said, "I am asking fifty thousand rupees."

The moneylender said, "Since people are saying all kinds of things about the house, can you not give it to me for twenty-five thousand rupees?"

The old man said, "No, fifty thousand rupees is the price. I won't take one rupee more or one rupee less. I will sell it to whoever wants to buy it, but that is the price. I am a sincere man, and someday people will realise this. Now they are saying that it is a haunted house, but someday they will see that it is a very good house."

The moneylender said, "I believe you, I believe you. It is not a haunted house. But won't you give it to me for twenty-five thousand rupees?"

The old man said, "No, I won't give it to you for less than fifty thousand rupees." The old man knew that it was the moneylender who had been spreading the rumours, but he didn't tell him.

Finally the moneylender said rudely, "Then take this fifty thousand rupees! Now it is my house!

The servant of the old man overheard the conversation and was very happy that the moneylender had finally bought the house. The servant said, "Since this moneylender has given such a hard time to my master, let me make some trouble for him."

The servant secretly followed the moneylender back to his house. There he heard the moneylender tell his assistant, "Look, I have bought this house for fifty thousand rupees. Now I am going to tell the rich man from the neighbouring village that he should come and buy it."

Then the old man's servant went to the rich man's house in the neighbouring village and said to the rich man, "I tell you, that is a haunted house. Everybody knows it. Don't be a fool. Don't buy that house."

When the moneylender went to the rich man and offered to sell the house to him, he said, "You wanted to buy it for a hundred thousand rupees, but I am ready to lower the price a little. I can give it to you for a lower price."

The rich man said, "No thank you! I have heard that it is a haunted house. I have heard this from someone who is very reliable, very sincere, very honest and very simple. I am not going to buy a haunted house — never, never!"

### MRC 98. *The Master answers the disciple's question*

There was once a spiritual Master who had quite a few disciples. People often used to give him money, property and so forth. The Master was very nice and honest, and he would give the money to one of his rich disciples to save it for him. When he had accumulated a large amount, the Master was planning to open up a hospital for the sick and elderly that would be free of charge.

One day somebody gave the Master a very large amount of money. The Master wanted to give the money to the rich disciple who was saving it for him, but the disciple was sick and he could not come to the Master's house. The Master said, "Let me go to his house and give him the money. I want him to keep it."

The Master asked one of his disciples to put the money inside a bag and then carry it while they went to the rich disciple's house.

The disciple said, "Master, something has been bothering me for a long time."

The Master asked, "What is it?"

The disciple said, "In the battle of Kurukshetra the Pandavas won. Many people think that it was because of Sri Krishna that Arjuna won. I don't agree. I think that even without Sri Krishna Arjuna could have won. Please tell me who is right? Am I right or are my friends right?"

The Master said, "Today I am not in the mood to answer that question. It is a very serious and complicated question, a very good question, but some other day I will answer it. Now let us go to my disciple's house."

The Master and the disciple were walking and walking. After some time they came to a forest that they had to pass through to get to the other disciple's home. By now it was getting dark. The Master said, "Who knows what will happen? Find a big stick in case we are attacked by animals or hooligans!"

The disciple found a very thick stick which he started carrying in case anything happened. O God, in fifteen minutes' time they were attacked by a hooligan with a gun. He said to the disciple, "Where are you going? Just drop the bag at my feet."

The disciple was trembling, but the Master was not afraid. The Master turned to the hooligan and said, "I am saving this money because I want to open up a hospital. Do you not think it is a good cause? Will you excuse us and not take our money?"

The hooligan laughed and laughed. He said, "You fool, you fool! How can a fool like you have so much money? Don't waste my time. Just drop it at my feet and then go away. I will not kill you. You two are fools."

The disciple was still trembling and trembling. The Master said, "All right, then put it at his feet. What can we do?"

Then the Master said to the hooligan, "Tomorrow I will not be able to show my face. My disciple will tell the world that I surrendered to you because I don't have any spiritual power or occult power. True, I don't have occult power, but still it will be a terrible disgrace for me. Please do me a favour. Just kill me with your gun. Then the world will think that I just happened to be killed because I came into this dangerous forest. It is better to be killed by you than to have to show a humiliated face to my disciples tomorrow."

Again the hooligan laughed and laughed. "I have a gun, true," he said, "but inside the gun there is no bullet."

Then the Master shouted to the disciple, "Use your stick!" Both the Master and disciple beat the hooligan mercilessly. Then they continued on with the money to the rich disciple's house.

The Master said, "Now you see! Who was needed more in the battlefield — Arjuna or Krishna? You were Arjuna; you had the stick. I was Krishna; I was the one who played the trick on the hooligan. Now look how we escaped!"

The disciple said, "O Master, now I see that Krishna was needed to give wisdom to Arjuna. It was you who asked me to find the stick, and it was you who afterwards played the trick on the hooligan. You warned me and then you played a trick. Now I know that Krishna played all kinds of tricks to save Arjuna in the battle."

### MRC 99. *The beggar's trick*

There was a beggar who was very kind and, at the same time, very wise. He used to beg and, again, he used to help other beggars and old people. But sometimes, when people were nasty, he would play tricks on them and deceive them.

One evening he stopped in front of a small shop and picked up an Indian rupee that was lying on the street. The owner saw him and shouted, "You! That coin was mine, mine! I dropped it there."

Some other people said, "No, no, you are such a rich man. How can you say that coin was yours?"

The shopkeeper started shouting at the beggar, "You have to give me the money. Otherwise, I will have you arrested."

The beggar said, "Can you not be nice to me? I am a beggar, whereas you are a rich man. Can you not at least give me half? I picked it up and you say it is yours. Since I didn't see you drop it, I am not sure whether it is yours or not. And even if it was yours, you lost it. Since it is now evening, you would have closed your shop and gone home. Before you returned in the morning, someone else would have found it and taken it. You would not have got anything. So please give me at least fifty paisa."

The rich man said, "All right, take it," and handed the beggar fifty paisa. The beggar gave him the rupee and left.

The next day, very early in the morning, the shopkeeper saw his wife searching for something in front of the shop. He asked her, "What are you doing?"

She said, "Oh, I am just looking for something."

He said, "I know, I know, you fool! You are so careless. You lost a rupee."

The wife said, "That is right. How did you know?"

He said, "Yesterday a beggar found it. I gave him fifty paisa and took the rupee back. I left it in the shop. You take it. It is yours."

The wife was very happy and ran to get the rupee. But when she picked it up, she saw that it was counterfeit. She said, "What is this?"

The husband said, "What has the beggar done? What has he done?"

What had happened was that the beggar had found the real coin that the shopkeeper's wife had lost. But because the shopkeeper was so nasty to him, and because he had heard from others that the shopkeeper was deceiving people and cheating them in so many ways, the beggar played a trick on the shopkeeper. He kept the rupee that the wife had actually dropped and gave the owner a counterfeit coin.

When the shopkeeper discovered what the beggar had done, he cursed the beggar. But the beggar had really given him a good lesson. Because he was an unkind shopkeeper, he got this kind of treatment.

### MRC 100. *The coat and the donkey*

There was once a very clever man whose wife was very stupid but had a very, very good heart. One evening, when the husband was not at home, the wife was working in front of the house. She had a fire burning so that she could see what she was doing.

It was very cold that night, and someone approached her and asked if he could stand by the fire to warm up. The man was shivering, so she said, "All right. You stand here." Then she asked him, "Where do you come from?"

He said, "I come from Heaven."

She said, "You come from Heaven? Oh, have you any news about my father?"

He said, "Yes, yes, your father and I are roommates. I know him very, very well."

She said, "What is my father's name?"

The rogue lived near her village, so he knew her father's name. When he said the name, the woman was so delighted.

She said, "Oh, yes, yes! That is right. How is my father?"

The man said, "Your father is fine, but in Heaven it is also very, very cold. What he needs is a good, thick coat."

She said, "He needs a thick coat? What can I do? Are you planning to go back to Heaven?"

He said, "Yes, tonight I am going back to Heaven."

She said, "Can you do me a favour?"

The man said, "Certainly."

The woman went into her house and brought out her husband's brand new, very beautiful, warm coat and gave it to the man. "Please, please, take this and give it to my father," she said.

He said, "Of course, I will give it to your father. He will be so grateful to you and so proud that you still care for him."

She said, "Oh, my father was so affectionate to me. This much I can do for him. And my husband also liked my father very much. So there will be no problem."

So the man went away with the coat. Soon the husband came home. His wife was so excited. She said, "Look, look, I have done something very great today."

He said, "What have you done?"

She said, "Somebody who came from Heaven told me that my father is suffering from the cold there. When I heard it, I felt very sorry for my father. So I gave him your new coat. My father loved you so much and you also loved him. So I thought you wouldn't mind."

The husband became very pale. Then he started walking out of the house. The wife said, "You are not going to leave me!"

The husband was so mad. He said, "I am not going to leave you? I have already left you! You are a fool! I am going away and I will not come back unless and until I have found a greater fool than you."

The wife started crying and crying. Then she started praying to God, "O God, I have lost my husband. Please let him find a greater fool than I. I don't think I am really a fool. I am a sincere person with a good heart. But my husband does not trust my good heart; he thinks I am a fool. Only my father in Heaven can appreciate me. He had a big heart and I inherited his big heart."

Meanwhile, the husband set out in search of the rogue who had stolen his coat. He was walking very, very fast, hoping to catch him. After some time, all of a sudden he saw someone a few metres ahead of him wearing his coat. He said, "Ah, now let me see what I can do."

He followed the man secretly and watched him enter into a small house. The man left the coat there and then went away. Then the husband approached the house. In front of the house was a donkey. The husband began looking at the donkey with tremendous devotion and bowing down to it.

The lady of the house came out and said to him, "What are you doing? Why are you bowing down again and again to the donkey?"

He said, "Only a few months ago I lost my brother-in-law. He had been very, very kind to me and I had been kind to him. My brother-in-law's face looked exactly like your donkey's. That is why I was so moved by the donkey and why I am showing it all my affection. I am talking to him by nodding, since I don't know donkey language.

"Will you do me a favour? Will you allow me to take this donkey to my house just for tonight? I want to show it to my wife, since she was so fond of her brother. She misses him like anything and every day sheds bitter tears over him. If I could show her this donkey, she would be able to see her brother's face. Perhaps the face of this donkey can give her some consolation."

The lady said, "All right, take it. But tomorrow morning please bring it back."

The man said, "Definitely, definitely I will return it tomorrow."

Then quite unexpectedly the woman said, "This donkey is our favourite animal. It is very cold out tonight, so let me put my husband's coat on it to keep it warm." Then she brought out the coat and put it on the donkey.

The lady said, "Tomorrow, when you bring the donkey back, please don't forget to bring the coat. Otherwise, my husband will be mad. Just a little while ago he came in and told me that it was a very good coat that he had bought for a very cheap price.

My husband will be very mad if he loses it. So please bring it back."

The man said, "Definitely I will bring it back. When I return the donkey, I will bring back the coat also."

So the man took the donkey and the coat. After covering only a short distance he freed the donkey and went away with his coat. The donkey went back to its owner's house and started braying in the street. When the owner came back, he said to his wife, "What is the donkey doing in the street?"

The wife said, "You don't know what happened! Somebody came here who was miserable because he lost his brother-in-law. The brother-in-law looked exactly like this donkey." Then she told him the whole story. Finally she said, "But look at this rogue! He has not brought back the coat!"

The husband said, "What coat?"

She said, "Since it was cold, I gave him your new coat for the donkey to wear. He promised that he would bring back both the donkey and the coat tomorrow morning. He has returned the donkey, but he has taken away the coat."

The man was furious, but what could he do?

So the first man succeeded in finding a greater fool than his own wife. Even if the woman had not given him the coat he would have accomplished what he had set out to do. He could have taken the donkey and sold it, and with the money he could have bought another coat. But quite unexpectedly the lady gave him the coat, so he didn't even have to go to the trouble of selling the donkey. He just left it and went away with his own coat.

# PART II

# AMUSEMENT I ENJOY
# ENLIGHTENMENT I STUDY

# AMUSEMENT I ENJOY
# ENLIGHTENMENT I STUDY

## BOOK 1

AIE 1. *The court jester's most painful joke*

There was once a king who was extremely fond and proud of his court jester. Each time the court jester said something witty, the king burst into roaring laughter. The king used to give this court jester special rewards whenever he surpassed himself in saying something that was extremely funny and at the same time deeply meaningful.

One day the king decided that on the following day he would not laugh, no matter what the court jester said. He took an oath that he would remain very serious, even to the point of sadness, throughout the entire day. He would not allow even a smile to escape from his lips.

When the next day dawned, the king summoned his ministers and went out early in the morning for a ride on his horse. The king and his entourage were aimlessly riding through the king's estates when, all of a sudden, they saw the court jester on his horse. He was not coming in their direction; it appeared that he was going somewhere else.

The king wanted to catch the court jester's attention, and so he called out, "Hey! Hey!" The court jester brought his horse to a halt and walked towards the king. The king said to him, "You are so short, you are so thin, you are so slight — you do not seem to be strong at all. But your horse is so strong, so stout, so beautiful and powerful. How do you keep him so beautiful, powerful, strong and stout? What is the secret to his excellent condition?"

The court jester said to the king, "I feed my horse, your Highness, but *you* feed me. This is the difference between my appearance and that of my horse."

The king could not laugh; he could not even smile. Indeed, he fulfilled his oath, because he felt absolutely sad and miserable for the rest of the day. Then, on the following day, he increased the salary of his court jester.

AIE 2. *In search of incomparable beauty*

One day a young boy returned home from school. As he entered his house, he saw on the floor a beautiful necklace. Immediately he cried out to his mother, "Mother, Mother! Where did you get this from?"

His mother came hurrying into the room. As soon as she saw the necklace, she said, "O my God, I must have dropped it when I came home from work. Such an expensive thing, such a beautiful thing! You know that every day I go to work for a rich, elderly woman. Today she was so pleased with me that she gave me one of her necklaces. The problem is that when *she* wears this necklace, she looks so beautiful, but I am sure that if *I* wear it, I will not look as beautiful. Physically she is much more beautiful than I am, and when she wears these gems they add so much to her beauty. Just by wearing her necklace, I will never be able to equal her in beauty."

The young boy felt sincerely sorry for his mother. The next day, when he went to school, the teacher happened to say to his pupils, "The sky is so beautiful, the sun is so beautiful, the moon is so beautiful, the stars are so beautiful. God's creation is so beautiful, but God Himself is infinitely more beautiful. That is why He was able to create such beautiful things — sun, moon and stars. If you look around at Nature, you will see that everything is so beautiful. Why? Precisely because God Himself is much more beautiful than His own creation."

The boy said to himself, "This reminds me of the necklace belonging to the rich woman. My mother says that when the rich woman wears it, she looks exceptionally beautiful, because she herself is most beautiful. In the same way, God must be much more beautiful than all the beautiful things He has created. Let me go to the Beautiful One. Let me go to the Source of all Beauty. I want to see with my own eyes God the all-Beautiful."

The young boy did not return home that evening. Nobody could find him. Hours became days and days became months; still he was missing. Years passed by. His family all believed that he had met with some kind of accident and gone to the other world. They were totally heartbroken and grief-stricken.

Many years later, a letter arrived at the mother's home. It read, "Mother, you told me about the beauty of the rich lady. The next day, when I heard about God's Beauty from my teacher, I was deeply inspired to search for God. Now I have found God. Mother, I have realised God. Now I do not need any earthly beauty, because the source of all Beauty has come to me."

At first the mother cried and cried for her lost son, but then she became extremely happy in the knowledge that he had found God, the only Beauty.

### AIE 3. *Business unexpectedly restored*

A certain businessman went bankrupt and lost his business. The reason for his downfall was that his workers had deceived him. This businessman was actually a very kind-hearted man, so his workers had taken advantage of him and betrayed him by stealing money from the business. Their greed had led to the complete collapse of the business and, as a result, the businessman was very miserable.

He said, "Now that I am no longer rich, what can I do?" Then he decided to go to his dearest friend and borrow some money so that he could start afresh. To his surprise, this friend refused. The friend said, "If you climb up a mango tree and you happen to fall down and break your legs, will you immediately start climbing up the same tree again?"

The businessman answered, "Yes, I will try to climb up the tree again, but I will be more careful this time, more cautious. I still want to pluck mangoes, but I will not take any risk the second time."

The friend said, "No! Once you fail you should not try anymore. The next time you will meet with a much more serious accident and you will die. Anyway, since you have come to me, how much money do you want?"

The businessman replied, "I need 5,000 rupees to start again."

His dearest friend said, "Oh no, my business is not doing so well either. I cannot part with that amount. But since you are my friend, let me give you five rupees as a gift. You do not have to return them. Just take them and be happy."

Instead of 5,000 rupees, the businessman received only five rupees from his friend. Sadness and depression descended upon him as he made his way back home. He did not know what to do or where to turn. His wife asked, "Why are you so sad?"

The businessman said, "I have every reason to be upset! When I was rich, I used to give money to charity. Now that my business has failed, everybody looks down upon me. Once upon a time they used to appreciate me, salute me — even honour me. Now those same people will not even look at me! They are mistreating me so badly, as if I had committed a sin! I went to my dearest friend and begged for a loan of 5,000 rupees to open my business again. And what did he give me? Five rupees! This is what our friendship is worth."

Then the wife asked, "Do you have other friends like him?"

Her husband said, "Yes, I have three or four more whom I once thought of as my good friends."

"Then can you not go to them and beg for a loan?" asked the wife.

The businessman said, "No! Am I a fool? They will also treat me the same way. I do not want to be humiliated by them."

"Then what are you planning to do?" asked the wife.

"I do not know what I can do now," said her poor husband. "For the rest of my life I will feel miserable because I cannot properly support you and our children. I see no hope for the future."

The businessman's little son had been quietly listening at the door for a few minutes. Now the small boy stepped forward and asked, "Father, do you have only four friends?"

"No, my child," said his father, "I have hundreds of friends in this city. Over the years I have helped many, many people in their hour of need. I am sure they have not forgotten."

The son said, "Father, can you give me a list of all your friends?"

"That is an excellent idea!" exclaimed the businessman's wife. "Do give us the list."

Then the father started telling them the names of all the people whom he had served in one way or another and his son wrote them down. By the time the list was complete, it contained more than one hundred names! The little boy put the list in his pocket and went out of the room.

The following day, without saying a word to the businessman, the mother and son went from door to door, visiting all these friends. To each one the little boy said, "You know my father is a kind-hearted man. He has helped so many people. Now he has lost his business. His workers fooled him, but he has not done anything wrong personally."

Each of these people, who knew from experience that the businessman was very kind and good, offered the boy a little money to take home to his father. Lo and behold, in one day the mother and son were able to collect more than 5,000 rupees! When they returned home and gave the whole amount to the father, he could not believe his eyes.

This story teaches us that if you lose something and you want to regain it, then you must proceed step by step — slowly, steadily and unerringly. On the outer plane, if you have lost all your worldly possessions and you want them to be restored, you must not expect immediate results. Start slowly, and eventually you will reach the same level once more. And on the inner plane, once you fall down, do not expect to regain all your divine qualities overnight. That is not the right way. Start again at the very beginning, and you will once more reach the highest height. This is the lesson that the little boy and his mother taught the businessman.

### AIE 4. *The theory of cat-illumination*

This story is about a spiritual Master who used to roam from place to place. He did not care to have disciples, for he believed that disciples only create problems. In his wanderings, he came to a particular village where people started following him. They wanted to offer him their devotion, but he said, "No, no! I do not want your devotion. I only want to pray and meditate in peace. If you can spare a small hut, then I will be happy to stay here for some time. I want to remain in solitude so that I can pray and meditate. While I am praying and meditating, I shall definitely pray to God to bless you and your village. This much I can offer, but I cannot accept disciples."

The villagers were so happy that the spiritual Master had agreed to stay with them for some time. They wanted to give him a big house, but he would not hear of it. He said, "Oh no, I want to lead the life of a hermit. For that I need only a small hut."

The villagers complied with his request. Soon the spiritual Master took up residence in a small hut on the outskirts of the village and immersed himself in prayer and meditation.

One young man from the village remained near the Master day in and day out. He told the Master, "I want to serve you, I want to serve you unconditionally."

The Master said, "If you can bring me food from time to time, well and good. Otherwise, I will depend on the kindness of the villagers. But I will not go out. I want to remain inside this hut."

The young man said, "I will look after all your earthly needs. I want to be your disciple. Each day I will eat at my parents' place and then I will bring food for you. After you have eaten, I will stay here and pray and meditate in your presence for a few hours before going home."

The spiritual Master accepted the services of this young man, but to the other villagers he said, "Please, please, do not bother me. I have not yet realised God. Once I have realised God, I shall really be able to help you, but now is the time for me to pray and meditate."

The villagers obeyed the Master and allowed him to live in solitude. Meanwhile, the young man was serving the Master most devotedly and faithfully. One day the spiritual Master had a vision. A luminous figure came to him and said, "I am your Guru. I am now in the Himalayas. You should come to the Himalayas and pray and meditate most seriously."

Immediately the spiritual Master decided to leave the hut. He said to the young man, "I must go. My call has come. I had a vision of a most luminous being, and I really feel that he is my Guru. He has asked me to go and join him in the Himalayas, so I shall be leaving this place."

The young man begged and begged the Master not to go, but the Master was determined. When the villagers came to know about the Master's decision, they also begged him to change his mind, but to no avail. He told them, "I have got the call. I must go."

Then the young man said, "In your absence I would like to preserve this place, this little hut where you have prayed and meditated for so many hours. Will you allow me?"

"Do whatever you like," said the Master. "I cannot think of these things right now. I am getting ready for my journey."

Shortly afterwards, the Master set out for the Himalayas and all the villagers bade him a sad farewell. The young man lovingly preserved the hut. Every evening he would hold a puja there and many people used to come to pray and meditate.

After a long journey, the spiritual Master reached the Himalayas. He found a cave and there he stayed for many years in deep meditation. He did not meet his Guru, but he felt that his Guru was inwardly helping him and guiding him. He was longing for his God-realisation, but although he saw light everywhere and he was full of inner joy, God did not bless him with realisation. After a long time, the figure of his Guru appeared before him once more. This time the Guru said, "Now I would like you to go back to your hermitage."

After the figure had vanished, the Master said to himself, "I no longer have the hermitage." Then he remembered the young man. "Oh, perhaps my disciple is still there. He promised that he would preserve it. Anyway, let me go, since the command has come again. After so many years my Guru has appeared before me again, and I must listen to him."

So the Master left the Himalayas and made his way on foot back to the village. By this time he was quite an old man. At last he arrived at the place, but it was difficult for him to recognise it as the same village, for it was now thriving and very prosperous. He could not understand how the village had improved to such an extent.

The Master went in the direction of his former hut and there he saw a crowd of people. To his astonishment, he saw that some people were holding up cats and announcing a particular price for each one. The spiritual Master could not believe his eyes and ears. People were selling cats! And other people were eagerly buying them! The spiritual Master could not understand this strange behaviour and he wondered why it was happening so close to his former hut. Was this the place to sell cats? As he approached the crowd, he heard people calling out things like, "This one is strong," "This one is healthy," "This one will do better meditation."

The spiritual Master was so puzzled. How could cats practise meditation? It was really a mystery. Then he decided to look for his disciple. Perhaps his disciple could give some kind of explanation. But the disciple was not to be found in the Master's old hut. The Master came to learn that the disciple now had a very nice house. There he invited the villagers to come to pray and meditate in comfort. He himself was leading a very comfortable and luxurious life.

The Master enquired where the disciple's house was and went there. As soon as he saw his old Master, the disciple showed him tremendous respect and love. Although this disciple was now rich and prosperous, his sincere devotion came to the fore when he saw his Master standing at his door.

When the Master saw that his disciple was indulging in a life of luxury, he became disgusted. "What are you doing here?" he said.

"Master, forgive me," pleaded the disciple. "When you left I practised the spiritual life most sincerely for a few years, and then temptation entered into me. I wanted to have worldly possessions. But now that I have seen you again, I will once more start leading a life of prayer and meditation. I do not need this life anymore."

"Do you know anything about the cats?" asked the Master. "Why are people selling them near my hut? That is a spiritual place, not a market for cats! And why are they saying that the cats will do excellent meditation? How can a cat meditate?"

Now it was the disciple's turn to look puzzled. He said, "Master, do you not remember? You had a cat. You used to play with the cat. And when you were about to meditate, you used to take a piece of rope and tie the cat to a post inside the hut. Then, when your meditation was over, again you used to play with the cat. I remember it so clearly. Master, I told the villagers that if they also kept a cat, they would have very high meditations. You used to have such high meditations after playing with your cat. I felt that just because you had such affection for your cat, God showed you His boundless Affection through your meditation. Master, I have looked after your cat all these years. I keep it by my side when I meditate and I, too, have had such high meditations! I know it is all because of the cat. I told the villagers my experiences and that is why they all want to keep cats. I saw how high and how deep you used to go in your meditation, and I realised it was all due to your cat."

At that moment a cat strolled into the room. It was simply enormous. "I am seeing your cat," said the Master, "but I would like to see my cat once more. Please show it to me."

"Master, can you not recognise your own cat? I have fed it and taken care of it for so many years," said the disciple.

The Master was astonished. "This cannot be my cat," he said. "It is so huge!"

"Master, I assure you, this is your own beloved cat. I have such affection and fondness for it, but if you would like to have it back, I am ready to give it to you here and now. I will get another cat to help me in my meditation."

The Master said, "You kindly keep the cat. I do not need it. For so many long years I have tried to realise God. Now I see why I have not succeeded. I was so deeply attached to the cat. It is no wonder that I failed! I do not need a cat to enter into my highest meditation. In the Himalayas I had very high meditations. I have learned my lesson. Now I understand why my Guru asked me to come back to this village. I had to free myself from this attachment to my cat. I shall not stay here any longer. I shall return to the Himalayas and this time I am determined to realise God — without any cat, without any bondage, without any attachment.

"Alas, so many years I have wasted because I had this kind of affection and attachment for a cat. Now I know that if you are not attached to anything, you will realise God sooner than if you pay all attention to a cat or dog instead of your own prayer and meditation. You can have pets, but if you are really attached to them, then God-realisation will always remain a far cry."

### AIE 5. *The uncivilised student*

Every day a young man went to his university library to study. His final examinations were fast approaching and he was very anxious to get high marks, so he was determined to read as much background material as possible. Each day he went to the library early in the morning and returned late at night. He was always very modestly and decently dressed and he did not create any problems for the library staff.

Unfortunately, on one particular day something went wrong with this young man, and he came to the library wearing only his underwear. He had completely forgotten to put on his outer garments! His chest was bare and he was not wearing any trousers or shoes. He was so preoccupied with his studies that these things had slipped his mind.

When the head librarian saw the young man entering the building, he became absolutely furious. He rushed up to the student and cried, "What are you doing? So many people come here to read — both men and women — and you are wearing only your underwear! What will they think? This kind of behaviour is unacceptable!"

But the student did not feel ashamed of his appearance at all. He said, "It is my eyes that read the books, not my clothes. I have come here to study with my eyes. What does it matter what I wear? My clothes will not be able to read on my behalf!"

What the young man said was very true, but his argument served only to increase the anger of the librarian. The librarian said to him, "Whatever you want to wear in your own home while you are studying you can wear, but this is a civilised place. Here you have to observe a certain dress code."

The student vehemently objected to the librarian's strict rule and before long their argument descended into a physical fight. The librarian was trying to push the young man out of the library and he was resisting in every way. Soon the two of them were wrestling on the ground.

An old man came up to separate them, but he was rudely beaten by both parties. The librarian struck the old man and told him that it was none of his business, and the student also directed some blows at the poor fellow. Both of them claimed to be in the right. The librarian felt that it was his duty to punish the student, and the student felt that nobody should be able to prevent him from studying at the library, regardless of how he was dressed.

By this time, a crowd of people had gathered. Finally, they managed to separate the librarian and the young man. These onlookers said to the student, "Please explain to us why you came to the library today without proper clothing. This is not your normal appearance."

The young man said, "It is very simple. I must sit for my examinations very soon and I am so worried. Do I have time to think about mundane things like clothing? This morning I came running to the library so that I would be able to have a few extra minutes to study. I did not intend to create a commotion."

Then one elderly woman said, "Tell me, young man, if you had seen somebody in the street running to and fro completely naked, what would you have done?"

The student said, "I would have thought that the fellow was insane. Perhaps I would have cursed him."

"You would not have run to join him?" continued the old lady.

"Never, never, never!" said the student. "I would have run in the opposite direction."

The old lady looked at him compassionately. "Then what are you doing here?" she said. "Is this not exactly the same sort of thing? Like me, so many people have come to the library today to read and study. We are all wearing proper clothes. If you appear dressed like this, almost naked, then we will all be forced to run in the opposite direction! Is it fair? So where does your argument lead you? Your eyes do the reading, true, but this is a civilised society. People will be horrified by your behaviour."

"I do see your point," said the young man, "but again and again it happens that when I am in a rush, I completely forget about external things. I do not have the time to look civilised. I am only concerned about my examinations."

Then the old lady became stern. She said, "Young man, if you have no time to be civilised, then I wish to tell you that you will never become civilised by reading books. Civilisation is something inner. It is the inner goodness of an individual. You may become a great person by reading books, but you will never become a good person unless you pray to God to give you the light to do the right thing at every moment. Right now, you are assailed by worries and anxieties. You are afraid of failing your examinations, and this fear has made you insane. But you do not see that this insanity itself will never allow you to pass your examinations. It is an obstacle on your path. Only if you are calm in mind and body will you pass the examinations. If you are so worried about the examinations that you do not have time to wear proper clothes, then you will definitely fail. I am absolutely sure of it."

The young man saw the wisdom in the old lady's advice and thanked her profusely. He went home to put on proper clothes and then he came back to the library with a humble attitude. The librarian was waiting for him at the entrance. Very happily he said, "Now my library welcomes you."

The young man answered, "Your library is really illumining me." The librarian and the young man embraced each other and from that very day they became lifelong friends.

### AIE 6. *A tricky fellow will always remain a tricky fellow*

There was once a very tricky fellow. He tried to fool everybody, but sometimes he was caught and exposed. He used to tell people, "I do not mean what I say and I do not say what I mean." That was his line of defence.

As time went on, this fellow began to lose his mind. He would constantly forget important things and do stupid things. This disturbed him greatly, so he went to consult a doctor about his condition.

He said to the doctor, "Doctor, I am so alarmed. Something is wrong with my brain! I am in serious trouble, because I do not know what I am saying. When I say something, I do not mean it; and when I mean to say something, I forget what I am about to say. Can you cure me, doctor? I promise you that once I am cured, I will give you thousands and thousands of rupees."

So the doctor began treating this fellow and, in the course of time, he fully regained his memory. The doctor said to him, "You do not have to return for any more treatments. You are completely cured. Now kindly pay me the large sum of money that you promised."

The patient simply shrugged his shoulders. "I told you before you began treating me that when I say something, I do not mean it! I told you this long ago, and today I am most seriously telling you the same thing once more: I did not mean what I said." And he left the doctor's clinic without parting with a single rupee.

There are people on earth who will take help from you, but their meanness, their roguishness, they will never give up. To the very last, they will remain unkind and cruel. They may fool you for some time, but sooner or later you will come to realise their tricky nature.

### AIE 7. *A comedy of greed*

There were two thieves who were extremely good friends. One night it happened that they came to the same house at the same hour to steal. Just as one thief was about to carry his ladder through the front gate, the other thief arrived with his bag of tools. They could not make any noise, because they did not want to wake the residents of the house, so in whispers they had a wonderful fight. The one with the ladder said, "I came a few seconds before you, so I have the prior claim. It is my right to steal from this house!"

The other thief whispered back to him, "You can go in if you want, but I am telling you that I will wait until you are inside the house, and then I will create a noise to wake up the residents so you will be caught. Make up your mind! Do you want to be caught, or do you want us to steal together? We are both expert thieves. We can be partners!"

So the two of them agreed to combine their talents. They quietly opened the gate and went into the front garden of the house. By nature, these two thieves were of different types. The one carrying the ladder was fast and nimble. The one with the bag of tools was slow and methodical.

The one with the ladder placed it carefully against the side of the house and said, "I will climb up and look through the window on the second floor to see if the owners are asleep. If they are asleep, I will drop a coin. As soon as you hear the sound of the coin, you will know that it is safe for you to climb up. Then we will go in through the window. If we both enter together, we shall be able to work very quickly. Then we will leave the same way. I do not want to go in alone because it will take me too long to collect all the valuables."

After they had agreed on this plan, the first thief climbed up the ladder and looked through the window. He saw that the occupants of the room were fast asleep, so he took a coin out of his pocket and dropped it onto the pathway below. He heard it make a slight sound and then he waited for the second thief to climb up the ladder. He waited and waited. Five minutes, ten minutes, fifteen minutes passed by, and still there was no sign of his partner. Then he began to get annoyed. They had to complete the job under cover of darkness, and dawn was fast approaching. He was in a difficult position. He could not call down from the top of the ladder for fear of rousing the people inside and being caught.

Finally, after waiting a long time, the first thief decided to come down and see what was happening. At the foot of the ladder he saw the other thief kneeling on the ground. With utmost disgust he said, "What are you waiting for? Why did you not climb up the ladder when I gave the signal? Are you deaf as well as stupid?"

The second thief answered, "I heard the signal, but I have been looking for the coin. I heard it strike the ground, so I have been searching and searching for it."

The first thief said, "You fool! Before I dropped the coin, I tied a long piece of string to it. After the coin touched the ground, I pulled it up again. Did you not see the string?"

How greedy these two thieves were, all for the sake of a little coin! The one on the ladder did not want to part with his coin, so he tied a string around it. And the one on the ground ruined their chances of robbing the house because he wanted to find the coin. This small amount of money was so precious to these two that they did not hesitate to try to take it away from each other. Such was the friendship of the two thieves!

### AIE 8. *What faith can do*

A young man was in great distress. His mother had been suffering from cancer for a long time, and her condition was now extremely grave. He knew that it was only a matter of months before she would pass behind the curtain of Eternity. Many, many doctors had given her different treatments, but all had failed.

One day, one of the young man's friends said to him, "I know how much you care for your mother. Medical science has not been able to cure her, but there is someone who can cure her. A few hundred miles from here there lives a particular sage. He definitely has the occult power and spiritual power to cure your mother. Let me make enquiries as to the name of his village. I will give you directions so that you can find this sage."

The young man eagerly accepted his friend's advice and in a few days he set out for the remote village of the spiritual Master. When he arrived at his destination, he found that the spiritual Master had gone to another village because he had a very high fever. The Master had heard that in the other village there was a medical doctor who would be able to cure his fever.

Since the young man had already travelled so far, he decided to go on to the other village in search of the great spiritual figure. He arrived in the village only to find that the spiritual Master had just passed away! All the young man's hopes were crushed. The poor fellow began crying helplessly because he felt that now his mother would never be cured.

The son of the spiritual Master happened to see the young man crying in the street. He said, "What is wrong with you? Why are you crying so bitterly? Are you crying for my father? You did not even know him. Why are you so grief-stricken?"

The young man said, "Yes, in a sense I am crying for your father. Your father was such a great man. He had so much occult power and spiritual power. My mother is dying of cancer. I came to your place to beg your father to cure her. There I discovered that your father was not feeling well, and for that reason he had come to this village. Now I have come here, but it is too late. Your father has passed away. Now there is no hope for my mother to be cured."

The young man was swimming in the sea of sorrow. The son of the spiritual Master was astonished. "You fool!" he said. "If my father had this kind of spiritual power and occult power, do you think he would have come here to see a doctor? He was suffering only from a fever. If he had had any power at all, he would have cured himself!"

The young man was shocked. He said, "My friend told me that your father was a great spiritual Master with tremendous power. I had such faith in your father! Because of that faith, I came to your place, and now I have come here. I am so unlucky! Had I arrived just a day or two earlier, I feel he could have cured my mother."

This time the son could not stop laughing. He said, "This blind faith of yours is so ridiculous. I know my father. He did not have the powers that you ascribe to him. He came here to get a remedy for his fever. He was just an ordinary man."

The young man simply said, "I had faith in my dearest friend, and my friend had faith in your father. Now my mother will definitely die. What more can I do? Let me go home and take care of her for her few remaining months on earth."

The young man went all the way back to his own village, where he expected to find his mother sick in bed. Instead, he saw his mother doing housework. With utmost surprise and delight he said, "Mother, Mother, what is this? For months you have been bedridden. Now you are moving about with such energy all of a sudden. Why? Why?"

His mother said, "I do not know what the reason is. One day, while you were away, I woke up and it seemed that I had got a new life. I felt so much better! I got up and began moving around without any pain. For the last few days I have been cooking and cleaning the way I used to do. I feel that in a few weeks I will be completely recovered. It is a miracle! What have you done? Where did you go?"

The son started shedding tears of joy and gratitude. He said to his mother, "This is what faith can do! I had faith in my friend and my friend had faith in a certain spiritual Master. This miracle is all due to the power of faith."

### AIE 9. *The ambitious priest*

There was once a village priest who was highly educated and fully conversant with all the sacred scriptures. Because he was so erudite, he was the priest for several villages. Everybody appreciated and admired him.

This priest came to hear that the king was looking for a priest for his temple. The village priest was deeply interested. He felt that he had all the qualifications to become the king's personal priest. Without a doubt, he was the most learned priest in the land. He could recite all the scriptures without any mistake. He felt certain that he would be offered the position.

With absolute confidence, he sold his house and property. Then he entrusted all his duties to a junior priest. He told this junior priest, "Now you must fill my position, because I will soon be appointed as the king's priest. I will not be coming back to this village. I will live in the palace and I will become rich, very rich, overnight. I will be the king's mentor. He will seek my advice at every moment and the whole world will appreciate me, admire me and adore me. Even here, in this village, you will hear about me quite often."

So the priest collected his remaining belongings and made the journey to the capital, where the king had his palace. The king had proclaimed a date on which he would examine all the religious leaders and priests and make his choice. This particular priest arrived in good time for the examination. As he approached the city gate, he saw that the city was in mourning. Then he learned that the king's mother had passed away just two days earlier. When he asked about the forthcoming examination, he was told that the king had postponed it indefinitely because he was mourning his mother's passing. The king had not set any new date for the examination, but he had said that it would be at least a few months before he would be ready to make the appointment. In the meantime, the position would be vacant.

The poor priest was so disappointed. He had to find somewhere to stay while he was waiting. Weeks and months went by and still there was no announcement from the king. The priest found that it was very expensive to live in the city and his supply of money soon dwindled to nothing. Since he could no longer afford to stay there, he decided that the best thing was to go back home. Somehow he managed to make the return journey.

When the village people saw the priest returning penniless, they jeered and mocked him. They said, "You greedy fellow! You left us because of your ambition to be the king's priest. Now we have appointed somebody else to take your position. Here there is no place for you. You sold your house and property. We do not want you to come back here. You have shown us that beneath your spirituality there is nothing but greed, greed, greed. Take your greed somewhere else!"

### AIE 10. *The lesson of the hungry dog*

Once there were two neighbouring kings. They were friends, but at the same time there was considerable rivalry between the two. One day one of the kings went to visit the other. The host king was much more powerful and important than his guest. His army was much larger and, as a result, he was much wealthier. He was not at all hostile to his guest, but in the back of his mind there was always the fear that one day this neighbouring king might surpass him in wealth. The poorer king, on the other hand, felt that his was a hopeless case. It seemed that he would never be able to match the splendour of his friend's palace or the strength of his army. He was jealous of his friend, but he knew that he could never equal him, let alone defeat him.

The host king received his friend with utmost courtesy and the two sat down to talk. The guest said, "You are my true friend. You have made me feel so welcome here in your palace. Now may I ask you a serious question?"

The host king answered, "Any question that you have, whether it is serious or not, I will try to answer. We are friends, so it is natural for us to help each other."

"Tell me," said the guest, "how did you acquire such a huge army? You have so many soldiers, elephants and weapons. How did you become so powerful?"

"You do not know?" said the host. "Tell me, have you ever seen a hungry dog following its master?"

"I have not, but I can easily imagine it," his guest replied.

The wealthy king continued, "The secret is that if you keep your dog hungry, the dog will follow you. I keep my army hungry, so they all follow me. I do not give them a proper salary, proper nourishment or proper uniforms, so they all follow me. They feel they will eventually get a high salary, good food and all kinds of benefits, so they stay with me. They want to get a promotion. That is my trick!"

The poorer king listened very thoughtfully and did not make any further comment. He spent the night at his friend's palace and returned home the next day. On the way back to his kingdom, what should he see but a dog following its master! The king got down from his horse and started walking behind the dog and its master. After some time the king felt very sorry for the dog, so he gave it a large piece of bread.

O God, as soon as the dog had devoured the bread, it started following the king, and not its real owner! The king gave the dog a few more pieces of bread, and the dog followed him all the way back to the palace. The king immediately got the point.

The next day, the king asked his spies to go to the army of his friend and give each soldier a very large amount of money on his behalf. Lo and behold, the soldiers all decided to join the army of this generous king. In a few months' time, the army of the poorer king became so strong that he was able to attack the neighbouring king and defeat him badly.

When the wealthy king saw the attacking army, he said to his opponent, "These are my own soldiers! How ungrateful they are! They have betrayed me to fight on your side. What has made them go against me?"

Then he began to curse the so-called poorer king. "You are such a rogue! In the name of friendship I invited you here a few months ago, and now you have taken away all my soldiers. How could you do such a thing?"

"You yourself taught me," came the answer.

"I taught you?"

"Yes. You told me the story of the hungry dog. You said that if you keep a dog hungry, it will always follow you with the hope of getting something to eat. On my way home from your palace, I saw a dog following its master and I tested your theory. I gave the dog a piece of bread and then it started following me. In the same way, you were not giving a sufficient salary to your army. I gave them money and now they all have become loyal to me. I learned this lesson from you, so you cannot blame me at all!"

Indefinitely we cannot torture any living creature, whether it is a little dog or a human being. If we do so, we are bound to meet with the consequences eventually, for cleverness and unkindness are no match for wisdom-light and justice-power.

# AMUSEMENT I ENJOY
# ENLIGHTENMENT I STUDY

## BOOK 2

## AIE 11. *The disadvantages of desire-fulfilment*

Once there was a great singer who had been performing in public for many years. Unfortunately, all of a sudden he lost his hearing. At first he felt miserable, because he thought he would no longer be able to continue his profession, but he soon found, to his surprise, that he could still maintain the same high standard when performing.

The singer prayed and prayed to get his hearing back. One night, after quite a few years, a luminous being appeared to him. The being was able to speak without using words. It said, "Do you want to regain your hearing?"

The singer said, "Oh, yes! For the last ten years I have not been able to hear at all, but before that I could hear perfectly. When I was able to hear, some members of the audience would criticise my singing and some would appreciate it. On the whole, it seemed to me that more people appreciated me than criticised me. Right now, although I cannot hear their opinions, I feel that my audience is much more critical. How I wish I could have my hearing back!"

The luminous being said, "If you want to get back your hearing, I have the power to restore it to you, but I cannot promise that people will appreciate you more." The luminous being blessed the singer, and right then and there he got back his hearing.

Early the next morning, the singer was rudely awakened by the sound of loud voices. His wife and their two sons were having a serious altercation. The poor singer found that his morning peace was completely shattered. That very evening he was supposed to give a most important performance. For the rest of the day he practised, and then he went to give his concert. During the performance everything seemed to be normal, but at the end there was no applause. Not even one person clapped!

The singer was extremely puzzled. He said to himself, "What is this? When I was deaf I could not hear the applause, but I could see that people were clapping. Now I can hear, but I am experiencing the same silence!"

The audience did not know that the famous singer was no longer deaf, and they were all wondering why his singing had changed overnight. They said to each other, "My God! He has lost his singing capacity completely. What a wonderful singer he was in the past! Recently also he sang well, but tonight's performance was simply abominable!" The audience members were so sad and disappointed that they did not clap at all for the singer.

Unavoidably, the singer heard the complaints of his listeners, and he went home that night completely downhearted. He said to his wife and children, "Now I have come to realise that when I lost my hearing, it was a great blessing. I have had my hearing back for only one day, and already I am deeply regretting it. Early in the morning I was forced to listen to the sound of my own family quarrelling and fighting. And this evening's performance went so badly that the entire audience remained silent after my performance."

For a few moments the singer remained silent. Then he continued, "O God, everything that You do for us is for our own good. I have learned my lesson. Now please take my hearing back! I do not want to hear anymore. One day is enough! I do not want to hear unkind and undivine things about others and I do not want to hear negative things about myself. When I was deaf, I was happy in my own world. I do not want to hear anything! O Lord, do come and take my hearing back!"

But, alas, God did not come to his rescue. The poor singer was compelled to listen to constant criticism. Ultimately he was forced to abandon his singing career because everybody said that he had lost all his capacity.

When this singer started his journey, it was full of promise. Even after he had lost his hearing, his achievement was not adversely affected. On the contrary, it became more and more glorious. Then, when the singer got back his hearing at a ripe old age, he became utterly miserable. His forward march took an about-face. Why? It was all because of his desire-prayers. For years and years he prayed to God to give him back his hearing, and eventually God fulfilled his desire. When God fulfils our desires after our repeated requests, sometimes it is to our greatest disadvantage!

### AIE 12. *The city of Lavanya Puri*

Many years ago there was a city named Lavanya Puri. In that city people lived very, very happily. They were kind and courteous to one another; their businesses prospered and in every way they were making progress. The residents of other cities used to appreciate and admire Lavanya Puri and try to model their cities along the same lines.

God knows how or why, but after some time it happened that twenty hooligans from a distant tribe decided to enter Lavanya Puri and create trouble. At night these hooligans would destroy stores and plunder houses. They would attack and beat the men and torture the women. This gang quickly became notorious. Unfortunately, nobody was able to catch them and prevent them from doing their undivine deeds.

Eventually the Mayor of the city imposed a curfew. During the day everybody was allowed to move around freely, but after sunset nobody could come out of their house. The Mayor said to the people, "We can see that these hooligans are torturing us ruthlessly in so many ways during the evening. Therefore, it is wiser to stay at home with our families at night. Perhaps these hooligans will leave our city if everyone is home at night."

So the curfew was enforced and nobody could venture out at night. People were unable to visit the homes of their relatives; they could not go out to eat; they could not go to the temple with offerings. All activities were stopped. One by one, businesses began to fail. The restrictions of the curfew were causing tremendous suffering, but there did not seem to be any alternative. On the one hand, the citizens were terrified of the hooligans; on the other hand, they were disturbed because they could not carry out their normal evening functions.

When the Governor of the province came to know about the situation in Lavanya Puri, he wrote a polite letter to the Mayor. He said, "I congratulate you on the curfew. You have done very well. People are not suffering anymore from unwarranted attacks. But now I wish to offer you another type of wisdom, a higher wisdom. Just because of twenty criminals, the whole city is being forced to suffer unbelievably. Why should the good citizens of your community be the ones to suffer? They are innocent. It is the bad people, the intruders, who should be made to suffer. I am advising you to change your policy. Now, it is time to be very strict. Kindly make an announcement that from now on if any hooligans appear, they will immediately be arrested and put into jail, and eventually they will be hanged for the crimes that they have committed.

"Let all the citizens come out of their houses at night and move around as usual. If anybody sees those hooligans in the streets, they should report the news to you immediately so that the police can come and arrest them. Everybody should be on the lookout. Now let us see if those hooligans will dare to do their work!"

The Mayor respectfully accepted the advice of the Governor and everything returned to normal. In fact, thousands of people came out into the streets that very night in the hope of catching the hooligans. When the hooligans saw that there was no possibility of continuing to plunder and steal from the citizens of Lavanya Puri without being caught and hanged, they lost all their courage. As soon as the citizens went home to sleep, the hooligans escaped as fast as their legs could carry them.

### AIE 13. *The boatman's way of teaching*

There was a boatman who was very, very kind. Every day he used to ferry passengers across the river in his boat. Everybody liked him and they all enjoyed the time they spent on his boat crossing from one shore to the other.

One day a young man came up to the boatman and said, "I would like to be your apprentice. I wish to learn from you the skills needed to be a boatman. You are so kindhearted. Will you please teach me?"

The boatman said, "I am more than happy to teach you. Now, if you sincerely want to learn how to be a boatman, the first thing you will need is patience. So many passengers cross the river every day. Some will smoke, some will talk about undivine things, some will have animals or baskets of vegetables. There are many things that can go wrong, so you have to be very careful. You have to have patience."

The young man listened to everything the boatman said and watched as the boatman began to get his boat ready for the day. Two or three minutes later the boatman said, "If you really want to help me, you will need patience. So many people smoke, so many people say undivine things, so many have huge bundles or goats with them. You have to be very, very careful at every moment. Today you can just watch me. Later I will definitely be able to teach you."

After a few more minutes the boatman started the same lecture all over again. "You have to be so careful! People may smoke or say undivine things. They may be carrying heavy loads. You will need so much patience."

Finally the young man said, "I have heard all this, old man! Three times you have told me exactly the same thing. Do you think I am deaf? Do you think I am an idiot? For God's sake, when are you going to get on with the business of teaching me how to operate the boat?"

The kindhearted boatman looked at the young man sadly and said, "Look, I have only repeated my advice three times, and you have already lost your patience. With this level of patience, do you think that you will make a good boatman? I am sorry, I do not want you to work for me."

The young man fell at the feet of the boatman and said, "Forgive me, please forgive me! You are right! You are right! Will you not give me a second chance?"

The boatman said, "No, I cannot take you back today. In a few weeks you can come back. When you return I will tell you exactly the same thing, but perhaps by that time you will have learned some patience. God knows how many times you will have to listen to my lecture, but if you succeed, then I shall take you as my apprentice."

The young man agreed to the boatman's conditions. He said, "The next time I come, please examine me again. I will try my best to pass your examination."

A few weeks passed and one morning the young man appeared at the bank of the river again. The boatman was so happy to see him. This time the old man was inspired to give his lecture at least twenty times. Each time the young man listened patiently and said, "I am so happy and grateful that you are advising me. I really want to become an excellent boatman like you."

At the end of the day the old man said, "Now you have passed your examination. I shall keep you as my apprentice. You may come back tomorrow, and then I shall begin teaching you how to operate the boat."

## AIE 14. *The way to the highest Heaven*

There once was a group of spiritual seekers who used to meet together to pray and meditate. They were all well advanced along the path to God-realisation. They all had one aim in common and that was to enter the highest Heaven after leaving the body. So they were praying and praying to God to be allowed to dwell in the highest Heaven.

One day the seeker who was the most advanced said to the others, "Let me enter into deep meditation and see how we will be able to go to the highest Heaven. Perhaps I will receive an inner message that will help us make faster progress."

So this seeker entered deep within to try to discover the shortest road to his goal. All at once he saw a beautiful goddess in front of him. He bowed to the goddess and said, "I am searching for the way to reach the highest Heaven. My friends and I have been praying and meditating for so many years. When we die, we would like to enter the highest Heaven. Is there any special passage which is extremely fast?"

The goddess gave the seeker a mantra and told him to repeat this particular verse many times. Then she said, "Now go and teach this sloka to your friends. Let them learn it from you and practise it every day. I do not want you to go alone to the highest Heaven."

When the seeker had finished his meditation, he taught his friends the mantra and together they repeated it countless times. They were all extremely pleased with the mantra and they begged the advanced seeker to tell them how he came by it. But the seeker remained silent, so everybody concluded that he had received it from within and did not want to take the credit.

They told him, "You are so modest, so kind. We feel that since you are more advanced than we are, your own soul gave you this message. That is why you are reluctant to tell us. Your humility is preventing you." Still the seeker just kept quiet.

Many years passed. One evening the seekers were all meditating together when the same goddess appeared. This time everybody could see her. She said, "You have all prayed and meditated here on earth for many long years. Now the time has come for you to leave your physical existence behind and go to Heaven. I have come to show you the way."

The goddess went to each seeker in turn and showed that person the way to Heaven. At last she came to the advanced seeker. But instead of showing him Heaven's door, she said, "You are so ungrateful! I will not allow you to go with your friends. Why did you not tell them that I gave you the mantra? You allowed them to believe that you received it from deep within yourself. You became so full of your own self-importance!"

Suddenly the goddess disappeared. The advanced seeker found that he could not go to the highest Heaven, although all his friends had gone there. Alas, he was forced to start all over again, chanting the mantra that the goddess had taught him long, long ago.

### AIE 15. *The welcome song*

A new Governor came to a particular state. He was very kind, good and learned. The citizens of the state held a ceremony to welcome the new Governor and sang a song highly appreciating him. One particular singer, the leader of the choir, sang the song again and again, and the Governor was extremely pleased. The citizens proudly told him, "We have performed this song in honour of your appointment. It was composed by our leader.

We are deeply honoured that we have been able to sing it for you."

The following day the Governor sent for the leader of the choir, and the singer hurried to the Governor's office. The Governor said to him, "I understand that you composed the song which was sung yesterday in my honour. I would like to offer you some money as a gift. I was so moved by your song."

The singer asked, "How much money would you like to give?"

The Governor mentioned a certain amount and the singer said, "It is not worthwhile to take money from you."

The Governor increased the amount, but still the singer said, "It is not worthwhile."

Finally the Governor said, "Kindly tell me how much you want. I shall gladly give you the full amount. By the way, I would be so pleased and happy if you could sing the song one more time."

The singer said, "All right, I shall sing the song for you once more."

He sang the special song of welcome very soulfully and beautifully. The Governor was deeply pleased. Again he said to the singer, "Please tell me how much money I should give you. This song was composed specially for me and I would like to show my gratitude in a practical way."

Then the singer was compelled to tell the Governor the truth. He said, "Alas, alas, this song was composed for all those who come to our state as Governors. When the first Governor came, we sang that song. Each time another Governor comes, we perform it for him."

The new Governor was completely shattered and disillusioned. In a very sad tone of voice he said, "Oh, it is for everybody. It is a general song."

"Yes," said the singer. "We sing the same thing for everyone who comes here to serve as the Governor."

The Governor was so disheartened that he was not inspired to give any money at all to the great singer, and the singer quietly left the room.

### AIE 16. *The doctor-swimmer*

This is a story about a village doctor. This particular doctor was very successful in his profession. He had an excellent reputation and people used to come and seek his help from far and wide.

One evening a young man arrived at the doctor's place from a distant village and cried, "My father is dying, my father is dying! Please come and cure him! You are so famous. You can cure any disease. You have to help my father!"

The doctor said, "I am glad that people appreciate my treatments, but how can I know in advance whom I can cure? I can only try to the best of my capacity."

The son said to the doctor, "No, no! I know you can cure my father. Everybody says that your treatments are one hundred per cent successful."

Finally the doctor said, "All right, let us see. Kindly take me to your father."

There was no proper transportation to the young man's village, so he and the doctor covered the four miles on foot. When they arrived, the doctor examined the patient and gave him some medicine. Then he waited to see if the medicine would take effect. Unfortunately, in two hours' time the patient took a serious turn for the worse and died.

There were some local village doctors present. Their advice and remedies had been passed over because the son had placed all his faith in the famous doctor. Now they began saying, "We were on the verge of curing the patient when this new doctor came! Obviously he gave the wrong medicine to your father, or the dose that he gave was too powerful. That is why your father died. Had you listened to us and followed our advice, your father could have gone on living for many more years. We could definitely have cured him. In fact, by the time you came back, he was already making some improvement. Why did this new doctor have to interfere?"

At this point, the son was also regretting that he had brought in the famous doctor. Now he became absolutely mad and furious. He and the members of his family, along with some of the villagers, grabbed the poor doctor and threw him into the deepest part of the river. It was late at night and there was nobody nearby to rescue the doctor. Fortunately, he did know how to swim. The water was extremely cold, but the doctor swam and swam until he reached the shore. From there he started walking, and finally, early in the morning, he came home.

The doctor arrived at his home to find his son studying medical books. The son had always wanted to become a great doctor like his father. Now the doctor said to him, "My son, do not study anymore. You do not have to study right now."

The son said, "Why, father? You have always encouraged me to follow your profession, and now all of a sudden you do not want me to study. I cannot understand."

The father said, "Before you start learning medicine, I want you to become an excellent swimmer. If you can be an excellent swimmer, then definitely you can become a good doctor. You have to know that your life comes first." Then he told his son how he had saved his own life the previous night. The doctor said, "I could not save the life of the young man's father, but I saved my own life by swimming. All my medical knowledge became useless when my own life was in danger. At that time it was only my knowledge of swimming that saved me. So, my son, first learn how to swim. Then you can think of giving medicine to others!"

AIE 17. *The king disobeys his own decree*

One day long ago a king went up to the roof of his palace. From there he could look out over the whole city. To his wide surprise he saw that down below, in the street, all the citizens were singing and dancing. They were wearing brilliant and colourful costumes and they looked most spectacular. Naturally the king thought that they were all appreciating and admiring him, so he was very pleased with them, especially when he saw that they had gone to so much trouble to wear beautiful costumes.

Unfortunately, the king had a very critical side to his nature. The more he looked at the costumes, the more unsatisfactory he found them. He said, "I know they are getting joy from wearing all the colours of the rainbow. However, since I am the one they are trying to please, I feel my own joy should come first. I must get joy in my own way and not in their way."

So the king went downstairs and summoned his minister. He told the minister, "You can make an announcement that I am very pleased with the singing and dancing that was held today in my honour, but I will be more pleased if, from now on, all the citizens wear a kind of uniform. It has to be the same colour, but there should be one design for men and another for women. Right from tomorrow, everybody will wear the same thing. This also applies to me and to the queen. Everyone will be equal, and you people will be able to talk to me in exactly the same way that you talk to each other. Everyone will be able to talk and mix freely and openly, without any distinctions of rank or wealth. According to me, that will make an ideal kingdom. I want everybody to be equal, equal, equal."

So the decree went out. The poor people were very happy that they would be wearing the same uniform as the king and the members of the court, but the members of the court and all the wealthy citizens were unhappy to the extreme because now they would look just like the poorest people in the kingdom. The queen was especially unhappy because she would not be able to wear her beautiful gowns and jewels. She would look just like a maidservant.

But the king was supremely happy and he was convinced that his attempt to create an ideal society would be a success. The next day the king put on his uniform and went in search of his wife. He saw quite a few women in the palace, but he found it difficult to tell which one was his wife, since they were all wearing exactly the same kind of dress. He said, "What is happening? My queen is so beautiful, so dignified. Now everybody looks practically the same. I cannot distinguish her from any of the other women or attendants in the palace."

When the queen saw that her husband could not recognise her, she was deeply hurt and she went back to her own room. Meanwhile, the king went in search of his minister. He found the minister chatting with some friends. When the king approached, the minister did not bow down or show him any kind of outer respect. What is more, the minister was wearing exactly the same kind of uniform as the king. This was too much for the king. He grabbed the minister's arm and said, "How dare you ignore me when I approach you! I am the king. You and your friends are wearing the same outfit as I am wearing. There is absolutely no difference between your uniform and mine. I can see that you are all trying to make fun of me!"

The minister was horrified, but he thought perhaps the king was trying to test him in some way. So he said very casually, "You yourself told us to dress like this. If there is anyone to be blamed, it is you."

Nobody had ever spoken to the king in that manner before. His anger knew no bounds. He said, "What right do you have to challenge me in this way? You are speaking as if you were my equal. That is intolerable! My word is law in this kingdom."

The minister mustered up his courage and said, "O King, in your decree of yesterday you gave us all the authority to feel that we are as great and as powerful as you are. That is why you told us to wear the same uniform. You wanted everybody in your kingdom to be on an equal footing, including yourself. Furthermore, you told your ministers and others not to treat you any differently than they treated each other. That is why, when you approached me a few moments ago, I did not show you any special respect. I was talking with my friends. If you wanted to interrupt us, you should have apologised first. But you simply grabbed my arm and demanded my attention, the way a king would. You are the first one to disobey your own decree. Now perhaps you will realise your own stupidity!"

When the king received this serious scolding from his minister, he came to his senses and gave up his idea of having an equal society. He said, "Let everyone behave the way they have been behaving all along. Let them dress in whichever clothes they choose, let them mix with their own friends and let them once more show proper respect to their king and queen. I have recognised my stupidity!"

### AIE 18. *The turtle that bragged*

Two little fish met together in a stream and began bragging to each other. The first fish said, "I am so beautiful, so exquisite in every way. Look at my colours! See how I am shining! I am literally perfect!"

The second fish said, "I have a much more subtle beauty than you have. You look so gaudy! I am much more elegant. And what is more, the lake where I live is far superior to yours!"

The first fish was shocked. "How can your lake be superior to mine? It is so puny and shallow. My lake is as vast and deep as an ocean! Your claims are all exaggeration."

The second fish began to defend itself in a spirited way. It said, "Your lake has no character. Mine is smaller and more charming. People appreciate it so much. There is really no comparison between my lake and yours!"

The two fish continued bragging and then started fighting about their respective claims. There seemed to be no end to their argument. Finally, one of them had a brilliant idea. It said, "Let us find a judge who will be able to tell us truthfully who is actually the more beautiful and who lives in the nicer lake."

The fish agreed to go and ask a turtle to be the judge. The turtle said, "Let me hear both sides of the case and then I will decide."

So they explained everything to the turtle and repeated all their claims. The turtle listened patiently and then said, "All right, before I tell you who is the more beautiful, listen to me carefully." Then the turtle stretched out its neck and legs and said, "Look at me! God has given me such a beautiful, thick body. My legs are so strong and beautiful. I feel that even God's Legs may not be as beautiful as mine! And see how long my neck is! Now look at my eyes. I cannot see my eyes, but when I think of them, I know they must be like sparkling jewels. I cannot imagine that there can be anything more beautiful than I in God's entire creation. Without a doubt, God has made me His most beautiful creation."

The little fish were aghast. They said to each other, "We chose the turtle to be our judge because we thought that it would be impartial. We thought that it would truthfully be able to proclaim which one of us is more beautiful. We never imagined that the turtle would think of itself as the most beautiful of all God's creations. Now we have come to learn that everybody has the right to feel that he himself is beautiful and perfect. It is a matter of individual belief."

Then they said to the turtle, "We shall not go to any other judge. You have really taught us something. We are so grateful to you for illumining us by bragging and bragging about your own beauty. Your self-appreciation is no match for ours, but we have learned something most important about beauty from you. The best thing is for everything in God's creation to live happily believing that it is the most beautiful of all. Bragging only creates problems which have no solution. Now let us all go back to our own homes and live peacefully."

### AIE 19. *The court jester says something new*

In ancient India, most of the kings had court jesters. Sometimes the fame of these court jesters spread far and wide, especially if they were extremely clever, witty and imaginative. The job of the court jester was to make everybody laugh, but if he was also very wise, then everybody was able to profit from his humour.

This story concerns a particular court jester who was renowned for his unique sense of humour. One time he was asked to entertain a visiting king. He said many, many funny things and composed some very witty verses. Everybody enjoyed his performance immensely.

The visiting king was very, very pleased. Finally he said to the court jester, "Say something new, something absolutely new! If I really enjoy it, then I will reward you with some gold coins. I have in my pocket one hundred gold coins. I will give you twenty if you can say something which has never been said before."

The court jester said, "For twenty gold coins it is not worth my time to exercise my brain. For such a small price I do not want to reveal something absolutely new and humorous which my king and others have not heard."

The visiting king said, "All right, I will increase it to fifty gold coins. Now at least say something new which your king has never heard."

The court jester's own king was observing everything in silence and waiting to see what would happen next. The visiting king continued, "I am offering you half of my gold coins, and still you do not want to tell me something absolutely new?"

The court jester said, "No, still I do not feel it is worthwhile."

Finally the visiting king said, "All right, here is my bag containing one hundred gold coins. It is all that I have with me. You may keep the entire amount if you tell me something new. Is this acceptable?"

The court jester took the bag of coins and said, "If I keep these gold coins of yours, then you and I will be equal. Previously, you were offering this amount and that amount as if I were a beggar. That is why I did not feel it was worth my while. You were only tempting me by raising my reward. But now that you have given me all your wealth, I do not have to beg anymore. You have given the highest price, which is everything that you have. Now I do not need your money. Take it back."

And the court jester handed the bag of coins back to the visiting king. This king was puzzled. He said, "What do you mean?"

The court jester said, "I do not need your money because I am pleased with you. You are ready to give me everything you have, whereas my own king does not give me all that he has. Not by any means! He has so much wealth, but he is very miserly with his gifts." Then the court jester began to elaborate on the defects of his own king. He criticised his king mercilessly. Instead of getting angry, the king laughed and laughed.

Then the visiting king asked, "So, what is the new thing that you are saying?"

The court jester explained, "The new thing that I am saying is that my king is miserly. Whereas you are ready to give me everything that you have, my king finds it very difficult to part with his money. He is closefisted to the extreme. Once in a while, with great reluctance, he may give me one gold coin. But he would not dream of giving me one hundred gold coins!"

Then everybody laughed and laughed. The visiting king laughed because the court jester had flattered him and said unkind things about his own king. And the host king laughed because his court jester, as usual, had conveyed the truth in a very humorous way by making fun of his own king. Both the kings agreed that the court jester had succeeded in saying something absolutely new.

### AIE 20. *A little boy and his drum*

A little boy was bragging and bragging to his young friends that he was getting so much money from his drum. With this money he could afford to buy ice cream, pastries and all kinds of delicious things.

One of his friends said to him, "That means you must play so well! You are a born drummer. One day I would like to hear you play. I have no money, but please play for me."

The little boy said to him, "You do not have to worry about paying me. I am your friend. As a matter of fact, you can come to my house tomorrow. I will give you free ice cream and I will play for you."

The following day the young friend who had been invited came to the house of the budding musician. To start with, the little musician brought out some ice cream and the two friends sat eating quite happily. The drum was on the floor beside them. When they had finished eating, the eager guest pointed at the drum and said, "Now can I hear you play?"

"No, it is not necessary," said the musician very proudly. "Without playing the drum, I make so much money! My parents, my brothers and sisters and all my relatives give me money on the condition that I do not play my drum. I can easily make so much money by not playing."

His little friend was curious. "If you play, what will happen?" he asked.

The budding musician looked very serious. "If I play," he said, "perhaps my parents will turn me out of the house!"

### AIE 21. *A child after his own heart*

A court jester had a little child. He was very, very fond of his child. Whenever the child wanted anything, his father would immediately give it to him. He indulged the child in every possible way. His position as court jester brought him lots of money and he was able to fulfil all the wishes of his son.

One day the child was caught doing some kind of mischief in the house. His father scolded him a little and sent him out to play. Then the father felt miserable because he had been so strict with his little child. He went in search of the child, only to find that he was again doing the same thing. This time the father gave the child a slap. Afterwards the father felt so sorry for giving his son a slap that he gave him a rupee.

The little child said to his father, "You are so kind to me. I did something wrong, so you gave me a slap, but now you have given me a rupee. Can you sign a contract?"

"What kind of contract?" asked the father.

The little child explained, "Every day I will do something wrong. You will give me a slap to punish me and then you will give me a rupee."

The court jester was greatly amused. He said, "All right, all right!"

One day the court jester allowed his child to accompany him to the palace. The king was extremely fond of the court jester and his family, and he was very pleased to see the child. He said to the child, "So, are you learning jokes from your father?"

"Yes, I am learning many jokes," said the child with tremendous confidence.

The king smiled and said, "Then you may begin today by telling me some of your best jokes. If you can tell me at least one good joke, then I will invite you to come to my court once a week to entertain us."

"Yes, I can tell you a good joke," said the child eagerly. "My father says to me that you are very, very kind to him. He has never seen anybody as kind as you are."

The king was very pleased. "Did he really say that?" he asked.

"Yes, he did," answered the child.

"I am very glad to hear it," said the king, "but this is not actually humour. There is no joke behind it."

The little child immediately said, "There is no joke behind it because right now it is incomplete. But if I complete the joke, you may be displeased with me, so it is better to stop here."

"What could make me unhappy with you?" said the king. "I am telling you to finish your joke."

"All right," said the child. "My father has also told me that the queen is infinitely more generous than you are! So if the queen comes to know that you are employing me one day a week, she will definitely pay me much, much more than you will give me."

The court jester was very embarrassed and uncomfortable, but to his great relief the king started laughing. The king said, "Oh, this is real humour! Unfortunately, the queen is not here today, so I am giving you much more than what I will normally give you because I want to give you the queen's share also. I would definitely like you to come here to the court once a week on a regular basis, and I do hope that one day you can surpass your father!"

Then the king handed the little child a small pile of rupees.

### AIE 22. *The retired military officers*

Four retired military officers used to meet together to discuss the glorious adventures of their youth and to brag about their bravery and heroism. One afternoon, when they were all taking tea and chatting together, one of the officers said that in a certain battle he met an enemy soldier face to face and cut off both the man's legs.

The second officer said that he had exactly the same experience, except that in his case he had found himself face to face with two enemies, so he had cut off four legs.

The third officer said to them, "Why did you cut off their legs? Surely it would have been better to think of their heads!"

Now the fourth officer, who had been silent all along, suddenly opened his mouth. "Stop, stop, stop!" he said. "They did not get the chance. I cut off the heads of those three enemy soldiers long before these so-called heroes arrived upon the scene!"

# AMUSEMENT I ENJOY
# ENLIGHTENMENT I STUDY

## BOOK 3

## AIE 23. *A son's sacred promise*

There was once a prosperous villager. One day he said to his son, "When I die, I have made arrangements for you to have all my wealth. Please promise me that you will do two things: you will give money to charity, and also you will erect a monument in my memory. Only these two things I am asking of you. The rest of the money you can spend as you like."

The son said, "Definitely, Father, I will build a monument in your honour and I will give money to charity, the way you do. You have always been so kind and generous to the poor and the sick. Now let us not talk about it any further. It is such a painful topic."

A few years passed and then the villager fell extremely ill. The best doctors were called in to treat him, but to no avail. They were able to keep the villager alive for three more months, but then he died. His possessions and money passed to his son, as he had planned. But when the son began to examine his father's financial situation, he discovered that so much money had been spent on his father's medical treatment that he died with next to nothing to his name.

The son felt very sad, but he wanted to keep the promise he had made to his father. He did not know how it would be possible now that he had no money, but he was determined not to break his sacred promise. Somehow he would fulfil his father's loving wish.

A few days later the son went to a market where people were sold as slaves. He pinned a sign on his back that said, "I am ready to be a lifelong slave," noting a certain wage that he wanted to receive each week. It was a very low amount, but he thought that if he could save the money, then gradually he would accumulate enough to erect a monument to his father. At the same time, he would be able to offer a little money to the poor on a regular basis.

A certain merchant saw the young man and agreed to his terms, so the young man went to work for him. He used to work very, very hard. With the little money that he earned, he helped the poor and kept something aside for his father's monument.

One night the young man was not feeling well at all. Suddenly a beautiful lady appeared before him and began to treat him. After treating him, she gave him some money and then left. The lady gave him money again the following night, and then again the next night. In this way she was adding more and more to his meagre savings. One night he said to the lady, "I am a poor man, but I do not want to take any more money from you. Whatever money I receive from my master is more than enough for me."

"No, no, no," said the beautiful woman. "I want you to accept this money. You are a good man, a very good man."

The beautiful woman continued coming to see him. One night she said to him, "I want to marry you."

The young man was shocked. "Marry me? But I am so poor and you have so much money! What will people think? And I have promised my master that I will serve him all my life. I cannot break our agreement. It is impossible for me to marry you."

But the beautiful woman would not accept his refusal. She said, "I have already dealt with everything. I asked your master how much money you would have to pay if you left him now. He told me a certain figure and I gave it to him, so you are not under any obligation to him. You are free to marry me if you wish. If you do not believe me, tomorrow you can go to your master and verify what I am saying."

The next morning the young man went as usual to work for the merchant. When he saw the merchant, he asked, "Is it true that somebody came to see you concerning me?"

"Yes," said the merchant. "I have received money for you. Now you are free to go home."

So he married the beautiful lady and they went back to his village to live. When he arrived at his old house, he was unable to recognise it. It had become like a palace! His wife was so wealthy that she had transformed it in advance. He was very happy as he and his wife began their life together. Everybody appreciated the new couple. They were both kindhearted. Now the young man was able to fulfil his promise to his father most satisfactorily. His wife allowed him to draw as much money as he wanted from her bank account. He built a beautiful monument for his father and he gave lots of money to the poor.

A few years passed by and the young man and his wife were blessed with a child. The young man was filled with joy, but he noticed that his wife was a little sad, and he tried to reassure her. He said, "We have been so happy together. Now that we have a son, I promise you that my love for you will not decrease. Since you came into my life, I have been filled with joy. Nothing will change! My love will remain the same. Please, please, do not be sad!"

His wife said, in a very sad voice, "I know your love for me will remain, but my time is over. I am not an ordinary woman. I am a nymph. I came from a higher world because you are so kind and sincere. You wanted to keep the promise that you made to your father; you wanted to fulfil your dearest father's wish. When he died, he could not leave any money for you. You were under no obligation to keep your promise, but you were prepared to undergo suffering and poverty all for the sake of your father's wish.

"There is another world, an inner world. When human beings like yourself have very sincere and devoted wishes, we come from that inner world to try to help them fulfil their wishes so that they can be happy. That is why I came to you. Now I have played my role in your life. You have fulfilled your promise and I have given you a son who will love you the way you loved your own father. My time is over. Before I go, I will tell my maidservant how to care for the child properly so that you will not have to worry. Please, please try to be happy when I am gone. If you meet someone else and you would like to marry that person, I will have no objection. Your new wife will have my good wishes, love and blessings."

While the young man watched in stunned silence, his wife gave some instructions to her maid and held her child for the last time. Then, with a final farewell look at her beloved husband, she disappeared forever.

### AIE 24. *The farmer illumines the king*

One day a king rode out through the main gate of his city to go hunting. As he passed through the gate, he noticed that the boundary wall around the city was crumbling. This boundary wall had been constructed many years before to protect the city from attack. Now, in some places, large gaps were beginning to appear.

The king felt very sad that the boundary wall had fallen into such a state of disrepair. He said, "If I use all the funds in my treasury to repair the wall, how will I be able to keep my subjects happy? They are expecting me to be very kind and generous. If I have to pay for the wall, I will not be able to hold any special celebrations for my people. I do not know what is more important. Something has to be done soon."

The king continued on, deep in thought. At last he came to a little farm. He saw that the farmer was busy putting a fence around his tiny plot of land. The king looked inside the fence to see what was so precious to the farmer. Here and there he saw a vegetable growing, but otherwise the plot of ground was filled with weeds.

The king asked the farmer, "What are you doing? You have not even removed the weeds! Is this the time to be putting up a fence?"

The farmer came over to the king and very respectfully said, "O King, forgive me, but I have to disagree with you. I feel I must do first things first. If I do not put up a good fence first, then stray cows and other animals can come and destroy my plants. I want to have many, many different kinds of vegetables. Without a fence they may all be ruined. If I put up a strong fence first, I can remove the weeds at any time and plant my vegetables. First I have to provide protection for my plants, and then I can think about when to remove the weeds and what seeds to sow."

The king at once saw the wisdom of the farmer's philosophy. He realised that he should also take care of his boundary wall first, so that his subjects would be safe, and then only should he think about how to make his subjects happy.

## AIE 25. *Wisdom came late*

There was a cook who worked for a rich man and his family for many years. Because of his excellent food preparation, he was able to earn lots of money. When he had saved a considerable amount, the cook said to his employer, "I wish to leave your service and return to my own village. I have saved enough money to buy a nice house and live comfortably. Every week I shall give some money to charity. I have worked hard for many, many years and now I want to lead a simple life and share my money with the other villagers. In this way, I feel I shall be able to please them and also please God."

The cook put all his money in a bag and swung it over his back, along with another bundle containing all his belongings. Then he set off walking with his heavy load. His own village was quite far away and it would take him several days to reach it. After some time, he saw a man riding a horse. The man asked him, "Where are you going?"

The cook said, "I am going home to my native village. Now it is getting dark. I am planning to spend the night in my uncle's house a few miles from here. Then in the morning I shall continue my journey. But if you want to do me a big favour, since you have a horse, you can take my bag and leave it for me at my uncle's place. If you can do this for me, I will be so happy."

The man on the horse said, "Am I a fool? Am I a fool? Such a heavy bag you are carrying and now you want my poor horse to bear it?"

The cook felt very sad that this fellow would not help him by taking the bag. His shoulders and back were really aching under the weight of both the bag and the bundle. But he could not persuade the man to change his mind. The horseman said, "You go your own way! I will have nothing to do with you!" And with that he rode off.

As the horseman was riding away, a sudden thought occurred to him. He said, "What a fool I am! Who knows, perhaps inside the bag that fellow had some valuables. He told me he was going home to his own village, so I am sure that bag contained all his savings. What a chance I missed! Perhaps even now it is not too late. Let me go back and tell him that I have changed my mind. I am ready to do him the favour of taking the bag to his uncle's place. Depending on what I find in the bag, I may take away only some of the valuables and leave the rest for him, or I may keep the entire contents."

So he turned his horse around and rode back in the opposite direction. At last he saw the traveller moving very slowly under his heavy burden. The horseman called out, "My friend, I am sorry I was rude to you before. You asked me to do you a favour and I refused. You must think that I am such an unkind person! Please give me a second chance. I shall gladly take the bag to your uncle's place."

In the meantime, the traveller had also had second thoughts. When the man on the horse rode away, he said to himself, "My God, I was such a fool! I have so much money inside my bag. What would I have done if he had stolen the bag? I took him to be an honest fellow, but I could easily have been mistaken."

When the man on the horse asked for a second chance, the traveller said, "Oh, no, no, I have changed my mind. I can manage by myself. Now I do not need you at all!"

The man on the horse began cursing himself. "Wisdom always comes too late!" he said.

In both cases, wisdom came late, but in the case of the traveller, he was still able to prevent his bag from being stolen. If the horseman had immediately agreed to carry the bag, then he would have been able to take all the traveller's money.

How stupid they both were!

### AIE 26. *"I do not want to be anybody's slave"*

This story is about a farmer. He himself was illiterate, but he wanted his only son to be well educated, so he kept aside all the money that he earned and sent his son to school and university. The son was a very brilliant student, and eventually he got his university degree.

After receiving his degree, the son came back home to his father's farm. The father was extremely pleased with his son. He said, "I am so proud of you! You did so well in all your examinations, and you have earned a university degree. But now I would like you to do some agricultural work."

The son was surprised and shocked. He said, "Father, what are you saying? You made so many sacrifices to send me to university so that I could do higher studies, and now you want me to do simple agricultural work? You yourself did not go to school, but you valued education so much that you spent all your money on the best schooling for me. And now you want me to do farming like you? What is the reason, Father?"

The father said, "All right, all right, I am sorry. I made a mistake. Since I spent so much money on you, please go and get a good job. If you do not want to help me at all, I will not mind, as long as you are happy. You may go. I wish you good luck." Then the father added, "I have a rich friend who works for the king. You can go to his place and ask if he can help you to get a job at the king's palace."

The young man returned to the city and went to see his father's friend. The friend was very, very kind to the young man and invited him to spend the night there. He promised to take the young man to the king's palace the following morning and help him get a job.

The young man was so happy and excited. He liked his father's friend and he was looking forward to working at the palace and utilising all the knowledge that he had acquired. Perhaps, eventually, he would even become the king's minister!

The night was still quite young, and so the older man said, "Let us play a game of dice to pass the time." They began playing and for some time they were enjoying themselves immensely. All of a sudden, quite late at night, a messenger came from the king. He said to the older man, "The king has summoned you. You must come at once." The man dropped his dice then and there and immediately got ready to leave. He apologised to the young man and said, "This is what happens."

The young man could not understand at all. He said, "Where are you going at this hour? Can you not go and see the king tomorrow morning?"

His father's friend said sadly, "Oh, yes, tomorrow morning! If I do not go now, not only will I lose my job — that I do not mind — but the king may chop off my head! I have no choice but to go immediately. This is what happens when you work for a king. One moment the king may be nice to you, but the next moment he may be very strict. He may even punish you mercilessly. I do not want to lose my head for the sake of a good night's sleep."

The young man realised he was not meant for that kind of life. Before the friend returned home the next morning, the young man went back to his father's farm. He said to his father, "You encouraged me to go to the king and get a job, but I do not want to be anybody's slave. The best thing is for me to stay here and help you with the farming. I want to follow your profession so that I can enjoy freedom. If I work at the king's palace, I will be at his beck and call. Here I can do everything in my own time."

Needless to say, the father was extremely happy and deeply relieved that his son had given up his ambition to work for the king.

### AIE 27. *The king's secret examination*

Once a king and his minister went out of the palace incognito to visit the subjects of the kingdom. When evening fell, they approached a cottage and knocked on the door. The owner came to the door and the king said, "My friend, we are travellers and we would like to take rest here overnight. Will you allow us?"

The owner asked, "How many are in your party?"

"Only we two," answered the king.

"All right, you may stay," said the owner. So the king and his minister entered the house and spent the night with the owner and his family. In the morning they thanked him for his hospitality and went on their way.

The following evening they stopped at another cottage and asked, "May we spend the night here?" This time the owner immediately said, "Yes, come in, come in, come in! You can definitely stay with us. By the way, how many of you are there?"

"We are two," replied the king.

"Very good, come in," said the owner. The king and the minister passed the night in the cottage and, in the morning, they returned to the palace. Then the king asked his minister to go back to the second cottage and bring the owner to the court. The king wanted to give him a very large amount of money.

"Both of them gave us shelter, your Majesty," said the minister. "Why are you rewarding only one of the householders? What about the other one? Kindly tell me the reason."

The king said, "There is a great difference between these two subjects of mine. The first one asked us how many we were. After he found out that there were only two of us, he invited us to come inside and stay with him. The second one immediately welcomed us to stay and only then did he enquire how many of us there were. He offered us shelter first, before asking any question. Therefore he is much more hospitable than the other fellow, and I would like to reward him for his kindness. Do you see the difference?"

Now the minister did see the difference and he was very grateful to the king for illumining him.

## AIE 28. *The king's clever new recruit*

A young man went to one of the king's ministers and begged, "Please, please give me a job at the king's palace!"

The minister said, "I will give you a job tomorrow, on one condition."

"What is that condition?" the young man asked, a little nervously.

The minister explained, "A few months ago I gave a job to a young man like you, and now that fellow has become the king's confidant. He has gone so high in the court that he does not care for me at all. He is so ungrateful! Now, I want you to become dearer to the king than this fellow is, so that you can get rid of him. If you can get rid of him, I will be very, very happy. That is my condition!"

"I am sure I will easily be able to get rid of him," said the young man. "I am quite clever. I will definitely find a way to make him lose the king's favour."

So the minister fulfilled his promise and gave the young man a job at the palace where he would attract the attention of the king. The young man immediately began looking for an opportunity to discredit the minister's previous protégé who no longer cared for him.

One day the king was engaged in a serious battle. Somehow it happened that the young man, the new recruit, saved the king's life. The king was so pleased with him that he said, "Today you have done me the greatest service: you have saved me from death. Please tell me what you want. I will give you anything you want."

"I can ask for anything?" said the young man.

"Anything at all," said the king.

The young man immediately declared, "I would like to marry the minister's daughter. She is so beautiful! I would like to have her hand in marriage."

"That is so easy!" said the king. At that very moment he ordered the minister to give his daughter in marriage to this young man.

Afterwards, when the minister and the young man were together in private, the minister said, "I am so puzzled. You could have asked for anything. You could have asked to marry the king's own daughter. Then you would have become a member of the king's family. Why did you ask to marry my daughter?"

The young man smiled at the old minister and said, "I want to marry your daughter because I know that if I marry her, you will not be able to bring in someone else to throw me out of the king's inner circle! Otherwise, now that I have become so close to the king and the king is so fond of me, you may be tempted to appoint somebody else to get rid of me. You gave me my job on the condition that I get rid of another of the king's favourites. So far I have been unable to fulfil my promise because this fellow has such high standing in the court. He is the king's confidant, and he does a very good job. Indeed, I do not think I will be able to get rid of him. Seeing that I did not keep my word, you may try to introduce someone new to bring about my disgrace. That is the thing I want to avoid. Only by marrying your daughter will I escape your punishment!"

### AIE 29. *The right prayer, the wrong goddess*

In a particular village there were two very wealthy families. The wives were close friends. The husbands believed that it was their wives who had brought prosperity to their families, so the husbands were very pleased with their wives and proud of them. Before they married, these two men had not been at all rich.

Then, when they got married, all at once their circumstances changed for the better.

There was another woman in the village who was extremely curious to know the reason behind the sudden material prosperity of these families. One day the two wives invited her to come and have tea with them. She took the opportunity to ask them to explain what had made them so wealthy.

The first wife said, "In my case, it is very simple. I prayed and prayed and prayed to the goddess of poverty. I begged this deity not to come near me. I said, 'O Goddess, I really want my husband to become rich, so kindly do not visit our house.'"

The second wife said, "I prayed and prayed and prayed to the goddess of wealth. I said to her, 'Please, do come and abide in our house.' I had a special mantra which I repeated over and over. This goddess did listen to my prayers, and she blessed my family with her prosperity."

The first wife added, "I also had a special mantra, which I repeated for the goddess of poverty. She heard it and she very compassionately stayed far, far away from our house." Each wife was more than happy to teach her special mantra to the woman, and the woman was very happy and grateful.

The woman returned home and started praying and praying, using both the mantras together. Unfortunately, after repeating the mantras thousands of times, sometimes she got a little confused and mixed them up.

One day, while the woman was praying, the goddess of poverty and the goddess of wealth both came to her at the same time. She did not realise that she had invoked both of them. They came to find out what she actually wanted. They both looked most beautiful and radiant. Even though the goddess of poverty was not dressed as elaborately as the goddess of wealth, her face was full of light. The goddesses asked the woman to choose which one should stay and which one should depart.

The woman looked from one to the other, mesmerised by their beauty. Finally she said to the goddess of poverty, "You look more beautiful to me. I want you to stay with me and bless my family." To the goddess of wealth she said, "You are beautiful, true, but your beauty is not as deep, so I would like you to go. By going, you will make me happy."

Then the goddesses asked the woman, "Do you wish us to obey you immediately?"

"Oh no," said the woman. "Now we have talked for so long. Let us start from tomorrow." To the goddess of poverty she said, "Tomorrow please come back and stay with me." And to the goddess of wealth she said, "From tomorrow on, please do not come to me again. I do not need you."

So the goddesses disappeared and the woman was very happy because she had resolved everything to her satisfaction. Within a short space of time, she thought, she and her family would become extremely prosperous. She did not realise that she had made a terrible mistake. She simply had no idea that she had banished the goddess of wealth from her house forever. It had not occurred to her that the goddess of poverty would also be very beautiful and compassionate, so she had not thought to ask their names. She assumed that the more beautiful one would be the goddess of wealth.

Alas, alas, the following day the goddess of poverty came and blessed the woman by making her poorer than the poorest. When the woman saw how everything in her life was being transformed for the worse, she asked the goddess, "What happened?"

The goddess said, "I am the goddess of poverty. It was I whom you invited to stay with you. The other being was the goddess of wealth. You asked her never to come back again. This unfortunate mistake was all due to your greed. Now your family will be forced to suffer from poverty. This time, if you really want to help them, you can start praying again, but instead of praying for outer prosperity, you can pray for inner prosperity. If God is pleased with your sincerity, He will shower upon you His infinite Peace, Light and Delight."

AIE 30. *The miserly zamindar*

There was a village zamindar who was very, very rich and, at the same time, very, very miserly. He would not give away any money, even for a good cause. Others who were infinitely poorer than he was would give money to improve conditions in their village. They would always raise funds for a special project. But they never dared to ask the zamindar to contribute because they knew in advance that he would refuse.

One time the villagers were trying desperately to gather enough funds to repair the village school. A young man who was a teacher at the school said, "I will compel the zamindar to give a donation. He is the richest one among us. He should set an example."

All the other villagers told him, "It is impossible, impossible! You will never be able to bend him. We have tried in so many ways. We have flattered, we have begged, we have demanded — nothing has worked. He does not care for others. He is determined to hoard all his wealth."

The young man said, "Let me try. I will take up the challenge."

The young man went to the zamindar's house and knocked on the door. The zamindar opened the door just a little and said in a very rough and rude manner, "Why are you here? I have told people not to bother me."

The young man said, "I have come here for a special purpose."

The zamindar barked, "If it is a question of money, I can tell you now that I will never, never give money to any of your village projects."

In a very sympathetic voice the young man said, "You are absolutely right to keep your money, and I have made it very clear to the villagers that they must not expect you to give money here, there and everywhere. I told them that you are not an ordinary man. Ordinary people, like them, give money only for one reason: to be flattered. They want everyone to appreciate and admire them because they feel they have given such a large amount. They give only for their own glory. But I know that you are far, far beyond name and fame. You are the zamindar of our village. Nobody can be more important or powerful than you are. That is why you do not need to get name and fame by doing charitable work. The others badly want name and fame. They feel that just by giving a little money, even an insignificant amount, they will become extremely popular. But, in your case, you do not have any wrong motives. To me, you are like a great sage. You are above worldly flattery, and that is why you do not give money."

The zamindar was so surprised and pleased by the young man's speech that he came out and stood in the open doorway. All his hostility had vanished. He said, "Can you tell me once again why I do not give money?"

The young man replied, "You are far, far better than the villagers because they give with a purpose, a motive. They are dying to be appreciated, admired and adored. You do not give money because you do not want to go down to that level. You are beyond name and fame, far beyond it. I wanted to come here to tell you that I have realised your true height, your true goodness."

The zamindar said, "You have understood me perfectly! I do not care for the adulation of the villagers. That is why I do not give money. Since you are the only one to arrive at the truth, let me give you a little money. Do whatever you want to do with this money. If you want to give it to your friends for the development of the village, you can, but remember, I am far beyond name and fame. If you give them this money, you must also tell them the truth that you have realised. Unlike them, I am not giving this money to you with any ulterior motive. I do not want to glorify myself. I am just giving the money unconditionally. Go and tell them this truth."

The young man thanked the zamindar profusely and rushed to tell the other villagers the good news. On the way, he counted the money and discovered that the zamindar had in fact given him a very large amount. When he showed the villagers, they were astonished. The young man said, "My method of flattery worked! By giving me this money, the zamindar wanted to prove that he was above name and fame, but he made me promise to tell everybody where the money had come from. Indeed, he is above name and fame!"

### AIE 31. *The value of a dhoti*

There was a businessman who owned a secondhand shop where he used to sell clothes, mostly dhotis and punjabis. He would buy secondhand clothes and then re-sell them at a higher price. One day a man came to sell him a dhoti. The dhoti was all wrapped up in a towel. Before taking the dhoti out of the towel, the man said, "Please tell me how much you charge for a new dhoti."

The businessman said, "Did you not see the sign above my shop that says 'secondhand'? I can sell you a very nice secondhand dhoti, but I do not know the price of a new dhoti. If you are looking for a new dhoti, you have come to the wrong place."

The customer said, "I find it very hard to believe that you do not know the price of a new dhoti. You may not buy or sell them, but are you sure you do not know?"

The shopkeeper said, "Actually I do know."

"Then how much does a new dhoti cost?" asked the customer.

The shopkeeper said, "It is 20 rupees for a new one. When I buy a secondhand dhoti, I usually pay 5 rupees and then sell it for 10 rupees. I have a very good selection of secondhand dhotis, but you will not find a new dhoti here."

The customer said, "As a matter of fact, I have not come here to buy a new dhoti. I asked you the price just out of curiosity. And I am very glad that you have told me that the cost of a new dhoti is 20 rupees."

"So what have you come here for?" asked the shopkeeper, who was beginning to grow a little suspicious.

"First, let me clarify what you have told me," said the man. "You buy dhotis for 5 rupees and you sell them for 10 rupees?"

"Yes," said the shopkeeper uneasily.

The man said, "All right, then can you give me 5 rupees for this one?" He unwrapped the dhoti that he was carrying in the towel and placed it on the counter.

The shopkeeper cried, "Five rupees? I cannot give you 5 rupees for this ancient relic! The border has completely faded! You do not have to unfold it. I can see at once that it is not in good condition at all. Had it been in good condition, I would have handed you 5 rupees immediately. And I could have sold it for 10 rupees without any difficulty. But in this case it is impossible. For a dhoti like this, the most I can give you is 2 1/2 rupees."

The man said, "Two and a half rupees! Oh no, it is worth much more than that. Look at it carefully and see for yourself."

The shopkeeper unfolded the dhoti and held it up, only to discover that worms had enjoyed a feast on this garment. There were a number of places where the worms had eaten right through the fabric. Furthermore, it was quite stained. "This kind of dhoti I do not want!" he exclaimed. "I am prepared to offer you 2 rupees, but no more. If you do not want to sell it for 2 rupees, then get out of my sight. Do not waste my time anymore!"

The customer did not seem at all upset. He continued to remain very calm. "Only 2 rupees?" he asked.

The shopkeeper said, "Yes, 2 rupees," and he took the coins out of a small bag and handed them to the man.

The man said, "The money from the sale of the dhoti is yours, not mine."

"How can it be my money?" the shopkeeper asked. "I have agreed to buy your dhoti, even though it is in such bad condition. Now, for God's sake, just take the money and go. All this talk is only confusing me!"

The man said, "Listen to me. You have a big shop. This particular dhoti was hanging near the door. On the way in, I just grabbed it and wrapped it in a towel. I stole it from you. If I had not stolen it, you would have sold it to some innocent person for 10 rupees. Now you are prepared to offer only 2 rupees because you see for yourself that it is stained, the border has faded and worms have eaten into the fabric. The true value of this dhoti is 2 rupees, not 10 rupees. You are such a rogue! For years and years you have been deceiving people, but you cannot deceive people forever. Sooner or later, you are bound to be exposed. In this case, it was you yourself who said that this dhoti could not be worth more than 2 rupees. So, you keep the money. You deserve it!"

### AIE 32. *The thief's illumination*

There was a confirmed thief who used to steal every night. His wife was very, very honest. She used to beg him, "Please do not steal, do not steal!"

Her husband would reply, "If I do not steal, if I do not practise my profession, I will not be able to support you."

The wife's answer was, "I will be able to support both of us. I can go out and work. I can clean old ladies' houses. We shall easily be able to manage. Please give up this dishonest life!"

But the thief said, "No, no, it is beneath my dignity for you to go out and do maid's work."

"It is beneath my dignity to have a husband like you who steals!" said the poor wife.

Then the husband threatened his wife. He said, "If I hear you say once more that it is beneath your dignity, then I shall thrash you. It is a husband's duty to support his wife by any means."

So the situation continued. Every night the thief used to steal, and every night his wife used to cry and beg him to give up that kind of work. Finally the husband thought of a solution that would bring a little peace into their marriage. He said to his wife, "From now on, I shall keep whatever I steal someplace else so that you do not have to be reminded of the stolen goods. I will tell you that I am just visiting my friends when I come and go at odd hours. Then you can imagine that I am living a different kind of life."

His wife said, "Why are you trying to fool me? I shall never forget for a moment what kind of life you are leading."

But the husband was determined to put his brilliant plan into effect. For a few weeks he kept all his loot at the house of one of his friends. This fellow's wife did not mind at all. Her husband was also a thief and she did not find anything wrong with his calling. Sometimes the two thieves would work alone and sometimes jointly. Then, after a few months had elapsed, they would resell the stolen property and make lots of money.

One morning the first thief returned home full of sadness. He told his wife that when he went to his friend's house that evening to store some things that he had stolen, he discovered that his thief-friend and his wife had left the village. And they had taken with them all the things that the two thieves had stolen for the last few weeks! This fellow was left with nothing.

His wife said to him, "Now you can see how much people suffer when their valuables are stolen from them! In your case, these things were not even yours to start with, but still you feel so miserable. Surely those who have had their own things stolen feel infinitely more miserable that you do at this moment!"

Suddenly the thief saw that his wife was right. He had not even thought about the suffering his actions would cause others. He touched his wife's feet and said, "You have illumined me. I shall give up this life of stealing. But do not worry. You will not have to work as a cleaner. I am going out to look for a job as honest as you can ever imagine!"

### AIE 33. *The money-lender and his rogue-friend*

There was a money-lender who loaned the sum of 100 rupees to one of his friends. The friend said that in one month's time he would, without fail, return the money. But when the time came, this friend did not return the money. He insisted that he did not have 100 rupees.

Actually, this friend had a reputation in the village for borrowing money and never repaying it. But, since the money-lender happened to be one of his close friends, the money-lender had thought that this time the fellow's promise was sincere. Unfortunately, it seemed that his friend had no intention of returning the money. No matter how many times the money-lender begged him to return it, he simply refused.

Now that the rogue-friend had accumulated a considerable amount of money, he decided to go to the market and buy a cow. He did not know that the money-lender was following him secretly. He examined all the cows at the market but did not find any cow that satisfied him. He said, "Bad luck, bad luck! Some other day," and began walking back to his village.

The money-lender continued to follow him. All of a sudden, from behind a bush, a bandit appeared with a knife. He grabbed the rogue-friend and said, "You look like a wealthy man. Drop your wallet here! Otherwise, I will stab you without any hesitation!"

The fellow cried, "Do not kill me! I am dropping my wallet right here where you can see it." As he turned to run away, he saw the money-lender behind him and screamed, "Here is your money! Now come and take it."

The money-lender said he did not want to fight with the bandit, so he, too, ran away.

The bandit grabbed the wallet and disappeared into the bushes.

The following day, the money-lender wrote a note to his friend who had not returned the money. The note said, "You borrowed 100 rupees from me on the condition that you would return it in one month. Now four months have passed, so I have added the interest to the original amount. It was I who hired the bandit to steal your wallet. There was no other way for me to get back my money, so I have added his fee to what you owe me. You had more than enough money in your wallet to cover everything. The money that is left I am returning to you. I have taken only what is justly mine. What a rogue you have turned out to be! You had so much money in your wallet, but you could not return the amount that you borrowed from me four months ago. I am sorry our friendship had to come to an end in this way."

If this friend had kept his promise and returned the money on time, there would have been no interest and no robbery, and his friendship with the money-lender would have been preserved.

Because of his insincerity, he was compelled to suffer such heavy losses.

# AMUSEMENT I ENJOY
# ENLIGHTENMENT I STUDY

## BOOK 4

### AIE 34. *The thief's advice to the king*

A king went on a short trip with a few of his ministers and a small entourage. They decided to camp in a particular town for the night and then return home to the palace in a leisurely way the following day. The king's tent was in a very nice location, and the others in his party placed their tents all around him. All of a sudden, in the middle of the night, there was a great commotion. People began calling out and running to and fro. The king came out of his tent and asked, "What happened? What happened?"

One of his ministers replied, "We saw a thief stealing things, and now we cannot find the thief. We are searching the camp."

The king became furious. "Here I have so many ministers and guards," he said, "and you cannot find a single thief? You have to find him! Otherwise, tomorrow morning I shall punish you all!"

There was no sleep that night for those who had travelled with the king. They searched and searched, but the thief was nowhere to be found. Day dawned and still there was no sign of him. The ministers were so sad that their excursion had been ruined, and they were all afraid of the king's punishment.

In the morning, the king assembled everyone and said, "What have you done? You are all supposed to protect me. I have entrusted you with my safety. Is this how you carry out your job? If the thief had wanted to kill me, he could easily have done so. It seems he had no trouble entering our camp and stealing things. He may have been carrying a knife or some other weapon. This experience could have been infinitely worse. I am so disappointed and disgusted with all of you! Let us go back to the palace at once."

The ministers and guards were all absolutely miserable as they stood listening to the king in silence. Just as the king finished his speech, they heard somebody sneeze very powerfully. The sound came from a very small tent belonging to one of the guards who had been absent the entire night looking for the thief. The guards rushed to the tent and looked inside. They saw that in one corner somebody had rolled himself up in a blanket. It was the thief! The guards dragged him before the king and waited for the king's command.

The king said, "You have to punish this thief!"

At that moment the thief spoke up. He was trembling because he thought that his life could be measured in minutes, but he found the courage to say, "O King, please give me a moment of your precious time. I want to tell you something."

The king's fury had not diminished. He said, "You! You should be thrashed to death. The whole night you did not allow us to sleep, and now you have to tell me something! All right, what is it?"

The thief said, "O King, I have done you a big favour."

"You have done me a favour by coming here to steal?" asked the king.

"Yes," said the thief. "O King, just think of what will happen when you go back to the palace! The local people will all laugh at you when they hear this story. They will say that you are surrounded by stupid ministers and useless guards. I am nothing but a poor thief, but I was able to enter your camp all alone and forty of your people could not find me. This story will spread like wildfire throughout the kingdom. One thief was able to outsmart forty of the king's men! People will not only say that your guards are useless, but they will also begin to say that you must be stupid to keep them. So you see, I am giving your guards dignity and I am giving you dignity also by allowing myself to be caught. When I sneezed, the guards came to know my hiding place and they were able to catch me. Now people will say that the king's guards are so alert and so efficient that they were able to catch the thief. And they will admire you also for keeping such excellent guards. But had I not sneezed, I could easily have escaped. Then you would have had to return to the palace without the thief. You would have been so embarrassed and ashamed. So I do not think I deserve punishment. On the contrary, I deserve a reward because I have done you a big favour."

The king saw that the thief was speaking the truth. He said, "You are right. Because of this unfortunate incident, my guards and I would have become a laughing stock. Please tell me what reward you would like from me."

The thief said, "O King, I do not need any outer reward. I only want you to be strict when you appoint your guards and ministers. Do not keep these people. Either give them a last warning right now or dismiss them all. You deserve people who are infinitely better."

### AIE 35. *The money-lender and the drunkard*

There was a money-lender who used to lend money on very strict terms. At the same time, he was a good and sincere man, so people liked him and they always returned the money promptly.

Once the money-lender loaned some money to a drunkard. He did not realise that the fellow was a drunkard, so he gave him a large amount of money. This drunkard refused to return any portion of it. Weeks ran into months and months ran into years, but the money did not materialise.

The money-lender would send his assistants to the drunkard's house to collect the money. No matter what hour of the day they rang the bell, even if it was late in the evening, the drunkard's servants used to say the same thing: "He is not at home! He is not at home!" Sometimes they used to say that he was staying with relatives. During the day they would always claim he was at work.

"Where does he work?" asked the money-lender's assistants. But the answer was always the same: "We do not know."

One day the money-lender's patience reached its limit, and he decided to go personally to collect the money. Just as he arrived in front of the house, the drunkard happened to be returning home. The money-lender screamed, "You have to give me the money!" But the drunkard ran and hid inside the house. The guard at the gate told the money-lender, "No, no, that was not my master. That was somebody else. My master is not at home, so it is useless for you to wait here. Kindly come back some other time."

The money-lender knew that the guard and the drunkard's other servants were all trying to fool him. He said, "Do you take me for an idiot? With my own eyes I saw your master run into this house. I know his face well. I am not going to leave until he comes out. If he does not come out, I will call the police and they will arrest him."

Still the drunkard remained inside the house. The money-lender had no choice. He called the police and told them that the man inside the house owed him a very large sum of money. The police arrived and asked the drunkard to come out. Then they began to question him. They said, "This money-lender claims that you borrowed a large sum of money from him and you have not repaid it. Is it true?"

"No," said the drunkard. "I have never seen this man before and I do not know what he is talking about."

One of the policemen said, "You do not know this man? That means he must have made a mistake."

"Do not believe him!" shouted the money-lender. "I tell you, this is definitely the same man to whom I loaned a large sum of money several years ago."

"What has become of you?" said the drunkard. "Here you are, shouting in the street and causing a scene. You do not believe me when I say that I am not the man you are seeking and yet, just yesterday, you believed my servant when he told you I was staying at a relative's house. A low-class person like my servant you believe, and a high-class person like myself you disbelieve. Is your standard so low that you believe only the words of low-class people? I am really insulted! Somebody else has borrowed this money from you. Go and look for the actual culprit instead of wasting my time and the precious time of these police officers."

The money-lender looked at the drunkard and realised that he could never win against such an unscrupulous fellow. He said, "You say that you are high-class and you are incapable of lying. If that is so, then you remain with your so-called height. It is beneath my dignity to come and ask you for the money anymore. If this is what it means to be high-class, I do not want anything to do with it. You can go back into your house, get drunk and do whatever you want. I shall never mix with your type again."

### AIE 36. *King Shivaji and the Muslim princess*

King Shivaji spent most of his life fighting against the Moghuls and the expansion of the Moghul Empire. Sometimes Shivaji and his brave soldiers won against the huge Muslim army, and sometimes they lost. But everybody respected and admired Shivaji. Although he lived on earth for only 52 years, he became a truly great man in every way. He was a hero and a patriot without equal throughout the length and breadth of the Indian sub-continent.

It was not to oppose the Muslim religion that Shivaji fought against the Moghuls. On the contrary, he had a deep love and appreciation for all religions. He once said that Hinduism and Islam are manifestations of the same divine spirit, and he used to encourage everybody to practise their own religion.

Once somebody wanted to examine Shivaji's religious tolerance, so he threw a Koran at Shivaji. To a Muslim, the Koran is as sacred as the Upanishads, the Vedas and the Bhagavad Gita are to the Hindus. Shivaji took the Koran and held it very devotedly and respectfully. Then he happened to see a Muslim standing at a distance. He called for the man and presented him with the book very soulfully, saying, "Please take this book. It is your most sacred text. When I hold our Gita, I feel it is so sacred that I must become very prayerful and spiritual. When I hold your Koran, I have the same experience. Now you should take this book and revere it."

Shivaji often encountered the Muslim troops in battle. Once his Maratha soldiers defeated a certain division of the great Muslim army. Shivaji's commander was supposed to bring the defeated Muslim leader before his king, but before he did so, he brought the Muslim leader's daughter. Shivaji's commander said, "O King, now that you have defeated this Muslim leader, you are entitled to seize all his possessions. That includes his daughter. I would be so happy if you would take her as your wife."

King Shivaji said, "I should marry her?"

"She is such a beautiful young girl," said the commander.

King Shivaji looked at the girl and said, "It is true. I have never seen anyone as beautiful as you are! How I wish my mother could have been as beautiful as you are! If my mother had been beautiful, then perhaps I would have had more beautiful features."

As a matter of fact, Shivaji was quite handsome and very strong. He only lacked a little in terms of height. While looking at the girl, he continued to think about his mother.

Finally Shivaji's commander interrupted his reverie. He said, "O King, either you can marry her or you can give her in marriage to your son."

Shivaji not only was brave, but he also had many, many spiritual qualities. The fate of this young girl now lay in his hands. He said to his commander, "Let me pray and meditate."

After meditating, Shivaji said, "What has this young girl done to me that I should take her from her family? Her father is my enemy, true; but if I take her away and marry her, or if I ask my son to marry her, will she be happy? At this very moment the poor girl is so afraid that I may kill her father or put him in jail for life. Again, she feels that I may mistreat her and take her as my maid instead of marrying her in a proper way. No, I cannot add to her sorrow. I have conquered her father. That is more than enough for her to bear without being taken away from her near and dear ones."

Then Shivaji asked somebody to bring lots of gifts, and he gave them to the young girl. He said to her, "You will not be harmed. You can go back to your father. And you can tell him that I am not going to arrest him or put him into jail. I want him to remain with his family so that the affection between father and daughter will grow and grow. I do not want to come between you. Go back to him with all your affection and love. When your father sees you, he will be so happy. And you can tell him that these gifts are the gifts of a father to his daughter."

The young girl asked, "What do you mean when you say that these are a father's gifts?"

Shivaji explained, "I did not want to marry you, and I did not want my son to marry you. In a way, I am your father, for only a father can have this kind of affection for a daughter. I have defeated your real father, but how can I take you away from him and destroy the affection that you have for your father and your father has for you? I cannot do that. I will allow him to return to his home, and you are free to go with him. The fact that your father lost to me in battle does not give me the right to come between him and his beloved daughter. So you take these gifts and go back to him, with all the blessings and love of someone who feels for you as a father feels for his daughter. Go, my child."

AIE 37. *China's ancient wisdom preserved*

The First Emperor of China was the first person to unify the country. Under his rule, the wealth and power of the separate states came into the hands of the central government. The First Emperor was very anxious to maintain his power. He said to his Prime Minister, "Even now I find that some people are cherishing opposing ideas. Where do these opposing ideas come from? How do they circulate?"

The Prime Minister said, "O Emperor, these ideas are embedded in our ancient books, which are known as the five Classics, and also in the works of Confucius and others. When people read these philosophical works from the Golden Age of the past, they learn about benevolence, righteousness and other moral precepts. That is why they criticise you."

The First Emperor said, "I clearly see that the only way to extinguish these ideas is to burn all the books. Not only the books, but also those found reading the books must be burned!"

The Prime Minister, who was extremely ambitious, immediately agreed. He said, "That is an excellent idea! We shall keep aside only medical books and books about growing crops. All others will be burned to ashes. If anyone is found reading those ancient classics, we will burn a mark on that person's face and send him to the frontier to build the Great Wall. In this way, the old works will lose all their prestige in the minds of the people."

The Emperor was very pleased with the recommendations of his Prime Minister, and he issued orders for them to be carried out. Those who did not comply with the regulations received the terrible punishment of being branded on the face.

In spite of these brutal measures, some books did manage to escape destruction, for the priests very carefully hid them in the walls of houses. Some priests even committed the books to memory. When the First Emperor's reign came to an end after just fifteen years, those priests were able to write out the old classics word for word. In this way, the ancient Chinese wisdom was preserved. Even now, the Chinese culture is taken as one of the world's most precious sources of wisdom.

### AIE 38. *The superlative fool*

There was once a superlative fool. Nobody could be compared with him, for his stupidity knew no bounds. Wherever he went, people would poke fun at him and make his life miserable. Finally, the poor fool went to the king. He showed the king his sad face and said, "Your Majesty, please help me! Everybody is saying I am the worst possible fool. Nobody takes me seriously. Is there any way you can change my reputation?"

The king sympathised with the fool and said, "All right, let me examine you. If I find that you have some wisdom, then nobody will dare to call you a fool again." The king thought for a few moments and then said, "I have a wife, as you know. People call her the queen. My wife is very, very beautiful. I have a daughter who is also extremely beautiful, and talented as well. She has a younger brother who is the prince. Although he is still a child, he is already quite strong. So these are three of the members of our family. But we actually have four members. Can you tell me who the fourth member is?"

The fool was stupefied. He said, "How do you expect me to know? Have I been inside your palace? Do I know your family members personally?"

The king felt genuinely sad, for the fool was even more dull-witted than he had imagined. He said, "The answer is so simple: I am the fourth member of the family." Then the king added, "Although you could not pass my examination, let me see what I can do for you."

The fool was so happy and proud that he had been permitted to have an audience with the king and also to know the answer to the king's riddle. He was dying to show off his knowledge, so he went to see his dearest friend and said, "I have a very beautiful wife, an excellent daughter and a very strong and powerful son. There are four members in our family. Can you tell me who the fourth member is?"

The friend said, "Of course I can! You are the fourth member."

"Oh, no," said the fool, "you are wrong, you are wrong!"

The friend said, "In what way am I wrong?"

The fool replied very dramatically, "The king has told me privately that he himself is the fourth member of the family. I cannot tell a lie. The fourth person is the king!"

Eventually the king came to hear what the muddleheaded fool was saying, and he felt that the time had come to fulfil his promise to the fool. The king appointed a very learned member of his court to give this stupid fellow as many free lessons as he wanted. Not only would they be free of charge, but each time he attended a lesson, he would get some gold coins from the king. In this way, the king hoped to have one less fool in his kingdom.

## AIE 39. *The goddess and the businessman*

There was once a very rich businessman. Every morning before going to work in the city, he would pray to the presiding goddess of his family. He always prayed for the same thing: the increase of his material prosperity. Finally, after many years, he said, "At last I am satisfied. I have so much money! I have a beautiful house and so much property. Now I do not have to pray to the goddess anymore; I do not need her."

Soon afterwards, the goddess appeared to him in a dream and said, "Because you prayed to me for so many years, I gave you your present prosperity. Now you have become so ungrateful. Everything that you have, you will lose!"

The businessman became extremely worried and frightened. "O my God, O my God," he repeated, "what have I done? If she really has this kind of power, I will become destitute!" Then he pleaded with the goddess, "Please, please give me another chance! You have been so kind to me over the years. Now I want to perform a magnificent puja in your honour. I will spend thousands and thousands of rupees. I will bring all my relatives from different villages and everyone will see how I worship you! You just have to give me a little time to make the necessary preparations."

The goddess agreed to the businessman's proposal. She said, "You do not have to perform this puja overnight, but in a few months' time you must do it."

The businessman promised to begin making the arrangements immediately. The goddess was very pleased that he would soon worship her with great pomp. She did not withdraw as she had threatened to do. On the contrary, she continued to bless the businessman and his family every day.

Days ran into weeks and weeks ran into months, but still the businessman did not even begin making arrangements for the puja. He postponed the event indefinitely. Finally, the goddess became disgusted. Once more she appeared before him, and this time she said, "You told me that in the near future you would worship me with a very elaborate puja, but I can clearly see that you have done nothing. Your promise was empty. Now I shall leave you permanently!"

This time the businessman was not at all frightened. He told the goddess, "If you go, then I will tell the whole world that you are a liar."

"I, a liar?" asked the goddess, greatly surprised.

"Yes," continued the businessman. "You assured me that you would stay with me for some time. You are a divine being. You have to honour your promise."

"But weeks and months have now passed," said the goddess.

"Do you not know that we mortals are full of weaknesses?" said the clever businessman. "I am just an ordinary man. It is in my nature to tell lies. But you are supposed to have compassion for humanity. You are supposed to have patience to help us overcome our weaknesses. That is why we worship you. You have all the divine qualities in infinite measure: forgiveness, patience, compassion, wisdom. Alas, we can only offer you our imperfections."

The goddess decided to give the businessman yet another chance. She said to him, "Do you think you will be able to worship me on a daily basis once again? Can you give me your sincere promise?"

"Daily I shall worship you," said the rogue-businessman in his most devoted voice.

For a few days, he did honour his promise and he worshipped the goddess before going to work in the city. Then, somehow, he managed to forget about her. He became very irregular in his worship and eventually he ceased to worship her altogether.

Once more the goddess appeared before the businessman. This time she came with her power-aspect. She cried, "You are such a rogue! You are full of greed, insincerity and dishonesty. I have decided to withdraw from your life once and for all. I will be the presiding goddess for those who love me and value me. But I do not want to remain a goddess for you. You stay with your money-power, since you are more than satisfied with it. But, I tell you, after I go away from you, all your money-power will disappear and you will become a street beggar. That is what you deserve!"

At this, the businessman was really horrified. He said, "How can you curse me like this? Only ordinary people curse others. But you are a goddess! I shall let the whole world know that you have come down to this level. How do you dare to claim that you have any divinity at all when you hurl your curses at innocent human beings like me?"

This time the patience of the goddess had run out. With a stern voice she said, "For you, I do not want to remain a goddess. I will definitely be there for those who love me and value me. I will go to them and I will help them inwardly and outwardly in countless ways. But in your case, from today you will see how your fate has changed!"

Then, in the twinkling of an eye, the goddess disappeared.

### AIE 40. *Thieves by nature*

There were three thieves who had completed their jail terms and were due to be released one particular evening. At the appointed hour they passed out of the prison gates and found themselves in the street. Since it was already quite dark, they decided that instead of going back to their respective homes, they would spend the rest of the night just outside the walls of the prison.

It was a cold night and the three emancipated thieves lay down on the ground close to one another. One of their jailbird friends who had been watching them from the window of his cell saw that they had no blanket, so he handed his own blanket to the guard and asked him to go and give it to his three friends. The guard willingly agreed. He was deeply impressed by the selflessness and kindness of this particular prisoner.

The guard offered the three men the blanket and then he went back to his station. In a few minutes' time, he observed that the thief who was sleeping on the far right had tugged the blanket to such an extent that it covered only him, and not the other two. He was sleeping comfortably, but the others were shivering.

After another thirty minutes had passed, the guard saw the man in the middle grab the blanket and wrap himself up in it very tightly. Now the other two were cold and miserable.

The guard waited to see what would happen next. Another thirty minutes passed and he saw the thief on the extreme left reach over and pull the blanket quite violently. Then he covered himself from head to toe and went to sleep. This kind of pulling and tugging went on all night.

When morning finally dawned, the thieves got up and started to leave for their homes. All of a sudden, the guard came over and arrested all three. He said, "I can see that you are not going to change your nature. You three are thieves to the very core!"

He put them back into jail and then he went to the cell of the sympathetic prisoner who had donated his blanket. The guard said to this man, "You have a good heart. You are extremely kind and sympathetic. You have shown that your thieving days are over. Therefore, I am allowing you to go free. You may gather your things and leave today. But, alas, your friends have not learned their lesson at all!"

## AIE 41. *The minister's test*

One day the king summoned his most trusted minister. This minister had served the king for many years, and the king deeply valued his wisdom and advice. When the minister came before the king, the king looked at him compassionately and said, "I am extremely grateful to you. You have rendered devoted service to me for many long years. Now you are growing old. I do not wish you to discontinue your work, but I would like you to take an assistant, somebody whom you can train to do your duties. Please select somebody who is as honest as you are. As you know, I am so proud of you. Your honesty has saved me time and again. So do not take anybody who is dishonest."

The minister interviewed many of the young men in the kingdom and finally he chose three whom he believed to have all the right qualities to be his assistant. Above all, they seemed to be honest. The minister informed the king, "Your Majesty, I have three candidates for you to choose from."

The king said, "No, you choose."

The minister replied, "O King, I would prefer that you make the choice, since you are the one who wants me to have an assistant. I personally do not want an assistant."

The king said, "I feel it is for your ultimate good. You are no longer a young man. As the years go by, I am sure you will depend on this assistant more and more. But I would like it to be somebody of your own choice."

Finally the minister agreed to select one of the three candidates. He asked each one to come to his home at a particular time. He said to them, "This evening I will have something very special to tell you."

When the first candidate arrived at the minister's home, the minister invited him into his private room. The room was in total darkness. The minister took a gold coin from his robe and flicked it into the air. As soon as it dropped on the floor, the minister said to the young man, "The king has asked me to send you to his palace immediately."

The young man had started to feel for the coin in the darkness, but the minister whispered, "Do not delay! You risk the king's anger."

The young man immediately ran out of the house and did not stop until he reached the king's palace.

When the second young man arrived, the minister followed the same procedure. He took the candidate into his private room, which was completely dark, threw the gold coin onto the ground and then told the young man that the king was calling him. Like the first candidate, this one also ran at top speed to obey the king's wishes. He was so happy and proud that the king had asked for him.

Finally the third candidate arrived for his appointment. Once more the minister threw the coin and made his dramatic announcement. This time the candidate did not heed the king's urgent summons. He continued to search for the coin on the ground. After about five minutes, he did find the coin and he gave it back to the minister. The next day, the minister brought all three candidates before the king. The king asked him, "Have you decided which candidate you will choose?"

"Yes, I have made up my mind," said the minister.

"Which one?" asked the king eagerly.

The minister pointed out the candidate who had spent so much time searching for the gold coin.

"How did you manage to choose this one?" enquired the king.

Then the minister recounted to the king the whole story about the test. He added, "Now I am more than happy to have an assistant because I see this one will do an excellent job. And when the time comes, he will replace me as your minister. I know that he will take care of your kingdom honestly and carefully. He will serve you most devotedly because he will give everything its proper value. The other two ran away for name and fame. They wanted to enhance their own glory. But this one valued the gold coin that I had dropped. He searched and searched for it until he found it. He did not want it for himself. He immediately returned it to me. In the same manner, when he becomes your minister, he will preserve your kingdom and everything in it. He will care for it in every way. That is why he is the best candidate."

The minister smiled at the young man whom he had chosen. With sad faces, the two candidates who had failed the test bowed to the king and left the room.

### AIE 42. *The hermit's peace-boon*

There was a hermit who lived in a cave far removed from the hustle and bustle of village life. One day a villager came to his humble abode and asked, "Can you please make me peaceful? I have a successful business in the village. I have wealth, I have everything; but how can I have peace?"

The hermit replied, "Do you have any idea how you can attain peace?"

"Oh, yes!" said the villager without the least hesitation. "If I have more prosperity, I am sure peace will dawn in my life."

The hermit said, "Granted! If you feel that more prosperity and more name and fame will bring you peace, then your wish is granted. When you return home, you will see that my boon has already taken effect."

The villager returned home and, to his great surprise, he found that his wealth had literally doubled overnight. For a few years he was very happy. Then something prompted him to return to the hermit again.

The hermit recognised him and asked, "What do you want this time?"

The villager answered, "I am still seeking the same thing. I want to be happy and peaceful."

"Then how do you want me to help you?" asked the hermit.

The villager looked a little embarrassed. Finally he said, "Someone has moved to our village who is infinitely richer than I am. He has really disturbed my peace! I feel that if I can defeat him in wealth, then I will be happy and peaceful once more."

Again the hermit said, "Granted! I will give you the capacity to become richer than your rival, immediately."

The villager returned home and discovered that his wealth now far surpassed that of his rival. The hermit had arranged everything to the villager's utmost satisfaction. Once more he could be truly happy and peaceful.

Unfortunately, after a few more years another businessman who was exceedingly rich came to live in the village. Once again, the villager's supremacy was challenged, so he went back to see the hermit.

"Please, please," begged the villager, "tell me what I must do! I tried to get peace in my own way by amassing more and more wealth, but that peace never lasts. Somebody always comes along and ruins it. Now I would like to hear from you how I can become really peaceful. I have been coming to you for so many years, but I have never asked you for *your* advice. If it is not too late, please illumine me."

The hermit said, "That is what I have been waiting to hear from you! Here is my advice to you: if you give away all the wealth that you have, you will be flooded with peace. And if you become my disciple, I will be able to offer you joy and happiness."

The villager immediately prostrated himself before the hermit and said, "I want to become your disciple. I do not care for earthly riches anymore. I want only inner wealth. Please allow me to stay with you, or allow me to build a small cottage next to you so that I can pray and meditate with you every day. The atmosphere around you is full of peace and harmony. What a fool I was not to notice it before! I want to be your devoted disciple. Please grant me initiation."

The hermit said, "Granted! I accept you as my disciple. I will give you all the peace of the inner world."

Lo, the villager found immediate peace, happiness and fulfilment at the feet of the hermit.

AIE 43. *In search of an infallible man*

There was once a king whose favourite minister passed away. The king was anxious to fill the vacancy, so he interviewed several young, well-educated men. Finally, he narrowed his choice down to two candidates. To these two he said, "I would like you to answer this question: can one become infallible?"

One of the young men replied, "O King, it is not possible to become infallible. Human weakness is such that we are always prone to making mistakes. But, if God wishes, He can create someone who is infallible right from the dawn of his life. That special soul will be born without imperfections."

The second young man then gave his opinion. "As human beings, we do have inherent weaknesses, true. But I believe that one can become infallible in this life by praying and meditating. If God showers His choicest Blessings upon us, then we can become infallible."

The king said, "All right! One is saying that we become infallible on the strength of our prayers and meditations, and the other is saying that it is somehow pre-ordained; one must be infallible right from the beginning of his life. I would like to see such a person. Please go and find me a person who is infallible."

The young man who had made this assertion left the palace and went in search of an infallible person. A long time passed by and still he was not to be found. Eventually he returned to the palace and he was forced to admit defeat. The king said to him, "Since you have not found anybody who is infallible, do you think there is a possibility that you are the one?"

The young man said, "Yes, perhaps I am one of those very few who are infallible."

"Thank you! Definitely you are," said the king. Then to his attendant he said. "Please bring the other young man, the one who said that with God's Grace, and by praying and meditating, one could become infallible. He is the right one to get this post. I do not need someone who is bloated with pride and self-importance. I need someone who is humble and sincere. Then only can I have confidence that he will make the right decisions for my kingdom."

### AIE 44. *The excellent dal*

This story is about a very happy family. It consisted of a husband and wife and their two children. The son helped his father with the family business and the daughter was still at school. When the son came of age, his mother wanted him to get married.

The son said, "Why, Mother, why?" If I bring a wife home to live with us, you two will quarrel and make the entire family miserable. Right now we are all so happy together. But if you and your future daughter-in-law are at daggers drawn, then we will have serious problems."

But his mother remained firm. "No, I really want you to get married. I promise I will never be unkind to my daughter-in-law. I will never scold her or quarrel with her — never, never, never! I am getting old, so I need somebody to help me with my household activities."

Her husband had been following the conversation. He said to his wife, "Do you promise that you will never scold your daughter-in-law?"

"Yes," she said, "I promise. I will treat her as my own daughter."

So the son got married to please his mother, but alas, his mother totally forgot her promise. She used to find fault with her daughter-in-law at every moment. She would blame her for every mishap in the household, and then the daughter-in-law would cry and cry. The son suffered badly because his mother was making his wife's life so miserable. His sister also suffered when their mother would scold the daughter-in-law in season and out of season, without rhyme or reason. They all felt sorry for the new member of the family. They saw that their mother had become a neurotic and impossible old lady. The daughter-in-law tried desperately to please her, but to no avail.

One day the mother's brother was coming to visit the family. She was thrilled that her brother would be visiting after a very long time, and she wanted to feed him a most delicious meal, so she prepared quite a few dishes. The last item was dal. By then it was getting late, so the mother put the pot of water and dal on the stove and said to her daughter-in-law, "Look, Sita, I must go and take my bath in the Ganges before it is dark. I have put the dal on the stove. Let the water boil. Then, when the time comes, you will add some salt. I have already put in the other spices. You will only add the salt — without fail! Do not forget. You are quite often unmindful and careless. I do not want to scold you right now. I do not want to ruin the atmosphere, since my brother is coming after such a long time. We are so fond of each other! Nobody can ever imagine how close we were when we were young. I am only asking you to do this simple job. Do not disappoint me!"

The mother left to bathe in the Ganges. In a little while, Sita found that it was time for her to put salt in the dal, and she did so, very carefully and accurately. Then she was free to leave the kitchen and complete some other household jobs.

After five minutes had elapsed, Sita's sister-in-law entered the kitchen. She was always very sympathetic to Sita. When she saw the pot of water boiling on the stove, she said to herself, "Perhaps my sister-in-law has forgotten to do her job. Poor girl, she is so nice! My mother always scolds her. My mother is too old to change her nature. Now, in case Sita has forgotten, let me save her."

So the sister-in-law put some salt in the pot and went away. She was so happy that she had saved poor Sita from yet another scolding.

In a few more minutes, Sita's husband happened to pass through the kitchen. When he saw the pot of water and dal boiling on the stove, he said, "I know my mother will behave in such an undivine way if my wife forgets to put salt in the dal. In fact, I am sure Sita has forgotten; otherwise, she would be here looking after the pot. I really love my wife and I am so sad that she has to put up with my mother day in and day out. Let me add the salt on her behalf." So Sita's husband took some salt and added it to the pot. He was sure that he had saved his wife from a terrible scolding.

Finally, the mother came back from bathing in the Ganges. As usual, she was convinced that Sita had forgotten to do her job. When she saw that the pot of dal was still on the stove, all her worst fears were confirmed. She said, "My daughter-in-law is so undivine! She is useless, useless! She does not even have the common sense or wisdom to turn off the stove. I am sure she has not set foot in the kitchen since I left; otherwise, she would have turned off the stove by now. As to adding salt, it is out of the question! As usual, I have to do everything myself." With that, the mother added a generous portion of salt to the pot.

Later in the evening, the mother's brother arrived and the whole family sat down to enjoy the feast. After the honoured guest had eaten, the mother asked her brother, "How did you like the meal?"

Her brother answered, "Everything was simply excellent!"

"But which dish did you like the best?" his sister asked.

"Without a doubt, the dal was absolutely the best," he replied.

The mother became a little sad at this reply. The dal was the only dish which she had not prepared by herself from beginning to end; the matter of the salt she had left to her daughter-in-law. Then she consoled herself by saying that, since her daughter-in-law had forgotten the salt, she herself had actually been the one to give the dal its final touch.

She asked her brother, "Was it only the dal that you liked, or did the other dishes appeal to you also?"

Her brother said, "I did like them, but the dal was very special."

The mother was so flattered. She asked her brother if he could elaborate a little. He said, "The reason your dal was so special is that now I do not need to take salt for ten more incarnations!"

"What do you mean? What do you mean?" cried his sister in dismay.

He replied, "I am saying that for this incarnation and for nine more incarnations I shall not have to take salt."

"I cannot imagine what has happened," said his sister pitifully. "Since you are our guest, I served you first. I have not even tasted that dish. We were all waiting for you to eat before we started. How could my food be so horrible?"

She went on moaning and holding her head. Meanwhile, her brother had to leave the table and go outside. Alas, from the dinner table they heard him vomiting. The whole family was so sad. The mother asked her daughter-in-law, "Sita, did you put salt in the dal?"

"Yes, mother," replied Sita, "how could I disobey you? I did add salt — but I only added a small amount."

Then the daughter confessed, "Mother, I thought that Sita had forgotten the salt. Sometimes she is unmindful, but we love her because she is so kind, so affectionate, so compassionate. I wanted to save her from your anger, so I added some salt on her behalf."

Sita smiled gratefully at her sister-in-law. Then Sita's husband said, "Mother, I am also to blame. I did not want you to insult my wife, which you so often do. I wanted to spare her, so I also put some salt in the pot."

Then the mother said quietly, "I also added some salt, even though I had asked Sita to do it. When I came back from my bath, I saw that the pot was still on the stove after such a long time. I thought Sita's common sense would have told her to turn off the stove. So I came to the conclusion that she had not been in the kitchen at all, and I, too, added salt. Please forgive me, Sita."

The mother was deeply mortified that her food had made her brother violently ill. She was also embarrassed that this had happened only because the other members of the family were trying to save Sita from her endless scoldings. At that very moment she took an oath that, from that day on, she would love and care for Sita as her own daughter — and this time she did keep her promise!

## AIE 45. *The magnificent coat*

There was a shopkeeper who used to sell very beautiful garments. He had many customers who deeply appreciated the special fabrics and beads that he had to offer. One day a young man was examining the coats in the store and he came across a most magnificent coat. It was so smart and so exquisite in every way. It was made of the finest silk. Even though the price was quite high, the young man finally decided to buy the coat.

The shopkeeper highly praised the young man's selection. "When you wear this coat," he said, "you will look like a real king. In fact, everybody will take you as the king!"

The young man was very pleased. He was anticipating the dramatic effect he would create with his new coat. He paid for it and then put it on, so that he could wear it home. As he was walking along, he began to attract a tremendous amount of attention. Everybody was admiring his new coat.

Then, all of sudden, a disturbing thought flashed across the young man's mind: "When I am wearing the coat, people say that I look like the king. But I cannot wear it all the time. On those days when I do not wear it, will I not look like an ordinary commoner? People may begin to make fun of me, saying that one moment I am the king and the next moment I am a commoner. Why should I create more problems in my life? The best thing is to return the coat!"

So he retraced his steps to the store and returned the magnificent coat.

# AMUSEMENT I ENJOY
# ENLIGHTENMENT I STUDY

## BOOK 5

## AIE 46. *The three questions*

There was a young traveller who had been walking for hours and hours. Finally the day was drawing to a close and he was becoming extremely tired. At last he noticed a small hut. Entering the hut, he saw that the owner was cooking something over a fire.

The traveller asked, "Could I please pass the night here with you?"

The owner answered, "Certainly! I am always glad to offer hospitality to travellers. You have come at the right time. I am cooking and I shall soon be able to offer you a most delicious meal. Just wait a little.

"By the way, I shall ask you a few questions. If you can answer them, I shall be very happy. If you cannot answer them to my satisfaction, I tell you, I may not give you shelter and I may not allow you to eat anything. In fact, I may even punish you!"

"I am to be punished?" responded the traveller. "What kind of hospitality is this?"

"The questions will be very simple," the host assured him.

The traveller said, "All right. If the questions are simple, I shall agree to your condition. It is quite dark outside and I do not know where I shall find another hut to pass the night. And you are tempting me with a most delicious meal. But mind you, the questions have to be very simple and straightforward."

His host repeated, "Yes, yes, the questions will be so simple, so simple."

Just as the host was preparing to ask the traveller the first question, the traveller saw that a cat had strolled into the hut. The cat had a bandage on its tail, but this did not seem to bother it at all.

The host pointed at the cat and said, "My first question is: what is this?"

The traveller was deeply relieved to hear such an easy question. He said, "It is just a cat. I feel sorry for it because it is forced to wear a bandage on its tail. Perhaps it is injured."

The host said, "A cat? How dare you say this is just a cat! This is Agni. I gave it the name Agni, and now you have to say it is just a cat!"

So he gave his guest a very smart slap as the punishment for his wrong answer. Then the host showed the traveller a jug containing water. He asked, "What do you think I have inside the jug?"

The traveller replied, "That is easy! It is water."

"What an insult!" shouted the host. "You are saying that this is water? No, for me it is life itself that is inside this jug! It can never be mere water." Again he gave the traveller a smart slap.

Even after punishing the traveller, the host was still exclaiming, "My very life exists inside this jug and he has to call it water!"

Finally the host said, "I have one more question."

"If your third question is like the first two, then after the third question I will leave," said the poor traveller.

His host said, "If you can answer the third question, then I will forget your first two deplorable answers. You will be able to stay and eat the most delicious meal that I am preparing and you can spend the night here."

Then the host indicated the roof of his house and asked, "What is this?"

"It is a roof," said the traveller.

"Roof!" cried the host. "You fool, I am showing you the height of my house!" For the third time he gave the traveller a very painful slap.

By now the traveller was extremely disgusted and angry. He said, "This is too much, too much! O God, what is happening to me? Why should I endure this for the sake of a meal and a place to spend the night? I do not need these things. I am going away this very moment!"

The traveller gathered his belongings and marched out of the house. At the foot of a large tree nearby, he stopped for a few minutes to recover himself. He lit a cigarette and threw the matchstick on the ground. Then he started smoking. To his astonishment, he noticed that the cat had followed him. The cat went up to investigate the matchstick. Unfortunately the matchstick was still smouldering. Suddenly, the bandage on the cat's tail caught fire. In a frenzy, the cat ran back to the hut and climbed onto the roof. The roof was made of straw and it was soon consumed with flames.

The owner of the hut rushed out and cried, "What have you done? What have you done?"

The traveller said, "I have not done anything. It was your Agni who did it! Agni is the god of fire. He wanted to show you his true nature. He is revealing himself to you. Agni is like that. He rewards his devotees by showing his power. Now, for God's sake, take your jug of 'life' and save your hut!"

But it was too late. The hut was burned to ashes, and the traveller went on his way. What a bad fellow the owner was!

### AIE 47. *The proud student*

At a special boarding school for young boys, examination time was fast approaching. One particular boy was reading far into the night, when all the other boys were fast asleep. Most of them were planning to get up early in the morning to study because they felt that was the best time.

The student who remained awake was so happy and proud that he alone was studying at that hour. He felt that he would do much better than all the others. After some time, one of the senior teachers passed by and noticed that this boy had kept his light on. He asked the boy, "What are you doing?"

"As you can see, I am the only one studying for the examination," replied the student in a very superior manner. "Others are fast asleep, snoring. But I am so proud of myself! I have been studying for hours and hours."

The teacher said, "Yes, I suppose you can be proud of yourself, but I have to say that I am ashamed of you!"

"Why? Why?" asked the boy.

The teacher said, "You should go to sleep like your friends."

"You do not want me to do well?" asked the boy, puzzled.

The teacher told him, "I do want you to do well, but you are so full of pride that I do not see how it is possible. I am telling you, your pride will ruin you. It is far better for you to sleep like the other students than to go on studying with this attitude. Those who are sleeping are doing the right thing. They will get up in the morning with new inspiration and enthusiasm. You go and join them; otherwise, I can clearly see that your pride will be your destruction!"

### AIE 48. *The tell-tale plants*

A young man had just graduated from medical school. Fortunately, his family was quite wealthy and he was able to open up a clinic of his own. Outside the clinic, he put up a big sign saying "Qualified Physician" and listing all his degrees and diplomas.

The very day the clinic opened, the doctor was standing in the doorway when he saw a most respectable-looking man approaching. The man was very well-dressed. The doctor was so happy. He took it as a sign of good fortune that his first patient should be someone very wealthy. He watched the man approach the clinic and read the sign very carefully. Then the man looked at the outside of the clinic itself.

All of a sudden, the man turned around and started walking away. The doctor ran after him and cried out, "Why are you leaving? You have come to the right place! I am the doctor who is mentioned on the sign and my clinic is now open. You can rest assured that I will do the needful for you. I am very well-qualified. Please come back for a consultation."

The man said, "I was coming to your place to get treatment, but I am leaving because of certain plants that you have placed right outside the door of your clinic."

"Yes," said the doctor, very confused, "I placed them there for decoration."

"May I ask when you last watered them?" enquired the man. "In case you have not noticed, all the plants are dying. They are dying because of your negligence, and for no other reason. You could have saved them if you had given them water, but you did not care for the lives of these innocent plants. Why then should I expect you to care for my human life? No, you are indeed a horrible doctor!"

"People will come to me so that I can give them life," protested the doctor. "They are not coming to see some stupid decorations."

At this point the man became really angry. He said, "You are the last one to be qualified to care for human lives. Take care of your plants first! Then you can think of human beings. I am disgusted by your callous attitude! You have no genuine concern or compassion for God's creation; otherwise, you would immediately have seen that your own plants were dying."

Then the man turned and left without another word.

AIE 49. *The coconut vendor*

There was a shrewd old man who used to sell green coconuts on the street. He had quite a few regular customers, one of whom was a little girl. Every day she would come and buy a coconut for her father. He was not doing well physically and he believed that coconut water would help to improve his condition. All the coconuts had a fixed price, no matter what their size. Sometimes there was a great difference in the size, but the old man always charged the same. What is more, whenever the little girl came with her rupees, he would select the smallest possible coconut for her to take home. She could not understand why he always gave her the smallest one.

One day, after he had handed her a particularly small coconut, she became brave and asked the old man, "If you are saying the price is the same for all, why do you always choose the smallest one for me? My father is asking me why I bring home such small coconuts. He says he has never seen them this size. I told him that you do have big ones, but you keep those for other people. So he has asked me to tell you that he is prepared to give you more money so that I can take home a larger one."

The old man said, "Oh, no, no! You are right. They are all the same price. But tell your father that I have a heart of compassion. You are such a little girl. If I give you a big one, it will be too heavy for you to carry. Your home is quite far away. So I was only showing my concern for you. I am sure your father will understand. I give you the smallest one so it will be easier for you to carry."

The little girl returned home and told her father what the old man had said by way of explanation. The next day, her father said to her, "This time I want you to look in the baskets and select a very big coconut. First you pick up the coconut and then you give the old man the money. But do not give him the full amount. Just give him a few rupees and keep the rest in your pocket."

The little girl ran to the coconut vendor and found a huge coconut in one of his baskets. She grabbed it and then quickly gave the man a few rupees, saying, "I am going. Here is your money." The old man was very surprised by her behaviour. When he started counting the coins, he discovered that she had not given him the full amount, so he ran after her. She was going quite slowly because the coconut was so heavy. The old man grabbed her and screamed, "You rogue! You little thief! You took my best coconut, and you did not give me the full amount!"

The little girl began to scream with fright. Then the old man let his monkey loose and it jumped on the girl to bite her. There was such a commotion on the street that many people gathered to see what was happening. Finally someone summoned a policeman. He rescued the little girl from the monkey and the old man. Then he questioned the old man and asked the girl, "Why did you deceive this man? He says that you have not given him the full amount for your coconut."

The little girl said, "For weeks and weeks I have been buying coconuts from this man. Every morning I come here. But he always gives me the smallest ones because he says that it is too difficult for me to carry the large ones. The price is exactly the same, but I get only half the amount of coconut water from the small ones. I told my father last night, and he said to me, 'Since the old man is so kind to you, I want you to give him less money. When he catches you, just tell him it is for his own good that you have done it. Tell him that you also know how to be kind. If you give him the full amount, he will have to spend such a long time counting all the coins. He has many, many customers to serve, so if you give him less money, it will take him less time to count and then he will have more time to help others.' That is what my father told me to do. Now may I keep this coconut and go? I am sure my father is waiting for me."

The policeman took the little girl to one side and said, "Your father is a wise man. You did the right thing. Now you can go home with your coconut."

Then the policeman severely scolded the coconut vendor for cheating the little girl day after day.

### AIE 50. *Alexander the Great and the pirate*

There was once a pirate who was notorious to the extreme. He used to sail here and there, plundering small boats and raiding villages along the coastline. He would torture people and then make off with their valuables. It was very difficult for people to resist him because he had all kinds of guns and knives. Everybody was afraid of him.

Nevertheless, there came a time when the people were able to trap this scoundrel and make him their prisoner. They brought him before the mighty Emperor, Alexander the Great. It was almost certain that he would be hanged for his misdeeds.

Alexander the Great said to him, "Now that we have caught you, are you not ashamed of the life you have led? You must know that you will receive a most severe punishment. Before you are condemned, I would like to give you the chance to ask for forgiveness from all those whom you have injured. I cannot restore their valuables, because you have already disposed of them. But if you beg these people to forgive you, I feel it will give them some consolation."

The pirate said, "I do not want to be punished. I do not want to be forgiven. But there is something that I would like to say."

"What do you want to say?" asked the Emperor.

The pirate looked directly at the Emperor and said, "If you feel that I should be ashamed of the life I have led, then I want to tell you that you should be infinitely more ashamed of what you are doing."

No one had ever spoken to the Emperor in this manner before. He was profoundly shocked and disturbed. "Go on," he said to the prisoner.

The pirate continued, "You and I are doing the same thing. We are leading exactly the same kind of life, only I am doing it in a very small measure. I may rob a few individuals and trading boats here and there, but you are doing it on a wide scale. How many countries you have conquered! How many lives you have needlessly destroyed! How many valuable treasures you and your soldiers have plundered! I tell you, it is you who should be ashamed, not I!"

The Emperor remained quiet for some time, lost in thought. Then he said, "You have spoken the truth. But for me it will be extremely difficult to change my way of life. In your case, since you are an individual, it will be infinitely easier for you to change. I have decided to give you enough material wealth so that you can give up this life of piracy. You can make a fresh start. I know that I also need the transformation of my nature, but I am starting with you because it will be easier for you to do it. In my case, gradually, gradually, I will try, but I fear it will prove too difficult."

This is how Alexander the Great came to free the notorious pirate.

### AIE 51. *The old lady who acted in self-defence*

In their march across Asia, Alexander the Great and his soldiers invaded a new country. There they found everything to be lush and prosperous. One village lay right across their path. Alexander's soldiers entered the village and immediately started pillaging everything in sight.

One soldier entered into the cottage of an old lady and began threatening her with his weapons. He said, "Give me all your coins and jewels!" While he was brandishing his weapons and frightening her, a large gold coin fell out of his tunic. He did not notice that it had dropped to the ground, but the old lady immediately pointed to it and said, "Look, look! That is your own money that you have dropped!"

The soldier snatched up the coin and said to her, "Now give me all your money!"

The old lady responded, "I showed you the coin that you dropped. I do not have that kind of money. What little money I have, I keep in that corner over there." She showed the soldier where to look for her money and he grabbed it. Then he said, "You are a crafty old lady. I am sure you must have some more money hidden somewhere."

She said, "All right. I can see it is no use lying to you. I do have a secret hiding place. Come with me and I will show you where I have kept all my savings."

The old lady led the soldier outside. In the garden was a deep, empty well. She said to him, "I have kept my savings under a rock at the bottom of the well. If you go down, you will easily find the bag of coins."

The soldier came near the well and bent over to see how deep it was. As he did so, the old lady gave him a mighty push. The soldier was caught off guard and he tumbled down into the well. There he met his death.

The soldier's comrades had seen him go inside the cottage and they were wondering why he did not appear again. They confronted the old lady and she told them, "I threw him down the well and he died. He was such a bad fellow! I am not ashamed of what I have done."

The soldiers were furious. They seized the old lady and brought her before the Emperor. The Emperor asked the old lady, "Why did you take my soldier to the well? Did you really have money hidden there?"

"No, I did not have any money there," she said truthfully.

"Then why did you tell a lie?" asked the Emperor.

She said, "He was such a bad fellow that I was afraid for my life. He was threatening me with his weapons and forcing me to give him the little money that I had. His own gold coin he dropped. I could have kept quiet, but I showed him where the coin had rolled. Still he was suspecting me of having more money, so I fooled him. I told him that the money was at the bottom of the well. When he took a close look inside the well, I pushed him and he fell to his death."

"Are you not repentant now that this man is dead?" asked the Emperor.

"Yes," replied the old lady, "but I feel that bad people should pay their karma. I did not want him to die, but I thought he should be punished. If he had lived, he would have gone on torturing helpless people like me."

Alexander the Great said, "You are right. Now let me give you back all the money that he stole from you."

The old lady gratefully accepted some money from the Emperor.

"Now take more money," the Emperor said.

"More money?" she asked.

"Yes," said the Emperor. "I want to reward you because you informed him that he had dropped his own coin. You could easily have kept it for yourself. He did not even notice that it was missing. So you deserve more."

Alexander gave her a second purse of coins and said, "I assure you that my soldiers will not harass you anymore."

## AIE 52. *Belated sincerity*

There was a certain king who liked to display his wealth. From time to time, he used to invite neighbouring kings and other noble personages to visit his palace so that he could show off his latest acquisitions.

Once it happened that he obtained a most extraordinary diamond ring. It was extremely expensive, but he felt that it was worth the price because it was the largest diamond that he had ever seen. The king was filled with innocent, childlike joy and he invited twelve of his friends to come and see his new treasure. These friends were all kings in their own right.

When they arrived, the host king took them into one of his private chambers. There the ring was displayed on a golden plate. The visiting kings greatly appreciated the ring, and they stayed in the room chatting and praising the excellent taste of the host king.

All of a sudden, the king's minister noticed that the diamond ring was missing. The minister looked around the room and thought, "Here there are no common thieves. These are all kings and great figures. This matter must be handled very carefully."

So the minister approached his king and quietly whispered to him that the ring had been stolen. The minister asked, "What should we do?"

The king immediately replied, "I do not wish to embarrass my guests. Their happiness and goodwill matter more to me than the ring. Kindly forget about the ring. I shall find another one in the course of time."

The minister said, "My King, I cannot allow this shameful crime to be dismissed. Please allow me to try something. I promise I will not embarrass your guests. I shall be as tactful as possible."

With a movement of his head, the king gave permission for his minister to try to recover the diamond ring in a diplomatic way. The minister began by addressing the gathering: "O great kings who have assembled here, you are all friends of my king and you have enjoyed his hospitality many times. Unfortunately, something has happened in this room today which is not the action of a friend. The diamond ring is missing. Perhaps one of you picked it up to examine it more closely. Perhaps someone removed it out of curiosity as to what would happen. Perhaps someone played a joke. And, again, perhaps it has truly been stolen. Since nobody has left the room, I can only assume that it is here somewhere.

"I am now going to extinguish the lamps for two minutes. If you are in possession of the ring, for any of the reasons I have mentioned, please return it to its place on the gold plate during these two minutes. In this way, nobody will be exposed and nobody will be embarrassed. Otherwise, if I command the palace guards to search you, it will be a most embarrassing and humiliating situation for the king in question. Are you all in agreement with this method?"

The kings were profoundly shocked at the disappearance of the ring and they immediately agreed to the minister's solution. The minister extinguished the lights and waited for two minutes. When the lamps were re-lit, everybody looked in the direction of the gold plate — only to discover that now the gold plate itself was missing! Nobody had anticipated this new development. The minister was particularly upset. He realised that now he had to catch not only one thief, but perhaps two.

With a sad smile, the host king brought the gathering to a close and they all retired to their respective rooms for the afternoon. The minister went at once to the queen to report to her all the untoward events of the day. The queen was absolutely furious. She confronted her husband and said, "This kind of friends you have! They must be searched, each and every one, before they are allowed to return to their own kingdoms."

The king replied, "No, I will not allow them to be searched. One of my friends has definitely stolen my ring. If my diamond has stolen the heart of my friend, what can I do? You stole my heart. That is why I married you. I stole your heart, so you married me. Similarly, somebody prized this diamond so much that he had to steal it — and the gold plate as well. Let that person be happy in his own way. I have no intention of embarrassing him."

The king and queen had a serious disagreement on the subject, but the king was adamant in his point of view and he would not issue the command for his guards to search the guests.

Later that evening, the host king and his guests enjoyed a magnificent banquet. Most of the kings were quite happy and cheerful, but there were three or four who were quite miserable. One was the culprit himself. The others were close friends of the host king who felt miserable that his joy had been blighted by this unthinkable act.

When the evening ended, the host king made a short speech. He said, "My friends, soon you will all be departing for your own kingdoms. Before you go, I would like you to know that I value my friendship with you all infinitely more than I value a diamond ring and a silly golden plate. These things I acquired only the other day. But you have all been my lifelong friends. I want to maintain the harmony, peace and friendship that exists among our kingdoms. So, if you have taken the diamond ring by mistake, do not worry at all. I shall not hold it against you."

The following day, all the kings returned to their respective kingdoms. Shortly afterwards, the king who had actually stolen both the diamond ring and the gold plate, and hidden them in his tunic, had a vivid dream. He dreamt that he saw the queen of the host king shedding bitter tears. She was inconsolable because the diamond ring had not been recovered and also because the culprit had not been caught and punished.

This dream made such a deep impression on the king who had stolen the ring that he had a change of heart. He decided to return the ring and the plate, but he was ashamed to confess his crime. He summoned his minister and asked him to offer some advice in this embarrassing situation. The minister said, "Your Majesty, you may leave it to me. I will find a way of returning these items secretly."

The minister then rode to a neighbouring kingdom. He wrapped the ring and plate together securely and sent them by special post to their true owner. When the parcel arrived and the king and his minister saw the postmark, they could not believe their eyes. The ruler of that kingdom had always been truthful. The king said, "How could my friend do this kind of thing? I know his nature. He is such a good, honest man."

But the minister was convinced that that particular king was guilty. He showed the queen the evidence of the postmark and she became absolutely furious. She wrote a very strong letter to this king accusing him of the crime.

The innocent king sent back an urgent letter saying, "Please believe me when I say that I did not steal your diamond ring and gold plate. I am being blamed because the parcel was sent to you from my kingdom, but I assure you it has not come from me. How I wish the real culprit would confess! I would be so happy and relieved to have my name cleared. But if he does not come forward, what can I do? You will be forced to think the worst of me. At least my dear friend has his ring and plate back."

Meanwhile, the king who had actually stolen the ring and plate asked his minister how he had managed to return them to their real owner. When the minister described his escapade in the neighbouring kingdom, the king was taken aback.

"You idiot! Why did you do that?" he cried. "You could have gone to a place where there was no king. You could have gone far, far away. Why did you have to go there? You know that that king's reputation is unblemished. If you had had a brain in your head, you would have posted the package from somewhere else. Now nobody will be his ally! I cannot allow that to happen. I am the one who stole the ring. Now, before anything else happens, let me go and confess what I have done to the innocent king who has been accused."

So the guilty king paid a visit to the kingdom of the innocent king and told him the whole story. When he had finished, he said, "I have told you the truth because I do not want you to be accused unjustly. Now you can punish me in whichever way you want. My minister played the trick on you, but it is I who have to take the responsibility. And I will allow you to inform our friend that it was I who stole his precious things. I do hope that one day he will be able to forgive me."

The innocent king said, "No, I cannot do that. Since I have been accused, let me remain guilty. As a matter of fact, I know that I am guilty only in the eyes of the queen and the king's minister. The king himself has written me a letter of consolation and sympathy saying that he does not believe I was the thief. I am happy to let things stand as they are."

The minister of the guilty king said, "I believe I can solve this problem."

His king asked, "What do you propose?"

The minister continued, "You will write a letter to the king saying that you can clearly see that he has an enemy. That enemy went to the kingdom of this innocent king to post the parcel. Tell him that the king who has been accused has played no part in this heinous crime."

The guilty king said, "But then people will ask me how the ring came into the possession of an ordinary man, since it was definitely one of the kings who stole it. No, your plan is not at all satisfactory. I do not see that it offers any solution."

While they were debating which course of action to follow, the guilty king reached an inner decision. Suddenly he announced, "My friend, I do not want you to suffer anymore. I stole the ring and the plate and I shall now go to the king's palace and make a full confession. That is the only way to put an end to all these accusations."

He departed before his minister could say another word and rode swiftly to the host king's palace. There he related everything exactly as it had happened and begged his friend's forgiveness. He said, "I am the thief and you may punish me as you see fit. I not only stole the ring and the plate, but I asked my minister to help me avoid embarrassment. Then he had the reprehensible idea of placing the blame on your dear friend. I wanted to return the ring and the plate because in my dream I saw your queen shedding bitter tears, but I did not have the courage to do so personally. My weakness has caused so much suffering for you and your friend."

When the queen heard the confession of the guilty king, she started crying. She said, "We have the diamond ring. We have the gold plate. Now we have the thief. I am so proud of you, for at last sincerity has dawned in your life."

The ending of the story was so sweet. The king and queen were most grateful to the guilty king. Not only did the queen forgive him, but she deeply appreciated his sincerity — his belated sincerity.

From this story we learn what greed can do. You may be a king, but if greed enters into you, then you may behave no better than a common thief.

## AIE 53. *Friendship on earth*

Friendship is such a strange and wonderful thing! When friendship is formed in Heaven, it never dies. On earth, friendship dies before it even takes birth. This is the difference between friendship in Heaven and friendship on earth.

This story is about two village friends. One of them borrowed twenty rupees from the other to buy a dog. He went to the bazaar and chose a dog that he liked. Unfortunately, after a month had passed, the dog fell ill and died. Now it happened that this fellow was supposed to return the twenty rupees to his friend at the end of the month, but he kept postponing and postponing his obligation.

Finally, the friend to whom he owed the money came to his house to collect it. He was saved because his wife answered the door and said that he was not at home. The friend came back the next day and the next, but the answer was always the same: "He is out."

Now a third friend entered the picture. He knew that the rogue-friend was deliberately avoiding the one who had given him the loan. So he said to the rogue-friend's wife, "This time when our friend comes to collect what you owe him, I am going to inform him that your husband is at home. Then you will be in serious trouble. So the best thing is to return the money."

The wife cried, "Please, please, do not tell him! Here — I am giving you one rupee as a bribe."

So the third friend accepted the bribe and went away. The next day he appeared again and made the same threat. Once more, the wife gave him one rupee as a bribe. Like this, twenty more times he came and twenty more times he received money from the wife to remain silent. Each time the loan-giver came to collect his money, the wife said the same thing: "He is out."

One day, fortunately or unfortunately, the friend who had given the loan and the one who had received it met face to face on the road. Their meeting was unavoidable. The fellow who had borrowed the money became extremely frightened. In a pitiful voice, he began pleading, "Please, please, give me another chance! This time when you come to my house, I will definitely be there and I will give you the full amount."

"I have already received the money," said his friend, smiling.

"How is it possible?" asked the rogue.

"Our mutual friend has given it to me," said the friend.

"Surely you are pulling my leg!" said the rogue.

"Not at all," answered the friend. "Every day he threatened your wife that he would inform me that you were actually at home when she said you were out. So she started giving him one rupee after another as a bribe. Eventually, he was able to pay me the complete sum: twenty rupees. And he also earned a commission!"

### AIE 54. *Retribution for the village scoundrel*

In a particular village there lived a young man who was wicked to the backbone. Everybody brought complaints against him, but his nature remained unchanged.

One day this scoundrel found himself with nothing to do. None of his friends were available and he could not think of any way to kill time. As he was lounging by the roadside, he saw the village pandit passing by. The scoundrel took a sharp rock from the ground and aimed it at the pandit. It struck his forehead and the wound began bleeding profusely. The scoundrel did not bother to run away since he was far stronger than the elderly pandit. Instead, he just stood nearby and laughed and laughed.

Then, to the scoundrel's wide surprise, the pandit began calling his name most affectionately and compassionately. He approached the old man cautiously. In spite of his pain, the pandit managed to give him a smile. "I am so proud of you, so proud of you!" he said. "You have such perfect aim. I am a poor man and I have only one rupee with me, but I wish you to take it. I want you to know that I appreciate you. Who cares if I am bleeding! This bleeding will soon stop. The most important thing is that you have shown your remarkable skill. In two hours' time, the village chief will pass by. If you can repeat your performance, I assure you that he will give you a far greater reward. I can give you only one rupee, but he is a very rich man."

The village scoundrel was now listening very intently to the wise words of the pandit. The pandit continued, "I am sure the chief will also reward you with a job in his palace. He has countless enemies. There will be a great advantage for him in keeping you by his side. You will be able to protect him by aiming at anyone who attacks him. So you should wait here and show the village chief your capacity. I am sure he will be most impressed."

The scoundrel was extremely pleased with the pandit's advice. He resumed his place by the roadside and selected a stone that was to his liking. After some time, he saw the village chief approaching with some of his attendants. The scoundrel took careful aim and threw his stone straight at the chief himself. It struck the chief in the head and he fell to the ground. Luckily he was not seriously hurt. The chief's attendants immediately grabbed the scoundrel and thrashed him to death. In this way, the pandit with his infinite wisdom was able to rid the village of this abominable scoundrel!

Nothing can surpass wisdom. Wisdom can solve any problem in our life. In our Indian villages, there is a kind of wisdom that we call village wisdom. This wisdom says that when you see a tiger, you should not try to fight it. Just climb up a tree. The tiger will roam around at the foot of the tree for some time, but how long can its patience last? Eventually it will go away, because it is beneath the tiger's dignity to wait indefinitely.

In my own case, I used village wisdom with my pet monkey, Madhu. He used to bite me mercilessly, but he would never bite my mother and he would never bite an infant who was crawling. It seems that anyone over the age of ten became his perfect victim. Then somebody told me that monkeys will never bite someone who is dead. So that is how I used to escape. When I saw Madhu coming towards me, I would fall down, stop breathing and pretend to be dead. Then he would come and examine my body, but he would not bite me. So many times I escaped by using that method! Unfortunately, it worked only if I fell down when he was forty or fifty metres away. If he was released just ten metres away from me, then no matter what I did, he would bite me very nicely!

That is how I was able to use our village wisdom.

### AIE 55. *The father-in-law loses his worker*

A grocery shop owner hired his son-in-law to work for him. This relative used to work hard, but he was quite greedy. All day long he would take food from the shelves and eat it. His father-in-law used to say, "I am giving you a proper salary and I am prepared to give you some food, but do not steal food from me! Because of your appetite, I am not able to make any profit."

"I am not stealing," the son-in-law objected. "I am your family member, your son-in-law, and I am hungry, so I am eating just to satisfy my appetite. Why should you deny me food?"

The poor father-in-law did not know what to do, so he went to see the village sage. This sage was said to possess tremendous occult power. After he had heard the whole story, the sage said, "I will give you a special kind of medicine. If you give the medicine to your son-in-law secretly, he will not feel hunger at all."

The shop owner asked, "How much money are you asking for your fee?"

"You have to give me 200 rupees," answered the sage.

The shop owner said, "This treatment is very expensive, but I know that if my son-in-law continues like this, he will ruin me. So the best thing is for me to pay you."

The shop owner returned home with the medicine, which he was supposed to add to his son-in-law's meal. The next day, he sent a regular meal from his house for his son-in-law. Before sending it, he added a dash of the medicine. The son-in-law ate the meal and did not experience any more hunger for the rest of the day. The father-in-law was very happy. The next day, he did the same thing. Still the son-in-law did not suspect anything. His father-in-law even asked him, "Why are you not eating? You will fall sick!"

But the son-in-law just continued working. At the end of the week, the shop owner gave his son-in-law his salary. The son-in-law counted it and said, "What shall I do with this meagre salary?"

"What do you mean?" asked the shop owner. "You have never objected to it before."

"That was because I was able to eat as much as I wanted to," replied the son-in-law. "Now that I do not have the same appetite, I will be able to work elsewhere and earn much more than the amount you are giving me. Why should I stay here in your tiny grocery shop when I can work in a big shop or business? Do you take me for a fool? From today on I shall look for another job!"

The father-in-law tried to save money by preventing his son-in-law from eating, but ultimately he was the loser because his son- in-law found another job and then there was nobody to help him run the grocery shop.

### AIE 56. *The rogue-businessman is exposed*

There was a very wealthy businessman who happened to be an unbearable and unthinkable rogue. He used to employ workers and tell them, "I will give you a very, very high salary, but you will receive it only at the end of each month. You must work very hard. If you please me, I will give you a very high salary, plus some baksheesh."

One by one, each worker failed to meet with the businessman's satisfaction. They never received the money that was due to them. Why did this occur? Two days before the end of the month, he would tell each worker to do something absolutely absurd and impossible. To one he would say, "You have to run twenty miles to the next village and pick up a parcel and then run the twenty miles back again." Some poor workers could not walk even half a mile, let alone run twenty miles! To others he would say, "You have to swim in the river for three hours without stopping." On one occasion, he even gave a worker a tabla and told him, "You have to play this tabla to my satisfaction. If I do not like your performance, then you will not receive any salary from me."

So these kinds of demands he used to make just before the end of each month. In that way, he did not have to pay anybody's salary. But his fate was about to change. It happened that a very smart young man came to work for him. This young man worked very, very hard. One day before the end of the month, the rogue-businessman said to him, "Look, I am giving you two glass tumblers. One is very small and one is quite large. Now you have to put the large one inside the small one."

The young man took the larger tumbler and dashed it on the ground. Then he collected all the little pieces of glass and put them inside the small tumbler. The businessman was furious and gave the young man a punch. He demanded that the young man pay for the broken tumbler. He even threatened to kill the young man for his insolence.

The poor worker had not even received his salary and here he was expected to pay for the broken tumbler. He said, "I have not received the salary that you promised me when I began working here."

The businessman said, "Why should I give you a salary when, on the last day of the month, you could not perform your job satisfactorily?"

The young man was compelled to leave the place empty-handed. He went to the village judge and placed the case before him. The judge summoned the wealthy businessman and said to him, "Why are you not giving this young man his salary? He has worked for 29 days prior to this."

The businessman replied, "Why should I give him a salary? I told him that I would pay him only if he worked for the whole month to my satisfaction. On the last day he deliberately broke an expensive glass tumbler belonging to me. It is he who should pay me!"

The village judge asked the young man, "Why did you break it?"

The young man replied, "He asked me to put the big tumbler inside the smaller one. I could not do it without breaking the big one. He tells all the workers to fulfil this kind of impossible demand just before the end of each month so that he does not have to pay them. I realised long ago that he is insane, but if I started spreading the news in the village, who would believe me? That is why I decided to do something striking. I wanted his case to come to the attention of the authorities. So many workers before me have suffered because he has not paid them one rupee. It is time he was brought to justice."

The village judge said to the wealthy businessman, "Right in front of me, you have to give this young man his salary plus a substantial bonus, or I will throw you into jail!"

So the businessman had to give a very large sum of money to the young man. From that day on, nobody would work for him because they all knew in advance that he was an unpardonable rogue!

# AMUSEMENT I ENJOY
# ENLIGHTENMENT I STUDY

## BOOK 6

AIE 57. *An idle man changes his nature*

Once there was an extremely idle man. He never did anything, either for the betterment of the world or for himself. He only wallowed in the pleasures of idleness. Then one day, for some unknown reason, he changed his attitude. He said, "Right now, everybody is hating me because I do not contribute anything to the village. I need to do something with my life."

He did not even know how to go about looking for a job, so he went to the king and explained his situation. He told the king, "I am notorious for being lazy. I am sure nobody will want to give me a job. Will you not give me a chance? If people see that I am working for you very conscientiously, then perhaps they will stop despising me."

The king said, "Certainly I shall give you a job. Tomorrow morning you can come back and I shall give you some tasks."

The idle man returned to the palace the next morning and the king asked him to do some errands. He did them quite happily. However, the following day he came late. The day after that, he came even later. And he formed the habit of leaving the palace two hours earlier than everybody else. So it went on, day after day.

Finally, the matter was brought to the attention of the king. The king said, "This fellow wanted to turn over a new leaf. Now he has fallen into his old way of life once again. He always arrives late and he leaves before the actual finishing time. Laziness is in his nature."

After many months, the king asked the idle man, "What are you doing, coming and going at any odd hour you choose? How do you expect me to tolerate a worker like you?"

The idle man said, "O King, every day, early in the morning, I go to the temple and sing and sing for two or three hours.

Then I come here to work. As soon as I can, I leave here and go back to the temple to sing."

Upon hearing this, the king's minister became furious. Privately he said to the idle man, "The king appointed you specially. He gave you a job here, not at the temple. Instead of going to the temple to sing the Glory of God, you should come to the palace and sing the glory of the king!"

So the idle man came to the king's palace early the next morning and started singing the glory of the king very loudly for about two hours. The first day, the king was amused. Then, after two or three days, the king grew irritated. He said, "Did I give you this job to flatter me or to do the needful? Get out, get out!"

"O King, please, please listen to me!" cried the idle man. "It was your own minister who advised me to sing here. I used to go to the temple to praise God's Glory. As a result, I was usually late in coming to work. So your minister said I should praise your glory, since you are the one who gave me the job and you are paying me."

The king looked at his minister and said, "In one sense, you have shown your cleverness. At least he is coming to work at a regular hour now. But, again, you are so stupid! Did I ask him to sing my glory? No, I only asked him to do some small jobs here and there."

Then the king said to the idle man, "I shall keep you on one condition: you must remember that, for you, duty always comes first. From now on, you must work here for six hours every day. Those hours will be fixed. During that time, you must not sing God's Glory or my glory. Afterwards, you can do anything, go anywhere and sing anything that you wish."

The idle man agreed to the king's condition and he changed his nature completely. He became a man of duty.

## AIE 58. *A saint by day and a thief by night*

Every day a young girl had to fetch water from the village well. She came of a good family and she used to wear a very nice sari and a beautiful necklace. One day, as the young girl leaned over the well to draw water, her necklace fell into the well. She did not know that the clasp had somehow become loose. Helplessly she watched as her necklace disappeared out of sight. Needless to say, she was extremely sad and miserable.

After returning from the well, the young girl went to see someone who had the reputation of being an excellent swimmer. Other villagers had told her that he was the only one who could dive to the bottom of the well and bring up the necklace. Unfortunately, this man was a rogue. After the young girl had begged him to help her, he said, "First you have to give me five hundred rupees. Then only shall I find your necklace." He knew that her parents were quite wealthy and he saw an opportunity to make a considerable amount of money from this adventure. When he quoted his fee, the young girl was horrified. She said, "Five hundred rupees? It is too much, too much!"

The rogue replied, "Nothing is too much for you! If your father comes to learn that you have dropped your necklace, I am certain he will give me as much as five thousand rupees just to make you happy."

"No, no, you are wrong," she said. "Instead of giving you five thousand rupees, my father will scold me for my negligence and carelessness."

No matter what she said, the rogue refused to reduce his exorbitant fee. Sadly, she went home. The following day she returned to the well and sat there. She thought perhaps she would get some inspiration as to how she could recover her necklace. Soon she saw a vagabond approaching. She knew that this particular man happened to be a thief. It was common knowledge to everybody in the village that he was responsible for committing many robberies, but nobody had been able to catch him red-handed. He was extremely smart and tricky.

As soon as the thief was close at hand, the young girl began screaming and wailing, "I have dropped my necklace in the well! Is there anybody on earth who can help me?" She did not address the thief directly, but she wanted her words to reach his ears.

The thief merely passed by without paying any attention to her. The young girl began following him. She was screaming, "If you cannot help me, is there anybody whom you can recommend?"

The thief said, "What do you expect me to do? I do not know how to dive, and I do not know anyone else who can dive. I cannot help you at all."

The young girl showed great annoyance at his callous attitude. As a last resort, she said, "If you can do it, I will give you three hundred rupees."

The thief pretended that he did not care for her money at all. Like a saint, he was far above it. He paid no attention to the girl's pleas and nonchalantly went away.

Later that day, the young girl spoke to some of the other villagers who had come to the well. She told them, "I was so desperate to get my necklace back that I even asked the thief to help me. He did not pay any attention to me. But, who knows? Perhaps he will come under cover of darkness and try to steal the necklace."

The villagers saw their chance to catch the thief red-handed at last. Quite a few of them came to the well that evening and hid at various places. They made themselves completely invisible. Lo and behold, in the middle of the night, the thief came and jumped into the well. After a few minutes, he found the necklace. Then he climbed out of the well and started to run away.

Suddenly all the villagers emerged from their hiding places and grabbed him. They thrashed him soundly and confiscated the necklace from him. The next morning, they gave it back to the young girl. She was deeply grateful to them, and they were also most grateful to her for helping them to catch such a notorious thief!

## AIE 59. *The Master's burden*

There was a spiritual Master who always used to cut jokes. On his path, he liked to use humour to a great extent. He would pray and meditate with his disciples but, after the meditation was over, he would entertain them by cutting jokes or by asking the disciples to say amusing things. This spiritual Master was always cheerful, self-giving and very, very happy.

Finally it came to pass that the Master fell ill. He was running a high temperature and all kinds of diseases attacked him. Day by day, his case got progressively worse. The disciples asked him, "Master, Master, what has happened to you? Why are you suffering so much?"

In a weak voice, he said, "Do you think it is an easy task to take on the burden of four men? Do you think it is an easy task to give away the burden of four men?"

To the disciples, it seemed that the Master was talking in riddles. They could not understand him at all. With each passing hour, they became more and more alarmed at the Master's condition. That very day, he left the body.

Now, this particular Master had only four disciples. They placed his body on a stretcher to carry it to the place of burial. As they all grasped the stretcher, they suddenly realised the meaning of the Master's words. He had carried them; he had taken their burden. Then he wanted to give up the responsibility, but he found it difficult to unburden himself. It was too much for him to carry the burden of these four disciples. Finally, he left the body and they were compelled to take care of themselves.

So many spiritual Masters have developed serious illnesses from taking on the burden of their disciples. Sri Ramakrishna declared that he developed cancer because of the imperfections that he had taken from sixteen disciples. The Saviour Jesus Christ also took on the sins of his twelve disciples.

Sometimes the disciples do not believe that the Master has taken on their weaknesses and imperfections. Even if they are attacked by a headache, they say, "Here is the proof that you have not taken away all my problems. If you have really taken them, why am I still suffering?"

What can the poor Master do with this kind of disciple? Sometimes he escapes by saying, "You do not realise that you would have suffered infinitely more. Because of my intervention, your sufferings were much, much less than they would have been."

And what does God do? He hears from Above the Master's story and the disciple's story. Then He says to the Master, "You rogue! It is I who have taken away all your disciples' problems, not you." And God tells the disciples, "You are also rogues! Can you not see that your sufferings are next to nothing in comparison with what you deserve?"

### AIE 60. *The rich man's "service"*

There was a man who was exceedingly rich. He was actually an upstart who had accumulated his money in a very short space of time. He was extremely proud of his wealth and he always used to look for any opportunity to parade it in front of his neighbours. During the day he would act in a very arrogant manner, and at night he would remain awake making noise. He would open the drawers of his desk and then bang them closed deliberately. Or he would yell at his two dogs so that they would begin barking incessantly. Sometimes he would sing as loudly as possible. In every way, he tried to draw the attention of the villagers to himself so that they would constantly be reminded of his wealth.

His poor neighbours could not sleep. Every night the same thing would happen. The rich man would get the inspiration to make as much noise as possible. The whole day was not enough for him. At night also he had to prove that he was busy taking care of his house and all his financial affairs.

This went on, month after month and year after year. He made everybody's life miserable, but his neighbours did not dare to raise any complaints. They were afraid that he would use his wealth to bring harm to them or to their families, so they remained silent.

One day a relative visited the wealthy man's nearest neighbours. As usual, when evening set in, the rich man started his clanging and banging, opening and closing all the doors unnecessarily. His dogs were barking hysterically and he was singing tuneless songs at the top of his voice.

The visiting relative next door listened to the commotion in disbelief. He said, "Uncle, why do you allow this man to behave in such a way? What right does he have to disturb the whole neighbourhood?"

His uncle replied, "He is very, very rich, so we cannot silence him. He will not listen to our requests. We have to surrender to him."

The relative was very smart. He told his uncle, "I am sure that from today he will surrender to you. I will make him surrender."

The next morning, he went to the wealthy man and said, "I am a relative of your neighbour. I am just visiting for a few days. I have come here to express my gratitude to you on behalf of all your neighbours. How I wish I could have a person like you as my neighbour! We need someone like you in our village."

"You need me?" said the rich man, in a surprised voice.

The relative continued, "Absolutely! Last night I heard you moving around and making noise. My uncle tells me that you do this every night. You have no idea how helpful this noise is! In other neighbourhoods, they have thefts and so on. But here it is completely safe because you are doing the work of ten guards. No other guard is needed. How selflessly and tirelessly you are performing this service for the sake of all your neighbours! They are so grateful to you because they can sleep in peace every night. Alas, in my vicinity we have no one like you who is prepared to do this kind of service on a regular basis!"

The rich man had a very mean streak. As soon as he heard what this young man had to say, he thought to himself: "O my God, I have been such a fool! Here I was, showing off every night how great I am and all the time I have been saving them the expense of hiring a night guard. Why should I do this kind of unpaid work for them? If they cannot afford to have a guard, is it my fault? Let them solve their own problems. I am not going to help them by making noise anymore!"

### AIE 61. *The priest who changed his profession*

There was a blind man who used to go every day, early in the morning, and sit near a certain temple. He would place a small container in front of himself, and then he would begin crying most pitifully, "I am blind! Please take pity on me."

Many devotees of the cosmic gods and goddesses would start arriving at the temple at an early hour to perform their worship. In India, we believe that one can gain merit by praying and meditating early in the morning before entering into the hustle and bustle of life.

As these devotees passed by the blind man, many of them would place some annas and even rupees in his container. They felt that the cosmic gods and goddesses would be pleased with them if they could help this poor, unfortunate man.

This went on for a number of years. The blind man was always to be found in his place near the temple, and every day he would receive enough money from the kind-hearted devotees to buy his food and have some comforts in his life.

Eventually a new priest got a job in the temple. This priest observed the blind man and saw that people were very generous towards him. The priest said to himself, "Every day this blind man earns so much money just by sitting there. I am sure he is very sincere, but who is to know the difference? Someone could easily earn the same amount of money just by pretending to be blind. I work so hard for the temple, but I earn a mere pittance! Let me give up my profession and become like this man. I will go to another temple and pretend that I am blind. I will cry and cry as this one does, and I am sure people will shower their money upon me."

So he left his job as the temple priest and went to another village. There he dressed in some rags and took up his position outside the temple. He closed his eyes and began crying helplessly, using the same pitiful voice that he had learned from the man who was really blind. Many devotees were coming by on their way to the temple and he was very happy to hear the sound of the coins that they were dropping into his container.

The priest of this temple also happened to pass by. He, too, was moved by the cries of the blind man, but when he looked at the blind man, something did not seem to be right. The priest could not explain what it was. So he continued on inside the temple to commence the puja. At the same time, he decided to secretly observe the blind man and, from time to time, he glanced at him through the temple doorway.

After two or three hours, people stopped coming to the temple. Morning prayers were over and there was usually a rest period until the evening prayers began. The priest was watching the blind man and he saw him suddenly open his eyes and grab his container of love-offerings. He tipped the whole amount onto the palm of his hand and then very nicely hid it in one of his pockets. Then the so-called blind man replaced the container in its original position, closed his eyes and started his pitiful wailing once again. By now it was around ten o'clock in the morning and very few people were coming to worship. Even then, the blind man continued his performance. Greedy people are like that. They do not want to miss even a single rupee.

Day after day, the temple priest watched this charade. He prayed for the illumination of the blind man, but to no avail. Finally, the priest could tolerate it no longer. One day he stood in front of the beggar and said, "Oh, I see that you are blind. That is why you are earning so much money!" Then he gave the blind man three smart slaps. The priest continued, "Every morning you have been fooling the sincere devotees who come to pray and meditate here at this temple. I have been watching you for a long time. I have seen you open your eyes and count your money. Then you hide it in your pocket. But you cannot fool me! I know that you have perfect vision."

"Is that so?" asked the blind man. "Then tell me, can you see a house about one hundred metres away?"

"Yes, I can see one," said the priest.

"What colour is it?" asked the blind man.

"It is green."

"Green?"

"Yes."

Then the blind man asked, "What else do you see?"

"I see a few coconut trees around the house."

"Ah," said the blind man, "that is what I cannot see at all. That proves I am blind! You can see so far — you can see not only the house, but also the trees around it. But, poor me, I am so blind, so blind! All those things in the distance are hazy for me."

Then the temple priest became really furious and gave the beggar a few more slaps. The beggar cried, "I am calling the police!"

"All right," said the priest, "you call the police! In fact, I myself will call the police to come. Now tell me the truth: whose house is it over there? It is newly built and I suspect that it has something to do with you."

The beggar said, "It is my house. It is not a crime to own a house. I was able to build it with the money that I have earned from begging."

"Now I am definitely taking you to the police station," said the priest. He took all the beggar's earnings for that day and was about to drag him to the police station.

Then, all of a sudden, the priest changed his mind and set the beggar free. He said to himself, "Let me remain inside the temple and try to be a sincere priest. Then people will appreciate me. If I do not do my job properly, then people will treat me in the same way that I have treated this fellow. Insincerity can strike in any profession. Whether he is just pretending to be blind or I am just pretending to be a good priest, it is all the same. The best thing is for me to become sincere and spiritual in every way so that I do not share his fate."

AIE 62. *Cincinnatus the farmer*

In olden times the Romans were always trying to expand their Empire. They would make their army as strong as possible so that they could continually fight with other countries and conquer them. Once it happened that the Emperor himself was on his way to join his army. He wanted to lead his army to victory. The Emperor and his personal guards camped for the night at a hidden place. Unfortunately, some spies came to know where they were and the enemy was able to surround them. When morning dawned, the Emperor saw that he and his small troop of guards were trapped. Escape was impossible.

The enemy soldiers did not dare to touch the Roman Emperor until they had received instructions from their leader, and so they prepared to wait in that place for a few days. Meanwhile, a farmer from the area came to learn of the Emperor's dire predicament. This farmer had tremendous loyalty to the Emperor. He decided to try his best to save the Emperor, even though he had no weapons and no military training.

The farmer gathered some other farmers and villagers and told them his plan. He said, "Tonight, when darkness falls, we will begin work. I want you all to come on foot, very quietly, carrying large logs. Some of you can make several trips while the others start building a solid wall around the enemy. We will divide ourselves so that we can completely surround them. There must be no gap in the wall. They are not expecting any counter-attack, especially not from a group of simple farmers. So we shall do this while they are resting. Our Emperor will suffer for only one day and one night. Then we shall free him!"

With these spirited words, the farmer inspired all the villagers to work through the night. Soundlessly, they built a wooden wall around the enemy. Then the farmers took up their positions at various places with rocks and other simple weapons to attack the enemy.

When morning came, the enemy soldiers found that they were now prisoners. They ran to and fro, looking for some means of escape, while the villagers pelted them with stones. Seeing the situation, the Roman Emperor gathered his personal guards and launched his own attack on the enemy. When the enemy realised that they were being attacked on all sides and there was no way to cross the wall, they were compelled to surrender.

The name of this brave farmer was Cincinnatus. How authentic the story is, we do not know; but it is very entertaining and, at the same time, inspiring.

### AIE 63. *The Brahmin's lie*

Ramesh was the son of a Brahmin. He was a very good student and he had a few extremely close friends. One of his friends was a young girl. She was the daughter of a farmer and she did not have any education, but Ramesh liked her very much. He wanted to marry her, but he was afraid of breaking the news to his parents because he knew they would be horrified. In India, Brahmins are the highest class. This farm girl came of the lowest caste. Ramesh knew that his parents would not approve of his marrying someone from the lowest caste, so he became sadder and sadder day by day.

Ramesh spoke about his situation to several of his other friends and they said, "Go and tell your father. Who knows, he may change his mind when he sees how much you care for this girl."

Ramesh said, "No, he will never give up his old ideas. Let me play a trick on my father. That is the only way he will agree to this marriage."

"What kind of trick?" they asked.

Ramesh said, "I will bring my girlfriend home to meet my parents and I will tell my father that she belongs to our caste."

"That is an excellent idea!" his friends responded. "There is no reason for your father to doubt that she is also from a Brahmin family."

So Ramesh brought his girlfriend home and introduced her to his father. He said, "Father, we like each other very much and we want you to give us your blessings so that we can get married. You do not have to worry. She also belongs to our Brahmin caste."

As soon as Ramesh had spoken these words, his girlfriend cried out, "Oh, no, no, no! How can you say that? I am of the lowest class. I am not of the Brahmin class at all. I come of a Shudra family. We are only farmers. I do not know why Ramesh is trying to deceive you."

"My son, how can you tell me this kind of lie!" cried the father. He was absolutely shocked and horrified by his son's behaviour.

But the worst was yet to come. Ramesh's mother was so deeply shocked by this revelation of her son's character that she had a heart attack and died then and there.

In spite of his suffering, the poor father then said to the farmer's daughter, "You are a true Brahmin because you had the courage to tell the truth. I am going to visit your father and beg him to allow you to marry my son."

So the Brahmin went to the farmer and said, "You and your family are true Brahmins. My son and I are Shudras. In spite of this vast difference in our caste, will you allow your daughter to marry my son?"

The farmer could not believe his ears. He knew that the Brahmin had deliberately reversed their castes. He asked the Brahmin, "Why are you pretending to be of a lower class?"

The Brahmin replied, "Whoever tells the truth is first-class. It is the duty of Brahmins to tell the truth. My son deliberately lied to me, but your daughter told me the truth. Therefore, yours is the true Brahmin family."

The farmer saw that the Brahmin sincerely wanted this marriage to take place, and so he gave his permission.

Ramesh married his girlfriend and they were very happy together. The Brahmin was also happy at first. Then he began to feel miserable because he had lost his wife. He felt that his life was empty. One day he said to Ramesh, "My wife has died. I hold you fully responsible. You are the culprit who had to tell me a lie. Now there is nothing here for me. What is the use of staying on earth?" Then he had a heart attack and died.

Ramesh was completely shattered by his father's death. He said, "Because of my one small lie, my mother died and now my father has died. What is the use of my staying on earth? I know that I shall never be happy in this life." Then Ramesh himself had a heart attack and died.

After her husband's passing, the poor wife went back to her father's place. She cried, "Father, Father, what have I done? By telling the truth, I have become responsible for my mother-in-law's death, my father-in-law's death and now the death of my beloved husband. What is the truth worth if it can destroy so many lives? Why did I have to open my mouth?"

"No, my daughter, you did the right thing," said her father. "Brahmins are expected to tell the truth, but Ramesh consciously told a lie. Now he and his mother and father have all had to pay the price of that one lie. You told the truth. Therefore, you did the right thing. Do not let this experience ruin your life. You are still very young. If you want to marry someone else, I will find somebody suitable from our class. I really want you to find happiness."

His daughter looked at him sadly and said, "Ramesh loved me and I loved him, but I did not know he was going to tell a lie. Life is full of suffering. I do not wish to marry again."

So the young girl remained a widow.

### AIE 64. *Paying for a beating*

There were two men who were deadly enemies. They hated each other and, at the same time, there was constant rivalry between them. Eventually, it came to the point where one of them engaged a professional wrestler. This wrestler was huge and extremely powerful.

The employer said to the wrestler, "Here, take these hundred rupees. Now I will be so grateful if you can wait on the street where my enemy lives. When he comes home from work, I want you to beat him up. He has been torturing me for so many years. The time has come for him to be humbled."

The wrestler said, "Definitely I will beat him up, since you are giving me a hundred rupees. Soon he will receive a sound thrashing from me."

The following day, the man who had employed the wrestler was coming home from the market. He saw the wrestler waiting for him outside his house. He thought that the wrestler had some good news for him and so he hurried in his direction. Alas, when he came near the wrestler, the wrestler threw him to the ground and started beating him mercilessly.

As the man was lying flat on the ground screaming and kicking, he managed to cry out, "What happened? I gave you a hundred rupees to thrash my enemy and now you are giving me the same treatment! You are so bad! Why are you doing this?"

The wrestler replied, "Why? I was waiting for your enemy on the street, according to your instructions. He saw me as he was approaching his house and asked me what I was doing there. I told him that you had offered me a hundred rupees to give him a beating, so he immediately offered me four hundred rupees if I would beat you up instead. He gave me much more money than you did for the same job. So I accepted his offer and now I have done my job. But I do have a conscience. Because of my conscience, I am returning your one hundred rupees."

The wrestler took one hundred rupees out of his pocket and gave them to his victim, who was lying on the ground in utmost pain. He kept the four hundred rupees that the second man had given him.

### AIE 65. *Stick to one god*

There were two friends who were very spiritual. One of them eventually became a great seeker, but for some time he used to do something that seemed to indicate that he did not have any real depth: every day he would worship a different cosmic god or goddess. This seeker became very well known, and many people would ask him to pray to the cosmic gods or goddesses on their behalf. He did it quite happily. He used to tell them, "If you like Lord Krishna, then I will pray to Lord Krishna. If you like Shiva, then I will pray in front of Shiva's image. If you like Mother Kali, then I will worship Mother Kali. It is up to you. Most sincerely I will pray on your behalf. But I cannot guarantee the results."

So, people would give him money and then ask him to pray on their behalf for the deity of their choice to bless them and solve all their problems.

The seeker's friend heard that he was making lots of money by worshipping this god and that god. This friend was not at all well known, although he was also an excellent seeker. He realised that his dear friend was doing something which would seriously affect his own spiritual progress. So one day he came and dug five deep holes in front of his friend's house. The great seeker came out and said, "What are you doing? Why are you digging so many holes? Is one not enough for you?"

His friend stopped digging for a moment and said, "I am making these holes with the hope that, from one of them, water will spring up."

The seeker said, "What do you mean? How will you know that any hole has water if you do not dig it deeper than all the others? My friend, I advise you to concentrate on only one hole!"

The friend smiled and said, "You have to give me this piece of advice? Every day you are praying to a different cosmic god or goddess with the hope that one day one of them will be pleased with you. By constantly changing, you are not giving the proper amount of time to any one of them. That is why I have dug these holes in your garden. It is high time for you to realise that if you want results, you have to stick to one god or goddess."

This was how the friend taught the great seeker a most significant spiritual lesson.

### AIE 66. *The matchsticks*

Two friends went to a village market and sold their wares. They were returning home quite satisfied when one friend said to the other, "Let us rest here for a few minutes and smoke. I have only one *cheroot*. Do you have anything?"

The other one said, "Yes, I have two matchsticks."

"Then let us share the cheroot," said the first one.

He held the cheroot while his friend tried to strike the first matchstick. For some reason, it did not strike. Now there was only one matchstick left. The first man said, "If this one does not strike, we will not be able to smoke at all. Everything depends on this matchstick."

The other fellow closed his eyes and started praying with folded hands.

The first friend said, "Why do you have to pray to God for this trivial thing?"

The second one replied, "I do not want to take any chance. I am praying to God in case something happens to this one also and it does not strike."

When his prayers were over, he tried the last matchstick. Again nothing happened. There was no flame. The first friend said, "Why did you bother to pray? Look at the result! Prayer is useless. When we pray, God never grants us our prayer."

The second friend said, "No, He did listen. But when I prayed, God told me something."

The first friend was curious. "What did God tell you?" he asked.

The second friend said, "God told me that at this place, all around us, is a large quantity of straw. It is extremely dry. If the matchstick had worked, we would have used it to light the cheroot and then we would have thrown it on the ground, the way we always do. Then the straw would have caught fire. Right beside this area is a beautiful park. That park would have been destroyed. And the park contains so many little animals and birds. All of them would have perished. You know that God is so fond of birds. If we die, God may not care; but if little innocent birds or animals die, then God will feel absolutely miserable. That is why God told me that He was not going to allow us to strike the match successfully and smoke the cheroot."

Perhaps the first friend was secretly jealous that God had not spoken to him also. Outwardly he said, in a mocking tone, "I see! God cares more for his little birds and animals than He does for human beings! Then we should also become birds and animals. From now on, let us pray to God to change us into birds and animals so that He will care for us!"

The second friend remained silent, but in the inmost recesses of his heart, he was deeply grateful to God for not allowing the destruction of the park and all the little creatures dwelling there.

### AIE 67. *The clever poet and the wise poet*

In a particular region there were two noteworthy poets. One was extremely clever and popular. His poems were very witty and amusing. The other one had much more depth, but his poems were not widely known. Once it happened that the local zamindar wanted to honour all the poets, and so he said that they should come to his palace on a particular day and read their poems.

The serious poet said, "So many poets will join this competition. I know that my clever poet-friend has been flattering the zamindar constantly of late. Naturally the zamindar will make him stand first, so it is useless for me to go."

The competition took place. Many poets came and, as the serious poet had predicted, the clever poet won. He was showered with tremendous adulation and lots of material riches. Soon afterwards, the clever poet visited the serious one. He said, "Did you hear that I have won a huge sum of money? In front of so many other poets, the zamindar appreciated and admired my poems the most. I am now the most revered poet of the land!"

The serious poet felt sorry, but not because he had not joined the competition. He felt sorry because he knew that the clever poet's poems were not all that good. It was only by flattering and flattering the zamindar that he had won first place in the competition. "I have to find a trick to make this boastful fellow learn some humility," he said to himself.

After the clever poet had finally finished bragging, the serious one said to him, "I will recognise your talent only if you get appreciation from a particular zamindar."

The clever poet said, "Definitely! Just tell me his name and I will go and read my poems to him. I am sure he will be deeply impressed by my command of language, my striking images, my use of metre and so on. I may even be inspired to write a special poem just for him!"

The serious poet continued, "I am telling you, if he says that you are an excellent poet, only then will I feel that you are really superlative. He is the only one whose opinion I value. He is a great person and he is very well educated."

Full of confidence and self-assurance, the clever poet went to the zamindar that the serious poet had mentioned. This zamindar agreed to listen to a selection of his poems. So the clever poet started to read them out in a ringing voice. Now and then he glanced at the zamindar to get a little appreciation. On and on he went, until he had read out thirty poems, but still the zamindar did not offer any appreciation. Then, at one point, the poet got a faint smile.

He said to himself, "I have read out so many poems and all I have received in return is a faint, fleeting smile! What kind of man is this?"

He continued reading a little longer, but it was obvious that the zamindar was not impressed in the least. Finally, the poet stopped reading and said to the zamindar, "That concludes the poems that I brought with me. I have read out so many for you. Will you not do anything for me?"

The zamindar reached for a piece of paper and wrote "fifty rupees." Then he gave the note to his secretary. The secretary handed the poet the sum that the zamindar had indicated. When the poet received the small sum of coins, he was badly insulted.

The zamindar whom he had flattered had given him so much money and this one had given him next to nothing.

He said to the secretary, "Can you not give me some more? After all, I have travelled quite a distance to come here and read my poems."

The secretary answered, "It is not up to me. I can only do what the zamindar commands me to do."

So the clever poet went back to see the serious poet. He was filled with depression. He said to this other poet, "I read out all my best poems for him. They are all so nice. But he gave me only fifty rupees in payment for my trouble! I tried so hard to get an iota of appreciation from him, but he did not utter even one word."

The serious poet said, "I told you, if you get appreciation from him, only then will I admire you. Otherwise, I will not. I hold his appreciation in very high esteem."

Humbly, the clever poet asked the serious one, "Did you ever get appreciation from this particular zamindar?"

"No," replied the serious poet, truthfully.

"Then why did you send me?" asked the clever poet.

The serious poet said, "I sent you because you think that you are the greatest poet of all."

The clever poet said, "Now I do not feel that I am the greatest. Had I been really great, then surely I would have received some genuine appreciation and admiration from that zamindar. No, I have come to realise that I am only an ordinary poet or even a budding poet. I was clever enough to fool our zamindar with my empty flattery. But flattery is not poetry. This zamindar has opened my eyes. According to him, my poems were worth only fifty rupees. I am grateful to you, my friend, for illumining me in this way."

Then the serious poet embraced the clever poet and said, "My friend, I beg you to forgive me. I have fooled you. There is a very simple reason why the zamindar to whom I sent you did not speak: he is mute. He can not utter a word, so that is why he did not appreciate you!"

Instead of getting angry, the clever poet laughed and laughed. He said, "You have really opened my eyes this time! You have defeated my cleverness with your wisdom. I promise that I will give up my silly flattery and try to write poetry that is beautiful, deep and meaningful in every way."

# AMUSEMENT I ENJOY
# ENLIGHTENMENT I STUDY

## BOOK 7

## AIE 68. *The king seeks wise advice*

There was a king who had a very wise minister. This minister had been advising the king for many, many years and he was now quite advanced in age. When the minister felt that his death was approaching, he said to the king, "I shall not be able to serve you much longer. I am deeply concerned about who will advise you when I die. I have given the matter much thought and I would like to request you to bring three young men to the court after my passing. Each one should be wise. After observing these three young men for a while, please appoint one of them to take my place as your chief minister."

Soon afterwards, the old minister did pass away. The king badly needed to find a replacement for him. Remembering the old minister's advice, the king sent for three very wise young men. They came from various parts of the kingdom. When they arrived, the king said to them, "I have a serious problem and I would like you to advise me what course of action I should follow. There are two neighbouring kings who are always quarrelling and fighting. One of them is definitely much stronger than the other in terms of his wealth, his army and the size of his kingdom. But the weaker king compensates by holding many spectacular celebrations. The problem is that both of them want to have me as their friend, their ally. Each one has written to me that he will be so glad if he can have me as his friend. Now what should I do?"

One of the young men immediately answered, "O King, the answer is so easy! You should take the side of the stronger one. If anything happens to you, if anybody attacks you, then the stronger one will help you."

The king listened to this advice in silence and then asked the second candidate, "What do you recommend in this case?"

The second one said, "O King, he is wrong! People who are strong and rich cannot be trusted. Quite often their character is not good at all. When you first become their friend, they promise that they will help you if you find yourself in unfortunate circumstances. But this kind of person never actually comes to your rescue. When you are in need, the people who are wealthy and powerful always invent excuses. They say they have no time to help you or they have something more important to do. My advice is not to go to the stronger king. Offer your friendship to the weaker one. Those who are weaker usually have good hearts."

Once again, the king did not pass any comment on the advice that had been offered to him. Finally he asked the third young man, "Where do you stand? Are you in favour of my becoming friends with the stronger king or the weaker one?"

This young man said, "O King, this is my advice: do not go to anyone, good or bad, weak or strong. Now both of these kings want your help and friendship, but I feel that you should not go to either one."

"Then what should I do?" asked the king. "I do not want to remain all alone, without any friends."

The third candidate continued, "You will not remain alone for long. Tell both these kings that you will become their friend on the condition that they themselves become friends first. If they resolve their differences, if they stop fighting and become friends, then only will you become their friend. Otherwise, if you choose to become friends with the stronger one, he may fool you. When you need his friendship, at that very moment he may desert you. And if you make friends with the weaker one, he will not have the capacity to help you, even though he may have a good heart. So the best thing is not to choose either one, but to encourage them to become friends first. If they become friends, then you do not have to worry. The three of you will be peaceful neighbours."

As soon as he heard this advice, the king knew that he had found a worthy replacement for his old minister. He said to this young man, "You are the right one!"

### AIE 69. *The treasurer's integrity*

There was a king who was extremely powerful. At the same time, he had a most compassionate heart. He was very concerned because every day he received countless complaints against his ministers. He was simply shocked by the charges that were brought against these men, whom he had taken as his trusted advisors. At the same time, the king received tremendous appreciation for his treasurer. The treasurer was held in very high esteem by everybody.

One day the king decided to find out for himself why everybody appreciated the treasurer, whereas his ministers were subject to so much criticism. The king waited until evening and then went to the treasurer's room in disguise. He knocked at the door and the treasurer invited him inside. The king said, "You do not know me. I am a new member of the king's court. But I have not come to see you on official business. I have a personal problem. I shall be so grateful if you can help me solve my problem."

The treasurer said, "Please sit down. I am doing something very important, but in half an hour I will be through and then I can listen to your problems."

The king waited patiently for half an hour while the treasurer went on with his business, adding up columns of figures. When he finished his job, he turned to speak to the stranger. But first he turned off the electric light and lit a small lamp.

The king said, "May I ask why you turned off the electric light and put a lamp in front of it?"

The treasurer replied, "It is my duty. I am the king's treasurer, so I cannot exploit government money. The electric light is paid for by the king, so I use it when I am doing official business. But this is my own lamp. From my home I bring oil for it that I pay for with my own money. I use this lamp when I am dealing with things of a personal nature. Yours is not an official visit. You have come here with a personal problem, so I cannot use the electric light. I can use only my personal lamp."

The king was deeply moved by his treasurer's integrity and sense of duty. He himself had not commanded the treasurer to use his personal things while dealing with personal matters. It was the treasurer's own high standard that was compelling him to be so strict. Aloud, the king said, "Forgive me, but I cannot stay any longer. While sitting here, I have solved my problem. Now I have something else very important to do. But I shall come another time."

The treasurer said, "All right. Please come another time. I shall be ready for you."

The following day, the king went to the treasurer's office again. This time the king was wearing his royal robes. The treasurer was delighted to receive the king in his office.

The king said, "I have heard so many reports about your wisdom. Now I have come to see you personally. Mine is not an official problem, a problem of state. It is absolutely personal and private. I would like to discuss it with you. Please tell me, what kind of treatment will I get from you?"

The treasurer said, "O King, if it is a personal matter, then I will give you personal treatment and not royal treatment."

"What do you mean?" asked the king.

The treasurer explained, "If it is a personal problem, a family problem or something of that nature, I will treat you as an ordinary man. I will advise you in exactly the same way that I would advise an ordinary person. I will not treat you as the king at that time. I hope that you will not be offended."

The king was most pleased. He said, "This is what I expect from everybody. You have shown that you are truly a man of duty, a man of integrity and a man of honesty." Then the king offered to give him 20,000 rupees.

The treasurer said, "O King, how can I take even one rupee from you? It is my duty to serve you. Indeed, it is my duty to help any human being who asks me. If people feel that I have some wisdom, then I shall give it freely. I do not need any reward. Why should I charge for this kind of service? By your grace, I have enough money to meet with my expenses."

"Surely you are my best friend!" exclaimed the king. "You know the true meaning of duty. You are the right one to take care of my treasury and also to advise others. Now I see why everybody appreciates you and admires you. Duty must always come first in our lives. I am so happy that I have someone like you in my kingdom."

### AIE 70. *A mother-in-law is reformed*

We all know how bad mothers-in-law can be! They are famous for torturing their daughters-in-law. There was one mother-in-law who took an oath that in her own life she would not allow this maxim to prove true. When her son reached the age where she felt that he should get married, she encouraged him to look for a wife. She vowed to be extremely, extremely kind to her future daughter-in-law.

The son said, "Mother, why, why? You are happy with me and I am happy with you. Why do we have to bring somebody else into the picture? You are still young enough to do the housework. Even when you are older, we shall have maids who can do your work and look after the two of us. If I marry now just so that you will have someone to help you with your work, then it will only create disharmony. You will torture the poor girl and I will feel miserable."

The mother said, "No, I promise I will not behave in that way! If you find a wife and bring her here to live with us, I will be very kind and compassionate to her. Just wait and see."

The son surrendered. He said, "All right. To fulfil your wish, I shall start looking for a wife. But I know my problems will start on the very day I bring her home to live with us."

The son found a very nice girl to marry and she came to live with him and his mother. True to her word, the mother-in-law was extremely kind and affectionate to her new daughter-in-law. She would not allow the young girl to do any hard work in the house. All the cooking and cleaning the mother-in-law did herself. She tried to make her new daughter-in-law happy in every possible way. The daughter-in-law could not believe how kindly she was being treated. Before her marriage, she had heard so many bad things about mothers-in-law that she was frightened to death. Now she found that her own mother-in-law was just the opposite.

Usually the mother-in-law prepared excellent meals for her son and daughter-in-law. However, one evening, while the son and his wife were eating together, the son said, "Today the food is not as good as it is on other days."

His wife said, "I am sorry that today Mother did not cook as well as she usually does."

Her husband got the shock of his life. He exclaimed, "You do not cook my meals for me?"

"No," said the wife, "your mother does everything."

"My mother?" asked the son. "Then what are you here for? Who asked you to marry me if you were not willing to do any work around the house?"

"You asked me," said the wife, pitifully.

"But why did you agree, if you do not even know how to cook?" shouted the son."While I am at work, my poor mother has to do everything! And you have remained silent the whole time! When I think of how my mother must have been killing herself, my heart breaks."

By this time the wife was sobbing. She said, "I wanted to cook for you, but Mother would not allow me to do anything. What was I supposed to do? She insisted on doing all her own work and mine also."

Then the son became furious. He said, "My old mother has to do everything for you and you will not even lift a finger to help her with the cooking! You should have found a way to help her!" Then he got up and left the room.

The wife stayed in the room. She was utterly sad and depressed. After some time, her mother-in-law entered and found her looking miserable. With utmost compassion, the mother-in-law asked, "Why are you so sad, my child?"

The daughter-in-law remained silent. She did not want to bring any complaints against her husband and she could not blame her mother-in-law for being so kind. Seeing her weeping eyes, the mother-in-law thought, "The poor girl has not seen her parents for so many months. Perhaps that is why she is sad. She is still a young girl and it must be difficult for her, living in a strange place. I should have been more thoughtful."

So the kind mother-in-law made all the arrangements for her daughter-in-law to visit her own parents in their village. When the time came for the girl to leave, her mother-in-law said, "Now you please go and be with your parents. After a short time, I will send someone to bring you back again. I know what it is like for you. I was also quite young when I was married and I used to miss my parents so much. In fact, I used to go quite often to visit them. I had forgotten that it can sometimes be very lonely for a new wife. I should have sent you long ago. Now please, please go."

So the mother-in-law forced the young wife to go back to her parents' place for a few weeks. On the one hand, the wife was happy that her husband would not be able to scold her anymore, but on the other hand, she was sad that her mother-in-law had to continue doing all the work.

When the wife arrived at her parents' home, she observed the situation there. Her brother had recently married and his young wife was now living with them. Every day, from morning until night, this girl was being scolded and harassed by her mother-in-law. Nothing this girl did seemed to please her mother-in-law. Her mother-in-law was constantly saying, "Could you not have done this correctly? You could have done this properly. You could have done that infinitely better!" The visiting daughter felt really miserable. She said to herself, "How can my own mother be so bad? I see that this girl is trying to do everything as perfectly as possible, plus she is trying desperately to maintain a cheerful attitude, but my mother is only scolding her and criticising her."

One morning she said to her mother, "Mother, why are you behaving like this? You know that I also have a mother-in-law now. My mother-in-law is so kind, so compassionate, so self-giving. But if news had reached your ears that I was being treated the way you are treating my sister-in-law, if you had heard that I was being scolded and insulted mercilessly, how would you have taken it?"

Her mother answered, "I would have gone there myself and scolded your mother-in-law. I would have asked her what right she had to scold and insult my daughter unnecessarily."

Her daughter said, "Exactly! If I had been mistreated, you would have become extremely upset. You would have gone to challenge my mother-in-law. Now look at your own case. How my sister-in-law is suffering from your constant scoldings! If she goes and tells her mother how you are torturing her, what will happen? Naturally her mother will come and berate you. Perhaps she will even take her daughter away with her. So now I am begging you to stop treating her like this. Please give her the work that she is supposed to do and take her as your own daughter, the way my mother-in-law has taken me as her daughter. Try to offer her all your love and kindness. If you want happiness in your life, then take your daughter-in-law as your own daughter."

The mother saw the truth of her daughter's words and from that moment on she wholeheartedly embraced her new daughter-in-law as her own daughter. Meanwhile, her true daughter returned to her husband's house and convinced her mother-in-law to allow her to help with the household chores in every possible way.

So this is how one mother-in-law, by being good, was able to make another mother-in-law good also. When one person in this world is good, automatically that goodness spreads to others.

### AIE 71. *Give money and lose friendship*

Once there were two friends. One of them was going out of town for a while, so he gave a large amount of money to the other one for safekeeping. He told his friend, "I must go to another country for some time. I know that it is not good to take excess money abroad. I shall take only enough to defray my expenses. You kindly keep the rest of the money safe. You are my good friend, my very close friend. You are the only one I can trust with my savings."

The second friend said, "That is a very good idea. I shall definitely keep your money safe, and when you return you can come and ask me for it. It is very risky to carry a large amount of money with you when you are travelling. So many unfortunate things can happen."

So his friend entrusted him with his savings, which amounted to two thousand rupees, and then he left on his voyage. One month later he came back, and the very next day he went to visit his friend. The two friends were so happy to see each other. Then the first friend asked to have his money back.

The second friend opened his eyes wide. "Money!" he exclaimed. "When did you give me money?"

The first friend could not believe his ears. He said, "The day before I left, I gave you two thousand rupees for safekeeping. Please do not joke with me! Now that I have returned, I need this money badly."

His friend began laughing. "Two thousand rupees! When did you ever have two thousand rupees to start with, you liar?" And he went on scolding and ridiculing the friend who had given him the money.

The other friend cried, "How can you deceive me like this? Before I gave you the money, we were such good friends. I did not give you this money as a loan or a gift. When I gave it to you, I made it clear that I would be coming back for it. Since I was going abroad, I did not know where else to leave it. You promised to keep it safe for me."

He was begging and pleading for his friend to return the money, but the friend only said, "What a liar you have turned out to be! You never gave me any money, and here you are accusing me of stealing it. This is what happens when you go abroad: all the undivine forces enter into you. Now you have destroyed our friendship!"

The first friend could not see any way to get his money back. It was impossible to reason with this deceptive fellow. In desperation, he went to the village court and told the judge the whole story. The judge believed him and immediately summoned the culprit. When the culprit appeared, the judge said to him, "Now tell me the truth! Are you in possession of his money? Are you keeping it from him?"

The culprit answered, "Oh, no, no, no! I would never steal somebody else's money. The problem is that he went abroad. While he was away, some bad forces attacked him. Now he is talking like a lunatic and he has ruined our friendship."

The judge asked the first friend, "There was no witness when you handed him the money?"

The friend said, "No, I did not consider having a witness because he was such a good friend of mine. I did not even ask him to sign a piece of paper. It was beyond my imagination that he would fool me in this way. Still I do not understand how it is possible for him to go on deceiving me."

The culprit added, "There was definitely no witness. Here is the proof that I did not receive money from him!"

The judge remained silent for a minute. Then he took a long bamboo cane and started to threaten the culprit with it. He commanded, "Give him the money back or I will give you a thrashing that you will never forget as long as you live!"

"But I have not taken the money!" cried the culprit.

The judge proclaimed, "I know for certain that there were twenty-five witnesses. They have come to me with the true story. Some were inside the house and some were standing in the street. I can prove that there were twenty-five witnesses."

When the culprit heard that the judge could produce twenty-five witnesses, he started trembling violently. Then he fainted and fell to the floor. When he opened his eyes, he saw the judge bending over him. Very sternly the judge said, "Now give him the money or I shall kill you here and now!"

When the judge uttered these words, the friend who had given the money began shedding copious tears. He begged the judge, "Please, please, do not kill him! I do not want my friend to be killed or beaten. Let him tell lies. Let him deceive me. I do not need my money. I want you to spare his life!"

So the judge dismissed the case, and the friend who had given the money did not get it back because he had such a good heart. First the judge wanted to punish the culprit, then the judge even threatened to kill him. The twenty-five witnesses that the judge spoke about were his own invention. They did not actually exist, but he fabricated the story in order to frighten the culprit into making a full confession. When the unfortunate traveller saw that the judge was going to thrash his friend, he said, "Please spare him! I do not need my money. My friend's life is much more important."

### AIE 72. *Solving half the problem*

There were two childhood friends. As they grew older, one of them became very, very rich. The other one led a simple, ordinary life. He did not acquire any wealth or property. One day the poor man came to see his wealthy friend. He said, "I am truly glad that you have become very rich. We started our journey together. God did not grant me wealth, but I am really happy that He has blessed my dearest friend with material prosperity. I am very, very glad."

His friend replied, "I have become rich, true, but I have such a serious problem."

The poor man was shocked. He said, "How can a man in your position have a serious problem? Poor people, like myself, can have problems. But rich people do not have to have any problems at all. Your money can solve all your problems."

His friend responded sadly, "No, money alone cannot solve all the problems of the world. It is not possible."

"Why not?" asked the poor friend. "What kind of problem cannot be solved by money?"

The rich man explained, "In my case, I have been suffering for such a long time from back pain. You cannot imagine what kind of suffering I endure! I have tried so many expensive doctors and treatments, but nothing can cure me. My money is practically useless when it is a matter of curing my pain!"

The poor man said, "I have practised medicine for some time. I am not a qualified doctor, but I know a considerable amount about your kind of problem. How is it that the real doctors cannot cure you? I can easily cure you."

"You can cure me?" asked the rich man.

"Certainly," replied his friend. "I am astonished that you have not been cured by now. As soon as I start giving you a special medicine, I assure you that at least half of your problem will disappear."

"All right," said the rich man eagerly, "you can try. How much money do you need from me?"

The poor man said, "Unfortunately, I will need a considerable amount, because I have to go to a different town to get the medicine. I can start my journey tomorrow. I cannot guarantee that I will be able to solve your problem fully, but at least half your problem will be over."

The rich man was ready to believe his friend, for he had implicit confidence in him. He felt that as soon as he started the new treatment, his pain would be reduced by at least half. Perhaps it would even disappear completely. He reflected that even if his pain were reduced by only a quarter, he would be satisfied. So he gave his poor friend a large sum of money to go and purchase the medicine.

Every month from then on, the friend sent him medicine. One month, two months, three months, four months, five months, six months passed by, but the rich man's back pain remained the same. It was not going away at all.

Finally the rich man went to see his poor friend and said, "You have been sending me medicine for such a long time, but I have to say that my pain is still the same. I am suffering so much. What can be done?"

His friend said, "I told you that half your problem would be solved, and it *has* been solved."

"What? I do not understand," said the rich man.

"It is so simple," responded the poor man. "You see, I needed money badly because I had accumulated huge debts. I charged you lots of money for the medicine. Now, for the last six months, I have been paying off my debts with your money. By this time, I have reduced my debts by half, so we can say that half our problem is over. You and I are one. Therefore, my problem is your problem. I told you that half your problem would soon be over, and my words have come true. I am so happy now, and I know that you will be happy in my happiness!"

### AIE 73. *The critical travellers*

A man owned a huge and splendid mansion. Indeed, it was the most beautiful mansion in the entire town. One day this man was picking up some grains that had fallen on the ground in front of his house. At that moment, five travellers were passing by. Seeing the wealthy man performing this trivial task, they called out to him, "Sir, it seems that you are very rich. Why then do you have to carefully collect those tiny grains from the ground as if they were pieces of gold?"

The wealthy man looked up and replied, "It is not good to waste anything. By the way, it appears from your dusty appearance that you have been travelling for a long time."

"Yes," said the travellers. "We have been travelling for many days and our destination is still quite far."

The wealthy man said, "Perhaps it will do you good if you come and eat at my place. I am sure that a nourishing meal will give you the strength and energy to proceed to your destination."

"That is a splendid idea! You are so kind," said the travellers eagerly.

The wealthy man opened the gate and said, "Please come in."

They all went inside the house and the wealthy man invited them to be seated at the dining table. He said, "Please do not mind waiting for a short time. I am asking my servants to prepare most delicious food for you."

As the travellers waited for their meal, each one was imagining what kind of dishes they would be served. They were all extremely happy and excited. Finally, the servants appeared carrying trays which they placed before the travellers. On the plates was not rice or any kind of vegetable. Each plate contained only a few pieces of gold.

The travellers were deeply dismayed. They asked their host, "What have we done? How do you expect us to eat gold?"

The wealthy man said, "You valued gold so much while I was collecting the grains that I have given you gold to eat. You did not feel that the grains were of any importance. You thought I was a fool for picking them up. It did not occur to you that perhaps we might want to eat the grains. So now I am giving you gold, since you value it infinitely more."

The travellers got the point of the rich man's gesture, and they felt ashamed and embarrassed for having mocked him earlier. Their host continued, "Even if you are rich, you must value things that are around you. Gold has its purpose and grain has its purpose. You were laughing at me when I was collecting the grain, so I gave you gold to eat. Do not try to find fault with people in season and out of season. It is always advisable to be sure of what you are saying."

The rich man saw that the travellers were genuinely sorry for what they had done, so he asked his servants to bring them real food to eat. This time they ate to their heart's content. As they were finishing their meal, their host appeared once again and said, "I am showing you my compassion and concern because I feel it will help you to make progress. That is why I gave you real food. Now you are ready to continue your journey. Try to value each and every thing that you see and do not find fault with others."

With a new illumination the travellers went on their way.

### AIE 74. *The rich disciple's poor choice*

There was once a spiritual Master who had many, many disciples. Most of them were not rich at all. They led very simple lives and somehow they managed to meet with their earthly expenses. But one disciple was extremely, extremely wealthy. This particular disciple was a merchant. Strangely enough, the life he lived was even more austere than that of the poorest disciples. This was not because he was more spiritual than those disciples; it was because he was the most miserly person imaginable. He was only interested in hoarding his money. He would not keep any proper furniture or valuable things in his house. He did not spend money on clothes and he never invited his fellow disciples for meals. Sometimes, if he happened to buy something in the market, he would punish himself for having spent a little extra money by skipping a meal. To compensate for the most trivial purchase, he would not eat! Yet, in spite of his ungenerous nature, the Master tolerated this particular disciple.

After many years, there came a time when the Master gathered all his disciples and said to them, "My days are numbered.

Now I am telling you all: do not worry about the future. God took care of me and He will also take care of you. I came as your teacher, but the real Teacher is God. He is the One who will act in and through you. So do not cry, do not weep. God will take care of you."

In spite of the Master's compassionate words, all the disciples started crying helplessly. Then the Master said, "All right, I am ready to bless each and every disciple. Come one by one, my children, and I shall give you my last blessings. Since this is my last chance to see you all, I am ready to give you whatever you want. You have only to ask me."

There were about forty disciples present. One by one, they all stood before the Master to receive his blessings. Each one said the same thing: "Master, I need only your blessing. I do not need anything else in my life. Now you will be leaving. Your blessing is the most important thing. Nothing else matters in my life."

Finally, it was the turn of the last disciple to come for the Master's blessings. This happened to be the wealthy merchant. The Master offered him a most compassionate smile and said, "Now, my child, tell me what you want. I shall fulfil your dearest wish."

The merchant-disciple said, "Master, you know that I am rich, very rich, but I would like you to give me a special mantra which I can repeat to increase my prosperity. This is my last request to you. Today you have promised to grant all our wishes. Now please grant me this wish!"

The Master said, "Here I am dying and you are only thinking of how to accrue more money, more gold? You have so much material wealth! Why do you need more, for God's sake?"

The merchant-disciple replied, "Master, I feel that one day I will be able to give all my wealth to charity. Right now I am collecting and collecting as much money as I can, but it is for a good cause. A day will come when I will be able to give it all away so that many people will benefit from it."

All the other disciples were literally shocked that this disciple could be thinking of increasing his wealth at such a time. But the Master simply said, "Oh, I see. All right, I am giving you a special mantra. This mantra will transform a certain kind of iron into gold." Then the Master picked up a piece of iron that was lying on the ground and said, "Look, I can prove it to you. I will say the mantra and then, as soon as I touch this piece of iron, it will become gold."

The Master chanted the mantra and then touched the piece of iron. Before everyone's eyes, it was immediately turned into gold. Then the Master taught the mantra to the merchant-disciple. When the disciple learned it, the Master said, "In the future, whenever you need more gold, you have only to obtain some of this kind of iron and chant the mantra. Then you will be able to transmute the iron into gold just by touching it, the way I did. But do not forget the mantra. Now I am giving you one more piece of iron to take home."

The merchant-disciple was extremely happy that the Master had granted his wish. He left the Master's home and went to the market, where he thought he would buy a large quantity of iron to keep in reserve so that whenever he needed gold, it would be available immediately. When he came to the ironmonger's shop, he found that the price of iron had gone very high. It was much more than he had expected to pay. The disciple said to himself, "My God, even yesterday the price was much lower than this! How could it have gone so high in one day? The best thing is for me to use my wisdom. I know that nobody will buy it at this price. Eventually this greedy ironmonger will be forced to lower the price again. I can wait until then. I already have the piece of gold that the Master created and the second piece of iron that he gave me."

So the disciple waited for a week or two. Then he went back to the market fully prepared to buy a considerable quantity of iron. To his greatest sorrow, the price had gone still higher. The disciple was so upset and dismayed. He said, "What is this? Now the price is even higher! I am not going to pay such a ridiculous price!" And again he went home empty-handed.

After an interval of two more weeks, he returned to the ironmonger's place, only to find that the price of iron had risen even higher! This time, the disciple became furious with himself. He said, "Why did I not buy it when I had the chance the first time? How stupid I was! Even though the price was quite high, it was next to nothing in comparison with the amount of gold that I would have been able to produce. Now the price is so exorbitant! I refuse to pay such a high price. Luckily, I have the other piece of iron that the Master gave me. Let me transmute that into gold and then I can wait indefinitely to buy some more iron at a cheaper price."

The disciple returned home and took out the piece of iron that the Master had given him. He was all ready to say the mantra but, lo and behold, he found that he had completely forgotten it! Not a single word came to his mind. In vain he struggled and struggled to recollect what the Master had taught him. Because he had only been thinking of buying that particular kind of iron at a cheap price, he had forgotten the mantra altogether. Now what was he to do? He was utterly miserable. "What have I done?" he cried. "I cannot transmute this piece of iron into gold and I cannot obtain more iron because of the outrageous price. I am at a complete loss. O Master, you fooled me! You knew that this would happen."

The rich man's fellow disciples came to hear of his accusations against the Master and they said to him, "The Master did not fool you. He only illumined you by exposing your greed. We all asked the Master for his blessings. Now he is not in the physical anymore, but we are all living so happily with his blessings. We feel that he is taking care of our spiritual lives. But you had to ask him for gold. How greedy you were! Perhaps by now you have learned your lesson."

The merchant sighed, "Alas, I have lost both my Master and my mantra."

The poor fellow died in utter misery because he had lost the things that were dearest to him in his life. This was how the Master punished him.

### AIE 75. *The honesty certificate*

There was a Muslim who was very, very rich. At the same time, he had a very good heart. Once a year he would offer unlimited gifts to the poor. He would distribute money, lengths of fabric and food unreservedly. Everybody was most grateful to him for his kindness and generosity, especially the poor people in the village.

One particular year, many poor people came to this Muslim on the day he was going to make his charitable offering. They formed a long line outside his house. The Muslim stood behind some tables which were piled high with grains, fabrics, fruits, spices and many other necessities. As each person came up to him, the Muslim would put certain things inside a bag for that person. He told everyone not to open up the bags there, but to wait until they arrived home.

One particular beggar waited in line very patiently. When it became his turn, the rich man put only one thing inside the bag. Then he gave it to the beggar. This particular beggar was extremely poor. He and his wife lived in dire poverty. When he returned to the tiny hut in which they made their home, he opened up the bag and saw that the Muslim had placed a single gold coin inside it.

The beggar immediately said, "O my God, this kind-hearted man has made a mistake. Instead of putting a little rice or something else inside our bag, he has put in a gold coin. I am sure he did not do it deliberately."

His wife said, "No, you fool, you fool! We are so poor. Do you not see that God has given us this coin to relieve our suffering?"

Her husband disagreed. He said, "No, no, God is not like that. He does things in a different way. If He wants to improve our condition, He will give me the opportunity to do some kind of work. In the past, this rich man has given us rice, dal and new pieces of cloth to wear. I am sure he did not intend to give us a gold coin. I have to return it."

The wife cried, "You cannot! You must not! It is God who has given this piece of gold to us in and through the rich man. This coin will provide us with enough food for many, many months."

The husband replied, "I do not believe in this kind of God. Very soon the rich man will feel sorry that he has made such a serious mistake. We have to believe in God's Dispensation. God has given money-power in abundant measure to this man and not to me. So I have to be satisfied with my poverty, the way he is satisfied with his wealth. I must go back to his house and do the needful."

Although the wife continued pleading with her husband, he refused to listen to her. He took the gold coin and walked back to the rich man's house. There he very humbly returned the coin to the rich man. The rich man was extremely pleased and moved. He had never met such a sincere, honest man.

He said to the poor beggar, "I deeply appreciate your honesty. Now, this time I am giving you a hundred gold coins. I am telling you exactly how many I am putting inside the bag so that you do not think I have made a mistake. Kindly take them. I assure you, you do not have to bring them back."

This time the beggar unmistakably knew that the rich man wanted him to keep the gold coins. He bowed to the rich man, offering all his gratitude, and departed with his bag. When he entered his hut carrying the bag, his wife said, "Again you have brought the bag! Now this time what did he say?"

Her husband replied, "He himself has said that we should keep it. And he has increased the amount from one gold coin to one hundred gold coins!"

He opened up the bag and showed his wife all the coins. Needless to say, she was astonished and delighted. Her husband said, "You did not want me to go back, but I went. And this is what happened! Instead of one gold coin, we now have one hundred. We do not have to worry about food and clothing again. When you conquer greed, you get this kind of result."

The wife said, "Yes, yes, I can see it. You were one hundred percent correct. Please forgive me for doubting you."

So the beggar and his wife lived very happily. But the story does not end there. While the rich Muslim was giving the one hundred gold coins to the beggar, a merchant happened to be passing by. He was not poor in the least. He had a very nice house and he was extremely prosperous. When he saw the Muslim counting out the gold coins for the beggar, he hid and watched the exchange. Then a brilliant idea struck him. He thought to himself, "Tomorrow I will come to this Muslim's house in the guise of a poor man. I will put on dirty, filthy clothes and stand in front of his door. For bringing one gold coin this beggar has received one hundred. If I put fifty gold coins in my bag and give them to the rich man, I am sure he will reward me by giving me much more than one hundred in return. I can easily afford to take fifty gold coins from my business for one morning. I will tell exactly the same story as the beggar. Who ever thought there would be such an easy way to gain instant wealth!"

The next day the merchant went to the rich man in the guise of a beggar. He handed the rich man a bag containing fifty gold coins and said, "Yesterday, by mistake, you gave me this. I cannot imagine that you intended to give me fifty gold coins."

Then he waited eagerly. He was full of expectation that he would receive a substantial amount of money from the rich man. Meanwhile, the rich man was surprised. He could not remember having given this particular beggar fifty gold coins. What is more, even though the beggar was absolutely dirty and unkempt, he was wearing a costly ring on his finger. The rich man wondered how a beggar came to be wearing such a ring, and he began to grow a little suspicious.

Now the time had come for the beggar to ask for more gold coins. He said, "With utmost sincerity I have come here to return your money. Now will you not give me any reward?"

The rich man beckoned one of his clerks and requested him to bring a special piece of paper. When the clerk brought it, the rich man asked him to write down that the beggar was an honest man. Then the rich man gave the piece of paper to the beggar.

"You are not giving me money?" cried the beggar-merchant in dismay.

The Muslim said, "Oh no, I am giving you something much more valuable. I am so pleased with you that I am giving you an honesty certificate. Money I can give to this person and that person. But because of your exceptional honesty, I want you to have this special certificate!"

AIE 76. *The king's washerman*

There was once a king who was very, very kind and compassionate. He was a real father to the poor and needy, and he always found ways to please each and every subject in his kingdom.

The king had a personal washerman. At the end of the day, this washerman would take the king's garments home to launder them. But the king did not know that when the washerman arrived home, he used to put on the king's garments and walk around his village showing off. All the villagers were deeply impressed that the washerman had such expensive clothes, so they used to salute him and offer him tremendous respect. Some of them thought that, since he was working for the king, perhaps the king had rewarded him for his services by giving him these magnificent clothes. At the same time, others suspected him. They wondered where he had acquired such costly garments.

So the washerman lived a dual life. During the day he was an ordinary worker, and at night he would pretend that he was a king. It was extremely gratifying to him when all the villagers admired him. Indeed, they were on the verge of worshipping him.

Unfortunately, everybody has enemies and this washerman was no exception. One of his enemies from the village went to the king and complained that the washerman was wearing clothes which were worthy of a king. He hinted that these clothes might even belong to the king himself.

The king could not believe it. "How could my own washerman do this?" he exclaimed. "All right, let me see what I should do. You return to your village and I will take care of the matter."

That evening, the king put on the dress of a hermit and went in disguise to the village where the washerman lived. Before long he saw the washerman parading through the streets wearing the very clothes that he himself had worn earlier that day. All the people in the village came out to see the washerman and to offer him their admiration. But the hermit did not pay any attention to the washerman at all. On the contrary, he ignored him completely.

This made the washerman very angry, and he began to berate the hermit. He said, "How dare you ignore me? Can you not see who I am?"

The hermit replied very calmly, "No, I do not know who you are."

The washerman became disgusted. He said, "If you just look at the garments I am wearing, you will see that I am the king!"

This speech failed to impress the hermit, who slowly walked away. The washerman followed him and started scolding and insulting him. He said, "You have no respect for the king. Stop and salute me properly!"

Suddenly the hermit turned and threw off his ochre robes to reveal his kingly garments. "*I* am the king!" he pronounced in a powerful voice.

When the washerman saw the real king standing before him, he was frightened to death. He immediately fell at the king's feet and begged for forgiveness. Then he said, "One moment ago, you were a hermit. Now please bless me and give me some peace of mind."

"What do you mean?" asked the king.

The clever washerman went on, "Only a hermit can ignore a king. You were wearing a hermit's garments and I was wearing your garments. But a hermit is infinitely higher than a king. You were acting like a real hermit, a spiritual renunciate. Now I want to worship you, so you have to bless me."

The king did not ignore or rebuff his washerman's flattery. He gave him a compassionate smile and said, "From tomorrow on, you have to work at the palace. You have to wash my clothes there, not here."

So the washerman's flattery worked and, to his great relief, the king did not punish him.

# AMUSEMENT I ENJOY
# ENLIGHTENMENT I STUDY

## BOOK 8

### AIE 77. *The feeling of humility*

This is an authentic story. There was an extremely great spiritual Master whose sincerity was most admirable. From time to time, he could not meditate to his satisfaction. So, in order to meditate well and reach his own highest height, he did something unique: he used to get up from the place where he was meditating and look for somebody of the lowest caste — a sweeper or cobbler — and then he would go and embrace that person. He himself came of a Brahmin family, which is the highest caste. After embracing that person, he would return to his place of meditation and enter into his absolutely highest meditation.

Sometimes he did something else. He would rise from his meditation spot and find somebody who was very unspiritual and unaspiring. Then he would fall flat at that person's feet. Afterwards, he would return home and once more have a very deep meditation.

Why did he do this? Because it gave him a feeling of humility. For years and years he had meditated so well that pride had entered into him. His mind had literally become a pride-desert. So, in order to regain his highest meditation-height, either he would embrace a lower caste individual or he would fall at the feet of someone whom he had considered to be undivine to the extreme. He felt that when humility enters into the mind, one's meditation immediately becomes both high and deep.

This is so true. Here in the West there is no caste system, but there are various other ways to feel humility and to reach your highest meditation.

If you consider someone in your spiritual family to be infinitely less spiritual than you are, then try to feel or think of your Master's compassion and our Lord Beloved Supreme's Compassion in tolerating that particular person on the spiritual path. That person, according to you, may be the worst possible disciple. You may absolutely deplore the undivine qualities that he or she embodies. But if you can imagine the Compassion-Tears of the Supreme for that particular person, and if you can become one with those Tears, immediately you will be identified with the Compassion of the Supreme. At that time, you will find that your meditation has once more become very high and deep. Why? Because the Supreme's Compassion-Tears for that other person, which you are imagining and also identifying with, are also entering into you. They are entering into your mind, which is not aspiring on that particular day, and into your wrong, undivine thoughts.

There is another way which, at one time, Swami Vivekananda tried. That way is to remember your three highest meditations. If you have been following the spiritual path for many years, by this time I am sure you have had high meditations on many occasions. Consciously recall to mind the three times in your life that were absolutely the highest. Imagine the particular day, the place where you sat and how you meditated. Remember what you felt in your heart and in your entire being. Enter into the joy that you are imagining.

Then concentrate on that imagination. Take your imagination as a material object that is right in front of you. Make your imagination into a tennis ball or something small that you can keep right in front of your eyes. You do not have to keep your eyes open; only concentrate, concentrate!

In a few minutes, I assure you, you will be able to reach your highest meditation — but only if you want to. There are many days, even months and years, when you do not want to have your highest meditation. You go to the meditation hall, but you allow yourself to think of other human beings, or what you are going to eat, or what happened on the previous day. Countless times you have not had the eagerness to do your best meditation.

If one day you really want to do your best meditation but, for some reason, are unable to, then you can try what I have said. If you have sincerity and eagerness, then definitely you can bring forward your best meditation with your imagination, for imagination is a reality in its own right.

### AIE 78. *A mother's heart*

There was a rich woman who came from a very prominent family. One day the woman entered into the kitchen to get some milk for her child. There she saw her two daughters striking the maid mercilessly. "We have caught her stealing milk," they explained.

The maid was crying pitifully. "I also have a little child. My child is five years old and today I do not have any milk for him. If I take this milk home, then I will be able to feed my child this evening. Otherwise, he will have nothing."

When the rich woman heard this, she became furious with her daughters. She said, "What are you doing to our poor maid? How can you beat her? I am a mother and she is also a mother. You know how much I care for your little brother. Soon he will start crying for his milk. If this maid takes his milk, my heart will break that I have no milk to give him.

"But this maid also has a heart for her child, and if she cannot give him milk, she too will feel miserable. So I am ready to give her the milk. I know that I can easily send you to the market to buy more milk to replace what she has taken. But she does not have money enough to buy fresh milk, or perhaps she will not have the opportunity to buy it on her way home after work. So let her have the milk. She needs it much more than I do.

"If we want to make ourselves happy, we have to renounce our own desires and always make other people happy first. By allowing her to take the milk, I shall be infinitely happier than if I punish her for stealing."

This compassionate woman was the mother of the spiritual Master in the previous story.

### AIE 79. *The saint's humility*

Once there was a saint who had quite a few disciples. His disciples loved and adored him from the very depths of their hearts. One day, the saint was meditating all alone at the foot of a tree. While he was in deep trance, a man approached him. This man was full of pride and haughtiness. He kicked the saint and commanded him to get up. Since the saint's trance was broken, he stood up.

The man placed a heavy load on the saint's shoulders and said, "Today my servants are not available. It is beneath my dignity to carry this heavy load myself, so you have to do it for me. I can clearly see that you are just a lazy fellow. You were only sleeping under the tree. Anyway, I shall give you some money and afterwards you can have a nice meal."

The saint most obediently followed the man and carried the load to the destination, which was the man's home. The man told him, "Wait here until I come back. Then I will give you some money and food." So saying, the man went inside the house.

The saint stayed there, not because he wanted money, but because he was extremely tired from carrying such a heavy load and he needed rest.

In the meantime, the saint's disciples were looking for their Master. They had not found him in his usual position at the foot of the tree, so they had begun searching for him here, there and everywhere. Eventually they found him in the next village sitting by the roadside outside a large house.

They asked, "Master, what are you doing here?"

At that very moment, the man emerged from his house and said, "What are all you people doing here outside my house? This man is my servant. He has just carried a heavy load for me and he did a very good job."

When the disciples heard these words, they became furious and rushed to attack the man. The saint shouted at them, "What are you doing? What are you doing? Do not hurt this man! God wanted me to have more humility. Therefore, I have carried his load cheerfully. God wanted me to shine bright, brighter, brightest. To my sorrow, I am not physically strong, so I am totally exhausted. But in a few minutes' time, I will regain my strength and go back with you."

Even after hearing the saint's humble and compassionate words, the haughty man showed no remorse. The saint's disciples said to the man, "You are a real scoundrel. Just because we are obedient to our Master, we are not going to thrash you. But we could easily do so."

The man got frightened and ran indoors. The saint said to his disciples, "My children, God wanted me to learn something today, but it seems that you do not want me to learn it."

One disciple said, "Forgive us, Master. God may want you to learn something but, at the same time, we are also sure that He wants us to teach that scoundrel a lesson. God is acting in and through you in one way and He is acting in and through us in another. This is the philosophy that you have taught us. Please forgive us."

The Master gave his disciples a powerful smile. What else could the poor Master do?

AIE 80. *Burning with grief*

There was once a spiritual Master with tremendous occult and spiritual power who lived in the Himalayas. He had a particular disciple who lived many hundreds of miles away. This disciple also had some occult power, though not as much as his Master. When the disciple meditated, he would reach the very highest plane. For that reason, he already had some disciples of his own.

This disciple had a wife and two children. But instead of earning money to support his family, he used to spend all his time in meditation. His wife scolded and insulted him mercilessly, day in and day out, and this made him extremely sad.

One day the husband's Master came down from the Himalayas to visit him, bringing two other disciples. The Master observed the family scene in his disciple's home and he saw that the wife was really bothering his disciple. When this disciple was able to meditate in peace, he had the highest inner experiences, but when he came down to the ordinary level once more, all his time was wasted in quarrelling and fighting with his wife.

The Master decided to take the wife away with him to the Himalayas. Very politely, he said to her, "Now that we have come to see you and your husband, can you not go to the pond to fetch some fresh water for us? The water you have is not fresh and we are so thirsty. Can you bring the water at once? We will accompany you to the pond."

The wife had such respect for her husband's Master that she immediately went with him and the two disciples to the pond to fill her pitcher with water. On the way, the Master used his occult power and made her physical form extremely subtle. Then the Master took her with him to the Himalayas.

Soon the disciple's son and daughter noticed that their mother was missing and they began searching and searching for her. "Where has Mother gone?" the daughter cried. "She left here with the Master and she did not return." Then the daughter began to curse the Master.

The disciple realised intuitively what his Master had done and he began laughing and laughing. "How compassionate my Master is!" he exclaimed. "My wife and I were quarrelling incessantly. The Master does not want us to fight, so to give me a little peace of mind he has taken your mother to the Himalayas. I know he will take good care of her, and while she is gone I will be able to meditate without any interruptions."

At first the children could not believe that their mother was safe and happy. Their father tried to console them, but to no avail. Finally, he said, "You do not believe me, but I know it is true. I am her husband. If I am quite happy, then why should you be worried? When the time comes, you will believe me."

At last the daughter said, "All right. If Father says that Mother is safe, then I will accept it."

Three or four weeks later, the mother reappeared. She was wearing the cloth of a renunciate. When her children saw her, they were overjoyed. "Mother, where did you go? What have you been doing?" they cried.

The mother replied, "I went to the pond with the Master and his two disciples to bring water. Suddenly, I saw that I was flying with them in my subtle body. I was enjoying it so much! I went with them to the Master's hermitage in the mountains and he took such good care of me. I was very happy there. But after some time I began missing my children, so Master brought me back home.

A few years afterwards, the mother suddenly died. The son cried for a few hours and then somehow managed to control his grief. But the daughter was absolutely inconsolable. Even after two weeks, she was still crying pitifully and missing her mother at every second.

Her father tried to comfort her. He said, "Dying is just like going from one room to another room. Someday I will go there and you also will go there. The bell will ring for us, as it did for your mother. At that time, when you go to the other world, you will be able to see your mother again. But for now you have to live in this world."

Unfortunately, the daughter did not want to hear her father's philosophy. Her tears continued to flow unceasingly. Finally, her father said to her, "Come to me."

She went close to her father and he placed the palm of his hand on her head for a few moments. When he removed his hand, she saw that it was severely scorched. She asked her father how it had happened. He told her, "I had to take your grief away somehow. You could not have gone on living with the grief that you were feeling. It was burning you like fire."

So the father took away the grief from his daughter and she was able to live on earth for many more years.

### AIE 81. *He really cared for his mother*

The disciple in the previous story eventually became a very great spiritual Master in his own right. This is another story about him.

For some reason, his mother became completely insane. She used to scream and strike people. One day, some of the village boys started to thrash her and beat her ruthlessly. At that time, her son was at least four hundred miles away. He was meditating with his disciples. Suddenly he felt intense pain and his back became covered with red marks.

While his mother was being struck, she had invoked her son. Inwardly the son heard her call and he immediately left to visit her. After many days of travel, he arrived at her village home. There he found his mother crying. She told him her sad story.

Then she added, "I am sure you will still be able to see the marks on my back where those boys struck me."

"Mother, you do not have any marks," said her son.

"Is it true? How is it possible?" she asked.

"You can see my back," he replied. Then he took off his kurta and showed her that his back was covered with red marks.

While the mother was being struck, she was screaming at the top of her lungs. At the same time, she was invoking her son. Inwardly, her son heard her cry for help and, on the strength of his identification with his mother, he took the attack on his own back.

When his mother saw how badly his back was hurt, she realised that he really cared for her. In this way, the son was able to console the mother.

### AIE 82. *Who is an atheist?*

There was once an atheist-dentist who was extremely proud of his discovery that God does not exist. He used to brag to all his patients about his great discovery. Outside his clinic and also inside the room where he treated patients, he placed huge signs that said:

GOD IS NOWHERE.

There were some devout elderly ladies coming to him for treatment who were horrified by his philosophy. They would say, "How can you say there is no God?"

He would answer, "I am telling you the truth. If you feel that there is a God, then you can go to another dentist instead of bothering me!"

What could the poor elderly ladies do? They were suffering from tooth pain and needed treatment. Inwardly they were furious with him, but outwardly they needed his help.

One day a woman brought her little daughter to this dentist. This little girl was suffering from a very bad toothache. The woman had been telling her daughter that God is everywhere and that He is all Kindness, all Compassion and all Forgiveness. So she was afraid that when her daughter read the sign saying that God is nowhere, her daughter would be so upset that she would leave the dental clinic and not allow the dentist to treat her.

Mother and daughter arrived at the clinic and sat down in the waiting room. The little girl stared at the dentist's famous sign. Then she very loudly read out:

GOD IS NOW HERE.

The mother was overwhelmed with joy that the child had misread the sign. Even the other patients in the waiting room were happy and amused. Nobody corrected the girl or told her that she was stupid. They did not want to destroy her happiness.

Then the little girl said, "Mother, you told me that God is everywhere, but you never told me where God actually is. The sign says that God is now here. That means that the dentist is God. Since God is here, please take me to a flower shop so that I can get flowers for God. You told me that if I see God, immediately I should give Him flowers. So you have to take me to a flower shop!"

The mother took her daughter to a nearby flower shop, and the daughter got beautiful flowers for the dentist.

When the girl gave the dentist the flowers, he said to himself, "I do not believe in God, but this little girl has made me into God Himself. For once in my life I have made someone truly happy. If I can make this little girl so happy, then I must try to make other God-believers happy also. I do not have to become another God, but at least I can become a God-believer!"

So the dentist separated the letters on the word 'nowhere' so that the sign really did say:

GOD IS NOW HERE.

Then something entered into his mind and he was afraid and embarrassed that his patients would think that he was claiming to be God. "They will say that I am going from one extreme to the other and laugh at me."

Finally he decided, "It is better for people to laugh at me than to be angry with me. Let them laugh at me to their heart's content because I am claiming to be God."

Then he took a picture of the little girl and put it alongside his own picture. Underneath he wrote: "This little girl says I am God."

People were very amused by the little girl's realisation. But, as a matter of fact, nobody thought ill of the dentist or inwardly mocked him. They felt that it is better to take yourself as God than not to believe in God at all. People who were very spiritual even felt, "If the dentist wants to say that God is now here, we will not mind. God is in everyone."

In this way, everybody was happy. And who made them happy? The little girl and her discovery!

### AIE 83. *The difference between a stark atheist and a staunch God-believer*

Once a disciple said to his Master, "How horrible atheists are! God is so kind, so compassionate, so forgiving. Without God's Presence, no human being can live on earth. How can atheists be so cruel to God?"

The Master replied, "My son, that is your way of thinking."

The disciple said, "Master, please illumine us. What do you think of an atheist?"

The Master said, "The difference between an atheist and a God-believer like you is very simple. You are a talker and an atheist is a doer."

The disciples were surprised and shocked by the Master's statement. Then the Master told the following story:

There happened to be a very, very old man who was a street beggar. One day the old man came to an atheist and asked him for money. The old beggar said, "Sir, if you help me, God will be so grateful to you and so proud of you. Then God will bless you and give you more outer riches."

The atheist said, "Shut up, shut up! I do not believe in God and I have nothing to do with God. If you have anything to do with God, then go to Him for alms and do not bother me."

The beggar replied, "I know that God exists, but at this moment I do not know where He is. Otherwise, I would have gone to Him and asked Him for a little food and money to lead a very simple life."

The atheist said, "You believe in God, but you do not know where God is! You have spoken all about God's Goodness, Kindness and Compassion, but He is not giving you the material things that you need. I do not believe in God at all, but if I give you money, then I shall become your God, your real God. The one who is kind to you and compassionate to you is the real God. The other God is hiding. God alone knows where He is!" Then the atheist gave the old beggar a large sum of money.

After telling this story, the Master said to his disciples, "You always brag about your good qualities, but if this street beggar had come to you, you would have given ten reasons why you could not help him. You would have said, 'Oh, I do not have enough money. I have to buy something special on this particular day,' and so forth. For so many reasons you would have refused to help the poor old man who needed money and food so desperately.

"Although the atheist did not believe in God, he helped the beggar. So he became the real God at that time. This is the difference between a stark atheist and a staunch God-believer, like you."

AIE 84. *A question of faith*

Two ladies went to a spiritual Master. One of the ladies asked the Master a question on behalf of her friend. She said, "Can you tell us whether her son will pass his examination? He will be sitting for it very soon."

The mother of the boy also showed some interest in hearing what the Master would say.

The Master meditated for a few moments and said, "Oh, he will do very, very well!"

A few weeks later, the results appeared: that particular boy had failed his examination. As a result, the lady who had asked the question stopped coming to see the Master. "What a useless Master!" she said. "His prophecy was all wrong!"

But the boy's actual mother came back to the Master. When the Master saw her, he said, "Please tell me about your son's examination."

"Unfortunately, he failed," the mother said.

"And where is your friend?" asked the Master.

"My friend lost all faith in you because your prophecy did not come true and my son failed," said the lady.

"Then why are you still coming here?" asked the Master. "After all, it was your son who failed."

"I come because I see something in you," said the lady. "I feel something in you. Who cares for my son's personal failure? He can easily sit for the examination again. But the joy that I get when I look at your eyes and your feet is indescribable. I come here for joy and not for prophecies."

Then the Master blessed her and said, "You are my real disciple."

The useless friend had used her mind to judge the Master. She did not want a Master who could not see even two weeks into the future. But the boy's mother came back to the Master, even though he had been wrong. As a matter of fact, the Master did know in advance that her son would fail the examination, but he had wanted to see the strength of her faith in him.

We all need this kind of faith. You can call it blind faith. Faith itself is blind, true! But again, blindness is all oneness, all oneness.

### AIE 85. *The spiritual lesson*

Two disciples were meditating in front of their Master. The Master's eyes were wide open and he was looking soulfully at one of the disciples. He was not looking at the other disciple at all. But this other disciple was still gazing at the Master most devotedly with folded hands.

The disciple on whom the Master was meditating assumed that the Master was ignoring the other disciple because that person was very bad. He became angry that such an undivine fellow was even being allowed to meditate in front of the Master. This is what was going on in the mind of the disciple on whom the Master was intensely meditating.

Meanwhile, the other disciple was thinking, "Master, I am so grateful to you for looking at him and not at me. You are teaching me how to conquer my jealousy. In your presence, I have no jealousy. So I am sending you my gratitude for looking at him."

When the meditation was over, the Master stood up from his chair and went over to the second disciple and blessed him. "You have shown me what gratitude is," the Master said. "Even though I did not look at you, you remained in a soulful and devoted consciousness." Then the Master scolded the first disciple mercilessly because he had become so proud and haughty.

### AIE 86. *The wrong prayer to the wrong person*

There were two women who were very close friends. Both of them had a happy family life as well as material prosperity. Another lady observed how fortunate these two friends were and she longed for the same wealth and happiness. So she asked them, "How is it that you and the members of your families are blessed with such inner and outer riches?"

One of the friends told her, "For years I prayed and prayed to the goddess of misery. One day the goddess came and I said to her, 'Now that you are pleased with me, please go away and never come back!' The goddess listened to my prayer and she has never returned."

Then the other friend said, "I prayed to the goddess Lakshmi to give me wealth, beauty, prosperity, harmony and all other divine gifts. I, too, prayed for years and years. One day she came to bless me and I begged her, 'Please do not leave me! Please stay with me forever.' The goddess Lakshmi listened to my prayer and stayed with me."

When the third lady heard these stories, greed entered into her. She said, "Let me invoke both the goddess of misery and the goddess of prosperity. When both of them come, then I will be able to ask them for the proper boons."

So she began praying most fervently. At long last, both goddesses came together to bless her. The lady was so excited and delighted to see both goddesses at once that she became confused. She said to the goddess of misery, "You are so kind. Please stay here with me forever." To the goddess of prosperity, she said, "You can go away! Now that you have come to bless me, I am asking you to leave. I never want to see you again."

So the goddess of prosperity went away and the goddess of misery stayed with her for the remainder of her life.

This lady had wanted to get double benefit by invoking both goddesses at once. But when greed enters, wisdom disappears. In her excitement, she offered the wrong prayer to the wrong person. Always we have to be careful when we pray. Otherwise, we may make the wrong choices.

### AIE 87. *Tomorrow never comes*

This is a story about people who think that there will always be another opportunity tomorrow to do what they did not do today. In Spanish, they say *mañana,* but mañana never comes.

There was once a rich man who was extremely miserly. People in his village used to hate him because he did not give anything to the poor and the needy. He was also very unkind to children. In every way, he showed his stinginess.

This man used to promise the villagers that he would give all his wealth to charity when he died. He told them, "Now I do not want to give you any money, but in my will I will give so much money to you."

The village people did not believe him at all. They knew that he was miserly to the core, so they had no confidence in his will.

One day the rich man went out shopping. It began raining very heavily and he took shelter at the foot of a tree. He was joined there by a pig and a cow.

These two animals started conversing. God opened up the man's third eye so that he was able to understand their language.

The pig said to the cow, "Why is it that human beings are so unkind to me? You only give them milk and they appreciate you so much. I am utterly sick of hearing about cow's milk! As if there was only cow's milk and nothing else in God's entire creation!

"In my case, I give three things at least: ham, bacon and bristles. I give so many things, but all I ever hear is 'cow's milk, cow's milk!' They all appreciate you and admire your bounty. Do they ever mention my name? No! Even when they eat what I have to offer, they do not show me any gratitude."

The cow listened to the pig's long list of woes and then she offered him her wisdom-light: "In my case, while I am alive human beings get milk from me. It is extremely nourishing and they like it very much. But, in your case, it is not like that. Only after your death do they get the benefit. When you want to do something good in this world, you have to do it while you are alive, not after you have left the body."

The cow's philosophy touched the rich man's heart. He went home and gave away all his riches to the poor. He no longer cared to wait for the evening of his life to arrive in order to become a good person. Then he was admired, adored and loved by everybody.

### AIE 88. *Practising what you preach*

There was once a brilliant student named B.M. On examination day, he and his colleagues were taking their English exam. The teacher was moving to and fro watching them. At one point, the teacher saw B.M.'s pen drop to the floor. The teacher immediately picked it up and gave it to B.M. The student again started writing.

The teacher said, "How is it that you have not thanked me?"

The student said, "Why should I?"

The teacher could not believe his eyes and ears, for this particular student had always been excellent in his behaviour and conduct. He asked the student, "How is it that today you are behaving so undivinely? Before today, I have only seen your divine nature."

The student said, "Sir, you have always taught us to help others immediately whenever they are in need and never to expect any reward, not even a 'thank you'. Then only, you said, would we be blessed most powerfully by the Heavenly Father."

The teacher immediately shed tears of delight and said to the student, "I am so grateful to you and proud of you for helping me to practise what I preach."

### AIE 89. *God is in everyone*

There was once a very poor family. The father was a tailor who could barely support his wife and son. When the father became a victim of cancer and died, the poor mother found it very difficult to support her eight-year-old son. There were no relatives who could help. She used to tell her son, "God is kind. He is giving us a special experience. God will change our fate." Then, O God, the mother also fell very sick!

The young boy was very upset, and the mother tried to console him. "God is so kind, He hears all our prayers," she said.

The son asked, "If I write a letter to Him, will it reach Him?"

The mother said, "Yes, if your letter is sincere, then God will respond."

He asked, "What is the address?"

She said, "You just address it to Heaven."

The son wrote, "Dearest Father, my earthly father passed away a short while ago and now my mother is very sick. We do not know what we did wrong in our previous lives to deserve this fate and we have not consciously done anything wrong in this life. Please help us." It was addressed to the Supreme Father in Heaven.

He went to put the letter in the mailbox, but because he was very short, he could not mail the letter. Then a tall man came by. The boy said, "Can you help me?"

The man said, "Certainly!" The man looked at the letter, addressed to God in Heaven. He asked, "Can I read your letter?"

The boy said, "Yes."

The man did not have the heart to laugh. He started shedding tears, and then he gave the boy some money.

The boy said, "But you are not God."

The man said, "No, but did your mother not teach you that God is in everyone? Can I come to your house to see your mother?"

The little boy said, "Alas, how will we feed you?"

The man said, "Do not worry. I am just coming to see your mother because she is sick."

The man was a member of an organisation that did good things for mankind. He called a special meeting and read out the letter in the meeting. The members were deeply moved, and they all came to see the lady. They said that every month they would send contributions to the family.

So if you have faith in God, this kind of thing happens.

### AIE 90. *The king's surprise visit*

From time to time, George V of England used to enjoy walking along the street incognito. He especially liked to go to the villages. Once he was supposed to go to a particular village to meet with the local people and give them advice. Everybody went to that particular village to get advice and blessings from the King, but the King did not come. Instead, he went to another village and was moving around in disguise. He saw a lady working in the field and asked, "You are working all by yourself. Do you not have dear ones to help you?"

She said, "Yes, I have dear ones, but today they have all gone to see the King."

He said, "The King?"

She said, "Yes, are you such a fool that you do not know? The King is speaking in a nearby village, but I have five children. If I go to see the King and do not work, then tomorrow we will not have any food to eat. Who wants to see the King? For me, duty comes first."

When George V heard this, he immediately gave her a large sum of money. He told her, "When your friends come back, you tell them that since you could not go to the King, the King came and talked to you."

She was dumbfounded!

### AIE 91. *The great man*

There was once a man who was physically, vitally, mentally and psychically strong. When he was young, he used to play American football. In the course of time, he entered another field and became famous. One day, just for the fun of it, he came to play football with his old colleagues. They could not believe that such a great man had come to play football with them.

A thousand people came to watch because he was the greatest man in his country. During the game, this man collided with someone else and fell down. Immediately all the other players came to see if he was hurt. But he smiled at them and assured them he was all right.

In case you do not know who he was, he was John Fitzgerald Kennedy. He won over the American people with his heart-power, vital-power and mind-power.

### AIE 92. *Benjamin Franklin's price*

This is a story about Benjamin Franklin. He was many things combined in one frame.

Once a young man went to Benjamin Franklin's bookstore and started browsing. After a long time, he selected a book that he wanted to buy. He asked Franklin's assistant the price. The assistant said, "One dollar."

The customer said, "The price is too high. Can you not ask your boss? He is in the other room at the printing press. Perhaps he will lower the price."

So Franklin came out and the man asked him the price of the book. Franklin said, "A dollar and a quarter."

The customer said, "Your assistant said a dollar and you have to say a dollar and a quarter? Please be serious and tell me what the price is."

This time Franklin said, "A dollar and a half."

The man asked, "Why do you keep raising the price? Please be serious!"

Franklin said, "I am serious. Do you not see that you are wasting my time? The price of the book is one dollar. But because you are wasting my time, the price of the book has to go up."

The man understood and bought the book for a dollar and a half.

### AIE 93. *The Swiss captain and the Emperor*

When Switzerland was ruled by France, a Swiss army captain asked the French Emperor for a large sum of money for the military. The Emperor told the treasurer to give him the money, but the treasurer said, "Do you think it is wise? They are not French people. Why spend so much money on the Swiss army?

Instead of giving the money to the captain, let us build a long and excellent paved road."

The captain said, "I do not deny that this road is a splendid idea. But what about the countless Swiss soldiers who have sacrificed their lives for you? Instead of a road, can we not have a river flowing with the blood of the Swiss soldiers who have offered their lives for the French Emperor?"

The Emperor was very pleased and very embarrassed at the same time. He scolded the treasurer and said, "Give him the money immediately!"

The Emperor had quite a few swords. His most treasured sword he gave to the Swiss captain for his wisdom and brave words.

# PART III

# LIFE'S BLEEDING TEARS AND FLYING SMILES

# AUTHOR'S INTRODUCTION AND DEDICATION

LTS 1. *Author's introduction*

These are not my own stories. These are ancient stories. I do not claim even an iota of originality. The original authors are buried in oblivion, but the successors are following in the footsteps of their predecessors with gorgeous embellishment. I, too, have indulged lavishly in my own way of embellishment. Long live my humour-wisdom-flooded predecessors, who loved anonymity.

May these tales liberate us from the heavy dryness of the mind, and may they transform the dryness of the mind into an ever-blossoming fountain-ecstasy.

— Sri Chinmoy

LTS 2. *Dedication to first 73 stories (volume 1 to 5)*

On the most auspicious occasion of my brother Mantu's 73rd birthday on 17 November 2000, I am lovingly and gratefully dedicating to him 73 stories. They will be published in several volumes.

LTS 3. *Dedication to additional 100 stories (volume 6 to 12)*

On the most auspicious occasion of my brother Mantu's 73rd birthday on 17 November 2000, I lovingly and gratefully dedicated to him 73 stories, which were published in five volumes. Now, I have decided to continue the series by writing an additional 100 stories dedicated to him. These 100 stories will be published in seven volumes, for a total of twelve volumes.

# LIFE'S BLEEDING TEARS AND FLYING SMILES

## BOOK 1

## LTS 4. *The good man and the jealous man*

There was once a good man, a very good man. He was learned, very learned. He was pious, very pious. In everything he used to see good. Our tendency is to see bad in everything, but his way of life was to see everything good, good, good, good. Inside everything there is good. In everything there is gain. There is no such thing as loss — it is all gain. Inside each happening, each incident, there is something good and divine. This was the man's way of looking at the world.

Many people were extremely jealous of this man's good qualities. One man in particular was jealousy incarnate. He used to hate the good man because he had so many admirers and adorers. The good man also had enemies, but his admirers, adorers and lovers were infinitely more in number than his adversaries.

Eventually this man, who was very good in every sense of the term, became old. Age descended upon him, and he lost his eyesight. Day and night he would spend his time praying to God.

One day, the good man's worst enemy, the jealous man, came to see him. Inwardly he was so happy to see the good man in such poor condition. Mockingly he said to the good man, "I am awfully sorry that you have lost your eyesight! But, O great philosopher, professor, you used to say that everything is for your good. Now you are blind. Is this also for your good? What kind of gain do you get from this loss? You have lost your eyesight! Answer me!"

The good man replied, "Either I can pray to God to give you the answer, or God has already given you the answer!"

The jealous man exclaimed, "Do not bring God into the picture! It is between you and me. Tell me, what gain do you get from the loss of your eyesight?"

The good man said, "Can you not see that because I have no eyesight, because I have no vision, today I am so fortunate that I do not have to see your face? You are so undivine. Because God is so kind to me, He does not want me to see you. That is why He has taken away my vision!"

A few months later, again the bad fellow came to visit the good man and said, "You are so old. You cannot move around. You cannot see anything. What good is it that you have become so old that you cannot see, you cannot move around, you cannot even walk? How can you say that everything is for your good? Does it make any sense?"

The good man replied, "Yes, everything is for my good. Here is the proof: it is you who are coming here to see me. I did not have to go to your place. Because I cannot walk now, it is you who are coming and touching my feet. Because I am lame, you are compelled to come to me. True, you are not coming with a good motive — you have come here to make fun of me. But you were compelled to come here because your jealousy forced you. As for me, I did not have to go to you. My goodwill, my kindness, my way of prayers did not have to go to see you!"

### LTS 5. *The weak can be wise, the strong can be fools*

In one village there were a few notorious boys who used to torture men and women alike while they were walking along the street. In various ways these rogues would torture the villagers. They would beat people up, tie them up on the street and do all kinds of terrible things.

One day the village scholar was walking along the street. He was well respected because he had studied spiritual scriptures. These boys wanted to make fun of him, so when he was passing by, one of the boys threw a stone at him. The stone struck his forehead, and he started bleeding profusely. The boy who had thrown the stone got frightened, and all the boys started to run away.

The great scholar said to the boy who had struck him, "Come here, come here! I have something very nice to tell you."

The boys could not believe that this scholar was so kind, compassionate and forgiving. So all of them came back. The scholar said, "I am so happy that you have someone among you who has such good aim. I tell you, one of these days I will ask the zamindar, the village chief, to walk along this street. He will definitely be pleased to see what good aim you have because he needs a few hunters. I can see clearly that all of you will be very good hunters. The zamindar will be so pleased with the one who is able to throw a stone most accurately that he will want his daughter to marry that person."

A few days later the zamindar was going somewhere, and he and his bodyguards took that particular street. The boy who had thrown the stone was waiting on that street. He was so happy because he thought that he would be able to marry the daughter of the village head. When the group passed by, this fellow came very near and threw a stone at the zamindar. The boy was caught immediately by the bodyguards, and they put him and his whole gang in jail, instead of asking him to marry the zamindar's daughter.

From this story we learn that a weak person can be wise, and a strong person can be a fool.

LTS 6. *Physically strong but mentally weak, physically weak but mentally clever*

There were two friends going to the market to buy and sell things. One of them was physically very, very strong and the other one was physically weak, but they were good friends. The weaker one said to his friend, "Can you give me ten rupees? I need money badly because I have to buy things."

The other one said, "Certainly I can give you ten rupees, but I do not give anything without security."

The weaker one had on his back a big load of merchandise that he was going to sell at the market. He said to the stronger one, "You give me ten rupees, and I will give you some of my merchandise. You can take that as security."

So the weak fellow took the ten rupees, and the fellow who was physically strong started carrying the load. When they came to the market, the weaker one said, "You gave me the money, and now I can return it. Give me back my merchandise."

The weak one gave back the ten rupees that he had received from the strong one, took his merchandise back and started selling it. The strong one had carried the whole load! So, one who is physically strong can be mentally weak, and one who is physically weak can be mentally very clever.

### LTS 7. *The kindhearted neighbour*

There were two friends. One of them borrowed ten rupees from the other and promised that on a certain date he would return the money. But when the time came, he did not return the money. Time after time when the other fellow went to his friend's place to get back the money, the friend's wife would say, "He is not at home."

The friend was actually inside the house, but the wife would come to the door and say, "He is not at home. Sorry! Please come some other time."

This fellow was so disappointed. He said, "He was my good friend, but now he is not returning my money. What kind of friendship is this?"

A kindhearted neighbour knew that the wife was telling lies. He knew that the man was hiding inside, so he got angry at the family. He said to the wife, "The next time this fellow comes, I am going to tell him that your husband is inside. Then he will go in and catch your husband, and your husband will have to give the money."

The wife begged him, "No, no! Please, please do not do that!"

The neighbour said to the wife, "Whenever your husband's friend comes here, if you do not give me a rupee, then I am going to tell him that your husband is inside the house. Just give me one rupee. Otherwise, if this fellow comes here and I know your husband is inside the house, I am going to tell him the truth!"

From then on, every time the friend came, the wife would tell him that her husband was not at home, and then she would give the neighbour a rupee. The friend came many times, and each time the wife said that her husband was not there. Finally, the wife felt miserable, because the neighbour had received more than ten rupees. The husband did not know that his stupid wife was giving the neighbour a rupee not to tell the friend that the husband was inside the house.

A few months later, the fellow who had borrowed the money came upon his friend unexpectedly in the street. He said, "When you come to my place, I promise I will give you back your ten rupees."

The friend said, "I have already got back the money."

"When?" the first one asked. "When did you get it?"

The friend said, "Every time I went to your house and your wife said that you were not there, your neighbour compelled your wife to give him a rupee. Now I have got back all ten rupees from your neighbour!"

LTS 8. *Imaginary service*

There was a rich man who was very miserly. He did many, many bad things. He committed many sins. Then, finally, he repented. He said to himself, "People say that if you take a dip in the Ganges, all your sins will go away. The Ganges is quite far from my place. I want to be purified, but at the same time, I do not want to spend the money to go to the Ganges."

One day he heard that one of his neighbours was going to the Ganges. He had also committed many sins, but he was not rich. He was going to bathe in the Ganges so that he would be purified of all his sins. When the rich man heard that his neighbour was going to the Ganges, he gave the man some money and said, "I am not feeling well. You take this money. First you will bathe for your own purification. Then once more you will dive into the Ganges in my name. Remember me! I am giving you money so that you can dive into the Ganges in my name."

The neighbour said, "Definitely I can do that."

The man said, "You have to think of me. The first time you will bathe for yourself so that you will be purified of all your sins. The second time think of me, and then my sins will all go away. I will have no more sins! I will be purified while remaining here."

The neighbour agreed completely. But a few weeks later the rich man saw that his neighbour had not yet gone to the Ganges. He asked, "Why are you not going? What have you done with my money?"

The neighbour said, "I spent it."

"How could you spend it without going to the Ganges?" the rich man asked.

The neighbour said, "I imagined that my pond was the Ganges. I entered the water and had a very good swim. Then, the second time I went swimming, I thought of you. You gave me the money, and I spent it because I purified you of your sins. I imagined that the pond right in front of my house was the Ganges. You told me to imagine you, so I uttered your name and imagined you. And I imagined more: I imagined that my pond itself was the Ganges. The second time I swam in my pond, I thought of you. I did your work, so I spent your money."

LTS 9. *The father's sacrifice*

An old man became very sick. His son was a doctor. The son gave medicine to his father, but he could not cure him. The father was dying, and the mother was absolutely miserable. The mother said, "Alas, our son is not a good doctor. Let us find another doctor."

It happened that a good doctor from another village heard about the illness of the old man. This doctor came to see the old man and told him, "I will be able to cure you."

The mother said, "Please, please, cure my husband!"

The father was extremely sick, but he immediately jumped up and said, "No, no! I am feeling better. My son is giving me medicine and I am getting well. Soon I will be completely all right and I will be able to move around. You are so kind, extremely kind. If I really feel sick, I will definitely call you. You are so generous and so kind."

The doctor said, "All right. When you need me, you can send for me." Then he went back to his own village.

The mother said to her husband, "What have you done? What have you done?"

The father said, "You fool! If people from our village come to know that this doctor has cured me, then they will all go to him and not to our son. His business will prosper like anything, and our son will have no job. Our son will be in poverty. How can I allow that? It is better for me to die. I am ready to give up my life."

Then he said to his son, "Please, please, become a good doctor. Study more, practise more. I am giving up my life for you."

The mother was crying and crying because her husband was about to leave the world.

After begging his son to become a very good doctor, the father died. The mother was so miserable that she had lost her husband. Look at the father's sacrifice for the son!

### LTS 10. *Gifts for the other world*

An elderly couple had a maidservant who used to do their housework, and both of them were so pleased with her. She was extremely devoted to them. All of a sudden, the maidservant got a serious disease and passed away. The couple was so miserable because they had taken her as their own daughter.

One day an old beggar came to their place to beg for alms. The man was not at home, so the elderly lady opened the door. She said, "How are you?"

The beggar said, "I am fine. I just came back from the other world."

The lady said to herself, "What is the other world?" Since the beggar looked so thin and weak, the elderly lady thought that he had been about to die and then he had recovered. Perhaps his case had been very serious. Although he had not died, he was so weak. She thought that the other world meant Heaven. She said to him, "You are coming back from the other world?"

The beggar said, "Yes."

The lady said, "Have you any idea about our maidservant? She died all of a sudden and we could not do anything to save her."

The beggar said, "Died? Your maidservant? As a matter of fact, I married her! We were married in Heaven."

The lady asked, "You were married in Heaven?"

The beggar said, "Yes, I married her."

The lady said, "Oh! Here I have many things for her, her garments and so many valuable items. Will you be able to take them to her?"

The beggar said, "Certainly! I am married to her after all. I just came here to visit. I am going back again to the other world."

The elderly lady gave the beggar all the personal belongings of the maidservant and all the expensive things she and her husband had given the girl over the years because she was such a good worker. The man started carrying everything away. On the way he met with the husband, who was riding home on his horse. The husband got off his horse and said, "What are you doing? Why are you taking these things?"

The beggar said, "Your wife has given me the order to take them. I am only listening to your wife."

While he was talking, the beggar started running away with all the clothes and gifts. The old man jumped on his horse and chased him. He thought that since he was chasing the other fellow on a horse, the fellow would drop everything. But instead of dropping everything, the beggar kept carrying all the items. Finally the beggar found a tree. He left all the things on the ground and climbed up the tree.

The elderly man was so furious. He said to himself, "I will be able to take these things home, but since this fellow is such a rogue, I want to beat him up!" He left the horse at the foot of the tree and started climbing up. He said, "I want to punish him! I am not going to wait for him to come down. I am going to climb up and punish him. Then I will take back all these things. My stupid wife has given them to him, but I shall take them back."

When he started climbing up, the beggar came down quickly from the other side of the tree.

The beggar said, "I am carrying these things to your maidservant in the other world!" Then he grabbed all the expensive things and put them on the horse. When the elderly man saw that the beggar had put all the valuables on the horse and was about to ride away, he came down from the tree and said, "Wait, wait, wait! I have a special message for you."

The beggar said, "What is the message?"

The elderly man said, "Those silly gifts are from my wife. But tell our maidservant that this horse is from me. It is my gift. I am giving her my own horse as a gift because she was such a good worker."

### LTS 11. *Money or freedom?*

There were two friends. One was very happy, and the other one was always sad and miserable. One day the first friend asked the fellow who was always sad, "Why are you nowadays so often sad and depressed?"

He answered, "The salary that I am getting is not enough. I have a big family. I have a wife, children and so many expenses. I am so sad that I do not have enough money."

On that very day the sad fellow's wife went to the kindhearted friend and said, "Can you not do something for my husband? We have such a big family, and he is always sad and depressed because he does not have enough money."

The friend answered, "Definitely, definitely! I will go to his boss. His boss is my friend. I will tell his boss to give him an important job so he will make more money. But he will have to spend a few more hours working every day."

The wife said, "As long as he gets more money, he will gladly do it."

The wife made the arrangement without the husband's knowledge. When the husband went to work the next day, he got a promotion. He was transferred to a very good job in another section. Now he was making lots of money and bringing it home to his wife. Then again he started feeling sad and depressed. One day the boss said to the unhappy worker, "I have given you such a good job. Why are you sad, why are you so depressed? You are making lots of money."

The man said, "This work is too much for me! I have no holidays and I cannot go anywhere."

The boss said, "Which one is better — your old, simple job or your new, important job?"

The man said, "The first one! I did not have enough money, but even with the little money I had, I used to go wherever I wanted to go. Now I have money, but I am not allowed to go anywhere because I have got so much responsibility. I do not want so much responsibility! I do not need so much money. I will be satisfied with just a little money as long as I do not have too much responsibility. Then I will be able to go wherever I want to, whenever I wish."

### LTS 12. *The judge's punishment*

An innocent man went to a church. While he was taking his seat, he made a lot of noise. The priest was furious because the man was disturbing others who were praying around him. The priest came up to the man and said, "How could you make so much noise?"

The man said, "I could not avoid it. I stumbled, and that is why I made the noise."

The priest said, "You have ruined the prayers of so many sincere seekers! I am taking you to the judge immediately. The judge will punish you!"

The man said, "If I have done something wrong, I will accept whatever punishment I deserve."

The priest took the man to the judge and explained what had happened. Then the priest went back to the church.

The judge was furious. He said, "How could you disturb the prayers of so many seekers? You should be punished."

The man said, "I know I have committed a crime. Whatever punishment you give me, I will take."

The judge said, "You have to give fifty cents."

The man said, "I do not have fifty cents. I have only one dollar."

The judge said, "You have to give exactly fifty cents. I do not have change."

The man said, "I do not have any change either."

Finally the judge said, "All right. Listen, fellow. Give me the dollar. Now go back to the church and again make noise. Fifty cents extra you have given me. Since I do not have change, you will be allowed to make noise once again. You have got my permission. If the priest says anything, tell him that you have got my permission to make noise once more." The judge was so kind.

### LTS 13. *The two thief-rivals*

There was a town where every night some houses were being robbed: either one house, two houses or three houses. People were suffering like anything. God alone knew how many thieves were responsible for these crimes. The mayor said, "Whoever can catch the thieves will receive 10,000 rupees from me."

Everybody was looking and looking for thieves to catch. There were actually two thieves who were stealing every night. Sometimes it happened that burglaries took place at two locations at the same hour. These two thieves were rivals. They knew each other well and were jealous of each other. Each time they met, the two rivals would brag about their accomplishments. They were always competing to see who had got more expensive things.

After the mayor's announcement, one thief said, "I will put on very nice gentleman's clothes. My wife and I and our whole family will go to the mayor's office. I will be able to tell the mayor who the thief is, and my wife will be the witness. My wife will cry and cry and say, 'I know the person.' Then I will tell the mayor, 'I also know the person. We will be able to tell you who the thief is. He is so bad!'"

The thief and his wife went to the mayor's office with their big family. The thief had put on a very nice dhoti and the wife was dressed very simply and religiously, with a tilak.

They were very happy that they would be able to tell the mayor who the culprit was and get the reward. When they arrived, the guard said, "The mayor is busy right now. Please wait here in this office." The entire family went into the office. The wife and all the children were ready to serve as witnesses when the father told the mayor who the thief was.

Then all of a sudden, the other thief arrived with his family. They had also come to tell the mayor who the thief was. With the hope of getting 10,000 rupees, the two culprits and their families had come to tell the mayor who was responsible for all the crimes.

As soon as they saw each other, the two rivals both screamed, "He is the thief, he is the thief!"

The first culprit shouted to the second one, "You are the thief, you are the thief!" The second one screamed, "You liar! You are the thief!"

Both of them were screaming and shouting, and all their family members started crying. There was such a big commotion. What did the mayor do? He put both of these wonderful rivals into jail and sent all the relatives home.

## LTS 14. *The special cap*

One man had a business making caps. At night he used to make very, very nice caps by hand, and during the day he would sell them. People knew this was the place to buy caps for their families. They felt he was a very nice, honest man with a good business.

For some time he used to spend about two hours every night working on one particular cap, making it as beautiful as possible. This went on for two or three months.

The children asked their father, "For whom are you making this special cap? Every day you are working, working and working on this one. You are selling the others right away. What are you going to do with this one? How much will you charge?"

The man said, "I will tell you later who is getting this cap. Let me finish it first."

He continued working at night for a couple of months more. During the day he would sell the other caps that he had made. He had many customers, but it seemed that no one was getting the special cap.

One day the man said to his family, "I have been making this cap only for myself."

The family members said, "What! For yourself?"

The man said, "When I die, you will put it on me. I have to take something to God as a present. That is why I have been working so hard on this cap. If God asks, 'What have you brought for Me?' I will give it to God, and God will put it on Himself. God has given me this profession, making caps. I have never been idle. God will be so pleased that I have worked very, very hard, plus I am bringing this special cap for God. So, when I die, please put this cap on me. When I go to God, I will give it to Him, and He will take me to the highest Heaven."

When the man died, the children did put the cap on their father in his coffin so that he could bring it to the highest Heaven. Something very nice he wanted to take to God as a gift.

### LTS 15. *Flattery works*

One fellow borrowed money from another fellow, and he was not returning it. One day the fellow who lent the money said to the other one, "Please, please, listen to me. I am not asking you for the money back. I have something important to tell you. A few days ago I saw a man exactly like you. It was not a dream! His eyes were as beautiful as yours, and he was as tall, as stout, as strong and as kindhearted as you are. How I wish both of you would meet together one day!"

He was very nicely flattering the fellow who had borrowed the money. He said, "You are so good. You are absolutely so handsome and so powerful. You draw such attention. How I wish in this lifetime I could see both you and this other man together! I know you would become very good friends, excellent friends."

The other one said, "This fellow is as good as I am? That means I have to see him!"

The first one said, "I tell you, one day I will see him again somewhere, and then I will bring him to you. Both of you will be so happy."

The man said, "All right, all right! I did not want to give you back your money, but now your flattery is melting me like anything and giving me so much joy."

Then he returned the money.

## LTS 16. *Pay for your pride*

A villager was going to town riding his horse. On the way, the horse became very restless and absolutely unruly. The villager could not keep the horse under control, so he came down and with great difficulty fastened the horse to a tree.

Then he saw that a policeman was also going to town on his horse. The policeman's horse was about to pass very near his own horse. He said to the policeman, "Please, please be very careful! My horse is extremely restless. I cannot control him. Please do not come near my horse."

The policeman cried, "My horse has to be afraid of your horse?" The policeman jumped off his horse and allowed his horse to fight with the villager's horse. Many people, including lots of young boys and girls, came to watch and enjoy the fight. In spite of being tied up, the villager's horse killed the policeman's horse.

The policeman got furious and took the villager to the town chief. The policeman said, "My horse was killed by his horse."

The man had already warned the policeman, "Please, please do not come near my horse," but it was beneath the policeman's dignity to listen. What could the man do?

The judge said to the villager, "Now tell me what happened. How did your horse kill his horse? What happened?"

The villager was so mad and furious. Inwardly he was brooding. He said to himself, "I warned the policeman!" But outwardly he remained absolutely silent.

The judge said, "Idiot! You will be fined since it is all your fault that your horse killed the other horse."

The villager was getting punishment, but even then he kept quiet. The judge said, "What is wrong with you? You cannot open your mouth and tell me what actually happened? Are you dumb?"

The policeman said, "He is not dumb! He warned me so many times that his horse was very unruly, restless and dangerous, but I took my horse there anyway!"

Then the judge said, "Fine, fine. Now I see that you are the idiot!"

The policeman's horse was killed, but because of his stupid statement, the judge fined him 100 rupees. He told the judge, "This fellow warned me, but I did not listen." So the judge said, "Pay for your pride — 100 rupees' fine!"

Then the judge took the money and gave it to the innocent villager.

### LTS 17. *The punishment*

There was a man who sold fruit. One day he was selling bad mangoes. Some people bought his mangoes, and then they became furious when they discovered that the mangoes were absolutely rotten and smelled very bad. These customers brought the man to the village chief and made complaints against him.

The village chief said to the man, "The rest of the mangoes you have to eat yourself. All the mangoes you have to eat!"

Then the accused man said, "Let me go to somebody higher than you. Let me see what he says."

When he went to a higher authority, the authority said, "If you do not want to eat the fruit, then the people who are angry with you should beat you up. They should whip you 30 times. Since you do not want to eat the rotten mangoes, the people who have made the complaints should whip you at least 30 times."

The man said, "The first one says I have to eat all the rotten mangoes and the second one says I have to be whipped 30 times! Now let me go to the absolutely highest authority."

He went to the highest authority, and the highest authority said, "You do not have to eat the fruit. You do not have to be beaten or whipped. Just pay 50 rupees. Then it will be all settled. Pay me 50 rupees, and I will distribute the money to the people who have made complaints against you. Now, you make the choice. Do you want to eat the rotten mangoes, do you want to be whipped, or do you want to give the money? Choose whatever punishment you want. It is up to you."

The man said, "I am ready to eat the mangoes."

He started eating the mangoes, and immediately he began vomiting. The judge said, "Whatever you start, you are supposed to complete. You were supposed to eat all the mangoes. You have failed, so now you should be whipped 30 times."

Those who had made complaints started whipping him. After 15 lashes, the man was about to faint. He said, "I cannot bear this punishment!"

The judge said, "Then pay the penalty: 50 rupees."

The man had exactly 50 rupees, so the judge took the money and distributed it to the people who had made complaints against him. Look at the fate of this fellow! First he ate half of the fruits that were so bad. Then he was punished by being whipped fifteen times — half of the sentence. Finally he had to give the full amount of the fine. Then the judge distributed the money to the people who had accused him.

The moral is that if you do one bad thing, you can easily be punished by everybody beyond what you deserve.

### LTS 18. *The miserable thief*

There was a very, very bad thief. He used to go to work during the day and at night he would steal. He used to commit thefts all the time and torture so many people. So many expensive and valuable things he stole! He learned how to steal from his father. His wife was dead against it, so when his father died, she was inwardly quite happy. Outwardly she cried because her father-in-law had died. But inwardly she was happy, and she started begging her husband, "Please, please, do not follow your father's ways any more. People know that you are stealing, although you are not being caught. Everybody knows that you steal! I am your wife, and I feel miserable when they accuse you. Still you are not being caught. Please promise that you will stop. Otherwise I am going to leave you and I am going to leave our three children with you. You take care of them! I cannot go on like this any more."

Finally the husband said that he would not steal any more. The wife was so happy that he was giving up stealing.

One day the husband came home from work absolutely miserable. The wife said, "What happened? Why are you so miserable? You cannot even talk properly. What happened?"

He said, "You know, when I used to steal, I hid everything in my friend's house. I used to keep all my loot there. Now my friend has taken all the things that I stole, and I do not know where he has gone."

The wife said, "Look, is this not your fate? Many people's things you stole, and now you are miserable because someone else has taken these things away. Just think of those people who had their own things stolen by you! They were the actual owners of those things. Do they not feel infinitely more miserable? See how sad you are! Can you not think of the loss and the sadness of those people who were the actual owners of all those valuables? Again, I am begging you, never steal."

Then the husband promised that he would never, never steal again. Because of his sadness and his sufferings, he gave up stealing. What a nice wife he had! The wife gave such good, moral advice.

# LIFE'S BLEEDING TEARS AND FLYING SMILES

## BOOK 2

### LTS 19. *The special mark*

There was a very, very rich family. When a little baby was born into the family, the mother was so happy to see the child. The father was also very happy with their firstborn child. The mother and grandmother both noticed that there was a mark a little above the child's left eye. When the grandmother saw the mark, she said, "This is a sign that he will become a very, very great king."

The mother immediately had such faith in this old lady. She felt that old people know everything. When the mother-in-law says something nice, everybody believes it. The mother-in-law was such a wise old lady. She felt that the child would become king.

But the father said, "Who cares for my mother's opinion? She is just an old lady. What does she know about these things? Let me go and bring the astrologer."

The village astrologer came and cast the child's horoscope. Then he said, "No, no, he will not be a king. He will be a very, very great scholar and philosopher."

The wife said, "I believe what the child's grandmother says. I know she is right. He will be a king when he grows up."

The husband said, "I have brought the astrologer. The astrologer is saying that the child will be a great scholar, a philosopher and a learned man."

The wife said, "Let us bring a palmist to see what he has to say."

The palmist looked at the child's hand and said, "Oh no, he will be a very, very famous singer."

They all had a difference of opinion. The old grandmother said one thing and the mother believed it. Then the husband had to go and bring the astrologer, and the astrologer said something else. Now the palmist came into the picture and said that the child would be a great singer. Everybody said something different. One said he would be a king, one said he would be a great philosopher and scholar, and the third one said he would be a great singer and musician. Still the mother and father were so happy that they had got this little baby. Everybody in the family was very happy.

At that moment an old beggar came to the house for alms. The grandmother, who had predicted that the baby would become a king, was giving some rice to the beggar. All of a sudden she saw a mark over his left eye, and she fell down and fainted. Everybody said, "What happened, what happened?"

When the grandmother opened her eyes, she pointed out the mark on the left side of the beggar's forehead. Then everybody cried and cried and cried, "Alas, alas, alas!" The beggar had the same mark that the little baby had! Just a few moments ago they were all full of joy. Now everybody in the family felt miserable. They were swimming in the sea of sorrows because the beggar had the same mark. First the son was going to be a king, then he was going to be a great scholar, and finally he was going to be a wonderful singer. All their predictions were smashed when the beggar appeared.

### LTS 20. *The mysterious box*

A villager went to the zamindar and said, "I would like to buy two acres of land from you. Please allow me to buy this land. I will not be able to pay the full amount immediately, but on an installment basis I will pay you."

The zamindar said, "No, no, no! I will not allow you to do this. Either give the full amount or I will not allow you to buy this plot of land from me."

The villager was very sad that he did not have the full amount. The zamindar wanted only 200 rupees, but the villager could not give that much at once. This poor fellow wanted to give 10 rupees at a time until he had paid the full 200. He was a sincere man.

A few months later, the same villager came to the chief and said, "Yesterday I had a dream. In the dream I saw two acres of land at a particular place. I saw that one of your ancestors had dug a hole in the ground and buried a box there. Inside the box there were gold coins. Now I am telling you so that you can dig up this box. I will be there to watch you. If my dream does not prove to be true, then you do anything with my life. You can beat me up or do anything else."

The zamindar was so greedy. He said, "No, no, no, I will forgive you, I will forgive you. If I see the box, then I will be so happy. But even if I do not get the box, since you have given me such a piece of good news, I shall forgive you, even if there is nothing there."

The zamindar and a few of his people all went with this villager to the particular place he had seen in the dream. The poor fellow said, "Let me dig it up. It is your property, so you will take the box. Only let me get the joy of digging it up, because I had the dream."

The zamindar said, "Do it, do it!"

The zamindar was thrilled that he would get the box of gold. The villager started digging in front of the zamindar, and soon he found the box. On the top of the box was written, "Please open me one year after the day you discover me if you want to get the full amount. If you open me before one year, you will be disappointed. But after one year if you open me, you will be the happiest person on earth."

The zamindar said, "One year! That is nothing."

The zamindar was so happy. What did he do? Immediately he wrote down this message, "You do not have to give me 200 rupees for the plot of land. I am giving it to you free. You take this plot of land; it is yours. I am taking away the box."

The zamindar gave the villager the two acres. He took away the box, and the villager got the land free. He did not have to pay anything. The zamindar was so happy and so proud that he had given away the land free of charge.

The zamindar was not supposed to open the box for one year. It was written on the box, "If you open me one year after the day you discover me, you will be the happiest person."

But the eldest son of the zamindar miscalculated. After eleven months, he thought one year had gone by. He was so greedy that he wanted to cheat and deceive his father. He thought that he would open the box, take out a small amount and give the rest to his father. The father had kept the box somewhere secretly, but the son knew where it was. So, although only eleven months had passed, the son opened the box. When he opened it, he saw that there was nothing inside.

Suddenly, the father came into the room and said, "You idiot! It was written that one year should elapse. Why did you open the box? If one year had gone by, then there would have been something so valuable inside!"

Now the zamindar was miserable because he had lost the money and he had lost the land. But the poor fellow who received the land said to the zamindar, "I have borrowed money from my friends. I am giving you 200 rupees. I will pay back the money to my friends little by little."

The zamindar took the 200 rupees, and the man kept the land. The man had already started plowing the land, and he would soon be able to give the money back to his friends. Greed, greed, greed! How much suffering greed can create!

## LTS 21. *The king's astrologer*

A king wanted to have an excellent astrologer in his court so that, before he did anything, he could ask the astrologer's opinion and the astrologer would be able to tell him what to do. He made an announcement for all the excellent astrologers in his kingdom to come to his palace. Then he would test them and he would choose one to be his personal astrologer.

Many astrologers came because they wanted to be the king's astrologer. The king himself knew quite a few astrologers. But one particular astrologer did not come. The king said, "Practically all the astrologers have come from all over my kingdom. How is it that this particular one has not come? Where has Ram gone? He is also an astrologer."

Ram did not come, but the others all came. They were all ready to be examined by the king. Finally, the king sent for Ram, the great astrologer. The king asked, "Why did you not come? All the other astrologers have come. What is wrong with you?"

Ram said, "O King, forgive me, forgive me! I will say something that will annoy you, but I am telling you anyway. You have to forgive me first, before I say anything."

The king said, "I will always forgive you. Say whatever you have to say."

Ram said, "These astrologers are all idiots. They have come here with the hope of becoming your personal astrologer. I know that you are going to ask me to take the job. You are going to appoint me because any question you ask me, I will be able to answer. If you ask these idiots any question, let me see if they can answer it. I was absolutely sure that you would choose me, so I did not want to be with these idiot-astrologers. It is beneath my dignity to mix with them. I do not want to be examined along with them. You can examine me privately or do anything you like. What kind of astrologers are they if they do not know that I will get the job? If they do not know even this much, are you going to keep them with you permanently? O King, is it fair that you are going to keep these idiots here when they do not even know who is going to be appointed for the post? They have come to you for the highest post, and even this much they do not know!"

The king was very pleased. He threw out all the other astrologers and appointed Ram to be his astrologer. All the others felt miserable. Ram was such a rogue! The others all had to go home full of humiliation.

### LTS 22. *The drunkard and the goddess*

There was a drunkard who used to drink and drink and drink and make his wife and children all absolutely miserable. Also, he used to torture people. There was a forest near his house. When people would go to the forest to enjoy themselves, he used to go there and torture them. He was heavily drunk, so he would beat them up. In every way he would torture everybody. He was very, very strong, and everybody knew that he was a horrible, horrible drunk.

One day the drunkard saw a most beautiful lady in the forest. The drunkard said he wanted to beat her up. Now, she happened to be a divine goddess. The goddess immediately showed her power, and he became frightened because the goddess had so much power. He had thought she was just a beautiful lady.

The goddess said, "Now look here, I can easily kill you, easily! But with my infinite compassion I am telling you to give up drinking. You are torturing your wife, your children, your father, your mother — everybody. You are torturing your family, and you are torturing innocent people who come to the forest. Why are you doing this? Give up drinking! Give up, give up! I am telling you, if you do not give up drinking, one day you will suffer terribly. You will have a very short life, and your family members will feel sad when you meet with an untimely death."

The man said, "But I have been doing this for such a long time. I cannot get rid of this bad habit."

The goddess said, "No! You should and you must! And if you do not, then you will soon be punished. You will see your fate."

After saying this, with her spiritual power the goddess created a swimming pool right in front of them. The man was so happy, because the swimming pool was filled to the brim with wine. He said, "Every day I will be able to come here and drink!"

The goddess said, "All right, every day if you want to drink this wine, you can do so. Since you are such a rogue, since you are such a bad fellow, you will never keep your promise. You drink and drink. I am going away."

Then the goddess went away and left the swimming pool full of wine. The drunkard said to the swimming pool, "Today I am taking an oath. I will drink wine to my heart's content. I will be so heavily drunk that I will enjoy myself tremendously. Then I will never, never come near you again. I will totally give up drinking. Today I will drink as much as I can, because there is so much wine here. Then, after today, I will not drink any more in this lifetime."

This was the promise that he made to the swimming pool. Then he became totally drunk. The wine was so tasty that he was overjoyed. He went home and told his wife and children that he had drunk so much that from the very next day he was giving up drinking altogether. They were so thrilled that he promised to give up drinking.

A few days later he went back to the swimming pool and saw that still there was so much wine left. In fact, it was absolutely filled to the brim. Again he started drinking. The goddess came and said, "Look, you promised to the members of your family that you would not drink any more. What happened? How is it that you are drinking again?"

The drunkard said to the goddess, "Mother, you are a goddess. Tell me, have you ever heard of a drunkard keeping his promise? I am a bad person, but you are such a fool. How can you believe a drunkard? I am a bad fellow, that everybody knows. But I will tell everybody that you are a fool. You are a stupid goddess!"

The goddess felt sad that she could not change his nature. Then the goddess said, "All right, I will do something."

She immediately used her spiritual power, and the swimming pool disappeared. Then the man started crying and crying and crying because there was no more wine for him. The goddess said, "If you cannot keep your promise, you will see what happens. I am telling you that soon you will die if you do not keep your promise."

The man said, "No, no, no, I will not drink any more! Please forgive me, forgive me!"

The goddess said, "No, you will never keep your promise. I gave you an opportunity."

The man said, "But my family will suffer."

The goddess said, "Your family will not suffer. Your family is miserable because you are such a horrible drunkard. Nobody will miss you. Now you can go and tell everybody that I am a fool and you are a bad fellow."

### LTS 23. *The zamindar and the hermit*

Two village zamindars had a quarrel and then started fighting. They brought their supporters to join the fight. They fought for a long time, and on both sides people were very, very badly injured. Finally, everybody left the place of the battle, near a forest, except one of the two village zamindars. He was so badly hurt that he was unconscious. His people all left because they did not want to be beaten by the other side. They left this zamindar alone and senseless. Nobody came to help him.

In the forest there lived a hermit. The hermit came out of the forest and started strolling and moving around. Suddenly he saw the man lying down, practically dead. He brought water for the man, fanned him and washed his face. Finally he revived the zamindar. He was so happy that the zamindar was revived, and the zamindar was also very happy.

The zamindar said to the hermit, "Please, please, take something from me. If you come to my house, I will give you something."

The hermit said, "I am a hermit. I have everything, absolutely everything. I have the sun, I have the moon, I have fruits to eat. I do not need anything at all."

The zamindar said, "My pride is hurt. I took an oath that in this lifetime I would never be indebted to anybody. I said that I would only give and give, and I would not owe anything to anybody. You are a hermit. You have nothing, like a beggar. I am a zamindar. I am so rich. You have to come to my place. I will give you whatever you want so that your poverty will disappear."

The hermit said, "No, no, no, I do not need anything."

The zamindar said, "But I am indebted to you."

Then the hermit said, "All right. In the future, if I need any help, I will come to you."

The zamindar begged him, "Please, please, you must come now. Otherwise, I will remain indebted to you. I do not want that. My pride will be hurt. I am so rich. My people, my children, my friends, my guards — all have left me. They betrayed me because they were being beaten by the enemy. All my dear ones deserted me because they did not want to be attacked and beaten mercilessly. Now you have come here to rescue me. I am so grateful to you."

The hermit said, "When I am in need, I will come to you."

The zamindar was proud, but he was a good man who really wanted to help the hermit. A few years later when the hermit became very, very old, he started suffering from this disease and that disease. Then he remembered that the zamindar had promised to help him, so he went to the zamindar's place. The guard knew that the zamindar had once upon a time been helped by the hermit. The guard said, "He is now taking a shower. After the shower, he will come and see you."

The hermit waited near the zamindar's meditation room. After finishing his shower, the zamindar went to his meditation room. With folded hands he knelt down and started praying to God, "Give me more wealth, give me more name, give me more fame! Please give me more people, more strength." For all these things he started praying.

The hermit said to himself, "I came here to beg this zamindar to give me some medicine or to find a doctor to cure me. Now I see that he is begging God to give him this and give him that. I have only one desire: for my disease to be cured. He has so many desires! He wants money, name, fame and everything else. He is such a beggar!"

The hermit started to go away very fast. The zamindar came out of his meditation room and asked the guard, "What did he want?"

Then the zamindar saw that it was the hermit. He started running after the hermit saying, "Why are you going away? You did me such a big favour when I was dying, when I was practically dead. Now you have come to my place, and I am so happy. Please, please, please tell me what you want!"

The hermit said, "No, I will not ask you for anything."

The zamindar said, "You came here, and I still owe you so much. Do you want me to remain indebted to you all my life?

If you take my help, I will be so happy and so grateful. Then I will know that you helped me, and now I am helping you."

The hermit said, "You have already helped me."

The zamindar asked, "How could I have helped you? You have not taken anything from me."

The hermit said, "Look, I am a hermit. I pray to God every day for my illumination. Here I am seeing that you are also praying to God for what you need. You have taught me that there is only one Person who can give us what we need. You have everything: you have name, fame, money and property. But you have gone to the one Person who is infinitely richer than you and infinitely stronger than you for help. You have gone to the Highest, and you have taught me today that for everything we must go to the Highest. I came to you, but you gave me the lesson that you are nobody in comparison to God. You have taught me to go to the Highest, so I am going to the Highest.

"You do not owe me anything because you have given me the real illumination: always, for everything we have to go to God. To cure my disease I am going to God, and this lesson I got from you. Going to God for everything is the best way in our life. This lesson I have learned from you. You have everything, but you still need more things from God for your fulfilment. In my case, I have been praying for so many years, and I should have realised this. But this lesson I got from you, so you do not owe me anything.

"I helped you, true. For that you owed me something, but now you have illumined me by showing me that for everything we have to go to God. Now you do not owe me anything. Both of us are equal."

LTS 24. *God's Hour*

There was a hermit who was sincerity incarnate and purity incarnate. He lived in a small forest. From nearby villages people used to come and get inspiration and aspiration from him. They had tremendous love and devotion for him. He used to pray for hours and hours, and they used to watch him worshipping. They used to bring him the bare necessities: bananas, milk and other simple things that a truly spiritual person eats. A very simple life he led. This went on for ten or twelve years.

A young boy from a neighbouring village observed the hermit and said, "Ah, they all worship him. Let me go and be with him. Then people will worship me also."

The young boy had never prayed or meditated. He came to the hermit only to be worshipped. The hermit accepted him as his disciple. He was all the time wondering when people would start admiring him and worshipping him because he was now with the hermit.

A few months later, sincerity dawned on the young boy. He started praying and meditating very sincerely, and in this way he went on for two or three years. Then the hermit said, "I have to leave this place. I want to go away from here because here people are bothering me. They are disturbing my meditation and my peace. I have to realise God. If I stay here, I will not be able to realise God, so now I am going away."

The boy, who was now about 17 or 18, had become very sincere. He said, "Please, please take me. Master, I came here to be worshipped by others, but now you know how sincerely I am praying to God and praying to you for illumination."

The Master said, "No, no, you are too young. You pray here for a few years. Then, like me, you will also follow a higher spirituality. At that time you can go wherever God takes you."

The boy started praying and meditating very sincerely. Villagers continued coming, but they were not worshipping him. They were watching him to see whether he was sincere or not. Finally they were quite pleased.

In his possession the boy had only two loincloths. One day he saw that a rat had eaten into one of them. Then the poor fellow had only one loincloth left. When the villagers came to know about this, they gave him a very large supply of loincloths and food.

One of the villagers said, "Rats may come again and destroy your loincloths. The best thing is for you to have a cat. A cat will kill the rats."

So the villager brought the young hermit a cat. The hermit was very happy. But now that the hermit had a cat, the problem was that the cat needed milk. When the villagers brought milk for the hermit, he used to share it with the cat. But sometimes the villagers did not bring milk for him. When he did not have milk, he would go to the neighbouring villages and bring milk for the cat. This was what was going on, but the hermit was still praying sincerely.

Finally one of the villagers suggested, "If you have a cow, then you will not need anything. Why should you have to go anywhere for milk? If you have a cow, you can stay here and pray and meditate."

This particular villager was kind enough to bring the young hermit a cow. Now, the cow needed grass, but there was no grass nearby. The poor fellow had to take the cow to some neighbouring fields every day. The zamindar came to learn of this situation. He felt sad, because the hermit was a nice fellow. He was acting like an idiot, but he was very sincere. The zamindar gave the hermit a very large plot of grassy land, so he did not have to bring his cow anywhere else to graze. The hermit had admirers, and they used to take the cow to his field to graze.

Then a farmer came and said, "This is such a vast field! Allow me to plow this field, and I will be able to get a bumper crop."

The hermit allowed the farmer to plow the land and grow all kinds of grains. Then one of the villagers said, "You have everything, but who will take care of you?"

The hermit said, "True, now I am responsible for so many things."

The villager continued, "Who is going to take care of you when you have to manage your land and your cow and everything else? You should get married."

The zamindar had a beautiful daughter. Since the hermit was a very sincere man, the zamindar proposed that he marry his daughter. The zamindar said, "Do not worry, your spirituality will not descend."

So the hermit married the zamindar's daughter. In the course of time they had three or four children, and the children were all nice. Very, very happily the hermit was living.

Finally the hermit's Guru came back. He could not recognise his disciple's cottage. By this time it was no longer a cottage. It had become almost like a palace, and the grounds around it had beautiful gardens.

The Guru asked his disciple, "What has happened? What has happened? How could you fall like this?"

The hermit said, "You left me, so I did not know that all these things were temptations. One by one I accepted them, and people were advising me and saying that I would not fall. Now what has happened? What am I going to do?"

The Guru looked into the young man's eyes and saw that still he had sincerity in him. He said, "All right, are you ready to give up your wife, your children and all your property?"

The disciple said, "Immediately! I do not need them."

The Guru said, "Then come with me. Follow me."

The disciple followed his Master, even though his wife and children all became miserable that he had left them.

First the boy was curious. Then he became sincere. Then stupidity entered into him. Temptation came from all around him, and he did not realise it. Then again he was awakened. Again he accepted the spiritual life, and he no longer cared for his family. He left everything behind when God's Hour struck for him.

### LTS 25. *The unlucky baby*

A young couple were on their way to the temple early in the morning when they saw a very little baby crying in the street. Nobody knew who had left the baby there. They were very kindhearted people. The wife lifted up this baby and started showing it all her compassion and affection. The husband also liked the baby.

There was a note on the child saying, "Take this unlucky baby. One day you will become very lucky." The couple understood this to mean that they should take this helpless baby. They were full of compassion and affection, so they took the child home.

In a couple of hours the couple discovered that the baby was blind, and they felt miserable that the child could not see anything. They did not have any children of their own, so they said, "This is our fate." The baby was very cute, and they were showering their affection, sweetness and fondness on her.

For several years the husband and wife lavished their affection on the child. Then the couple had their own children. The wife gave birth to one son and one daughter. They were very, very beautiful and very affectionate children. Now the parents were so miserable. In a rush they had taken the little blind baby from the street, and now they could not do anything about it. It was too late.

The wife was so fond of her own children that she started neglecting the child they had adopted. Every day she became more miserable and she stopped paying any attention to the adopted girl. The husband also finally took his wife's side. He saw that his own children were so beautiful and so smart. Finally the husband and wife both wanted to get rid of the adopted child.

One day the husband became very, very brave. By that time the adopted child was five years old. He said, "Today I will take her to a desolate place. I will spend the night with the child, and then I will leave her there."

The wife was so nice to the adopted child in the beginning, but now she was only for her own children. She was so happy that they would be able to get rid of the adopted one.

The husband took the child, and they slept at a particular place where there were no people anywhere nearby. They had a good night's sleep. Early in the morning, he started to leave the child. Then his heart was making him feel miserable. He said, "This is a helpless child. What am I doing?"

Again he thought of his own children: "They are so sweet and beautiful. Who needs this one?"

When the day dawned, the child woke up and started crying, because she was not hearing her father's affectionate voice. When he was halfway back to his house, the father was feeling miserable: "Such an innocent child! So helpless! What have I done? What have I done? What have I done?"

His heart was killing him, so he went back. In the meantime, the child had started playing with some pebbles all by herself. When the father came back, he saw that in the child's palms there were five small diamonds. He was so thrilled! He grabbed the child and took her back home with the diamonds.

The note had said, "Take this unlucky baby. One day you will become very lucky." Now the father was so happy. When he brought back the child with the diamonds, his wife was also so happy. They had become rich overnight. Then both of the parents started treating this blind girl very, very nicely and affectionately because she had made them very rich.

So, this is what happens. Compassion comes, and then it disappears. Then affection rules. Finally compassion again comes forward. When compassion comes back, God's Grace descends.

### LTS 26. *Fear of the great occultist*

There was a villager who declared that he had tremendous occult power, and many people believed him. If you say you are an occultist, some will believe it and some will not believe it. If you say you are a doctor, some will believe it and some will not believe it. Then, if your powers do not work or if your medicine does not work, you are in trouble.

Some villagers had tremendous admiration for the so-called occultist, while others did not believe him. Many people hated him. When he went to the market, everybody used to give him anything that he wanted for free. Some people gave him things out of fear that something would happen, because they believed he was a great occultist, while others used to give him everything free out of admiration.

One day the occultist went to a shop to get something. This particular shop owner hated the occultist. He was not afraid of him, and at the same time he did not believe in his occult power. The occultist grabbed something, and the shop owner said, "You have to pay."

The occultist said, "No, I do not pay anybody. Do you not know who I am? I am the greatest occultist."

The man said, "I do not believe you."

"You do not believe me? All right, tonight you will see what happens inside your stomach. Tonight, I am telling you! Give me what I want!"

The shop owner said, "Nothing will happen. I will not give you anything!" Then the occultist went away.

When the shopkeeper went home, he told his wife and children what had happened. He was laughing. He said, "I tell you, I will be able to prove that he is a rogue. He does not have any occult power."

Unfortunately, the wife and children got frightened. They said, "Something will happen, something will happen!" The shopkeeper himself did not believe it, but the fear of his wife, his children and also some neighbours entered into him. Then the poor fellow started getting a severe pain in his stomach. Look what imaginary fear can do! He started vomiting, and he was suffering and suffering. The pain was only increasing hour by hour, even minute by minute.

His dear ones, friends and neighbours came to his side, and they were so furious. They said, "How could the occultist punish him like this?"

Then they all went to the great occultist. They said, "You are so bad! Just because he did not believe you, why did you punish him?"

The occultist said, "I told him that if he did not give me what I wanted, something bad would happen. Why did he not listen?"

The relatives, friends and neighbours got so furious that they were about to strike the so-called occultist and beat him up. Then the occultist cried out, "I do not have occult power, I do not have occult power!"

They asked, "Then how did it happen? If you do not have occult power, why is he suffering?"

The man said, "Believe me, believe me, I do not have occult power! I was telling lies all along. Some people believed me and some hated me, but I am telling you that I do not have occult power."

They said, "Then why is our friend suffering?"

The man said, "I am praying to God to cure him. I am praying to God!"

They said, "You do not have to pray to God. We are doing it." Then they thrashed him and threw him out of the village. Once he was out of the village, all the pain of the poor fellow who was suffering disappeared.

Look what fear can do! The man had no occult power. His claims were all false, but fear is like that. There is an Indian story in which the father tells his son, "Tigers kill people." A few hours later the older brother hangs a picture of a tiger on the wall. The little child asks, "What is it?" When the older brother tells him it is a tiger, the child gets frightened and faints just because he has heard that tigers kill people.

If an occultist tells you something and you do not believe it, then you are in trouble. Again, if you do believe it, you are also in trouble. The man did not believe in the occultist, but his wife and children got frightened. They said, "Something will happen!" All their fear entered into his stomach, and then he suffered like anything. The best thing is only to pray to God, and never to deal with occultists. Never go near occultists! Either out of fear or out of something else, you will be in serious trouble.

## LTS 27. *The absent-minded professor*

There was a history professor who was very good and very kind. The students all liked him. One very hot day he came to the class and taught the students. The students were very pleased. When the class was over, one by one the students left. Only one boy was still collecting his books. He was a little bit late in going out. He saw the professor desperately searching, searching and searching for something.

While going out, the boy asked, "Please tell me if anything is missing."

The professor said, "Yes, yes, I am missing something! Today it is so hot. You saw that I took off my jacket, I took off my tie and I even took off my wristwatch. Now I have got my jacket and I have got my tie, but my wristwatch is missing."

"Your wristwatch is missing?" the student asked.

"Yes," said the professor.

The boy said, "Sir, look at your right wrist."

"Oh," cried the professor, "It is there! How could it be? Every day I put the watch on my left wrist, but I forgot that today I put it on my right wrist. I was looking at my left hand, so I did not see it."

The boy started to go away, but the professor wanted to give the boy a ride home in his car. He said, "Today you have saved me from embarrassment."

"What kind of embarrassment?" asked the student.

The professor explained, "I would have gone home, and even at home I would have continued searching for my wristwatch, because I was not aware that it was on my right wrist. What an embarrassment!"

The boy said, "My house is very near, Professor."

The professor thanked the boy profusely, because at home also he would have searched for the wristwatch, in front of his family. He would have still missed his wristwatch at home, and he would have continued looking for it. Absent-minded people are like that!

### LTS 28. *The return ticket*

There were two friends. One of the friends was rich, and one was poor. The rich one said to the poor one, "I have only one daughter and no son. You know I have so much money and property. Please find a very handsome and wise young man for my daughter."

The friend said, "You are so miserly! Even if I find someone, you will not give your money to your son-in-law. You will not even give money to your daughter."

The rich one said, "What shall I do with my money if I do not give it to my own daughter?"

The poor one said, "No, you are so bad that you will ask people to put your money in your coffin when you die. You know that if you want to go to Heaven, you have to buy a ticket."

In a few months' time, the poor friend brought two young men to his rich friend and said, "Now you choose a husband for your daughter. I have brought these two young men. It is up to you to make the choice."

The two young men had come together by train from a distant village. One of them had bought only a one-way ticket and the other one had bought a round-trip ticket. The man asked them several questions, and then he decided whom to choose. He said to the fellow who had bought only a one-way ticket, "You go home. I do not need you."

This fellow said to his friend, "I have to go now. He has chosen you. Since you are not going back, can you not give me your ticket? Mine was only a one-way ticket, whereas yours is round-trip. Can you give me the other part of your ticket so that I can go home happily?"

Then the rich man said, "No, no, I have changed my mind!" He said to the second young man, "You go home with your round-trip ticket."

Then he asked the first young man, "Why did you buy a one-way ticket?"

The clever young man said, "I knew that if you chose my friend and I had to go back, I would be able to ask my friend to give me his return ticket. Again, if you chose me, I would not need to buy another ticket."

The rich man immediately said, "You are the right person to marry my daughter!"

### LTS 29. *God wants everybody to be happy*

There were two friends. As always, their friendship was founded on rivalry. One of the friends was rich and one was poor. Their friendship was good on the outer level, but inwardly the poor one was jealous of the rich one. The rich one was also jealous of the poor one because the poor one had many, many good qualities which the rich one did not have. Both of them were jealous of each other.

One day the rich friend wanted to go to the market to buy a horse. The poor one said, "You do not have intelligence! You will not be able to buy a horse. I tell you, when you go there, you will be puzzled, and you will not be able to buy a horse. You do not have a brain! They will give you a useless horse, and you will only waste your money."

The rich one said, "All right, let me see my fate."

He went to the market and bought a very, very nice-looking, smart horse. While he was bringing the horse back home, the zamindar saw the horse. The zamindar said, "This is such a beautiful and strong horse. How much did you buy it for?"

The man said, "I bought it for 600 rupees."

The zamindar exclaimed, "For only 600 rupees you bought this horse? I like him so much! You have to give the horse to me for 1,000 rupees."

"But I like the horse," the man said.

"No, I am the zamindar. You have to sell him to me."

So the man sold the horse to the zamindar for 1,000 rupees and went back home. Then the friend came to his house and said, "You see, I was right! Where is your horse?"

The rich man said, "I could not buy one."

The friend, "I told you, you idiot, that you should have taken me along when you went to buy the horse!"

The poor friend was so happy because his prediction was right. He thought that the rich friend could not buy a horse because he had no brain. The rich friend remained absolutely silent. Finally, the rich one said, "You are right, you are right." But he knew that he had made 400 rupees profit. In this way God made both friends happy. The poor one thought that the rich one was an idiot, and therefore he could not buy a horse. The rich one was actually so smart that he got 400 rupees' profit. The poor one, who was jealous, was so happy that his friend had not succeeded in buying a horse, and the rich one was happy because he had made so much profit. In this way both of them became happy. God wants everybody to be happy.

### LTS 30. *The house alarm*

A young man got a job as an assistant to a thief. The young man wanted to learn how to commit theft.

The old thief said, "If you do well, I will give you lots of money and you will become very, very rich. Then you can give up this profession."

The young man said, "That is what I want. I do not want to commit theft all my life. I want to make some money and then give up stealing."

The older man said, "That is fine. You can do that."

The first day the boss said, "Go to this particular house and break in. That family is very, very rich, but be careful! If you find that they are awake, then you have to be extremely careful. Very, very carefully you will go."

The young thief went to the house. As soon as he entered into the house, the alarm went off, and he was caught and badly thrashed. Then he went back to his boss absolutely miserable. The boss asked, "How did this happen? Did you not hear the alarm?"

The young man said, "Yes, I heard the alarm."

The boss asked, "Then why did you not run away?"

The young man said, "I thought the alarm was meant to wake them up, and not to catch me! I thought it was an alarm clock. You told me to steal, so I went there to steal. I was sure that the alarm was meant for them, not for me. So I entered into the house and I was caught."

## LTS 31. *The storm*

A husband and wife had a small child only three or four years old. The parents were very, very happy with this beautiful little child.

One day the father was engrossed in reading a novel. He was getting so much joy from the story. All of a sudden the child started crying. The mother was ironing clothes, cooking and doing all kinds of work in the house, so she was unable to pay attention to the child.

The wife said to the husband, "Please, please take care of our child. He is bored. You are just reading, but I am working. I am unable to pay any attention to him. At least take him out for a few minutes. Perhaps the fresh air and the sun will do him good."

The husband was not listening. He was still reading, reading and reading. Then the child started crying very loudly. The wife said, "Please take him out! I am doing all this work. You are doing nothing! You are just reading."

The husband said, "What? How can you ask me to take him outside? It is thundering and raining heavily. A storm is raging, and you are asking me to take our child outside? He is our only child. He will fall sick and die. Do you want our child to be killed in this storm? Can you not see? The trees are all trembling. Are you a fool? At a time like this I have to take our only child outside?"

The wife said, "All right." Then she took the child outside. The sun was shining brightly. The mother stayed outside with the child for a few minutes until he became very calm and quiet. Then she brought the child back inside.

The father said, "How could you take our child outside when it is raining so heavily? Such a storm is raging!"

The mother said, "You idiot! Where is the storm?"

The father said, "I can prove that it is raining heavily outside."

Then he showed her the book. He said, "It is written here." In the novel it said that it was raining very heavily. He showed it to his wife to prove that the weather outside was so bad. That was why he did not take the child outside.

### LTS 32. *The zamindar's temple*

There was an honest, simple man. Everybody liked him because of his honesty. One day his house was robbed. He was very, very sad. But because he was very honest, his friends gave him money, clothes and everything else that he could possibly need. His friends were so kind to him that he soon had much more than he had originally lost.

One of the honest man's friends, who was quite rich, became very, very jealous. He said, "Let me also tell people that my house has been robbed."

That night he took his belongings outside his house, dug a hole and buried all his valuables, money and expensive things under the ground. Then he started crying that his house had been robbed. But because he was so rich, people were not showing any interest. He was not a good man, whereas the first one was a really good man. Nobody gave him any money, but he kept on crying and crying as if he had lost everything.

Then he did not know what to do. People were all watching him. He was miserable. He was only waiting for the day when he could dig up his valuables. He said, "Since my friends are not giving me anything, I will bring everything back into the house."

Now it happened that the zamindar wanted to build a temple. The zamindar said, "I have done many, many bad things in my life. Now I have to build a temple so people can come and worship. I will also go there to worship."

Since the zamindar could do anything he wanted to do, he gave some money to the rich man and said, "I am buying this plot of land." The rich man was totally lost. What could he do?

The zamindar wanted to build the temple immediately, so he started digging. All of a sudden he found so much money! The money that he had given to the rich man was nothing in comparison.

The zamindar said, "Look at this! Already God is so kind to me. God knows that this temple is for Him. I am building a temple, so God is giving me this gift because I am doing such a good thing."

The zamindar took away all the valuables. He felt that God was so pleased with him because he was building a temple for people to worship. The zamindar got the money and the rich fellow who wanted to fool people lost everything. So if you want to fool people, you also can be fooled.

### LTS 33. *The adopted son*

There were two brothers who lived in two different villages. The two brothers were very close to each other. One day the younger brother came to visit the older brother. He saw that the older brother had adopted a little boy. He said, "What have you done? Have you not heard that adopted children always turn out to be very bad? People say that they destroy the whole family."

Because the older brother did not have any children of his own, he had adopted this child. The older brother said, "No, I think my case will be an exception."

The younger brother said, "There is no exception."

A few days later the younger brother went home. The older brother was lavishing and lavishing affection and compassion on his adopted son, treating him absolutely like a prince. And every day the son was becoming more and more notorious in every way.

One day the elder brother decided he would visit his younger brother. When he was almost at his place, the older brother saw that the younger brother was now living in a very small house. The older brother said to the younger brother, "What are you doing here? You had such a big house. What happened?"

The younger brother said, "My son is so greedy! He took all my money and everything that I had. Then he kicked me out, so I am staying in this small house. You see, even my own son has misbehaved so badly. I cannot imagine how much you will suffer since you adopted a son. My own son has thrown me out of the house, and he has taken all my property. He is enjoying his own life with his wife and children. So I can scarcely imagine how much you will suffer!"

The older brother said, "No, no, I am not suffering at all."

The younger brother said, "How is it that you are not suffering?"

The elder brother said, "I was sick for quite a few days. Then my adopted son did something so good."

"What did he do?"

"He gave me poison, and I died. Now I am so happy in Heaven. My adopted son was torturing me like anything. Then, when I fell sick, he wanted to get all my money and all my property, so he put poison in my food and I died. Now I am so happy!"

How could this happen? The subtle body of the elder brother had come to visit the younger brother, taking exactly the same form as the physical body. Every day the adopted son had been torturing his father. Finally, the adopted son had given him poison and killed him. The father was so happy in Heaven, whereas on earth he had been absolutely miserable.

# LIFE'S BLEEDING TEARS AND FLYING SMILES

## BOOK 3

LTS 34. *One rogue punishes another rogue*

There was a young man whose father, grandfather and great-grandfather were all thieves. Everybody in his family was a thief, save him. He did not want to be a thief. He said, "I have no desire to be a thief. I want to be an honest man."

His father said, "You fool! Just once if you commit a theft, you will get so much money. Then for the rest of your life you will not have to worry. Otherwise you will have to work eight hours a day for years and years. You can see that in our family, we do not work. Only a few times we have stolen money and valuables from people. Now we are so rich."

The son said, "No, no, I do not want to steal even once in my life. It is not good. I want to pray to God and I want to be happy in a different way. I do not need this material wealth."

The father said, "You have to steal!"

They had a fight, and then the son left the father. The son went out to look for a proper job. One man who was quite rich asked the son, "Do you want to work for me?"

The young man said, "Yes, I will work for you."

The young man did not know that this rich man was another thief. The rich man said, "Look, now that you are working for me, I will make you very, very rich in a few days' time if you listen to me."

The young man innocently said, "Yes, I will be happy to do as you say."

The rich man said, "I want to have you as my assistant. I will teach you how to rob people and steal things."

The young man said, "O my God! My father is in that profession!"

"What is your father's name?" the rich man asked. When the young man told him, the rich man said, "You are the son of that thief? That means you are another rogue! I am sure you have come here to do something bad, to play a trick on me, and you are planning to steal my money!"

The rich man remained silent for a minute. Then he said, "I will see if you are an honest man or not. I will examine you before I throw you out. Today I am not going to steal. Today I am going to the market. I will buy two small diamonds, and then I will see what I can do with these diamonds."

When the rich man went to the market to buy the diamonds, he came upon his best friend and worst rival, who was another rogue. This fellow had more money, so he bought four diamonds. The first rich man did not have enough money to buy four diamonds, so he bought only two.

He came back and said to his new assistant, "Look here, I am going to my friend's place. You will come with me. I will enter into a long conversation with him. First I will show him the two diamonds that I bought, and then I will ask him to show me the four that he bought. When we are deep into our marathon conversation, in a very tricky way you will take away those four diamonds of his."

"I will?" cried the young man.

The rich man said, "You have to do it. Otherwise, I will tell the whole world that you came to me with a big plan. You are such a bad fellow! I know your father is smarter than I am. He has sent you here to play a trick on me. I will punish you!"

The young man said, "I am not going to carry out your order. I am going away."

The rich man said, "No, you have to stay."

The young man said, "No, I am resigning. I have not stolen anything, so if you want to, you can dismiss me for disobeying you."

The young man went to the fellow who had bought the four diamonds and narrated the whole story. He said to him, "Look, this is what he himself told me he will do, so be careful!"

This smart man said, "All right, I will teach him a lesson."

The young fellow went away and again started looking for a job. Alas, wherever he went, he had such bad luck.

A few days later, the man who had bought the four diamonds went to his rival and said, "We two are such good friends. I will now be going to visit some other friends for two or three weeks. Kindly keep these four diamonds for me. When I come back, please return them to me. You see, I have sealed them inside this box. If you would like to have a commission from me for doing this service, I will gladly give it."

The first rogue said, "Commission? How can I take money from you? We are such good friends! I will keep this box safe. You take your time and come back whenever you like."

The second rich man said, "I have decided that since you will keep these diamonds so safe, I will definitely give you some money when I come back. At that time, please take money from me. If I were to give these diamonds to somebody else for safekeeping, they would definitely be stolen. God knows what any other person would do to me."

After three or four weeks, the second rogue came back and asked for his diamonds. The one who was keeping the diamonds said, "Since you are taking them away, can I not see them just once?"

The man said, "Certainly you can see them. Let us open the box."

When the fellow who had kept the diamonds opened the box, he found that there were only four pieces of glass inside. He said to the second rogue, "You fooled me! I kept this box so safe for you. Why did you do this?"

The second rogue said, "What was in your mind originally? What did you tell that young man? You said that you would bring him with you to my place, and we would enter into a marathon conversation. Then you wanted him to steal the diamonds. He came and told me everything! That is why I fooled you."

This is how the second rogue exposed the first rogue.

### LTS 35. *Punishment pays*

A father and mother were both extremely fond of their child, who was only six years old. They were a very, very happy family. One day the child did something wrong and the father was very upset, so he gave the child a smart slap. Then the child cried and the father felt absolutely miserable. The father tried to console the child by giving him four rupees.

When the child got the money, he started crying more loudly and pitifully. The father said, "Why are you crying? I gave you a slap, but now I am consoling you. I will not slap you any more. Why are you still crying?"

The son said, "I am crying more powerfully and pitifully because I have to ask you something."

"What do you have to ask me?" the father said.

The son said, "Will you promise me that each time you give me a slap, you will increase the amount of money you give me?"

"What?" cried the father.

The son said, "I did something wrong, and you gave me a slap. Now I will do something even worse. Each time I do something worse, will you not give me another slap and more money?"

The father said, "What are you saying?"

The son said, "I want to be punished by you every time I do something wrong. Each time my crime will be worse, so you can give me a harder slap if you wish. I will not mind at all. But you have to give me a larger amount of money, too."

The father said, "What kind of son do I have? He is ready to be slapped for money. Why did I make the mistake of giving him money the first time? Each time he wants the slap to be harder. He does not mind being slapped if he receives a larger amount of money!"

LTS 36. *Thief-husband and thief-wife*

One day a husband brought home a most expensive sari for his wife. The wife said, "Ah, this is so beautiful! I have never seen this kind of sari. Where did you buy it? How could you afford to spend so much money?"

The husband said, "You know, I steal things."

The wife said, "You steal? How can it be?"

The husband said, "I stole this particular sari from the market. I went to a shop and I stole it."

The wife said, "Do I have to keep a stolen sari?" After a few moments, she smiled at her husband and said, "Never mind! I am so proud of you. You are such a smart thief. You know, I also steal."

The husband said, "You steal? What have you stolen?"

The wife explained that she had stolen so many things. The husband stole only at night. The poor fellow worked the whole day and at night he stole simple things. But the wife used to steal during the day when everybody went out. She would invite some neighbourhood friends to her place and cook for them. Then she would tell them, "I am just going to the market to buy more vegetables and other supplies because I want to make a better meal. Kindly stay here."

While her friends were at her house, first she used to go to the market and buy the supplies she had mentioned. Then she would go to the homes of her friends who were visiting her and steal their valuable things. But she did not bring the things to her house. She used to hide them in another place. Then she would bring home the vegetables and other things from the market.

On this particular occasion, the wife showed her husband some of the things that she had stolen over the years. The husband could not believe it.

Then the wife said, "You are a thief and I am a thief. It is not good for us to stay for a long time in one place. We should move."

From then on, every three or four months they would move from one place to another. They accumulated so many things. Four or five times they moved to different places. In each place, the wife invited people to come to her house to eat. The people who were invited felt so sad that this nice lady was moving away, because she would always welcome her neighbours to come and eat. Then, when they went home, they found that their jewels and other things were missing. But they did not blame the wife because she had gone to the market, and she had brought back more vegetables. Nobody could catch her.

As soon as the husband and wife came to a new village, they would go to the neighbours and start talking to them. They said that they were so happy to come to a new place, and they wanted to establish friendship with their neighbours. So it went on.

After some time, instead of stealing during the day, the husband and wife started stealing in the evening. Of the two, the wife was the smarter. They would invite some neighbours, and both the husband and wife would entertain them. Then, all of a sudden, the wife would be missing. The guests would think that the wife had gone to attend to some urgent matter. After some time, the wife would come back.

One time the wife went to a particular house to steal things, but she was unable to break open the door. She was very smart and she tried in so many ways, but she was unsuccessful. Then she said, "Since I have taken the trouble of coming here, let me at least take some ripe mangoes." She had carried a lantern with her, so she was able to see mangoes in a tree. She climbed up the tree and plucked quite a few nice mangoes.

One of the neighbour's sons was very alert, and he saw what happened. He was watching everything from the window of his house. When the wife went back home, she put the mangoes in a room where nobody would see them. The guests were all eating. Then all of a sudden, the neighbour's son came to the door. The wife said, "What are you doing here at this hour?"

The husband continued, "We have not invited you. Why did you come?"

The son said, "I do not need an invitation."

They said, "What? How is it that you do not need an invitation?"

The son said, "I came here to give these people a message."

All the neighbours stopped eating and asked him, "What are you doing here?"

The young man pointed at the wife and shouted, "She is a thief!"

They said, "How can it be?"

He said, "She has stolen mangoes from your garden. I saw her."

The neighbours were extremely shocked. Then they said, "All right, let us see if she has really stolen these things."

Then the neighbours ransacked the whole house. In one corner of a small room the couple had hidden all their stolen goods. The neighbours found so many things of theirs that had been stolen, and they also found things that they knew this couple could not afford. Why were the husband and wife hiding all these things? It could only be because they were stolen goods.

The neighbours thrashed the husband and wife mercilessly. Then these two stopped stealing. They gave up stealing altogether. They said, "We will not do it any more! It is just not worth it." From then on, they began to lead better lives.

LTS 37. *Lord Indra and his consort*

A good man and a bad man were neighbours. One day the bad man said to the good man, "You have to develop artistic qualities. You have to go to some good clubs and learn about culture, philosophy, spirituality and many other things."

The good man was hesitant. He said, "No, no. For me it is better to stay at home and read religious and spiritual books."

The bad man said, "At least come to my club once and see what it is like. You are bound to learn quite a few things that are necessary in human life."

So the good man agreed, and together they went to a club. They read aloud from religious and spiritual books and discussed all kinds of things. After the discussion, they started drinking. They had such wonderful cultural, religious, spiritual and philosophical discussions, and then they started drinking!

When the good man came home, his wife could not believe her eyes. She could not recognise her husband. She cried, "What have you done? What have you done? I cannot recognise you!"

He said, "I have drunk wine."

The wife became furious. "How could you do this?" she shouted.

The husband said, "My friend told me it is good. Lord Indra used to drink nectar. His nectar and our wine are the same thing. We do not have nectar, but we do have wine. It is the same thing."

The wife was extremely mad. "No, no, you cannot drink! You must not drink!"

The man said, "All right, I promise not to drink any more."

Alas, once you drink wine, you are caught. When his neighbour again invited him to go to the club, the man said, "My wife will be furious. What am I going to do?"

The friend asked, "Tell me frankly, did you enjoy it?"

"Yes, I enjoyed it, but now I will have a fight at home. I will have a war!"

The neighbour said, "No, no, no, this time nothing will happen. You just come with me. I assure you, nothing will happen."

The good man went to the club again. He enjoyed philosophical, spiritual and all other kinds of discussion. When he came back home with his friend, heavily drunk, his wife was waiting. She said, "You promised not to do this!" Then she announced that she wanted to leave him.

The good man said, "No, this time my promise is definitely sincere. I will never, never go there again!"

The wife said, "Why did you tell me a lie? You said last time that you would never go there again!"

He said, "But even Lord Indra himself told many lies."

She said, "So are you another Indra that you can lie to your heart's content?"

The husband said, "Indra told many, many, many lies, and Indra even stole a cow. I have never stolen anything, so Indra went one step ahead of me. Indra was a thief, whereas I am only a liar. Indra has taught us how to tell lies. If Indra, the cosmic god, can tell lies, what is wrong with a human being telling lies?"

The following day was a holiday for the husband, so he did not go to work. His wife was really devoted to him. Every morning she would cook breakfast for the husband. Then she would cook lunch and dinner. Usually she cooked breakfast around eight o'clock in the morning. But on this particular day it became eleven o'clock and then twelve o'clock, and the wife still had not made breakfast. What was she doing? She was sewing a garment for herself. Finally the husband asked their son to tell his mother that it was getting very late and he was extremely hungry.

The mother said to the son, "Please, please, my son, my darling, do not be involved in our fight. Please only watch and enjoy what is going on."

The son said, "I do not want to be involved in your quarrel and fight, Mother. You please take care of it."

Soon it became one o'clock and then two o'clock. Still the wife was not giving the husband any food, and he was getting furious. Finally he said, "What kind of wife are you?"

The wife said, "You have become another Indra, so am I not Sachi, Indra's wife? Since you are Indra, definitely I am Sachi. Who can tell me that Sachi ever cooked? She had many, many servants and maids to cook for her. Now you should get some maids, because I cannot cook any more. I am Sachi now. I will do whatever I want to do. Since you have become another Indra, you can have some maids to serve you. You can have some cooks to prepare your food. Let them cook for you, because from now on I will do whatever I want to do. I am a queen, after all. Indra was a king, and a king has to have cooks and all kinds of servants. I am a queen, so I will do whatever I like. I am not going to cook for you any more."

The man was so sad and disturbed to hear his wife's words. He said, "I will never, never go with my friend to that club again. I will remain really devoted and faithful to you. This is absolutely my solemn promise."

The son was overjoyed that his parents had become reconciled. From that day on, the wife cooked and did everything for the husband as usual, and the husband kept his promise. He did not go to that club any more. This was how the wife taught her husband a lesson.

## LTS 38. *What ambition can do!*

A village priest was very proud of himself because he was conversant with the shastras and with countless religious books. He had read all the spiritual scriptures. In his own village and all the nearby villages he was the supreme authority. He had a big family, and everybody was very good to him because he was a nice man. All the villagers respected him, admired him and adored him. Quite often they offered him presents because he had brought such prestige to their village.

One day the news came that the king wanted to appoint a new priest for the royal family, and that the king himself would make the choice. This particular priest said, "Here in my own village I am appreciated and admired, but I am eager to have a better position. I am sure that the king will definitely select me because I am the greatest scholar. When it is a matter of religion and spirituality, I have no equal. Once I go to the king's palace, I shall never come back here again."

The priest sold his house, and he and his wife and children set out for the king's palace. They were so happy that they would be going to live in the king's palace. The whole family believed that the king would definitely select that priest. The priest himself was absolutely confident that the king would choose him. Having sold everything they owned, now the family had enough money for the journey.

Alas, on the very day they arrived at the king's palace, the king's youngest son passed away. The king was utterly grief-stricken. He said, "I shall never be able to overcome this loss."

Previously the king had wanted to have his own priest and to build a very big temple that would be most beautiful, extremely wonderful and supremely glorious. On that day, though, the king took an oath that as long as he continued to suffer from the loss of his youngest son, he would not build a temple and he did not need a personal priest. So the king did not appoint the priest who had come to see him. The king said, "I do not need a priest. If ever I erect a temple, then I will need a priest. At that time I will invite you to come here. I will examine you, and I will tell you where you stand."

So the great scholar had to go back to his village, but now he had no home! Something more, when he left, he was replaced by somebody else. Now those people who loved him, appreciated him and admired him once upon a time no longer cared for him. They said, "Because of your ambition, you deserted us. We do not need you any more. Our new priest is good enough for us."

So the priest lost his job and he did not get it back. He lost his house and his property, and he became poor and miserable. This was the reward of his ambition.

### LTS 39. *What greed can do!*

There was a very, very rich man. As he was rich, even so was he miserly. His wealth and his stinginess went together. He had an only daughter, a very beautiful girl. He did not want to spend any money on his daughter's marriage. His daughter and his wife liked a particular boy who was very nice and well-educated, but the rich man did not want to give his daughter to this fellow. He was waiting for someone who would give him thousands of rupees for permission to marry his daughter. He was not ready even to buy two garlands for his daughter and his future son-in-law. He did not want to part with even five rupees.

One day the rich man went to the market to buy groceries. He saw some of his friends inside a bakery. They were eating sweets, especially *ladoo,* and they were so happy and so thrilled. The rich man was dying to have some ladoo, but he did not want to spend any money. He was hoping that one of his friends would be kindhearted enough to give him some ladoo, but no one offered him any sweets. He was so miserable. He was dying to eat some ladoo because, according to his friends, it tasted so good.

Finally, the rich man decided that he would buy the ingredients and make the ladoo himself. He went to a shop and bought everything that is needed to make ladoo.

Then the rich man said to himself, "If I make the ladoo at home, I shall have to share it with my wife and daughter." He did not want to do that. He said, "I will tell my wife that I have an urgent piece of business tomorrow, and I will come home only late at night. I will say that they should not wait for me. They should eat without me, and I will come back in the evening."

He took the ingredients and went quite far from his home. Then he started making ladoo. He was so happy because his preparation was becoming very tasty. Then two hooligans happened to pass by. They said, "What are you doing here? This is our property!"

The hooligans thrashed him, and right in front of him they ate all the sweets he had made! Then he was so miserable. He could not enjoy any of his own preparation. He went home very sad.

When he came home, the rich man thought that, seeing his miserable face, his family would show him sympathy. Instead, his wife and daughter were in the seventh Heaven of delight. He said, "I am miserable. How can you be so happy?"

He did not tell them why he was miserable, but they said, "We can tell you why we are so happy."

When the rich man had gone away for the whole day, the wife had immediately arranged for their daughter to get married. On that very day she and the young man got married. They were so happy that they were in the seventh Heaven of delight.

So, for a little ladoo, the rich man had to give away his daughter. His daughter was happy, but the poor fellow did not get any money from the marriage, and he could not even eat his own ladoo preparation.

Look what greed can do! Greed meets with such unbearable punishment. If you are miserly, then your suffering never, never ends. If you lead a good life, eventually you will get your due reward.

### LTS 40. *The daughter-in-law's wisdom*

This is a story about a good father who had a bad son and a wise daughter-in-law. The father was a religious man. He and his wife had only one son. The son was doing well in his studies, so the father wanted the son to study in the town. Although he was not rich, as a villager he had some land, so he sold a plot of land to pay for his son's education. His son studied and studied and studied and then did well in his examination. He became a scholar and afterwards he became very, very rich.

Then the father wanted the son to get married. Once again the father was ready to sell his property so that his son could be happy, happier, happiest.

Now the son became very happy and very rich and prosperous. He lived in the town, while the poor father and his wife remained in the village. Eventually the son got married and he and his wife had a child. When the time came, the son was able to send the child to a good private school because he was now very rich. In every way the son was doing well. Then, from the village, news came that his father was very, very sick. But the ungrateful son did not want to go to see his father. He said, "Who cares what happens to my father? He is an old man and his time has come. It will be a waste of time for me to go and see him."

In the village, the mother was miserable that she and her husband had spent so much money and sold their property for the higher education of their son, and the son had become such a rogue. The son never came to see them.

Finally the father died. Even then, the son did not come from the town to observe his father's obsequies. The poor mother was left with only the neighbours to help her perform the funeral rites. Then the mother was all alone.

In the course of time, the rich son wanted his own son to get a higher education. But his wife said, "Now look here. I do not want our son to have a higher education. He has earned his high school diploma. That is enough. Now he should look for a job."

The husband said, "My son should get an ordinary job? No, no! He has to be well educated! He has to be a great scholar like me. He has to become very rich. At this time if he gives up his studies, if he no longer goes to school, he will have no future."

The wife pleaded, "Can you not see what you have done to your father? Your father did so much for you, but you did not care for him at all. Then he became old and he died. Will our son also not behave like you? He will become very well educated, rich and prosperous. Then, when you become old, he will do the same to you as you did to your father. He will live with his own wife and son very happily, and he will not pay any attention to you. Can you not learn from your behaviour? What you have done to your father, your son will also do to you."

After listening to his wife's words, the rich man felt some pangs in his heart. He agreed to go to the village with his wife to see his mother. When he set eyes on his poor, old mother, he began crying and crying. His mother told him, "Son, at last you have come! Better late than never. Finally some wisdom has dawned in your life."

Then the mother embraced her daughter-in-law and said, "You have so much wisdom! Now you have given wisdom to my son. Otherwise, my son would have suffered the same fate as his own father did when he became old. My son would also have suffered at the hands of his own son."

The mother thanked her daughter-in-law profusely for taking care of her grandson's future life. Indeed, this wise daughter-in-law had saved the whole family.

### LTS 41. *The king and the washerman*

There was a very kindhearted king. Everybody was pleased with him and grateful to be in his kingdom. Whoever worked for the king was very happy with him, and the king was also happy with his subjects.

The king had a special washerman. This washerman used to collect clothes from the king's palace during the day, and at night he used to wash them. The following morning he would bring a fresh supply of clothes for the king. The king was very, very satisfied with him.

The washerman had a big family, and the king gave him an adequate salary. But at night, after washing the garments, this audacious fellow used to put on some of the king's garments and walk around in the street to show off. People used to think that he belonged to a royal family. They would salute him, and he would be bloated with tremendous pride and joy. Then again he would wash and iron the garments very nicely and bring them back to the king the next day.

One day the king said, "Let me see if my people are really happy in my kingdom. Let me see what kind of life they are leading — if they are thieves, vagabonds, hooligans or good, simple people." So he went out of the palace in the guise of a mendicant. All of a sudden he saw his own palace washerman parading along the street in a splendid outfit. The king pretended he did not see this fellow and started walking away.

The washerman screamed, "Hey! Everybody shows me respect. What are you doing? Can you not see that I come of a royal family?"

The mendicant-king said, "Who cares?"

The washerman cried, "Who cares? I will punish you! Can you not see I am royalty?"

When the washerman came closer to the mendicant, he saw that it was the king. Then he realised what he had said. Desperately he caught hold of the king's feet and started crying and crying, "Forgive me, forgive me, forgive me! I have been doing this at night all along. Then I wash and iron your clothes and take them back to you."

The king laughed and laughed and laughed. What could he do with this fellow?

### LTS 42. *The three hooligans and the lamb*

There were three very, very bad hooligans who had settled in a nice village. The hooligans began torturing the villagers ruthlessly. Nobody could go anywhere. Not only at night, but in the daytime also, if the hooligans happened to see anyone, they would harass that person. They did not care whether it was day or night.

One villager had a lamb. He wanted to bathe in a pond, so he tied the lamb to a tree. He had a long bath and he was very, very pleased. But when he came out of the pond, he saw that his lamb was missing. While he was bathing, he had seen those three bad fellows roaming around. He had thought that since his lamb was tied to a tree, nothing would happen. But in fact, those three had untied the lamb and taken it home. Then they cooked it and ate it.

The owner suspected those three bad people because he had seen them while he was in the water. He went to the hooligans' place and confronted them. They told him, "We had nothing to do with your lamb."

Naturally the owner could not find the lamb, because they had cooked it and eaten it. So the owner went to the village zamindar and made a serious complaint that these three hooligans had taken his lamb.

The zamindar asked, "Where is the proof?"

The hooligans said, "There is no proof. If we had taken the lamb, then it would have been at our place. But it is not there."

The villager was so miserable that he had lost his lamb. The zamindar said, "This man was telling me that the lamb was near a pond, and it was tied to a tree."

One of the hooligans said, "Can you imagine? We did not go near that pond! We did not even see a pond. Where was the pond? We did not go near a tree either."

The zamindar pretended that he was convinced that the three hooligans had not gone near the pond. The other two hooligans were very happy that the first one had been able to convince the zamindar. Then the zamindar said, "Near the pond there was a tree. Did you see that tree?"

The second hooligan said, "We did not see a pond. We were never near a tree. How can this fellow say such things? There was no tree, there was no pond, and we definitely did not see his lamb."

Both the first and second hooligans seemed to have convinced the zamindar. Then the zamindar asked the man who had lost his lamb, "Now tell me how many days ago this happened."

The man said, "It happened three days ago."

The zamindar said, "Today is Tuesday. That means it was on Saturday. At what time do you think it all happened?"

The man said, "It was in the evening. I was going to the pond to take a bath. It was Saturday evening."

The zamindar said to the third hooligan, "Tell me, what were you doing on Saturday evening?"

The hooligan said, "Saturday evening? In our village there is no Saturday, so how could we do anything on that day?"

In this way the zamindar caught the three hooligans. He said, "If there is no Saturday, then you should have one!"

Then he asked his people to thrash the three hooligans and put them into jail. But first the zamindar fined the hooligans fifty rupees so that the poor villager who had lost his lamb could buy another one.

### LTS 43. *The chase*

There was a jeweller who was very, very bad. He had a worker who was very nice. This worker asked the jeweller if he would give him a small loan.

"Loan?" said the jeweller. "I never give loans."

The man said, "Then I am not going to work for you any more because I need some money for my daughter's marriage. I am a sincere worker. If you do not give me a loan, I shall go away."

The jeweller wanted this fellow to continue working, so he said, "I will tell the whole world that you have stolen jewellery from my shop."

The worker cried, "I have stolen jewellery?"

He was so disgusted that he started running away. The jeweller chased him. They passed by an old man who was selling some fruits. The worker ran to a nearby house and climbed up on the roof. The jeweller ran after him. Suddenly the worker fell down from the roof on top of the old man, and the old man was badly injured. Then the old man's son started chasing the worker. The poor worker was an innocent fellow. He was only running away from the jeweller. But now there were two people chasing him. The fellow was running and running, although he had not stolen anything.

As he was running, the worker happened to see a camel. He wanted some protection because he was losing his balance. He reached for the camel's tail, but the camel had no tail. The jeweller and the son of the old man were very near him. Now the owner of the camel saw him and also started chasing him. So the three of them were all chasing the innocent man.

The man ran and ran and ran until finally he dashed against a house. Alas, it happened to be the zamindar's house. The zamindar was having breakfast with his wife and children. They were in the seventh Heaven of delight. But the wife got frightened when she saw so many people running towards their house, and she fainted.

The innocent man said, "Help! Save me, save me!"

The jeweller came up to the zamindar and said, "He has stolen my jewellery!"

The zamindar said, "This fellow has frightened me. I see that you have been chasing him. First give me one hundred rupees. Then only will I take up your case."

The jeweller gave him one hundred rupees. Then the second fellow came up to the zamindar and said, "My father was badly hurt by this man. What kind of punishment will you give him?"

The zamindar said, "Now, you go to your father's place. This fellow will stand exactly where your father was standing. Then you go on top of the roof, and from there you will jump on top of him." The son would jump onto the innocent man, and then he would injure the poor fellow the way the father had been injured when the man was running away. The zamindar told him, "Go and jump on him! This is my judgement."

The son said, "But I will break my legs!"

The zamindar said, "Why? When he jumped on your father, your father's legs were broken, but nothing happened to this man. In the same way you will go up to the roof and jump down on him."

The son said, "Oh, I do not want to do that!"

Then the third man came up to the zamindar with his camel. The zamindar asked, "What is wrong with you? And why is there no tail on your camel?"

The man said, "There is nothing wrong with me or with my camel. I was only watching the situation."

The zamindar said, "But you also ran."

The man said, "I was curious to see what was happening. Nothing has happened to my camel. My camel never had a tail. I was not actually chasing this man. I was just curious to see what was happening and why they were running."

In this way the innocent man escaped the zamindar's punishment.

### LTS 44. *The pond*

There was no rain for a long time, so a small village had run short of water. The villagers were suffering from the scarcity of water. The king came to know of it, and he ordered his minister to create a pond. The minister then ordered his assistant to make a pond. The assistant in turn asked his assistant, and that assistant asked his own assistant. Finally, one of the workers in the village was ordered to dig a pond and then there was plenty of water.

The king wanted to see if the pond was in good condition and if it was full of water. Others all followed the king to see the pond. The king was very, very pleased inwardly, but outwardly he said, "This is a very bad job. This pond is not good at all." The king showed great displeasure. He said, "The water will one day run out of the pond." So many defects the king found in the pond.

Then the king became angry with his minister. He said, "Now, minister, tell me what happened. I gave you a job, and you did not do it satisfactorily."

The minister pointed to his assistant and said, "Your Majesty, I asked him to do it because I was very busy."

The minister's assistant pointed to his own assistant and said, "I asked him to do it because I was very busy. I have so much to do."

Like that it went on and on. Everybody was blaming his subordinate in turn. Finally the king came to know which fellow had actually dug the pond. This poor village worker came before the king shaking.

The king asked him abruptly, "Did you dig this pond?"

The poor man said, "Yes, my boss asked me to do it. He gave me specific instructions. I did it, and my boss was satisfied."

The king said, "But I am not satisfied. I am the king. Whether or not your boss is satisfied is irrelevant. I am the one you must satisfy."

The man said, "Your Majesty, if you are not fully satisfied with my work, then please punish me in whichever way you want to punish me."

Then the king started laughing. After a few moments, he took out a bag containing a thousand rupees and gave it to the man. The man was astonished. He said, "You were mad at me. Now you are giving me money. I do not understand this at all."

The king said, "No, I am very, very pleased with you. You are an excellent worker. But I wanted to find out who was actually responsible for digging the pond. Because I found fault with them and scolded them, the others all said that they were not responsible. Each one, in turn, passed the responsibility to somebody else. Poor man, you are the last one in the line, so they thought that you would be punished. On the contrary, I am so satisfied that I am giving you one thousand rupees."

Then the king fined each and every one of the worker's superiors one thousand rupees, right from his minister on down, because each one said that he was too busy and somebody else should do it. The minister, his assistant and his assistant's assistant, everybody, was fined. The worker received one thousand rupees, and the others were fined one thousand rupees. After the king collected all the fines, he presented the entire amount to the poor worker.

The king said to him, "If I had said that I was very, very pleased with the pond, the minister would have been the first one to say: 'I did it. I did it.' He would have claimed all the credit. But my minister is such a rogue. He went to somebody else, and then that person went to somebody else, and so on. I wanted to know who had actually dug the pond so that I could reward that person. I am so happy to have an excellent worker like you."

### LTS 45. *The king's treasurer*

There was a bandit who used to steal things from here, there and everywhere. His wife was miserable that he was doing this kind of thing. One day the bandit told his wife, "I will give up this profession. The time is fast approaching when I will give up this kind of thing."

His wife begged him, "No, no, please give it up at this very moment. We do not need more money. Enough, enough! Please, please do not rob people any more."

The bandit decided that the following day would be the last day he would steal in his life. On that day he would steal something very expensive and then he would stop stealing forever. So he went to rob the house of the king's treasurer. At night he secretly hid in one room. The treasurer came home late in the evening, bringing lots of gold coins.

The treasurer said to his wife, "Today I have completed my task. I am so happy. I wanted to have ten thousand gold coins. I was stealing them little by little from the treasury and now I have the full amount. The king has such faith in me that he will never imagine that I am the one who has stolen this large sum. Still there is so much wealth in the treasury. There are literally millions and billions of gold coins remaining, so the king will never discover what I have done. He is very pleased with me, so I do not have to worry."

The treasurer was so excited that now he had ten thousand gold coins. At that point, the bandit, who was hiding in an adjacent room, burst into the room and said, "Do not attack me!"

The treasurer asked, "What are you doing here?" He was furious with the intruder.

The bandit said, "I have come here to change my life."

The treasurer said, "What are you talking about?"

The bandit explained, "I have been stealing all my life. I thought that today I would become the richest person. Since you are the treasurer, I thought I would be able to steal a large quantity of money from you. I told my wife that this would be the last time I would steal. So I wanted to do something spectacular. Now I am seeing that you are just another thief, like me. We have the same profession. A beggar does not go to another beggar to get money. It is absurdity on the face of it. He goes to somebody who has money. In your case, I am seeing that I am a mere thief, but you are also nothing but a thief. So it is beneath my dignity to steal anything from you. In which way are you better than I am?"

The treasurer was very nervous. He said, "Will you report this matter to the king?"

The bandit replied, "No, I do not feel inclined to tell the king that you have been stealing from him."

The treasurer wanted to guarantee that the bandit would remain silent, so he added, "Can you not take some money for yourself from here? I have got so many gold coins. There is more than enough for both of us."

The bandit said, "If you tempt me, then I shall go to the king immediately! I want to give up stealing. My wife has been begging me and begging me to give up this way of life. Today I am going to tell my wife what happened — that I was going to steal from someone who himself was stealing. I am now listening to her. From this moment on, I am giving up stealing."

In spite of the bandit's sincere vow, the treasurer did not believe him. He was afraid that one day the bandit would change his mind and inform the king. So the treasurer gathered together all the ten thousand gold coins and secretly put them back in the treasury. If the bandit told the king that the treasurer had stolen the coins, then he would be able to say, "There is no proof." The treasurer would be able to show the king that the full amount was there.

The bandit had promised his wife that this would be the last day he stole anything and on that same day he had this unique experience. Needless to say, he never stole anything again.

### LTS 46. *The lost rupees*

There was once a very good worker. He used to work very, very hard during the entire day. At the end of the day he would go to his boss and receive five rupees. For his whole day's work his salary was only five rupees. One day his boss gave him a ten-rupee note and said, "Give me five rupees change."

The worker said, "I have no money to give you change."

The boss said, "Then I cannot pay you."

The worker pleaded, "Can you not give me the ten rupees? You know that tomorrow I will definitely come. You can pay me for tomorrow in advance."

The boss said, "No, no, no, I do not trust you."

The worker said, "I have worked the whole day from early morning until now. On a daily basis you give me five rupees. Today you have a ten-rupee note. You know that tomorrow I will come and work. Can you not give it to me?"

The boss said again, "No, no, I do not trust you. You may not come."

The worker was very, very sad that this had happened. The boss said, "Tomorrow you come and at the end of the day I will give you five rupees for today and five for tomorrow."

The worker said, "But today I have to buy food for tomorrow. I entirely depend on your five rupees to eat."

The boss said, "Are you arguing with me?" Then the boss gave him a very smart slap.

The man was so miserable. He was not getting any money, and then he received this kind of treatment. At that moment, a friend of the boss, a jeweller, passed by. He asked, "What is happening? Why is that worker crying?"

The boss said, "He is a rogue. He has finished working. I have only a ten-rupee note. He is unable to give me five rupees back, so I did not give him his salary for today and, what is worse, now he is arguing with me."

The friend asked, "He is not arguing. He is simply stating his case. He is such a humble man. But I can easily solve this problem. Give me the ten-rupee note."

The friend took ten rupees from the boss and gave him a five-rupee note in return. The boss gave the five-rupee note to the worker. Then the friend said, "I owe you five rupees."

The boss asked, "When will you give me the five rupees that you still owe me?"

The friend said, "When the time comes, I may give you back your five rupees. You are such a bad fellow. This man is a very sincere worker and you were refusing to pay him. The more I think about it, the more I am determined not to give you back your five rupees."

Then the boss said, "All right. I am not going to force you to return my five rupees. It is better to keep our friendship than to get my five rupees back."

### LTS 47. *Singing the king's glory*

The king needed a very, very good worker to do some special tasks in the palace. The minister found the perfect worker. This worker was very sincere, very nice looking, very honest and so forth. But he had one bad habit: he used to come to work late. So the king scolded the minister: "What kind of man is he? He is coming late to work every day. Does he not value his job in the palace?"

The minister was very embarrassed. He went to see the worker and said, "I got you the job and told the king that you were such a nice man and a good worker. Why are you behaving in this way? Why do you come late to work every day? How can you justify it?"

The man replied, "Early in the morning, I go to the temple, and there I praise God. I sing God's Glory for hours and hours. That is why I arrive late."

The minister said, "This is what you do? Then when you come to the king's palace, why do you not sing the king's glory?"

The fellow came the following day to work and started singing the king's glory. He was extolling the king and praising him to the skies. The king observed the worker for some time. At first he was amused. Then after half an hour or forty-five minutes the worker was still going on with endless singing. He was not working at all. He was only singing the king's praises. Then the king became exasperated. He gave the man a slap and demanded, "What are you doing?"

The man said, "What can I do? The minister asked me to sing your glory."

Then the minister was summoned. The king asked him, "Why did you tell this worker to sing my glory?"

The minister said, "He told me he comes late each day because he sings God's Glory in the temple. I told him that if he came and sang your glory for a little while, you would be pleased. But I did not think that he would be only singing your glory and not working at all."

The worker said in his own defense, "God created me. That is why I go to the temple every day and sing God's Praises and Glory."

The minister said, "God created you, and God also wants you to live on earth, to work honestly. By praising God constantly, how will you be able to support yourself? If you wanted to praise God all day long, why did you accept this job? There is a time for everything. If you go to the temple early in the morning, you can praise God before you come to work. Then you will come to the palace punctually and work here. At the end of the day, you will take your salary and buy what you need. In this way, everything will have its proper time. Come to work on time. Before you come to work, go to the temple and sing God's Glory. Then after finishing your work here, you can again go to the temple. But, in the meantime, you must work."

When the king heard such sound advice and saw that this worker was going to listen, he gave a large amount of money to the minister. He was such a wise minister! The king also gave a bonus to the worker.

The minister was right. The following day the worker arrived at the palace on time. He had already gone to the temple and offered his praises to God. Then he came to work because he was getting money from the king. Before starting work, he sang the king's praises for a short time, and then he started working.

So the king was pleased with this worker and the minister was pleased with him. Definitely God was also pleased with him because he was doing the right thing.

## LTS 48. *The spiritual Master's burden*

A spiritual Master had many, many disciples. When old age descended upon him, he became extremely frail. His disciples were worrying and worrying! "O God," they cried, "We have such a great and good spiritual Master. Do not allow him to die. We do not want to lose our beloved Master."

They were all begging the spiritual Master, "Please take some medicine to improve your health."

The spiritual Master would not take any medicine. He said, "My time has come. I do not want to take any more medicine. If it is God's Will for me to leave this body, then I am fully prepared. If I continue to live on earth, then I will have to take the burden of so many people. But when I die, only four men will have to take *my* burden. I am very, very sorry for those four men who will have to bear my burden."

The disciples asked, "Why are you saying that only four people will have to take care of you? There are so many people here who are extremely devoted to you. We will all take care of you if anything happens to you." Then they all started crying.

The spiritual Master said, "I do not need all of you. I need only four people."

The disciples could not fathom why their Master was making a special point of saying four people. Finally, the Master said, "You fools, when I die, my coffin will be carried by only four men. I am feeling sorry for them because they will have to carry my lifeless body to the burial ground. Here on earth I took the burden of so many people. But when I die, only four men will have to bear *my* burden."

# LIFE'S BLEEDING TEARS AND FLYING SMILES

## BOOK 4

## LTS 49. *The stolen diamond*

A very, very rich man had a diamond shop. His assistant was extremely sincere and devoted. This worker asked the owner for a loan so that he could make preparations for his daughter's marriage.

The owner said, "No, no, I do not give loans. You are a good worker. I give you a salary, but I cannot give you a loan. I do not trust people, so I do not give loans."

The worker was miserable. He was worried that although his daughter was still beautiful, she was getting old. In a few years, who would marry her? He said to himself, "What can I do now?" He was thinking of going to some nice, kind-hearted man to borrow money.

Later that day, a wealthy man came to the shop and wanted to buy a most beautiful, most precious diamond. While he was selecting the diamond, the owner suddenly had to attend to an urgent matter, so he said to his assistant, "You take care of him. I have to leave now."

The worker accepted the rich man's payment and put the diamond in a small package. Meanwhile, a very old friend of the rich man saw him in the shop and came inside. They embraced and talked to each other for a long time. Finally, the rich man and his old friend went away together. When he left, the rich man forgot to take the diamond.

The boss had left, so the worker was the only person in the shop. The worker said to himself, "At this time in my life I have to do something so important. My daughter is supposed to get married." What temptation can do! He said, "Now this is the time for me to act. The owner has left, and the rich man has forgotten to take his diamond. He is so rich. Nothing will happen if he does not get this particular diamond. He will be able to buy another diamond."

The worker put the diamond, which he had already packed nicely, in his pocket and started walking to a nearby pawn shop to sell it. He was practically at the pawn shop when his conscience started haunting him. He said to himself, "I have been honest all my life. What am I doing? My daughter wants to get married, and I badly need money. If I can sell this diamond, then my daughter will have a beautiful wedding and she will be very honoured. She will be so happy, and her husband will be so happy. All right, just once in my life let me do this, although I know it is very bad."

When the worker reached the pawn shop, he discovered that his pocket had a hole and the diamond had fallen out! He said, "O God, You have saved me, You have saved me, You have saved me!" Then again, he was extremely afraid of what would happen the next day. His conscience was bothering him ruthlessly. He said to himself, "All my life I have been such a nice, honest man. Now what have I done? I have lost the diamond, so tomorrow I will be punished. This is the result of my wrong action! I did something bad, so now God will punish me. Anyway, let me see what my fate will be, now that I have become so bad."

The worker went to the temple next door to the shop and started praying and crying: "God, save me, save me, save me! What have I done? What have I done? Now I will be blamed by my boss. He will not believe me, no matter what I say. And I will also be blamed by the rich man."

The worker decided that if sincerity had any value, then he should tell the whole story to his boss and to the fellow who had bought the diamond. He said, "Let them punish me. How could I become so bad?"

Early the next morning, the rich man who had bought the diamond started walking toward the shop. All of a sudden, he saw a young man pick up something from the street. It happened that this young fellow was the servant of the assistant who had stolen the diamond. This assistant had gone to work, and the servant was carrying a special message from the assistant's wife, asking him to buy something on his way home.

The rich man said to the young servant, "Let me see what you have found."

What did he see? It was exactly the same diamond that he had bought the day before! The rich man told him, "This is mine! I dropped it yesterday." He was sure that he had dropped it while he was walking with his dearest friend.

The servant did not question him because he was a very rich man. The rich man said, "I am taking my diamond, and I am giving you a very large sum of money." Immediately he gave ten thousand rupees to the servant.

The servant said, "What shall I do with this money?"

The rich man said, "You deserve a reward. Just take it." Then he continued walking.

The servant said to himself, "My master is so nice, so kind to me. He is dying with worries about his daughter's marriage. I like him, and I also like his daughter so much. Let me give this money to my master."

Meanwhile, the assistant in the diamond shop was dying of anxiety. He opened the shop, but then he said, "My boss will come late today. Now let me go to the temple and pray again."

Again he went to the temple to pray to God for forgiveness. He said, "God, tell me what to do. My boss will be furious, and the man who bought the diamond will also be furious."

The servant saw his master entering into the temple to pray. He went up to his master and said, "I have such good news, such happy news!"

The assistant said, "What kind of good news?"

The servant said, "You see, your wife asked me to bring you a message. On the way, I found something in the street. I did not see you in the shop, so I was about to go back home when I found you here in the temple. Now let me give you some good news: I have received some money out of the blue, and I am giving it to you." Then the servant gave his master the money.

The assistant asked, "How did you get this money?"

The servant said, "I found a diamond in the street, and the owner came up to me to claim it. He said that yesterday he bought it from the shop where you work, and on his way home he dropped it. Since I found it, he was so pleased with me that he gave me ten thousand rupees. What do I need this money for? You are so kind to me. Your wife is also so kind to me. You have made me so happy by accepting me as your servant. Therefore, I am giving you the money."

Look how God saved this fellow! On the way to the pawn shop to sell the diamond, he lost it. His own servant found it, and the man who had bought it retrieved his diamond. The servant was amply rewarded and he gave the entire amount to his master. Later, when the daughter came to know what had happened, she hugged the servant and said, "You have saved me! Now I will be able to get married."

The assistant went back into the temple, crying and crying and crying with gratitude to God. When his boss came to the diamond shop, he saw that it was closed. Finally, the assistant arrived with his servant.

The boss asked, "Why are you late today? What have you been doing? Why are you crying?"

The assistant said, "Today I was in the mood to pray because God is so kind to me." He was still crying out of sheer gratitude to God for saving him.

The assistant was about to tell the whole story. He was going to be very frank about what he had done, but the servant stopped him. The servant said, "I found a diamond in the street on my way to the shop. A rich man came up to me and said it was his, so he gave me a large amount of money. He said he had dropped the diamond in the street."

The owner of the diamond shop was quite pleased. Then his sincere assistant said, "Please, please, I want to tell you the whole story."

He confessed the whole thing. The owner of the diamond shop was simply shocked. He said, "How can you be so bad?" Then he fired the assistant.

Soon the rich man came to learn that the assistant had been fired. The rich man himself went to give the assistant a very, very large amount of money. He said, "You are an honest man. You did one thing wrong out of desperate necessity for the sake of your daughter's marriage. Now you can open up a diamond shop of your own."

The marriage did take place, and the man opened up a shop with the money that the rich man had given him. Soon he also became very rich.

Bad people can do many bad things every day and it does not bother them. But when good people do one bad thing, their conscience tortures them so much. They really suffer until they have rectified their mistake.

### LTS 50. *The great philosopher*

There was a great philosopher. He had acquired name and fame, but he wanted to renounce everything. He said that name and fame did not bring him inner joy.

One day the great philosopher was swimming in a pool. The swimming pool was dirtier than the dirtiest, but he was getting tremendous joy. The philosopher was in his own world. After some time, a minister came from the king's palace and said to the philosopher, "You have to come with me now. The king wants you to come and stay at the palace, so you have to come immediately. The king wants to utilise your wisdom."

The philosopher said, "Please tell me, does the king have a turtle in his palace?"

What kind of question was this? The king had summoned him, and the philosopher had to ask if the king had a turtle! The minister started laughing and said, "This kind of philosopher the king will keep in his palace? All right, I shall tell you. Yes, the king has one turtle, and he keeps it in a very beautiful glass container. When people come to visit, they ask to see the turtle and we show it to them inside the glass container."

Then the philosopher said, "Look here, I do not want to be in the king's showcase. I am also a turtle, and I am satisfied with this swimming pool. Even if it is dirty, here I am enjoying my life. Here I am my own boss. In the palace I will not be my own boss. The king will utilise me at his sweet will. He will ask me all kinds of silly questions. If I do not answer, he will be upset. Again, if I answer the questions correctly, then he will try to show off by telling the whole world about me."

The minister said, "I do not want to hear your philosophy. You have to come with me. The king has called for you. What the king wants to do with your life, the king alone knows. It is not my problem."

Then the philosopher said, "I want to have peace of mind. With great difficulty I have entered into the spiritual life, and I have given up studying philosophy. I shall not answer questions with regard to philosophy. Just as there is no peace in politics, there is no peace in philosophy. Philosophy is in the mind. Let us bring Sri Ramakrishna into the picture. Sri Ramakrishna said that in the Vedic era, people used to pray for years and years to have *darshan*, the direct vision of God. But nowadays people can buy a book for ten rupees to learn about *darshan*, which is the Sanskrit term for philosophy. Now that I have entered into the spiritual life, I am so happy. I am getting peace, peace and peace. I do not want to lose my peace, so I do not want to go to the palace."

The minister said, "You have to come! Otherwise I will arrest you."

Then the philosopher said, "All right, take me. You may take my body, but you cannot take the real me." Again he started giving his philosophy!

The minister brought the philosopher to the king, and the king asked him a few questions. After each question the philosopher said, "God alone knows, God alone knows."

The king became annoyed. He said, "God alone knows? Then where is God? And how do you know that God alone knows?"

The philosopher said, "I know that God alone knows."

"Then prove it," said the king. "Where is God?"

The philosopher said, "I am searching for Him. Once I find Him, I will bring Him to you."

Then the king said, "You are a hopeless case! Go back home. Find God first, and then bring Him to me."

Then the great philosopher was released and allowed to go back home.

### LTS 51. *The teacher and the student*

Once a teacher said to a particular student, "You have to form a sentence or a few sentences containing the words 'something' and 'everything'."

The student thought for a long time. He said, "I am finding it difficult to form a sentence using both 'something' and 'everything'."

The teacher said, "I will help you out in case you cannot do it."

The young boy finally gave his answer: "An executive is he who is supposed to know something of everything."

The teacher clapped enthusiastically for the student.

Then the young boy gave another example: "A technician is he who knows something perfectly, whereas a barber is he who knows everything imperfectly."

The teacher was very happy.

Finally the student said, "There is something of truth in the statement: 'A lawyer ruins everything'. There is more truth in the statement: 'A doctor butchers everything'. And there is one hundred per cent truth in the statement: 'My little dog eats up everything'."

The teacher was so thrilled with her brilliant student. She said, "I did not know all these things. I am the one who posed the question, but you have answered it to my full satisfaction."

### LTS 52. *A widow is the answer*

A teacher asked his student, "Can you show me someone who is both 'bereaved' and 'relieved'? I am sure you know the meaning of these two words. If somebody dies, you are bereaved. And if you have some pain, when the pain goes away, you are relieved."

The clever student said, "Your question is so easy. I know a certain widow. Let me bring her here. Because her husband has passed away, she is bereaved. Again, since she had no love for her husband, she is greatly relieved!"

### LTS 53. *Two grandmothers*

Two grandmothers met to chat together. One of them said, "Please, please, I have to tell you something very significant about my granddaughter. It is so cute, so cute."

The other grandmother said, "All right, what is it? If you want to tell me about your granddaughter – how beautiful and how good she is, and how she has done something very great and significant – I shall listen to you without fail. But there is one condition: you have to listen to all my stories about my twenty grandchildren."

The first grandmother immediately said, "In that case, I have changed my mind. I do not want to tell you about my granddaughter. Let us change the topic!"

### LTS 54. *The theft of the five mangoes*

There was an old man who had stationed himself on the sidewalk of a busy street. There he was selling very ripe and delicious mangoes to the passersby. He did very brisk business and soon five mangoes were all that remained. Suddenly a young man came and snatched away the mangoes without paying. The old man cried, "What are you doing?"

The young man haughtily replied, "Look, I am the servant of a very important person. If you do not believe me, you can ask anybody. My master lives in a splendid tent near the palace. He is such a great man. So why should I have to pay you for these mangoes? On the contrary, you should be very proud that I am taking your mangoes for my master." So saying, the young man left the vicinity with his stolen goods.

The old man cried bitterly. Then he decided to take his case to the king because he knew that the king was extremely kind-hearted. As soon as he appeared before the king, the king asked,

"Please tell me why you are crying. What has happened to upset you so badly?"

The old man replied, "I am crying because five of my mangoes were just stolen. One young man came and took them for his master. He said that his master is a very great man and I should be proud to provide mangoes for him free of charge. He also told me that this master of his lives near your palace in a most beautiful tent."

"Then I can easily trace him," said the king, and he sent his bodyguards to search for the tent of that important person. If they found even one mango inside, then it would be taken as proof of the old man's story.

The bodyguards went out of the palace and easily located that particular tent. Inside it were the five mangoes, still uneaten. When they reported their discovery to the king, the king summoned the owner, who happened to be a very wealthy man. The king asked him, "Do you own the five mangoes that my guards found inside your tent?"

The rich man said, "Yes, they are mine."

The king asked, "Then where did you obtain them?"

"Oh, I do not know," answered the rich man.

"If you did not buy them, who did?" continued the king.

"My servant presented me with these mangoes," said the rich man. "I have no idea what he paid for them or where he bought them."

The king said, "I would like to speak with your servant."

"Your Majesty," said the rich man, "I have sent my servant on an errand."

The king asked, "When will he return?"

"It may take a little time," said the rich man, "but I assure you, I have not stolen these mangoes. As for my servant, I simply have no idea whether he paid for them or not."

The king said, "I believe you. You are innocent, but your servant is so bad. Now listen to me, kindly return the mangoes to this old man. Still you deserve more punishment. I order you to be the slave of this old man for five days — one day for each mango. Whatever he asks you to do, you have to do immediately. And if he makes any complaint against you, then I will punish you further."

So for five days the rich man and not his servant had to be the slave of the old mango-seller. Anything that this old man asked him to do, he had to do.

After a few days, the servant-thief completed his errand and came back to the tent. He saw that his master was not there and he made enquiries as to his whereabouts. In this way, he came to learn what had befallen his master. The servant immediately ran to the street where he had first seen the old mango-seller, and there he discovered his master doing some menial work.

"You rogue!" said the master. "I gave you money to buy mangoes for me, but you told this poor man that you did not have to pay because you were my servant. Since I am such an important person, you told him that you were entitled to take the mangoes for me. Then this old man lodged a complaint with the king himself. Now I am being punished for your misdeed! Tell me the truth — do you still have the money I gave you for the mangoes?"

The servant quickly produced the money. Then the rich man asked the mango-seller, "If I pay you for the five mangoes, will you allow me to go back to my home?"

The mango-seller said, "I cannot make any decision on this matter. It is in the king's hands. I would not have dared to make you my slave, but the king has ordered it. If you want to be released before the end of the five days, you must ask the king."

Since the rich man was still the old man's slave, his servant went to the king on his behalf. The servant cried and cried. He confessed to the king, "I did have the money, but I did not want to part with it. Therefore, I told the old man lies."

The king said, "Now the punishment will be that you have to be the old man's slave for five months. For each mango, you have to be a slave for one month. You will start when your master has completed his five days. On that day, you will go and take his place as the old man's slave and he will be free to go home. One thing more I am adding — if you come back before five months has ended, then you will be his slave for five years. And if I receive any complaint from the old man against you, then the term of your punishment will increase even more!"

So the master completed his punishment of five days, and the servant became the slave of the old man for five long months. During this time, he performed all his tasks very, very well. At the end of five months, the king asked the old man, "Did this fellow listen to you all the time?"

The old man said, "Oh yes, he always listened to me. He was very obedient."

The servant was then released and the king gave five hundred rupees to the old man.

### LTS 55. *A peaceful solution*

There were two brothers who were constantly fighting and quarrelling. The younger brother instigated these fights. The elder brother was good in every way, but for his own protection he had to fight against his younger brother. Outwardly the neighbours condemned this family fight, but inwardly they all enjoyed it.

The elder brother had a servant who was extremely pious. One day the elder brother saw this servant leaving the temple in a prayerful mood. The elder brother said to him, "I see that you have been praying. Please tell me what it is that you need.

You are such a good person. Whatever you need, I will gladly provide. I can see that you have been praying so sincerely."

The servant said, "I was praying so sincerely for you."

The elder brother was surprised. He said, "For me? Why do you need to pray for me?"

The servant replied, "I was praying for your victory. Next time you will defeat your brother in such a way that he will never come to fight with you again. I was praying also for your brother's death."

"My brother's death!" cried the elder brother.

"Yes," said the servant. "He is so bad. He harasses you all the time."

The elder brother became furious. He said, "I am simply shocked to learn that you have been praying for my brother's death. You must not go to the temple any more with this kind of prayer. Granted my brother has been torturing me for years and years, but he does not deserve to die because of his behaviour."

The servant bowed and the elder brother entered into the temple and began praying. When he emerged some time later, the servant was still standing in the same position waiting for his master. The servant asked, "Will you please tell me what you were praying for just now? Can you tell me?"

The elder brother said, "Yes, I can tell you why I prayed to God. My younger brother thinks that I am richer than he is. Truth to tell, I do not know whether he has more money or I have more money. I was praying to God to make both of us happy. If my brother wants to have more money or property from me, I will be equally happy. By taking this money or property from me, if he becomes happy, then I will also become happy. I do not want him to attack me any more. So I am prepared to give him whatever he wants."

The servant said, "O master, how can you offer this kind of prayer? Do you not see that he is fooling you? The truth of the matter is that he has much more money than you do, and yet he is telling you that he has no money. He is trying to take away all your money."

The elder brother said, "All right. I am going once more to the temple to pray. This time I will pray for something else. Then I will come and let you know the result."

The elder brother entered into the temple and began praying: "O God, I do not need my money or my property. Let my younger brother take away everything that I have. I do not even need a servant. I only need You. It is You alone who will give me peace and happiness."

All of a sudden, this elder brother heard a loud noise. This loud noise was actually made by the servant and an assistant, but inside the loud noise, the elder brother saw only light, light, light. This light gave him the answer to his prayer. He came out of the temple and sent the servant to his younger brother's house, requesting his brother to come and visit him. The younger brother was extremely suspicious. He thought that his elder brother might do something, so he began making preparations to go and fight.

The servant said, "Come with me peacefully. This is a totally different thing."

The younger brother believed the servant and he went to see his elder brother. Immediately his elder brother embraced him and said, "My brother, my brother, in terms of material wealth and property, I do not know whether I have more than you have or not. It is of no consequence to me. You can take my money, my property, everything. Only let me go peacefully. I shall become a sannyasin. Let us both be happy in our own way. You want to be happy with my money-power. So be it. You may take it all. I have found my money-power in God. He is my real wealth."

So the elder brother became a sannyasin. And what did the servant do? He followed his master and entered into the spiritual life.

### LTS 56. *I need only God*

There was once a wealthy man who was quite advanced in years. In the course of time, he passed away and his son inherited all his money and property. Unfortunately, this son used to smoke and drink and lead an undivine vital life. Soon he had squandered all his father's money. Because of his desperate financial situation, he could no longer drink or smoke or enjoy his pleasure-life. He was so miserable because he had acted so foolishly and so unwisely.

One night this young man had a dream. In his dream, a most luminous being came to him. He said to this being, "Ah, you are God. I am sure you are God Himself."

The luminous being said, "No, I am not God, but I have come from God. I have been sent by God to help you."

The son had been cursing God for not stopping him from drinking and smoking and living an undivine life. He felt that if God had given him some common sense, he would not have behaved in this manner. Because he had been cursing and insulting God, God sent this particular angel to him.

The angel then asked him, "Do you want to have all your money and property restored to you?"

The young man replied, "Yes, I want to get back my old way of life."

The angel said, "All right. From now on, for one full year, you have to do something. If you can do it successfully, you will get back all your wealth. You will be able to lead your old pleasure-loving way of life. This is what you must do: you must not tell a lie for one year and you must stop smoking."

The young man said, "How can I smoke? I have no money!"

The angel said, "All right. Smoking is taken care of. Now tell me, do you have anger?"

The young man answered, "Yes, I have been literally cursing God day in and day out."

The angel told him, "Then this is what you must do for one full year: you must stop telling lies and you must never be angry with anybody under any circumstances. Then everything you have lost will be restored to you."

One full year passed by. True to his word, the man did not tell a single lie and he did not get angry with anybody. Then he asked himself, "Did God's angel tell me a lie? One year has gone by since the angel visited me. In which way has the angel fulfilled his promise? Where is my long-lost wealth? Where are my former days of happiness? They have not been restored to me."

That night the same angel appeared to the man. The man was furious with the angel. He said, "You have told me a lie! I have not told a lie for one year and I have not done anything bad. How is it then that I am not getting back my property, my money and everything else?"

The angel said, "True, they have not come back, but tell me, when you had so much material wealth, were you happy?"

"Yes," the man said, "I enjoyed it to the fullest extent."

"And now," said the angel, "what is happening?"

"I cannot enjoy it," said the man, "because you did not keep your promise."

The angel went on, "Tell me frankly, do you think it will be possible for you to think of your life in a different way?"

"What do you mean?" cried the man. "I do not understand."

The angel continued, "Previously, you enjoyed the world in a special way. You fell in love with material prosperity and you craved worldly pleasures. Now, can you not fall in love with yourself?"

"What are you saying?" cried the man. "Please explain what you mean."

The angel explained, "There are two ways to derive joy. One way is through possession and another way is through renunciation. Once upon a time you possessed many things, but you misused them and you lost everything. Now you do not have anything, but you do have a heart, a beautiful heart."

"Is it true? Do I have a beautiful heart?" asked the man.

The angel said, "You not only have a beautiful heart, but also a most beautiful soul."

"What will happen now?" asked the man.

The angel replied, "If you continue to bring to the fore this most beautiful heart and soul of yours, then you will find that in a few years' time you will gather many disciples. These disciples of yours will be at your beck and call. They will listen to you at every moment, they will obey you unconditionally and in every way they will make you a real prince. True, you have lost your material wealth. But, I assure you, you will gain so much spiritual wealth if you just fall in love with your soul and with your heart."

The man was wonderstruck. "Is it true?" he asked.

"Yes," said the angel. "Just be fond of yourself because you have such a beautiful heart and beautiful soul. I am telling you, very soon you will have so many disciples and these disciples will do everything for you. You will be like a prince."

The man followed the angel's advice. He did not smoke or drink and he led a very good life. He became extremely spiritual. Almost overnight, disciples began to flock to him. He was very happy that his disciples were obeying him in every way.

Alas, alas, in a few months' time these same disciples started making his life miserable. They began making complaints against each other and displaying so much jealousy and insecurity.

For a few months, the man had enjoyed his newfound life as a Guru. Then, when his disciples started fighting and quarrelling, the idea of guruship no longer appealed to him. This time, however, he did not curse God. He prayed to God most sincerely, "O God, when I squandered all my wealth, I cursed You because You took away everything. I could no longer smoke or drink to my heart's content. Now it seems that You have cursed me by giving me all these undivine disciples. O God, please, please, can You not save me?"

Once again in a dream God's messenger appeared. This time the luminous being said to the man, "Indeed, you are caught. You cursed God because you were unable to lead your old life. Now you are saying that God has cursed you by giving you such bad disciples. Make up your mind. What would you like to do now?"

The man said, "I will not curse God any more and I do not want God to curse me any more. Please, please inform God that I am renouncing this whole world. I do not want to drink and lead that wild life any more, and I do not want the name and fame of a Guru. I need only God."

### LTS 57. *Where is God?*

There was a teacher who taught a class of young boys. One day he asked his students a very simple question: "Can you tell me where God is?"

Quite a few students raised their hand. One said, "God is in Heaven."

Another boy stood up and said, "God is everywhere, except in hell."

A third boy stood up and said, "My mother told me that God is only in good people, not in bad people."

A fourth student stood up and said, "God is in everybody. My grandmother has taught me that God is in everybody, good or bad."

Still another one stood up and said, "My grandfather has told me that God is everywhere and in everybody. Even in hell, God is there."

The teacher said, "All right, all of you have given excellent answers. Is there anybody who has anything new to say?"

Finally one little boy stood up and said, "Teacher, they are all wrong. I know where God is. God is in our kitchen! Every morning my father comes into the kitchen and says to my mother, 'My God! Are you still cooking? It is so late!'"

### LTS 58. *The stupid judge and the clever judge*

A courtroom was filled with convicts who were waiting to be tried, and also with lawyers, prosecutors and spectators. A judge was presiding over everything. One after another, cases were being heard to determine who was guilty and who was not guilty.

A murder case came up. The accused was a young man who was very thin but spirited. He was seated behind his lawyer. The judge asked this young man, "Tell me, how could you kill someone with only one blow? Many witnesses have said that it took only one blow to kill the deceased. They say they saw you give him one hard blow and then he fell down on the ground unconscious. Shortly afterwards, he died. With one single blow, how could you do that?"

The young man replied, "Your Honour, may I show it to you?"

In the courtroom, some people began roaring with laughter. Others became frightened and quickly left the building, while others were very curious to see the young man's technique. And what did the judge do? The judge ran away!

Then the accused jumped over the bench and started chasing the judge! He soon caught the judge and the judge begged him, "Please, please do not harm me! I dismiss the charges. I will not punish you. You are free, you are free. Do not hurt me!"

The young man said, "No, I want to show you how it can be done."

The poor judge fled for his life. He knew that if the young man demonstrated his technique, then his own life would end. In the meantime, another judge had come to replace this judge. The new judge ordered quite a few guards to go and bring the culprit back into the courtroom. Still there were many spectators remaining in the courtroom. They were eager to see how the new judge would deal with the case.

When the culprit was brought back, the judge said to him, "Now you can demonstrate how you killed your victim."

The young man said, "No, I will not be able to show it."

The judge said, "I am ordering you to show us your technique." Then the judge held a mirror in front of the young man and said, "You will strike this mirror and not any human being. In this way I will be able to see what you do and I will also be able to see your own face reflected in the mirror."

The young man struck the mirror with tremendous force and smashed it. But his hand was badly hurt and it began bleeding profusely. The judge said, "You deserve this kind of punishment. You have killed someone and you will go to jail. But first I wanted you to feel the suffering of your victim." Then the guards took the murderer away.

This is how two judges tried the same case. The first judge was stupid — he ran for his life. The second one was wise — he made the murderer inflict the injury on himself.

### LTS 59. *The faithful spouses and the unfaithful spouses*

There was a man who loved to play golf. One day the wife of the golfer was crying and crying and crying. A neighbour came and said, "Why are you crying?"

The wife said, "This time my husband has left me for good."

The neighbour was shocked. He said, "What?"

The wife sobbed, "Four times he has left me, but he has always come back. Now this is the fifth time."

The neighbour reassured her, "He will come back again. If he told you four times that he would leave you, and then he came back, the fifth time also he will come back."

The wife said, "No, this time he will not come back."

The neighbour said, "How do you know this?"

She said, "Because this time he has taken his golf clubs. That is a sure sign that he will not come back any more!"

The neighbour said, "If he does not come back tomorrow, let me know."

The next day the neighbour came and found the wife still crying and crying. All of a sudden she stopped crying. The neighbour asked, "What happened? All of a sudden you stopped crying."

The wife looked at him and said, "You are so handsome. I want to marry you."

He said, "I am already married. How am I going to marry you?"

The wife said, "I do not care for my husband at all! Let him not come back. I am praying to God, 'Let him not come'."

The golfer's wife and the neighbour fell in love, and they were both praying to God that the golfer would not return. The neighbour stayed with the golfer's wife and they were both extremely happy. This went on for about a week. The neighbour's wife did not know that her husband was just next door. He had told her that he was going out of town on business for a week. The wife was absolutely sure that he was going away for a week, and then he would come back. She did not suspect him at all.

One week passed, and the neighbour's wife started worrying that something had happened to her husband. Next door, the golfer had not returned, so the golfer's wife and the neighbour were very happy together. They were absolutely in love.

After three weeks, the golfer came back and discovered the neighbour living in his house. He immediately started beating up the man. He said, "What right do you have to live in my house?" Then he kicked the neighbour out onto the street.

The golfer's wife said to her husband, "I do not want to remain with you any longer. I love this man and I want to marry him."

The poor golfer said, "Can this be my wife?"

In the meantime the neighbour had no choice but to return home. His wife heard the whole story. She told him, "You are such a rogue! I will not take you back."

So the unfortunate neighbour could not marry the golfer's wife because her husband had badly thrashed him and kicked him out. Then his own wife did not accept him back because he was so undivine and unfaithful. So he had lost on both sides: he lost his wife, and he lost his lover. Meanwhile, the wife of the golfer did not want to remain with her husband any more. She said, "No, I love our neighbour far more than I love you."

Her husband said, "You are so unfaithful! It is much better for me to remain a bachelor. If your love is for our neighbour, then I do not need you. I do not want to be with you any more.

In fact, I do not need marriage any more. All women are like you."

The two couples went to a judge to help them resolve their situation. The judge said, "What is all this about?"

The golfer explained that he did not want to keep his wife because she was so unfaithful. The neighbour's wife explained that she did not want to take her husband back because he was unfaithful to her.

The judge said, "This matter is so easy to settle." He asked the wife of the golfer, "Do you still love your neighbour most?"

She said, "Yes, yes, I love him so much."

Then the judge asked the neighbour, "Do you still love the wife of the golfer?"

The neighbour said, "Yes, I still love her."

The judge said, "Then you two should get married." Then the judge turned to the neighbour's wife and asked her, "Will you not be happy to have a faithful husband?"

She said, "Yes, I need a faithful husband."

The judge asked the golfer, "Will you not be happy to have a faithful wife?"

The golfer said, "Yes, that is why I do not want to remain married to my wife any more — because she has been unfaithful."

The judge continued, "Then can you not marry your neighbour's wife? She is faithful and she wants a faithful husband. You are faithful and you want a faithful wife. Such being the case, can you not switch? You be faithful to your new wife and your former wife can be faithful to her new husband. At least with one person you should be faithful."

The golfer and the neighbour's wife saw the wisdom of the judge's suggestion. They said, "Let us get married."

So the unfaithful pair got married, and the faithful pair got married. This is how the judge wisely solved the problem.

LTS 60. *The mother-in-law's insult*

A young girl had been recently married. She was always afraid of staying alone. She wanted to be with her husband, but she could not accompany him to his office. So whenever her husband was at home, she was always nearby him, feeding him and so forth. She was absolutely so fond of her husband and he, in turn, was very, very happy that his wife was so fond of him.

One evening, the husband returned home and saw that his wife was crying and sobbing. He asked, "What has happened? What has happened?"

His wife said, "Your mother has insulted me so badly."

He said, "My mother? How can it be? My mother is not here. She lives hundreds of miles away. How can she insult you? Did she call you on the telephone?"

The wife said, "No."

He asked, "Did you call her for anything?"

The wife said, "No, I would not dare to call her."

"Did she call you?" the husband asked again.

The wife said, "No, she did not call."

Now the husband was really puzzled. He asked, "Then how could she insult you so badly?"

The wife said, "A letter came for you from your mother, so I opened it."

The husband was shocked. He said, "You opened my letter?"

She said, "I am your wife. We two are one. So I am entitled to open your mail."

He said, "This is true. Now tell me, what has my mother written?"

The wife said, "Your mother has written how much she loves you, and how much she is missing you."

"Then where does the insult lie?" asked the husband.

The wife said, "In a postscript she says, 'Dear Linda, please do me a big favour and give this letter to my darling son Patrick'. What an insult! What an insult! Throughout the whole letter she has repeated how much she loves you, and she has not mentioned my name at all. Then at the very end, she had to add this postscript. Can you imagine! She knew that I would read the letter before you. As if I would not have given you the letter! Your mother does not trust me in the least. How can I live with you when my mother-in-law does not trust me at all?"

The poor husband said, "What am I going to do? I am not responsible for what my mother says."

The wife continued, "In her letter she has said again and again, 'Dear Patrick, darling, you are so good. Nowadays you have no time to think of me, but before you got married you were always thinking about me. Now you are all the time thinking of your wife. You never think of me.' She used the word 'darling' over and over. Your mother calls you darling. I lost my mother at a tender age. My mother is not here to call me darling." With that, she burst into a fresh flood of tears.

He said, "But I call you darling, I call you darling."

She said, "You call me darling, but your mother calls you darling, and my mother is not here to give me that kind of affection."

The husband said, "What can I do? Your mother has passed away. How can I bring your mother back here? If you want a mother's affection, then you have to start pleasing my mother."

The wife said, "I do so much for your mother whenever she comes here. I try to please her, but she has never liked me, and she says she will never invite me to come to her place."

The husband said, "Who cares? If she does not invite you, then I am not going to her place."

Then his wife became so happy that her husband would not go to his mother's place if his mother did not invite her as well. She was very, very happy with her husband's loyalty to her.

In silence the unfortunate husband said, "Alas, alas! O God, why did You create both mothers-in-law and daughters-in-law on earth? Could You find nothing better to do with Your precious time?"

## LTS 61. *The kind mother-in-law*

One mother had two married daughters. The husbands of these daughters were not so nice to their wives, and the mothers-in-law were simply unbearable. They tortured their daughters-in-law unimaginably. These two daughters suffered and suffered and suffered in the hands of their mothers-in-law.

Now the mother also had a son. When her son got married, she took an oath that she would be an exception. Everybody knows that mothers-in-law are bad everywhere. But this woman wanted to be an excellent, super-excellent mother-in-law. From the beginning, she was extremely, extremely kind to her daughter-in-law. Anything that was difficult or heavy or time-consuming, the mother-in-law would do herself. She would not allow her daughter-in-law to do it.

The mother-in-law would say to her, "No, you are still a young girl. A day will come when you will have to do everything yourself. I am an old lady. My time will soon come and I will die. When I die, then you can do everything that I am doing, but not now."

Even when the daughter-in-law wanted to cook, her mother-in-law told her, "No, no, no! I have been cooking for my son since he was born, so I know what he needs and what he likes. I will look after the cooking, and when the time comes, I shall show you how to cook. Now you do other things. You can bring flowers and put them on the shrine and you can do a little bit of dusting around the windows and doors. Just do some easy household chores."

The daughter-in-law was deeply moved that her mother-in-law was so kind to her and everything went on very harmoniously in the house. This young wife used to watch her husband eating his food. The husband was always very, very pleased, and the wife was also very pleased that her husband liked the food. One day the story changed. The husband said to the wife, "I am so sad that today your preparation is not up to its usual standard. Not even one curry is good."

The wife was very sad. Then the husband asked, "What happened to you today? Why is the food so bad?"

The wife finally said, "Unfortunately, I am not the one who cooked your food."

The son said, "You have not cooked today?"

With tremendous hesitation, the wife replied, "Your mother cooked."

He said, "My mother cooked?"

The wife went on, "Your mother cooks every meal, every day."

"My mother cooks?" the son cried. "Then what do you do? Why do I need a wife? You allowed my mother to cook at her age? I do not need you. Get out of my house!"

His wife pleaded, "Your mother does not allow me to cook. I want to cook, I want to learn from her, but she does not teach me. She gives me only very light jobs." Then she started crying and crying.

The husband was furious. He began screaming at her, "Why did you not tell me that my mother has been cooking all the time?"

She said, "Your mother asked me not to tell you. Otherwise, I would have told you. Every day you have been appreciating your food and I have been getting the credit because your mother asked me not to tell you. Today you do not like the food. I could easily have said that I cooked. I could have taken the blame. Then you would have been very happy. Now what am I going to do? I have been sincere in telling you that your mother cooked. It is not that I am finding fault with your mother. She has been so kind to me. Your mother is so sincere. She would be furious if I told a lie. I was afraid that if I took the blame, she would ask why I told you a lie. So I revealed that your mother cooked the meal, which is so true."

The wife was weeping profusely. The mother-in-law heard the commotion and entered the room. When she saw the wife's tears, she became furious. She said to her son, "Luckily, your father is not here. Otherwise, I would have asked him to thrash you. Your wife is so nice. She is not my daughter-in-law. She is my real daughter. My own daughters who are married are suffering so much in the hands of their husbands. Their mothers-in-law are also so bad. They are literally unbearable. How badly my two daughters are being treated. Now you have also started torturing my daughter. She is absolutely like my real daughter. I will leave the house if you ever scold her again."

The son said, "Mother, you do not have to leave the house. I promise that I will not scold her."

But still the young wife continued crying and crying. Her mother-in-law said to her, "You are a young girl. Perhaps you are missing your own home. You go for a few days to your mother's place. Your mother will give you so much affection."

The girl said, "No, no, you are so kind to me, so affectionate to me. My mother is in no way more affectionate to me."

The mother-in-law said, "I am sure that is the best remedy. After all, she is your true mother. In a few days' time we shall send for you, and you can come back. Nobody can replace one's mother. Your mother will show you much more affection than I can ever show you."

Again the girl insisted, "No, no, you have so much affection for me. Your affection is absolutely equal to, if not more than, that of my own mother."

The mother-in-law said, "Believe me, I know. I am not your mother, but your mother will have more affection. You go. I will bring you back very soon."

So the young wife went back home. On the way, she was saying to herself, "If I go home crying and crying, then my mother will notice my tears and she will curse my mother-in-law. My mother will immediately think that my mother-in-law has been torturing me and making my life miserable. She does not know that my mother-in-law is so kind, so affectionate and so compassionate." So the young wife dried her tears and arrived at her mother's house with a happy face. Her mother was so thrilled to see her daughter again and she began questioning her about her husband and mother-in-law. The young girl was saying very, very nice things about her mother-in-law and about her husband also. She said, "He is so nice, so kind, so loving." She fooled her mother with regard to her husband by not revealing that her husband had asked her to get out of the house. But when she said that her mother-in-law was so good, it was the truth.

Now her brother had recently married a young girl and they lived together with his mother. Unfortunately, his new wife was being treated mercilessly by her mother-in-law. The daughter liked her new sister-in-law very much and they soon became close friends. In the evening, they would sit together and talk and talk and talk. The daughter soon noticed how her mother treated her daughter-in-law, so she tried her best to console the young wife. She also spoke to her mother directly. She begged her mother, "Please, please do not scold her. She is only a young girl. She has joined our family and she has nobody but us. It is not good to scold her."

Then her mother would say, "Do I have to learn from you how to behave in my own house? I tell you, she is useless, useless. We have gained nothing but a useless girl in our house."

The daughter saw that her brother's wife was very, very, very good. This girl was very kind, full of concern and she worked extremely hard. But no matter how hard she worked, her mother-in-law was not pleased at all. So she would cry before her husband's sister, and the sister would console her and encourage her to be patient.

One day the daughter said to her mother, "Mother, if my husband's mother, my mother-in-law, also treated me as ruthlessly as you are treating this young girl, what would you have thought of my mother-in-law? How would you have reacted?"

At once her mother replied, "I would have thought that she was a tyrant. I would have hated her. In fact, I would have gone and thrashed her. I might even have kicked her for daring to mistreat my daughter, my darling."

The daughter said, "If you are saying that you would have beaten up my mother-in-law if the circumstances were reversed, how can you justify your behaviour? The way you want to treat my mother-in-law, will you not be treated in exactly the same way by the mother of this girl who has taken shelter in your house?"

Her mother said, "Oh, that will never happen. Her mother is gone. She is dead."

Her daughter was shocked by her mother's callousness. She said, "Are you not a Hindu? Do you not believe in religion? Have you not read the scriptures? Her mother's soul is seeing from Heaven that you are torturing her daughter day in and day out! She is definitely alive in Heaven. Do you never feel her heart's tears?"

Her mother was melting a little. In her heart she was deciding whether or not to scold her daughter-in-law any more. Each day she began to show a little more kindness to her daughter-in-law and soon the entire situation in the house was transformed.

One day the daughter saw through the window that her own mother-in-law was approaching the house. The husband was also missing his wife, but again he had pride. He knew that he had scolded her so mercilessly and he was afraid that perhaps his wife had told her mother how badly he had scolded her for the food and also for not cooking his meals. He felt that if he came to his mother-in-law's place, his mother-in-law would scold him severely.

His mother had said, "No matter what happens, I am going to fetch your wife. She has to come back. I have been very, very nice to her. Even if they insult me, I am prepared to go because my love for her far exceeds all my problems with your mother-in-law."

So she went there, and the young girl came running up to her, asking, "Why have you come, why have you come? I would have gone back. You only had to send for me. You did not have to come yourself."

Her mother-in-law said, "You were not coming back, so I have come to take you."

Then the good mother-in-law went inside and saw that the bad mother-in-law had changed completely because of her daughter. This mother-in-law changed the other mother-in-law through her own daughter-in-law. Both the families were now swimming in the sea of joy.

The first mother-in-law and her daughter-in-law returned to their place, and the husband was so happy that both his mother and his wife had come back home. They all lived happily together. Both the families were now genuinely happy.

This story shows how one person can be the instrument to make others good and to make everybody happy.

### LTS 62. *The hundred-year-old lady*

There was a lady who was one hundred years old. Before she reached the age of sixty, she did not want to observe her birthday. When asked about her birthday, she would lie about the date so that people would not celebrate it. She would say, "Oh, my birthday is long since passed." But from the age of sixty, for some reason, she became very eager to observe her birthday. Every year people gave her all kinds of beautiful gifts, and she was very, very happy.

After she reached the age of ninety, people started giving her only household things. They gave her everything that she could utilise in the house because she could no longer go out, and she did not need nice clothes.

Then when she turned one hundred years old, she said to quite a few relatives and friends, "This year, I need only one thing from each and everyone."

They all asked, "What is that thing? We will give you anything you want."

She said, "I need only a kiss from each of you."

So everybody kissed her. Then they asked, "Why do you need a kiss? Is it because you feel that soon God will call you?"

She said, "No, no, no! God is not going to call me in the near future. But if I receive a kiss from you instead of a household object, then I will not have to wash so many pots and pans and other things. I will not have to dust the things that you give me for the house. Now I have to get up and dust them regularly. Every day I have to clean them and wash them. Now I do not want any new things to clean and wash. If you kiss me, then you will not create any more work for me. There is no dirt on my face that I have to wash off. Now I am so happy."

One of her friends said, "There is something that will give you more joy than a kiss, and you will not have to wash it."

The old lady said, "What is it?"

Her friend answered, "It is a fond embrace."

"Let us try it then," said the old lady.

So they all started embracing this very thin old lady with utmost love and affection. Afterwards, one of them asked her, "Now do you see the difference between being kissed and being embraced?"

The old lady said, "Yes, I am getting far more joy from being embraced."

One of the ladies in the group said, "I know of something else that will give you much more joy than either being kissed or embraced."

The old lady asked, "What is it? I want to have that thing. Before I die, I want to have it. Of course, I am not going to die today or tomorrow. Tell me, what is it?"

The other lady said, "I have a spiritual Master. If this spiritual Master looks at you and blesses you, you will receive tremendous joy."

The old lady was not spiritual at all, but she was looking for new things that would give her joy. The kiss gave her joy, and the embrace gave her more joy. So the old lady said, "Can you go and request him to come here? I want to see your spiritual Master."

The spiritual Master came and looked at her and blessed her. When he was blessing her, she was so thrilled. She fell flat at the spiritual Master's feet and died then and there. At first everybody was very sad that she had died. Then they were so happy because the spiritual Master said, "As soon as her soul saw me, the soul said to me, 'Now that I have been blessed by a true spiritual Master, there is nothing remaining here on earth for me. Only in Heaven will I get infinitely more joy. If I go to Heaven, I will receive infinitely more joy than you have given me. Therefore, with your permission, I am leaving behind this mortal coil'."

### LTS 63. *The grey hair*

Once a middle-aged lady was scolding her daughter severely. She was saying, "Is there any day when you listen to me? I have never seen anybody on earth as disobedient as you are. All the time you are moving around with your boyfriend and misbehaving. You are making my life miserable. Each time you disobey me, I get new grey hairs."

The daughter said, "Now I know why my grandmother's hair is all grey!"

The mother said, "What do you mean?"

The daughter replied, "It is because you were so 'obedient'. That is why my grandmother's hair is so grey!"

The mother became furious and wanted to strike her daughter for her insolence. The mother said, "Stop, stop your foul tongue or I will strike you."

The daughter boasted, "I am stronger than you. You will not be able to touch me." The girl was really much stronger than her mother, so the mother could not carry out her threat.

The mother went on, "You are such a bad girl. Now I am telling you why my mother has all grey hair. It is because my brother was very, very disobedient. It was all due to my brother that this happened."

The young girl went to her maternal uncle — her mother's brother — and said to him, "Is it true that you are such a bad person? It seems to me that you are a very good person, but my mother claims you used to be so disobedient. You used to torture my grandmother. All her grey hair is due to you. My mother says so."

Her uncle said, "Your mother is saying that?"

Then he went and challenged his sister. He said, "You liar! You can ask the neighbours what kind of boyfriends you had. I did not have any girlfriends. When the proper time came, I was married according to our parents' wishes. I was not like you. You had so many boyfriends."

Then the mother and her brother had a huge fight. Who was telling the truth, the mother or the brother? Finally the mother said to her daughter, "There is only one person who can tell the truth, and that is your grandfather. Let us go and see your grandfather. He will tell us the truth."

When the daughter asked her grandfather, he said, "Your grandmother got grey hair because it is hereditary. I am your grandfather, but I do not have grey hair. I have all dark, black hair, but she has grey hair because she inherited it from her father's side. Her mother did not have grey hair."

The grandmother said, "No, it is all lies. Now I shall tell you all the real reason. Your grandfather did not listen to me. He led a very bad life. He would come home late. Only God knew what was going on. It is all because of your grandfather's bad life that I have grey hair. I used to worry and worry, about him for hours and hours. It is from his bad life that I got all this grey hair!"

# LIFE'S BLEEDING TEARS AND FLYING SMILES

## BOOK 5

LTS 64. *Who can be admitted into Heaven?*

Three men died on the same day. They went to Heaven and they were all waiting for Saint Peter to open the gates to Heaven so that they could enter. One of the men had been a doctor, another an engineer and the third a consultant. Unfortunately, Saint Peter was very, very busy on that day. While they were waiting for him to come, the three men became very anxious. They were worried about what would happen to them if he did not accept them into Heaven.

At long last Saint Peter came. He announced, "Today there are not enough vacancies in Heaven, so I can take only one of you. I cannot admit three new souls today. Whoever is the most important of you three, I will take."

The doctor immediately said, "Clearly, I am the most important. Why? Everyone knows that God created Adam, and from Adam's side God removed one rib and thus created Eve. This happened right at the beginning of creation. Adam came into existence directly from God, but through a doctor's surgical operation on one rib, Eve was created. I am the most important because God depended on medical skill to start His creation."

The engineer protested, "No, no, not at all! Before Adam and Eve were created, this universe was full of chaos and confusion. First God had to create the earth, and for that God needed an engineer. An engineer created the world. Therefore, I am the most important."

Now the third one, the consultant, spoke up. He said, "No, no, no! God needed a consultant to decide where and how He would position the earth in the universe. There was so much chaos and confusion, it is true. But before God actually created the earth, He needed the help of a consultant to remove all the chaos and confusion and come up with a good design. So the consultant was the one who was needed most."

The doctor claimed that he was the most important. The engineer claimed that he was the most important. Then the consultant claimed that he was the most important. Now Saint Peter was in trouble. Since he could not decide whom to choose, he went to God. Saint Peter said to God, "I have three new candidates for Heaven. Kindly tell me whom to choose."

God said, "Throw them all out! I am telling you how the creation actually took place. Before I created the world, I had the Vision of this creation. But even before this Vision, my omnipotent Will-Power existed. My omnipotent Will-Power existed long before anything else. With this I started. My omnipotent Will-Power was and shall forever remain the most important thing on earth and in Heaven. So throw these three out. Do not allow these liars — the doctor, the engineer and the consultant — to enter into Heaven."

So none of the three could enter into Heaven.

### LTS 65. *When God was called as a witness*

One day a thief was seen stealing valuables from a house. Three members of the family witnessed the theft. The thief took the valuables and ran away, and the members of the family chased him. Unfortunately, the thief ran so fast that the members of the family could not catch him. Since they knew who he was, they brought the case to the village court. There were many cases before the village judge, but when the thief came before the judge, he was not at all afraid. In fact, he was very confident.

The judge said to him, "You are accused of theft. Have you stolen anything?"

The thief said, "Where is the proof? I do not have anything." The thief had carefully hidden the stolen things at his place, and nobody could find them. The thief continued, "They are telling lies. I have not been near their house."

The judge said, "You say they are telling lies. I am telling you that if we find the stolen goods at your place, then for ten years you will be in jail."

The thief said, "But I have little children at home. They are so young. If I go to jail, who will take care of them?"

The judge said, "If you want to take care of them, go and bring what you have stolen."

The man replied emphatically, "No, I have not stolen anything."

The judge said, "You have not stolen anything? Are you saying that these three people are telling lies?"

The man said to the judge, "Your Honour, three people are saying that they observed me while I was stealing. On the word of three people, you are ready to put me in jail? It is a joke! I can easily bring one hundred witnesses who will say that they have not seen me stealing at all."

The judge asked the three plaintiffs, "What should we do?"

They said, "Your Honour, how could one hundred people have been inside our house on that night to observe him stealing? It is simply impossible."

The man said, "No, they need not have been inside the house. You say that I was running away with the loot, and you were chasing me. How is it that nobody saw me in the street running away? I can bring hundreds of people from the village who will say that they did not see me running away. If your story were true, would there not have been one person at least to see me while I was running away?"

The man argued so powerfully in his own defense that the judge could not decide the case. The judge felt miserable. He said to the three plaintiffs, "I am so sorry. In one sense, he is right. Nobody saw him running away from your house. So I cannot decide whether he is guilty or not guilty."

Then the judge continued, "The thief is challenging you to find your stolen property. If you find it, then I will definitely punish him. But he is saying that he has not taken it. You three are witnesses to the crime, but he can bring one hundred witnesses who will say that they have not seen him stealing. What can I do? Let us pray to God, and God will give us illumination. If God comes here in person, then God will show us where the thief has actually kept the stolen things."

Since God did not appear in court in person, the case was dismissed. God Himself was definitely the prime Witness, but how could He come?

### LTS 66. *What I need is money*

There was a young student who was very sad and miserable. His friends and colleagues asked him, "Why are you so sad?"

The student said, "I am so sad because I wrote to my parents to give me money so that I could buy a wristwatch. And what have they done? They have sent me a wristwatch."

His friends were puzzled. They said, "What is the matter? You wanted money to buy a wristwatch, and your parents have sent you a nice wristwatch."

The student said, "Oh no, no, no! That is not what I wanted at all. Each time I ask them for something, they usually send me money to buy that particular thing. Then I use the money in my own way. Last time I asked them to give me money to buy some books. Immediately they sent me money. They said they did not know which books I needed, so they gave me the necessary money. Of course, I spent the money in my own way.

"The previous time, I told them that I needed notebooks and a small tape recorder. They sent me money, and I used that money for some other purpose. At night I enjoy going to the movies or I buy other things with their money. Always I use the money for my own pleasure. But this time I cannot do that. They have given me the actual wristwatch, so what am I going to do? I am so miserable. It is not what I wanted at all. Now I have to think of something else which they will not be able to send, so that they will give me the money.

"I need money more than anything else. I am supposed to study for my examination, but many text-books I do not have because I used the money for other things. Who wants to study? But it is good to remain a student. As long as I am a student, I can ask them for money. Now I have to think of something else that they will not be able to send. I asked for a wristwatch, and they have given me a wristwatch. What I need from my parents is only money."

This is how the young student deceived his parents.

### LTS 67. *The cheater*

One day two friends were relating all the village gossip. One friend said, "I feel so sorry for Peter. He is a good person, but when it comes to horse races, his horse always loses. So I feel very, very sorry for him."

The other one said, "You feel sorry for Peter? Do you not know that he is a real rogue? Whenever we play cards, he shuffles the cards in a tricky way in order to win. Since he cannot shuffle the horses, he loses all the time. You feel sorry because his horse loses every time. I do not feel sorry for him at all. He deserves to lose. There he cannot shuffle, whereas when he plays cards, he shuffles the cards dishonestly and defeats everybody."

The first one said, "I never knew that Peter was such a rogue. I will tell him that everybody knows what he is doing."

The first friend was sympathising with Peter, but the other one felt that Peter deserved to lose money at the horse races. The first one went to his friend Peter and said, "Peter, I never knew that you were such a bad fellow. I have come to learn all about your cheating at cards. Since you do this kind of thing, your horse deserves to lose."

Peter became furious and said, "Tell the fellow who says that I cheat at cards that God has given me a brain. I have more intelligence and more talent than any of you. That is why I defeat you all. Who asked you all to be idiots? You deserve to lose to me. Unfortunately, my horse does not have brains. I have been trying so hard to give him some brains so he can defeat the other horses. I am praying and praying to God that one day my horse will also be very clever the way I am clever. Just wait! When I do tricky things while playing cards, none of you can catch me. But someday my horse will acquire my intelligence. Then my horse will defeat all the other horses."

The friend said, "All right, then let us wait. I am waiting for the day when your horse will have your brain!"

### LTS 68. *The humble politician*

A politician came out of his office only to find many, many voters screaming at him and hurling insults at him. They were berating him at the top of their lungs. He said to these angry voters, "Why are you behaving like this? What have I done?"

The voters said, "You rogue! We do not want you to represent us. You are no good."

The man said, "I am no good? What have I done?"

One voter was so mad that he screamed, "I am going to stone you."

Then he threw a stone at the politician. The politician bent his head, and the stone flew by without striking his head. The politician said to the unruly crowd, "Look, here is the proof that I am a good person. You are all saying I am a very, very bad person. No, I assure you I am a good person. Other politicians always keep their heads straight. They never bow to anybody because they feel they know everything; they believe they are perfect. They are sure that they will make you all happy. In my case, I am not like that. I am modest, I am humble. When you threw the stone, it did not strike me. Why? Because of my humility. When I bowed to you, your stone did not strike my head."

An old lady happened to be there. The politician went to the old lady because she had a reputation for being extremely honest. All the others were watching. He said to this old lady, "Please tell me, who will you vote for?"

She said, "Young man, I do like you, but I want to tell you that you are my second choice."

Everybody started roaring with laughter and saying, "Oh, he is the second choice, second choice!"

The politician was miserable. He thought that he had convinced the crowed that he was a very humble man, if not the most humble man.

Then the old lady said, "My first choice is anyone who is not a politician!"

### LTS 69. *The rogue ascetic*

There was a village where people were extremely worried because there had been no rain for a long time. They were suffering from a severe drought. The farmers could not produce any crops in their fields, and everybody was suffering so much.

An ascetic happened to come to the village. He observed the plight of the villagers and said, "Why do you have to worry? Just bring some money and gifts and I will worship God. God will definitely listen to my prayers. Anything that you give me, I will accept, but it has to come from honest people. If you are dishonest, then do not bring me anything. I am a very pure person. I do not want to have anything to do with impure and insincere people. Only my sincere prayer will reach God. So if you are dishonest or insincere people, then do not bring me anything. Only honest people should bring gifts."

Naturally everybody was of the opinion that he was honest. So the ascetic received a great deal of money and many gifts. He told the villagers that he would use some of the gifts to do a very, very special puja. The ascetic said, "I will have to pray for three days privately and secretly in my hut. Nobody should watch me. Then when I come out, it will be the signal that I have finished."

All the villagers waited outside the ascetic's hut for three days and three nights, but there was no speck of rain, not to speak of a torrential downpour. The villagers became furious and many started crying. They had given the ascetic so much money and so many gifts, but it had all come to nought.

Finally the ascetic emerged. He told the villagers, "Did I not tell you that it would work only if you were all sincere and honest? What can I do? I have prayed for three days. Obviously you are not honest. That is why my prayer was not granted. Even if I pray for ten days, nothing will happen because there are dishonest people who have given me gifts. I have never seen a village where people were so bad!"

When they heard this, the villagers cursed the ascetic. They wanted to retrieve their money and valuable things and they even went to the extent of thrashing him. They thought that perhaps he had hidden some of the money, but when they could not find it, they finally kicked him out of the village.

## LTS 70. *The old man's prayers for the king*

There was a king who became very, very sick. His queen was extremely worried and his sons, the princes, were also very worried that their father would die. For months and months the king suffered, and it seemed his days were numbered. He was almost like a dead man.

Finally, after many months, the king's health changed for the better and he managed to come to the court for the first time. Everybody was so happy and delighted that the king was getting better. All were in the seventh Heaven of delight, specially the queen and the princes. They were shedding tears of joy.

While they were all celebrating, the gatekeeper of the palace opened the gates for some courtiers to enter, but an old man came inside instead. This man was old, but he was quite fast. The gatekeeper chased him, but the old man ran and fell flat at the king's feet, saying, "O King, I am so grateful to you."

The gatekeeper began apologising profusely to the king. He said, "Your Majesty, for five days this old man has been loitering near the gates. I suspected him, but I never thought that he would be so smart as to come through the gate when I was distracted. With your permission, I will now stop chasing him and start thrashing him."

The king said, "Wait, wait. Let us give this old man a chance to tell his story."

The old man said, "Your Majesty, we heard in our village that you had fallen very, very ill. I am extremely devoted to you. Like me, there are many, many villagers who are so devoted to you. You are such a kind-hearted king. Where will we find another king like you? For the past few months we have been praying and praying. Along with many others, I prayed to Mother Kali: 'Divine Mother, please, please, cure our king. He is so good. We will never be able to find another king who is so kind-hearted, so compassionate, so forgiving.' We prayed and prayed, and Mother Kali listened to our prayers. Four or five days ago, I received the message that you were getting better. I was so happy. I offered prasad to Mother Kali, and I have brought some prasad for you."

The old man had brought the prasad in a small bowl inside a dirty, filthy bag. He dropped the bag, touched the king's feet and ran away. Everybody was shocked. The bag was dirty and filthy and it had a terrible odour. Some members of the court wanted to chase the old man because they believed he was a rogue. But the king held a different opinion. He said, "Where can you find such a nice person? I know he is telling the truth."

Then the king told the gatekeeper, "I am giving you ten thousand rupees. Run as fast as you can and catch him and give him the money. If you cannot give him the money, then I will fire you. What kind of gatekeeper do I have?"

The gatekeeper took the money and ran after the old man. When the fellow saw that he was being chased, he cried, "I am outside the gate. Why are you still chasing me?"

The gatekeeper screamed, "Wait, wait, wait! The king has given me something for you."

The old man did not believe him. He thought that the gatekeeper would thrash him, so he did not stop. The gatekeeper had to run very fast to catch him. He gave the old man the bag of coins, saying, "This money is for you from the king." Then the gatekeeper returned to the palace.

The king told the members of his court, "Look, this old man has brought me stale food, but to me it is like nectar. He is poorer than the poorest. Five days ago he cooked this simple village food and offered it to Mother Kali. It smells bad, true. But his heart is made of beauty. His heart is full of love. His heart is full of fragrance. Do I have any person here like him? His heart is made of beauty, love and fragrance. I can feel it. I can see it.

He is the one who really cured me. He and others from that village who really love me cured me. It was not your prayers. You only worried, and some of you perhaps were secretly happy because you thought that soon I would pass away and you would be able to exploit my kingdom. I need people like this old man. His heart is all beauty, all fragrance and all love for me."

### LTS 71. *Mother Kali's boon*

One day a middle-aged man entered into a temple. He was looking at the statue of Mother Kali and crying and crying and crying. For some time the priest watched the man. Then the priest told him, "It is too much. You are making so much noise and disturbing everyone. Get out! Get out of this sacred place. Others have to pray and meditate in silence. You are ruining the atmosphere."

Then the priest dragged the man outside with the help of some other worshippers. When the man was outside the temple, again he started crying. The priest became extremely irritated. He said, "Now you have to leave these precincts. Do whatever you want to in the street, but not near the temple."

The man continued to cry and cry, so they took him about a hundred metres away from the temple. Some strong men remained with him to prevent him from re-entering the temple.

All of a sudden Mother Kali appeared in her fiercest aspect holding her sword. Those who were guarding the man got frightened because she looked at them with such powerful eyes. Then she turned to the man, full of compassion and full of love. She changed her mood completely. Mother Kali frightened those guarding the man, and then she was full of love, affection and concern for the man himself.

Mother Kali said to him, "Now tell me, my son, why are you crying?"

The man said, "I am crying because one of my friends has become a magistrate. One has become a doctor, and another has become an engineer. All of them have become very, very famous. Poor me, I am nothing. I studied with them, but now they have become so famous in their own fields, and I am nobody. I do not think I will amount to anything, so I am crying. I am so grateful to you, Mother, for coming. What am I going to do with my fate?"

Mother Kali asked him, "What do you want me to do?"

He said, "Please give me one boon."

"What boon?" Mother Kali asked.

The man said, "I am so jealous of my friends who have become so great in their own fields. I am so embarrassed to see them. They invite me to come to their homes, but they are such big shots that I do not dare to accept. In my case, I do not even have a wife. I tried to find one, but nobody wants to marry me because I am not successful."

Mother Kali asked, "Do you want to have a wife?"

The man said, "No, now that you have come, I want to die here and now, in front of you."

Mother Kali said, "No, no, your time has not come. Please ask me for something else. Any desire you have, I will fulfil. I do not want you to die, but I am ready to fulfil any other desire. Tell me what you would like to have, what you would like to be."

The man was thinking and thinking. Mother Kali continued, "Do you want to be another doctor or another engineer or another very important person? Anything that you want I will grant you."

Still the man was thinking and thinking and thinking, but his mind was not functioning. He said, "Already there is a doctor, there is an engineer, there is a magistrate. What else can I become?" Nothing was coming to his mind.

Mother Kali said, "What am I going to do? I am ready to fulfil your desire, to grant you anything you want, but you have to name something."

The man said, "I do not know what I want to be. I only know that my friends have all become so great."

Mother Kali said, "My son, in life there should be a goal. You earned your degree, but you did not pursue any field. They wanted to become a doctor, engineer, magistrate and so forth. In your case, you had no goal. You have the arrow, but there should be a target. If you do not aim the arrow at the target, how will you reach your destination? You have become the arrow, but you have no desire to go to the destination, the target. Always you have to have a goal. Then you have to become the goal. This is what your friends did. In your case, you did not want to become anything. Now I am telling you that it is not too late. There is still a chance for you."

"Oh no, it is too late," lamented the man.

"It is not too late!" insisted Mother Kali.

Then the man said, "Only give me this boon: I want to die because it is too late for me."

Mother Kali said, "No, you can make a successful career."

He said, "No, Mother, I want to die at your feet."

Mother Kali said, "At my feet? Then where do you want to go?"

The man said, "I do not want to go anywhere. I will die at your feet and go wherever you take me."

Mother Kali was full of compassion and affection for this soul. She said, "All right, I bless you. I will take you to the highest Heaven." Mother Kali touched him, and he died. Then she disappeared.

Those who were passing by said, "What is happening? This noisy fellow is not crying and screaming any more?" They came closer and saw that the man was dead.

Those who had seen Mother Kali appear thought that she had looked at him with the same kind of anger and destructive power with which she had looked at them. They said, "We knew that he was a bad fellow. But he was also an idiot. He did not run away. That is why the Mother Goddess killed him. He deserved it."

None of them wanted to take the dead body away. Everybody wanted to leave without taking care of this body.

Suddenly Mother Kali appeared. Once again the villagers all ran away. They were frightened to death. Then Mother Kali used her occult power and took the body away, flying in the sky. When the villagers came back, the body was not there and Mother Kali had also vanished.

The villagers thought that this man was very bad, but as it happened, he was the one to receive all Mother Kali's love, affection and concern.

### LTS 72. *The loan*

A villager needed a loan. He went from door to door, but nobody would lend him money. Finally he went to his landlord and asked, "Please, will you lend me three thousand rupees?"

The landlord said, "Why? Is there nobody else who can give you three thousand rupees?"

The villager said, "Certainly, I can borrow money from anyone, even from the worst possible miser."

"Then why have you come to me?" the landlord asked.

The villager explained, "I have come here because you are very noble, kind-hearted and pious. I want to show off that I can take money even from a great landlord. It is only to boost my ego. Since you are so great, I will be able to tell others that I have taken a loan from a truly great man."

The landlord said, "All right, since you have come here and since you are flattering me, I could give you three thousand rupees. But, instead, let me see if you can borrow money from the worst possible miser. You have to keep your promise. Go and borrow three thousand rupees from the worst possible miser in the world and then bring the money here and show me."

"What will you give me if I do this?" asked the villager.

The landlord replied, "If you can bring back the money from the worst possible miser, I will give you this golden bangle, which is worth four thousand rupees. By selling this bracelet, you will be able to return three thousand to the miser and keep one thousand rupees for yourself."

The villager agreed. Then he said, "I can tell you who I think is the worst possible miser, but do you have anyone particular in mind?"

The landlord replied, "Yes, I know who he is." The landlord and the zamindar of a far-off village absolutely hated each other. The landlord told him the name of that person.

"Go to that village," the landlord continued. "The village zamindar is so miserly. If you can bring money from him, I will be very proud of you."

"But that miserly zamindar's place is so far away," complained the villager. "Can you not do me a favour? Will you not give me the bangle first and send one or two of your bodyguards to accompany me? I am sure I will be able to get the loan from that miserly zamindar. If I cannot borrow the money from him, you will get your bracelet back."

The landlord agreed to the villager's proposal and gave him both the bangle and the bodyguards to accompany him. Then the villager set off to fulfil his task.

They travelled very far. When they finally reached their destination, the villager immediately went to see the zamindar.

"What do you want?" the miserly zamindar asked.

The villager showed him the bangle and said, "If you give me ten thousand rupees, I will give you this most valuable bracelet."

The miser examined the bangle and said, "It is so beautiful. Ten thousand rupees I am giving you immediately." The zamindar was such a greedy fellow that right away he agreed to buy the bangle for a very high price. Although the first landlord had said it was worth four thousand rupees, the miserly zamindar thought it was worth much more. He was sure he would be able to sell it for at least fifteen thousand rupees, so he eagerly gave the villager ten thousand rupees.

Once the transaction had been completed, the villager said to the bodyguards, "Look, I came to your boss for a loan of three thousand rupees, but he sent me here to see if I could borrow from this man instead. Now I am ready to give you three thousand rupees to bring back to your boss, according to our agreement."

The bodyguards exclaimed, "You rogue! You sold the bangle to get the money. But you were supposed to borrow the money. Only if you could borrow the money and bring it back to our boss would you be entitled to keep the bangle. Those were the terms of your agreement."

The man said, "What is wrong? I am not supposed to give back the bangle. Your boss did not have any objection if I showed the bracelet to anybody. The main thing was for me to get the money. He told me that if I could borrow money, then I could keep the bangle. That is what I have done."

The bodyguards were furious. They said, "But the bangle is not with you any more. You have just sold it. You were supposed to borrow the money without giving the zamindar anything."

While the guards were arguing between themselves, the villager secretly told the miserly zamindar how his landlord had called him "absolutely the worst miser in God's entire creation." The zamindar, who hated the other landlord, immediately wanted to prove that he was not a miser and that his enemy was a fool.

He said to the villager in front of the bodyguards, "All right. Take your bracelet back. The money is a loan." He was so smart. He knew he would be able to get the bracelet back from the villager.

The villager turned to the two bodyguards and exclaimed triumphantly, "You see that I have borrowed the money from this good zamindar. Now the bracelet is mine. But since he has lent me such a large amount of money, out of generosity, I am giving him the bracelet to keep. I only wanted three thousand rupees from your boss, but he ordered me to go and bring the money from the worst possible miser. Your boss chose this zamindar. I did not. So now I have succeeded in getting the money. It is up to me what I do after that."

The miserly zamindar and the villager were now very nicely in collusion.

The villager said to the bodyguards, "Look, I have the bangle with me. Here is the proof that this good zamindar has lent me the money and not purchased the bangle."

"Yes," agreed the miserly zamindar. "I am confirming that I lent him the money. He did not sell me this bangle."

The bodyguards were still arguing that it was not a loan. Because the zamindar wanted to keep the bracelet, he and his servants began striking the bodyguards mercilessly.

Finally, the villager said to the bodyguards, "Once and for all, I am requesting you to take the three thousand rupees. Either go back to your boss and show him that I have lived up to our agreement, or split the money and keep it yourselves."

The prospect of keeping the money for themselves was too tempting for the bodyguards. They divided the money equally and did not return to their boss.

They were all such rogues. Instead of borrowing the money, as he had agreed to do, the villager sold the bangle to the miserly zamindar. Rather than giving the three thousand rupees to their boss, the bodyguards kept it for themselves.

The first landlord was the worst possible fool. He wanted to make fun of the villager by asking him to get a loan from his worst enemy. But the landlord did not get any satisfaction. On the contrary, he lost everything. He lost his money because his bodyguards decided to keep it for themselves, he lost the bracelet because the villager sold it for ten thousand rupees, and he lost his bodyguards because they never returned. So he was, indeed, the real loser.

### LTS 73. *God listened to his prayer*

There were two Russian friends who happened to meet on the street. They went to have a cup of tea, and they were chatting.

The first friend said, "You must be so proud of your sons. One son is a doctor. One son is a lawyer. One son is a musician. You must be so proud!"

The other friend replied, "Yes, I am happy with those three sons. But I am truly proud of my fourth son, who lives in America. He has his American citizenship. He is now retired and receives a pension. From that he is able to send me money on a regular basis. With that money we are able to save the whole family from starvation.

The next day, the first man went to the post office and made friends with a postal worker there. He told him about his friend who received money from his son in America on a regular basis. He proposed, "Let us intercept his letters, since they contain money for his family."

After that, every month, whenever there was a letter from America, the postal worker used to give it to this man. There was always money in it. The man used to give a little money to the postal worker, and the rest he would keep for himself.

This went on for one month, two months, three months. The father was not getting any money from his son in America, and he was becoming so sad and miserable. The son in America was also sad that his father was not thanking him for any of his letters. Although the father was worried, he did not write to ask his son what was the matter. He just waited.

After some time, the father finally sent his son a letter saying that he was not receiving any letters from him and asking if everything was all right. The son was sad and furious. He did not know where the money was going, whether it was being stopped in America or Russia.

Time passed by and one day the two friends again met in the street. This time the father of the son in America was so sad. His friend, the rogue, asked, "Why are you so miserable? What has happened to you?"

The father said, "I do not know what has happened to my son in America. He is not writing to me or sending me money any more. I do not know what is wrong with him." He started crying and said, "I have no idea whether he is even alive or not!"

The heart of the rogue was touched by his friend's sadness. "Let us pray to God for your son," he said.

The father replied, "But we are communists. We do not believe in God."

The rogue said, "No, when we are in danger, we can pray to God and God will save us. I am praying to God on your behalf, but will you start praying to God yourself?"

The father answered, "All right. If I again start getting money from my son, I will definitely believe in your prayers, and I, too, will start praying to God."

Then the rogue went back to the post office and said to the postal worker, "We have enough money now. Let us not steal any more. From now on, whenever a letter from America comes, you should send it to the right person."

When the father again began to receive letters from his son in America, he was so happy, so relieved and so surprised at the same time. He told his rogue-friend, "God has listened to your prayer! Now I am also going to become a devotee of God. I shall pray like you."

So the father started praying to God — if there is a God — since God had listened to his friend's prayer!

### LTS 74. *The Russian bank workers*

There were once three workers in a bank in Russia. One day, one of the workers was fired because he had come late to work. Not only was he fired, but in those days in Russia if you came late to work, they would put you in jail. So he was thrown into jail.

On another day, the second worker came early. As a result, the manager of the bank suspected he was a spy, assuming he had come early to see if he could send some news or some sort of message to America. Otherwise, he thought, there was no reason for him to come early. So that worker was also arrested and thrown into jail.

The third worker always came on time. One day, the bank manager asked him, "How do you always come on time?"

The worker answered, "It is because I have an American wristwatch. It keeps perfect time."

The manager said, "How is it that you have an American wristwatch? I do not have an American wristwatch. Communism means that all are equal. How can you have this wristwatch and not me? No, it is not good. I will have you thrown into jail for three months because you are not following communism. After three months, when you come back, I will give you back your wristwatch." So the third worker was sent to jail without his wristwatch.

All three workers ended up in the same jail together.

The first worker said to the others, "What is this? I came late to work once and I ended up in jail! Look at my fate!"

The second worker exclaimed, "What about me? I came to work early and because of that I have been thrown into jail! Does it make any sense?"

The third worker said, "My case is the worst! For wearing an American wristwatch I have been put in jail! Because I wanted always to be on time for work, I used an American wristwatch which keeps the correct time, whereas Russian wristwatches do not."

They all said to each other, "Now what shall we do?"

The three workers were all of the same opinion. They decided that since it was due to the policies of the bank that they were now in jail, they would rob the bank at the earliest opportunity.

All three agreed that once their jail terms were over, they would go back to the bank and cry and cry to have their jobs back. They felt that the manager would be very happy to give them back their jobs because he would feel badly that they had undergone imprisonment. On their first day back, they would all go to work at the same time. The best thing would be for them to go as early as possible. Then they could easily rob the bank. Afterwards, with the money they stole, they could go to a real spy. They would offer the spy a little money and ask him to help them to go to America, the land of the bold and the land of the gold.

When their jail sentences were over, the three workers went back to the bank crying and crying, and the manager did give them their jobs back. Then, as planned, they robbed the bank. Next, they went to see the spy to give him money so that he would make arrangements for them to go to America.

The spy said to the three workers, "You have given me money. Let me see what I can do for you. I am sure my friends in America will take care of you. I will make the arrangements for you."

Overjoyed at the prospect of going to America, the three workers eagerly gave the spy even more money. Still they had some left for their journey to America. They were very happy.

Alas, after taking the money from the workers, the spy went directly to the manager of the bank and told him everything. The bank manager was furious and immediately had the three arrested and sent back to jail. The spy was honoured by the bank and received a cash reward from the bank manager, while the three workers ended up in jail again — this time indefinitely.

### LTS 75. *The German friend and the Russian friend*

A German man and a Russian man were very good friends. But friendship is made of nothing, if not rivalry.

The German man had four or five children, and the Russian man also had four or five children. They lived on either side of a small river which divided Russia and Germany. Even though they lived in two different countries, their houses were so close to each other that they could even speak loudly to each other from one side of the river to the other.

The German friend used to go fishing on his side of the river, and the Russian would do the same on his side. They would often come at the same time. Smiling at each other, they would start fishing on their respective sides of the river.

One day, when they were both fishing, the German man caught many fish one after another. But his poor Russian friend did not catch any fish although he was just across the small river. It seemed that on the Russian side there were no fish, while on the German side there were so many fish! The German friend was catching fish again and again and again.

The Russian friend was so miserable. He said, "Why am I not catching anything, while you keep catching one fish after the other? Please tell me, what is the secret?"

The German man said, "My Russian friend, you are such a fool! Do you not know that in your country, you are not allowed to open your mouth? In our country we are allowed to open our mouths, and we do so as much as we like. In your country even the fish are afraid of opening their mouths! If they do not open their mouths, how will you catch them?"

The Russian friend said, "My German friend, how right you are! It seems the only way I will ever be allowed to open my mouth is to go to Germany. But how shall I get there?"

The German friend replied, "Do not worry. I will come to help you. One evening I shall swim across. Do you know how to swim?"

The Russian man said, "No, I do not know how."

The German friend responded, "No harm. I will carry you on my back and take you to the German side."

The Russian man said, "That is fine. You will save my life. You are so compassionate."

The Russian fellow was so grateful to the German because he was prepared to smuggle him into Germany. Alas, while the Russian man was eagerly waiting for his German friend to cross the river, the German man was swimming very happily and making a great deal of noise. He was making so much commotion that he could not escape the attention of the guards who were patrolling the shore on the Russian side.

"What is that?" the guards exclaimed. Seeing the German man swimming towards them, they kept quiet, and when the German reached the shore, they grabbed him.

"What are you coming here for?" they asked.

The German man replied, "I came to save my friend."

The guards said, "You came to save your friend? Now we are arresting both of you!"

So, if you have an open heart, you suffer. And if you make fun of someone, somehow God punishes you. At first, the German man was making fun of the Russian for not being able to catch any fish. Then, he became so sympathetic and tried to save the Russian, in spite of the fact that the Russian man did not even know how to swim. Then, unfortunately, both of them were caught.

### LTS 76. *The size of the communist party*

In a primary school in Russia, one day the teacher asked the students, "Can you tell us the size of the Communist Party?"

Some students stood up and said, "It is so vast. It has countless people."

Then another group of students stood up and said, "It is more than countless. It is infinite."

Everybody was satisfied except one boy.

The teacher said to the boy, "Now there are two groups. One has said the Communist Party has countless people, and the other said it is infinite. What do you want to say?"

The young boy said, "I want to say that the size of the Communist Party is five feet, eight inches tall!"

Some of the other students laughed, some were shocked and some were furious at the boy's answer.

The teacher asked the boy, "Why do you say such a thing?"

The boy replied, "My father is a communist leader. He is six feet, two inches tall. Every evening when he comes home from work, he says, 'I have had enough of the Communist Party. I have had it up to here.' Then he points to his chin, which is about five feet, eight inches high when he is standing up! He says, 'I am not going to be a member of the Party any more.' But again the following day he goes back to work."

Everyone in the class was shocked because the boy's father had spoken against the Communist Party. The other students wanted to thrash this boy. But the teacher said, "No, no. If all of you thrash him, he will die." So the teacher did not allow the students to beat the boy.

After school, the teacher took the boy home and said, "From tomorrow, you will not be able to come to school. Otherwise, those unruly children will surely thrash you."

The following day, the teacher felt compelled to go see someone very high-ranking in the Communist Party and report to him how a child in his class had told them his father's words against the Party.

Meanwhile, the child was at home crying because he would not be able to go to school for a while. He did not know that his teacher was reporting his father to the Communist Party.

The parents were very concerned and asked their son, "What have you done that you are not allowed to go to school?"

The boy told his father, "When the teacher asked me what was the size of the Communist Party, I said that you always say that it is up to your chin — five feet, eight inches tall. For that, I cannot go to school." The boy was so miserable.

No sooner had the boy uttered these words than the police came to the house, arrested the father and took him to jail. The child and the mother were crying and crying.

On hearing what had happened, the teacher felt sorry for what he had done. In a short time, he was summoned by the communist leader, who asked him, "How could you have kept such a bad student? Why did you not examine him previously?"

The teacher told him, "He is just a little boy. That day I had asked the students about the size of the Communist Party. He just repeated what he had been hearing from his father."

The high-ranking communist leader said, "Have you nothing else to ask your students? Look what you have done! When the boy's father's jail term is over, he may create real problems for us. He is very talented. We are afraid that he will become a spy and send reports to America about us. Since you have done this, we have to take revenge on you. Since you are the problem-maker, you also have to serve time in jail."

So the teacher was thrown into jail.

This story shows that at that time in Russia, nobody could open his mouth without getting into trouble.

# LIFE'S BLEEDING TEARS AND FLYING SMILES

## BOOK 6

## LTS 77. *The miser's just punishment*

There was a man who was very rich and, at the same time, extremely miserly. He would not spend money even for the basic necessities of life. Even when he had to go to the market, he would walk. He was ready to cover the distance of three miles in the hot sun to save the few rupees that a carriage would cost. Everybody in the village knew that he was the wealthiest person and the worst possible miser. His reputation had spread far and wide.

One day the miser was on his way to the market. As usual, he was proceeding on foot. There were many carts and carriages passing by. One cart stopped and the driver said, "Come in, come in! You do not have to walk all the way. Just give me a rupee and I will take you there in half the time. Instead of walking, you can afford to give me a rupee."

"One rupee? No! I can afford only half a rupee," said the miser.

"Half?" cried the driver. Then he said, "It is beneath my dignity to deal with a poor man like you."

"You are calling me a poor man? Do I look like a poor man?" said the miser. He was furious with the driver. "I am the richest man in this district," he said. "I am carrying three thousand rupees with me at this moment!"

When he made this astonishing revelation, the driver of the cart said a few unkind words to him: "Three thousand rupees you are carrying, and you cannot even give me one rupee!"

Then both of them exchanged harsh words. The miser was so proud of his wealth that he said he had three thousand rupees in his pocket. Still he did not want to part with one rupee. He was only prepared to spend half a rupee to go to the market.

A hooligan happened to be nearby and he overheard the whole story. As soon as the cart driver left the scene, this hooligan came and grabbed the miser. The miser was absolutely helpless. In a rough voice, the hooligan said to him, "Now, give me all your money or I will kill you here and now!"

The miser emptied his pockets and the hooligan found that this richest man had only one hundred rupees and not three thousand rupees as he had boasted. This hooligan had been so happy at the prospect of getting three thousand rupees but, instead, he was able to steal only one hundred rupees.

The hooligan said, "Since you do not have three thousand rupees, I have something for you!" Then he slapped the miser extremely hard. Another slap followed and finally a third one.

The first slap was for being the richest man and at the same time being so stingy. Then another slap the miser received for being so proud of his wealth. The third slap was for telling a lie. He was such a rogue! So three slaps he received from the hooligan.

Finally the hooligan said to him, "Had I known that you had only one hundred rupees, I would not have taken the trouble of coming to you." Then he took the one hundred rupees and left the miser in the street, still smarting from the three slaps.

### LTS 78. *The dishonest son-in-law*

Three friends were on their way to the market. One of them was very, very intelligent, and the other two had tremendous respect for him. On their way they found a bundle. They picked it up and, out of sheer curiosity, they opened it and found a large sum of money inside.

One of them said, "It is not good for us to keep this money. Let us go and give it to the village zamindar."

The second one said, "Yes, we should be honest. The poor fellow who has lost it is now miserable."

The intelligent one said, "You fools! Why should we do that? We three need money badly. It is our good fortune that we discovered the bundle, and it is somebody else's bad fortune to lose it. Why should we be responsible for his bad fortune? We should be grateful to God for our good fortune. Let us divide the money. Let us all take equal shares."

Now, how long can good qualities last? The good qualities of the first two friends surrendered to the bad qualities of the intelligent man. Sometimes good qualities last only for a few seconds.

The three friends divided the money, and each one received a very large sum. They went to the market and got the things they needed, and still they had lots of money in their pockets.

When the intelligent man returned home, he saw his mother-in-law at the door, crying very bitterly. He and his mother-in-law were on very good terms. So when he saw his mother-in-law crying and crying, it absolutely broke his heart.

He said to her, "You are like my own mother. You are full of affection and love for me. You know that I am so fond of you. I will do anything you want me to do."

His mother-in-law said, "Then please, please, can you take me to the police station nearby?"

"What has happened?" he asked anxiously.

She explained, "I was coming to your place, and I was bringing with me lots of money for you, because you are like my real son. For my daughter I was bringing a most expensive diamond ring. Now, unfortunately, I dropped my bag and I cannot find it. I do not even know where I dropped it. Let us go at once and inform the police. After that we can search for it ourselves. But I do not think that we will find it.

The son-in-law began to shed bitter tears. He did not have the heart to tell his mother-in-law what he and his friends had done. He simply said, "All right, let us go to the police station first."

Both of them went to the police station and reported the missing money, but the son-in-law knew in the heart of his heart what he had done. He said, "I feel so sorry about your loss. I have a little money, please accept it." He did not tell her that he was the culprit. He merely said, "This little money I would like to give you."

She said, "Why? I do not need money from you. I came here to give *you* money. I do not need it for myself. It is very kind of you to offer it, but I do not need it. I only feel miserable that I am unable to give you the money I had intended to give. Such a large amount I brought with me to give you."

Where is comedy in life? It is full of sadness.

### LTS 79. *A moment of Brahma's time*

There was a great devotee of Brahma. He had been praying and praying for years to Brahma. Brahma was very pleased with his devotion, and so Brahma appeared before him.

This devotee said to Brahma, "Lord, why are you so unkind to me? It has taken so many years for you to come to me. How hard I have been trying to please you so that I can have my desires fulfilled!"

Brahma replied, "My son, for you it has been years and years. For me, it has been only a matter of a moment, a second. Our one second is equivalent to your thirty or forty years or even more. So, what can I tell you?"

The devotee said, "O Brahma, in that case, please tell me, one rupee of yours will be equivalent to how many rupees of ours? Since your one second is our thirty or forty years, then for your one rupee, how many rupees will we get on earth?"

"Millions and billions of rupees," said Brahma, "but, unfortunately, I never thought that you would ask me for money. Because you have been praying to me so sincerely and I am a spiritual being, I thought you would ask me for spiritual things."

The devotee said, "O Brahma, can you do me a favour? I shall wait for you here, if you go back to your abode and bring me a large amount of money."

Brahma smiled and said, "Fine, my son, fine! Kindly wait here. I shall come back in a moment!"

The devotee was filled with happiness that in a moment Brahma would return with millions of rupees.

Now, Brahma was gone and it was taking him years and years to return, because Brahma's moment was equal to so many years of earthly time. Brahma was taking his own time to make the fellow rich. So the poor fellow was waiting and waiting in vain for Brahma's return.

### LTS 80. *The village fool*

There was a fool in one particular village. He was absolutely the worst possible fool. Everybody made fun of him. So the fool went to the village chief. He was crying and crying, "People are always making fun of me. Please give me some intelligence."

The village chief said, "Definitely I will inject some intelligence and wisdom into you. This will be your first lesson. Listen carefully. I had three sons plus my wife. Now, my wife died of a heart attack, one son died of cholera, another died of a brain defect and the third one died in a car accident. All of them have passed away. They were very, very close to me. They lived for me and I lived for them. Out of five, only one person remains, and that person will be the next to die. Can you tell me who that person is?"

The fool answered, "How can I know the answer? You are saying that your family members were so dear to each other. Intimate things you used to share with one another. You never involved me in your private family discussions, so I do not know what went on between you and your wife and children, and I do not know who will be the next person to die."

The village chief said, "You cannot answer such a simple question? Since I am the only one left, am I not the one who will die next?"

"Oh, yes, I am sorry," stammered the fool. In this way he received wisdom from the village chief and left full of gratitude to him.

Then the fool went to his friends, bragging about his new-found wisdom. He said to them, "I am asking you a question. You have to answer it correctly." Then he said exactly the same thing as the village chief had said to him: "I had three sons plus my wife" and so on. He described how each one had died. Then he asked them, "Now, who will be the next person to die?"

They all immediately said, "It will be you, you idiot!"

"No, no!" he cried. "You are all fools. The village chief, who is the wisest of all, told me that *he* would be the next one to die!"

Then the villagers laughed and laughed at the fool's wisdom.

### LTS 81. *The stolen bundle*

After committing a theft one night, the thief left all the stolen things in a bundle on the road. He had stolen many expensive items, but he did not take them with him. Early the next morning, the people who lived in the house found the bundle near their house. When they looked inside, they discovered that it contained their own stolen property.

Two villagers happened to pass by while they were examining the contents of the bundle and the owners told them what had happened. One villager said, "This bundle is so heavy! Although the thief was able to bring it out of the house, he knew that he would not be able to carry it home because his house is quite far. That is why he abandoned it here."

The other villager said, "No, it is not that. Perhaps he heard some noise and got frightened. That is why he dropped the bundle and ran away."

Now a third villager came and joined the discussion. He said, "You fools! It is not that he was weak or he became frightened, not at all. After stealing the items, the thief was going away. All of a sudden, he saw God in front of him. He was so thrilled when he saw the Beauty of God. Then God appealed to his conscience. God said, 'What are you doing? Do you not know that stealing is very bad? If you behave like this, if you steal any more, I will punish you.' Then God added, 'My son, in due course I will make you very, very rich. Do not steal from anyone.' So the thief listened to God and he left everything behind. He has faith that soon God will make him very, very rich. This is what actually happened."

The three villagers, plus the people who lived in the house, wanted to resolve their difference of opinion. They said, "Let us go and see the wisest person of all, the village chief. Come!"

They all went to the village chief and told him their stories. Each one had his own version. The village chief happened to be very kind and generous. He reflected for a few moments and said to them, "I believe the one who said that God appeared before the thief."

The other two villagers said, "In that case, if we leave the bundle here once again at the same place, then we, too, will be able to meet with God. God will appear again."

The village chief said, "I am not sure whether God will appear or not. I feel the best thing is to take the bundle inside where it is safe and then pray to God that He will appear before you."

One of the villagers vehemently disagreed. He said, "No! God will appear only at exactly the same place. That place is the luckiest place. God will appear only where we found the bundle."

The village chief said, "I have no idea if God will come again or not. I only feel that this version has some truth in it, that God came and awakened his conscience and that is why he went away without the stolen goods."

One of the people who lived in the house took the bundle into his room and began praying to God to appear before him. But, in spite of his fervent prayer, God did not appear. The two villager-friends said, "See, we told you that your room is not the right place. It has to be outside in the street where we found the bundle. Then only God will appear."

The man was eager to see God, so he placed the bundle containing all his expensive things in its original place. Then he started praying to God to come and stand before him. His prayer was most sincere. Alas, after a few hours he fell asleep. His two villager-friends were watching him. They saw that he was lying down in front of the bundle fast asleep. So these two rogues came and took the bundle away. The poor fellow lost everything.

The man went to the village chief, but the chief said, "I told you that I was not sure whether God would appear at the same place or not. Why did you leave your valuable things outside your house? Everybody wants to see God, but again, God gave us common sense. If you do not use your common sense, you will get this kind of unfortunate experience time and again. God is inside a mad elephant, true, but why should you go and stand in front of a mad elephant? The mad elephant will simply destroy you. Similarly, if you do not use common sense in your aspiration, you will only get this kind of unfortunate result."

### LTS 82. *The callous logician*

There was once a kind-hearted spiritual Master. He had three disciples. One was an ayurvedic doctor, one was an astrologer and the third one was an expert in logic. One day an elderly man came to this Master and pitifully asked him a question. He said, "Please illumine me. My daughter wants to marry a certain young man. I like him, but I am anxious. What do I know about the future? Please tell me whether or not they should get married."

The spiritual Master replied, "They are both good people. Both of them are very, very nice, and it will be a very happy marriage, but I see that in a few months' time your daughter will lose her husband. The marriage itself will be good, but then something will happen and your son-in-law will die."

"Oh no!" cried the elderly man. "Then I do not want this marriage to take place."

The spiritual Master said, "Wait, let me ask my disciples if they can be of any help."

The astrologer-disciple concentrated on the problem and said, "Yes, it is true. This young man will soon die."

The ayurvedic doctor-disciple quickly said, "No, he will not die. I have medicine. When he falls sick, immediately inform me and I will cure him. Your son-in-law will not die."

The elderly man was so happy that his son-in-law would not die.

The third disciple, the one who dealt with logic, kept quiet. He did not say even one word. The wife of the spiritual Master said, "Why do you have to keep that third disciple? He contributed nothing. He was silent. We do not need him. We need only the astrologer and the ayurvedic doctor."

The spiritual Master said, "No, we need all three."

The young couple got married and were leading a happy life. Then, in a few months' time, the husband fell seriously ill. Fortunately, the ayurvedic doctor was able to cure him.

Still the wife did not care for the third disciple, but the spiritual Master said, "Let me think of a way to show you that we need this fellow also." In front of the wife, he took a tiny insect and put it into his mouth. Only his wife knew it was a dead insect. Then he pretended that he was dying because he was suffering so much from this insect. The astrologer-disciple cast the spiritual Master's horoscope and said, "O my God! You are destined to die."

Then it was time for them to eat. It was the custom of the three disciples to eat together. The astrologer and the ayurvedic doctor said, "We will not eat until we can cure our Master. We have to cure him." They would not eat even one mouthful. The third disciple, the great logician, started eating heartily. Seeing this, the wife of the spiritual Master began scolding him ruthlessly.

"Clearly you have no concern for your Master," she said. "You see, the other two are not eating. They want to cure him. And what are you doing? Thinking of your own stomach!" The logician calmly went on eating.

Then the spiritual Master said, "At a time like this, logic is needed. We all saw that this insect is tinier than the tiniest. It is not going to kill me. But the other two are so stupid. They were convinced that I was going to die. I simply pretended that I was dying. Actually I would not have died from this kind of thing. So here logic is needed."

The wife said, "I do not need that kind of logic. If my husband is suffering, even if he pretends that he is dying, the disciples *must* show their love and concern."

Then she said to her husband, "Now you decide. Either your wife will stay with you or you can keep your third disciple."

The spiritual Master said to his wife, "I cannot afford to lose you."

So the disciple who was supreme in logic was thrown out of the Master's ashram.

LTS 83. *The king's ambassadors*

A king needed ambassadors for two different countries. So the minister found two well-educated men and brought them to the king for his approval. The king was very, very pleased with the minister's choices, and he confirmed their appointments. The king said to one ambassador, "I am sending you to this particular country. Although the people there are under my rule, I want to strengthen my friendship with them. I want them to be more loyal to me. I wish you to strengthen our relationship."

The king gave the ambassador a very nice present to give to the head of that particular small country. Then he gave identical instructions to the second ambassador and also entrusted him with a very expensive gift to give to the king of the second country. The king said to both of them, "Once you reach your destination, do not stay there for more than two days. After two days I want both of you to return. Give the gift and come back."

The two ambassadors left the palace to fulfil their commissions. One of them covered some distance, and then he turned back. When he came before the king, the king asked, "What happened? Why did you not go?"

The ambassador said, "O King, you have to forgive me. As I was travelling to that country, some ideas entered into me. You told me that you are infinitely more powerful than that ruler, and you want to strengthen your friendship. If you are so strong, what kind of friendship do you need with that country? Since they are already devoted to you, why do you have to strengthen your friendship? I am afraid they will misunderstand you when I go and tell the king that you want to strengthen your friendship. He will be shocked. He is already like your slave. So why do you have to strengthen your friendship? He will never expect your friendship. He will only expect commands from you. So I have come back to you in case you want to change your opinion."

The king said, "Change my opinion? I gave you an order and you did not obey me. What right do you have to question my orders? I do not approve of your disobedience, but before I take any action, let me wait and see how the other one fares."

Two days passed by and still the second ambassador had not come back. When he gave the expensive gift to the king of the neighbouring country, the king was so happy that he begged the ambassador to stay a few days more. The ambassador was enjoying himself immensely. He was given almost a royal reception. With difficulty, he took his leave after four days and returned to his own kingdom.

When this second ambassador appeared before the king, the king asked, "What happened?"

The ambassador replied, "O King, I have strengthened your friendship with that ruler immeasurably. He was so pleased, so happy. He treated me like another king, and he begged me to stay there because you gave him such an expensive gift. So I stayed there an extra four days."

The king became furious. He said, "I need an ambassador like the first one. On the one hand, ambassadors are bound to listen to the commands of the king. On the other hand, if they feel that something the king has said on the spur of the moment is unwise, then it is their supreme duty to bring it to the notice of the king. That ambassador did the right thing by returning to the palace. I am so superior to the rulers of those countries. Why do I have to strengthen my friendship with them? I do not need it. Did I not tell you to come back in two days' time? You stayed there an extra four days! This is how you listen to my command?"

The king dismissed the ambassador who lingered and enjoyed himself in the neighbouring country. Then the king said to the entire court, "We kings give orders to our ambassadors, but they can also give us advice on occasion and we shall consider it. After weighing the pros and cons, we shall either accept the advice or not. In this instance, I fully accept the advice of my first ambassador. That is the kind of ambassador I need."

### LTS 84. *Two impossible fools*

There were two real friends. Each one had one servant. One day the friends were talking to each other and they said, "Let us have a competition to see which of our servants is the worse or the better of the two."

As it happened, both the friends were blessed with impossible fools for servants. Fortunately, the fools did not mind that their bosses used to make fun of them.

The first friend said to his servant, "I am giving you a rupee. Please go and buy the most beautiful, most expensive diamond from the jewellery store."

The fool immediately said, "Easily." He agreed to go at once.

Now the other friend said to his servant, "Please go and see if I am walking in my garden."

The garden was at least a mile away from the house and the boss was inside the house with the servant when he gave the order. But this fool rushed away to see whether his master was walking in the garden.

So one servant went to buy a diamond with one rupee and the other one went to see if his master was in the garden. On the way, they met each other.

The first fool said, "My master is so proud of me. Today I am going to the market, and there I will buy a very nice diamond for him."

The second fool said, "My master is so proud of me. I am sure I will be able to find him in his garden."

Both of them were so proud of themselves.

After some time they came back to their respective masters. The first one said, "Master, you always make fun of me. Today I am making fun of you!"

At first the master pretended that he was very angry. He said, "You? Then try."

The first servant went on, "Master, I went to the market to buy you a diamond, and all the people were laughing at me because today is Sunday. Why did you send me on Sunday? You knew that the shops would be closed. Otherwise, I could easily have bought the diamond for you. But they were all laughing at me because you had sent me on Sunday." That was the wisdom of the first fool.

The second servant went to the garden to search for his master. There he saw somebody else walking, but it was not his master. This man said to him, "What kind of master do you have? He is such a fool. You tell your master on my behalf that he is a fool! He is now at home. How can you find him in his garden?"

This fool came back and said, "Master, every time you make fun of me. Today I am making fun of you. Somebody has told me that you are here. Since you are here, how can you be in the garden?"

Both the masters were so pleased with their servants. They said, "All right, we agree that both of you have now become extremely wise." Then the servants started laughing and laughing.

The two masters said, "Since you have both passed your examinations, we shall look for brides for you. We shall find a suitable girl for each of you. We will be responsible. We need some relaxation and enjoyment. We will find two girls who will be of your type to keep us happy."

### LTS 85. *A Brahmin priest teaches two thieves*

A Brahmin priest went to the house of a family to perform spiritual rites. He completed the rites and was going back home. His clients had given him a considerable amount of money as well as other expensive things because they were so pleased with him. He was carrying these things in a bag on his shoulder.

On the way, two bandits appeared out of nowhere and attacked him. When they demanded his bag, the clever priest said to them, "Take it, take it. You deserve it. In fact, if you take it, I will be so grateful to you. You have come to make me a good person. I do not need this money because I have stolen it."

The two thieves were surprised. They asked, "You have stolen it from where?"

The Brahmin priest pointed in a certain direction and said, "A short distance from here I saw a cart full of money, jewellery and expensive things. I did not see the owner anywhere. So I surrendered to temptation and stole these things. I was carrying them home before anybody discovered the loss. They are not my things, so you can take them. You will be saving me from a terrible sin."

As soon as the two bandits heard that there was a whole cart full of valuable items where the Brahmin priest had filled his bag, they left him with his bag and ran in the direction he had indicated. In the meantime, the Brahmin went back home with the money and gifts that were rightfully his.

### LTS 86. *A thief in the well*

A young girl was fetching water from the village well. As she was bringing up the water in the bucket, she was not careful enough, and her earring fell into the well. The young girl began to panic. How would she retrieve it?

In that particular village there was one man who was an expert diver. The young girl immediately thought of him and she went and asked him if he could dive into the well and find her earring. The diver told her that it was quite possible, but when he quoted his fee, it was exorbitant.

The young girl told him, "I cannot afford to hire you."

All the neighbours were extremely sympathetic to the young girl's plight, but they did not come to her rescue. She did not know where to turn.

Evening fell. A thief happened to pass by the well in the midst of the commotion. Everybody knew that this fellow was a thief, but nobody had been able to catch him in the act. He paid no attention to the girl's crying and weeping and continued on his way.

Finally, the girl returned home and the neighbours also went home. Late that night the thief came back to the well and very quietly entered into the water. He took a breath and dove to the bottom, but came up empty-handed. He tried again and again, but it was taking time for him to find the earring in the dark. After repeated unsuccessful attempts, he used a very bad word, a curse word. The neighbours woke up and came to the place saying, "Who is shouting there?"

They discovered the thief inside the well searching for the earring. The neighbours pulled the poor thief out of the well and thrashed him soundly. Then the neighbours became very sympathetic to the young girl and gave money to her to pay the expert diver to bring up the earring. She hired him and eventually he brought out her earring.

### LTS 87. *The king and his two ministers*

There was a king who had two ministers. One was named Bhola and the other one was Kala. According to the king's subjects, Bhola was extremely bad and Kala was extremely good. Bhola had the reputation of being extremely tricky, cruel and undivine. He used to torture all and sundry. If someone applied for a job in the palace, he used to harass them and compel them to give him a large bribe. Kala was very, very honest, but Kala also used to receive very bad treatment from Bhola.

Because of Bhola's misdeeds, one of Kala's friends decided to punish Bhola. This friend was named Raghu. He spread a rumour that soon he was going to marry the king's daughter. The king came to hear the rumour and he became furious. How could Raghu dare to make such a pronouncement? Raghu did not hold any important position in the court. As far as the king was concerned, Raghu was just a silly fellow.

The king asked Bhola what he should do. Bhola said, "What kind of audacity this Raghu has! He should be hanged!"

Then the king asked Kala for his advice. Kala said, "Raghu is a silly fellow, but he is harmless. Why pay any attention to this kind of thing?"

The king's anger could not be appeased so easily. He felt it was beneath his dignity to have his daughter mentioned in connection with Raghu. So the king took Bhola's advice and ordered Raghu to be hanged. Raghu was brought to the king's court and sentenced. As he was about to be taken from the court,

Raghu said, "Please, please, your Majesty, do allow me to tell you why I said that I would marry your daughter."

The king said, "You may tell your story."

Raghu said, "This all happened in a dream. In my dream I married your daughter."

The king said, "It was only a dream?"

The king looked at Bhola to help him decide what to do. Bhola said, "Even in a dream we do not dare to do this kind of thing. How could he have a dream that he is marrying your daughter? He should be hanged."

Kala was so miserable. He said to the king, "How can you take a dream like this seriously? We have so many dreams, but nothing comes of them. And now you are ready to hang him!"

At this point Raghu interrupted. He said, "Please, please, allow me to complete my story."

The king said, "What more do you have to say?"

Raghu went on, "I saw in my dream that another king who is your rival came and attacked you. In the dream that particular king forced me to marry your daughter. You were killed in the dream and then that king told me that I would marry your daughter. I saw all this quite clearly."

The king was shocked. He said, "How could it be? How could I be killed?"

Raghu said, "No, in the dream I saw that this king killed you. Still the story does not end there."

The king asked, "There is still more you have to say?"

Raghu said, "Yes. When you were killed, immediately Kala killed himself because he has such love for you. But what did Bhola do? He started criticising you ruthlessly. In this way he became very dear to the king who killed you. This Bhola is such a rogue! He always flatters you. But when the neighbouring king killed you, Bhola immediately started flattering the other king in order to secure a very high post."

The king became absolutely furious. He said to Bhola, "You rogue! So this is what you will do after my death! Kala will kill himself because of his love for me, but you will only criticise me." Then the king decided to give Kala a very high post. At the same time, he decided to have Bhola put to death. Bhola pleaded, "Please, please, do not kill me! Do not kill me!"

The king said, "Then you have to leave the country. I will no longer keep you in my country. Go and join that other king."

So Bhola was dismissed and Kala was given a high post. Then the king said, "Now, what am I going to do with my daughter?"

Kala said, "Your Majesty, it is up to you to decide who is worthy of your daughter. Since you have asked me for my opinion, I wish to say there is somebody who really brought to your notice what kind of nature Bhola had. Bhola was fooling you all the time and he made so many people angry. So if you want to honour an honest man, then I would like to suggest Raghu. I am not advising you. This is only my humble suggestion. If you want to honour an honest man, then he is the one. Raghu is so nice. In his dream he saw everything, and that is how you found out the real nature, the true nature of Bhola."

The king said, "You have such love for me. I should listen to you. When you saw that I was killed, you said, 'There is nothing left for me here' and you immediately killed yourself. What a difference from that rogue Bhola! I shall never forget what you did. I accept your suggestion. Let my daughter marry Raghu."

### LTS 88. *The court jester wins the bet*

This story is about two kings. One king had a court jester who used to make fun of everything. This court jester had many, many, many good qualities and the king was very fond of him. Again, he had one bad quality: he loved gambling. The king tried so hard to correct his nature, but the court jester was incorrigible in that respect. He was always gambling.

The king said, "Since I am unable to be strict with you, I am sending you to the neighbouring king, who is my friend. He is very, very strict. He will teach you to give up this passion for gambling. Then I will take you back, because I am so fond of you. You will not be able to make fun of my friend. He is a very serious type."

The court jester said, "No matter how serious your friend is, I will turn him topsy-turvy in ten minutes."

The king said, "All right, I accept your challenge. If you are successful, I promise I shall give you one thousand rupees."

The court jester immediately said, "Can you not give the money to me now? I am absolutely certain I will be successful."

"I am absolutely sure that you will *not* succeed," said the king, "because my friend is so serious. He is not like me. You will not be able to fool him with your wits."

The court jester departed for the kingdom of the neighbouring king. Unbeknownst to him, his king sent an advance message to this other king. The message was: "I am sending you my court jester. This fellow has many, many good qualities and I am very fond of him. Only one bad quality he has, and that is his love of gambling. Please be strict with him and transform his nature. Then you can send him back. I shall be very grateful to you if you can do me this favour."

In due course, the court jester arrived at the palace. As soon as he was presented to the king, he said to him out of the blue, "I would like to challenge you."

The king said, "What! What kind of challenge? Do you know that I am a king?"

"All right then, let us call it a bet," said the court jester.

"What do you want?" asked the king.

The court jester had promised his own king that he would turn this king topsy-turvy within ten minutes. So he said to the king, "I want you to do a head balance."

All the people who were around the king became furious. They said, "What kind of audacity is this! Our king has to do a head balance at your request? It is simply absurd!"

Fortunately this particular king used to practise hatha yoga from his childhood. He was intrigued by the request and said to the court jester, "What will you give me if I can do it?"

The court jester said, "First do it. Then I will tell you."

The king said, "No, no, I am a king. You have to behave well! I will not allow you to trick me."

So the court jester said, "I will give you one hundred rupees. That is my promise."

The king said, "I do not trust you. Give one hundred rupees to one of my ministers now."

The court jester took out one hundred rupees and handed them to one of the ministers with the understanding that the minister would return the money if the king could not do a head balance.

The king came down from his throne and did a head balance very, very nicely. Then the king said to the court jester, "I do not need your hundred rupees, but I am keeping this money to teach you a lesson, because you have this bad habit of gambling. Always you are wasting your time and energy. My friend has told me that you have many good qualities, but your love of gambling is a serious defect. So now your hundred rupees I will not give you back. I hope this has taught you a lesson!"

Then this king wrote a letter to the first king and related the whole story. He concluded, "Your court jester lost to me and I kept the money deliberately. He did not think I could do a head balance, but I was able to do it very well. Now he has learnt a lesson. I am sure he will no longer enjoy his gambling."

When the first king received this message, he started laughing and laughing at how easily the court jester had outsmarted his friend. Then he wrote back to his friend, "Yes, he has lost his bet with you, but he has won his bet with me. He told me that in ten minutes he would turn you upside down. Now you have written that you did a head balance at his request for a mere one hundred rupees. He lost only a hundred rupees to you, but he gained one thousand rupees from me. That clever fellow has won nine hundred rupees, plus he has not been cured of his love of gambling!"

### LTS 89. *The hermit's only possession*

A spiritual man was leading a very simple life in the forest. He had a small hut and he used to pray day in and day out. One evening he was meditating near his hut when two thieves saw him. According to their own standard, they thought he was not a good person. They wanted to teach him a lesson. So they entered into his little hut. There they did not find any material object except a plate. They said to one another, "How can someone live with only a plate? There is no food, no furniture, nothing — only a plate. That means he is doing something undivine. He goes somewhere else to eat at night and during the day he pretends that he can live without food. Here is the proof that he is not a sincere seeker."

One of the thieves grabbed the plate and put it inside his bag. The other one felt a little sorry for the spiritual man. He said, "Who knows, perhaps this man is sincere after all. Here in this forest there are some fruits. Perhaps he lives on fruits or during the day perhaps he goes to the neighbouring village and begs for food. I do not want to be involved in stealing this plate."

The other thief was adamant. He said, "No, I strongly suspect that this so-called seeker is up to no good." So he stole the small plate and the two thieves left the vicinity. Meanwhile the seeker did not have the slightest idea of what was going on.

After covering a long distance, the culprit saw that his friend (the one who was not in favour of stealing) was very, very happy. He asked his friend, "Why are you so happy?"

The friend replied, "I am happy because I know that seeker is a sincere person. We are not. We are both bad people. We make our living by stealing from others. But today is an exception. Today I feel that I have not done a bad thing. But you have done something wrong. You took his plate. If somebody is very prosperous, we can steal from that person. But that hermit is so poor. He is leading such a simple life. His only possession was that plate. So I am happy that today I am not the culprit."

Then the other thief said, "I also want to be happy like you. Let me return the plate." So the second thief went back to the hermit's hut to return the plate. When he arrived, he saw that the hermit was once again meditating right in front of his doorway.

The thief approached him and said, "I have come to return this to you."

The hermit looked at the plate and said, "Whose is this? Give it to the owner."

The thief was puzzled. He said to himself, "This is the same hut. It was from here that I took the plate. Now why is the hermit saying, 'Give it to the owner'? What does he mean?"

The thief tried to make the situation very clear. He said, "I stole this plate from your hut. Are you not the owner?"

The hermit said, "No, I am not the owner."

"Who is the owner then?" asked the thief.

"The actual owner is either you or God. It is between you and God," said the hermit.

Still the thief did not understand. He asked, "What do you mean by 'between me and God'?"

The hermit replied, "Today I am the happiest person. Why? Previously I had only one possession — a plate. I used to feel miserable because of that plate. I wanted to renounce everything, but I could not give up that plate. I used to take it with me when I went to nearby villages to beg for food. Today at long last I can say that I am a true renunciate. I have given up everything. I do not have anything. So kindly take the plate. It is yours, since you have taken the trouble of stealing it. And if you do not want it, give it to God."

The thief asked, "Where can I find God?"

The hermit replied, "God is everywhere. If you throw it away, God will make sure that somebody will find it, and that person will be the right person. He will be the rightful owner of the plate. I am no longer the owner of this plate."

This story shows us that if you deal with a good person, you immediately learn something good.

### LTS 90. *The seven-year-old defeats the scholar*

There was once a great scholar. He was very proud and haughty. In argument, he used to defeat the rest of the scholars. Those who were defeated by him had to pay a penalty. On a monthly basis they had to send the scholar either money or material objects. This went on for a long time. Nobody could defeat him.

One day a little boy saw his teacher sad and miserable. He was only a seven-year-old child. He asked his teacher, "What has happened to make you so sad?"

His teacher said, "I have to pay my next instalment to the greatest scholar and today I do not have any money. My payment is due and he will be so angry with me if I do not pay him on time."

The little boy felt miserable. Something within him prompted him to say, "I will be able to solve the problem of this bad scholar who is torturing everybody."

Something within prompted this little boy to challenge the greatest scholar. He asked his teacher to take him where the greatest scholar was currently residing. The teacher became frightened. He said, "I cannot take you. You are a little boy. How are you going to challenge such an expert on the scriptures?"

All of a sudden the teacher and the little boy heard an enthusiastic noise. The greatest scholar was passing by on a palanquin, and his admirers and adorers were singing his praises. It was his practice to go from village to village in this way and challenge the local scholars.

When the little boy heard the commotion, he went running into the street and stood directly in front of the greatest scholar. People could not account for it. "What is he doing?" they asked.

The little boy ignored them. In a loud voice he said to the greatest scholar, "You have to stop! Stop! I have to ask you a question and you have to answer me."

All the villagers were highly amused.

Then the little boy collected some sand from the street and closed his fist. He said to the greatest scholar, "Please tell me how many grains of sand there are inside my palm."

The greatest scholar could not reply. He did not know the answer to the child's question. Some of the villagers became frightened, some were amused and some started clapping because the greatest scholar could not accurately say how many grains of sand were inside the little boy's palm.

Then the boy said, "Since you have lost to me, all the other scholars, including my teacher, do not have to pay you their penalties. They are freed from their debt."

All the scholars agreed. They said, "Why should we pay you? This little boy is greater than you are. You could not answer his question."

Soon news of what had happened reached the ears of the king. The king had tremendous admiration for the greatest scholar. He was astonished to hear that the greatest scholar had been defeated.

The queen said to the king, "I would like to see this little boy who defeated the scholar."

The king replied, "I still cannot believe that it is true."

The queen said, "I believe it. Let us invite both of them — the so-called greatest scholar and this seven-year-old boy who has now surpassed him. Let us hear them debate and we will decide for ourselves."

So the pair were summoned and all the scholars in the kingdom, plus thousands of their friends and relatives, gathered at the palace to witness the debate.

When the queen saw the little boy, in silence she poured all her affection, love, sweetness and fondness into him. She said to herself, "This little boy has to win."

Meanwhile, when the king saw this upstart, he began laughing and laughing. He said, "I cannot imagine how this little boy is going to defeat the scholar!"

The queen said emphatically, "He is going to defeat him. In my heart I know it."

"Let us wait and see," replied the king.

The debate began. First of all, the greatest scholar said to the little boy, "It is beneath my dignity to ask you questions. You can ask me any question and if I can answer successfully, which I shall easily do, I shall apply this hammer to your head to teach you a lesson." Then he brought out a hammer from his garment.

Everybody was shocked. They were afraid that he would kill this little boy. But the little boy was not frightened. He said to the scholar, "I am going to make three statements, and you have to prove that in each case I am wrong. My first statement is: I am my mother's only child. The second statement is: our king has committed no sin. The third statement is: the queen married only the king. Think it over and see if you can refute these statements."

Now, the greatest scholar had listened to the statements with increasing dismay. The little boy was known to be the only child of his mother. It was the simple truth. How could he deny the truth? The second statement was much trickier. In order to win the point, the scholar had to prove that the king was full of sin. If he did so in front of so many people, he would lose his job — and perhaps his head! But the third statement was by far the trickiest of all. He had to prove that the queen had married someone else other than the king. He ran a tremendous risk by even discussing such a subject. So the greatest scholar was forced to admit that he could not disprove any of the statements. He hung his head in shame.

Then the queen said to the little boy, "My child, in order to win the debate, you yourself must disprove the statements."

"That I shall gladly do," said the little boy. "In one of our scriptures it is written that if a mother gives birth only to one child, then she is as good as childless. If she is blessed with only one child, then she is considered unmarried, a virgin. So according to the scriptures, my mother has no child."

What he said was absolutely true, but the scholar had not remembered this scripture passage.

The little boy went on, "My second statement was that the king is free from sin. That is also false. The king has accrued no sin personally. Everybody knows this truth. But if he is a real king, he has to identify himself with the sins of all his subjects. A real king is full of oneness, oneness, oneness. We are all his subjects and we have committed so many sins. If he is a real king, which he is, then he has to establish his oneness with all of us. Since he has to share our sins, we can say that the king is also full of sin."

The king was not pleased with this answer at all, but the queen said, "What the child has said is absolutely true. What kind of oneness can you claim to have? You always brag that you have such sympathy for your subjects. Such being the case, you are also full of sin."

The queen fully supported the little boy, so she was determined to justify him. Then came the third statement, which was the most difficult, that the queen married only the king. The queen was so eager to hear what the little boy would say. Everybody felt that here he would certainly fail.

Again the little boy drew from the scriptures: "It is an ancient tradition," he said, "that when a wedding takes place, the bride is first married to the five cosmic gods. Then only does she marry an earthly human being. So our queen was already married five times to the five principal cosmic gods. Therefore, how can she say she is only married to the king?"

The queen knew that what the child said was absolutely true. In the marriage ceremony, first the priest invokes the five main cosmic gods to marry the bride. Then she takes a human husband. So the queen immediately embraced the child and she said, "I am not going to allow you to go home. Your parents and everybody in your family have to come and live in the palace."

Then the queen said to the king, "I want you to say the greatest scholar has been defeated in front of the whole world. Now we shall keep him as our slave, our lifelong slave."

So the greatest scholar had to stay there in the palace and perform the duties of a slave and the little boy was given the greatest honour. The king said that when the time came, this little boy would marry the princess. His whole family became members of the royal family.

His questions were so difficult to answer, but his third question in particular absolutely puzzled the queen! So we see that bad people will eventually be punished.

### LTS 91. *Children ride free*

A father, mother and two children went to the market to do some shopping. When their shopping was over, the whole family was coming back home. It was a distance of four miles. Because the children had walked to the market with their parents, now they had become a little bit tired. The father saw that a horse-drawn carriage was returning from the market. It had brought some people there and they were now engaged in shopping, so it was coming back empty.

The father hailed the carriage and asked, "How much will you charge to take us home?"

The carriage driver said, "For you one rupee, for your wife one rupee, but children can ride free of charge."

Immediately the father said to his children, "Jump into the carriage. You can ride for free. Your mother and I can walk."

The carriage driver said, "What? It was understood that all of you would ride home with me!"

The father said, "No, you did not say that if all of us went, the children would ride free. You simply said that children are free, whereas my wife and I are supposed to pay. So we do not have to pay."

Now confusion arose. The carriage driver did not want to take the children free of charge and the father did not want to pay. What is more, the children did not want to descend from the carriage. The father said, "If you agree, we can strike a compromise. Instead of paying one rupee each, I will pay you a quarter and my wife will pay you a quarter. Between us, my wife and I will give you half a rupee, and our children will ride for free. If you agree to this compromise, then we shall use your services."

The carriage driver said to himself, "I am dealing with rogues, but I want to prove that I am superior to them. It is better to have something than nothing. If I do not take them, if I go home without any passengers, then I will get nothing. The best thing is to take these two rogues. At least now I am getting half a rupee." So he took the husband and wife plus their two children home from the market.

### LTS 92. *The superior friend*

This is a story about three friends. One friend was always bragging that he had so much knowledge, so much wisdom and so much wealth. He asserted his superiority in every way. His kind-hearted friends said, "It is true. You are wealthy and we are poor. But do not brag, do not brag. Boasting is not good." In spite of this, the friendship of these three was in very good shape.

One afternoon all three friends were on the bank of a river under a tree. The two kind-hearted friends advised the boastful one, "It is true, you are wiser than we are, you have more wealth than we have, but it is not good to brag. You will invite some calamity." Unfortunately, their friend did not heed their advice. He continued his endless boasting. But they forgave him because they wanted to maintain their friendship.

As they were chatting about various topics — "cabbages and kings" and so forth — a young man happened to pass by. He looked very strong and smart. Out of curiosity, they asked him who he was and he answered, "I am the wisest man in this district, and I am also the strongest. Everybody appreciates me, admires me and adores me. It is very strange that you have not heard about me."

They were puzzled because they had no idea who he was. They did not know anything about him. Then the friend who was very proud of his knowledge, wisdom and wealth said to this young man, "Would you like to answer one question?"

The young man answered, "Certainly! I will answer any question you have, since I am the wisest man."

The boastful friend continued, "Now you are seeing me and my two friends. Please tell us which one is giving you more joy. You are looking at us, but all of us cannot give you the same kind of joy. Somebody has to give you more. Which one of us is it?" He was sure that he would be the one chosen because he was clearly superior in every way.

The young man said, "Now, this is a most difficult question. I cannot answer it immediately. I have to examine you one by one. I shall ask you a question with regard to money. This will determine the outcome. Please tell me how you deal with money."

One friend said, "It is good to have money. Money enables us to buy material things, so in that sense, money is keeping us alive."

The second one said, "True, money is necessary, but money quite often creates problems for us. When we misuse money, we suffer."

The third friend, the richest one, said, "I have lots of money, but I am not attached to money at all."

He wanted to prove that he was rich, and at the same time that he was spiritually great.

He went on, "I have plenty of money, but I am not attached to it in the least. If anybody wants to take away my money-power, I will not mind."

Again he was showing off to this man that he had tremendous wealth, but he was above it.

The young man said, "Unfortunately, I am now on my way to the town, so I cannot give you an immediate decision. Tomorrow, if you happen to be here, I will tell you which one I have selected. Or, if you wish, I could come and see you. Where do you live?"

The friends answered, "We also have houses in town."

"You have houses in town?" said the young man.

"Do you want to be our guest?" asked the three friends. "We each have our own house."

The young man said, "All right, if you will allow me, I will gladly be your guest. With each one I shall spend a night, so I will be spending three nights altogether, and then I will be able to give you my answer."

The young man started reciting slokas from the Vedas, the Upanishads and other sacred books. He was showing off how he was the greatest pandit. The three friends were deeply moved that they would receive knowledge and wisdom from him.

Then the two kind-hearted friends said, "Here is our dearest friend. He is the one who has so much material wealth and who is so learned. We feel in all sincerity that he deserves to have you as his guest first. Then you can come to our places to stay."

The young man agreed to this proposal. He said, "Let me be at his place today, and tomorrow and the day after I shall come to your homes."

The young man accompanied the boastful friend to his home. This particular friend was very, very kind to him and showed him tremendous hospitality. Together they talked and talked far into the night. Alas, the boastful friend was tempted to show off. He showed the young man where he kept his safe and his expensive things, such as diamonds and gold.

The young man said, "I am not interested in these kinds of things. I am only interested in the Vedas, the Upanishads and physical strength. For me, the body and the spirit must go together. It is good that you have so much wealth. God is indeed kind to you. But, unfortunately, I am not interested in material wealth. I am only interested in my own physical strength and in reading the scriptures.

The boastful friend was a little bit sad that this young man was not interested in material wealth and could not appreciate his expensive things. But he enjoyed talking with the young man immensely. After some time, the young man declared that the following day he did not have to stay at the other two places, for he was planning to announce that of the three friends he had chosen this one.

"You are giving me tremendous joy," he said. "I do not think that I will get the same kind of joy from the other two. I am ready to declare you the winner."

The boastful man was so happy and so proud that he was chosen before the other two had even been examined. Then both the host and his guest retired for the night.

Now, the young man merely pretended that he was fast asleep. He even started snoring. The richest man was sleeping soundly. This young man was actually a rogue of the first water. When he was certain that the rich man was fast asleep, he emptied the safe and took all the jewels. As he was leaving the house, he saw that the rich man was still fast asleep. He said, "How can he sleep like this?" Then he kicked the rich man a few times. In case his victim woke up, he was ready to run away. He said, "I am infinitely stronger that this stupid fellow. He will not be able to do anything." He gave the rich man a few extra hard kicks, but still he did not wake up. Then he left with the stolen things.

Early the next morning, the rich man woke up. He immediately noticed that the young man was missing and the door of the safe was wide open. The rich man said, "What has happened! He has taken away everything!"

He rushed to his friends and cried, "I have nothing. I have nothing! Everything has been stolen by that rogue. I am now bankrupt!"

The two friends tried to console him. They said, "We begged you not to brag. We knew that you would invite some calamity and now this is what has happened."

The rich man stopped crying and said, "God has really blessed me today. Although you two were my friends, inwardly I used to look down upon you because I was infinitely richer and more learned than you. In every way I felt superior. I told that young man that, despite having great wealth, I was not attached to it. You two said that money is necessary and then again money can create problems. In my case, I was showing off, but in the heart of my heart, was I not attached to my money? I was so proud of my money-power. God has really saved me from my pride. Now I can truly claim you two as my friends. My friendship with you has proven to be infinitely more important than my attachment to wealth."

# LIFE'S BLEEDING TEARS AND FLYING SMILES

## BOOK 7

## LTS 93. *The shopkeeper and the dwarf*

There was once a shopkeeper who loved to play practical jokes. One evening, as he was on his way home from work, he felt in a particularly humorous mood. He suddenly saw a dwarf who was shorter than the shortest and who was wearing a pair of glasses. The shopkeeper was overcome with the desire to make fun of this dwarf, so he called out to him, "My wife is a very good cook. May I invite you to come with me to my place tonight for dinner?" The dwarf agreed to the shopkeeper's invitation, unaware that the shopkeeper only had in mind to poke fun at him and laugh at his expense. So together they went to the shopkeeper's place.

At first, the shopkeeper's wife was very kind and hospitable. She made the dwarf feel right at home and so, as they sat around the dinner table, he kept on talking and talking and talking. The shopkeeper was feeling very happy and proud of himself that the dwarf's visit was such a success, and he felt that the time had come for him to start making fun of the dwarf. But the wife was getting annoyed with the dwarf. She thought to herself, "This fellow is talking so much and eating next to nothing. It is an insult to my cooking." She turned to the dwarf and said, "You do not want to eat? You do not care for anything?"

The dwarf replied, "I get such joy in just talking!"

The wife was so frustrated that she commanded the dwarf to open his mouth. He obeyed, opening his mouth wider than necessary, and the wife put a huge portion of cooked goat meat inside. Then she forced the dwarf's mouth shut so he had to eat it! What could the poor fellow do? He had no choice but to swallow the huge portion of meat. But, alas, there was a bone inside it. The bone got stuck in the dwarf's throat and he died immediately!

Now the shopkeeper felt miserable. He said to himself, "What am I going to do?" He was blaming himself for the dwarf's death. At the same time, he was worried that he would get into trouble. He said to his wife, "I have an idea. Let us cover his dead body and take him to the doctor. You follow me, crying and crying. We will tell the doctor that our son is sick and that we are afraid his case is very serious."

So the shopkeeper carried the dead body of the dwarf to the doctor's house. His wife followed behind him, crying pitifully. When they arrived at the doctor's place, the doctor and his wife were eating dinner together upstairs. Seeing that he had a patient, the doctor wanted to go downstairs immediately, but the doctor's wife insisted that he finish his dinner. "Sit down and finish eating!" she ordered. "I will go and see what they want."

The doctor's wife went downstairs and told the shopkeeper and his wife, "I am sorry, but you will have to wait. The doctor will see you, but you have come at an odd hour. He must finish his dinner first, and then he will come down." Then the doctor's wife went back upstairs, leaving the shopkeeper and his wife waiting outside the door.

The shopkeeper was truly a wonderful rogue. Recognising a chance to abandon the dead body, he said to his wife, "Let us put the corpse right up against the door. When the doctor opens the door, the body will fall down on the ground and roll down the staircase." Quietly, the shopkeeper and his wife put the body against the door of the doctor's house. Then, as the doctor still had not come down, they went home very peacefully.

When the doctor finally finished eating his dinner, he went downstairs and opened the door. In shock, he watched as the body fell tumbling to the foot of the staircase below. He ran down after it only to find the poor dwarf lying there, dead.

The doctor felt so miserable. He said to himself, "How could this happen?" The shopkeeper had informed the doctor's wife that the case was extremely serious, so now the doctor was blaming himself mercilessly for not attending to the patient sooner. He thought, "Now I will be in serious trouble!" But since it was late at night, he picked up the dead body and placed it back against his door. Then he went upstairs. The eyeglasses were still on the body of the dwarf.

It happened that this dwarf was the court jester of the king. One of the king's guards had been heavily drunk the previous day and had dropped his glasses on the ground and could not find them. Now, he happened to pass by the doctor's office and saw his own glasses on the dwarf's face. Still a little drunk, the king's guard began punching the dead man mercilessly.

A passerby saw what was happening and shouted, "What are you doing?"

The king's guard replied, "This man has stolen my eyeglasses! Look at this! They are mine!"

"But why are you punching a dead body?" the man cried.

The guard was immediately arrested and taken to the king. He said to himself, "Now I will be punished; I will be hanged."

The doctor came to know that this guard was going to be hanged and he felt absolutely miserable. He felt that it was he who had killed the dwarf, and his conscience was bothering him terribly. So, at the last moment, just as the guard was about to be hanged, he ran to the king and made his confession. "It is not this man's fault," he exclaimed. "I am to blame!"

The king was very pleased with the doctor's confession. While he was considering what kind of punishment to give the doctor, the first culprit, the shopkeeper, came to know what was going on and his conscience started bothering him. He ran to the king and said, "No, no, no! I am to be blamed! I was the one who brought about the death of this dwarf! I was the one!"

Then the shopkeeper's wife cried out, "No! I am the culprit, I am the culprit! I put a piece of goat meat into his mouth and forced him to eat it. There was a bone inside the meat. It got caught in his throat, and he died immediately!"

In this way, all of the culprits made their confessions.

Then the king exclaimed, "I never thought that I had such sincere people in my kingdom! You all could have escaped, but one by one you have all confessed." The king was so proud of all of these sincere people that he declared, "I shall not punish any of you. Instead, I shall give all of you rewards! You all deserve to be rewarded."

So the king gave rewards to each and every one. Then the king said, "We should admire the court jester most of all, because even after his death he has made us laugh. He has made us all laugh even after leaving this world. Such an excellent jester!"

### LTS 94. *The king's stolen treasures*

Once there was a very rich king who was very, very proud of his wealth. None of his fellow kings in the surrounding kingdoms were as rich as this particular king, and he used to enjoy showing off his wealth to all of them. Quite often, he would hold exhibits where he would display his collection of diamonds and other most expensive and most valuable treasures for all to see.

On one such occasion, all of the king's friends and colleagues were assembled to view the king's wealth, including his most expensive diamond, which was prominently displayed on a plate of gold. All of a sudden, the unthinkable happened: the diamond disappeared. The minister had to report to the king that his most expensive diamond was gone. Upon hearing the news, the king was sad, mad and furious. "I cannot understand it!" he exclaimed. "I consider all these people to be my friends! How could they steal from me?"

The king's minister was a very, very wise man. He replied, "O King, let us not embarrass them. Let us simply say to them, 'Please, please, we do not want to search you. You are our friends. It would be an unbearable embarrassment. The best thing for us to do is to turn off the lights. Then, whoever has taken the diamond will kindly put it back on the plate.' These people are kings, after all!"

The king agreed to the minister's plan. They turned off the lights, certain that the culprit would place the diamond back on the golden plate. But alas, when the lights came back on, to their great surprise, they saw that the plate itself had now disappeared!

The king said to his minister, "I cannot believe it! In the dark, the same person who took the diamond has now removed the plate, and he himself has disappeared!"

The majority of the kings attending the exhibit were very, very honest. They were so embarrassed by what had taken place. Some of them left the palace to try to chase the thief. Others felt it was beneath their dignity to be in such bad company, so they, too, left the palace. But some of the kings remained out of sheer curiosity, hoping to see the thief when he was caught. They were such stupid fellows! Two groups of kings had already gone and the culprit had fled, yet they remained.

After some time, the thief was found and caught by a small group of the kings. "I will not surrender this diamond or this golden plate unless you pay me for them," he declared shamelessly. He quoted a price that was considerably higher than that which the very rich king had originally paid. One of the kings offered to pay the thief the sum. "Fine!" said the thief. "But I will only relinquish the diamond and plate on the condition that none of you will reveal my identity." All of the kings assured the thief that they would keep it a secret amongst themselves. Then he took the money and ran away.

This thief was such a rogue. He began informing his friends that it was not he who had stolen the diamond and plate, but that he had seen these expensive things in the hands of the very king who had bought them from him! So they all went off in search of the other king.

Meanwhile, the very rich king came to learn who the first thief was. He had him arrested and thrown into jail. The thief told the king, "I have neither the diamond nor the plate. I sold them to somebody else for a higher price than even you paid for them." So the rich king sent his guards to search for the second culprit.

With great difficulty they found the king who had bought the treasures. Unfortunately, he no longer was in possession of them. His son, who was very greedy, had taken both the diamond and the plate and disappeared. The father was caught and thrown into jail, but the son was nowhere to be found. "If in one week your son does not come back on his own and return my valuables, you will be hanged," the very rich king declared.

The poor fellow did not know where his son had gone. He was crying and crying in his jail cell. His wife was praying and praying to God for their son's return by the appointed day. Otherwise, she would lose her husband.

The son was quite far from the scene, but somehow he felt his mother's heart-rending cries. So he came to the rescue of his father, returning the diamond and the plate to the very rich king. "Please, please, release my father!" he said. "I am the one who stole these belongings of yours. Do anything you want with my life. My father is innocent."

"Your father is innocent?" the very rich king replied. "Who bought these things when they had been stolen from me? True, your father did not steal them, but was he not the culprit who bought them from the thief? He knew quite well that they were mine. Why did he buy them, instead of telling me where they were?"

The son replied, "O King, I was the last person to have them in my possession. Therefore, I am the one who is guilty. I am giving them back to you — both the plate and the diamond. Please, please, punish me any way you see fit, but release my father."

When the very rich king saw his plate and diamond returned in excellent condition, he was simply thrilled and overjoyed. He said to the son, "Do not worry, I do not want to kill anyone. I just wanted to get back my most precious treasures. You and your father are free to go and do whatever you like. I am releasing you both. You will not be punished because both of you have kept my precious possessions in such good condition."

### LTS 95. *The man who ruined the street*

One day a gentleman was driving his car. Alas, at a certain point, his car got stuck. The street was muddy and full of big potholes, so the car could not go any farther.

A strong man happened to be nearby and saw that the gentleman was in difficulty. He asked the man if he needed help and he said, "Certainly, you can help me. I would be very grateful. You look so strong!"

The strong man lifted up the rear of the car and placed it on his shoulder. He was showing off how strong he was. Then he pushed the car forward, freeing the car so the gentleman could easily continue his journey. As the gentleman was about to leave, the strong man extended his hand to signify that he wanted a tip for his efforts. The gentleman was very pleased, so he said, "Oh, you have worked very hard. I could not have managed it myself. You are so strong!" Then he offered the strong man a fair amount of money. The strong man was delighted.

All of a sudden, a lady came running up to the gentleman and said, "Yes, he has worked very, very hard. My husband has worked very, very hard, and he deserves the money. In fact, he deserves even more, because every night he takes a bucket and collects water from the swimming pool. With that water, he ruins the street! That is why every day people are in serious trouble when they try to drive here!"

What kind of wife was this! The husband was simply furious with her. The gentleman said to himself, "What am I going to do? How can I change this fellow's nature?"

In the meantime, the strong man's teenage son arrived on the scene. He had heard his mother talking and was very angry. "How can you expose my father like this?" he cried.

The mother replied, "Expose him? It is beneath my dignity to remain his wife! How can he do this kind of thing? Every day he gets money in this way and I find it very difficult to bear. With this money he buys our groceries and all the other things that we need. But he is so strong. Why can he not go out and do some honest work?"

The gentleman was very kind. He said, "All right, if your husband does not want to work, why do you not come and work at my place? My wife will be very kind to you. She is quite old. You can help her with the housework and I will pay you."

At this, the strong man became furious with the gentleman and said, "My wife will work at your place? How dare you suggest such a thing!"

The wife replied, "I am ready to do it. I see that he is a very kind-hearted gentleman." To the gentleman she said, "I will be happy to work at your place."

But the strong man said, "No, I will not allow you to work."

The son always took his father's side. He said to his mother, "You cannot work." Both father and son felt that it was beneath their dignity for her to go and work at somebody else's place.

Again, the gentleman said to himself, "What am I going to do? This strong man is not going to change his nature, and they need money." To the husband and wife he said, "I have no idea how I can solve this problem."

Then the teenager said to the gentleman, "I know the answer. If you give my father a very large amount of money, he will stop ruining the street."

But the wife cried, "No, no! Do not trust my son and do not trust my husband!" The wife herself did not trust her own son and husband.

The gentleman said, "All right, somebody has to be brave."

The wife was very sincere and brave. She wanted to work at the gentleman's place, but her husband and son would not allow her to do so.

Now the boy saw tears in his mother's eyes and he realised that she was suffering very deeply. So he said to the gentleman, "I can solve this problem. I will work at your place. I can even work as your servant. I will do whatever you want. Then if you give me a large amount of money — whatever I deserve — I will not allow my father to do the kind of mischief that he does. Every night he goes out with a bucket and collects water. Then he deliberately ruins the street so that he can take money from kind people like you."

Then the father and son began to fight. The father exclaimed, "Look, I cannot give this up. I have formed a habit. Even if you get money from this gentleman, even if you go out and work, how can I get rid of this habit? It is impossible! Right now, money is not the problem. I have money, but I cannot get out of this habit!"

The gentleman said, "Let me go to an astrologer and see if he can tell us how you will be able to give up this profession of ruining the street as well as the joy of all the drivers who pass this way."

The gentleman left and came back with an astrologer. The astrologer immediately cast the strong man's horoscope and said, "I can clearly see that you are going to die very shortly. In a month's time you will no longer be in this world."

The wife was very smart. She did not cry, nor did the son. The strong man said, "What is this? I will die in a short while, and even then you two are not crying? How can it be? Do you not realise that I will soon die?"

The wife turned to the astrologer and said, "Please, can you not see if there is any way to stop this from happening?"

The astrologer replied, "I can clearly see that if you do not ruin the joy of the drivers any more, then your horoscope indicates that you will be able to have a very long life."

"Then I am giving up the habit right from this very moment!" the strong man exclaimed.

From that day on, the strong man did give up his mischief. He never ruined the street again. So in this way the astrologer saved the family, the street and all the drivers who came by that way every day.

### LTS 96. *The so-called blind beggar*

There was once a rogue who used to beg on a street corner near a temple. Every day, he would spread his mat and sit there begging, while hundreds of people came to the temple. Of course, they came not to realise God but to fulfil their countless desires. They thought that if they gave alms to the poor, God would be pleased with them and their desires would all be fulfilled. The rogue knew this, so every day he would sit there and beg. He kept his eyes tightly closed and he would call out to everyone who passed by, "I am blind, I cannot see. Please help me!"

On their way back from the temple, after they had prayed and meditated, people would say, "Poor, helpless fellow!" Then they would put money on the mat for him.

One day, a very, very kind-hearted man passed by and put lots of money on the mat. Then, after he had gone about thirty metres, he said to himself, "Perhaps I should have given him a little more money." He turned and walked back so he could give the beggar even more money.

When the man returned to the spot, he was shocked to see that the so-called blind beggar had opened his eyes and had started counting his money! He obviously could see quite well! The man watched in disbelief as the beggar put the money into his pocket and again began to beg.

The man exclaimed, "Oh, so this is what is happening!" He had been so moved by this beggar that he had been ready even to ask others to give the fellow money. How pitifully the rogue had been crying, saying that he had nobody, he had nothing! How convincing was his performance! But then he had opened his eyes and started counting the money! He was not blind in the least!

The kind-hearted man was so disgusted. He said to himself, "He is such a bad fellow, but today I do not have the strength to do anything about it. Tomorrow I will teach him a lesson." Then he went home and told the story to his son.

The son was a strong young man. The next day, he went to the temple and prayed and meditated. When he came out, he passed by the beggar and put a large amount of money on the mat. Then he started addressing everyone who walked by, saying, "Please, please give something to this beggar! He is helpless, absolutely helpless! Please, please, let us all be kind to him."

The beggar's eyes were completely closed. He was so happy because he knew that he was getting so much money.

The young man said to the beggar, "I am so happy that I have been able to help you. How I wish God would give you back your vision! I will pray to God to restore your vision." Then he went about twenty or thirty metres away to hide. From what his father had told him, he knew what the beggar was going to do next.

Just as he had done before, the beggar opened his eyes and began counting his money. The strong young man ran up to him and cried out, "Rogue, rogue, rogue! You are not blind after all! Either I will beat you up or I will take away all your money!" He felt that it would not be good to beat the fellow near the temple, so he took all the money and ran away.

Now this so-called blind fellow started chasing the young man, shamelessly running with his eyes wide open! The young fellow ran directly to the zamindar's place. The beggar knew that if he followed, he would be caught there. So he stopped chasing the young man and disappeared into the crowd.

When the young man told the zamindar what had happened, the zamindar sent his guards to chase the beggar. They caught the so-called blind beggar and brought him back to the zamindar.

The young man said to the zamindar, "Sir, I am not a thief and I am not a liar. What I have been telling you is true. This rogue has fooled countless people, including my father, so I wanted to punish him. He has been fooling people for such a long time, so he deserves some kind of punishment. Quite frankly, I do not need his money. I did this only to catch him and teach him a lesson."

The zamindar was very, very pleased with the young man.

Now it was time for the punishment. The zamindar said to the beggar, "Tell me, are you going to give up this profession? If not, today you will be thrown into jail."

The beggar said, "I am ready to give it up, right from today!"

"Very well," the zamindar replied. Then he proceeded to divide up the money. Most of the beggar's money, a very large amount, he gave to the young man. He said, "You deserve it! Today you have transformed this fellow. Nobody else could have done it. This rogue has been taking people's money for such a long time. You caught him, so you deserve the money as a reward."

Then the zamindar took the remaining money and gave it to the beggar on the condition that he would go out and get a job. The blind man, who was not really blind, would have to find work. On that condition the zamindar allowed him to go free.

### LTS 97. *One smart dog for sale*

There were two friends. One friend was very rich. The other one was not so rich. His name was Abhoy. The one who had money-power was extremely haughty. He thought that he could buy the whole world with his money-power.

Abhoy told him again and again, "Do not be so cocksure. You cannot buy everything."

But the rich friend insisted, "I can buy anything."

One day both of them were going to the market separately and they met on the way. Abhoy was not actually poor, but in comparison to his rich friend, he seemed poor. Anyway, Abhoy had a dog. The dog was very nice-looking and very, very smart.

Abhoy's rich friend said, "Your dog is so nice and smart. Can I not buy it?"

Abhoy said, "Yes, you can buy it."

The rich friend offered him two hundred rupees, but Abhoy said, "Two hundred rupees? How can I sell you my dog for two hundred paltry rupees?"

The rich friend answered, "I have offered you more than enough. Now hand over the dog."

Abhoy said, "No. This is my most faithful dog. I am not going to sell it for even one paisa less than seven hundred rupees."

In India, seven hundred rupees is like seven hundred dollars. The rich man said, "Seven hundred rupees for your dog! Who wants to buy your dog for seven hundred rupees?"

Abhoy said, "Then you do not have to buy it. Am I asking you to buy my dog? You were the one who was eager to buy my dog."

The rich friend said, "Be reasonable. I have offered you two hundred rupees, which is more than enough."

Abhoy said, "I am extremely reasonable. I am always reasonable. I can easily sell this dog for seven hundred rupees."

The rich friend said, "I will give you two hundred rupees if you can sell the dog to anybody for seven hundred rupees."

Abhoy said, "Two hundred rupees you will give me? All right. I will sell my dog, and you will be the witness. Then you have to give me two hundred rupees."

The rich friend said, "When did I ever tell you a lie? I will definitely give you two hundred rupees if you can sell this silly dog for seven hundred."

The two of them went to the market and Abhoy led the way to his uncle's pet shop. Inside was a cage containing several most beautiful parrots. Abhoy said to the owner, "Uncle, uncle, your parrots are so beautiful! I have never seen such beautiful birds in my life. Where did you get them from?"

Then Abhoy and his uncle started talking about the history of the parrots, their markings and so on. At last Abhoy said, "I think you should get at least three hundred and fifty rupees for each parrot."

His uncle looked at him. "How will I get three hundred and fifty rupees?" he asked. "Who will buy a bird for three hundred and fifty rupees?"

Abhoy said, "Why do you have to sell them at a cheaper price? They are such beautiful birds. I tell you, someone should buy each one for three hundred and fifty rupees. All right, since I am so fond of these birds, I would like to buy the two birds from you. Will you sell them to me for seven hundred rupees?"

His uncle got the shock of his life. He immediately said, "Why not? Where can I find another person who will pay this price?" He was eager to sell them at that very moment.

Before Abhoy gave his uncle the money, he said, "There is one condition. If I buy your birds for seven hundred rupees, are you going to buy my dog for seven hundred rupees? My dog is so smart and healthy."

His uncle at once agreed. He said, "I like your dog very much. I will definitely buy it for seven hundred rupees. I deeply appreciate your dog."

Then Abhoy said, "Now let us exchange. I will give you my seven hundred rupees because I liked your birds first."

So he gave seven hundred rupees to his uncle and his uncle gave him the two birds. Abhoy was so pleased. Then he said, "Now you have to keep your promise. You are supposed to buy my dog."

"Certainly," said his uncle. "I really like this dog."

The uncle took the dog and returned the seven hundred rupees to Abhoy.

Meanwhile, the rich friend had observed the entire exchange. He saw that Abhoy had fulfilled the terms of their agreement.

Abhoy said to his friend, "Since I was able to sell my dog for seven hundred rupees, now give me your two hundred rupees."

The rich friend had to agree that he had lost the bet.

This was not the end of the story. The funniest thing is that after the transaction was completed and Abhoy was going home with the two birds, his dog started following him. Abhoy's uncle was chasing it, crying, "Now I am your owner. You have to stay with me. Come back!"

Abhoy said to his uncle, "I am telling you, you are now the rightful owner. I am not denying it. But what am I going to do? You take your dog and go home."

But the dog did not want to go with the new owner.

Abhoy said, "What am I going to do now? You take it. I have absolutely no objection. You have paid me for it."

Then he said, "All right, I tell you frankly, your two birds are not worth even fifty rupees, but I am generous. I will give you one hundred rupees for the birds and keep my dog."

Abhoy gave one hundred rupees for the two birds and said, "Now we are all happy. I have the birds, you have one hundred rupees and I have my dog back."

### LTS 98. *An old lady defeats Birbal*

One day the Emperor Akbar was galloping through a village and his bodyguards were following behind him. They were also mounted on horses. At one place Akbar saw a very old lady standing outside her cottage. She was holding a sword that was very old and tarnished. She was looking at the Emperor so pitifully.

The Emperor said, "Grandmother, what do you want with this sword?"

The old lady answered, "I do not want anything. Only I would like you to touch it and bless it. You are the Emperor. It is the greatest honour for me to have you bless my sword."

Akbar took the sword and blessed it. Then he returned it to the old lady.

Immediately the old lady started crying and wailing.

Akbar was puzzled. He said, "Why are you crying? I did not tell you that I was going to buy it from you. You did not tell me a price."

The old lady said, "No, it is not for that reason that I am crying. I was told that if the Emperor touches anything, it will turn into gold because our Emperor is so good, so kind, so compassionate. I gave you my sword. You touched it and examined it, but it has not turned into gold."

The Emperor said, "I cannot turn your sword into gold, but I can give you some gold." From his pocket he took out a handful of gold coins and gave them to the old lady. Then he said to his guards, "Here is someone who can outsmart my Birbal!" Birbal was the court jester and his wit and wisdom were renowned.

"Birbal has to accept defeat," continued Akbar.

"Birbal will never accept defeat!" said one guard. "He will find some way to outwit her."

"No, Birbal will be no match for this old lady," insisted Akbar.

Akbar returned to the palace and summoned Birbal to come at once. The guards said to Birbal, "The Emperor says that this time you will have to accept defeat."

"I will never accept defeat!" said Birbal. "Nobody can outwit me."

When Birbal came before Akbar, Akbar related the incident with the old lady. "See how easily she parted me from my gold," said Akbar. "Birbal, you could not have done better yourself!"

"Emperor, I am going to bring the old lady and also her sword to the court," replied Birbal. "Then we shall learn the truth."

The Emperor said, "I do not think the old lady will come."

"The old lady will definitely come," said Birbal.

"How will you bring the old lady?" asked the Emperor curiously.

Birbal said, "I can bring her just by telling her one thing."

Akbar said, "Say anything."

Birbal said, "Then will you forgive me?"

Akbar said, "When have I not forgiven you? And how many stupid things you have said over the course of time! Yet I have always forgiven you."

Birbal said, "I will tell the old lady that you are going to marry her!"

The Emperor said, "All right, since I have already told you that I will forgive you, I forgive you. Now go and bring her, if you can. But, I tell you, she is not going to believe you. She is not going to come."

Birbal said, "Emperor, I have another way."

"What is your new plan?" asked Akbar.

Birbal said, "I will tell her that the Emperor was not just. The Emperor did not give her enough money."

"I gave her so much money. How can you say that?" said Akbar.

"I know," said Birbal. "I will tell her that the Emperor had no respect for her sword."

Akbar said, "I did not have respect? I touched it very carefully, plus I gave her so much money."

"No," answered Birbal. "I will tell her that this sword belonged to her great-grandparents, her ancestors. When something comes down from your ancestors, when it has been preserved for generations, the value goes very high. When you yourself say anything about your father Humayun and your grandfather Babar, immediately you shed tears of joy, love, gratitude and pride that you came from their family. Your ancestors were so great and good. Similarly, if I say something about them, you get such joy. And when I tell you stories about your forefathers, even though you already know them, you become so pleased with me that you always give me lots of money, because it brings them to your mind. When you think of them, you feel such joy in your heart.

"I will tell her that, since this sword belonged to her ancestors, it is invaluable. Therefore, you must give her more money. Whatever you have given is not enough. She may not believe that you are going to marry her. But the idea that she deserves more money will definitely appeal to her. Like you, I am sure, she has such respect for her parents, her grandparents and all her relatives. So she will definitely come. I am confident that I will be able to bring her."

Akbar said, "All right, if you can bring her, I promise I will give her more gold coins."

As soon as Birbal left the palace to bring the old lady, Akbar started praying, "Allah, let me defeat Birbal this once! For me, it is nothing to give the old lady more money, but I really want to defeat Birbal."

In the meantime, Birbal was absolutely certain that he would be able to bring the old lady by giving her a lecture on her ancestors. He went to her village, but alas, she had disappeared. After she received the gold coins, she left her cottage and moved to some other place.

The neighbours said, "She has left. We do not know where she has gone."

Poor Birbal had to come back to the palace and accept defeat. And Akbar was so proud of himself that for the first time he was able to defeat Birbal!

### LTS 99. *The king's clever servant*

Once upon a time there were two kings who were great friends. Then they started enjoying rivalry. That was not enough: they wanted to exercise their supremacy. They fought and fought and fought, pitting their armies against each other.

During one particular battle, one king was on the point of defeating the other, but the neighbouring kings joined forces to prevent him from vanquishing his former friend. Then the winning king had a dream. In the dream, a goddess appeared before him and said, "It is not good to fight. You are my son and he is my son. All kings are my special children. If you who are the rulers fight, then how will your subjects, all my children, be peaceful? Do not quarrel, do not fight, do not declare war."

The king wanted to abide by the soulful request of the goddess. He invited his former friend to come to his kingdom for negotiations. He said to his friend, "Let us have peaceful negotiations. Once upon a time we were friends. Let us go back again to our old life of harmony and oneness. We should enjoy our friendship, and not quarrel and fight."

The other king, who had been on the point of losing the battle, was so surprised and happy. Both of them were in the seventh Heaven of delight now that they were becoming friends again.

It happened that on the day of their meeting it was very, very hot. A close personal servant of the host king brought two glasses of juice — one for each king. This servant was extremely loyal to his Master. All of a sudden, he became afraid. What should he do? Whom to serve first: his king or the king's guest? He thought that if he offered the juice to his king first, in order to show his loyalty, then the guest king would be offended. He would say, "This stupid servant does not know that the guest always has to be honoured first. I am the guest. How is it that he is not honouring me? He has no manners."

If he offered the juice to the guest king and not his king, then his king would be slighted. He would say, "Can you imagine? My own servant does not have any respect for me! How does he dare to serve somebody else before me? Perhaps he does not remember who is feeding him, who is keeping him here. I am the one! He is my slave. Is this how he shows his loyalty to me?"

Thus ran the thoughts of the poor servant. So many conflicting ideas were passing through his mind and he was struggling to find the correct solution. He was holding the tray and yet he did not know whom to serve first.

Then a brilliant idea flashed across the servant's mind. He went to his king and said, "My Lord, according to our ancient tradition, when two kings meet together, the host king himself gives some refreshment to the guest. I am a mere slave, so I feel that you should give this to your guest, because he is, after all, your guest."

So the host king gave the first glass of juice to his friend and he drank the second one himself. As he did so, he said to his friend, "How smart my servant has become! I simply cannot believe it."

The other king was also laughing. They were laughing together at the servant's clear solution to the problem. Then the guest king said to the servant, "Now tell me frankly. You came and gave these two glasses of juice to your Master and asked him to serve me. But while you were pouring the juice, whom did you think of? You know which glass you poured first. Whom did you think of at that time? And whom did you think of when you poured the second glass of juice?"

In this way, the guest king was trying to examine the servant.

The servant replied, "O King, I know everything about my own king. He has been so kind to me for years, so naturally I was thinking of my king only when I poured both the glasses of juice."

"You never thought of me?" said the guest king, pretending to be shocked. "You knew that there were two kings present. How is it that you never thought of me?"

The servant said, "Why should I think of you? Do I know anything about you? It is only that you happen to be my king's friend. You became enemies and now you are friends. You are his guest. That is the full extent of my knowledge of you. Since I know next to nothing about you, your name never occurred to me. That is the truth."

Meanwhile the host king was observing the situation and wondering how the story was going to end.

The servant added, "I always value the one who is good and not the one who is great."

"What do you mean?" asked the guest king.

The servant answered, "My king proved to you on the battlefield that he is good. He gave up his greatness. He could easily have defeated you. Had the other kings not intervened, you would definitely have lost. Yet my king was so kind-hearted. He not only renounced the victory, but he showed his generosity by inviting you here. He is truly good. And you are truly great in the sense that you accepted his invitation. If you are a really great man, you accept an invitation. But the good man is the one who comes first in our hearts. So my king is good; you are great. That is what I meant when I said that I always value the one who is good. And that is also why I only thought of my king when I was pouring the two glasses of juice."

Both the kings laughed and laughed because they had received a lesson on goodness and greatness from a simple servant.

### LTS 100. *The lazy son and the hard-working son*

There was an old farmer who had two sons. One was lethargy and idleness incarnate. He had a reputation as a good-for-nothing. His name was Samarendra, but you could say that nothingness was his real name.

The other son always worked very hard. This son used to help his father plough the fields, cultivate the crops and so forth. His name was Amarendra.

In the evening of his life, the old farmer distributed his lands, half to each of his sons. To the lazy one, the father said, "I am giving you an equal share of my property. So, my son, give up your lethargy. You should turn over a new leaf and work industriously."

Samarendra said, "Yes, yes, Father. Now I depend on you, but once you go to Heaven, I will become very active and dynamic."

His father was very pleased, but he did not trust him to carry out his promise. He said to Samarendra, "Half of the land I have given to you, but I wish to show you a particular place in one of the fields. When you are badly in need of money, just dig at that particular place. Under the ground I have hidden a large amount of money for you. Although you have proved to be a useless son, my fatherly affection for you is such that I wish to make sure you have no financial worries in the future."

The farmer's good son, Amarendra, received his portion of the land, but there was nothing secret hidden in his fields. Amarendra knew what his father had done for his brother, but he did not feel sorry. He said, "Father is always wise. He knows I am active, dynamic and industrious. Whatever happens, I will be able to manage."

Amarendra had such love for his father that he did not question his father's decision. He used to admire his father's wisdom all the time. Again, although his younger brother was useless, he had tremendous affection and concern for his younger brother.

At last the time came for the father to pass behind the curtain of Eternity. After his death, the younger one, as usual, did nothing by way of work. The older one was ploughing his share of the fields and getting a good harvest of grain, while the younger one allowed his fields to go to waste.

One day the younger brother came to his elder brother and said, "Please, please, please, it is getting late, brother. The season is nearly over. Will you help me plough my fields and do everything that is necessary? From next year on, I will be very careful to do all these things at the proper time."

Amarendra said, "It is already too late. The proper season is almost over. I *can* help you, but you will not get the same results as I will get."

Samarendra said, "No harm, no harm. Whatever help you can give me I will deeply appreciate."

Amarendra started helping his younger brother. Naturally, the crops that his own fields yielded were infinitely better than those of his younger brother. Samarendra said to him, "I see you have reaped much more than I have."

Amarendra replied, "I told you when to plough the fields and plant the crop, but you waited and waited. What can I do?"

Then Samarendra said, "Brother, you have the magic touch with regard to farming. Anything that you touch becomes golden. You get miraculous results. My land, I can easily see, is fallow. Nothing will grow there. It is useless. Father has given you the really good land and he has given me the bad plot of land."

Look at this ungrateful creature! Amarendra protested, "No, no! Do not say such things. Father has been very, very kind to you. You delayed and delayed unnecessarily. You did not listen to Father. That is why your results are poor."

Then Samarendra begged him, "Please, please, Amarendra, can you not exchange your plot of land with mine? Mine is useless, I can see. Can you not take it?"

The elder brother agreed. He was all compassion for his younger brother. He said, "All right, I will exchange my land with yours, but you should start ploughing when I start."

Then Amarendra took the so-called bad plot of land. He started working in the fields and transforming them. One day he came across the secret place where his father had said that there would be something hidden for the younger son. Amarendra uncovered the place and discovered a large amount of money that his father had intended for Samarendra. He said, "Father was always so wise. My younger brother is absolutely useless. Now he needs money desperately. Father always cared for him. Tomorrow morning I shall go and give him this money. I know that he is not going to do a day's work in his life. I am going to give him the money that I got from under the ground. It is rightfully his."

Amarendra went to his brother's place and discovered that overnight Samarendra had sold his new plot of land. He was able to sell the land at a very high price by displaying the results of his brother's labours. Then he disappeared. Amarendra was so sad because his younger brother could have had this extra money that their father had hidden for him. He searched for his brother, but his brother had completely vanished after selling the property.

The moral of the story is that good people are good to the end. Again, no matter how kind good people are towards bad people, sometimes the fate of a bad person cannot be changed.

### LTS 101. *Who deserves the money?*

There were two villagers who were simplicity and sincerity incarnate. Their names were Jadu and Madhu. Now, Jadu bought a plot of land from Madhu and started ploughing the land most diligently. He was very happy. One day, in a corner of the field, he discovered a small earthen container, and inside it there were gold coins. He went to Madhu and said, "I bought the land from you, but I was not supposed to get these gold coins. You take them. The land is mine, but it is not right for me to keep this money."

Madhu said, "No, the land belongs to you, so whatever is on it is all yours."

Between these two friends, neither of them wanted to claim the money. They even went to the length of quarrelling and fighting. Jadu insisted, "I want to be sincere. I discovered the money on your land. It is you who sold the land to me, so you deserve it."

Madhu replied, "You paid me for the land. How can I deserve any more money? No, it is yours."

Back and forth they went.

"I will not take it."

"No, you have to take it! It is your money."

"No, it is not. It is yours. It is your property."

A wonderful fight ensued between these two good souls. Finally, they went to the village chief and asked him to decide what they should do. The village chief was so pleased to find that in his village there could be people like this. He was so proud of them. He said to them both, "Do not quarrel, do not fight! You two are so good! I have never seen people like you. I can easily solve your problem."

Then he asked Jadu, "Do you have children?"

Jadu said, "Yes, I have a son."

The village chief asked Madhu, "Do you have children?"

Madhu replied, "Yes, I have a daughter."

Then the village chief said, "I have solved the problem. Now, it is my command that your son and his daughter must get married. I can easily see that they will both derive great joy from this union."

The two villagers stopped fighting immediately. They were so happy that their son and daughter would marry each other.

The marriage ceremony took place in due course. At the wedding, the village chief said, "This money that was found in the field shall be given to the newlyweds." So both the parties were very, very happy. The village chief had solved their problem.

## LTS 102. *A good day of hunting*

This story concerns a king and his minister. The king was a middle-aged man and the minister was an old man. The minister always appreciated, admired and adored the king. Only one aspect of the king's life he could not appreciate and that was the king's love of hunting. The king spent a considerable amount of time hunting. He knew that his minister was not in favour of this pursuit, but he did not mind. The minister was good in so many ways. He was so kind, loving and faithful.

One day, God knows why or how, the king invited the old minister to join him in a day of hunting. The minister was shocked. At the same time, he did not dare to disagree with the king. He wanted to please the king by all possible means, so he accompanied the king.

The king and his entourage, including the minister, spent the whole day hunting. Fortunately or unfortunately, they did not come across any animal. The king was extremely sad. In order to console him, the minister said, "At other times you were always successful. This time I carried bad luck. That is why no animal appeared. In the future, please do not take me if you really want to be successful in your hunting."

The king said, "Fine! I shall not invite you any more, if that is what you wish. Or do you want to come with me again?"

The minister said, "No, no! I am absolutely sure. I prefer to remain in the palace."

That evening the minister returned to his own home. His wife was very curious to know how the hunting went. She asked, "How many tigers and how many lions did you come across today?"

The minister replied, "I had an excellent day, a simply excellent day!"

"Tell me all about it," demanded his wife. "How many animals did you hunt?"

The minister said, "How many? Can you not see that I have come home so happy?"

"Yes," said his wife. "I am seeing that you are beaming with happiness. That is why I am asking you about your hunting expedition with the king."

"You fool!" exclaimed the minister. "Had I seen a tiger or lion, would I not have fainted immediately? I would have died on the spot! Then you would have felt miserable that you had lost your husband. I am so happy because I did not see any tiger or lion or any other animal. I am very happy and you should also be very happy that we did not see any animal. Because of that, you still have a husband!"

### LTS 103. *Who is the greatest fool?*

One day a horse trader brought a white horse to the king's palace. This horse was most beautiful. It was stronger than the strongest and smarter than the smartest. The king was very pleased with the horse, and he was eager to buy it immediately. He said to the horse trader, "I am offering you one hundred rupees."

The minister whispered, "O King, since you like this horse so much, in the future perhaps you would like to have more. The best thing is to buy ten white horses from this man."

The king asked the horse trader, "Do you have more?"

"Yes, I can bring you as many as you want," replied the horse trader.

Then the king asked, "How long will it take? If I give you money now, when will you be able to bring nine more horses?"

"In three weeks or a month I will be able to bring them," said the horse trader.

The king gave the horse trader one thousand rupees in advance to bring the other nine horses, and the horse trader departed. Now, the king was very pleased, and the minister was also very pleased, but the court jester had serious reservations.

This particular king was extremely fond of humour. A few days later he asked his court jester, "Can you bring to the court the worst possible fool in my kingdom?"

The court jester replied, "The worst possible fool? He is already here in your palace. Why should I go any farther?"

The king said, "Who is that fool? What is his name?"

The court jester said, "Without a doubt it is your prime minister. This fool asked you to buy nine more white horses. Your prime minister is such a fool that he encouraged you to pay for them in advance. This horse trader is *not* going to come back with nine more horses, that is certain."

The prime minister became furious. He said, "How do you know the horse trader will not honour his promise?"

The court jester said, "It is plain to see he is not going to come back." Then the court jester said to the king, "In three weeks' time I will be able to present to you the worst possible fool. If the horse trader does not bring nine more horses, then your prime minister is the worst fool in our kingdom, and if he does bring them, then he himself is the greatest fool. After being paid in advance, why should he keep his promise?"

The king was a little perplexed. Then the court jester continued, "But there is somebody else who is infinitely worse than either the prime minister or the man who brought the horse."

"Then where is he? Bring him here!" commanded the king.

The court jester said, "He is also already in the palace."

"Do not waste my time!" said the king. "I want to see how much joy I can get from him."

The court jester bowed to the king and said, "Your Majesty, you yourself are that fool. It is your own noble self. So now you can enjoy your own foolishness. How could you trust your minister? He is a fool! He believed the horse trader. And if the horse trader comes back, then that fellow is also a real fool. But to start with, you gave him the money in advance, so you are the worst fool!"

When the minister heard the court jester's speech, he got furious. He said, "If the horse trader does bring back the nine additional horses, what kind of punishment will you receive for your outrageous remarks?"

The court jester replied, "Whatever punishment you or the king decide, I am ready to receive. But if the horse trader does not bring these nine more horses, what will be your punishment, Prime Minister?"

The prime minister said most sincerely, "I will tell the king to fire me."

Then the king said, "All right, if the horse trader does not bring the horses, the minister will be fired and I will put my court jester on the throne for one day. For one long day he will be the king."

The minister repeated, "What will the court jester's punishment be if the horse trader really brings the horses?"

"Whatever you decide," answered the king.

The minister said, "We will bring the strongest man and he will strike the court jester one thousand times with a cane. This will be his punishment."

The king said, "I fully agree with this punishment. The court jester will be beaten by the strongest man one thousand times."

Now, the minister had the address of the horse trader and he secretly sent for him. The man came to see the minister and he was absolutely sincere. He said, "In three weeks those nine horses will arrive. It may take even less time. I am waiting for my son to bring them. Already I had seven white horses. I needed only two more. My son is bringing them from another village. Once he brings them, I will be able to appear before the king with all the horses."

The horse trader kept his promise. In two weeks' time he came to the court with nine horses. The king was so surprised and thrilled. The king said to his court jester, "Now who is the fool? Show him to me."

The court jester remained silent because he knew that he himself was the fool. Meanwhile the minister was still very angry because he had been so rudely insulted. He said to the court jester, "Now, this is your time to be punished! One thousand times you will be beaten with a cane."

The strongest man was summoned to come and give the punishment. The poor court jester suffered so much. Each stroke of the cane was more powerful. He was being thrashed ruthlessly.

After five hundred strokes, the king felt sorry for him and asked the strongest man to stop. The king said, "I hope you have learnt your lesson. In this world we have to trust people. If we do not trust people, there will be only calamity and chaos. Even if others fool us, we must trust them again and again. This is the only way to build trust in this world. I forgive you, but you must always trust people."

### LTS 104. *Do not touch gold, do not touch women*

There was a hermit who was absolutely pure. The nearby villagers built him a little cottage and they revered him deeply. They wanted to bring him fruits and other kinds of food every day, but he refused their kind offer. He said, "No, I shall beg from door to door. I shall come to your homes and there you will give me whatever I need."

The villagers were very happy with this arrangement and they served him most lovingly and devotedly. In the course of time, two young men came to the hermit. They wanted to become his disciples.

The hermit said, "No, no! You are both too young. Young people are not meant for spirituality. The spiritual life is all austerity. You come from good families, I can see. If you adopt this way of life, your parents will come and create problems for me. No, I cannot accept you as my disciples at the present time."

One of the young men, whose name was Kalo, said, "No, no, no, our parents will have no objection, we promise. We want the spiritual life."

The other one, Bhulo, added, "We need it desperately."

Finally, the hermit agreed. He said, "All right, you will have to face many austerities. Are you ready?"

The two aspirants were very, very sincere. They said to the hermit, "Whatever instructions you give us, we shall gladly abide by."

The hermit was silent for a few minutes. Then he said, "I am giving you two special instructions. Never touch gold and never touch any woman. This is the first instruction. My second instruction is never to be familiar with people. If you are familiar with people, then they will only expect things from you and you will expect things from them. So do not be familiar with others. Just keep a few acquaintances, but do not become familiar with them, and never touch gold and never touch a woman."

Both disciples took the hermit's instructions very seriously. Every morning the hermit and his two disciples would go out and beg from door to door for alms. Sometimes they used to set off together and then they would go to different homes and return to the cottage. Then they would eat the food they had received.

One particular day, as usual, the hermit and his disciples set out. They went in separate directions but remained in the same vicinity. Kalo was walking in the direction of the river. On the way he saw a little boy crying pitifully. He said to the little boy, "Why are you crying?"

The little boy sobbed, "I had a gold chain, but a man took it from me. My Master asked me to take it to the goldsmith and sell it. Then I was supposed to bring the money to my Master."

"Do you know who did it?" asked Kalo.

"No," said the little boy. "A man just grabbed it from me and went away."

"In which direction did he go?" asked Kalo.

The little boy pointed towards the river. "He ran that way," he said and started crying again.

"All right," said Kalo, "Come with me."

The little boy and Kalo ran and ran towards the river. To their great surprise, they saw the thief sitting on the bank of the river.

Now, it happened that Kalo was physically very, very strong. So he went and pushed the thief over and snatched away the golden chain. Then he gave the chain to the little boy. The little boy was so happy. He carefully put the golden chain inside his pocket and went on his way to the goldsmith.

Kalo was about to continue to various places to beg for food when out of the blue he saw a young woman approaching him. She was weeping bitterly. Kalo said to her, "Please tell me why you are crying."

She answered, "A friend of mine has brought me the message that my husband is very, very sick. He is now on the other side of the river. I have been waiting in this place for a ferry to take me there so that I can take care of him. Alas, I do not see any sign of the ferry. How am I going to cross the river? I am so worried. Perhaps my husband will not live until I reach him. I want to go to him immediately."

Kalo said, "Do you not know how to swim?"

The young woman replied, "I am a woman. In our village, women are forbidden to swim. It is thought that if they learn to swim, they will become smart, and the villagers do not like smart women. They like only simple and sincere girls." Then she went on crying pitifully.

Kalo said, "All right, then climb on my back. I will take you to the other side."

Kalo placed her on his back and he swam to the other side of the river. When they arrived, the woman was full of gratitude to him. Then Kalo swam back to the other side of the river.

It happened that when Kalo was chasing the thief with the little boy and when he was crossing the river with the young woman on his back, somehow Bhulo observed him. Bhulo saw both of the incidents with his own eyes. He could not believe that Kalo handled a golden chain and, what is infinitely worse, that he carried a woman on his back to the other side of the river.

Kalo spent a little more time begging for food. Then he returned to the cottage. In the meantime, Bhulo came home and said to the hermit, "You cannot imagine what Kalo has done today! He did not obey you at all."

The hermit said, "He did not obey me?"

"No, Master," said Bhulo. "You gave us instructions not to touch gold, not to touch women. And what has he done? I saw with my own eyes that he touched a gold chain on somebody's neck. Then he snatched it away and gave it to a little boy. And what is infinitely worse, I saw him place a young, beautiful woman on his back and carry her across the river."

The hermit said, "Kalo has done these things?"

"Yes," said Bhulo. "He has done these terrible things this morning."

Now the hermit was waiting for Kalo to return. Eventually he came back with his alms bowl and the hermit said to him, "Is everything all right?"

Kalo said, "Yes, Master, everything is all right, but something eventful happened."

The hermit said, "I would like to hear about it in detail from you later on. Now go and take a bath and then come back."

Kalo went to take a bath. The hermit said to Bhulo, "You are such a fool! I told you not to be familiar with anybody. Why are you becoming involved in Kalo's life? Let me see what Kalo comes and tells me."

In a short time Kalo came back and began his story: "I saw two persons this morning. The first one was a little boy. He was so miserable. He was crying and crying. Afterwards I saw a young woman. She was also crying and crying."

"And then what happened?" asked the hermit.

Kalo said, "I do not know what actually happened. I was there and yet I cannot even remember what I have done. I saw the boy crying pitifully and I know that I helped him, but I do not remember the details. I also remember that a young woman was crying and I helped her. But I cannot remember what I have done. I simply cannot remember."

Then Bhulo said, "How is it that you cannot remember what happened this morning? Who touched a gold chain? Who was carrying a beautiful girl on his back?"

Then Bhulo described the two incidents in great detail.

Kalo said, "My friend, I truly cannot remember all these things." He was not pretending. They had literally vanished from his mind.

The hermit said to Bhulo, "You rascal! Kalo has understood the meaning of my message. When I said, 'Do not be familiar with anybody,' I meant, 'Do not be attached to anybody.' If somebody is badly in need of your help, as those two badly needed Kalo's help, you should help them.

"In Kalo's case, he helped the boy to get back the gold chain, and he helped the young woman to cross the river. He was not attached either to the boy or to the young woman. He did them a big favour, but while he was doing the favour, he was keeping in his mind my instruction never to be attached, never to be attached.

"When I said, 'Do not touch gold, do not touch women,' what I actually meant was, 'Do not be attached to any material thing or any human being.' Look at Kalo's spiritual height! He cannot even remember what happened! He is not fooling me, he is not fooling himself. When he saw that those two were overwhelmed with sorrow and grief, he felt that it was his duty to be of service to them. So he served God inside them.

"I can see inwardly that he is not attached to the young woman or the little boy. He has fully understood my message. In the future, Bhulo, you should also try to find the inner meaning of my instructions. Then you will become an excellent disciple like Kalo."

# LIFE'S BLEEDING TEARS AND FLYING SMILES

## BOOK 8

## LTS 105. *Untimely fruits*

There were two kings. Throughout every year the more powerful one used to receive very, very expensive gifts from the inferior one, especially on the occasion of his birthday. There came a time when some subjects of the inferior king said to him, "You are in no way inferior to that king. You must not send him gifts any more, and you do not have to be loyal to him. We shall demonstrate your supremacy. We shall fight for you."

So the inferior king began preparing himself and his army to fight against the superior king. When the superior king heard about this turn of events, he said, "That fool is still in the world of preparation, while my army is well equipped. Let me go and challenge him before he is fully ready. I shall easily destroy his army."

The prime minister of the superior king did not agree. He said, "O King, this is not the time to attack. It is winter. At this time it will be difficult for us to defeat him and destroy his army. Let us wait for better weather."

The superior king became furious at this advice. He said, "To conquer someone, why should we depend on the weather? Any time is the right time. You have to go now. This is my order."

The prime minister surrendered and said, "All right. We shall get ready."

The following morning the king saw his son, the prince, standing in front of a huge mango tree. The prince himself was watering the mango tree. The king said, "My son, I thought you were extremely wise, but now I see that you are a fool. I am already old, and the time has come for me to retire. I thought that I would give my kingdom to you, but how am I going to do that? You do not have the wisdom to rule like a king."

The prince said, "Father, what is wrong? I am watering this mango tree to expedite the arrival of the fruits."

His father said, "It is the rainy season. Can you not see that it rains heavily each day? As a matter of fact, it may rain at any moment."

The prince said, "It is the rainy season, true. But if I water the tree in addition to the rain, then I will get the mango fruits sooner."

His father said, "How can it be? You will get the fruits at the proper time and not before."

The prince said, "Father, in exactly the same way, this is not the proper time to wage war. What the prime minister is saying is so wise. You think that in spite of the weather if you can attack your enemy quickly, you will be able to conquer him. No, you cannot. In this weather, your soldiers will suffer tremendously. They will suffer, and they may even be defeated, because very few soldiers will be able to enter into the other kingdom. Who knows, your enemy's small army may be able to destroy you. So if you, the king, are doing something untimely, why is it wrong for me to do something untimely? In winter if I am trying to expedite the arrival of the mangoes, will I be successful by watering the mango tree to get fruits sooner? No, it is absurdity on the face of it. In exactly the same way, if you go there, you will not be able to win. On the contrary, you are bound to lose."

The king said, "My son, today you have shown me what true wisdom is. I shall definitely follow your advice and postpone the attack. What is more, I shall give my kingdom to you in the very near future. You have laid all my fears to rest."

### LTS 106. *Who is superior: husband or wife?*

This story is about a husband and wife. As usual, they were on 'wonderful' terms! Each one tried to exercise his superiority. Day in and day out they would quarrel and fight, quarrel and fight. The husband always used to say that he had made the most deplorable mistake of his life by marrying his wife. And the wife said the same. Then she used to add that if she had not made this kind of mistake, by this time she would have married somebody who was richer than the richest. So it went on for years and years.

One day a very great and wise scholar came to their house. He felt sorry for this couple because they were constantly quarrelling and fighting. They appealed to him, "Can you not solve our problem?"

The scholar said, "How can I solve your problem? Both of you are so good to me. True, you fight like cats and dogs between yourselves, but to me you have been extremely kind. So whose side can I take? But I can tell you about a dream I had many years ago. That dream is applicable to you both. In the dream I saw that a husband and wife were going to a distant place. It was the home of one of their relatives. They were walking and walking. On the way, they became very tired, especially the wife. The husband also needed some rest. The countryside through which they were walking was full of banyan trees. They decided to take rest at the foot of a banyan tree. On this day, for some reason, the wife became very kind and generous. While her husband was sleeping on the ground at the foot of the tree, she raised his head and put it on her lap. Then she, too, started dozing.

"All of a sudden she woke up and saw that a branch was shaking. It was about to fall on her husband's head. She raised her hand and said, 'Stop, stop, stop!' and because of her command, the branch did not fall onto her husband. It did not even bend. So that is my story. Now you decide who was superior — the husband or the wife."

The wife immediately said, "Here is the proof! The wife was definitely superior. She was able to stop the branch from falling down. Otherwise, her husband would have been killed or seriously hurt. Inwardly, she was the stronger of the two. She was superior in every way."

Then her husband said, "Stop, stop! You are absolutely wrong. It was because the wife knew that her husband was her master that she did this. A wife has to be loyal to her husband. To save him is her duty. It is not that she was superior. It was her duty to save her master. He is her lord."

Both of them interpreted the dream in their own way. Thus the great scholar made both of them happy.

### LTS 107. *No homes for the idle*

There was once a king who was kind, pious and self-giving in every way. He felt miserable that while he was the king, there were many, many homeless people in his kingdom. So he said to his prime minister, "You must bring all the homeless people here to the court and I will see what I can offer them. I will definitely give each one a house in which to live. Each one will receive a house at the very least."

The prime minister went from village to village making the announcement, and on the appointed day countless homeless people came. When the king saw the long queue, he said, "How can I give so many people houses? O God, You gave me the heart to be of help to the poor people, but You have not given me the capacity. I made a promise and I want to keep my promise, but where is my capacity? I was so moved by the plight of these homeless people, but I never imagined that there were so many of them in my kingdom. What shall I do? I am unable to give them all shelter."

The king felt very, very sad that he was not able to keep his promise. Then the prime minister said, "Oh, no, no! You can still do it."

The king asked, "How?"

The prime minister said, "I will solve your problem."

"If you can solve my problem," said the king, "I shall remain eternally grateful to you."

The prime minister said, "O King, listen to my plan. As you know, when you own a house, you have to do jobs around the house. If you have a house, you cannot be all the time sleeping. You have to do some housework, or you have to go out to buy food or things to furnish the rooms. Everybody has to do some work in order to live in a house. So the best thing is to ask each homeless person to do a small amount of work. I will tell them that in the very near future, each one will get a house from you. Just outside the palace is a very small hill. Those who want a house should only go up the hill and come down. That is all. And you will be thrilled to see how many people are eager to have houses."

The king was very pleased with the prime minister's proposal. Again, he was feeling miserable at the same time. If all of them climbed up the hill, then he still would not be able to fulfil his promise.

The prime minister made a general announcement explaining the situation to the homeless citizens. Then he said, "Now all of you go." Alas, only ten or twenty people remained to climb up the hill. The rest all left. The king was simply shocked. He could not understand why so many people had disappeared.

The prime minister said, "O King, those vagabonds do not need a home. They are wallowing in the pleasures of idleness.

Only the ten or twenty individuals who have remained behind really want to live inside a home. They will do the needful."

The king was quite satisfied and convinced. He gave each of the people who had remained a large home. This was how the wise prime minister solved the problem. The other homeless people wanted the houses, but they did not want to do anything to earn them. Very few needed houses and deserved them. They were the ones who went and climbed up the hill.

In life, if you need something, you also have to deserve it. If you do nothing to deserve it, if you feel that something will come to you out of the blue, you will not value that thing when you get it. If we want to receive something from God, then we have to be fully prepared. We have to feel that it is our bounden duty to take care of that thing.

### LTS 108. *The farmer and the priest*

There once lived a very good and pious priest. One Sunday he told his congregation, "Next week I shall give an excellent sermon. It will be quite a long sermon, and it will be all-illumining. I believe it will help you all immensely. So do come and listen to my wonderful sermon."

The following Sunday, he came to the church. Alas, nobody was there except one old man! The priest could not believe his eyes. He had informed everyone in advance that he would give a wonderful sermon which would illumine them. How is it that the church was not full to overflowing? He was shocked.

He said to the old man, "I have prepared such an excellent sermon. Now you are the only one to hear it. Tell me, is it worthwhile to give the sermon to one individual?"

The old man said, "What can I say? You are a priest and I am a fool. I have come here to receive illumination from you."

Then the priest said, "It is not worth giving illumination to only one person."

The old man said, "Father, I have something to tell you."

"What is it?" asked the priest.

The old man said, "Father, I am a farmer. I have quite a few cows. Every day I go to the cow shed and take lots of fodder. But some days when I go to the cow shed, for some reason, only one cow has come to eat. There should have been many cows, but on that day there is only one cow. Still I do my job. I feed the one who has come. Then I go back home."

The priest understood the old man's point. That was his first illumination — not to count how many have come to hear his message. Even if only one person has come and that person is sincere, he should be taken seriously.

So the priest gave his long sermon to his audience of one person. Unfortunately, from time to time the farmer started sleeping soundly. At the end of the sermon, the priest asked him, "How did you enjoy it?"

The farmer replied, "I enjoyed it very much."

The priest persisted, "But tell me more."

The farmer said, "All right. I shall tell you my opinion. When I go to the cow shed with a lot of fodder and I see there is only one cow, I do not force that cow to eat all the fodder that I have brought. It would die. I bring a large quantity, but it is up to the cow how much it eats. I do not force it to eat beyond its capacity. In your case, you came with a large quantity of wisdom, but I was the only one to receive it. You delivered your entire sermon all the same. How was I going to digest the whole thing? How was I going to understand it? It was far beyond my capacity. I was literally dying while listening to your long sermon. To be perfectly frank, I have not learned anything."

The priest realised his mistake. That was his second illumination.

Now it happened that in a few years' time, both the priest and the farmer passed away on the same day. When they went to Heaven, St. Peter was waiting for them. St. Peter said to them, "What have you both been doing throughout your life?"

The priest said, "I have been preaching and preaching and preaching."

Then the farmer said, "I have been farming and farming and farming."

St. Peter said to the priest, "Oh, I remember you. You are a fool! For the fools Heaven's door is closed."

To the farmer, St. Peter said, "You are truly a wise man. Heaven's door is always open to the wise. Come inside."

Then he turned once more to the priest and said, "You go back to earth and change your profession. I want you to be a farmer and learn how to feed cows. Then you will acquire some wisdom."

Then to the farmer he said, "You stay in Heaven for a number of years. Then I will send you back to the world and I will make you a priest, so you can spread your wisdom. People come to church for wisdom. This fellow has no wisdom, but your wisdom has pleased me. You will go back as a priest and illumine people in your church."

### LTS 109. *We need money-power to live on earth*

There were two very close friends who lived in the same village. The time came when one of them, for some reason, had to go and live in a distant village. Inwardly the two friends maintained their love for each other, but outwardly they were unable to be together. Finally, after twenty years, the friend who had gone away returned home for a visit. Both the friends were so happy and delighted to see each other.

"Ahh!" one friend said to the other, "You look so nice! Twenty years ago you did not look so smart. You look healthy. How did you become so strong? As a matter of fact, you look younger after twenty years than you did previously! You look so much younger and very, very strong!"

The other friend said, "To tell you the truth, I suffered so much for nineteen years. Only last year something happened, and that made me very happy and very strong."

"What was it?" asked the first friend eagerly.

"Let me tell you the whole story," said the second friend. "I opened up a shop and it failed. Then I went into other businesses and failed. I only failed and failed in my attempts to make money. Then I decided that I would not think of money any more. I decided to live a very simple life. The moment I gave up the idea of becoming very rich, I was inundated with peace. Peace entered into my mind and my body. I immediately became healthier. I look so much better because I gave up the idea of becoming rich. If you give up the idea of becoming rich, you have no worries or anxieties. You become very peaceful, happy and strong."

The first friend said, "You are a radiant example! I should also do the same. I must not think of money and all kinds of material things. Then I will look younger and I will become stronger and happier. My difficulty is that my wife will not allow me to lead a simple life. My wife wants to be very rich. Now that I have learned from you about the benefits of leading a simple life, I also want to do the same. But I know the nature of my wife. My wife will be pleased only if I make lots of money. How I wish I was not compelled to earn so much money!"

"You have my complete sympathy," said the second friend. "I gave up the idea of becoming rich, but my wife now wants us to open a new business. She wants to become very, very rich. I know that she will not be peaceful and happy like me by leading a simple life."

The first friend said, "Both our wives want to become rich and we want only simplicity. What are we going to do?" Then he had a brilliant idea. He said, "I have the solution! Let the wives stay together. Since we do not want money, you and I will live together. We can be happy and peaceful in our own way and they can be happy in their own way."

So the two friends went and informed their wives of their wonderful proposal and the wives gladly agreed. Both the wives were quite smart and they felt that they would manage far better without their husbands. So the two wives lived together and the two husbands lived together. The two husbands had next to nothing. They survived on very little money, but they were very happy and they had peace of mind. Meanwhile, the two wives were struggling under the pressure of running their businesses.

In the course of time, the husbands became quite old, and they developed all kinds of ailments. Eventually they needed to go to the hospital for treatment. Unfortunately, the hospital did not want to accept them. The hospital authorities and the doctors said, "Unless you pay, we cannot treat you."

The two husbands said, "We do not have money. We are poor. We do not even have insurance. What are we going to do?"

But the hospital authorities were adamant. They did not want to accept them. Then the authorities asked, "Do you have any relatives?"

"We have wives," said the two husbands.

"What are your wives doing?" asked the authorities. "Can you not take help from them?"

"Oh no," said the two husbands. "We wanted to become happy by remaining poor. So we separated from our wives."

"But are you happy now?" asked the authorities. "You have all kinds of diseases. You badly need medical treatment and you cannot afford it."

The two husbands said, "We know we need medical treatment, but what can we do? We are helpless."

So the doctors went to the two wives and said, "Your husbands are suffering so much. Do you not feel obliged to help them?"

One wife said, "They are fools!"

The other wife said, "We do not care for them. They left us. They said they wanted to have peace. Let them have peace! Why should we be responsible?"

"But now they are both suffering from diseases. They are in dire need of your help," said the doctors.

Finally the wives began to feel sorry for their husbands, so they decided to pay their husbands a visit. When they saw their poor husbands, they said, "You fools! Who wanted you to become very, very rich? Not us! You had the wrong impression, so you left us. Now you have nothing. It is not good to be greedy, but as long as we are on earth, we need money for our basic daily needs. Now we have to save you. If we pay for your medical treatment, then only can you be cured."

So the wives paid for their husbands, and the husbands were cured. Then they went back to their respective wives, and both couples again started living a normal life.

The wives said, "We shall give you whatever money you need, and you will help us to run our business. We need money not only to keep you alive but also to keep both our families alive. We are not asking you to be extremely rich, but each of us should have the money that we need to live on earth."

So this was how the two husbands received illumination from their wives. In the beginning, both the wives did want to become very rich. That is why they gave up their husbands. But then wisdom dawned on them. They realised that too much money creates problems in our lives. We need money-power to live on earth, but we should not constantly cry for more wealth.

### LTS 110. *What anger can do*

There was once a very strict boss. People who worked under him were always afraid of him. He used to say, "I do not want any idlers in my office. They will be fired!" If anybody was slow, he became furious. If anybody was idle, he insulted them badly.

One day this boss saw one of his workers loitering outside in the corridor. What is more, the worker was enjoying chewing gum. The boss was infuriated. He marched up to the man and said, "I cannot tolerate this kind of behaviour. I want my workers to be very, very active and dynamic. What do you think you are doing? You are such a bad fellow. I do not want you to be in my office any more. By the way, how much money do you get? I have a little sympathy for you and for your family. Tell me, how much money do you receive?"

The worker said, "I get one hundred rupees a month."

"All right," said the boss. "I am giving you one hundred rupees. Now go and find somewhere else to work. One month's salary I have given. I have sympathy for you, but I cannot keep you here because you are a bad example to my other workers. Now kindly leave my office and never, never come back."

The man left and the boss was very, very happy that there was nobody in his office to idle away time. Then the boss went out for lunch. He had a very nice meal and after two hours he returned to the office.

As soon as he came into his office to work, he thought he saw the same man standing in the corridor eating something. He was consumed with anger. He sent for his assistant and said, "This fellow is so ungrateful! I gave him money for an entire month. I told him, 'Go out and find another job. I am giving you one hundred rupees so that you and your family will not suffer.' Now what is that bad worker doing here? He is ruining the atmosphere in my office. Others will follow his example and they will also become lazy. He should be punished! Bring him here."

So the assistant brought the man to the boss. The boss was so angry that he could not even look at the man. He exploded, "You are impossible! When I fired you, I gave you so much money! Why are you still here? What are you doing?"

The man calmly took a letter from his pocket and gave it to the boss. The letter was from a friend of the boss inviting him to come for dinner that evening. After reading the letter, the boss looked more closely at the worker and realised that this was not the worker he had fired. It was somebody who worked in his friend's office.

So this is what anger can do. At first the boss was very strict. He did not want anybody to be idle or to waste time. Then, when he fired the lazy worker, he was generous to some extent. He showed his compassion. Finally, when he thought the lazy worker was still lingering, he became so furious that he did not even look at the worker properly. He thought that it was the same person. His anger was so great that he could not see clearly. Anger does not allow us to see the right person or do the right thing.

### LTS 111. *The inveterate smokers*

There were two villagers who were very, very good friends. One day they were returning from the market. They found a short cut to come home, so they were very happy. On the way, one of them said, "I have to smoke. Really, I need it badly."

The other friend said, "I also want to smoke."

The first one, from his pocket, brought out an Indian cigarette. We call them bidis. Then he said, "Oh, I do not have matches."

The second friend said, "I have matches, but I have only two sticks, so we have to be very careful."

The second friend struck one stick against the matchbox. Alas, there was no flame — nothing! It did not catch fire. He threw the stick onto the ground. Now there was only one left. He closed his eyes and started praying to God that this time the matchstick would work. For two minutes he prayed most intensely. With his eyes closed he prayed and prayed and prayed. The first friend was so happy that his friend was praying to God. He was positive that this time God would definitely allow the match to light. The first time his friend did not pray; that is why the matchstick did not work, but this time he had done the needful.

After praying, the second friend opened his eyes. He was cocksure that this time it would work. Alas, it did not work. For a few moments both of them were so sad. Then they started laughing.

The first one said, "I saw such sincerity in you! The second time, while you were praying, how is it that God did not listen to your prayer?"

The second friend said, "This is why I say not to pray to God. God never listens to my prayers. He simply ignores them."

The first friend agreed, "It is true! God does not listen to my prayers either. For years and years I have been trying to give up smoking. I pray to God to help me, but God does not listen. Now today you wanted to smoke and He did not listen. Here is the proof that God does not listen to our prayers."

The second friend said, "Let us stop praying to God. Let us become atheists."

The first friend said, "Before giving up our prayer-life, let us go to the village priest. Perhaps the priest will have some advice."

They went to the village priest to ask his advice before they gave up praying. When they saw the priest, the first friend said, "For years I have been praying to God to help me stop smoking, but God does not listen. I just go on smoking."

The other one said, "I pray to God to enable me to smoke whenever I want to, but something always happens. Either I do not have the money-power or there is some other obstacle. Here is the proof: today I wanted to smoke, but God did not listen to my prayer."

The priest said to the second friend, "You say that God does not listen to your prayers. I tell you, God does listen to you. I shall prove it to you. You can come to my place to smoke any time. We shall enjoy smoking together. And do not worry about paying. I have plenty of bidis here. Just come whenever you want to smoke with me. You see, God is listening to your prayer. I am telling you that in the future you will never have any problem with smoking."

To the first friend the priest said, "In your case, it seems that God is not listening to you. But I will send a message to St. Peter to see what he can do about your problem. Come back and see me in a week or so."

This friend was so happy that the priest would speak to St. Peter on his behalf. After one week had passed, he came back, hoping to receive good news. He said to the priest, "Please tell me what St. Peter said."

The priest answered, "St. Peter says he is very busy. He has more important things to do than worry about your smoking."

The first friend was so disappointed and disheartened. He said, "Then I will not be able to stop?"

The priest said, "You *will* be able to stop."

The first friend said, "How will I be able to stop if St. Peter does not listen to my request?"

The priest said, "I will give you a piece of good advice. I gave your friend good advice and it is working very well. He can come and smoke with me any time. I am always available. In your case, I am telling you to start smoking as much as you can for as long as you can, as many times a day as possible."

The man was dumbfounded. He said, "I want to give up smoking, not to increase it! By smoking so many times a day, how will I be able to give up smoking?"

The priest said, "Just smoke and smoke to your heart's content. Then you will fall sick. If you fall sick, then how will you be able to smoke any more?"

### LTS 112. *Your problem is my problem*

There were two friends who were dearer than the dearest to each other. Because of various circumstances, they had not seen each other for a long time. One day, quite unexpectedly, they met in the street. One friend said to the other, "I understand that you have become very, very rich. Is it true?"

The second friend said, "Yes, it is absolutely true. I have acquired a very large amount of money. But what can money alone do? I have been suffering from back pain for many months. I have spent so much money going from doctor to doctor, but no doctor can cure me. Money cannot cure my back pain, and I have been suffering unimaginably."

The first friend said, "I tell you, I can make a very sacred and secret ointment. If you use it for three months on a regular basis, you will be completely cured. But the ingredients are extremely rare and very difficult to obtain. Plus, they are quite expensive. I have to go to so many places to get them. But if you are ready to give me the necessary money, I am ready to go to all this trouble. Your problem is my problem and my problem is your problem. If one of us can solve our problem, at least half of our problems will be over. I cannot guarantee that you will be cured completely, but I assure you that you will get considerable relief. I am happy to know that money is no object for you. If you send me one hundred rupees a month, I will send you the ointment. Then half our problems will be over."

So the rich friend sent one hundred rupees every month, and in return he received the ointment. He had such faith in his friend. Alas, alas, three months passed and his back had not improved at all. He was very sad and mad. He asked himself, "What kind of deception is this?"

One day the two friends met again on the street. The rich man was very angry. He said, "You took money from me, but still I am suffering severely from back pain. Your ointment is useless."

His friend said, "Did I not tell you that half our problems would be over?"

"What do you mean by half our problems? I do not understand," said the rich friend.

His friend continued, "I needed money desperately, so this is how I was able to get it from you for three months. I told you that your problem is my problem and my problem is your problem. Now my problem is over, which means half your problems are over. To solve the other half of your problems, I advise you to go to a good doctor."

The rich man was so shocked. He decided to punish his friend for being such a rogue. This rich man had various other ailments which were already being treated by an excellent doctor. Because of the doctor's medicines, the rich man's condition was improving very gradually. The rich man did not blame the doctor for his slow progress. He knew the doctor was trying his best and, besides, the doctor had never claimed that he would be able to cure the rich man completely.

The rich man went to this doctor and narrated the whole sad story to him.

The doctor said, "I know this fellow. He is also a patient of mine. He is such a rogue. Do not worry. I will teach him a lesson."

In the course of time, the rogue-friend fell sick. Now that his financial problems were over, he did not hesitate to go and consult the excellent doctor. The doctor examined him and prescribed certain medicines. When the patient received the bill, he found that it was double the normal amount. On his next visit, he said to the doctor, "How can your bill be so high? All of a sudden you have raised your fee!"

The doctor said, "Everything nowadays is more expensive. Just look around you. Is anything the same price? Even at the market, everything costs more. I need more money to pay my bills. If you do not want to pay the fee, go to some other doctor. Everybody says that I am the best doctor. But if you do not believe it, then go to some other doctor. I do not care. I do not need you as a patient."

Now it happened that the doctor's medicines were working and the patient was getting a little better. Since he was getting better, he did not mind paying double the amount to the doctor. So the doctor was getting much more money than usual by charging this particular patient double.

When the doctor had collected three hundred rupees extra from this patient, he informed him, "From tomorrow my fee will be reduced. I will charge you half the amount."

"Why?" asked the patient.

"You are such a rogue," said the doctor. "You took three hundred rupees from your friend for some useless ointment and now I am returning the money to him."

The doctor gave the money to the rich man and said, "Please take your money. You are sincere, but your friend is a real rogue."

Those who are rogues will eventually be caught. Today they may fool us, but tomorrow they are bound to be caught.

## LTS 113. *Doctor, cure thyself!*

There was a very great doctor named Ram. According to many, he was by far the best doctor. But he was extremely humble. He used to say to his patients and admirers, "It is your faith that cures you. I know that there are many doctors who are as good as I am, and also there are some who are far better than I am." His admirers and patients did not believe him. They felt that he was simply being modest.

One winter, it happened that Ram fell sick. His relatives tried to cure him, but day by day, he grew weaker and weaker. Clearly he was getting much worse, and the case was becoming very serious. In India and elsewhere as well, doctors usually do not take medicine from their dear ones. If they are a doctor, they prefer to go to other doctors.

Ram's son-in-law happened to be a doctor. But how could Ram take help from his son-in-law, who was so dear to him? The son-in-law said, "You will not take my medicine, I know, because I am your close relative, but I am suggesting another doctor. His name is Shyam. He is a very good doctor."

Ram said, "Oh, definitely. I thought of him when I first became ill. Quite often I think of him, but now I should go to see him."

Ram's son-in-law took him to that particular doctor. Unfortunately, Shyam was not at home. Ram asked, "Where has he gone?"

His family members said, "He has been very, very sick. Ten days ago he went to a nearby village to see another doctor. That doctor's name is Rabi. He has gone to him because he has faith in that doctor, and he does not want to treat himself."

Ram and his son-in-law said, "Then let us go to Rabi. Dr. Rabi is definitely a great doctor. Perhaps he is the best. Even Dr. Shyam has gone to Rabi."

Ram and his son-in-law travelled to Rabi's village. When they arrived, they saw all the village people crying. Ram said, "Ah, that means some patient has died."

They made inquiries, and the villagers said, "No, no, not a patient. It is the doctor himself who has died."

Ram and his son-in-law felt miserable. They realised that these were all Rabi's friends who had come to console Rabi's son. Rabi's son was so sad and heartbroken. He said to the two visitors, "You have come here? Just two days ago my father said to us that in a day or two he would go to see you to ask you for your medical advice. He was getting ready for us to take him to your place. Then all of a sudden he died."

Ram himself was dying and Rabi had wanted to come to him for advice! He told his son-in-law, "Bring me home. I am not going to any other doctor."

His son-in-law asked, "What will you do now?"

Ram said, "I am going to cure myself. I lost faith in myself. That is why I wanted to go and ask another doctor's opinion. We must always have faith in ourselves. The Indian theory is that if you are a relative, it is not good to accept treatment from that person. I do not agree with that theory. I have regained my faith in myself. You will see that in a few days I will be completely cured."

And Ram did cure himself.

## LTS 114. *The king's awakening*

There was a king who was very, very rich. He passed his time wallowing in the pleasures of richness. All the pleasures of the world he had at his command. To some extent, he was neglecting his kingdom, but he had amassed so much wealth that he did not care. He was extremely greedy. In spite of having so much wealth, he wanted to become infinitely richer.

One day a young man came to his palace and said, "Your Majesty, you are so good, so great, so kind. Your reputation for greatness and goodness has spread throughout the length and breadth of the entire country. But I want to inform you that there are three other kings like you. Of course, they are inferior to you in every way, but they do have some wealth. They may not be as rich as you are, but nonetheless they are quite rich. At the present time, they are neglecting their kingdoms; they are ruining everything. Would you not like to have their wealth by conquering them? You can easily conquer those three kings."

Since the king was greedy, he said, "Definitely, definitely! I shall ask my commander to get ready as soon as possible. He will go and attack these three countries and conquer them. Then they will all become mine."

The young man said, "It is a splendid idea. But you may take a few days to prepare."

The king said, "Yes, of course, I will take a few days."

The young man told him, "When you are ready, you will send for me. Summon me and I shall come and show you where these three kingdoms are." Then the young man disappeared.

In a few days, the commander of the king's armies was fully prepared. He came to the king and said, "Now please tell us who the young man is and what is his address."

The king said, "I completely forgot to ask him his name and his address because I was in such a state of excitement. What can I do? I never realised that I was such a fool."

The king's minister and his commander began consoling him. They said, "Oh, it happens to everybody. We all make mistakes. We are, after all, human beings. We ourselves have made that kind of mistake many, many times." They were sympathising with the king and minimising his mistake.

The king said, "Now you have to go and find him. I am sure he came from my kingdom. You have to find out who the young man is."

The minister and commander went on a wild goose chase. They were looking everywhere for the young man who had given the news. Nobody dared to come forward and say who was the one who had given the news about the other countries, and so their search was in vain.

The king was miserable. How could he have been such a fool? The minister and commander reassured him. They said, "One day the same person is bound to come back. Perhaps he thinks that you are going to take a longer time. That is why he is not coming. But we are all ready. Any time he comes, we shall take your army and conquer those three countries."

The king was so sad and miserable that he fell sick. He could not stop thinking of those three countries that he was supposed to conquer and the wealth that he would have acquired. Day by day the king's case became worse, until his days were numbered.

A very old man came to the palace and said, "I will be able to cure the king."

Nobody believed him. Everyone thought he was just a feeble-minded old man. They asked him, "Are you a doctor?"

The old man said, "No, I am not a doctor."

"Then how can you cure him?" they asked mockingly.

He said, "I am a man of prayer."

Everybody laughed. "A man of prayer? Do you have occult power? Do you have spiritual power?"

The old man said, "No, I do not have occult or spiritual power."

"Then how are you going to cure him?" they asked. "You do not have occult power or spiritual power. You are not a doctor. How can you cure him?"

The old man insisted, "I know I can cure the king."

The king was desperate for a cure. When he heard the old man's message, he said, "Forget about his so-called lack of occult power or spiritual power. Since he says he will be able to cure me, let me give him a chance before I die. You people have brought me all the doctors, and nobody can cure me."

The old man was brought to the king's bedside. He said, "I will be able to cure you, my King, but first you have to answer some questions. If you answer my questions correctly, immediately I will be able to cure you."

The king said, "Yes, I am answering your questions, before I die."

The old man said, "O King, you have a bed, a most comfortable bed, a king's bed. Do you not appreciate your bed?"

The king said, "I used to appreciate it, but not now. Now I am so sick. I do not find anything comfortable. Everything is miserable, miserable in my life. There was a time, for years and years, when I enjoyed my bed. It was so comfortable. But now I am extremely sick. Nothing comforts me."

The old man said, "All right. When you were very happy with your bed, at that time if I had brought you three beds exactly like the one that you have, would you have been able to use the four beds at the same time?"

The king said, "You fool! How could I enjoy four beds at the same time?"

The ministers and commanders were all getting annoyed with the old man. What kind of silly questions was he asking?

The old man continued, "Now you are wearing some clothes. Tell me, if I bring three sets of clothes for you all exactly the same, will you be able to wear them all at the same time?"

The king said, "What kind of absurd questions are you asking? How can I use four sets of clothes at the same time?"

The old man said, "All right, all right. O King, this is my last question. You have a crown. It is the most beautiful crown that people have seen on earth. Suppose I give you three more crowns exactly the same. Will you be able to wear these four crowns at the same time?"

The king became furious. "You idiot!" he exclaimed. "What kind of question are you asking me? How can I wear four crowns at the same time? Get out! Get out of my palace! Here I am on my deathbed and you are asking me absurd questions."

The old man said, "I am not asking you absurd questions. I wish to tell you that you have answered my questions most satisfactorily. You cannot enjoy four beds at the same time. You cannot wear four sets of clothes at the same time. You cannot wear four crowns at the same time. In exactly the same way, if you had conquered those three countries, how could you have enjoyed all those countries the way you are enjoying your own country? You could not have been in four countries at the same time. You can be only in one country — either in your own country or in another country. You could not have been in four countries simultaneously to enjoy their respective wealth."

Then the old man bowed and disappeared. Meanwhile, the king was awakened. From that moment on, the king's health began to improve and he was eventually cured. It was all because he now realised that he could not enjoy four countries at the same time. When the king had regained his health, he gave up his greed for the pleasure-life. He said that from that time on he would be satisfied with his own kingdom, with his own country, and he would pay very special attention to all his subjects.

LTS 115. *The girlfriend who illumined the whole world*

There was a seeker who was unimaginably curious. His great desire was to have occult power so that he would be able to show off. He used to pray to God only for occult power — not for peace, not for joy, not for any spiritual quality — only for occult power. He did not care for spiritual power at all.

God eventually came to him and asked, "What kind of occult power do you need?"

The seeker replied, "The occult power that people will be astonished by. Jesus Christ came back in three days' time, but Jesus Christ was dead. In my case, I will be happy if I can be buried alive so I can prove that I have more occult power than Jesus Christ. I would like to be buried under the ground for quite a few hours."

Because he had been praying to God for occult power, God said, "All right. I am giving you occult power."

The seeker immediately wanted to demonstrate his newly acquired power. He arranged to be buried alive for twelve hours. After twelve hours, the villagers were supposed to dig him out and he would emerge alive. The police were present to record that nobody would be responsible for him if anything unfortunate happened. Many, many villagers went to see the spectacle. Some people stayed and watched. They were curious to know whether he would come out alive. The seeker's mother, father, brother and other relatives and dear ones were also watching. Since they could not stay for the entire twelve hours, they would go back home for a short while and then they would come back again. They were also extremely curious as to whether he would come out alive.

After twelve hours had passed, people dug up the ground and uncovered the young man. To everybody's amazement, he was quite all right. Everybody shook his hand. Absolutely hundreds of villagers were applauding and admiring him. But he was looking and looking for someone in the crowd. His poor mother, who had been worrying and worrying for hours, was so happy, delighted and excited to see her son alive. She was absolutely sure that he was searching for her, so she came running to him and cried, "I know that you are looking for me, my son."

Then she embraced her son with such love and affection. The son said, "No, no, I am looking for somebody else."

The mother was shocked. She asked, "For whom?"

He said, "I am looking for my girlfriend."

The mother was sad and mad when she found out that her son was not looking for her. She said, "What is this? I have given my whole life for you. I am the one who gave birth to you, and you are so ungrateful! You love her more than you love me. I have sacrificed my whole life for you, and you love your girlfriend more!" She was so disgusted that she went home.

The young man continued looking, but his girlfriend was not to be found. She had been there earlier in the day, but she thought that this fellow was not going to come out alive. She was absolutely convinced that he would die there, and who wants to see a dead body carried out? She was afraid that if anything happened to him, then people would express pity for her. They would say, "Poor girl, she has lost her boyfriend." She did not want to be embarrassed, so she left the scene after only an hour or two.

This is what happens when we pray to God only for occult power. God may give us occult power to use to show off. There were so many people there, but the young man was not satisfied. He was not interested in those others. He was only thinking that if so many people came, his girlfriend would see his performance and she would be deeply moved. Then she would be more willing to marry him.

Alas, alas, he did not see his girlfriend. When he found her at home, she told him that she did not want to marry him. He said, "But I showed this performance of occult power! Were you not impressed?"

The girlfriend said, "No, I do not want to marry you. I want to marry either someone who is very rich, to make me happy here on earth, or someone who has renounced everything for God."

In the course of time, the girlfriend met someone very, very rich, and she married him. Alas, alas, she discovered that marriage-life was full of quarrelling, fighting and misunderstanding. It was a most unfortunate experience. She said, "I have made such a serious mistake by marrying this wealthy man!"

So she left her husband. Then she wanted to marry someone who had renounced the world. Now, if somebody has renounced the world, why should he marry her? Most probably, he has renounced the world after going through this kind of suffering, where the husband and wife quarrel and fight.

The girl went to someone who had renounced everything and asked him, "Are you happy?"

The renunciate said, "Yes, I am truly happy because I have renounced the world. Before this, I went through married life. Truth to tell, my wife made my life miserable. Every day we were quarrelling and fighting. The fighting never ended. I was miserable, so I renounced the whole world. Now I am absolutely happy."

The young girl said, "I also want to be happy. My experience of married life is the same as yours. It brought me only misery. Now I want to renounce the world."

The renunciate said, "Do not make the same mistake again. Renounce the world and pray and pray. You will find true happiness."

So the young girl did not look any more for a husband. Since she did not know anybody who was sincerely interested in the spiritual life and had renounced the world who would marry her, she herself gave up the world of desire. She no longer wanted to have a boyfriend or a husband. She only wanted to pray to God to realise Him. She made a firm resolution: no boyfriend, no husband, only God.

When she renounced the world, she became so happy. That same night, God came to her in a dream and said, "I am your Boyfriend. I am your Husband. I am your Father. I am your Mother. I am your All."

In one day she received realisation. God came to her in a dream and became a reality in her life.

The occultist's nature was not transformed in the slightest by his experience. It was his girlfriend who became divine. In the course of time, the occultist's mother came to know that her son's former girlfriend had now received illumination, so the mother came to her and saw that she was indeed totally changed. The mother knew her son was useless; he cared only for occult power. But when she saw the spiritual light radiating from the girl who was supposed to have married her son, she was so moved. Then she started praying and meditating with her son's former girlfriend. The mother became very spiritual, and the girl was able to help the mother make inner progress.

When the occultist observed so many changes in his mother, he also wanted to become a disciple of his former girlfriend. His girlfriend said, "I cannot take responsibility for anyone. God is my Husband, my Father, my Mother — my Everything."

The young man said, "I do not want to be your husband. I want you to be my Guru. You have received illumination. Now no more occult power for me! I am giving up this kind of display. I want you to be my Guru."

She said, "No, I cannot be your Guru. My Guru is your Guru. If you accept God as your Guru, I will accept you. But if you take me as your Guru, I cannot accept you. Once upon a time we were boyfriend and girlfriend. Now my Boyfriend is my Guru — God. If you accept God as your Beloved, then I will accept you."

The young man agreed to accept God as his only Beloved, and all three began to lead most spiritual lives.

So the girlfriend realised God first. Then her boyfriend realised God. Finally the mother realised God. All three realised God. It was the former girlfriend who gave the son and his mother God-realisation. So the girlfriend illumined the whole world.

### LTS 116. *The unchained lion*

There was once a very great artist. His fame had spread far and wide. Everybody admired him. He was by far the best artist in the country. Now, a circus happened to visit his town, and a few people told the owner of the circus all about the great artist. They said that this artist could paint a lion that would be exactly like a living lion. Unsuspecting people would get frightened when they saw the painted lion because it would be so lifelike.

The circus owner liked this suggestion very much. So he went to the artist and said, "Can you paint a living lion for me?"

The artist said, "Yes, I can, but I warn you that people will take my lion very seriously. Children will get frightened when they see it."

The circus owner was so delighted and excited. He said, "Oh! That is wonderful! How much will you charge?"

The artist said, "I will charge 2,000 rupees. But first I must ask, do you want the lion with a chain?"

The circus owner replied, "Yes, a chain will look nice. How much will you charge for the chain? Is it extra?"

The artist said, "With a chain it will be 4,000 rupees."

The circus owner said, "Without a chain, 2,000 rupees and with a chain it will be 4,000? For a chain it will be 2,000 extra?"

The artist said, "Yes. It is very complicated to explain. The whole body takes a short time to paint, but when it comes to the chain, it takes a very long time. There is so much detail in the chain. But if you are ready to give 2,000 rupees more, I will do it."

The circus owner asked, "If there is no chain, will it still look like a real lion?"

The artist said, "Certainly it will look like a lion! Who will care whether or not it has a chain if the body looks like a living lion?"

The circus owner said, "Then I am ready to give you 2,000 rupees for a lion without a chain."

So the artist painted the picture. The result was extraordinary. It was absolutely like a living lion. Everyone who saw it was deeply impressed. The only problem was that, although most of the grown-ups were very happy to see the painting at the entrance to the circus, some of the children became frightened when they saw the lion and they did not want to go inside. At a distance the lion seemed so living. These little children would see it and beg their parents to take them home again. So sometimes more people attended the circus because at the entrance there was a living lion, but sometimes the circus lost business because children were afraid and did not want to go inside.

One night there was a severe storm. It rained very, very heavily. Some of the circus tents were badly damaged while others developed leaks. Alas, the rain destroyed the painting completely. Only a few lines of the original painting were visible. The lion was no longer recognisable. So the circus owner became furious. He went to the artist and said, "You gave me a living lion and now the lion has completely disappeared!"

The artist said, "The lion has disappeared? What can I do? You wanted it and I painted it. I am not responsible for what happened afterwards."

The circus owner said, "No, I will not accept your excuses. You have to paint me another one."

"The same thing will happen," said the artist.

"Can you not paint one that will never disappear, even if it rains?" asked the circus owner.

Then the artist said, "It is your own fault! I told you, you need a chain for the lion, to tie it. You said, 'No, I do not need a chain, since the chain costs 2,000 rupees more.' It is your own fault because you did not want me to paint a chain. If I had painted the chain along with the lion, then the lion could not have disappeared. It would have remained."

The circus owner said, "All right. I am ready to pay you extra for the chain. Please paint another lion."

"Then you have to give me 4,000 rupees," said the artist.

The circus owner said, "I am ready to give the money if I can keep the lion."

The artist felt sad that he had fooled this gullible fellow. The first time the artist had used water colours. This time he used oil paints. He painted another lion, and this one was even more powerful and ferocious than the first one. Plus it had a very strong chain around its neck. So the circus owner was very pleased with his chained lion and the artist received the full amount. And, since it was an oil painting, the lion remained permanently at the entrance to the circus.

LTS 117. *The stolen bullocks*

There was a farmer who had saved up money for years to buy two very strong and powerful bullocks. Finally, he had the necessary amount and he was so happy to be able to buy a pair of bullocks to plough his fields. The day after he purchased the bullocks, early in the morning, the farmer yoked them to a plough and for two hours he ploughed his fields. Then he became tired, so he released the bullocks and allowed them to move around. Meanwhile, he sat at the foot of a tree to take rest. Alas, in a few minutes the farmer fell asleep.

Soon afterwards, a thief happened to pass by. He saw the two beautiful bullocks and he began to lead them away. All of a sudden, the farmer woke up and started screaming, "Those are my bullocks! What are you doing?"

The thief said, "These are *my* bullocks! They were roaming free and I found them first."

Then both of them started fighting. The thief claimed that he was the owner of the two bullocks and the farmer said, "They are *my* bullocks! I paid for them." The farmer started screaming at the top of his lungs, and the villagers all rushed to the scene.

The thief said, "Two days ago I bought these bullocks. Now I am taking them to my home."

The farmer said, "No, it is not true! I bought them! These are mine! Just last night I bought them."

An elderly villager said, "If they belong to you, then you have to prove it."

The farmer said, "How am I going to prove it?"

The villager said, "Was there nobody who saw you arrive with these bullocks?"

The farmer said, "Yesterday in the evening I bought them, and early in the morning I brought them here to plough my fields. Alas, nobody has seen me bring them here."

Then the thief said, "I bought these bullocks two days ago and I am taking them home to my village. If you come with me, I will be able to prove it."

The villagers said, "Where do you live?"

The thief answered, "I live quite far from here, but if you come with me, I will be able to bring forward witnesses to prove my story." The thief knew that he could easily fool the villagers. He would bring them some distance and then run away in the night, taking the bullocks with him. That was the plan in his mind.

Since the villagers could not settle the dispute, the elderly villager said, "Let us go and get our village doctor. He is very, very wise. Perhaps he will be able to solve the problem."

So they brought the village doctor to the field. The village doctor said to the thief, "Since you claim to be the owner, I am sure you have fed the bullocks."

The thief said, "Oh yes, I have taken good care of my animals."

The doctor continued, "What did you give them this morning?"

The thief said, "I gave them boiled rice, sweets and many, many things. I even gave them fried potatoes."

Then the doctor asked the farmer, "What did you give them?"

The farmer said, "I am a very poor farmer. With greatest difficulty, I saved up enough money to buy these two bullocks. This morning I gave them only grass. I did not have anything expensive to offer them. I only gave them grass."

The doctor said, "Now let me see who is telling the truth." He took some powder and put it into water. Then, after shaking the bottle, the doctor said, "All right. Now let the bullocks drink a little." As soon as the doctor put this drink inside the mouths of the bullocks, they both started vomiting.

The farmer became so miserable. He said, "O my God! My bullocks will die!" He was panicking because of the way the two bullocks were vomiting.

In the meantime, everybody could see that the bullocks had vomited only grass. There was no rice, no potatoes. So they immediately declared, "The farmer is telling the truth. The other fellow is a thief!"

The farmer was so relieved. He took his bullocks and started leading them away. Then the villagers started thrashing the thief. They beat him up mercilessly because he was such a liar. They wanted to punish him for his crime.

The doctor said, "Listen to me. This is not the only world. There is another world. In this world he has told a lie, and for that you are all punishing him. But wait until he goes to the other world. When he dies, in that world they will punish him far more ruthlessly than you are doing now. So the best thing is to leave him to be punished in the other world."

The villagers said, "Will he really be punished? Are you sure?"

The doctor was the wisest man in the village and they all respected him. He said, "I tell you, there is another world. People who do wrong things on earth receive punishment in two places. Here you have punished him ruthlessly. He is almost dead. But when he dies, there will be another punishment, and that punishment will be even more severe. So do not punish him any more. Let him return home."

The villagers listened to the doctor and allowed the thief to leave the place. They were so happy that in the next world also he would be punished for telling lies.

# LIFE'S BLEEDING TEARS AND FLYING SMILES

## BOOK 9

## LTS 118. *The treasurer's lamp*

There was a very kind-hearted king. In every way he was appreciated, admired, adored and loved by his subjects. Unfortunately he received complaints against two of his very high-ranking officers that they were accepting bribes. These officers were so close to him that he could not believe it. Then he said, "How can I trust any human being? These two were so close to me for so many years. Now they are misbehaving. I do not know how I can solve this problem. It will be very painful for me now to fire them. They have been with me for a long time, and it will create many problems for me."

Then he said, "All right. Let me have some consolation. They say that my treasurer is the most honest man in our kingdom. Let me see if it is true or if my treasurer is also of the same type. Two I have caught. I had such faith in them. Let me see if the treasurer also belongs to that group."

In disguise, the king went to the treasurer's place. He was dressed like an ordinary citizen. He said to the treasurer, "I need your urgent advice."

The treasurer could not recognise the king. He said, "Please wait, wait." The treasurer was busy working, so the king sat down and waited. After some time the treasurer said, "I am so sorry that you had to wait. But as you know, I am working for the king and I have to submit my report to the king tomorrow."

The king saw that his treasurer was not using electric light. He had only a kerosene lamp. The king said, "How can it be? This is how he saves my money? He is so kind-hearted."

That was not all. Right in front of the king, the treasurer lit another kerosene lantern, and he extinguished the one he was using previously. The king said, "Why did you not continue to use the previous lamp?"

The treasurer replied, "That one belongs to the king. When I do the king's work, I use that one. But now you have come here for private advice. How can I use the lamp that I use for the king's work? Yours is a private matter. My lamp is for my private use, and you have come here for private advice. What little I know, I will share with you gladly, but for this kind of thing I am not authorised to use the king's lamp."

The king was so pleased with the treasurer. Right in front of him, the king took off his mask and the rest of his disguise. Then the king embraced him and said, "You are, indeed, the most honest person in my kingdom. Now I know that I *can* trust another human being."

### LTS 119. *The goddess of truth triumphs*

There was a king who was extremely, extremely kind to his subjects, especially to the poor. He said to himself, "I am king. I have material wealth, but I have countless subjects to take care of. What can I do? They say a king can do anything, but it is not true. I am ready to give away everything that I have, but even then I will not be able to raise the standard of my kingdom."

Since the king felt that he would not be able to help each and every one of his subjects, he decided that early in the morning he would stand outside his palace. From whomever he saw first, he would buy something. Every day somebody different would come, since the king had made a general announcement.

This went on every day for years. The king would come out of his palace, and from whomever he saw first, he would buy something. If there were people behind that person, they would not be accepted — only the very first one. No matter what the first one had brought or what price he asked for, the king would agree. He never argued. The king said, "I have to be kind-hearted. Whatever my subjects ask me for is according to their conscience. Whatever they ask from me, I will give."

In this way it went on month after month, year after year. One day a very, very poor man came. He was extremely old. He had nothing important or valuable to sell. He said to himself, "I need money badly. I have become so poor in my old age. Let me see how kind the king is." With greatest difficulty he came and stood first in line early in the morning. His sandals and clothes were covered with dirt. The only thing he had to offer the king was a dirty, filthy cloth.

The king asked him, "You have come to sell this?"

The old man said, "Yes, this is my fate. It is the only thing I have to sell since I am so poor. If you do not give me money, soon I shall die."

The king said, "No, I do not want you to die. Tell me the price."

The old man named an exorbitant price.

The king protested, "The price is so high!"

The old man answered, "Yes, it is true. But if you give me the money, then I will be able to buy the things that I need and I will be able to eat."

The king said, "Oh, you are right, you are right, you are right! Whatever you ask for, I am giving you."

The king gave him the money, and the king was so pleased that he had been able to be of help to this poor man. The king was very happy and proud of his own generosity.

That night the king had a dream. In his dream the Goddess Lakshmi came and said, "I am leaving you! You are squandering your wealth, giving it to poor men. I have made you very rich, and these people are just fooling you. So I am leaving you."

The king said, "O Goddess, what can I do? This is the promise that I made. I want to keep my promise to buy from whoever brings something first. And I also made another promise that whatever price they ask, I will accept. The poor fellow this morning named an exorbitant price. I knew that his cloth was not worth anything, but I had to keep my promise."

The Goddess Lakshmi said, "You keep your promise, since that is so important to you, but I do not want to stay with you." Then the Goddess Lakshmi, the Mother of wealth, left.

Then came another goddess. This goddess told him, "My son, if you continue in this stupid way, then you will lose everything. If you lose your material wealth, then there will be no fame for you. Now you are rich. That is why you are famous. Once you lose your wealth, all your name and fame will disappear, so I do not want to stay with you." Then she, too, disappeared.

A third goddess came and said, "I am the goddess of honesty, but I clearly see that you are so stupid. Because of your stupidity, people will only fool you and take advantage of you."

The king said, "What am I going to do? I cannot break my promise."

The goddess said, "I know, so I am leaving you." The third goddess also left.

Then came the goddess of truth. This goddess started scolding the king most vehemently. She said, "Truth is one thing, but what about your wisdom? You are very kind-hearted and you have so many good qualities. But people will fool you and fool you if you do not exercise your wisdom. Then what kind of truth is that? You are only encouraging them to deceive you." The goddess of truth went on scolding the king.

Finally the king said, "Mother, you are the goddess of truth. If you do not value me, who will value me? By remaining faithful to my promise, I am trying to be truthful. If truth is not valued in this world, then what will be valued?"

The goddess of truth gave the king a broad smile and blessed him profusely. She said, "I was examining you, my son. You are my dearest son. If I had more people like you, then this earth would be inundated with truth. Do not worry. I am never going to leave you. You will continue to keep your promise, and I will be there with you all the time to help you. Truth has to be maintained all the time at any cost."

When the goddess of truth decided to stay forever, all the other goddesses came back. They said, "We know we will never be valued permanently. For some time wealth and honesty will be valued, but it will not last. But ultimately everybody will value truth. Truth will prevail."

India's motto is "Truth ultimately prevails" (*satyam eva jayate*). Truth will always win, so the best thing is to stay with truth.

### LTS 120. *The father's questions*

There was a very rich man who was also a kind- hearted philanthropist. He used to give alms to the 'have-nots' of society, and he also used to be very kind even to those who were quite prosperous. He was always giving, giving, giving. One evening a very nicely dressed elderly man came to his place. He said to the rich man, "It is getting dark and I have not reached my destination. Can you suggest to me a suitable inn where I can take shelter?"

The rich man said, "No, no. I do not know of any inn in this vicinity."

The wife of this rich man said, "Since there is no inn available, please come in. You can spend the night with us."

The kind-hearted rich man also agreed, saying, "Yes, yes, you stay at our place, and tomorrow morning you can continue your journey."

They fed this elderly man, and they were having a nice talk. They were quite comfortable with this guest and he told them all about his family and so on. At one point the guest said, "I have a son who is quite well educated, and I see that your daughter is so beautiful and loving. I would like my son to marry her. I hope you will accept this proposal."

The wife was overjoyed because she liked this old man very much. But her husband said, "First you have to answer my questions."

The elderly man said, "I will answer them with all the sincerity at my command."

The husband proceeded, "Do you have rats? Do you have cats? Do you have dogs in your house?"

The old man was surprised and a little offended. He said, "Oh no, I do not have rats. I do not have cats. I do not have dogs."

The rich man said, "Then I will not allow your son to marry my daughter."

The wife was furious. She said to her husband, "What are you talking about? Why do you need rats and cats and dogs?"

The husband said, "I cannot explain it. You will not understand."

The guest was extremely disappointed, but nevertheless he offered his gratitude to the rich man and his wife because they had allowed him to stay overnight. He thanked them profusely and told them he was sad that his son would not be able to marry their daughter.

When their guest went to bed, the wife said to her husband, "I am so angry with you for ruining everything! Now tell me, why did you bring in rats, cats and dogs?"

He said, "Try to understand. I want my daughter to marry a rich person. If this man were rich, then he would have fields and he would have grain. If he had grain in his house, then there would be rats. If he said he had cats, that would mean he would have milk in the house. So he does not even have milk. Otherwise, if there were milk, then there would definitely be some cats to come and drink the milk. And he says he does not have dogs. What kind of person is this? Is there any rich man who does not have a dog? So it is obvious that he is not rich, and I am not going to give my daughter to his son."

### LTS 121. *The brahmin and the farmer's daughter*

In a particular village there lived a brahmin family. The eldest son was very well versed in the Vedas, the Upanishads and other Indian scriptures. All the villagers had tremendous admiration for this young man. As time went by, the brahmin son fell in love with a farmer's daughter. He knew that his father would have serious objections to their marriage because of the difference in their caste. A friend of his said to him, "You are indeed a fool! Just introduce this girl to your father and say that, like you, she comes of a brahmin family."

The young man said, "Do I have to tell my father a lie?"

His friend replied, "Tell me frankly, which is more important in your life: not telling a lie or this girl whom you love with all your heart and soul?"

The young man said, "This girl is infinitely more important in my life than one insignificant lie."

The young man brought the girl to meet his father and said, "Father, you know, we are brahmins, and this girl is also a brahmin. I would like to marry her. Do you have any objection?"

Immediately the girl said, "No, no, no! I am not a brahmin, I am not even a kshatriya. I am fourth class. I am a farmer's daughter."

The father became furious. He said, "You lied to me? Brahmins are not supposed to tell lies. You are my son, and you told me a lie. I never expected that you would tell me a lie. This farmer's daughter is not even third class, and yet she was the one to come forward and tell the truth."

The old man said to the girl, "I am begging you to marry my son because you are the real brahmin here. You have told the truth, whereas my son is a brahmin by birth but not by nature. He has told me such a lie. Now I am begging you to marry my son because you are of a higher class. You have shown us how a real brahmin should behave. Please consent to marry him."

She said, "Yes, I will marry him, but first I have to take permission from my father."

The old brahmin went to the farmer's house and begged the farmer to give his permission for the marriage. The farmer said, "Oh no, no, no! If I allow this marriage, people will hate me. They will say I am an opportunist. I am fourth class. How can I come up to first class? People will be very displeased with me if I do this."

The father of the young man said to his son, "You have ruined everything. Now I want you to marry her because I see that you are low class and she is first class. Unfortunately, her father does not want her to marry you. What am I going to do?"

Then he said to the farmer and his daughter, "I beg of you, please reconsider. I will take full responsibility. If the villagers speak ill of this young girl because she has married a brahmin, I will tell them, 'No, it is I who begged them to get married because I wanted to raise the standard of my family. My son is such a liar, but a farmer's daughter had the courage to tell me the truth. So this farmer and his daughter are the real brahmins, and my son and I are shudras, the fourth class. Please lay the blame on me. I wanted them to get married because I have seen a real brahmin in this girl. There are many young people who tell lies and their parents cannot catch them. When they are in love, the boys say that they are brahmin or the girls say that they are brahmin. But in your daughter I have seen a real brahmin girl. And if people speak ill of me or my family, I do not care. I want them to get married."

The farmer was so moved by the words of the brahmin father that he allowed his daughter to marry the brahmin son.

### LTS 122. *Timely assistance*

Once, quite unexpectedly, a serious cyclone took place and caused tremendous damage. Everything was destroyed in the fields, and many, many people suffered as a result. When the king heard about the devastating effects of the cyclone, for a few days he thought over the problem. Then he said, "I have to do something. I am quite rich. I will help my subjects."

The king had a very wise minister. This minister came to the king and said, "Your Majesty, I am sure you have heard how people are suffering from the cyclone."

The king said, "Do you think I am wasting my time? I have already sent high-ranking officers to see what my subjects need. They will inform me whether those who are suffering want money or rice or both."

The officers returned to the palace in a few days and said to the king, "The victims want money from you."

The king said, "Then take as much as you need from the treasury and give it to them unreservedly."

The officers took a considerable amount of money and distributed it to all the people who needed it.

Now, the king wanted to hear reports from his subjects about his own kindness; he wanted to hear them sing his praises for having given them so much money. So in disguise, the king went to that part of his kingdom. He talked with many villagers and overheard many of their conversations but, alas, he did not hear his own name mentioned even once. It seemed that all the villagers were only talking about a particular merchant.

When the cyclone first took place and there was lots of damage, this merchant sent a large amount of rice and pickles for the villagers. He immediately delivered cooked rice and pickles because their ovens had all been destroyed. He gave ready-made meals. His house was not damaged because it was well protected.

So everyone was talking about that merchant. Everywhere the king went, he heard the same thing: "How kind the merchant is! He has given us so much rice. He has really saved us. Soon we will finish rebuilding our ovens and we will be able to cook for ourselves. But we shall eternally remain grateful to him for helping us when we needed it most."

Nobody was talking about the king's gift of money. He said, "How ungrateful these people are! I gave so much money to everyone, and nobody is talking about my gift. They are only talking about this fellow who gave them rice and pickles immediately after the cyclone took place."

The king returned to the palace and told his minister, "I am so disappointed and disheartened. How ungrateful these people are! So much money they have received from me through my officers. I am sure they did get money, but they are not talking about the money at all. They are only talking about the cooked rice and pickles that one merchant has given them. What is his gift next to mine?"

The minister said, "O King, for everything there is a right time. When the cyclone took place and destroyed everything, at that time they desperately needed food to survive. And you were so late in responding to their plight. After so many days you started helping them. When one gets timely help, then one is most grateful. Now the crisis has passed and they can manage. They have food, and they are starting to repair the damage. Your money-power will help them, true, but it did not save their lives because you delayed for so many days. When they needed help badly, at that time the merchant was the one who came forward and gave them food — rice and pickles. You have to give help in a timely way. Today if I am extremely hungry and I do not get food, then I may die. Even if I know that in a few days I will be given a banquet, it does not make any difference. Before that day comes, I may die. Whatever I receive today, I will eat, even if it is only rice and pickles. This is how those people were saved. They were given the rice on time."

The king was embarrassed and, at the same time, he was enlightened by the minister's words. Always we have to serve others in a timely way. If we give help not at the right moment but a few days or a few weeks later, then they will not be as grateful to us as they are to those who were timely helpers. Time is a great factor. When someone is hungry, that person will eat the simplest food. Otherwise, if he has to wait for three days until someone comes with his money-power to buy him a huge feast, by then he may pass away. If you are kind, show your kindness as soon as possible. Only then will people derive real help from you.

### LTS 123. *The disobedient bullock*

A farmer bought two bullocks to plough his field. The farmer was very happy with his investment. Unfortunately, one bullock was very undivine. It was extremely lazy and it would not listen to the farmer. Try as he might, the farmer could not tame it. Fortunately, the other bullock was extremely obedient. It did not create any problem. But because of the unruly bullock, the farmer was utterly miserable. He needed two bullocks to pull the plough, but one was very good and one was very bad.

One day another farmer approached him and said, "Can you help me? One of my bullocks is sick, and I have only one bullock to work in my mill. Please loan me one of yours."

The first farmer said, "Here, take this one." And so he got rid of the undivine bullock.

The second farmer said, "I am so grateful to you. I will borrow it only for two days and then I will return it."

The first farmer said, "Take your time."

The second farmer took the bullock to work in his mill. There the bullocks go round and round to produce oil. From coconuts, coconut oil is produced, and the machine makes a loud humming noise all the time.

The disobedient bullock was yoked to the mill. Then the bullock started misbehaving, and the farmer struck it very, very hard. When the bullock continued to misbehave, the farmer beat it ruthlessly.

After two days, the farmer's own bullock recovered and he returned the disobedient bullock to its owner. The bullock immediately resumed its old ways and the farmer could not control it.

A few days later, another friend of the farmer came to him and said, "I need a bullock to pull my bullock cart. One of my bullocks is sick. Can you loan me one of yours?"

The farmer said, "Take this bullock and keep it for as many days as you want to."

The bullock cart driver was kind-hearted. At the same time, he was so disgusted with the misbehaviour of this animal. It would not obey any command. So the bullock cart driver struck the bullock with a stick and beat it black and blue.

Finally, the mischievous bullock said to itself, "I will die if this treatment continues! This time, if I am returned to my owner, I will cry and cry. Then my owner will take pity on me. Perhaps he will give me another chance to plough the field."

After one week, the bullock was returned. It was in a miserable condition. Large tears were rolling down its cheeks. The owner felt sorry for the animal and said, "Let me give it another chance."

To his great surprise, when he gave the bullock another chance to plough the field with the other one that he had bought, the mischievous bullock became so obedient.

Punishment sometimes works. This mischievous, naughty, disobedient bullock needed this kind of punishment to become a good bullock. In life also, sometimes on rare occasions people need and deserve a shock. Then they may turn over a new leaf. We should always try to transform others' natures with love, but sometimes love fails.

In the beginning, Sri Krishna always showed his compassion aspect. Before the Battle of Kurukshetra, he showed only compassion, compassion, compassion. In his case, he gave a time limit to the undivine forces. He said, "Change your nature, change your nature." But when they did not change their nature, when his compassion-height did not work, then he used his justice-light. First he tried with compassion. Then, when compassion did not work, he found another way. He had to resort to justice. That was Sri Krishna's philosophy.

### LTS 124. *Two great poets*

There were two great poets. One of them used to brag all the time that he was by far the best poet in the country. The king definitely appreciated his poetry, and many, many minor poets were his great admirers. The second poet was absolutely a saint-poet, a seer-poet. He did not care for name and fame at all. He felt that whoever was inspired by his poems would read them. He wrote only for God, to satisfy his inner life.

The king wanted to have a poetry festival, so his minister recommended that the first poet be the one to preside over the poetry festival since he was so well known. The king summoned the famous poet and began asking him many questions. The famous poet was so smart and clever that he answered all the questions to the king's satisfaction. Then the king officially appointed him to be in charge of the poetry festival.

This festival lasted for a week. Many minor poets secretly bribed the famous poet so that they could read out their poems. The king attended the whole festival and he was very pleased to find that there were so many poets in his kingdom. He gave all credit to the famous poet who was in charge of the festival and rewarded him with one thousand rupees.

Now, because this famous poet was insecure and jealous of the seer-poet, he did not invite the seer-poet to participate in the festival. The king had asked him to invite all the poets that he knew, but the seer-poet was not invited because the famous poet was afraid that if the king heard the seer-poet's poems, perhaps he would say, "He is by far the best poet."

A few days after the festival, out of sheer curiosity, the famous poet went to the seer-poet and said, "I am sorry, I forgot to invite you. We had such a big poetry festival. Please forgive me. Next time when we have a poetry contest or poetry festival, I will definitely invite you. By the way, did you know that I was the one who presided over the festival? The king appointed me because I am the best poet."

The seer-poet said, "Yes, I have heard all about it. But, to tell you the truth, unless you receive a recommendation or some words of appreciation from a certain king, I will not be able to say that you are the greatest poet. This king is the best judge of poetry."

The famous poet said, "If I receive appreciation from him, what will you do?"

The seer-poet said, "If you receive his praise, then I will consider you to be the greatest poet."

The famous poet said, "I will easily get it. In fact, if I do not receive his praise, I will give you a thousand rupees."

The seer-poet gave him a smile but did not say anything more. He was in his own world.

The famous poet had many flatterers among the minor poets. They said to him, "Easily you will win the praise of that king! After all, our king has appreciated you so highly and that one is just a minor king. Our king is far greater than he is."

So the famous poet was literally brimming with confidence. He and his followers went to that neighbouring kingdom only to find that the king was absent. They waited and waited for hours. Finally the king returned to the palace. He felt sorry that these guests had been waiting for such a long time and he gestured to his wife to offer them something to eat.

The queen exclaimed, "These vagabonds? I have more important things to do than to give them food."

What could the poor king do? He had to go into the kitchen and cook a meal for them himself because they were his guests. The queen saw that they were useless people. But the king had a big heart. So he went to the kitchen, prepared some food and fed them.

After the meal, the famous poet started reading out his poems. After each poem he expected some comment from the king, but the king did not make any comment. One, two, three, four poems went by and still the king remained silent. Then it occurred to the famous poet that if this king came to learn that his own king had greatly appreciated his poems, he would also appreciate them. So he said, "I am now going to read the poem that my king said has touched the pinnacle-heights."

Still this neighbouring king did not say anything. He just smiled.

The famous poet was so disappointed. He did not receive any words of appreciation from that king. So he went back to the seer-poet and said, "I want to be sincere with you since many witnesses were there. I went to see the king you spoke of, and he did not appreciate me or say anything kind about my poems. So I am giving you one thousand rupees as I promised. You have won the wager." The famous poet was so miserable. He lost one thousand rupees plus he did not get the appreciation he felt he deserved.

One day a few followers of this famous poet decided to go and ask that particular king why he did not appreciate their idol's poems. First they started by begging him for a few words of appreciation. When they did not get any appreciation by begging, they started insulting the king. But still the king remained silent. Then the queen began insulting them and screaming, "Go, go, go! Do not bother my husband!"

When the famous poet's followers were about to leave the palace, a kind-hearted minister approached them and said, "I have seen everything that has taken place. Do you not know that our king is mute?"

The seer-poet had deliberately sent the famous poet to that king because he knew the king could not speak. Such was the seer-poet's cleverness.

### LTS 125. *In search of an honest treasurer*

There was a very kind-hearted king. His ministers and other high-ranking officers were all quite honest, but unfortunately his treasurer was a rogue of the first water. This treasurer used to steal money from the treasury regularly. When the ministers discovered that large amounts of money were missing, they made complaints to the king, and the king became very, very sad and upset. He said, "I am an honest person. I feel that everybody in my kingdom should be honest. I will not allow anybody to be dishonest. I will have to replace this treasurer with somebody who is honest to the core."

The ministers said, "O King, God alone knows where we will find that honest person for you."

The king said, "All right, until I find someone, I will do the job myself. Since it is my money, I will count everything. I will be the treasurer."

So the king assumed the duties of the treasurer. After he had been doing the job for weeks, months and finally a year, he felt that it was boring. He had so many important things to do apart from counting his money. The king asked his prime minister, "What am I going to do? I am wasting so much time with this mundane job. I am the king. I have to rule the country with all my concern and wisdom. Can you do this job in my place?"

The prime minister quickly said, "Oh no, no! I do not trust myself, in case anything goes wrong."

The king said, "Then what shall I do?"

The prime minister suggested, "Let us look for someone who is suited for this task. I have an idea, if you approve of it."

The king said, "You are the wisest man in our kingdom. I will always value your advice."

The prime minister continued, "Tomorrow morning I shall make an announcement. I shall say that the king needs a treasurer and those who want to apply for the post should submit their names."

The following morning the prime minister went to a section where there were twenty very high-ranking officers and made the announcement. Afterwards he said, "I do hope that all of you apply for this coveted post."

Nineteen out of the twenty officers submitted their names and their credentials. The next day, in front of the prime minister, the king read all the credentials of these nineteen candidates. He said, "I never knew that I had such qualified people in my kingdom! I should have offered them an even higher post."

Then the prime minister said, "Now, please tell me, O King, what will you do with all these applications? You need someone whom you can trust. You can have only one person. You do not need nineteen."

"Yes, it is true," said the king. "I do not need nineteen, but I am confused. They all have such high qualifications. Whom am I to take?" The king read and reread the applications. Finally he chose one. Then he said to the prime minister, "You have more wisdom than I have. Have I chosen the right person?"

The prime minister said, "I am so sorry, O King. You have to forgive me."

"Why?" said the king.

"You have not chosen the right person," came the answer.

"I have not chosen the right person?" echoed the king. "But you read all their credentials yourself. Each one was worthy. How could I have made a mistake?"

The prime minister said, "O King, in confidence I wish to tell you that these people are all rogues. Only the person who has not submitted his application is the right person."

The king was puzzled. He said, "How can he be the right person? He has not even submitted his credentials."

The prime minister said, "When I made the announcement, I told them how much salary they would get if they became the treasurer. I kept the salary exactly the same as whatever they are now getting as officers. I know a little bit about human nature. These nineteen are such rogues that when one of them gets the post, he will steal money. Money is such a dangerous thing that he will be tempted. So, like the previous one who stole your money, whoever becomes treasurer in his place will also steal money, because the salary is the same as what they are getting now. With the same salary they will not be satisfied. They will only steal money."

"Then what about the other fellow?" asked the king curiously.

The prime minister said, "The officer who has not come forward to submit an application is saying to himself, 'What is the use of having this job? The salary is the same. I do not need this job because the king will not give me a higher salary. I do not have the habit of stealing and, at the same time, I will not get a higher salary, so it is not worth taking this job.'"

The king saw the wisdom of his prime minister's assessment and he summoned the officer who had not applied for the post. He said to this man, "You are the right person to be my treasurer. My prime minister trusts you because you are indifferent to the fact that you will be handling large sums of money. Otherwise you would have applied for the post. Had I chosen someone else, that person would steal money. This is what the prime minister has said, and I trust him."

So the king appointed this man and he did not steal any money. The prime minister said, "You see, I was right." The king was so pleased that he raised the new treasurer's salary tremendously for his honesty. This man remained the king's treasurer for many, many years and he never stole anything.

### LTS 126. *The king's secret reason*

There was a king whose prime minister was very, very wise. He was also quite old. The king also had a very high-ranking officer or nobleman in his court. The king used to show this nobleman his drafts before he made any announcements. The nobleman was very, very proud that the king used to show him the drafts, and not the prime minister.

In the course of time, the prime minister died. This nobleman was quite inferior to the prime minister in rank. Still, he was hoping that he would be chosen as the new prime minister. Alas, the king chose somebody else. The nobleman was so sad. He said, "The king did not show his announcements to anybody else, not even to the prime minister. He showed them only to me. It is only just that I should be the prime minister."

The nobleman felt that a great injustice had been done to him. So he went to the king and said, "O King, how could you do this? The prime minister did not even know what you were going to announce in advance. I was the only one to whom you showed your drafts. I feel very, very sad that you have not appointed me to be prime minister. This is an act of injustice."

The king said, "An act of injustice? Shall I tell you the real reason why I showed those drafts to you? My previous prime minister was very well educated and also had tremendous wisdom. In terms of knowledge and wisdom, you are no match for him. Such being the case, why did I show the drafts of my announcements to you and not to him each and every time? The real reason, my secret reason, is that you are an idiot. I showed my announcements to you because I knew that if you could understand them, then all my subjects would understand them. If you could understand what I was trying to say, there would be nobody in my kingdom who would not understand!"

### LTS 127. *A father's last words*

There were two brothers, Sunil and Anil. Sunil was very kind-hearted, wise and self-giving, but Anil was an idiot. In every way he was a disgrace to the family. There came a time when Sunil and Anil's father was dying. Before their father breathed his last, he whispered something to Sunil. In a sinking voice, he said, "I would like you to take care of your younger brother. I know that he will not be able to sustain his life without your help. If he wants to leave you, please do not allow him to leave. He will be totally ruined. I have kept him under my constant guidance and affection, so please always do the same. You will play my role." Sunil nodded, and the father was so happy. He died peacefully.

Now, Anil's wife happened to be near her dying father-in-law. She was so curious as to what her father-in-law had said. In a few hours' time, Anil came home and they held the funeral service.

The following day Anil's wife said to him, "Just before your father passed away, he said something very, very important to your brother. I am sure it is about something secret. He has kept something hidden. He whispered it so that we women could not hear. But I am sure it is something with regard to his money or property."

Anil said, "I cannot ask my brother to tell me. My brother has been so loving to me. He has never, never deceived me, so I do not want to ask."

But his undivine wife would not let the matter rest. She continually reminded her husband about it. She said, "You are such a fool! When it is a matter of money, everybody becomes undivine. See, he is not telling you what your father said. So many days have passed by, and your brother is not telling you. Here is the proof."

The wife was nagging and nagging, so Anil eventually said, "All right, let me ask my brother." He was quite unwilling to do it, but his wife compelled him.

He said to Sunil, "My wife told me that father whispered something to you before he died. Can you tell me what it was?"

Sunil said, "Father told me to take care of you."

Anil asked, "That is all?"

"Yes," said Sunil. "That was his dying wish."

Then Anil told his wife, "It was nothing special. Father asked him to take care of me and he agreed. Father was right. Sunil is so wise and I am so useless."

The wife refused to accept this explanation. She said, "No, it is not true. It is something else, something very secret and serious. He is hiding it from you." She suspected that Sunil was not telling the whole truth. Then she began spreading gossip that before her father-in-law died, he said something very secretly. She herself could not hear what he said and now her brother-in-law was hiding it from his younger brother.

This was too much for Sunil's wife. Like her husband, she was also very kind-hearted. Although she did not actually know what her father-in-law had said to her husband, she was sure her husband was telling the truth, so she felt miserable. She said to her husband, "You have to do something. This is absurd. It is all lies."

Sunil said, "What am I going to do? I want peace, peace, peace." Then he said, "All right. If Anil feels I am hiding something, that father has told me of a secret place where he kept his money, then I will do something."

He told his wife, "Now, you have to save me. Give me all your jewellery, all your ornaments. I will go to the jeweller and give him the jewellery. Then I will take money from him as a loan. Once I earn more money, I will reclaim your jewellery."

His wife received a shock. She asked, "What are you planning to do?"

Sunil said, "I only want a little peace. If you also want peace, then give me all your ornaments."

His wife said, "All right. I want peace. Take them and do the needful."

So Sunil took all his wife's ornaments and went to the jeweller, who was a great friend of his. He said, "Please keep this jewellery as security and loan me ten thousand rupees." He told his friend that he needed the money to solve this problem with his brother.

His friend the jeweller said, "I shall gladly loan you the money, but I do not want to take anything from you as security." He was, indeed, a true friend.

The following day Sunil said to his brother, "My dearest Anil, I have something very special to tell you. But first you have to forgive me."

"I should forgive you?" Anil said.

Sunil said, "Yes, you see, I told you a lie about what our father said. Last night father came to me in my dream and he was scolding me so severely."

Anil asked, "Why was father scolding you?"

Sunil said, "In my dream father asked why I was hiding the secret from you. With his dying breath, Father told me that at a particular place in our courtyard, he had kept lots of money for you. He said I should tell you at the proper time. But I was hesitating and hesitating because father had said to tell you when the proper time came. I did not know what he meant. Then last night he said it was already time. He said, 'You should have told your brother Anil long ago.' Father scolded me for my selfishness, so that is why I have come to you now. I am begging you to please forgive me. Let us go and dig up the money and then you will take it. It is all for you."

Anil said, "Father came to me also last night, but he gave me a different message."

Sunil was so surprised. He said, "What was that different message?"

"Father also scolded me ruthlessly," Anil said. "He said that he did not tell you anything about money. His only message to you was to take care of me. He said that I have no wisdom and, if I leave you, I will be totally ruined. So Father told me that he begged you not to let me go."

Sunil said, "That is strange. Father asked me why I was not giving you the money."

Anil said, "And Father came and insulted me for suspecting you."

Sunil said, "I do not know what to do. What can I say now? Who is telling the truth?"

All of a sudden, his younger brother burst into tears and fell at the feet of his elder brother. He said, "In your case, I do not know who came to you. In my case, I do know who came. The jeweller came to see me last night and told me what you had done. Your friend scolded me and said that you could never hide anything from me, that you would never deceive your brother. Now let us go and return the money. In the future I will never, never listen to my wife. I want to remain here peacefully with you. Always guide me, guide my life."

### LTS 128. *Stealing Mother Kali's necklace*

There was a priest who was very, very pious. Everybody loved him and adored him. He had so many divine qualities. He was extremely simple and honest. In every way he was so nice, and all the villagers were proud to have him as their priest. But, alas, his wife was not so divine. She always tried to compete with the other village women. The priest used to spend his days worshipping Mother Kali in the temple. But his wife would always harass him. She would insist that he had to buy her this or buy her that.

"How can I?" he used to say. "You know I am a simple man, a poor man. How can a priest be rich? I cannot afford the things you are asking for. We should pray to God instead of desiring material things. There is joy only in praying."

The more the priest talked about the spiritual life, the more his wife would get angry. She did not want to hear his spiritual philosophy. The poor priest tried so hard to please her in other ways, but he could not fulfil her material desires.

One day this wife said to her husband, "I want you to bring me the necklace that Mother Kali is wearing. Since you cannot afford to buy me any jewellery, you have to bring me Mother Kali's necklace."

"That is blasphemy!" cried the priest. "How do you dare to ask for something so sacred? Alas, what have I done to deserve this kind of wife? How can I steal things from my dearest Mother Kali? First of all, I will not be able to steal from anybody, no matter who they are. How can you ask me to steal from Mother Kali's neck? I will not do it. It is impossible."

"You will not do it?" said the wife. "Then I am giving you two days to change your mind. In two days if you cannot bring me the necklace, I shall commit suicide."

The priest had studied the Hindu shastras, and he knew that suicide is the worst possible crime against the soul. He was faced with a serious dilemma. How could he allow his wife to commit suicide? Again, how could he steal from his Mother Kali, who was his life-breath? He did not know how to solve the problem. So he went to the temple and in front of Mother Kali's statue he began praying, "Mother Kali, save me! I have heard that suicide is the worst possible sin, and stealing is also a terrible crime. How can I take the precious jewellery from your neck just to please my wife?"

At that moment Mother Kali appeared before him and said, "You decide what to do, my son."

Then the poor priest said, "In that case, the best thing is for me to die at your feet at this very moment. I will not be able to solve this problem. Please allow me to die at your feet."

"No, no, you do not have to die," said Mother Kali. "You can take my jewellery. All the ornaments that I have, you can remove and give to your wife."

The priest was shocked. He said, "How can I do this terrible thing? What will people think of me?"

She said, "Nobody will think ill of you."

All at once other cosmic gods and goddesses began appearing. They said to Mother Kali, "What are you doing? You are allowing this priest to desecrate your statue."

Mother Kali said, "This is my decision. He is my most devoted devotee, so I want him to take my jewellery. I have sanctioned it. You have no right to find fault with him." Mother Kali scolded all of them.

Then the cosmic gods and goddesses said, "All right. What can we do? But this priest is such a bad fellow."

Mother Kali said, "He is not a bad fellow at all. He is in some serious trouble and I am trying to solve his problem. He is very devoted to me. I am very, very pleased with him." Then she said to the priest, "My son, there will be one condition."

He said, "Mother, any condition you wish to make, I am ready to accept because you are saving my life. Still I do not know how I will be able to show my face to anybody."

Mother Kali said, "About that you do not have to worry. I want you to tell your wife that if my jewellery is worn for more than three days, then whoever is wearing it past the third day will die. One day, two days, even three days are fine. Nothing will happen. But on the fourth day, the person who is wearing it will die."

The priest was mystified, but he had implicit faith in his Mother Kali. Very carefully he removed Mother Kali's beautiful necklace and carried it home to his wife. She was overjoyed. Then he told his wife Mother Kali's condition. The wife was now in serious trouble. She did not want to die in four days.

The priest said, "You wanted this necklace, so I have brought it for you. Now you have to decide what to do. I have played my role."

The foolish wife began wearing Mother Kali's necklace. Inwardly the priest was crying and crying, "It is blasphemy! O my Mother, O Supreme Goddess, my wife is wearing what is rightfully yours." But then he would console himself by saying, "All right. My Mother has sanctioned it. What can I say?"

At night, when she slept, the wife did not wear the necklace. She kept it right near her bed. It happened that on the second night a thief was inspired to break into the priest's house. The priest and his wife were fast asleep. The thief saw the necklace and stole it. He did not know that this necklace was from Mother Kali.

On his way home, the thief saw that the door to Mother Kali's temple was slightly ajar. He wondered, "What is happening? Why should the door be open?" He entered into the temple and noticed that somebody was hiding behind Mother Kali's statue. The thief crept behind the statue and found another thief lurking there. The first thief started striking the second thief. He said, "You have stolen something from Mother Kali, I am sure of it. Before, Mother Kali had a most beautiful necklace. You have stolen it!"

The second thief said, "No! I have not stolen anything!"

"You are hiding it somewhere," screamed the first thief, and he started beating the fellow who was behind Mother Kali's statue mercilessly.

As the two thieves were fighting, it became the third day. More than the third day, one could not wear Mother Kali's necklace. On the fourth day something would happen.

When the priest arrived at the temple the following morning, the two thieves were still fighting. He saw them and he did not know what to do with them.

Mother Kali appeared to him and said, "Go home!"

The priest said, "Mother, I have not worshipped you. How can I go home?"

Mother Kali said, "No, no. Go, go, go! Come tomorrow."

The following day the priest came and saw both the thieves lying dead. He said, "I know that my wife is responsible for these deaths. Mother Kali warned me that someone would die after the third day and this is what has happened. It is my fault for encouraging my wife." Then he went and lay down between the two thieves and begged Mother Kali to take his life as well.

Mother Kali said, "Get up, get up! You are absolutely innocent. These two were very bad. That is why they are dead. You will find my necklace in the pocket of one of the thieves. Now you can put it around my neck again. It has done its job."

The priest did as Mother Kali asked. Then he removed the bodies from the temple and gave them a proper cremation. Finally, with a heavy heart, he went home. Tears were streaming from his eyes.

His wife saw his condition and cried, "What has happened today?"

The priest said, "To please you, I stole Mother Kali's necklace, and now two people have died as a result." Then he narrated the whole story.

The wife was so ashamed. She said, "I will not do this kind of thing any more. I will be worthy of being your wife. From now on, I will live a very, very simple life. I will never ask you to buy me expensive things. I will be satisfied with whatever you bring for me. I will never break my promise. I will be your most faithful and most devoted wife." And she did remain true to her word from that time on.

## LTS 129. *Seekers, nuns, Masters — and ghosts!*

This story took place ten thousand years ago, at least! There was a spiritual seeker named Vivian. She was very, very sincere and she had a spiritual Master of the highest order. This spiritual seeker happened to have a friend who was a nun. Her name was Linda. This friend was extremely devoted to the Saviour Christ. In the religious community where Linda lived, there was another nun who always said things that were contrary to others' beliefs. Her name was Gail.

Vivian used to visit her friend Linda, and she would always say sublime things about her spiritual Master. She would talk about his inspiring activities and also about her own lofty inner experiences. Poor Linda was not getting any high experiences from her Christian faith. She used to pray very intensely to Jesus Christ, but she was not so happy in her spiritual life. Something was lacking. Gradually she was becoming a little bit weaker in her commitment because Vivian was convincing her to leave her path and join Vivian's path. So Linda was seriously considering this course of action.

One day Vivian went to visit Linda, and she found all thirty of the nuns there laughing and laughing. They were roaring with laughter. Linda was also one of those. Only one nun was not laughing at all and that was Gail. She was deliberately not joining the party. So Vivian asked, "Why are all of you laughing and laughing and what is wrong with Gail? Why is she so serious?"

They said, "Nothing is wrong with Gail. It is simply that she never believes us. We all have the same opinion with regard to some things, but she enjoys a different opinion."

Meanwhile, Gail continued to be very serious. She was acting almost like a snob. Vivian asked Linda, "Please tell me if something has happened to upset Gail."

Then Linda explained what had happened. Through their windows the nuns could see a cemetery. There, every evening they used to see ghosts moving around and they would get frightened. Every night without fail it happened. But Gail never believed it. She always said, "No, there are no ghosts." The others saw that there were ghosts, but Gail always scoffed at the notion.

The previous night Gail had said to them, "Prove it! Prove that there are ghosts."

The others said to her, "We can see them. They are making noise, they are crying and screaming. Can you not hear them for yourself?"

But Gail could not hear them. She simply ridiculed the others. Then she said, "I can prove that ghosts do not exist. I am going there! Give me three nails and a hammer. If there are ghosts, then I will drive the nails into them and bring back some blood to show you. And if I do not return with the blood of the ghosts, it will be the proof that there are none."

So Gail walked to the cemetery in the middle of the night carrying a hammer and three nails. At first she did not see anything, so she threw away one nail and then another. She was about to throw away the third nail when she saw a white marble headstone. It was not a ghost, but in the darkness it looked like a ghost. She said, "Perhaps this particular marble stone has fooled the sisters. It is very pale and shines in an unusual way."

So Gail started driving the third nail into the marble. Quite inadvertently, while she was hitting the nail, a piece of her garment happened to get caught under the nail, and she found herself entangled. All of a sudden, she panicked. She started crying and screaming, because she thought that this was actually a real ghost.

The other sisters had come to see what had happened to her, since she had not come home. When they saw how frightened she was, they all started laughing and laughing.

Somehow God had wanted to prove to Gail that there *are* ghosts. The other sisters told her, "No, no, this is not a ghost."

But she insisted, "No, I have been attacked by ghosts. I can still see them." Then she started seeing the other sisters as ghosts. She cried out, "You are all ghosts!"

This went on for a couple of hours. They could not convince her that they were not ghosts and, at the same time, that ghosts do exist in that cemetery. Poor Gail, first she was of the opinion that there were no ghosts. Then she started seeing everybody as a ghost.

So they all started praying to Jesus Christ to illumine her. Of course, Jesus Christ had more important things to do. He was taking care of countless others. There are many, many widows in Heaven who have lost their husbands, and they are praying to Jesus Christ to give their husbands joy. Similarly, there are many devoted husbands in Heaven who have lost their wives, and they are also praying to Jesus Christ to give their wives joy. So Jesus Christ was busy trying to please the husbands and the wives. He could not come to help them. They all became miserable, especially Gail. They were confused because the Saviour Christ had not answered their prayers.

As I said before, Linda's faith was becoming weaker and weaker because Vivian had been telling her about her own spiritual path. Vivian said to Linda, "I know how we can solve this problem. Tell all the sisters to come and visit my spiritual Master." So at Vivian's request, they all came to visit Vivian's spiritual Master, including Gail.

Strangely enough, when the nuns came to visit Vivian's spiritual Master, for the first time Vivian saw her Master in a different way. She did not see his face the way she always saw it. She saw the face of Jesus Christ. She could not believe her eyes. It was like looking at a different person altogether.

Now it was Vivian's turn to be puzzled. How could her Master be Jesus Christ? Meanwhile, her friend Linda and the other nuns all started bowing down because for the first time they were seeing Jesus Christ. For years they had prayed and meditated on the Christ, but they had not seen him. Now they were seeing him for the first time.

Vivian was confused. How could she pray to Jesus Christ? For so many years she had been praying to her own Master. It was difficult for her to accept that this person who was her Master had somehow become Jesus Christ. She had brought these people with the idea that they would be inspired to follow her Master. Now it appeared that she herself had become a disciple of their previous Master! She did not know how to overcome her confusion.

Vivian went back with the nuns to the religious community where they lived. There, in the chapel, was a large statue of Jesus Christ. Vivian went there to pray and to receive guidance. She was crying and crying while looking at the statue. She said, "I have lost my Master. I am finding it so difficult to feel my Master's presence. I brought some of your disciples to meet him. They saw my Master as Jesus Christ and I could not see my Master at all."

All of a sudden, Vivian looked up and saw her Master's face there. She could not believe it. It was such a vivid experience. When her friends had prayed to that statue, they had not received anything. But when she went there to pray to the statue, she vividly saw her own Master there.

Now Vivian was really confused. The nuns had seen Jesus Christ in her Master, and she had seen her Master in Jesus Christ. Confusion never stops! So Vivian and the nuns all started praying and praying for illumination.

One day they came to realise that the Master and Jesus Christ were one. Then the nuns all became disciples of the Master, because they all had dreams in which Jesus Christ came and advised them to follow the path of the spiritual Master. He told them that the spiritual life is always easier when you follow a living Master, because the living Master is a bridge between earth and Heaven. One can easily see this bridge and walk on it. Even an atheist can cross to the other shore on the bridge. This bridge is visible even to those who are spiritually totally blind.

So sometimes spiritual Masters who are not in the physical body come to their dearest devotees and ask them to go to a spiritual Master who is still alive. In essence, the spiritual Masters are all one, but it is easier to make very fast spiritual progress by following a living Master.

Many people come to a spiritual Master and then leave him because they confuse the message of the Bible and the message of the Master. They do not recognise that the essence of each Master's message is the same: love of God. If one can realise that all the spiritual Masters carry only one message — love of God — then there can be no conflict between any of the true Masters.

### LTS 130. *The policemen*

Four policemen were playing cards at the police station. They had nothing else to do. They were enjoying their card game, and they played for a long time. Then they became bored. All of them started complaining, "Life is so boring! For the whole week, there have been no fights, no murders, no accidents — nothing, nothing, nothing. We have had absolutely nothing to do. Sometimes when we have nothing to do, we enjoy relaxing. But now it has gone on for so many days that we feel restless."

The captain overheard their conversation and said, "Wait, wait! Human nature never changes. In a day or two, once again we will have to rush to save people."

As soon as the captain finished speaking, the phone started ringing. Then one calamity after another started taking place. Somewhere there was a burglary. Somewhere someone was murdered. Somewhere a gang was fighting. The phone did not stop ringing.

The captain said, "Look, I told you, human nature will never change. So let us rush, let us run to do the needful."

So all the policemen went in various directions to attend to their urgent duties. The captain was so wise: human nature never changes. That is why it is always compared with the tail of a dog. You can hold the tail and try to straighten it. But as soon as you release it, it curls.

### LTS 131. *Three lawyers*

There was a very distinguished family of lawyers: a grandfather, his son and his grandson. The grandfather founded the practice and he taught his son how to be a great lawyer. Now this son was teaching his own son how to become a great lawyer.

Previously the grandfather had said to his son, "The most important thing is to get money by hook or by crook. Always tell the client that the case is very easy to deal with, and you have dealt with infinitely more serious cases, so his particular case is nothing, nothing, nothing. Always show utmost confidence. Then if you lose, you will say, 'What could I do? I tried very hard, very hard. I thought it would be very easy, but there were some hidden complications.'"

The son said, "If the case is really complicated, if it is very serious, how am I going to tell my client lies?"

The grandfather said, "Then you are not meant for this profession. Do you want to become a lawyer without telling lies? My only advice is to give up this profession and do something else."

The son quickly said, "I will try my best to tell a few lies, but I cannot promise to tell lies all the time if I take up a case."

Now, with your kind permission, I would like to digress from the story a little at this point.

My maternal uncle, my mother's eldest brother, was a lawyer. He wrote to Sri Aurobindo and said, "Is there any day when I do not tell lies in my profession? What can I do now? I want to practise the spiritual life. Please advise me."

Sri Aurobindo wrote back, "You know how many lies you tell every day. Try to decrease the number. Your yoga will be to decrease the number of lies that you tell. Then when you feel really miserable that you are telling even one lie, I advise you to give up the profession."

The barrister who saved Sri Aurobindo's life, C.R. Das, was deeply involved in politics. Sri Aurobindo was also in the political sphere. Then Sri Aurobindo gave up politics and entered into the spiritual life. This barrister remained very, very close to Sri Aurobindo. There came a time when he wanted to follow Sri Aurobindo and practise spirituality. Sri Aurobindo wrote to him, "If you sincerely want God, if you really want to practise spirituality seriously, then you have to change your profession. To be a lawyer, to be involved in politics and to be a real seeker — these three things do not go together."

To come back to my story, here the son told the grandfather that he would try his best to tell a few lies. In the course of time, the grandson was about to obtain his legal qualifications. Then his father began giving him some advice based on his own experience. He said, "You do not have to tell all lies, but charge a very high fee. If others ask for one thousand rupees, you should ask for four thousand. Everybody wants to win the case. Who does not want to win the case? So you have to give them hope. Do not promise anything, but give them very strong hope that you will be able to win the case. And do not forget to charge a very high fee."

The grandson said, "All right. Since you and my grandfather are so successful, I will maintain the family tradition and charge high fees."

The son passed all his examinations. He had become a lawyer. He was now going into practice, and he was eager to apply his father's advice. He was fully prepared to charge a high fee. The very first day he came to his office with such hope that there would be some clients. No sooner had he entered into his office than somebody came in. He told the man, "Please take a seat."

Then he lifted up the phone and started screaming as if to a client, "How many times do I have to tell you? I am not meant for you. I am not going to take your case. I will not budge an inch from ten thousand rupees. You can go to another lawyer if that is how you feel. There are so many. You say that my fee is too high, but do you want to win the case or not? Now do not bother me any more!"

The young lawyer put the receiver back on the hook. Then he said to the man, "Now, please tell me, how can I help you? What do you need?"

The man said, "I do not have any particular need. I am just here to connect the phone."

# LIFE'S BLEEDING TEARS AND FLYING SMILES

## BOOK 10

## LTS 132. *The death of the miser*

There was a miser of the worst type. He had no match in his 'profession'. He lived to be an old man, and then one day he passed away. When his neighbours heard of his passing, they shed crocodile tears. He did not have any friends, but people who knew him came and outwardly expressed their sadness. Everybody showed signs of sorrow and grief, although it was not at all sincere. But, to their utter astonishment, the miser's wife was not crying, she was not sobbing, she was not shedding tears.

One neighbour came forward and asked her, "Why are you not crying at all?"

The wife did not answer. She remained quiet and calm. Then some of the neighbours said, "We do not know where the miser has kept his money, and his wife is silent. We shall have to collect money for his funeral. Now it is an act of charity."

When the neighbours started collecting money as an act of charity, all of a sudden, the wife burst into tears. In an absolutely pitiful voice she began lamenting the loss of her husband. One neighbour said, "What has happened all of a sudden to make you cry? You were calm and quiet and unperturbed. You did not suffer from your loss. Now what has happened to bring about such a dramatic change?"

The wife said, "The word 'charity' that you are using used to chase my husband away. Whenever he heard the word 'charity', he literally used to run away. Now I see that you are using the word 'charity', but my husband is not running away. He is lying here and he is not moving, so that means he is really dead. So I am now suffering. Before I did not believe that he was dead, but now I know that he is really dead, otherwise the word 'charity' would have chased him away!"

### LTS 133. *Deceiving Mother Lakshmi*

A villager was quite rich and prosperous. He knew that his good fortune was coming from his worship of Mother Lakshmi. This goddess gives wealth and prosperity, so he was extremely grateful to Mother Lakshmi. Unfortunately, for some reason, Mother Lakshmi became displeased with him. He had done a few undivine things, so in a dream Lakshmi came to him and said, "I am leaving you."

The villager said to himself, "If Mother Lakshmi leaves me, then I will lose my fortune. I will be totally ruined."

He said to Mother Lakshmi, "Mother, Mother, please do not go! But if you are determined to leave me, then please allow me to worship you one last time in this lifetime with all my heart. I shall cover your statue with gold. I shall spend thousands and thousands of rupees and invite all my friends, neighbours and relatives to participate in my worship of you. Please, please stay."

Mother Lakshmi said, "All right, if this is your last wish."

The man said, "Yes, this is absolutely my last wish. But until I worship you in that way, please promise to stay."

Alas, that red letter day never came. Mother Lakshmi was waiting and waiting. Previously this rogue had been quite regular in his worship early in the morning. Now he had given up his worship completely. He was not worshipping the Goddess Lakshmi any more.

Once again the Goddess Lakshmi appeared to him. This time she said, "You are a rogue! You are not even worshipping me, let alone making preparations for that special worship. Before you used to worship me quite regularly, but now you have stopped. What is wrong with you? How can I stay here any longer? I am going away."

The man said, "O Mother, I am just an ordinary human being. I am in the habit of telling lies. But whoever thought that the Supreme Goddess Lakshmi would tell a lie? You promised, Mother, that until I worship you in a grandiose manner, you would stay with me. True, I am taking my time. But since you have promised, you also have to wait for that time."

Mother Lakshmi said, "You rogue! Enough is enough! I am not going to stay with you any more."

So she left and almost immediately this rogue became very, very poor — utterly bankrupt. Then he started praying and praying to the Goddess Lakshmi to come back. At last the Goddess Lakshmi came to him once again in a dream. She said, "Opportunity comes only once in a lifetime. I will not give you another chance. You must stay poor to the end of your life."

### LTS 134. *Flattery catches the culprit*

There were two good friends who lived in the same village. One of the friends owned a beautiful cow. One day this particular friend said to the other friend, "I am now getting old. I do not think I will be able to take care of my cow any more. I feel that the best thing is to sell the cow, so today I am going to the market."

The other one said, "I like your cow. Why do you not sell it to me? I am younger than you, so I will be able to take care of it for many years to come."

The first friend said, "Fine, I am willing to let you buy my cow."

The price was quite reasonable: two hundred rupees. The cow seemed to be very strong and in good health. The younger friend paid two hundred rupees, and the owner gave the cow to his friend. This transaction happened in the morning. Alas, in the evening of the same day the cow died.

The friend who had bought the cow was furious. He said to the previous owner, "Something was wrong with your cow! I am sure it had some disease."

The first friend said, "No! How could I know that my cow had some disease?"

Both of them argued and argued. Their friendship completely disappeared. Finally they went to the village chief with their dispute. The friend who lost his two hundred rupees said to the village chief, "I am sure his cow had some disease that he was hiding from me. He wanted to sell it in the market, but I persuaded him to sell it to me. Then, in a matter of hours, it died. Now that fellow is lucky, and I am so unlucky."

The village chief asked the previous owner, "Do you think the cow had some ailment? I am not asking in order to punish you. I simply want to know the truth from you. You seem to be a very sincere person. In this village I have heard so much about your honesty. I will not believe anybody else, but I will believe you."

When the village chief flattered him in this manner, the previous owner confessed, "Yes, the cow had a disease. How can I tell you a lie?"

The friend who had bought the cow cried out, "See, I was right! When he sold me the cow, he knew perfectly well that the cow had a disease."

The village chief said to the first owner, "Here is the proof that I was right. You are such a sincere person. You have confessed to me that your cow was not all right, so I deeply appreciate your sincerity."

The man said, "I knew that my friend was a fool."

The village chief asked, "Why is he a fool?"

The man went on, "He believed me. He thought that I would not tell him a lie."

Then the village chief said, "How I wish I could also be as sincere as you and as clever as you."

The previous owner was so thrilled to be flattered about his sincerity and his cleverness. Then the village chief became serious and said, "You rogue! Granted, you did not know that the cow was going to die today, but you definitely knew that the cow was sick."

The man told the chief, "Yes, I knew."

The chief continued, "When you knew that you had a cow that was sick, how did you dare to fool your dear friend? Why did you sell him the cow? Why did you not tell him the truth first? I appreciate your sincerity. You told me the truth that the cow had some disease. But your roguish nature I cannot appreciate. You are not responsible for the death of the cow, but you are responsible for hiding the fact that the cow was sick."

Immediately the village chief ordered the man to return the money to his friend. What could the previous owner do? In front of the village chief he had to return the money. Then the village chief said, "Flattery can catch everybody."

### LTS 135. *The judge punishes the cow's owner*

This is another story about a cow. This cow was in absolutely perfect health. The owner was in need of money because his daughter was about to get married. In this particular village he had a friend who was quite rich. This friend liked the cow because it was very strong and smart, and it was producing a very large amount of milk. The friend wanted to buy the cow, but he thought he could buy it at a very cheap price because he knew that the owner desperately needed money.

The owner said, "No, I cannot give the cow to you at such a low price. You have to make a better offer." So their friendship ended.

A few months later, the owner took the cow to the market to sell it. Various people were negotiating with him to buy the cow when all of a sudden a young man came forward and said, "My father liked this cow. I must give this cow to my father as a present, no matter what your price."

The owner quoted a high price, but the young man was not at all shocked by the figure. He bought the cow in order to make his father happy. Alas, while he was bringing the cow home, somehow the cow escaped. The cow entered into a paddy field and utterly destroyed it. The owner of the paddy field became furious. He captured the cow and dragged it before the village council. The council was comprised of five or six judges. Every day the head judge changed. On that day the friend who had wanted to buy the cow at a very low price happened to be the head judge. He still felt that he had been insulted by his former friend because the friend had not sold him the cow.

When he heard that this particular cow had destroyed the paddy field, he recognised at once that this was the cow he had wanted to buy. He said to the owner of the paddy field, "I am ordering the owner of this cow to pay two thousand rupees. He is such a bad owner. He knew that his cow was notorious, so I am fining him two thousand rupees. One thousand will go to you to help you restore your paddy field, and one thousand will be an act of charity. We need money for the improvement of our village."

This judge was such a rogue. He knew the cow belonged to his former friend, and that is why he imposed such a heavy fine.

The other judges on the council said, "Is your judgement not too harsh? Can you not lower the fine?"

The head judge said, "No! If it had been my cow that had misbehaved, I would have gladly given two thousand rupees."

Then the head judge requested the owner of the cow to be summoned. All of a sudden, the young man came running into the room and said, "This is my cow! I bought this cow, and I was looking for it. I was bringing it home to make my father happy. I heard that my father was deeply interested in this particular cow, so I bought it at the market to please my father."

The head judge saw his own son standing before him. He said, "What have I done?"

The other judges said, "You cannot change your decision just because it is your son. You have to stick to your decision."

So the father and son had to pay the fine of two thousand rupees. The farmer whose field was destroyed by the cow got one thousand, and the other thousand was distributed by the judges for the betterment of the village.

### LTS 136. *The perfectionist*

There was a landlord who had quite a few servants, a wife and three sons, but nobody could please him. No matter how his dear ones and servants would do something, even if it was absolutely perfect, he would find fault with them. Nobody could satisfy him in anything.

One day it happened that a young man came to his village and said to him, "My father is very sick, and your village has a very good doctor, so I have brought him all the way here. Now he will be staying at the doctor's place. Once he is cured, my father and I will go back to our village. In the meantime, you are a landlord, and it is said that you are very kind, compassionate and hospitable. Would you please allow me to stay at your guest house?"

The landlord was pleased that this stranger was so unreservedly flattering him.

He said, "Yes, you can stay at my guest house, but I do not give anything free of charge. Although it is a guest house, I expect the guests to work on the premises at least for half an hour a day. If you agree to this condition, you can stay as long as your father remains in our village."

The young man said, "Definitely. I will be quite happy to work for half an hour a day."

So the landlord gave him a very minor job. It was very, very easy, and the young man did it. The landlord felt that since this guest was neither his servant nor his relative, he should not be strict with him. So he did not find fault with his work as he usually did with others. Somehow the young man pleased the landlord.

It happened that the landlord had to go to another village to do some business. It would take him at least two weeks to go settle his affairs and come back. So he said to the young man, "I shall be away for two weeks. I would like you to do me a big favour."

The young man said, "Definitely I will do whatever you wish because you have been so kind to me."

The landlord continued, "Here is a small house. It belongs to me. I do not like the colour of the walls at all. I want you to change the colour. I am giving you a box as a sample. The colour of this box and the colour of the walls should be exactly the same."

"Easily I can do it," said the young man confidently. Then he asked, "If I finish the job in one week instead of two, do I have to wait for you to return?"

The landlord thought, "This fellow is very sincere and I am not certain that I shall be able to come back in two weeks' time." He said, "All right, I trust you. You will do the job, and I will give you the money for the job before I go. Somehow I am very pleased with you, so I am giving you the money before you have done the job."

Then the landlord left for the other village. In the meantime, the young man's father had recovered and the time had come for them to leave the village. The young man did not want to waste two weeks painting the house, so he thought of an easy solution. The colour of the small box was red and the colour of the walls was yellow. What the young man did was buy a small quantity of yellow paint and paint the box yellow. The landlord did not say that the walls had to be exactly the same colour as the box. He only said that they should match. So the young man simply painted the box and, with the extra money that he had saved, he took his father home.

After two weeks the landlord returned. He was thrilled that the colour of the box and the walls was the same, so he began bragging to his wife about his excellent worker. He said, "At last I have found a man who could please me. See, the box and the walls are the same colour!"

His wife burst into laughter.

He said, "Why are you mocking me?"

She said, "You fool! Was the box that colour? Your box was red. See, he fooled you! He just changed the colour of the box to match the walls."

The landlord became furious. "How dare that fellow fool me!" he said.

He went to the doctor's house in search of the young man. The doctor said, "You are too late. The patient is cured. They have returned home." Then the landlord asked the doctor if he knew the whereabouts of their village. The doctor gave him the information. In the meantime, the landlord's wife was laughing and laughing.

The landlord sent his servants to that village and they brought back the young man. By this time the landlord's anger could not be contained. He said, "You rogue! Give me my money back! You have tricked me!"

The young man said, "I have spent it."

"How could you spend it?" asked the landlord.

"Do you remember what you asked me?" said the young man.

"I *do* remember," replied the landlord.

The young man said, "Then repeat what you told me."

The landlord said, "I told you that both the walls and the box have to be exactly the same colour."

"So, you are saying they have to be the same?" echoed the young man. "You did not tell me that the walls have to be the colour of the box. You just told me that they have to be the same colour. So I found the method that was easiest for me and I did it. I changed the colour of the box."

The landlord was still furious because he had been fooled. Then his wife said, "He did not fool you. It is you who are the fool. You did not tell him correctly what he was supposed to do."

The landlord's son also joined his mother's side. He said, "Father, it is true. You made the mistake."

When they came to hear of the young man's trick, the villagers all laughed and laughed. They said, "At last, this perfectionist has learnt his lesson. He always demands perfection from others. He was never satisfied with anybody, so God punished him. If you constantly find fault with everybody, then rest assured, one day somebody will fool you and it will be unbearable."

### LTS 137. *The loaf of bread*

There was a king who used to invite other kings to come to his kingdom on his birthday. He also used to invite his special friends and practically anybody who would like to come. He made it known that he would be happy if his guests could bring him gifts. Then whoever gave him the most valuable present was allowed to sit beside him on the throne for one day, his birthday. This practice went on every year. Now this particular year, the king's Guru came to the palace to celebrate the king's birthday. The king was overjoyed that his Guru was present. He said, "Nobody can give me any gift that is more valuable than my Guru himself. His presence is the greatest gift. He will sit beside me on the throne. Plus, he will tell me what I should do. First I will keep him beside me. Then I shall ask him to guide me. Whomever he chooses to sit next to him or whatever gifts he chooses for me to receive first, I will gladly obey his will."

Then the king very prayerfully invited his Guru to sit beside him, but his Guru said, "No, I cannot sit there because I am not the most valuable gift."

The king said, "Are you not the most valuable? Your very presence is the most precious thing in my life. You have come here out of your infinite compassion and affection."

"No, no, no," said his Guru. Then he went on, "Now I am telling you which gift is more valuable. I would like you to declare what the gift is and show the gift to everybody. Then I would like you to thank the person wholeheartedly."

The king immediately agreed. He said, "I will wholeheartedly thank the person, whoever he is, and also I will appreciate him most sincerely. I will give him a scroll with my gratitude inscribed on it."

Then the king's Guru gave the king a large loaf of bread and asked him to write some words of appreciation for the gift. Everybody started laughing. How could a loaf of bread be the most valuable thing? The Guru said, "O King, let me tell you the story and then you can decide. This morning a very, very poor man came here with this loaf of bread. He was afraid of giving it to you, so he gave it to me because I am a simple man. I told him that I am your Guru and that I would give it to you. He was very pleased because he believed me.

"Then he started to go away. I asked him to stay for the celebration, but he said, 'No, no, no! I do not fit in with the king's important guests, but I have such love, admiration and adoration for my king. That is why I wanted to bring him my humble gift. In order to get this loaf of bread, I have not eaten for two days.'

"I begged him, 'Stay, stay here! I will give you food.'

"The poor man said, 'No, no, no. I want to go. These are all very, very important people and I do not fit in. I cannot stay. I am going back to my village today. When I reach my home, I will be able to eat.'"

The king was so moved by his Guru's story. He showed the loaf to his friends and, at his Guru's request, he read out a special message of appreciation for the old man.

Then his Guru said, "Poor fellow! He has set out on his way. I am sure he is feeling very weak. Perhaps he will not be able to cover a very long distance. O King, kindly send your guards to find him and bring him here so that we can feed him properly."

The king immediately sent his guards in search of the poor man. They went out on horseback in the direction of the poor man's village. After covering two miles, they saw the man lying by the side of the road. They got the shock of their life to discover that he had died from exhaustion. With heavy hearts, they brought back the dead body and placed it carefully at the feet of the king.

The Guru said to the king, "You have to give this man a special honour. His body you have to bury in a very special way, in a grandiose manner. He deserves the highest honour."

The king answered, "Yes, I will do anything you ask. You are my Guru."

The Guru looked around the court and said, "These are all your friends. They give you gifts from their surplus. They do not make any sacrifice. Most of them are very, very rich, and they give in accordance with their wealth and prosperity. In terms of their true capacity, they give you next to nothing. But this old man has given you everything — his last loaf of bread.

If he had eaten that loaf of bread himself, today he would have had strength; he would not have died."

The king said, "My heart is breaking for this poor man. I will keep this loaf on my throne until it becomes very, very hard and only then, when it has become completely useless, will I throw it away."

His Guru said, "No! You have to keep that loaf of bread by your side as long as you live. This bread will reveal to you the meaning of sacrifice. You see, this poor man sacrificed his own life. He wanted to bring you a gift and he gave his life to fulfil that wish. You want appreciation, admiration and adoration from your friends and neighbouring kings. In addition, I want you to add something good to your life and that is an understanding of the meaning of sacrifice. So it is my wish that you keep this loaf of bread in a box here on your throne permanently. This bread embodies the message of sacrifice. This old man gave his life because he loved you so much. You can also make a most significant sacrifice from now on to show the citizens of your kingdom how much you love them. This is my wish."

The king listened with utmost devotion to his Guru's words. Then he bowed to his Guru and said, "O Guru of my heart and soul, I will do as you wish. I will abide by your soulful request."

### LTS 138. *The art of being a miser*

There was a gentleman who wanted to be 'initiated' into the fine art of being a miser by someone who was himself a great miser. Although this gentleman had miserly qualities, the great miser was infinitely better than he was in that 'profession'. One day the gentleman went to the supremely great miser and begged him to teach him how to become a very great miser. The supremely great miser asked, "What will you give me if I make you as great as I am?"

The gentleman said, "I will give you anything you wish."

The great miser said, "If you will give me anything, then I will make you even greater than I am in miserliness."

The master-miser took his disciple-miser to a grocery store. The master-miser wanted to buy a pound of flour. He asked the owner, "Is this flour in very good condition?"

The shopkeeper said, "Yes, yes. You can see for yourself. It looks like pure butter. And when you taste it, you will find it tastes like pure butter."

The master-miser said, "We will be back."

Then he and his disciple went to another shop where butter was sold. The master-miser said to the owner, "So, I have heard that your butter is by far the best."

The owner said, "Yes, it is absolutely the best. Can you not see that it is so soft, just like olive oil?"

The master-miser said, "Ah, yes, it does look like olive oil. All right, we will be coming back soon."

Then the master-miser took his disciple to a store where they sold all kinds of oil. The master-miser asked the shopkeeper, "Do you have olive oil?"

The owner said, "Yes, yes."

The master-miser said, "Let me see the best olive oil you have."

The owner brought out a jar of olive oil and said, "This oil is by far the best. Can you not see that it looks like pure water? It is so clear and so pure, just like water."

The master-miser said to him, "I can see that what you are saying is true. We shall come back."

Then the master-miser took his disciple home to his house. The disciple-miser sat before the master- miser, eager to hear his words of wisdom. The master-miser said to him, "Do you know now what is the most valuable thing? It is water. We started with flour, which looked like butter. Then we found the butter was like olive oil. Finally, we discovered the olive oil was like water. So you see, water is most important. Water symbolises life itself. Do we pay anything for water? No, it is free. Other things we have to buy, and they are quite expensive, whereas water we do not have to buy. See how much money we have saved in the course of one morning! Now I have given you my lesson. The most valuable thing, according to all the shopkeepers, is water, and we have plenty of water in the house. So let us drink water."

The master-miser and his disciple both filled their glasses with water and drank it together. Then the master-miser said, "I am very pleased with your devotedness. You have followed me all morning and you have grasped the essence of my teachings. I am sure you will now become a super-excellent miser."

The disciple-miser said, "Please ask me for anything in return. I will give it to you."

The master-miser said, "I told you that you will be able to defeat me in our 'profession'."

The disciple-miser said, "How can I ever defeat you? You have given me such good advice today."

The master-miser said, "How will you defeat me? I have a beautiful daughter, and you have a very smart, well-educated son. I want your son to marry my daughter. You will not have to give me even one anna, but I shall have to give you thousands of rupees for my daughter's dowry. Now, have I not proved to you that you are greater than me in miserliness?"

## LTS 139. *The bronze statue*

There was a villager who used to dive well. If anything dropped inside the well by accident, he would dive and bring it to the surface. The king was very pleased with him for his efforts and gave him a trophy. It was a bronze statue of a Greek soldier. The diver was very, very pleased with the statue and he brought it home.

His village head heard that the diver had received something special from the king, so he became jealous. He said to the diver, "Please, can you sell this statue to me? It is so beautiful. It is such a precious thing."

The diver said, "No, I cannot sell it. The king himself has given this to me, and it means so much to me. I really treasure it."

The village head said, "Next week I am inviting my friends to my house for a party. I want to place this statue on the table to decorate it. That is why I am asking to have it."

The young man said, "I cannot sell it to you, but I can loan it to you for a short time. For a week or so I can loan it to you, but then you have to return it. When your guests go away, you can return it."

The village head said, "Definitely, definitely I will give it back to you. It is just a temporary loan."

The young man gave the statue to the village head, and the village head secretly asked some of his workers to cast an earthen statue in exactly the same mould.

A week passed and the young man came to the village head to retrieve his statue. He trusted the village head so much that he did not suspect anything. The statue had been in a special box, and the village head gave the same box back to the young man. Then he thanked the young man profusely.

The young man said, "I am so happy that I was able to help you."

Then the great diver went home, only to discover there was no bronze statue inside the box. It had become an earthen statue. The diver cried out, "That rogue! He has cheated me!"

He rushed to the house of the village head and accused him of substituting an earthen statue for his bronze one.

The village head said, "No, no! Whatever you gave me, I have returned in its original condition."

The diver said, "How can it be? How can what was bronze now be earthen?"

The village head said, "It is so simple. I washed your statue a few times. Perhaps that is why it changed its colour. The bronze coating washed away. Now it is no longer bronze; it is earthen."

In silence the young man cursed the village head but, alas, what could he do? He returned home feeling very sad.

A few months later, the wife of the village head was fetching water from the well. She was using a most valuable bronze vessel. Alas, it fell into the water and immediately sank to the bottom of the well. The village head went from person to person begging them to dive into the water. A few of the villagers tried, but nobody was successful because the well was so deep. Only that particular diver was capable of doing it. Finally, the village head was compelled to resort to the young man who had received the trophy from the king.

When the village head approached him, the young man said, "Not today. It is too late. Tomorrow morning I shall come here to the well and help you."

The village head said, "Do you still remember that unhappy experience with the statue?"

The diver said, "No, no, I do not believe in cherishing that kind of unfortunate experience. I have forgiven you. I have forgotten everything. Now I am quite happy. As long as I was harbouring that memory, I suffered, but now I have forgiven you completely. That is why I am very, very happy to help you."

The village head was very relieved. He said, "I wish we could have more people like you in our village."

The following morning the young man was supposed to come and dive for the bronze vessel. But in the middle of the night he secretly visited the well. Nobody was there to see him. He dove into the water, found the bronze vessel and took it home.

The following day he went to the well as agreed. He approached the village head and said, "Now I have come to do your work. I shall do the needful."

The village head and his wife and children were extremely happy. They were confident that the young man would be successful. In front of them, he dove to the bottom of the well. Alas, all he brought up was an earthen pot. The village head cried, "No, no! It was not earthen. It was bronze!"

The young man said, "What can I do? That is the only vessel I could find. If you prefer, you can ask somebody else to dive, or if you want me to dive again, I can."

The village head's wife was crying and crying. Meanwhile, the village head was puzzled. He said, "How could this happen?"

The young man said, "It is most extraordinary, but if you want me to dive again, I can."

The village head said, "All right, all right, again try. This time you will get the other pot, I am sure."

The young man dove into the well, but this time he came up empty-handed. He said, "I have been trying and trying, but I could not find anything else at the bottom of the well. The earthen pot that I found the first time is all there is to be found."

The village head and his wife were so miserable that they had lost their bronze vessel.

That night the village head secretly came to the great diver's home and whispered, "Please take your bronze statue back."

He gave back the young man's real trophy. Then the diver very smilingly said, "Please take your bronze vessel."

You can say that this is a story of tit for tat, but in the end both of them finally became happy.

### LTS 140. *Friendship proved, friendship lost*

A husband and wife were very kind and devoted to one another. Nevertheless, something used to puzzle the wife. Why did her husband come home late at night? He was a very nice man. Some days he would say he had office work, which was true. On other days he would say he was visiting his friends. That used to create a little bit of unhappy suspicion in the wife's mind, although he was such a good husband. The wife was constantly arguing with herself as to why he would come home late.

One day the wife said, "Please tell me frankly, why do you have to come home so late? How many friends do you have?"

Her husband said, "Friends? In this lifetime, if one gets even one friend, it is enough."

She asked, "Then where do you go? Some days you say you work late at your office. On other days you come late without giving any reason. Why, why?"

He said, "I go and visit my acquaintances and others."

She said, "No, that is not right. You should come back home."

Eventually the husband said, "All right. In the future I will come back home after finishing my office work."

Still the wife was not satisfied. She said, "Can you not tell me how many friends you really have?"

He said, "I have only two friends."

"Only two friends?" she said.

"Yes," he said.

"What kind of friends are they?" she asked.

The husband replied, "One friend will never allow me to be poverty stricken. He is very rich, and he is very kind to me. If anything happens to me, he will come to my financial rescue. And the other one is a military officer. He will do anything for me. He will even give his life for me."

The wife said, "Oh, one will give his life and the other will give you money. Let me see those two friends."

Now real suspicion was entering into the mind and heart of the wife. Insecurity and suspicion were reigning supreme inside her. The husband took her first to the house of the very rich friend. It was true that this friend was very rich and at the same time kind-hearted. The rich friend introduced his wife, and the two wives had a very lovely talk.

The friend's wife said, "Now that we know each other, you have to come to our home so that we can become very close friends."

By now it was getting late. The rich friend said to the husband, "Where are you planning to go from here?"

The husband said, "I am going to take my wife to visit my other friend."

The rich friend said, "Here, take my car. You can return it tomorrow morning."

So the husband and wife went to visit the military friend. Unfortunately, that friend was involved in playing table tennis with some other friends. He was losing, so he could not pay any attention to his new guests. They stood watching him, but the military friend did not even say hello to the husband.

The wife said to her husband, "This kind of friend you have! He did not even say hello to you when he saw that you were waiting there. I can see how much he cares for you."

The husband said, "He was losing, so he was not showing his friendship. He was concentrating on his game. Otherwise, he is my real friend."

The wife said, "Your real friend! He cannot say hello to you, and you believe he is going to give his life for you! I like your rich friend. He was nice to me, and his wife was extremely nice. But this military friend is no good. You said that the first one would give you money if you were in need. I saw that he is kind-hearted. He has given his car for you to use. But I can never believe that this other one would give his life for you."

The husband said, "Just wait. Let us see who is right and who is wrong. Tomorrow I will go to see my friends. You will accompany me. I will tell a downright lie to my friends, and you have to be very, very serious. If you laugh, it will not work, so you have to be extremely serious."

The following day, when they went to see the rich friend, the husband said to him, "Can you imagine? Somebody is jealous of me in our office. That worker has said such nasty things about me, and the boss is furious with me. The boss will not even look at me. Previously he was so fond of me. Now my boss has fired me. How am I going to support my wife and myself? I have become destitute overnight."

The rich friend said, "Do not insult me! Am I not your friend? Do you have to worry? I do not want you to worry. Take this money. You do not have to work for that fellow. I am infinitely richer than your boss. I am giving you money, and you do not have to do any work. Only do not tell your boss that I have given you so much money. Otherwise, like a beggar, he will come to ask me for a loan. So I do not want him to know. But you do not have to go back to work for him. Take your time and look for a better job."

The wife could not believe her eyes and her ears. The rich man had proven himself to be a real friend.

Then the husband and wife went to the home of the second friend. This time also his friend was playing table tennis. The husband came in very hurriedly, almost panicky, so the friend stopped playing table tennis and said, "What has happened? What is the matter with you?"

The husband told the same story. He said, "Some fellow in my office has said such nasty, bad things about me. My boss is furious, and he has fired me. Now I have no job."

The military friend said, "No job? Who has spoken ill of you?"

He immediately put down his table tennis paddle and ran into his room where he kept his gun. He said, "I am going to kill him! For somebody to speak ill of my dearest friend is intolerable!"

He took his gun and started running towards the front door.

The husband cried out, "Stop, stop, stop!"

The military friend said, "No, I cannot allow anyone to speak ill of you without punishment. I will punish that rogue. I will absolutely kill him."

The husband said to his wife, "Look, look at this! Is he not taking a risk? If he kills the fellow, then others will kill him. Did I not say that one friend would give me money if anything happened to me and the other friend is ready to give his life for me? Here is the proof."

The husband and wife begged the military officer not to take action and then they came back home. Both the husband and wife started laughing and laughing. Then the husband and wife invited the military officer and the rich man to come to their house for dinner. Both friends came to their house, and they had a very charming evening.

Alas, the wife could not keep the secret. It is a woman's dharma not to be able to keep any secrets. The wife told her husband's friends what actually happened. She started bursting into laughter while recounting all the events of that evening. The two friends were shocked. Each one was wondering what kind of friend would do such a thing.

At the end of the story, the husband said, "I wanted to show my wife that one of you was ready to give his life for me if I was in danger and the other one would definitely give me money if I found myself in financial difficulty."

Unfortunately, the two friends did not find the story amusing at all. They became very sad and serious. The rich friend said, "If you can think of fooling us in this way, how can we trust you in the future? Now when you actually need money, I will be unwilling to give it to you."

The military friend said, "And perhaps when you find yourself in real danger, I will not be able to help you. I do not want you to make a fool of me a second time."

So the husband's friendship with the rich friend and the military officer ended because both these friends were very sincere people. They never thought that the husband would fool them.

True, the husband was able to prove to his wife that he had two real friends. But the story has a twist: if you tell lies to your real friends, you can lose them.

### LTS 141. *The greatest wrestler*

There were two men in a particular village who were deadly enemies. They constantly used to speak ill of each other. In every way they would try to defame one another. One day, the greatest wrestler in the land came to the village. Of the two enemies, the one that was richer invited the wrestler to stay at his house as his honoured guest. The wrestler accepted the invitation and his host treated him with such concern, love, joy and pride.

One day the host said to his guest, "Will you kindly do me a favour?"

The wrestler said, "Certainly! You have been so kind to me. I will certainly do you a favour."

The host said, "I am giving you two hundred rupees. I will tell you the name of my worst enemy. One day you have to thrash him soundly! Only do not kill him. If you kill him, some problems may arise. Keep him alive, but beat him black and blue!"

The wrestler said, "That is a very easy task. I will gladly do it." He fully agreed to the proposal and took the two hundred rupees.

A day or two later, the host had gone to the market to do his shopping and he was returning home in the evening. He was hoping that soon he would hear the news from the wrestler that he had beaten his enemy black and blue. These were the thoughts that were occupying his mind. All of a sudden, the wrestler appeared from nowhere and started thrashing him mercilessly.

The man cried out, "What are you doing? You are mistaken! I am the one who gave you the money. You are not supposed to beat me up! Can you not see who I am? I am your host and you are my guest."

The wrestler said, "I know you are my host. I am fully aware of that fact."

The host said, "Then what happened to our agreement? Why are you beating me instead of beating my enemy?"

The wrestler said, "For two reasons. I went to your enemy and told him that you had given me two hundred rupees to thrash him. Your enemy immediately gave me four hundred rupees to thrash you! Since he gave me double the amount, I am beating you and not him."

As the wrestler continued beating the poor fellow, he said, "Now I will tell you the second reason. Before coming here, I was an honest man. I was the strongest wrestler, but I never thought of beating an innocent person. In wrestling, it is justified to fight. If wrestlers challenge me, naturally I defeat them, because I am a better wrestler, I am the strongest. But you tempted me with money. You taught me dishonesty. You took me into the temptation-world. That is the second reason why I am beating you. You asked me not to beat your enemy to death, so I am not going to beat you to death. But I am making sure that you will remember this day!"

### LTS 142. *The rich and miserly farmer*

There was a farmer who was both rich and miserly. Everybody knew him as a rich man and everybody knew him as a miser to the extreme. This story took place at harvest time. The miser and his neighbouring farmers were in their respective fields. They were collecting the paddy. In the evening some village boys came and wanted to help the farmers. All the other farmers, out of compassion, love and concern, used to give some paddy to the little village boys, but the rich farmer never gave them anything. The village boys knew his reputation, so they would not come near him.

On this particular occasion, jealousy entered into the farmer. He said, "The other farmers are my neighbours. They are appreciated, admired and loved by the little village boys. I also deserve the affection, love and gratitude of those young boys." So he decided to be very generous. He invited a few of the boys to come to his fields. He told them, "Today I have changed my mind. You work for me, and I will give you more paddy than the other farmers give."

The boys started working very happily. In the meantime, in a very tricky way the rich farmer put some very good paddy in a basket for them, and underneath the good paddy he put lots of husk. After they finished working, the farmer gave the basket to the boys. The little boys were so happy. The quantity was larger than the quantity they had received from the other farmers. They went home and they were so eager to tell their dear ones that today they had changed the nature of the farmer. Because of them, the farmer had become so kind.

One of the boys' family members said, "Let us see what kind of paddy the rich man has given you." When he examined it, he found that underneath was all husk. The good paddy was only on the top. The little boys and their families were furious. They all wanted to go strike the farmer.

The oldest and smartest villager said, "No, do not do that. I have a plan. Listen to me. Put the paddy back in the basket in exactly the same way. Put the husk underneath and on top put all the paddy. Then you will go to this farmer's wife and tell her, 'Look, we have a large quantity of paddy and we are going to sell it at a very cheap price.'"

So the little boys went to the miser's house. The wife asked, "How can you sell such a large quantity at such a cheap price?"

They replied, "Because somebody gave it to us for free!"

She said, "Somebody gave it to you for free?"

"Yes," they said, "we were working for so many farmers and somebody gave it as payment. We do not know who."

The wife enquired, "You do not know the names of those farmers?"

The boys said, "There are so many farmers. One of them was so kind today. He gave us this for free because we worked for him. Do you want to buy it? We shall sell it to you at a very cheap price. Please tell us whether or not you want to buy it. We have a very short time because it is getting late. If you do not want to buy it, we shall go somewhere else to sell it."

The wife said, "Oh, such beautiful grain! Do not go, do not go! I will give you money." So the miser's wife gave the little boys money. At a cheap price she bought all the paddy.

After some time, her husband came home and she said, "Look, look! I have some happy news."

He said, "What?"

She said, "Look here! Such beautiful paddy! It is in excellent condition. Some little boys came and they were so sincere. They told me that they were given it for free, so they wanted to sell it to me at a very cheap price. So I bought this for you. I am sure that tomorrow you will be able to sell this at a very high price."

The farmer immediately recognised that this was the paddy he had given the little boys. He said, "What have I done?" He was so miserable! It was the farmer's bad karma to lose money because of the husks he had used to trick the little boys. He did not gain anything. In fact, he became the real loser.

### LTS 143. *When friends become rivals*

This story is about two friends who were also great rivals. One moment they were friends, the next moment they were rivals and the following moment they became worse than the worst enemies. When they were friends, they would invite each other to go shopping and do various things together. At such times, they were in the seventh Heaven of oneness-delight. But at other times, they would display their rivalry. One would invite ten of his friends to his house, including his worst rival, and then he would give them an excellent feast. Everybody would appreciate and admire the host. Then his rival would burn with jealousy. A few days later this rival would invite thirty of his friends and show off by offering them a superlative banquet.

So in this way their rivalry went on. Then when rivalry descended into enmity, they could not even walk along the same street. Plus each one would hire people to speak ill of the other.

Once one of them went even further. He said, "I have to punish this fellow. He is unbearable. I am absolutely sick of him."

He went to the market and saw a man who was selling monkeys. Then a brilliant idea flashed across his forehead. He said to the monkey seller, "I want to buy the most dynamic, mischievous and powerful monkey that you have. No matter what price you ask, I will immediately give it to you."

So he bought the most powerful and destructive monkey that was available and took it away with him. By then it was evening. Both the rivals had huge gardens with all kinds of flowers and fruits. He entered into his friend's garden and let the monkey loose. The rival's servant saw him, screamed and started chasing him. Then he saw that it was his master's friend, so he did not pursue the chase and afterwards he did not create any commotion or sensation.

In a day or two this monkey had destroyed all the flowers, plants and tender fruits in the garden. The owner was miserable. He knew who was responsible for this destruction. Meanwhile, the neighbours were afraid that this monkey would enter into their gardens and do the same. So the owner of the garden said, "Why should we all suffer? I will show him. Tit for tat!"

He went to the market and approached the same monkey dealer. He said, "Give me the strongest, most powerful, most dynamic and most aggressive monkey that you have. I will pay you a very high price for it." So he bought a very large and frightening monkey at a high price. Then he took the monkey and let it loose in the garden of his rival. In a very short time, this monkey destroyed everything inside the garden.

Now both the rivals were happy and miserable at the same time. They were happy because the other one's garden was completely ruined and sad that their own garden had also been ruined. In the meantime, the neighbours of both parties were afraid that their own beautiful gardens would be ruined by these wild monkeys. So the neighbours went to the village chief and lodged a serious complaint against both parties.

The village chief summoned the two rivals and accused them of using the monkeys to destroy each other's gardens. In the beginning both of them denied the charge. They claimed that they knew nothing about the monkeys.

Then the village chief became furious. He said, "Tell the truth! Otherwise I will put you into jail!" Then both of them confessed that they were the culprits.

The village chief said, "Now you will hear my judgement. First of all, I am sending for the monkey dealer." The monkey dealer arrived and stood before the village chief. Then the village chief said, "This is my final judgement. They will return the monkeys to you. You can keep them under control. But they have to pay you a very high price to take them back."

Everybody was shocked. The two culprits had already bought the monkeys. They had paid once. Now they were being asked to pay a second time. What is more, the chief said to the monkey dealer, "You may set the price as high as possible."

The monkey dealer said, "Four hundred rupees for each one."

The chief was very happy and said to the two rivals, "Return your monkeys to him. Then four hundred rupees each one will pay because you have been so bad. These monkeys are animals, but I wish to say that you two are man-monkeys."

So the punishment was that the two rivals had to return their monkeys plus pay a penalty. Usually when you buy something and you return it, you get your money back, but here they had to return the monkeys plus pay a high price as punishment. When people are bad, this kind of karma they incur and then they suffer. So be careful! If you are dealing with your inner monkeys, you will reap serious consequences!

## LTS 144. *The mother-in-law's inheritance*

There was a mother who lived with her son and daughter-in-law. This mother was illiterate. She could not read, and she could not even write her own name. But she desired to have a daughter-in-law who was well educated, since her son was well educated. So she was very happy that she had found a well-educated wife for her son.

Now this daughter-in-law was very proud and haughty. She felt superior because she was well educated, while her mother-in-law was illiterate. Usually the story is that mothers-in-law torture their daughters-in-law. In this case, the story was totally different. The daughter-in-law was always showing off, insulting the mother-in-law and ridiculing her because she was not learned. She even went to the length of scolding her mother-in-law. The poor mother-in-law was suffering so much. What a mistake she had made! She had wanted a well-educated daughter-in-law. Now she was at the mercy of the daughter-in-law.

The son was very sad and miserable. He was so devoted to his mother, and he used to scold his wife for treating her so badly. Then the husband and wife would have a serious fight. He did not know how to end his mother's suffering. This situation went on for years.

One day a letter came, addressed to the mother. The mother was very happy. Unfortunately, she could not read the letter. So she asked her daughter-in-law to read it out. The daughter-in-law immediately started insulting her mother-in-law. She said, "You are such an idiot that you cannot even read your own letter! For everything you need me."

When the daughter-in-law opened the letter and began reading it, she got the shock of her life. The letter said that a very, very distant relative of the mother-in-law had left her a very large amount of money in his will. The condition was that she would receive this money only when she learned to read and write. The letter also mentioned that in three months or so, the mother-in-law would succeed in learning to read and write. The feeling in the letter was one of genuine encouragement. The distant relative had said in his will, "I really want you to have my money."

When the daughter-in-law saw what a large amount of money was involved, an immediate transformation came over her. "So much money is at stake," she said. "You have to fulfil the condition. Will you give me some of the money if I teach you?"

The mother-in-law was so happy that at last her daughter-in-law was talking to her nicely. She said, "Definitely I will give you some of the money. As a matter of fact, I will give half to you and half to my son. Kindly teach me."

Now everything changed overnight. The daughter-in-law began showing such affection, love and respect to her mother-in-law. Sometimes she would teach her twice a day. The husband could not believe his eyes and ears! How kind and affectionate his wife had become. It gave him tremendous joy to see that the mother-in-law and daughter-in-law had now become the best of friends. The daughter-in-law needed money to buy things for the house and the mother- in-law was determined to keep her promise.

In three months' time the mother-in-law could read books and she could write her name easily. They were expecting that any day the lawyer of the deceased party would write another letter to the mother-in-law. Finally a letter did arrive. This time it mentioned the name of the person who actually left the money, and it was the son. He had played a trick.

His wife became furious. She felt she had been cheated. Then her mother-in-law said, "True, my son has fooled us, but I still have to keep my promise."

That night when the son came home from work, his mother said, "Now you have to borrow money from the bank. I want to keep my promise and give it to your wife."

The poor son said, "All right. Now that you and my wife are on excellent terms, I feel that it is well worth it." So he borrowed money and gave it to his mother. She then gave the money to her daughter-in-law and everybody was satisfied.

Then the mother made another request to her son. She said, "I want to open a school for illiterate people of my age. For elderly people I wish to have a night class. I am begging you to give me the money to do it. I know how I suffered in the hands of my daughter-in-law when I was illiterate. I am sure there are other mothers-in-law like me who are suffering and who will continue to suffer. So the best thing is to make the elderly women literate so that they are no longer at the mercy of their daughters-in-law." Her son agreed and this kind-hearted old lady opened up a school.

The daughter-in-law was happy because she had received so much money. The son was happy because his mother and his wife were now on very good terms. Everything ended happily because of the son's ingenious trick!

### LTS 145. *The gold necklaces*

There was a husband who was very, very good and a wife who was very, very bad. Day in and day out the wife would nag the husband to give her this or give her that.

The husband would say, "You cannot see that I am poor? I am having so much trouble making ends meet!"

The wife would answer, "You are not poor! You are stingy, that is all."

This went on until the husband was sick of it. It seemed his wife only knew how to beg for expensive things.

Finally the wife said, "If you give me only one thing, I will not bother you again. I want a real gold necklace."

The husband went to a jeweller and said, "To be perfectly honest, I have very little money, but my wife is begging me to buy her a gold necklace. What am I going to do? Please give me some advice."

The jeweller said, "That is easy. Take an imitation gold necklace."

The husband said, "But my wife will find out."

The jeweller said, "No, no, no! Only a jeweller can say whether or not it is imitation. Otherwise, for anybody else to recognise that it is artificial is next to impossible. Just tell your wife a white lie. You are quite safe."

The husband paid for the necklace and brought it home. There was a struggle going on between his sincerity and his insincerity. He said to himself, "My wife loves me so much, and although she nags me and nags me, I have to admit that I love her deeply. Such being the case, how can I tell her a lie? He presented the necklace to his wife and, with tears in his eyes, he said, "Please forgive me. This is only an imitation gold necklace that I am giving you. From now on I shall save money, and very soon I shall be able to afford a real one for you."

The wife was very deeply moved by her husband's sincerity and love. A few moments later she asked her husband, "Can I tell people it is real?"

He replied, "Say whatever you want to say, but I am telling you frankly, it is not a real one; it is imitation. I am sincere."

In a day or two the wife went to her parents' house wearing the necklace. As soon as her sister-in-law set eyes on the gold necklace, she became very, very jealous. She said to her husband, "Look, they were only recently married. Their marriage is only a few months' old, and already she has received a gold necklace. I have been married to you for five years and what have I received? Nothing! You are so bad."

Her husband said, "What can I do? I am only a very poor man. I have no money to buy you a gold necklace."

She went on, "I know it is because you are stingy. That is why you want to escape by inventing excuses." Then she started barking at her husband and berating him.

Finally the poor husband said, "All right, all right. I will get you one. Do not feel miserable."

He went to the jeweller and said to him, "My wife wants a real gold necklace, but I do not have enough money to buy one. Please tell me what to do."

This jeweller happened to be the same one that the other husband had visited. Once again, he gave the same advice. "You fool!" he said. "You can easily deceive your wife. Take this imitation necklace. She will not be able to tell the difference."

This husband was not as honest as the previous one. When he brought the necklace home to his wife, he told her, "This is a real gold necklace."

She was filled with joy. Like her sister-in-law, she could now brag that she had a real gold necklace. She wore it every day and proudly showed all her friends and neighbours. One day the husband's sincerity came forward and he told his wife, "I have to confess that it is imitation."

His wife became furious. Why had her husband fooled her? The first wife sympathised when her husband told her that the necklace was imitation. She knew he was poor, and he said he would save up money and buy her a real one. This husband also told his wife that he would save up money and one day he would definitely buy her a real one.

Now both the wives knew that their necklaces were imitation, but still they went on bragging, telling each other that theirs was made of real gold. And neither one of the husbands had the heart to disclose the truth.

Every day both wives went to bathe in a particular village pond. One morning, one wife entered the water to bathe, and the other wife happened to pass by the pond. As she was walking by, she saw that the wife who was bathing had left her necklace on a stone slab. The sister-in-law quickly exchanged the necklaces. She said to herself, "Since my husband has secretly told me that mine is imitation, let me exchange it. They look exactly alike. My sister-in-law will never notice the difference."

Later that same morning, the second one also wanted to bathe. Then the same idea entered into the first one. She said, "I know mine is not real. It is only imitation." Then she substituted her necklace for the other one. Now both of them were so happy because they both believed that their necklace was real.

But this happiness was destined to be shattered. The first husband — who was very sincere or very stupid — wanted his wife to come up to his standard. Since he was sincere, he expected his wife to be sincere. So he had to say at a family gathering, "The necklace I bought my wife is imitation."

Then the other husband came forward and said, "My wife's necklace is also imitation." So this is how the two husbands ruined all the joy of the two wives.

# LIFE'S BLEEDING TEARS AND FLYING SMILES

## BOOK 11

### LTS 146. *Perfect in telling lies*

There was once a very prosperous man who wanted his son to be well educated in every way. He approached a great scholar and said, "In three years' time I want my son to be a first-class scholar. He may not become as great as you are. You are the greatest scholar, and you have a lifetime of study behind you. But I do want my son to be an excellent scholar. Please teach him for three years whatever subjects you feel are appropriate. I will give you a salary on a monthly basis." And he promised a very high salary.

The son began going to the scholar every day and spending hours with him learning all kinds of things. For three years he studied with the greatest scholar. Sometimes when he came home, he would use bombastic words that his family had never heard before, and he would talk about philosophy, religion, science, literature, poetry and mathematics. The father was so pleased with his son's progress and the mother was very proud to have such a learned son.

At the end of three years, the rich man said to the scholar, "Has my son learnt everything that he is supposed to learn?"

The scholar said, "Yes, he has learnt a great deal. He is an excellent student. I am very, very pleased with him and very proud of him."

The father said, "I am also very proud of my son. He has become everything that I hoped he would become. To me, he is perfect. Do you see anything in his life or in his nature that is imperfect?"

The scholar said, "In all sincerity, I wish to say that I have never seen anybody like him. Thousands of students have passed through my hands, but I have never imagined that such a good, smart, intelligent student would come into my life."

The father was overjoyed at these words of praise, and he gave the scholar a large sum of money. The scholar was very pleased to receive so much money. Then the father repeated his question. He asked, "Tell me frankly, is my son perfect?"

The scholar replied, "I cannot say he is one hundred per cent perfect. No human being is perfect. Perhaps he has one or two small faults. We are all human beings after all. In each person you will find one or two faults, but in comparison to others, he is infinitely better than all of us."

The father was very, very pleased. He said, "All right. Let me ask him some questions." The father said to the son, "My son, have you ever neglected your studies?"

The son said, "No, Father, no."

"Have you ever smoked?"

"No, I have never smoked."

"Did you ever mix with any girl?"

"No. I devoted all my time to my studies."

"Did you ever go out to watch a violent movie, or did you go to a night club?"

"No, no, no!"

Then the rich man said to the scholar, "My son does not have a girlfriend. He does not smoke. He has not neglected his studies. He has not gone to any night club. My son is perfect, perfect. What do you think? Is he not perfect in every way?"

"Yes, your son is perfect," said the scholar, looking down at the ground.

"Then tell me once and for all if you have anything to say against him," insisted the rich man.

"I have nothing to say against him," said the scholar abruptly.

The rich man was eager to hear more praise of his son. He went on, "Can you not pass any opinion? Do you not agree with me that my son is absolutely perfect?"

Suddenly the scholar looked up and said in a different kind of voice, "Yes, your son is absolutely perfect. But I have to add something. He is absolutely perfect in telling lies! Since he has come to me, he has *never* studied. I begged him and begged him to study. And all the things that you asked — whether he has gone to bars or smoked or watched movies — it is my painful task to inform you that his answers are all lies. I tried in so many ways to persuade him to study, but he never studied. Now you can see for yourself that he is really perfect. Perfect in what? Perfect in telling lies. I am glad that you are taking your son back because these last three years have been a real torture for me. What could I do? I could not say anything. I was afraid that you would scold me and insult me for not teaching him properly. Desperately I tried to teach him, but he was determined not to learn anything."

The father was bewildered. He asked, "Then how is it that my son used to come home from time to time and speak about religion, spirituality, science and other subjects?"

The scholar said, "Please, please forgive me. You are a rich man, but you are not at all a wise man. You have not studied these subjects. You know about business matters, but when it comes to higher learning, you are an idiot. Whatever your son said was erroneous. There was nothing correct in it. He was just saying things at random. If you had asked people who know philosophy or religion or science to verify what he was saying, they would have laughed and laughed. But you are not learned, so it was easy for him to fool you by using bombastic words and facts that he had invented on the spur of the moment. Since you want to see perfection in your son, then I can only say that he is really perfect in telling lies at every moment."

LTS 147. *The old man shows the scholar God's existence*

There was a very nice man who thought of himself as something of a scholar. He used to give talks here, there and everywhere. Since he was very, very rich, he was able to buy whatever he wanted. Because of this, pride entered into him. He said, "Whatever I want, I can get. Why do I need God then? Everything is at my command."

Gradually, gradually he stopped believing in God because he felt he could manage without God. One evening he was giving a talk, and he wanted to prove the non-existence of God. He announced from the speaker's dais, "Previously I used to have absolute faith in God. Now that I am very, very rich and I have acquired so much wisdom, I have come to realise that there is no God."

People in the audience were simply shocked by this dramatic statement. Then the speaker said, "I can prove it. I am telling you that God does not exist. If God exists, I will give Him five minutes. In five minutes, He has to take my life away. I have openly declared that I am an atheist. I do not believe in God. Now let us see what kind of punishment God has in store for me if, in fact, He exists. I do not believe that He does. I am giving Him five minutes. Whether He comes here personally or not, He has to find a way to kill me. If He cannot kill me within the time limit, definitely it proves that there is no God."

Five minutes passed. Then it became ten minutes and fifteen minutes, but God did not appear to kill the speaker. He said, "See, here is the proof. I even gave God extra time. God does not exist, so we do not have to pray to Him any longer."

A very old man was in the audience. He stood up and said, "O scholar, your stupidity beggars description. You have declared that there is no God. Now I can prove to you that there *is* a God."

The scholar said, "Prove it, prove it! I do not think you will be successful."

The old man said, "Do you by any chance have a son?"

The scholar said, "Yes, I have three sons."

The old man continued, "Now suppose one of your sons speaks ill of you and insults you mercilessly in public, and another son is very kind to you, very devoted to you and full of love for you. He is so disappointed and disgusted that his brother is mis- behaving so badly. What if that good son brings you a gun and asks you to shoot his brother? Will you do it?"

The scholar said, "Shoot my own son? No matter how bad he may be, he is my son. He has the authority to speak ill of me. After all, he is my son, so who will take him seriously? If he speaks ill of me, even if he denies our connection, I will always be for him, and when I die, I will leave a great deal of money for him just because he is my son."

The old man said, "Do you not know that we are all God's children? Now you are speaking ill of God in an attempt to prove that there is no God. Poor God! He has so much compassion for you, for all His children. If He wants to kill you, He can do so in the twinkling of an eye. He does not need a gun. You, as an ordinary human being, have so much affection and compassion for your son. You would not kill him even if he spoke ill of you and insulted you in public. Here also, how can God kill you? God has so much love for you. There are so many people in this hall who will be eager to give God a gun at this moment to kill you, but God will never be able to kill you because of His love for you. God's Love for us is infinitely greater than a father's love for his son."

Immediately the great scholar started shedding tears. He withdrew from his pocket a large amount of money. He said, "I am going from one person to another. I am distributing all my money. How could I say that God does not exist? Forgive me. Take this money."

He gave all the money that he had with him and then he cried and cried in front of the audience. He said, "I beg all of you, please forgive me. I will never, never speak ill of God again. God *does* exist. I am a father. I know how much affection I have for my son. God's affection for me is infinitely greater than my affection for my son, so all of you have to forgive me."

### LTS 148. *The doctor rushes to cure the zamindar*

There was a village doctor who was very, very well known. He was extremely kind-hearted and compassionate. Again, he was very proud of his medical capacities. One day he was preparing to go to the town. He had to settle something with regard to his son's marriage, and he was in a terrible rush. As he was about to leave, a servant of the village zamindar came to him and said, "Doctor, doctor, my master is very ill. He is suffering so much. Please come and cure him."

The doctor thought, "Now what am I going to do? I have to go there."

The zamindar's house was quite far. If he went by ferry, it would take a shorter time than if he walked. The doctor hastened to the bank of the tiny river and asked the ferryman to take him. The ferryman saw that the doctor was in a great hurry, so this clever fellow said, "I am not in the mood to ply my boat today."

The doctor said, "What? The zamindar is sick. It is a matter of life and death."

The ferryman clasped his stomach and said, "I am not feeling well, I am not feeling well."

The doctor said, "What if I give you double the usual amount?"

"Oh, no," said the ferryman, "I am not at all inclined to go."

Finally the doctor threw down ten times the usual fare and said to the ferryman, "Take this and behave well. Otherwise, if you do not take me, I am going to tell the village zamindar how bad you are. Then he will take care of you in his own way."

The ferryman took the money and ferried the doctor across the river. Upon reaching the shore, the doctor went running to the zamindar's house and started giving him all kinds of medicine. People soon came to learn that the doctor had given the ferryman ten times more than usual, and they began speaking very highly of him. They were deeply impressed by how much he loved the zamindar. They said that they would punish the ferryman for being such a bad fellow. This message somehow reached the ears of the doctor's new daughter-in-law.

The daughter-in-law came to the doctor and said, "I did not know how great you are, how good you are! Everybody is speaking so highly of you. I am so happy that my father-in-law is such a kind-hearted man. You went to cure the village zamindar and paid so much money to the ferryman to take you there."

The doctor said, "You fool! You do not know the whole story. Already twice this year the zamindar has been very, very sick. He was literally on the point of death. Who cured him on those occasions? Nature. When I went there, nature had already done her job and he was improving. Two times this happened. So this time I rushed to his place because I wanted to get the credit for being a great doctor. I knew that if I could cure him, then I would have thousands of patients because the news would spread far and wide that I cured our village zamindar. That is why I rushed to his bedside."

The daughter-in-law asked, "But you did not do it because of your compassionate heart?"

The doctor said, "I do have a heart of compassion for the sick. That is why I am a doctor. But at the same time, I am wise. I knew that if I could get the credit for curing him, then I would increase my business. How I hate Nature! Twice before when he was sick, Nature cured him. I could not play my role. But this time I arrived before Nature could step in. It was I who cured him. And the reward will be that from now on I will have so many patients."

The doctor was right. When the news spread that he had cured the village zamindar, he gained many more patients.

### LTS 149. *The admirer changes the court poet's nature*

There was a great poet who was attached to a particular court. The king admired this poet tremendously, but unfortunately, the poet had a disagreeable nature. He was not at all amicable. He would not talk with others or mix with them. Everyone thought he was very rude and indifferent. They did not realise that he was extremely shy. Whenever the king requested him to read out his poems, he did so, and his poems were simply excellent. That is why the king was very, very pleased with him. But with regard to his nature, nobody was able to appreciate him, and they begged the king to replace him.

This court poet had a great admirer of his poetry who happened to work at the palace. This admirer felt sad and miserable that people were speaking ill of the poet. He felt that he had to do something for him. He said, "I have to change his nature by begging and begging him to be more friendly and sociable."

The court poet spent his days at the palace, and at night he would return home. One evening, when the poet's palace duties were over, this particular admirer went to his house. The poet's wife said, "My husband is not here. He has gone out. I have no idea when he is going to come back." She was only protecting her husband. He was actually there in the house.

On the second evening, the admirer came again and said, "Just for a few minutes I would like to speak to your husband."

The poet's wife said, "My husband is doing something very, very important, and he says he will not be able to see you."

Again, on the third evening, the admirer knocked on the poet's door. This time the poet himself came out and started insulting him. He said, "Why do you have to come and bother me? You see me at the palace. Why do you have to come here? I come here for peace. It is my home. Leave this place immediately. If you do not go away from my door, tomorrow I will make complaints to the king against you. I will tell him that you are bothering me unnecessarily. This is the third night that you have come here. I do not want to have anything to do with you." The great poet was extremely rude to this young man, who was his sincere admirer. Then he went inside the house and slammed the door.

The poor admirer felt miserable. He said, "Here I am desperately trying to change his nature so that everybody in the palace will grow to love him, and he is only scolding me and insulting me. What shall I do now? Perhaps people are right when they speak ill of him. He seems to be really a bad man. But I must change his nature. How can I do it?"

One day this young admirer went to another city and made arrangements to read out poems. The people in that particular city did not know what the famous court poet looked like. The young man stayed in a hotel, and when he registered, he wrote down the poet's name. Everybody was so excited to learn that the greatest poet had come to their city. Word spread like wildfire!

It happened that at the same time, the court poet received an urgent message that his brother had passed away. This brother happened to live in that particular city where the false poet was supposed to give his poetry reading. So the court poet went to that city. On the way, he said to himself, "It is getting dark. Why bother my family members at this hour? Tomorrow morning I shall see them. Now let me take a room in the hotel."

He went to the same hotel and wanted to register in his own name. The people at the desk started laughing at him. They said, "There is no vacancy. You can stay outside."

He said, "Do you know who I am? I am the court poet. Every day I go to the king's palace. Tomorrow I will make complaints against your hotel. The king himself will hear of it!"

They said, "Go and make complaints! You are such a rogue. There is no room for you here. You can sleep outside on the veranda. We can give you a pillow. You say you are the greatest poet. You are such a liar!"

He said, "I am a liar?"

"Yes, you are a liar," they said.

The court poet was outraged. He said, "How do you dare to call me a liar? I am the greatest poet in the kingdom."

They said, "Already the greatest poet is here in our city, and you are stealing his name. Tonight he will give a poetry reading. He is staying at this hotel, so you cannot fool us." They were about to beat up the famous poet.

The poet was curious to know the truth of the matter, so he said, "Please, please forgive me. I want to see the real poet."

They brought his admirer and the court poet said, "What are you doing here?"

The young man said, "I am going to do something here that will help you."

The court poet said, "What are you going to do? Why have you used my name?"

The young man said, "Tonight many people will flock to hear your poems. I will read them out to the best of my ability. Most of the people do not know what you look like, so they will think that I am the creator. Then afterwards I will give each member of the audience something nice to eat for taking the trouble of coming here to listen to your poetry. I will mix with everyone. I will be as kind, compassionate and affectionate to them as possible."

The court poet said, "What are you doing this for?"

The young man said, "Then the news will spread all around that you have changed your nature, that you are no longer the same rude, callous and indifferent person. I love you so much. I admire you, and I want others to do the same. I want the whole country to know that you are not a bad person. You are a very good person, but you keep your good qualities hidden."

Then the real poet started shedding tears. He embraced his admirer and said, "You have changed my life. From tomorrow on, I shall become as kind as possible to whomever I meet. I will always be kind to my dear ones, my friends and admirers. I will transform my outer nature."

### LTS 150. *The king chooses the strongest man*

Once a king wanted to have the strongest man in the kingdom work for him. The prime minister said, "There are three very strong men. Which one is the strongest, I cannot say."

All the three were commanded by the prime minister to present themselves before the king. The prime minister said, "It seems that they are equally strong. Some will say the first one is the strongest, some will say the second one, and some will say the third one. O King, please decide who is the strongest."

The king said to the three men, "My guards will take each of you to a different place in the desert. The distance from each place to the palace will be the same. You will be taken there by cart, and you have to return on foot. You have to prove that you are strong. To the one who reaches the palace first I will give three hundred rupees. The second one will receive two hundred rupees, and the last one will receive one hundred rupees. Now you go."

The first strong man said, "If I have to go there, please give me shoes. I will be walking on scorching sand, so I need shoes. Will you not give me a pair of shoes?"

The king was surprised by this man's audacity. "All right," he said, "I shall supply you with shoes."

Then the second one said, "Please, please, allow me to take your son, the prince, with me. If your son goes with me, I am sure you will send me to a place that is a shorter distance from here. You will not want him to endure a gruelling ordeal."

Everybody started laughing. One wanted to have a pair of shoes so that he could walk on the sand. The other one wanted the prince to accompany him so that he would not have to walk as far.

The king was a little bit amused. He said to the third one, "Now what do you want? Do you need something special? Or are you ready to leave?"

The third strong man said, "I am not ready because I am not going."

The king asked, "Why?"

The fellow replied, "It is not worth three hundred rupees to risk my life in the desert. Let one of the other two be the winner. I will not mind. O King, I do not need your three hundred rupees. I know you will take me far away. If I have to walk fast in the blazing heat, I will collapse. It is not worth the money. I am not going."

The king was puzzled. He had never encountered this kind of disobedience. He had so many soldiers. Easily he could order them to kill these men.

Then the king said to the prime minister, "What kind of men have you brought? They are so haughty! I am only trying to decide how to punish them."

The prime minister said, "Did I know their characters? You asked me to bring you the strongest man in the kingdom, and I was doubtful who was actually the strongest. People said that these three were very, very strong, so I brought all of them. But did I know that they would be so arrogant? Please forgive me, O King. I did not know they would be so bad!"

The king said, "I have been thinking over the matter. I have misjudged them. It is not arrogance that they are demonstrating, but something else. I need this kind of spirited man. I want this kind of independence."

Then the king awarded the first prize of three hundred rupees to the one who refused to go. The second prize of two hundred rupees he gave to the one who said he needed shoes. And the third prize of one hundred rupees he presented to the one who wanted the prince to accompany him.

### LTS 151. *The prince chooses the prime minister*

Once a particular king suddenly fell sick. Every day his ailment was getting worse and the doctors were quite alarmed. The prime minister advised the king, "Since you cannot attend to the matters of state, in your absence, let your eldest son rule the country."

The king agreed to the prime minister's proposal. He realised that his condition was deteriorating. Then, to everybody's wide surprise, after about four months, the king suddenly started getting better. In the meantime, the king had been asking for reports about how his son was coping with his responsibilities, and he had heard that his son was doing very, very well. Everyone said the prince was very kind to people and very just. All the citizens were highly appreciating the prince, so the king was very happy and proud of his son.

Then a calamity struck. The prime minister suddenly fell sick, and in two or three days' time he passed away. The king was very, very sad to lose his trusted adviser. Because he had been told that his son was so good, so wise and so kind-hearted, he asked his son to choose a new prime minister. The son brought three men to the court and begged his father to choose between them.

The king said, "No, I asked you to make the selection. You examine them in your own way and tell me which one I should take as the prime minister. I will abide by your decision."

The prince asked the first man, "What is five multiplied by two?"

The first man said, "That is easy. Five multiplied by two is ten."

The prince asked the second one, "What is five multiplied by two?"

The second one also answered, "Ten."

To the third one he said, "Now tell me your answer. Everybody is saying ten. Do you agree?"

The third one said, "Five multiplied by two is seven."

Everybody started laughing, but the prince was delighted with this new answer.

He said, "We all know that five multiplied by two is ten. But here we are getting something new, a new discovery. We must go forward with new discoveries. Why should we follow the old pattern and always say that five multiplied by two is ten. This is a new discovery. Five multiplied by two has now become seven."

"O my son," lamented the king. "What are you doing? How will I show my face?"

The prince said, "No, father, I like this man. And I tell you something else. Our previous prime minister was very weak in mathematics."

The king asked, "How do you know?"

The prince replied, "I examined him while I was ruling the country in your absence, and I found that he was extremely weak in mathematics, although he was good in other things, such as politics and literature."

The king said, "You liar! I dealt with him so many times over the years, and I know that he was excellent in mathematics. You are telling lies. You are ruining his good name."

The son said, "No, no, no! I tell you, Father, he was not at all good in mathematics." Then the son added, "I feel that his soul will be very happy if you appoint someone like him who is inferior in mathematics."

The king said, "I know he was good in mathematics. I dealt with him on financial matters so many times."

The king and the prince were having a serious altercation. People were so shocked that the king could not make the decision himself. He was still depending on his son. Finally the king became angry with his son. He said, "Now I know the truth. Everybody told me that you ruled the kingdom in my absence, but now I see that it was actually the prime minister who did it. He was so wise and kind- hearted. He advised you on each and every matter, and you merely listened to him. That is why our kingdom was ruled so well. It was the prime minister who did it."

The prince said, "No! The prime minister was an idiot!"

The king said, "I asked you to rule in my place when I fell sick. Before that, how many hundreds of times I dealt with the prime minister."

The son said, "You do not know, Father, but I am telling the truth."

Finally the king said, "All right, let us put an end to the matter. Although I know I am dealing with an incorrigible fool, I have to please you because you are my son. By pleasing you, at least I will get some joy, although your choice of prime minister is absurd. To make you happy, I am appointing this half-wit as prime minister."

Everybody cried out, "O King, what kind of justice is this? You are making someone prime minister who believes that five multiplied by two is seven? What will be the fate of our kingdom if you appoint a fool like this as your prime minister?"

The king said, "No, I want to make my son happy. Afterwards I will appoint someone to teach the prime minister arithmetic."

Then the king said to the new prime minister, "Tell me the truth. Do you truly believe that five multiplied by two is seven, or did you in fact know that five multiplied by two is ten?"

The new prime minister said, "I knew that five multiplied by two is ten, but I wanted to say something new. The other two candidates both said ten, so I said to myself, 'Why do I need to say the same thing?' Of course I knew my answer was wrong. But I want to be independent of others' ways."

The king asked, "Did you go to school or college? Can you bring me the certificates?"

The new prime minister went home and returned with certificates showing that he had a very high education. He was extremely well qualified for the post.

Then the king said, "To make my son happy, I had to become stupid and surrender to his absurd choice. Now I see that my son unconsciously chose the right person. To justify his choice, he told some lies about my previous prime minister, but I see now that he was so wise. This new prime minister will be such an asset to our kingdom. I wholeheartedly approve of my son's choice."

LTS 152. *The hermit's occult power*

There was a hermit who was spiritual to the extreme. He was spirituality incarnate in his own way. Eventually even the prince came to hear about this hermit. One day the prince came to the hermit's cottage and said, "Would you kindly teach me about spiritual matters?"

The hermit said, "You are a prince. You will only argue with me. Because your father is the king, I am sure you are not accustomed to obeying others. I am a humble man. You will only create problems for me."

The prince said, "No, I will not create any problems for you. I have come here with utmost sincerity to learn from you."

The hermit said, "All right. I shall teach you." Then the hermit said, "Do you know that I have tremendous occult power?"

The prince said, "I have not yet started my spiritual journey and you want me to have occult power? Today for the first time I have come to you to learn. I do not even know the alphabet and you want to give me the M.A. course? How am I going to understand it?"

The hermit said, "Oh no, it is quite possible. I can give you all kinds of occult power — I have that capacity. Do you want to hear what kind of occult power I have?"

The prince said, "If you want me to hear about these things, I will listen. But I feel it is only delaying my journey. I have to learn the first steps. You have to teach me how to pray and then how to meditate. I have to repeat God's Name. I have heard that these are the first things one must learn if one wants to enter into the spiritual life."

"Have you come to learn from me, or do I have to learn from you?" asked the hermit.

Then the prince felt sorry. He was afraid he had offended the hermit. He said, "All right, if you can give me the advanced lesson in one day, I have no objection. I will try to learn from you. Forgive me, forgive me. I do not want to argue with you any more. I have come to you with utmost humility, admiration and love."

The hermit said, "I am very, very pleased with your humility. Now let me tell you what kind of occult power I have."

The prince remained absolutely silent. He wanted to behave well. He did not want to argue with his master any more.

The hermit continued, "I can remain under the ground for five hours! Then I can emerge, and you will see that I am in perfect condition."

The prince showed tremendous astonishment.

The hermit went on, "Come closer! I shall tell you a secret."

The prince moved closer. The hermit whispered, "I can remain underwater for ten hours or even more!"

Once again the prince showed that he was absolutely astonished.

Then the hermit breathed, "Come still closer! This time I shall tell you something very confidential."

The prince moved closer than the closest to the hermit and the hermit softly said, "I can fly in the sky!"

At this, the prince could tolerate no more. He cried, "What am I doing here? I thought that you were a most spiritual person, a jewel of renunciation. But you are a mere miracle-monger!"

The hermit became absolutely furious. He said, "I knew that I could expect this kind of behaviour from you. That is why I was unwilling to accept you as a disciple. I refuse to teach you!"

The prince said, "All right. You will not teach me. Please forgive me for taking your precious time. Before I leave, I would like to give you a few lessons."

Now the hermit became really annoyed. He said, "I have to learn from you?"

"From me," said the prince.

"How arrogant you are!" said the hermit. "Tell me what kind of lessons I have to learn from a prince."

The prince saw a worm on the ground nearby. He dug a hole and placed the worm in the ground. Then he covered the hole with earth and said to the hermit, "You can stay underground only for five hours, but this worm can live for years under the ground!"

Then he said, "You can stay underwater for ten hours, but fish remain in the water all their lives."

Then the prince looked up at a bird in the sky and said, "See how the bird is flying! You say that you have mastered the art of flying, but for birds, flying is quite natural. Why should we pray to God to do what a worm, a fish and a bird can easily do? That is going backwards in terms of evolution. Our goal should always be ahead of us."

The hermit screamed, "I knew it, I knew it! You did not come here to learn. You are such a rogue! Go back to your palace. Only people who are very, very sincere will be allowed to come and learn from me."

The prince bowed and said, "How I am praying to God to send you a few really sincere students!"

### LTS 153. *The Kashmiri shawl*

A merchant made a trip to Kashmir. This merchant dealt in Kashmiri shawls. Among other purchases, he bought a very costly embroidered shawl and he took it home to Calcutta. When he told his wife the cost of the shawl, she said, "It is so expensive! Who will buy it? You have to make some profit."

The wife's brother also happened to be present. He said, "What have you done? You have wasted so much money! Now who is going to buy this shawl from you? I thought you were a smart merchant, but this extravagance proves otherwise."

Then the merchant interrupted him. "Enough, enough!" he said. "You are an idiot, and your sister is another idiot. I am in between two idiots."

His wife said, "Soon it will be proved who is the real idiot."

Her brother chimed in, "It is not difficult to see who is the real fool in the family!"

Then the merchant said to his brother-in-law, "Look here, you just have to do what I tell you to do. Then you will see that I have made a sound investment."

The brother-in-law said, "Anything that you want me to do, I will do, but I am absolutely sure that you are not going to get the price that you have paid for that shawl."

The merchant said, "All right, listen to me." Then he whispered something to the brother-in-law.

A few moments later the village jeweller was passing by the house. The jeweller was quite rich but, as usual, he was very stingy. The merchant called out to him, "Please, please come here."

The jeweller said, "I have no time now to come in. You know that I am not interested in your wares."

The merchant begged, "Please step inside just for a moment. I want to show you a very beautiful shawl."

The jeweller said, "I have no time for this kind of nonsense. I have to open my shop and start my business for the day. Do not bother me."

The merchant said, "I promise I will not bother you any more if you just come in for a moment."

The jeweller reluctantly agreed. "All right, all right," he said. "What bad luck I am having today just because I have seen you!"

Very carefully the merchant unwrapped the shawl and showed it to the jeweller. The jeweller said, "What is this? Why do I need a shawl? You know that I am very strict with my money. I do not waste it on luxury items."

The merchant said, "I know that, but this is such a beautiful thing."

"No, I do not want it," repeated the jeweller.

Then the clever merchant placed the shawl around the jeweller's shoulders and said, "Oh, you look so beautiful! Please, please do me a favour. You do not have to pay a single rupee. Wherever you want to go today, please go wearing this shawl, and then at the end of the day kindly bring it back. Or tomorrow I can even go to your shop and collect it from you. I will not charge you anything. I promise. You do not have to give me anything. It is unconditional."

The jeweller had been looking at himself in the mirror, and he could see that he looked quite smart. "All right," he said, pretending to be indifferent. "I will wear it."

"On your way home tonight you can give it to me," said the merchant. "Or the best thing will be for me to come to your shop and collect it. Why do you have to bother to come to my place again?"

So the jeweller continued on his way to his own shop wearing the shawl. He had covered only fifty metres when the brother-in-law suddenly came from another direction and knelt down before the jeweller. The jeweller said, "What are you doing?"

The brother-in-law said, "What am I doing? How fortunate I am today to meet you, Prime Minister! Are you coming from the palace?"

The jeweller said, "You do not know me?"

The brother-in-law said, "I do know you, Prime Minister, and I have heard so much about you."

"What makes you think I am the prime minister?" asked the jeweller.

The brother-in-law said, "Only the prime minister could have such an expensive shawl. Nobody else would dare to buy something so gorgeous, and I must say, it looks so beautiful on you!"

"I am not the prime minister," said the jeweller. "I am only a jeweller!"

"No, no, only a prime minister could buy this kind of shawl," cried the brother-in-law. "It would not look beautiful on any other human being. For some reason of your own, you are not revealing your true identity." Then the brother-in-law bowed to the jeweller most humbly and went on his way.

The jeweller immediately retraced his steps to the merchant's shop and said, "Tell me, how much are you asking for this shawl?"

The merchant named a price which was much higher than the price he had paid for it.

"Oh, that is nothing!" exclaimed the jeweller. Immediately he brought out the full amount from his pocket and gave it to the merchant. The merchant's flattery had worked so well that the jeweller was ready to give the merchant whatever price he wanted. Then the jeweller continued on his way, proudly wearing the shawl. Meanwhile, the merchant went to his wife and brother-in-law and said, "See! Now who are the real fools in the family?"

### LTS 154. *Talking too much, talking too little*

A husband and wife were like North Pole and South Pole. The husband talked too much and the wife talked too little. The husband was a kindhearted man, but he would always talk and talk. Friends would say, "Enough, enough! Do not talk any more. We cannot hear ourselves think!" But the husband could not curb his garrulous tongue.

One day his wife received an invitation. Her class friend was getting married and wanted her to attend the wedding.

The wife said to her husband, "My friend has invited me to her wedding."

Her husband said, "It is such an important thing in life to have a friend! How many people are fortunate enough to say that they have good friends? She is a good friend of yours, and we all need friends to exist on earth. God is our real Friend, but He cannot come all the time, so He sends a friend to us here on earth to help us live very happily." Then he went on giving a long-winded lecture on friendship.

The wife became more and more impatient. Eventually she said, "Now, stop, stop! Enough of your sermon!"

The husband really loved his wife, and he did not like to upset her. He said, "You should go. Here is a most expensive necklace. I bought it for you a day or two ago, but I forgot to give it to you. And here is an envelope with quite a large sum of spending money. You go and enjoy yourself at your friend's wedding."

The day of the wedding arrived and the wife went to the church. All her former classmates were so excited to see her, but she had taken a vow that she would be a woman of few words. Friends with whom she studied in school were shocked. Why would she say only very few words? She seemed almost indifferent to her friends. Everybody else was chatting, reminiscing about their previous school life, this and that, but she said next to nothing. They were all in the seventh Heaven of delight, but she was not.

Her friends suspected that something had gone wrong between the husband and wife. So they started criticising her husband. They told her how bad he was in so many ways, whereas she was so nice. Even then she was not happy.

In the evening, when the wedding was over, the wife wanted to return home. She saw that two of her friends who had studied with her at school were going home and they had their horse and carriage. But she did not want to ask them to give her a lift, and they did not want to take her. Since she had misbehaved, they did not want to do her a favour. They felt she had too much pride, so they drove away.

Then the wife saw that other wedding guests were going by in their vehicles. Alas, nobody wanted to help her. She was expecting someone to stop and take her home, but they all abandoned her to her fate. Finally the wife saw a taxi. She asked the driver, "Can you take me?" and she told him the address. The driver said, "I do not feel like going there. I am going in another direction."

"I will give you four times the regular fare," said the wife with tears in her eyes.

"All right," said the driver. She entered into the car and they went on their way. Before they had travelled even half the distance, the driver stopped the car and said, "Get out! Get out! I do not trust you. You are not talking."

The poor wife climbed out of the car. Then the driver said, "That is not enough. Give me all your money!"

She said, "My money?" Fearfully she produced her envelope and the driver took away all the money. Then he tried to grab her necklace and she began to struggle a little. At this moment, quite unexpectedly, another car approached from behind, so the taxi driver jumped in the taxi and drove away at top speed. The wife's necklace had fallen on the ground and it was broken. Her money she had lost. She was completely helpless. "Please, please help me!" she screamed to the second car, but the driver did not pay any attention. He went away. The poor wife was now stranded. She was compelled to walk all the way home. She arrived home in such a miserable condition. Her husband was also very miserable to hear what had happened to his wife. He was full of remorse. He said, "It is all my fault, my fault!"

"How can it be your fault?" asked his wife.

"It is my fault because I gave you so much money," he said. "And I gave you that gold necklace and encouraged you to go to your friend's wedding. It is all my fault, absolutely my fault. Please forgive me. In the future I will not advise you to do this kind of thing."

The wife said, "It is not your fault."

This unhappy couple had an old maidservant. She knew all about their marital problems. At this point in the conversation she coughed a little and said, "Please forgive me. You two are very well educated, whereas I am illiterate; I did not go to school. But may I give you some advice?"

The husband said, "Yes, you are like one of the family. What advice can you give us?"

She said, "Both of you have to change your nature. The one that does not speak at all has to speak more, and the one that speaks too much has to speak less. There should be moderation in every aspect of life. Speak whatever is necessary, but do not go beyond the limit." She turned to the wife and went on, "Your husband talks too much. That is why you took this oath to be a woman of few words. To compensate for his big mouth, you speak next to nothing. That is not the right thing to do."

Then to the husband she said, "You will continue to speak, but there should be a limit to your talking. Do not go to the extreme. Because you went to one extreme, she went to another extreme, and this is what happened."

So the husband and wife received excellent advice from the old maidservant, and they started adjusting the amount of their talking.

### LTS 155. *Writing to God for money*

There was a poor villager who was absolutely in dire straits. He needed money desperately, but nobody would give him any money. They would not even loan him money, so he was miserable. One day he wrote a letter to God about his sad plight. He took the letter to the post office and mailed it. There was no address on the envelope. It had only one word: God.

The postmaster said, "What am I going to do with this letter?" So he took it to the prime minister. The prime minister said, "I am not God. I am not authorised to open up the letter. But something has to be done, since I am the prime minister."

Then he asked the king whether the letter should be opened up or not. The king said, "Yes, you must open it and see what is written there."

The prime minister was quite happy that with the king's permission he could open up the letter. The letter read, "I am a very poor man. Nobody is here to help me. Dear God, will You not give me twenty rupees?"

The king was highly amused and the prime minister was also amused by this innocent request. The king said to the prime minister, "Only twenty rupees? Just add one more zero and send it."

The poor villager had put his return address on the letter. So the prime minister put two hundred rupees inside an envelope and sent it to him.

The poor man was very, very happy to receive this blessing-gift from God, but he noticed the prime minister's return address was on the envelope. So he wrote another letter to God. This time he said, "Dear God, I am so grateful to You for the money. Whenever I need money, I will write to You, but please do not involve the government because I am sure they will take some commission."

## LTS 156. *The miser meets with defeat*

There was a very, very rich man. As you might have guessed, he was the worst possible miser. He had many, many workers, but he would pay them next to nothing. Sometimes he would not give them any wages, but what could they do? It was so difficult to get jobs. Everyone hated this miserly boss. They all had complaints against him.

One morning a new worker arrived to apply for a job. The miser said, "Yes, I will give you a job, but I want to warn you in advance that I only pay my workers' salary on a monthly basis. If you are expecting to receive money on a daily or weekly basis, this is not the place for you."

Giving only monthly payments was the miser's way of defrauding his workers of their salary. He would always find fault with them, and then he would not give them the full amount at the end of the month. If they were entitled to one hundred rupees a month, he would say, "You made such and such a mistake and for that I am deducting fifty rupees. I will give you only fifty rupees this month." What could these poor workers do? They had to accept this injustice. But they used to curse the boss and they did not want to work for him.

The miser said to the new worker, "If you work well, I will give you the full amount plus a bonus. But if you do not do a good job, then your fate will be like these people. Your salary will be reduced."

The new worker said, "No, I will do a very good job."

He worked very, very hard for the whole month, better than anybody else. But the rich man was such a bad fellow. He deliberately tried to find something that this poor worker would not be able to do so that he would not have to pay him his full salary for that month.

Then the rich man had a brilliant idea. He said, "I have one last job for you this month. So far you have proved to be an excellent worker. If you can do this job, then I will give you a bonus of one hundred rupees or even more. Here are two bottles: one is small, the other is much larger. I want you to put the larger one inside the smaller one."

The worker said, "Inside the smaller one? Oh, I can do that. It is very easy."

The rich man said, "Very easy? Then do it in front of so many witnesses."

The worker dashed the larger bottle against the ground and broke it into pieces. Then he collected the pieces and put them inside the smaller bottle.

The rich man was infuriated. "What are you doing?" he screamed.

The worker calmly said, "Did you not tell me to put the larger bottle inside the smaller one?"

The rich man said, "Yes, I did."

"You did not tell me that I was not allowed to break it," said the worker. "You asked me to put the larger one inside the smaller one, so I did it. I collected all the pieces and I put them inside."

The rich man said, "At long last, I have met with my defeat."

Then, in front of everyone, he gave the worker one hundred rupees plus another hundred rupees as a bonus.

Then the miser's true nature came forward. He said, "You may take this money, but in the future I will not be able to keep you as my worker. You are fired. If I employ you, then every month I will have to give you the full amount or even more. These other workers are idiots. If I give them some difficult job, they will not be able to do it. Then I will not have to give them the full salary."

## LTS 157. *The prime minister's secret letter to the king*

There was a king who had a very old and trusted prime minister. The time came when this prime minister said to the king, "O King, I have served you for many years. Now I am too old to perform my duties. I need a replacement."

The king said, "I am so sorry to hear that. I do not know what I shall do without you. Will you still remain near me?"

The prime minister said, "Yes, if you need my advice, I shall be here. But I am unable to carry out my other responsibilities. Please appoint somebody else."

The king said, "With greatest reluctance, I am agreeing to your request. But you will have to come on a regular basis to advise me."

The prime minister bowed to the king. Then the king said, "I am asking you to choose someone to replace you."

The prime minister said, "All right. I will devise some kind of test to narrow down the field. Then you will easily be able to choose the most suitable candidate."

The prime minister was searching for someone to replace him. He found two young men who were extremely qualified. He said to those young men, "Look here, I have chosen you two out of so many candidates who want to replace me. But I cannot tell you which one will get the post. Between you two, the king himself will choose. Both of you appear before him. I am giving you a piece of paper. It is a letter to the king that I wish you to deliver to him. Each one will carry it half the distance. When you arrive at the court, kindly present it to him. But do not open the letter because it is something very private and personal."

The first one to carry the letter walked for some distance. He was quite alone, since the other candidate had gone on ahead to their meeting place. Before he had completed half the distance, he was curious to know what the letter contained. He opened it and read, "Your Majesty, whoever hands this letter to you must be killed."

Then the fellow said, "Since I have the first half of the journey, I will not be the one to give the letter to the king, but the other fellow will be caught. After I cover half the distance, I will give him the letter. Let him give it to the king. At least I am not the one to be killed. The old prime minister is such a rogue. I do not need his job. I do not want to have anything to do with him. God alone knows what will happen to me if I become involved in this kind of thing." So he resealed the letter, and when he reached the halfway point, he handed it to the second candidate without saying a word.

The other candidate was very sincere, faithful and devoted. He did not open the letter because the prime minister had said not to open it. When he arrived at the court, the court jester was waiting for him. The young man asked, "Are you waiting for me by any chance?"

The court jester said, "Yes, the prime minister has sent a message to the king that a young man is coming to give him a letter. If you wish, I can give the letter to the king or, if you prefer, you can give it to him yourself."

The young man said, "The prime minister asked us to give the letter to the king personally. I do not know where the other candidate is, but I feel I should hand it to the king. I have to obey the prime minister."

The court jester said, "All right. Come and give it to the king yourself, since you are so obedient. Otherwise, I could easily give it to the king personally."

The court jester brought the young man to the king and the young man handed him the letter. The king opened up the letter and said, "The prime minister has written that you must be hanged!"

The young man said, "The prime minister told us to bring the letter and not to open it on the way. I am so stupid. Now I will be hanged!"

Then the king started laughing and laughing and laughing. He said, "My prime minister is so wise. You are the right person to replace him. You are so obedient. The other fellow has disappeared. I am sure he secretly read the letter. Now I am appointing you to be my new prime minister."

The court jester also started laughing. He said, "I am saved. Otherwise, if you had given me the letter, then I would have taken it to the king and the king would have killed me. I am so lucky!"

The king smiled at the court jester. Then he said to the young man, "I am so pleased with you. You deserve to be the prime minister. I am sure you will be as great and wise as my former prime minister."

### LTS 158. *The king's statue*

There was a king who was very good, but he had one fault. He always expected appreciation, admiration and gratitude from his citizens. He was very kind and generous, but appreciation was needed in return. The citizens genuinely liked their king, and so appreciation was forthcoming. They built a huge statue of the king, and the king was so pleased. Every day they garlanded the statue and placed offerings before it.

One season, there was a scarcity of water in the kingdom. The king was very charitable, and he sent a large quantity of water to the villagers. Even then, it was not enough to meet their needs, so they looked for water using a diviner. They found that there was only one place were water could be found, and that place was under the statue of the king. When they informed the king, he said, "Oh no, you are worshipping my statue. That is what I want. You should be so grateful to me. Every day I am sending you such a large quantity of water. There is no need to disturb the statue."

One day the king went to visit his statue. He was shocked to find that it had been utterly neglected. There were no flowers at all. Around it, only bushes were growing. Everything was dirty and filthy. The king said, "How ungrateful these people are! I have been sending them a regular water supply. Even if it is not enough to meet with their needs, should they not be grateful to me? Why should they neglect my statue so shamelessly?"

The prime minister said, "O King, you have to know that water is life. They value their life more than your statue. It is quite natural. You are kind to them, and they are grateful, genuinely grateful, but when it comes to life, is not their own life infinitely more valuable to them than your statue?"

The king said, "Your words are all true. Let them remove my statue from here, and take it to another location. Let there be a well here in its place."

The villagers were so happy. They moved the statue to another place where there was no water. Then they built a well and it yielded enough water to supply all the needs of the village.

When the king went to see his statue in its new location, he saw that it was garlanded and the villagers had made such a beautiful garden all around it! They were burning incense and they were worshipping the king. He was so pleased and proud.

When the king fulfilled the villagers' need for water, they became so grateful to him. They literally adored him, whereas when he would not allow them to draw the water beneath his statue, they allowed his statue to fall into disrepair.

## LTS 159. *The lucky watermelon seed*

There was a moneylender who was very, very rich, and at the same time, very, very bad. He was an old man, but he was unbearably bad. One day a poor man came to him to ask for a loan. He said to the moneylender, "I do not know whether I shall ever be able to return the money to you. I shall have to wait for a windfall. I will be grateful if you can give me a loan. I do hope that my circumstances will change and one day I will have money."

The moneylender said, "Do not worry, do not worry. God is with you. One day God will give you money, and then you will be able to repay me." Then the moneylender gave him the money that he had requested. The poor man was so grateful that the moneylender had agreed to the loan even though he was not expecting any money in the near future. He took the money and used it for his family needs.

After two months the moneylender came to the poor man's house and said, "Now, do you need more money?"

The poor man said, "I am so embarrassed. I do not know when I will be able to give you the money that I have already taken. How can I accept more from you?"

The moneylender said, "No, no, you need money, so take it. Pay me back whenever you can. Forget about interest, we will come to some other arrangement. The point is that you need money badly. You have a son, you have a daughter, you have a wife, so I feel sorry for you. I have been very undivine in money matters all my life. Now, in the evening of my life, I want to be kind and generous to people, so please take the money."

The poor man took more money, and he and his family were so grateful to the moneylender.

One night the moneylender came and started banging on the door of the poor man's house. He was screaming, "You rogue!

I have loaned you so much money and you have not repaid even one rupee. Now all the money you have to give me back. Otherwise, I shall sue you."

The poor man said, "The first time I went to your place of business to take money from you, but the second time you came here on your own to give the money to me. You said you wanted to be so kind. All your life you have been so unkind to people, charging them very high interest. Now you have loaned us the money interest-free, and we are so grateful to you."

The moneylender said, "No, I do not want to be exploited by you. You have to return all the money immediately. Here is a bill stating on which day I gave you how much money."

The poor man looked at the huge bill and said, "What am I going to do? I am totally lost."

The moneylender said, "There is one way you can avoid paying me if you do not have the money. I want to marry your daughter."

The poor man was horrified. He said, "You are an old man!"

The rich man said, "What is wrong with that? I will treat your daughter like a princess, like a queen."

The poor man's wife started crying. The son became furious. He shouted, "This is why you loaned us the money! All along you were planning to have my sister as your wife!"

The moneylender said, "I do not want to enter into a discussion. Either give me the money or give me your daughter."

The daughter started weeping bitterly. Then the old moneylender said, "All right. I have a solution. Let us cut open a watermelon and take out two seeds: one white seed and one black seed. We will place those two seeds inside a bag. Then your daughter will place her hand in the bag and take out one seed. If she draws the black one, she has to marry me, and you do not have to pay me anything. If she draws the white one, then she does not have to marry me, and you do not have to pay anything. I want to be generous. Do you agree?"

The mother was crying. If her daughter selected the black seed, then what would happen? She would have to marry this old man who was such a shrewd rogue. The daughter said, "I am ready to accept these conditions. Now my father is suffering so much. I know that no matter which seed I choose, my father will not have to repay the money. So the best thing is for me to sacrifice myself."

The old man said, "You know, I will die soon. Then you will get all my money and property."

The young girl was ready to pick out a seed from the bag. Quite a few people had gathered to watch. In front of everyone, the poor man put one black seed and one white seed into the bag. Then, all of a sudden, the moneylender said, "No, we need fresh air." He picked up the bag and went towards the door. On the way he cleverly removed the white seed and replaced it with another black seed. Now there were two black seeds inside the bag. When everyone had assembled outside in the street, the moneylender said, "Let us pray that whatever God wants to happen will happen."

The young girl said, "Yes, let us pray. I am ready to marry you if I get the black seed, because I do not want my father to suffer any more. You will only torture him and sue him."

The old moneylender said, "Yes, you choose. Let others stand aside."

The old moneylender was looking this side and that side because he was so confident that the young girl would draw out a black seed. He was so proud that he would soon have this beautiful girl as his wife.

Now, while they were cutting the watermelon, the young girl had secretly picked up a white seed and hidden it inside the palm of her hand. When she saw that she had drawn a black seed, she quickly threw it away and produced the white one. She held up the white seed and showed it to everybody. "Look, it is white," she declared with greatest joy. Everybody was so thrilled at her good luck. Now she did not have to marry the old moneylender, and her father did not have to repay the money.

The old moneylender became furious. He said, "How could it be? How could it be?"

He went home cursing himself: "This proves I am an old man. What have I done? I thought that I put two black seeds inside the bag. Instead of that, I put one white and one black. This is my insanity. I should have checked more carefully that I was putting in two black seeds. Now I have lost not only the young girl, but so much money as well!"

Meanwhile, the poor man and his wife were overjoyed that their daughter was so lucky. When she told them what she had done, they were so proud of her intelligence-cleverness.

# LIFE'S BLEEDING TEARS AND FLYING SMILES

## BOOK 12

## LTS 160. *The rich man's act of charity*

There was a very, very rich man who was stingy to the extreme. Although he was mean-spirited, he was a good talker. He made everybody feel that he was a very kind-hearted man. In his old age, this rogue passed away. He had not done a single good thing in his life, and no one mourned his passing. After he left the body, somehow this rogue found himself at Heaven's gate, not at hell's door. In the Christian world, Heaven's gatekeeper is St. Peter. The rich man was confident that St. Peter would allow him to pass through because he had performed an act of charity on earth.

St. Peter said to him, "How is it possible that you are here? You are such a bad person! I can see you have not done anything good on earth. How do you dare to come here?"

The rich man said, "I am a bad person?"

St. Peter said, "Yes! Tell me, have you done anything good in your lifetime?"

The rich man said, "I have definitely done good things."

St. Peter said, "Just give me an example."

The rich man said, "One day I was walking along the street and I saw a very old lady. She was very, very poor, so I gave her a coin. That is charity, is it not?"

St. Peter said, "I cannot believe you. You are making this story up. You are a horrible person. I am sure you have not done anything good."

Then St. Peter sent an angel to look for the old lady in the realms of Heaven. The angel brought the old lady, and she said to St. Peter, "Yes, what this man is saying is true. I was about to cross the street and he gave me a coin. Unfortunately, just after he gave me the coin, I met with an accident, and I died."

St. Peter asked, "Where is the coin now?"

The old lady said, "I still have the coin with me." She brought out her coin and showed it to St. Peter. It was a small, worthless coin, absolutely old, dusty and disfigured.

St. Peter said, "This is your act of charity?" He was furious with the rich man.

The old lady said, "Do not be angry with him. He tried to help me. He gave me money, but I met with an accident while crossing the street, so I died. I know he is a good man."

Now St. Peter became really furious. He said to the old lady, "You are such a fool! Can you not see that he has tricked you? Nobody would have accepted this coin from you because it is so disfigured!"

To the rich man, he said, "Go to hell!" For one minute the rich man had been able to stay at Heaven's gate because he said he had performed an act of charity. Then St. Peter sent him to hell.

The rich man said, "What is this? You are sending me to hell without my money? If you want me to go to hell, then give me my money back. Why should I go without my money?"

St. Peter threw the coin at him, and the rich man picked it up and went to hell.

### LTS 161. *God smashes the learned man's pride*

There was a very, very saintly priest whom everybody was extremely fond of. A young aspirant came to the priest's hermitage and expressed his desire to practise spirituality. The priest said, "No, no, you are too young. I do not want to have you as my student."

The young boy said, "It is true that I am young, but if I start at this early age, then in the course of time I will become very, very spiritual."

The priest said, "I admire your philosophy. I accept you as my student, and I am blessing you so that you will become very spiritual." Then the priest started giving the boy lessons.

By the time the boy had grown up, he had learned the sacred scriptures, and he had read many religious books under the guidance of his guru. People came to know that this great scholar was well versed in the Upanishads, the Vedas and many other texts. His guru had taught him, but the young scholar reaped all the glory. His reputation even reached the ears of the king.

One day the king summoned this young scholar to his court. The scholar said, "No, I am not going to see him. He should be my devotee."

His guru said, "What are you saying?"

The young scholar said, "I do not need the king. If he needs me, then he should come here. He wants to receive some knowledge from me. Such being the case, why should I go to him? He has to come to me."

The guru was almost speechless with shock. At last he said, "The king is calling you. Do not ignore him. Knowledge means humility. I beg you to go to him."

The young scholar said, "No, no. It is the other way around. Whoever is hungry for knowledge has to come to the knowledge-giver. The king is hungry for knowledge, so he has to come here."

The guru burst out, "I am sick of you! Is this what I taught you? I am going away alone. You stay here. You can take care of my hermitage, or you can go home, whatever you want to do. The king is so kind. Everybody loves him. Now he wants to know something about religious matters. You should go to him. If the king had asked me, I would have gone. I taught you everything because I did not care for name and fame. But you do care for name and fame. That is why you are so proud and haughty. You should go to him, but you are not going. I can no longer stay here. I am going out on a pilgrimage." The guru took his walking stick and sadly left.

A few days later the young scholar was studying his books when he saw an elderly couple approaching. They were accompanied by a beautiful young girl. The elderly couple said to him, "Our daughter wants to study the Vedas and the Upanishads. You are known as a deeply spiritual person. Do you have any students who learn from you the way you learned from your guru? We are certain that your spiritual disciplines will not allow you to teach our daughter by herself. She is a girl, after all."

The young scholar said, "I am above all that. For me it does not matter whether it is a girl or a boy. It will not affect my spiritual height. If your daughter wants to study with me, I can teach her."

The elderly couple said, "But you are a saintly person. Are you sure that it is acceptable for you to teach our daughter?"

The young scholar said, "Oh yes. In fact, I will teach her for nothing. You do not have to pay any sacerdotal fee."

The elderly couple bade their daughter farewell and the scholar started teaching her. The inevitable happened. In two weeks the scholar had fallen in love with the girl. The parents were shocked. They suspected something of this type would happen. Again, they had such admiration for the young scholar that they trusted him. Soon they came to learn that their daughter was also in love with him. In a short time the scholar and the beautiful girl were married. Everything had gone wrong.

In the course of time, the young couple had a child. Previously, the scholar had had a few other students whom he taught, but now nobody came to him because he had fallen. A friend of his came to him and said, "You cannot support your family on your meagre earnings. Now you have a son to think of. Why not go to the king and give him your knowledge?"

The scholar went to the king and said, "Some time ago, you asked me to come and teach you the sacred scriptures. Now I am in such serious financial difficulty. Will you hire me?"

The king said, "Yes, I am eager to learn. How often do you want to come?"

The scholar said, "I will come once a month and reveal to you the wisdom of the Vedas, the Upanishads and other scriptures."

The next year the young couple had another son. The amount of money the scholar was receiving from the king was not enough. He said to the king, "May I come twice a month so that I may receive double the amount from you? Because of my second son, I need more money to meet with all my expenses." Alas, the king agreed to this new arrangement.

A year later the couple had another child. Once more the scholar went to the king. This time he asked, "May I come weekly so that I can receive extra money from you?"

As time went by, he had even more children, so he was obliged to go every day to the king's palace in order to support his family.

After many years, his old guru returned from his pilgrimage and he saw that his hermitage was overrun with children. He said, "What has happened? This was such a spiritual place! Now it is full of chaos. This is what you have done in my absence? Get out, get out, get out!"

The scholar said, "No, we shall not get out. This was your place, and you left it in our hands. We have made it beautiful. We have furnished it and added extra rooms. So you get out!"

The old guru said, "This is my fate. I did not want to teach you when you came to me as a young boy. I said, 'No, no, I do not want to teach somebody so young. You have no experience of the world.' But you begged me and begged me, so I surrendered. Now this is the result. I implored you to go to the king, but you did not go. At that time your pride did not allow you to go to him. But God will always find a way to smash our pride. Once upon a time it was beneath your dignity to go to the king. Now you are going like a beggar every day. You go there so you can support your family."

The scholar and his wife refused to give the guru back his hermitage. He said, "Do I need these outer things? You need a wife, you need children, you need everything. I need only God. Once again I am leaving this place. I shall be a religious mendicant and wander to and fro. I shall depend on alms for my physical existence. Whatever people give me, I will eat, and I will sleep under the trees. I will spend the rest of my life as I started — only thinking of God and praying to God."

### LTS 162. *The mysterious golden roses*

An old couple had a beautiful garden. At one particular place they planted a rose bush. This rose bush used to produce golden roses. The old couple used to work very, very hard in their garden and people used to deeply admire their golden roses.

One day the eldest son of the village chief was galloping by. From his horse, he saw the golden roses. He could not believe his eyes. So he reached down from his horse and grabbed a few roses. When he grabbed the roses, the whole bush came out of the ground. He did not know how it could have happened. Then suddenly the rose bush left his hands; he could not hold it. It was beyond belief. Since he could not account for it, the son of the village chief turned his horse around and again came back to the vicinity of the rose bush. When he came back, he saw the same bush with all its golden roses. Once more he grabbed some roses from the bush. Then he turned around only to see that there was no rose bush in the ground.

He felt compelled to solve this mystery. He went home and this time he brought his servants to destroy that particular plot of land. He said, "Some villagers are making fun of me."

So he destroyed the whole plot of land. The bush and everything else was gone, completely gone. Then the son of the village chief was very, very happy. He went home and began bragging about this incident. He told his friends of the mysterious experience he had had, which he was certain would not be repeated. His father was also surprised to hear this story. His father asked his friends for an explanation, but they could not give any proper answer. So once again this young man returned to the place. This time he brought his relatives and friends in order to show them the plot of land that he had completely destroyed.

Alas! When he arrived at the place, he saw the garden and the rose bush with its golden roses growing in the same position as before. How could it happen? The son of the village chief was so sad and depressed. He could not show off to his friends that he had destroyed this place.

As he was returning home, he met with an old woman. He said to her, "You are old, very old. You are supposed to have wisdom. Can you tell me why this has happened? I destroyed that plot of land. How is it that again there is a rose bush growing there with golden roses?"

The old lady said, "I cannot answer this question, but I know someone who will be able to answer it."

"Who is that?" asked the son of the village chief.

The old woman said, "I know of a dwarf who is really wise. I am no match for him. He will tell you the real reason why it happened."

"This dwarf will give us knowledge?" asked the young man doubtfully.

The old lady said, "If it is beneath your dignity to go to the dwarf, then do not go. In that case, you will remain ignorant, because I know I cannot answer this question. But if you sincerely want to be illumined, then you must go to the dwarf."

So the son of the village chief went to the dwarf with utmost reluctance. He thought that now he would hear some stupid answer from the dwarf. In fact, he was fully prepared for this.

The young man invited a few friends and together they went to see the dwarf. The young man explained his problem at great length. Then the dwarf said, "You cannot solve this problem? You have gone to schools and you have gone to college. You have studied many books. You are supposed to have knowledge, yet such a simple thing you do not know?"

The young man said, "Do not waste our time! Now, for God's sake, if you have anything to say, kindly say it."

The dwarf said, "This is such an easy thing! The couple who own that plot of land work very, very hard. They planted that rose bush and they also cultivate various crops. God is always pleased with people who work very, very hard. And what did you do? Merely for your own pleasure, you snatched the golden roses. God does not like that kind of behaviour. God only likes people who work very, very hard. God shows them His infinite Compassion and affection, and He gives them His own Pride. Because they were working so hard, God wanted to make them extremely happy. Therefore, He created this beautiful rose bush with golden roses. But what did you do? You just went there and destroyed it. God does not love people who destroy His creation. He loves people who build things. So, in the future, you have to work very, very hard. If you work very hard, then like this old couple, you will get astonishing results from your efforts."

The young man and his friends immediately recognised the wisdom of the dwarf's words. In silence, they saluted him and returned home.

## LTS 163. *Gratitude to the rescue*

A particular king observed that for two years the citizens of one town did not pay their taxes. The king became furious, and he blamed the negligence of his tax collectors. He summoned the tax collectors and said, "How is it that for two years you have not collected taxes from that town?"

The tax collectors explained, "In spite of our frequent visits to that town, the citizens have not been able to pay us any taxes. They are extremely poor. That is why we could not be strict with them."

The king did not listen to the excuses of the tax collectors. He fired them all. Then he sent his prime minister to collect the taxes from that town. The king also sent a large army to accompany the prime minister, in case anything happened to him.

When the people in that town saw a large army approaching with the prime minister, they became frightened. They all left the town because they knew they were in serious trouble. They felt it was safer to go back to their villages. Only one old man and his wife stayed behind in the town. When the prime minister arrived and saw only this old couple, he said, "Are you the only ones who live in this town?"

The old man said, "No, the others became frightened. Many people live here, but when they saw that soldiers were coming, they thought they would be killed, so they left. But my wife and I thought, 'We two are old. True, we have not done the right thing, we have not paid the tax. We deserve punishment, but if we die at this age, no harm. The time has come for us to die.'"

The prime minister said, "No, go and tell all the people that we shall not punish them and we shall not even ask them for taxes. Let them come back."

When the citizens returned to the town, they brought with them the papers to show that for two years they had not paid taxes. The prime minister did not even ask for the taxes, but they thought that since the prime minister was so kind, they would show him the papers to prove they knew exactly how much tax they owed.

The prime minister said, "What? Did I ask you to bring these papers?"

They said, "No, you did not ask to see them. We were told that you would not punish us, so we are very grateful to you. We have brought the papers to show you that we are fully aware of how much we have not paid."

The prime minister said, "Tell me the truth. You are all farmers. Why is it that you have not paid? Is it because you are not getting good crops from your fields? Or is it your habit to escape the taxes by fooling the king in some way?"

The citizens said, "To be perfectly frank, we get very good results from the fields, but we are all first-class liars. When the tax collectors come, we tell them lies."

Then the prime minister said, "All right. Give me the papers." Then he took all the papers and tore them up.

The citizens asked, "What is going to happen now?"

The prime minister said, "Nothing is going to happen to you. I am only asking one thing of you: you have to be grateful to the king. You have been very bad, but I am telling you, now you have to be grateful."

They said, "Oh, we are very grateful to the king. We shall always remain grateful to him. We will do anything he asks. If the king needs our help, we shall give it."

The prime minister laughed, "You are the ones to give help to the king? Here you have been fooling him for two years, and now you are offering to come to his aid whenever he needs help?"

They said, "This is our solemn promise. If ever the king needs our help in any way, we shall do the needful. We know that we are only ordinary people. The king has so many soldiers. Perhaps he will never need our help. But we want you to know that this is not just an empty promise."

The prime minister returned to the palace and the king asked him, "Did you collect the money?"

The prime minister replied, "No, I did not collect it."

"Why not?" asked the king.

The prime minister said, "I have collected something much more important."

The king asked, "What is this important thing that you have collected?"

The prime minister said, "I have collected their gratitude."

"What shall I do with their gratitude?" protested the king. "I need the money from their taxes. O minister, what have you done now? I thought that you were the wisest man. I fired the tax collectors because they did not do their job properly. Now you have joined their side."

The prime minister said, "My King, please give me a little time. I will be able to show you the power of gratitude."

The king said, "All right, all right. I am very displeased, but I will wait and see."

The prime minister was sure that one day something would happen to make his words come true.

A few months later, some enemies of the king came and attacked the palace. They had brought with them a huge army. When the king's soldiers saw such a vast number of enemy soldiers advancing towards them, all their courage vanished. They deserted the palace and left the king to his fate.

In the meantime, the citizens of the town received the message that the king was in serious trouble. Immediately they all gathered up their simple weapons and farming tools and set out for the palace. The king simply could not believe his eyes when he saw so many ordinary citizens coming to help him with such willingness and determination. His citizens' army attacked the enemies in a very spirited way and managed to chase them beyond the borders of the kingdom.

On that day the king was so happy, excited and delighted. He informed his prime minister that his prophecy had come true.

Alas, the prime minister died on that very day. The king felt very, very sad and, at the same time, he said, "This was the prime minister whose wisdom-flooded prophecy came true." After that he built a big monument in memory of this prime minister, who taught him that the power of gratitude has no parallel.

### LTS 164. *The elephant and the frog*

There was a bridge. On one side of the bridge was an elephant, and on the other side of the bridge was a frog. The frog said to the elephant, "Please wait. Let me cross the bridge first. Then you can come."

The elephant asked, "Why?"

The frog said, "If both of us cross together, then the bridge will shake uncontrollably. It may even collapse."

The elephant said, "I am an elephant. I am so heavy. I shall go first. You weigh nothing, so you can cross after me."

When the elephant started walking over the bridge, the frog also tried to cross. When they met in the centre of the bridge and passed by each other, the bridge began to shake. It was on the point of collapsing.

The frog said, "This is because of you! You are huge, but you have no brain. Can you not see what is happening now? This is all because you did not listen to me. I am going to curse you."

The elephant replied, "What can you do? You are a mere frog."

Then the frog jumped off the bridge into the water. The elephant was trembling in all its limbs. It knew that something serious was about to happen, but it did not know what to do.

The frog called out, "You are huge, but you have no brain. If you had listened to me, if I had gone first, then nothing would have happened." In this way, the frog went on insulting the elephant.

The elephant said, "Now you are in the water, so you are safe. But if you come here and challenge me, I will prove who is more powerful."

"Why do I have to challenge you?" said the frog. "You have already lost. You have no brain. You did not listen to me. Because you did not listen to me, the bridge is collapsing."

As the frog spoke, the bridge broke apart and the elephant was thrown into the rushing river.

### LTS 165. *The moneylender and the diamonds*

There was a moneylender who was very, very bad. He always asked for high interest payments from his clients. An old man started coming to him every day because he needed money badly for his daughter's marriage. Each day the poor fellow visited the moneylender with the hope that the moneylender would lower the interest, but instead it only went up and up. Unfortunately, this moneylender was the only one in the village who lent money.

One day the jeweller saw the old man going to the moneylender. The jeweller said to the old man, "Every day I see you going to the moneylender. How much money are you borrowing from him?"

The old man said, "I have not yet borrowed any money. Every day I go to his shop with the hope that he will lend me some money. He is ready to lend me as much as I need, but with very high interest. I cannot afford to repay the loan with that amount of interest."

The jeweller said, "If I come and beg him to lower the interest, it will not work. But do not worry. I will solve your problem. Come to my shop tomorrow before you go to his shop. I promise I will help you."

The next day the old man went to the jeweller's shop. The jeweller gave him four glass pieces which looked exactly like very expensive diamonds. The jeweller said, "Now you go and tell the moneylender that you found these in an earthen pot buried underground and you are absolutely sure that these are diamond pieces."

The old man went to the moneylender and said, "Today I have something to show you."

The moneylender asked, "What is it?"

The man said, "I had a dream. In the dream I saw that there was an earthen pot under the ground at a particular place. When I went to that place and dug under the ground, I found a pot containing these four diamonds."

The moneylender said, "Are these really diamonds?"

The man said, "I think they are diamonds. If you do not believe it, I shall take them to the jeweller. You do not know for certain and I do not know for certain, but I am convinced that they are real diamonds. If you do not want them, I am going to the jeweller."

The moneylender hastily said, "No, no, stay." After the moneylender looked closely at the glass pieces, he felt sure they were diamonds.

The old man said, "You keep the diamonds. I am asking for a lower interest on my loan and also for more time to pay you back. If I am unable to return the money, then you can keep the diamonds."

The moneylender said, "I will give you the money, and the interest will be very low."

The moneylender was extremely greedy. He thought that he would be able to sell the diamonds for a very high price. So he loaned the old man the money for his daughter's wedding, and the interest was next to nothing. In the evening, the moneylender secretly went to the jeweller and said, "Can you tell me if these are diamonds?"

The jeweller said, "I am very busy now. I cannot take the time to look at them. Come back in two weeks."

The moneylender said, "Can you not take a few seconds just to say if these are very expensive diamonds?"

The jeweller said, "I cannot give a proper opinion at this moment, but they look like diamonds. I will not be able to be one hundred per cent certain unless I examine them."

Then the jeweller smiled, so the moneylender took it as a sign that they were definitely diamond pieces. He took them home, and he was so happy that in two weeks' time he would get an accurate appraisal.

In the meantime, the old man who had borrowed the money had a marriage ceremony performed for his daughter. At the marriage many people gave him gifts in the form of money. When the marriage festivities were over, he went to the moneylender.

The moneylender said, "How was it possible for you to marry your daughter in such a short time? Only one week has passed since I saw you last."

The old man said, "It was so simple. You loaned me the money. That is why it was possible for my daughter to get married. Now I wish to repay the loan and collect my diamonds."

In the meantime, the moneylender had made exact replicas of the four glass pieces in order to fool the old man. Since he was sure that the ones that he had were diamonds, he happily gave the old man the false glass pieces. He thought that he had cleverly cheated the old man.

When the two weeks had passed, the moneylender went to the jeweller and asked him to examine the diamond pieces.

The jeweller said, "All right. Today I shall look at them very carefully." After looking at them for a long time, from every possible angle, the jeweller announced, "These are all glass pieces."

The moneylender was furious. He said, "Then why did you say they were diamonds?"

The jeweller said, "I did not tell you that they were diamonds. I said to come back in two weeks' time. I told you on that day that I had no time to examine them and in two weeks I would look at them closely. Now you have come back, and I have done my job. I see clearly that they are all glass pieces. They are not worth even one paisa."

So when we cheat others, we get what we deserve.

## LTS 166. *The woodcutter and the golden wristband*

There was a very, very poor woodcutter who had worked extremely hard for many years. Even so, it was difficult for him to make both ends meet. He also happened to be a genuine spiritual seeker. One day he was praying most soulfully to Mother Kali for some money-power. Although Mother Kali is the goddess of power, she has everything at her command. She can do things for us in a fleeting second that other gods and goddesses will take fifty, sixty or one hundred years to do. She is the mother of speed. She has all the capacities, including wealth.

In a dream, Mother Kali appeared before the simple woodcutter and said, "Although I am not usually invoked for money-power, since you are my great devotee, I shall help you."

The following day, early in the morning, the woodcutter was leaving his hut to go and work in the forest. Right near his house on the grass he saw a man's wristband, and it was golden. He was so thrilled. He said, "Mother Kali, you have listened to my prayer. I will be able to sell this for a large sum of money." He immediately offered all his gratitude to Mother Kali.

When the woodcutter looked at the wristband more carefully, he saw that at one place it was studded with a small diamond. He was beside himself with joy. He hurried to the jeweller's shop with his treasure. When the jeweller saw the wristband, he examined it in minute detail. At first he was surprised, but then he concealed his surprise very cleverly.

The jeweller told the woodcutter, "I do not think this is such an expensive wristband. It looks very beautiful, but I am sure it has glass inside it. I am ready to buy it from you, but today I do not have any money here in the shop. Please bring it tomorrow. Then I will buy it for whatever price you want. Since it is not very expensive, I do not think you will ask me for much, but whatever you want, I will give."

The woodcutter was very pleased that on the following day he would receive some money, and perhaps he would not have to work for a few months.

That night the jeweller hired some hooligans to give the woodcutter a sound thrashing. The poor fellow was beaten black and blue. The hooligans demanded, "Show us where you have kept the wristband." The woodcutter showed them where it was hidden. Then the hooligans bound the woodcutter and took him away along with the wristband.

The next day the jeweller took the woodcutter to the king. He said, "I have caught a thief. This fellow came to my shop yesterday. I had to do something urgent, so I could not pay attention to him. I just turned around for a minute and he ran away with this valuable wristband. It is from my shop that he stole it. My associates and I caught him and punished him. Now you can decide what additional punishment he deserves. This is such an expensive thing he has stolen from me!"

The poor woodcutter said, "I did not steal it. I was coming out of my hut and I found it on the ground."

The king was very, very serious. The king said, "Do you expect us to believe that you found this kind of thing on the ground?"

The king seemed to have taken the side of the jeweller one hundred per cent. He continued, "I must definitely visit your hut, woodcutter. You have such beautiful and expensive things lying about."

The woodcutter said, "Yes, yes, please, please come to my place. I need your blessings, O King."

The woodcutter was so miserable. He said to himself, "What kind of king is this? Here I am telling the simple truth, but he is not taking my side. He is taking the side of the jeweller." He was filled with sadness.

Then the king said to the jeweller, "Since this wristband was for sale in your shop, I definitely feel that you had a pair of them, not just one wristband. I am sure you had one more of the same kind."

The jeweller said, "Oh yes, you are absolutely right, I had one more."

"Then what happened to that one?" enquired the king.

"Oh, just three or four days ago it was stolen," said the jeweller.

"Another robbery!" exclaimed the king. "Do you mean somebody else stole the other one?"

The jeweller said, "Yes, somebody else stole it. I am so miserable. I forgot to tell you, O King, that one wristband was stolen by this rogue, but the other thief I could not catch. I do not know who has stolen it."

The king said, "Oh, I see. You are so unfortunate. I sympathise with you."

The king paused for a moment. Then he said to the jeweller, "Now get ready for punishment."

The jeweller was horrified. He said, "What? What kind of punishment will I get? Here is the thief."

The king said, "Four days ago I made a small excursion. I took some noblemen out for hunting. When we were returning to the palace at night, I accidentally dropped my wristband. I discovered the loss when I arrived home, but I did not know where I had dropped it. Now I see that I must have dropped it as I was passing by this poor woodcutter's place. It is definitely mine. The other one is still with me."

The king asked his men to bring him the other wristband. He showed it to the jeweller and said, "Here is the other one. You can clearly see that it is identical. That means that I am the one who stole the other wristband from your shop!"

Then the king said, "Now the punishment comes. Your first lie was that this woodcutter, such an innocent man, stole this wristband. Your second lie was when you told me that it came from your shop. The third lie was that the other wristband was also stolen from your place. Three lies! For each lie I will put you in jail for five years because I feel you have deceived many, many people this way. So five years, five years, five years — fifteen years you will be in jail." By now the king was very, very angry.

In the meantime, the jeweller's sons came to know of what was happening, so they came running to the palace. They said to the king, "O King, if we give you some money, will you reconsider your sentence?"

The king said, "Do I need money from people like you? I have given my judgement. It is final."

Then the jeweller's wife arrived on the scene. She said, "O King, please keep my husband in jail for the full fifteen years." The king could not believe his ears.

The sons were shocked. They said, "What are you saying, Mother? What kind of wife are you?"

She said, "Your father has been doing this kind of thing for many years, and his nature has to be changed. Only the most severe punishment will change his nature. I will not mind at all. Please keep him in jail for fifteen years, or give him lifelong imprisonment."

The king was very pleased with the wife, and at the same time he was amused. Everyone was wondering what the king would do. The king said, "All right, since you are such a wonderful wife, such a good wife, I shall keep your husband in jail only for five years."

Then the wife said, "No, no, no! Only five years? Then he will come back again and do the same kind of thing."

The king said, "I see your sincerity, but something is telling me that five years is enough. I shall pray to God on your behalf, and you will pray to God. After five years your husband will be released. Let us both pray to God that he turns over a new leaf and becomes a good person. I am sure that God will listen to our prayers."

So the jeweller received five years' imprisonment, and then he returned to his family. After he came back, he felt miserable for his wife, and he also felt grateful to the king for his good heart. So the jeweller gave up his old undivine life and became a very good person.

LTS 167. *The two wise prime ministers*

There was a king who suddenly developed a desire to overthrow a neighbouring king. This neighbouring king happened to be a friend of his. The first king had the desire to conquer his friend and take all his wealth. So the king spoke to his prime minister and told him of his desire. Then he said, "What is your opinion of it?"

The prime minister said, "He is your friend. How can you even dream of doing this to him?"

The king said, "No, this desire has taken root inside me. I want to be stronger than he is. I want to be mightier than he is. Friendship is one thing, but this goes beyond friendship. If I can surpass him in every way, then I will be really happy and proud."

The prime minister replied, "What can I say? You are the king. You must make your own decision."

"Tell me frankly," said the king, "do you think I will be able to win?"

The prime minister replied, "How can I say whether or not you will be able to win? First of all, O King, you are doing something wrong. Your friend has not done anything to you. He has not antagonised you or insulted you in any way. He seems to be your friend, and you have always claimed to be his friend. How can you treat a friend this way? But if you have the desire to conquer him, then I can only say this: first let us examine the intelligence of his prime minister."

"What kind of examination do you propose?" asked the king.

The prime minister said, "Let me examine him in a special way. Based on the prime minister's intelligence, I shall tell you what to do."

The king agreed to send a messenger with a most expensive gift to the other king, along with a message that was dictated by the prime minister. The prime minister said, "Messenger, go and tell the king that our king will be extremely happy and grateful if he can send two men. One will have to prove that he lives for death, and the other will have to prove that he lives for life."

"What kind of stupid question is this that I am asking the messenger to take to the other king?" said the king.

The prime minister replied, "Please, please listen to me. Let the messenger deliver the message to your friend and let us see if he abides by your request. If he can fulfil your request, then I will tell you what to do."

The messenger arrived at the court of the neighbouring king. This king was very, very happy to receive such a beautiful gift from his dear friend. Then the messenger said, "O King, I also have a special message for you. My king requests you to send from your kingdom two men: one who lives only for death and one who lives only for life."

Now, the prime minister in this kingdom was very smart, very shrewd. He said, "Do not worry, O King. I know the answer." He immediately summoned a doctor and a priest. The prime minister said to the messenger, "Here are our two representatives: a doctor and a priest. The doctor lives for life. He tries to keep life on earth. Everywhere people are dying, but the doctors try to conquer death. So this is the man who lives for life. He wants people to stay on earth as long as possible. The priest lives for death. When somebody dies, the priest arranges the funeral and performs all the ceremonies. When somebody dies, he has to do his job. So the priest lives for death and the doctor lives for life."

The priest and the doctor accompanied the messenger back to his own kingdom and he brought them before the king. The prime minister of the first king saw them and said, "Your Majesty, do not try to fight against that king. His prime minister is extremely intelligent. I tell you, if you try to conquer your friend, you will fail because his prime minister is very smart. So do not do it."

The king took the advice of his prime minister and decided not to try to conquer his friend.

Meanwhile, the same desire entered into the other king. He wished to conquer the first king. Desire does not stay at one place. Like a monkey, it goes from one place to another. Now the second king discussed his desire with his own prime minister, the one who was so smart. This prime minister said, "Let us put the same question to them. You shall send your friend a very expensive gift, and your messenger will beg for the fulfilment of your request. Two men we need: one for life and one for death. But they cannot send the same type of people. They have to send two people from totally different professions."

This prime minister thought that the other prime minister would not be able to fulfil their request, since the puzzle had already been solved. He did not see how there could be two answers to the same question.

In due time, the messenger from the second king arrived with a most beautiful and expensive gift. Then he delivered his message requesting the first king to send one man who lived for life and one who lived for death.

The first prime minister said, "It is so easy. Send for an undertaker. An undertaker lives for death. When somebody dies, it is his job is to take care of the body."

Then the first prime minister said, "Now, for life, bring me a spiritual seeker, someone who does very deep meditation. A seeker prays to God all the time for the fulfilment of God's Will. Here on earth everything is transitory. Even human life is fleeting. But a true spiritual seeker prays for Immortality, for immortal life."

So the prime minister found a very saintly person and an undertaker, and he sent them both to the other king. The prime minister of the second king said, "O King, this prime minister is very smart. His intelligence has defeated us. I urge you not to fight with that king because we are bound to lose."

So the two wise prime ministers both advised their respective kings not to fight. Each king gave up the idea of conquering the other one when he heard that defeat was unavoidable.

### LTS 168. *The king's friend becomes the prime minister*

Once a king asked a very dear friend of his to accompany him. The king said, "I want to go for a long walk. You come with me. We shall take a leisurely excursion."

The friend gladly accepted the invitation, and the two friends set out walking together. Along the way they saw somebody walking about twenty metres ahead of them. The king said to his friend, "You know everything. I have such faith in you. Can you tell me what this man's profession is?"

The friend answered, "Yes, I can easily tell you. He is a woodcutter."

"How do you know he is a woodcutter?" asked the king curiously.

The friend replied, "I can see he is looking at this tree and that tree. He is examining all the trees growing along the side of the road, so he has to be a woodcutter."

The king said, "He has to be a woodcutter? Since you know everything, can you tell me his name?"

"Easily I can tell you his name," said his friend.

The king was astonished. He said, "What is his name then?"

The friend said, "His name is Salim."

"How do you know?" asked the king.

"It is very simple," the friend said. "My name is Salim. When you called my name, he immediately turned his head. He thought that you were calling him."

The king said, "Are you sure?" He thought perhaps his friend was joking with him. Then the king asked, "Can you tell me what he ate half an hour ago?"

The friend said, "Yes, I can easily answer your question."

The king said, "How do you know? Have you ever seen him before?"

"Never!" said the friend emphatically.

The king continued, "You have never seen him, never talked to him? Then how can you say all these things with such authority?"

The friend told the king, "It is self-evident. The last thing that he ate was honey."

"Honey?" queried the king. "My friend, are you mocking me by any chance? Why should I believe that he ate honey? It is too far-fetched!"

"I know it is true," said his friend, "because I saw that there were bees buzzing around his lips. Definitely he has eaten honey. That is why with his palm he was trying to brush aside the bees."

The king said, "All right. Now I wish to find out the truth of the matter." He asked his friend Salim to walk ahead and request the man to stop. Salim caught up to the man and said, "Please wait. The king wants to speak with you."

When the poor man heard the very word 'king', he began trembling with fear. He thought perhaps he had done something wrong. But the king spoke to him very kindly and compassionately. The king said, "I have a few simple questions to ask you."

The man only nodded. He was a very, very humble man. The king said, "First tell me, what is your name?"

The man answered, "My name is Salim."

The king asked, "What do you do?"

The man answered, "I am just a humble and poor woodcutter."

Then the king asked, "And what did you eat last?"

The woodcutter said, "I ate only a little honey. I like honey very much."

Everything that the king's friend had said was correct. Then the king gave the woodcutter a very large amount of money and told him, "Do not worry. You have done nothing wrong. On the contrary, I am very pleased with you."

To his friend the king said, "Today you have really proved to me how intelligent a human being can be! You must work with me. I want to replace my prime minister. You are the one to be my prime minister. You have to listen to my request. From today on you shall be my prime minister."

### LTS 169. *The prime minister solves the guru's riddle*

There was a king who had a guru. The king would not do anything without taking advice from his guru, and his guru was kind enough to offer him advice on a wide range of subjects. As a matter of fact, on the inner level, the guru used to rule the kingdom, and as a result everything was peaceful and prosperous.

Once it happened that a vacancy arose in the court. The king wanted a very high-ranking officer for a special task and he begged his guru to let him know whom to take. The king asked his prime minister to nominate two candidates who had, according to him, both knowledge and wisdom. Then he planned to send those two candidates to his guru, and ask his guru to choose one of the two.

The prime minister selected two well-qualified, high-ranking officers, and both of them went to the guru for an interview. To one the guru gave a sieve, and to the other he gave a winnowing fan. The guru did not explain anything. He simply told them to take these objects to the king.

Both of them came before the king holding the objects. The king said, "What kind of puzzle is this? How can I know which one my guru has selected? Now I am in serious trouble."

He asked his prime minister, "Can you tell me the significance of the sieve and the winnowing fan?"

The prime minister said, "O King, this is a most difficult question! Please allow me to think it over." Then to himself he said, "I do hope somebody — some angel or cosmic god — descends who can help me solve this problem. It is beyond my capacity to understand the significance of the fan and the sieve."

When the prime minister went home, he saw that at one point his wife was using a winnowing fan, and then afterwards she was using a sieve. He noticed the difference between the two. When she used the sieve, he saw that the good things were passing through the wire. They were rejected, while the bad things were left on top. But when she used the winnowing fan, at that time the good things remained, while the bad things were all scattered. All of a sudden, the meaning of the guru's gesture became clear to him. He knew that the one with the winnowing fan would keep the good and reject the bad, whereas the one with the sieve would neglect or reject the good things and accept the bad things.

The next morning the prime minister hurried to the palace and said, "O King, your guru wants you to give the job to the one who brought the winnowing fan." Then he explained to the king why he had chosen this one. So the prime minister's wife illumined him. He did not have to go any further to look for wisdom. She solved his problem.

LTS 170. *One sister pleases the old farmer*

A farmer and his wife were returning from their relatives' house. They had to travel a considerable distance on foot. Along the way, an elderly man came up to them and said, "Can you do me a very great favour? Where are you going?"

They mentioned the name of the village that was their destination. The elderly man said, "I am supposed to take my three daughters to that particular village. We have relatives there. Now I have some urgent business that requires me to remain here. Will you be kind to me? Will you take my daughters to that village? Once you take them there, then they will find their way to the home of our relatives."

The farmer and his wife were extremely kind-hearted. They said, "Definitely we will take your daughters. It is not safe for them to travel alone."

So the three sisters started accompanying the farmer and his wife. Together they covered a long distance. At one point, because the sisters were young and spirited, they were walking a little way ahead of the old farmer and his wife. The farmer's wife whispered, "Please, please, I really want you to choose one of these young girls to be our son's wife. They are all beautiful and sweet-natured. I leave it up to you. You choose one, and I will be so grateful if you can make arrangements for the wedding."

Like many mothers since time immemorial, this farmer's wife was always thinking of her son's marriage! The farmer replied, "How can we do this kind of thing? That elderly man has placed all his trust in us. This is not the time to think of your son's marriage." And he scolded his wife severely.

But the wife insisted, "Please, please, do me this favour. I see these three are all very nice looking girls. And they are so well behaved. It will not be taking advantage of the old man if we ask for one of them to marry our son."

Eventually the farmer said, "All right. I will see which one is most suitable." With great reluctance he walked a little faster and approached the three girls. Then he said, "May I ask you two questions?"

They said, "Yes, yes! You are so kind to us. How may we help you?"

He said, "First of all, have you ever cooked with a wooden pot?"

The first girl answered, "No, no. We have never cooked with a wooden pot. Our parents do not allow us to cook."

The second added, "We have servants who do the cooking."

The third girl said, "I do not know how to cook with a wooden pot, but I can make such a pot."

The farmer asked curiously, "How can you make one?"

By the roadside there was a tree. The girl said to the farmer, "Just cut a small branch. I can make a pot from it."

The farmer had a knife, and with the knife he cut a small portion of a branch and gave it to the girl. Then she asked for the knife and they resumed walking. As she was going along, she was cutting and shaping the wood. She carved the wood into a pipe. The farmer said, "This is only a pipe!"

The girl said, "Yes, but you have only given me a small piece of wood. Had you given me a larger piece, perhaps I would have been able to make a wooden pot."

The farmer was so pleased that this girl was able to work with wood. They continued on their way. After they had walked a long distance, they came to a wood. The farmer said to the girls, "My village is still far away from here. It will take many more hours. Is there any way we could shorten the distance?"

The first girl said, "How can we shorten the distance? Whatever the distance is, it is."

The second girl said, "Here there is only one road. If there were three or four roads leading to that particular village, then we could say that one is the shortest. But there is only one road to follow. How can we shorten it?"

The third girl said, "No, there is a way to shorten the distance."

The farmer was very curious to know how she proposed to solve the problem. The girl said, "I have been told that I have a very haunting singing voice. If you wish, I can sing as we walk. While I am singing, you will be listening to the songs and appreciating my voice. You will see that the distance will become nothing."

So she started singing and they continued walking. When they reached the village, the farmer said, "You are so right. While you were singing, the time flew by." The farmer and his wife did not feel at all tired. Under normal circumstances, they would have been very fatigued after their long journey.

The farmer did not say anything, but inwardly he was very pleased with this girl. Then the farmer and his wife accompanied the girls to the home of their relatives.

Afterwards, on the way back to their own home, the wife said, "Now tell me which one you like."

The farmer said, "You fool! You do not know which one is the best? The one that answered both the questions correctly. She is the one for my son."

The wife said, "Then you have to get her."

"How am I going to do that?" asked the farmer.

A few days later the farmer went to the place where the three girls were staying, and he asked them if he could get in touch with their father. Since the farmer had been so kind to them, they gave him the address. The farmer went to their father's place and made his request. The father saw that the farmer was very sincere and very nice, so he agreed. In the course of time, the farmer's son and this particular girl got married and both parties were very happy.

### LTS 171. *The boat's passengers reject the rich man*

Once a river broke its banks and there was an unexpected flood. This flood was destroying everything in its path — trees, houses and farms were all being destroyed. One tiny village was in a serious crisis. All the villagers decided to go to a nearby village where the flood waters were not so devastating. There was only one boat, and they all jumped into the boat. The boat held only a hundred people. They knew that if they did not cast off as soon as possible, then they would be caught in the surging waters and they would drown.

As they were on the point of leaving, they saw two latecomers approaching the pier. One was the richest man in the village. He had a very bad reputation. He was extremely miserly and loaned money to the poor people at a very, very high interest rate. The other latecomer was a beggar.

The boatman said, "I am sorry. I can only take one more passenger."

The rich man was so haughty. He said, "Since I am so important, I am the obvious choice."

But the passengers in the boat did not want to take the rich man on board. They wanted the beggar. The rich man became furious. He said, "I have so much wealth and influence — and you want to save the life of an insignificant street beggar?"

The passengers said, "Yes. We want to take the beggar. We do not want you for two reasons. The first is that you are so rich. If you insist on bringing with you all your wealth, the boat may sink. The second reason is that you are so mean and miserly, whereas this poor man is very kind-hearted. God has made him poor. What can he do? If we take him, then he will appreciate us because we are charitable. He needs our charity and he deserves our charity. You have never shown any sympathy to us. Why should we show sympathy to you?"

The boatman took hold of the beggar and pulled him into the boat. The rich man was shocked to the core. He said, "I curse you all! When you come back, you will find that all your houses have been destroyed by the flood. You will have no place to live. Then, when you come to me for money, I will charge you very, very high interest."

The passengers said, "See! Now your true nature is coming forward. How bad you are! We will not come to you to borrow money. You are a very, very bad fellow."

A few days later, when the flood waters ebbed, the villagers returned, and they saw that their houses were all destroyed. The rich man's house was also destroyed and the rich man himself had drowned. His only son was lamenting his father's death. The son said, "My father had amassed so much money. Now what shall I do with it? Alas, I have lost my father. There is no one to guide me in these matters."

One of the villagers said, "Do you believe in the other world?"

The son said, "Yes, I do believe in the other world, but my father could not take his money there."

The villager said, "True, even though your father was so attached to his money, he could not take it with him. You also will not be able to take this money to the other world."

"Then where is my father now? Does anybody know?" asked the son in a pitiful voice.

One man stepped forward and said, "I know. I am a man of prayer. Your father is roaming between Heaven and hell."

The son asked, "What do you mean, roaming between Heaven and hell?"

The man continued, "Your father needs our prayers so that he can go to Heaven. Otherwise, he will be totally lost. At this point, even hell does not want him because he was so bad on earth, and Heaven does not want him because he led a useless life. He did not do anything good for mankind."

The son said, "All right. If I give you all the money, will you pray for my father?"

All the villagers nodded eagerly. The son said, "I want to distribute the money equally." But the son was unable to do so because somc bad people took more than the rest did. Then the villagers began fighting and fighting. They all completely forgot to pray. They just took the money and built new houses.

Meanwhile, the rich man was loitering in between Heaven and hell. His soul found no place to rest.

### LTS 172. *Which son should become king?*

There was a king who had three sons. Each son was very handsome, intelligent and kind-hearted. The king was extremely, extremely pleased with all his sons. The question was, who would be the king after him? Usually the eldest son becomes the king when his father dies, but the king had such love for all three. He asked his prime minister, "How am I going to name one the crown prince and not the others? By tradition, it should fall to my eldest son, but I do not want to deny the other two. They will feel sad if I do not treat them equally. Is there any way I can truly find out which one is the best of the three?"

The prime minister said, "It is a very difficult matter. How can I know what to advise you? Usually the eldest son has to be the king, but in this case you want to see who is most suitable in every way, since you love them all equally. All right, let me try to see if I can be of any help to you."

The following day the prime minister put on the garb of a sage. He donned ochre robes and disguised his face with a beard. Nobody could recognise him at all, not even the king. The 'sage' whispered to the king, "I am your prime minister. Do not tell your sons who I am. In this way, I will be able to see which one is the best of the three."

The king summoned his three sons and said, "A most venerable sage has come. If you have any question, any desire or any problem, please take this golden opportunity to discuss it with him. He will be able to give you invaluable advice."

The princes said that they were very pleased to see the sage, but they did not have any questions for him. Then the king said to the sage, "If you have any advice to offer my sons or if you have anything to tell us, please do so."

The sage said to the eldest son, "Suppose you become the king after your father leaves this world. What will you do?"

The eldest son said, "I will try to do good things. I will try to be good and kind in every way, and I do hope that my subjects will also be good and kind to me."

The sage said, "Excellent. But if you become the king, will you give me a little portion of your kingdom?"

The eldest son said, "Of course I will give you a small portion, since you are taking the trouble to advise us."

Then the sage asked the same question of the second son, "What will you do if you become the king?"

The second son said, "If I become the king, I will be very nice and kind-hearted to my subjects, but I will not expect anything from them. If they do not want to be nice to me, no harm. I will not be angry with them. I will do my job. I will try to become a good person. If they also want to become good, well and good; otherwise, I will not expect anything from them."

Again the sage asked, "Will you give me a little portion of your kingdom?"

The second son said, "Oh, definitely, definitely I will give you some land."

Then the sage came to the third son. The third son was asked the same question, "What will you do if you become the king?"

He replied, "If I become the king, I will be nice to everybody, and I will not mind if my subjects are not nice to me. But if any dispute arises, any conflict or argument, I will always be just. I will be nice to them and, if they are not nice, I will not mind, but I will be just. I will not be partial at all."

Then the sage asked, "Will you give me a small portion of your property?"

The youngest son said, "No, I will not give you any property."

"Why not?" asked the sage.

The prince said, "First of all, my father the king is still alive. While my father is still alive, where is my kingdom? God alone knows whom father will choose. We have no idea whether it will be my eldest brother or my middle brother. I am the youngest. I have the least chance. But since we are discussing this, if I were to be just, I would have to ask on what basis I should give you a portion of the kingdom. What have you done for me? You are simply talking to me. Anyway, what kind of discussion is this? Let father decide whomever he wants to be king."

The king had listened silently to the whole proceeding. Now he said, "My sons, I am so glad that you three came here and had such an illumining conversation with this wise sage. I am so happy, so pleased. Now you may go."

When the princes had gone, the prime minister removed his long hair, beard and moustache, and both he and the king started laughing. Then the prime minister said, "Now, do I have to tell you which one will be the best?"

The king said, "No, I saw and heard for myself. Definitely it is my youngest son. He will perform good deeds, but he will not expect anything from others. Again, he will be really just. Just because you were kind enough to chat with him, why should he feel obliged to reward you with a portion of the kingdom?"

The prime minister said, "You are absolutely right. Your third son is good and just at the same time. He should be the next king."

### LTS 173. *The death of the villager's son*

A villager's son was stricken with a most serious ailment. His father was inconsolable. He went from one village doctor to another searching for a cure for his son, but nobody could cure him. Finally the father brought his son to the best doctor in the town. This doctor tried various treatments, but the son's condition did not improve. One day the doctor said to the father, "I do not think I will be able to cure your son. You have only one option left: pray to God."

"I have been praying and praying," cried the father. "Do you think I have not been praying?"

The father felt that any day, at any moment, his son would die. This was his only son. His wife had passed away many years before, so he was both mother and father to the son.

Every day the father would enter his son's room in the hospital and kneel by his bed. Then he would start sobbing. Late at night he would go home, and then he would come back to the hospital again in the morning. The doctor felt genuinely sad that he could not cure the patient. He knew that in a day or two the patient would die. Eventually the hour of death struck. It was in the middle of the night, and the father had gone home. Death came and snatched away the son.

Although doctors are accustomed to seeing death, this particular doctor felt very sad. How could he tell the poor father that his son was no more? He felt that it would break his heart. For hours the doctor was inwardly preparing himself to give the father the message.

At last the father arrived at the hospital. The doctor saw that on that day, of all days, the father was so happy. In this kind of happy mood he had to hear the worst possible news. With utmost kindness and sympathy, the doctor said, "I am glad that today you are happy. I do not know why you are happy but, unfortunately, I have to give you some bad news. Please, please sit down. I regret to tell you that your son passed away."

The doctor looked at the father, but the old man was not shedding tears. He seemed quite normal. The doctor said to him, "Perhaps you are in shock. Otherwise, I cannot understand your reaction. You can come and see your son's body if you wish. Your son has passed away and you are not crying at all!"

The old man went to see his son's body. Even then he did not cry. Now the doctor could not fathom the mystery. How could a father be so indifferent to his son's passing? He said to himself, "He has been crying for weeks and weeks. Perhaps he has no tears left." Then the doctor started questioning the father. He said, "How can this be? For a father not to cry is most strange!"

The father said, "Last night I had a most significant dream. In my dream I was a king and my queen was so beautiful. I had five sons. These young princes were so smart, handsome, well educated and kind-hearted. Everybody appreciated me, everybody extolled my wife's beauty to the skies and everybody admired my children. As king, I was so great and powerful. Then in my dream I saw that one by one my wife died and all my sons died. I was so happy to have these five sons, but when they died, I did not cry. Why? Because I knew it was only a dream. Now, for only one son do I have to cry? This life is also only a dream. When we are in ignorance, we cry for every little reason. But in my dream, one by one, all my dear ones departed. At that time, I did not cry. So why do I have to cry now? Just because this is reality? Dream and reality are the same. This moment we call something reality and the next moment we call the same thing a dream."

So the doctor received spirituality's highest lesson from his patient's father.

LTS 174. *The wrestler-teachers*

There was a king who engaged in wrestling in his adolescent years and became an excellent wrestler. When he became king, he encouraged wrestling and gymnastics as well. He kept two extremely strong wrestlers in the palace and asked them to teach wrestling to the young boys of the court. The king was very, very happy to know that these young boys were developing their physical strength.

One day this particular king visited another king's palace, and there he saw that his host was giving utmost importance to education. There the young boys and girls were all studying a wide variety of subjects. The king said, "I should also give importance to education."

He spoke to his prime minister about the matter and the prime minister said, "Certainly! Education is absolutely necessary. Let us bring some well eduated scholars to teach our children."

The king said, "Actually, I was told our two wrestlers are not only strong, but also well educated. Early in the morning they conduct wrestling classes for a few hours, but for the rest of the day they are free. I feel they should give classes in other subjects. In that way we can save money."

The two wrestlers started teaching on alternate days. Quite a few students attended their classes. After a year had passed, the king said to his prime minister, "Go and see how much progress the students have made."

The prime minister went and saw that the teacher was in another world. He was sleeping and snoring with his head on the table. The students were just playing games. The prime minister approached one little child and said, "Tell me, who wrote the Ramayana?"

The student said, "No, I just drew a line. I did not do anything wrong!"

The prime minister asked another student, "Who wrote the Ramayana?"

The student started crying, "I have not written anything!"

Then the prime minister asked a third student, "Who wrote the Ramayana?"

The child said, "I am sure one of us did, but I did not do it. I am not the culprit!"

The prime minister said, "I can see how much you have all learned!" Then he went to the teacher and shook him by the shoulder. When the fellow woke up, the prime minister said, "What are you doing? You are supposed to be teaching these children. How is it that here nobody knows who wrote the Ramayana?"

The teacher said, "They do not know? They are lying. They definitely know!" Then he flexed his muscles and said, "I am sure one of them did it! I shall knock out their brains if somebody does not come forward and confess!"

The prime minister said, "Yes, yes. This is what you have taught them."

Sadly the prime minister went to the king and said, "O King, in one full year our children have not learned anything. Even the teacher does not know who wrote the Ramayana."

The king said, "How could such a thing happen? Everybody knows who wrote the Ramayana."

The prime minister said, "Your Majesty, this only proves that for everything we need the right person to teach us. Those two teachers know all about wrestling, and they have taught it very well, but about religion, history, science and other subjects, what do they know?"

The king realised that he had to hire qualified scholars to teach the children.

LTS 175. *Giving credit where credit is due*

A young boy was very sick, and his parents were quite alarmed. Every day he was getting worse. The poor mother was almost prostrate with grief. Finally she said, "The doctor that we have presently is useless. Let us take our son to another doctor." This doctor had tried a few medicines, but he could not cure their only son.

The husband said, "Give the doctor time. I am sure our son will be all right in a week or so."

The wife became annoyed. She said, "No, I do not want to listen to you. I have another idea. I say no more doctors. Let us go to an occultist instead. An occultist just gives a talisman, and it cures the person."

The husband said, "No, I do not believe in those things. It is all superstition."

The wife said, "You *have* to believe in them because this doctor is not able to cure our son."

The husband said, "The doctor told us that the cure would take two weeks. Now one week is over. There is still another week to go."

The wife said, "I do not want to listen to you. I do not want to wait even one more day."

"Please give me another chance," implored the husband. "I am going to the doctor, and I shall bring back better medicine for our son."

The husband went to the doctor to get better medicine. To his wide surprise, the doctor's wife said, "He has gone to the occultist for a talisman because he has been sick of late."

Then the husband proceeded to the occultist's house, not to take a talisman, but to meet with the doctor. When he arrived, he saw the doctor coming out holding a talisman. The husband said, "Doctor, what about my son? My son is not getting better."

The doctor said, "Oh, I have some new medicine." From his bag, he extracted a bottle of medicine and gave it to the husband. He said, "This new medicine will definitely cure your son in one week."

The man was so happy that he had been able to get some very powerful medicine for his son. With tremendous joy, relief and pride, he went home. He said to his wife, "Look, this is new medicine."

The wife said, "I do not need it, and I will not give it to him."

The husband said, "What? You cannot trust me? You cannot trust the doctor for one week? Just give it to our son and let us see. After one week, if he is not cured, then I shall personally go to the occultist and bring back a talisman."

The wife said, "You do not have to do that. I have saved you the trouble. I have been to the occultist, and he gave me a talisman. You can see it around our son's neck. And our son is definitely going to be cured in a week. I asked the occultist. He said that at the outside it would take a week. Otherwise, it will take only a few days."

The poor husband was caught between the two cures. Finally he said, "Let us have faith. You have faith in the occultist's talisman, and I will have faith in the doctor."

The wife became cross. "Still you have faith in that useless doctor?" she said. "Can you not see that our son's case is only getting worse? That doctor is nothing but a charlatan!"

With all the patience at his command, the husband said, "I told you, it is a matter of one week. Let us use the medicine."

But his wife was extremely stubborn. She said, "No! You have faith in your fake doctor. I will have faith in my real occultist."

The husband said, "All right. Let us stick to our respective faiths. In one week, when our son is completely cured, you can give all credit to the occultist, and I will give all credit to the doctor. Let us be happy by having faith in our own methods."

As fate would have it, the son was cured in a week. The wife proudly said, "It is all due to the occultist's talisman." And her husband privately said, "I know it is all due to the doctor's medicine."

## LTS 176. *God pleases everybody in his own way*

There was an elderly hermit who was sincerely spiritual. He used to pray and meditate for hours and hours every day. His wife also used to follow spiritual disciplines. This couple had brought up their only son in the forest. There they had a small hut where they lived with utmost simplicity. To the son, his father was like his spiritual preceptor.

One morning the prince of the kingdom went out hunting on his chariot. He followed a narrow path that led through the forest. For quite a few hours the prince did not see any game. Then, at a distance, he saw a beautiful deer jumping from one bush to another. The prince was very happy. He aimed at the deer and released his arrow. When his arrow struck the deer, this deer started crying in a human voice. It sounded like a young boy was crying.

The prince said, "My God, what have I done?" Then he drove his chariot to where the deer lay, and he saw a boy clad in deerskin. The arrow had penetrated his heart.

The prince was horrified. "Now what will happen to me?" he wailed. "The best thing is for me to jump into my chariot and depart as quickly as possible so that nobody will connect me with this murder."

So he jumped into his chariot and drove a considerable distance. As he was driving, his conscience began to torture him. He said, "I am such a rogue! My father is the king. He is so well known for honesty and kindness. I am his son. How can I be so bad? No, no, I must go back. Whatever the consequences may be, I must go. I must face them."

So he returned to that isolated place in the forest. "Somebody has to be the father of that little boy," he reflected. He searched and searched for some sign of human habitation. Finally he saw a tiny cottage in the midst of a dense grove of trees. With a fearful heart, the prince went and knocked at the door. An elderly man with a long beard opened the door and said, "What can I do for you?"

The prince said, "I do not need anything. Only please tell me, do you have a son?"

"Yes, I have a son," said the hermit, his eyes alight with love.

Then the prince said, "Can you adopt one son?"

"Why do I have to adopt a son?" said the hermit in a puzzled voice.

The prince said, "I am the prince, but I want to be your son."

"How can you be my son?" asked the hermit. "You are a prince. You belong in the palace and my son belongs here."

The moment of truth had come. The prince said, "Please, please forgive me. I have done something very, very wrong."

The hermit said, "What have you done? What have you done?"

The prince continued, "My crime is unforgivable. Whatever punishment you want to give me, I am ready to accept." While he was speaking, a young boy exactly like the one that he had killed came and stood beside the hermit. Then the prince said, "Do you have twin sons?"

"No, I do not have twin sons," replied the hermit.

The prince said, "I do not understand the meaning of this. I killed this boy a few hours ago. I am absolutely sure of it. Now what is happening? With my own eyes I am seeing him standing here. Definitely they are twins."

The father said, "No, no, no."

"Then how can it be?" asked the prince.

The hermit explained, "When you aimed your arrow at my son and killed him, immediately I got the message from within. Then I used my spiritual power and revived him. God has given me the boon that in my family nobody will die, either in an accident or in a normal, natural way. For countless years I prayed and meditated to realise the highest. God was pleased with me and, out of His infinite Compassion, He gave me wisdom-light in boundless measure. He also said that as long as I want to live, as long as my wife wants to live and as long as my son wants to live, we will be able to live here on earth. We can command our own death. Nobody will be able to kill us. I know you did not try to kill my son deliberately, but even if you had killed my son deliberately, I could have revived him. God has given me this power."

The prince was overwhelmed with gratitude to learn that the young boy had been returned to life. He said, "Please, please grant me my soulful desire. My father once told me that whatever I wanted, he would fulfil my desire."

The hermit said, "In that case, you can ask your father to fulfil whatever your desire is."

The prince said, "My desire needs the blessings of both you and my father. I want to ask my father to name your son as the crown prince. When the time comes, he will succeed my father as king. I do not want the throne."

The hermit said, "That is an absurd notion! My son has entered into the spiritual life. You should be the king at the proper time. All your life you have spent in the palace. You have listened to your father dealing with affairs of state. That is your way of life."

"I no longer want to have my old way of life," protested the prince.

"Then what would you like to do?" asked the hermit.

The prince said, "Whether you accept me or not, I am going to tell my father that I do not want to be the future king. I want to accept the spiritual life."

"You are creating a problem for me," said the hermit. "I am a poor man. When your father receives this news, he will think I am responsible for your change of heart. He will come and destroy my little cottage."

The prince said, "No, my father is a man of his word. If I tell him the whole story, he will understand."

So the prince went to his father and narrated the events of the day. He concluded by saying, "Now, Father, you have to fulfil my desire. Once you told me that whatever desire I have, you will fulfil. Now I want to go and become the disciple of this hermit, and you have to allow me. I will live a very simple life. Occasionally you can come and visit me if the hermit allows."

The king said, "If the hermit allows? I am the king!"

Very bravely the prince said, "True, Father, you are the king, but this hermit is in touch with God. He can easily smash the pride of any human being. Even if you are unwilling, he can compel you to come to his cottage. He can do anything. I know his power. I have seen what he can do. So do not boast that you are the king. His power far surpasses yours. I am respectfully requesting permission to leave the palace. Please make my younger brother the crown prince. He can be king after you. I will not mind at all. But please allow me to pray and meditate under the guidance of this guru."

The king said, "I will keep my promise. You may go, and occasionally I shall visit you."

So the prince left the palace and returned to the forest. From time to time his father used to come and visit him. The king would see such beauty, light, delight and divinity radiating from his son's face. He also saw that his son was so respectful and devoted to his guru. The king was deeply impressed by the transformation of his son.

Eventually the time came when the king himself said, "I want to be like my son. I shall also accept the spiritual life."

The hermit said, "What is this? How will people take it when they learn that their king has gone into the forest?"

The king replied, "Since my son accepted the spiritual life, I have observed how happy my son is inwardly. I want to be as happy as my son. I am so miserable at the palace. Every day I have to deal with teeming problems. There is no joy for me any more in ruling the kingdom. I want to join you and my son and live the life of a simple renunciate. That will give me the greatest joy. Let my younger son take care of my kingdom."

The king gave up his throne and came to join his son. He started praying and meditating and having deep experiences. Everybody was happy, and his youngest son was so proud that he had now become the king. He ruled the kingdom wisely and well. So God pleased everybody in his own way.

# APPENDIX

# PREFACE TO ORIGINAL EDITION

*Editor's preface to the original edition of* Is your mind ready to cry? Is your heart ready to smile?

The tales in this book, part of a collection that Sri Chinmoy has adapted from traditional Indian stories, have an innocent and childlike quality that appeals to the child in all of us. The stories have been performed as plays by Sri Chinmoy's students.

# BIBLIOGRAPHY

IS YOUR MIND READY TO CRY? IS YOUR HEART READY TO SMILE? (10 VOLUMES)

SRI CHINMOY:
–*Is your mind ready to cry? Is your heart ready to smile?, part 1*, New York, Agni Press, 1981.
–*Is your mind ready to cry? Is your heart ready to smile?, part 2*, New York, Agni Press, 1981.
–*Is your mind ready to cry? Is your heart ready to smile?, part 3*, New York, Agni Press, 1981.
–*Is your mind ready to cry? Is your heart ready to smile?, part 4*, New York, Agni Press, 1981.
–*Is your mind ready to cry? Is your heart ready to smile?, part 5*, New York, Agni Press, 1981.
–*Is your mind ready to cry? Is your heart ready to smile?, part 6*, New York, Agni Press, 1981.
–*Is your mind ready to cry? Is your heart ready to smile?, part 7*, New York, Agni Press, 1981.
–*Is your mind ready to cry? Is your heart ready to smile?, part 8*, New York, Agni Press, 1981.
–*Is your mind ready to cry? Is your heart ready to smile?, part 9*, New York, Agni Press, 1981.
–*Is your mind ready to cry? Is your heart ready to smile?, part 10*, New York, Agni Press, 1981.

Suggested citation key is MRC.

AMUSEMENT I ENJOY ENLIGHTENMENT I STUDY (8 VOLUMES)

SRI CHINMOY:

–*Amusement I enjoy enlightenment I study, part 1*, New York, Agni Press, 1997.

–*Amusement I enjoy enlightenment I study, part 2*, New York, Agni Press, 1997.

–*Amusement I enjoy enlightenment I study, part 3*, New York, Agni Press, 1997.

–*Amusement I enjoy enlightenment I study, part 4*, New York, Agni Press, 1998.

–*Amusement I enjoy enlightenment I study, part 5*, New York, Agni Press, 1998.

–*Amusement I enjoy enlightenment I study, part 6*, New York, Agni Press, 1998.

–*Amusement I enjoy enlightenment I study, part 7*, New York, Agni Press, 1998.

–*Amusement I enjoy enlightenment I study, part 8*, New York, Agni Press, 1999.

Suggested citation key is AIE.

LIFE'S BLEEDING TEARS AND FLYING SMILES (12 VOLUMES)

SRI CHINMOY:
–*Life's bleeding tears and flying smiles, part 1*, New York, Agni Press, 2001.
–*Life's bleeding tears and flying smiles, part 2*, New York, Agni Press, 2001.
–*Life's bleeding tears and flying smiles, part 3*, New York, Agni Press, 2001.
–*Life's bleeding tears and flying smiles, part 4*, New York, Agni Press, 2001.
–*Life's bleeding tears and flying smiles, part 5*, New York, Agni Press, 2001.
–*Life's bleeding tears and flying smiles, part 6*, New York, Agni Press, 2001.
–*Life's bleeding tears and flying smiles, part 7*, New York, Agni Press, 2001.
–*Life's bleeding tears and flying smiles, part 8*, New York, Agni Press, 2001.
–*Life's bleeding tears and flying smiles, part 9*, New York, Agni Press, 2001.
–*Life's bleeding tears and flying smiles, part 10*, New York, Agni Press, 2001.
–*Life's bleeding tears and flying smiles, part 11*, New York, Agni Press, 2001.
–*Life's bleeding tears and flying smiles, part 12*, New York, Agni Press, 2001.

Suggested citation key is LTS.

# POSTFACE

*Publishing principles*

This edition of *The works of Sri Chinmoy* aims to obey the Author's wish: scrupulous fidelity to his original words, use of typographical style by him selected, specific spelling choices, end placement of any editorial content (i.e. not written by Sri Chinmoy himself), particular treatment of some personal nouns in special cases, etc.

*Textual accuracy*

The text of this edition has been checked to ensure faithful accuracy to the originals. Although much effort has been put in proofreading and comparing different versions of the text, this print may still present a few lingering errors.

The Publisher would be grateful to be apprised of any mistypes via postal mail or facsimile, possibly with scan of the original page where the text is different. Please use original books only, specifying the year of publication. Online versions may be not as accurate and should not be considered authoritative.

*Acknowledgements*

The Publisher is very grateful to the late Professor Lambert and his équipe for his invaluable advice. For many decades Prof. Lambert conducted a small publishing house specialising in hand-made prints of philological edition of the classics. The standard of this edition would not have been the same without his scholarly advice.

The Publisher is also grateful to the international team of collaborators that spent countless hours proofreading and checking the current text against the originals.

Our deepest gratitude to Sri Chinmoy. His living presence can be felt breathing throughout his writings. It is a privilege to be involved with his works, in any form.

*Citation keys*

Citation keys are used throughout *The works of Sri Chinmoy* to allow accurate cross-reference of texts across titles and editions. Examples: EA 13, ST 50000, UPA 7.

*Sri Chinmoy Canon*

We could not use better words than Professor Lambert's, who kindly offered the name *Sri Chinmoy Canon*:

> «By defining Sri Chinmoy's first editions as *editio princeps* we chose to follow classical scholarship criteria, not because we consider Sri Chinmoy's work antique, but because we believe it is among the few post ‹classical antiquity› works to rightly deserve to be considered a *classicus*, designating by that term *superiority, authority* and *perfection*.
> «The monumental work Sri Chinmoy is offering to mankind is awe-inspiring and supremely pre-eminent in proportions and quality. It is manifest that Sri Chinmoy's work — which we feel right to call *The Sri Chinmoy Canon* — will be of profound help and source of enlightenment to anyone seeking a higher wisdom, truth and reality supreme.»
>
> *[Translated from French by M. G.S.]*

TABLE OF CONTENTS

*Composition typographique par imprimerie*
*Ab Academia Aoidon, Paris & Lyon.*

*Un grand merci à Prof Knuth pour*
*l'utilisation avancée de TeX.*

A LYON, LE 13 AVRIL LXXXVII Æ.G.

www.ingramcontent.com/pod-product-compliance
Lightning Source LLC
Chambersburg PA
CBHW031957040826
48979CB00043B/1684/J
*9780993308055*